Wings of Destiny

Other Books by Catherine Lanigan

Dangerous Love
Elusive Love
Romancing the Stone
The Jewel of the Nile
Bound by Love
Admit Desire
Sins of Omission
Web of Deceit
A Promise Made
All or Nothing
The Way of the Wicked
At Long Last Love
Seduced
Becoming
In Love's Shadow
The Texan
Montana Bride
Tender Malice
California Moon
The Legend Makers
The Evolving Woman: Intimate Confessions of Surviving
Mr. Wrong (available January 2000 from HCI)

Wings of Destiny

A Novel

Catherine Lanigan

Health Communications, Inc.
Deerfield Beach, Florida

www.bci-online.com

c.1

Library of Congress Cataloging-in-Publication Data

Lanigan, Catherine.
    Wings of destiny / Catherine Lanigan.
       p.   cm.
    ISBN 1-55874-690-0
    1. Earthquakes—California—San Francisco—History—20th century Fiction.
I. Title.
    PS3562-A53 W56 1999
    813'.54—dc21   99-37207
                                                    CIP

Publisher: Health Communications, Inc.
             3201 S.W. 15th Street
             Deerfield Beach, FL 33442-8190

Cover design by Andrea Perrine Brower
Book design by Dawn Grove

*This book is dedicated to my father, Frank J. Lanigan,
attorney and decorated war hero, who died on February 14, 1992,
and to all my ancestors who came before me,
who love me and guide me every day of my life.*

Acknowledgments

The creation of this book began over twelve years ago during lunch with my sister, Nancy Porter, at the Grand Canyon. We were there because both my parents were in the hospital in Flagstaff, Arizona. My father's heart attack caused him to die for twenty minutes, then to be revived and live again.

From that incredible spiritual experience of his, my destiny was shown to me.

There have been so many people who have loved this book and believed in it for such a very long period of time. Each of them has been a part of my life. Some still are. Others have gone on to their own destinies both on this earth and in heaven.

My vision of this story and its purpose has never faltered. I have always believed in it. I have such an abiding love for all of you who have breathed hope back into me and this book and who have been the wind beneath my wings.

To Mitch Douglas, my agent at ICM who first heard my story and encouraged me to write it down and to not be afraid, I will never forget you and your inspiration.

To Kimberly Cameron, Reese Halsey Agency, who worked so hard to sell this story and was refused so endlessly that discouragement nearly set in, I send endless love back to you.

To Charlotte Dial Breeze, who mothered me just as much as she nurtured yet another rewrite of this story, my heartfelt appreciation for everything you have done for me.

To Jodee Blanco, Blanco and Peace, the sister of my soul, who asked after reading *Wings of Destiny* how it was that I'd written about her life, I send gratitude and the continuing hope that all we have lovingly accomplished together is only the beginning. We have so much more work to do.

To Dianne Moggy, MIRA Books, my mentor, who has brought so many of my stories to the world, you are my friend and always in my prayers.

To Ellen Edwards, my past editor, whose genius continues to light my writing to this day, thanks for being the angel, second to the right.

To Page Cuddy, my first editor at Avon, who taught me in my first days of publishing twenty years ago that there's no such thing as coincidence, there is only destiny. We are still on our path, Page. God bless you.

To Amy Moore, Laura Shin and Martha Keenan, MIRA Books, my editors and teachers, you have blessed my words, and through my work with you I have been able to give this book the best of you all.

To my loving mother, Dorothy Lanigan, who, though always a supporter, researcher and cheerleader, had to dig deeper into herself to keep believing in the angels that would make this book a reality.

To my son, Ryan Pieszchala, who for so long was my only reason for living, always the light of my life, I want you to know my cup runneth over.

To my friends, Vicki Bushman, Stacy Stoker and Cherry Hickson, who have been there for the twelve-year haul, I want to thank you all for listening to the countless rewrites and for loving me through it all.

To my band of angelic friends, Sharon Reese, Terry Anzur, Wendy Birkenshaw, my countless bookseller friends, my supporters, love and thanks for all your encouragement.

To Michael Adamse, Ph.D., author of *Anniversary: A Love Story,* whom I dubbed my "archangel" for reading my manuscript, falling in love with it and becoming its champion, my thanks forever.

To Matthew Diener, my editor at Health Communications, Inc., whose brilliance has honed and refined my inadequacies into gems, I have more than appreciation; I am in awe.

To Kim Weiss, director of public relations at Health Communications, Inc., I will always honor your belief in me and in my desire to change the world, one life at time.

To Erica Orloff, my editor extraordinaire, whose intelligence and vast base of knowledge to come to this book "cold" and work miracles, even under pressure, astound me.

To Peter Vegso, president of Health Communications, Inc., who saw my vision and helped me to expand what I'd thought was beyond expansion, I have more than eternal respect and gratitude for you. You are a hero for so many, changing lives one book at a time. You have been and continue to be my muse and guide.

And, to Jim Alexander, my soul mate who encouraged me with his every thought and strength of his will to never give up. To always press on. To always believe in what we love.

Prologue

The
Rachel Papers

one

Under the water it rumbled on.

—S. T. COLERIDGE
"THE RIME OF THE ANCIENT MARINER," PT. VII, L. 33

San Francisco—April 17, 1906

After today, your life will never be the same, Jefferson Duke thought, leaning his ninety-one-year-old body on his gold-topped cane in the doorway of Barbara Kendrick's office at the *Call. But will it be for better or worse?*

Intent on editing her latest scathing report on the graft and corruption in the mayor's office, Barbara didn't notice him. Her brows crinkled angrily as her pencil flew across the page.

"Hold the pencil any tighter and it will snap in half, young lady," he said.

Jolted out of her thoughts, Barbara softened at the sight of her dear friend. Smiling broadly, she rose. "Jefferson," she opened her arms. "How good to see you."

He carried a thick leather valise under his left arm and so only raised his hand to her. She took his hand and kissed his cheek, noticing how frail he'd become of late. Silver dominated his once-golden hair, thinner now, but by no means balding. His six-foot, four-inch frame was bent with age, and he'd often commented how he despised growing old. Even with his grumblings, he was a man of dignity—a man she trusted and loved.

"Please, sit here," she offered a chair.

Lowering himself, he peered at her through gold-rimmed spectacles that magnified his jade-green eyes.

2

"Can I get you anything?" she asked, caressing his thin shoulder, remembering that even in her childhood, when he was in his seventies, he'd always looked twenty years younger. Today there was a veil of defeat in his eyes she'd never seen before.

Jefferson Duke was the oldest and richest founder of San Francisco, a man who founded learning institutions, orphanages and libraries. Jefferson brought the opera, symphony and ballet to San Francisco. As it was with any living legend, gossip surrounded him. Always intensely private, few knew him intimately, so the gossip was never confirmed or negated, only recycled periodically from decade to decade. In the end, none of it tripped him or slowed him down.

Jefferson had been a formidable force in commerce in his younger years. He backed politicians, served several years as state senator and was personal friends with every governor of California since 1837. When Theodore Roosevelt came to San Francisco, he was a guest of Jefferson Duke.

Barbara knew Jefferson better than anyone in San Francisco, but even to her, he remained an enigma, a puzzle without all the pieces.

"I'm fine," he said, placing the valise on her desk with great care.

"You look marvelous, Jefferson," she lied.

"I look like hell," his raspy voice grumbled affectionately. "You, my little missy, are a most delightful sight for these myopic eyes." Despite his age, his lined and wrinkled face radiated merriment. "Even so, you're more than a little worried over that piece you're writing."

"True." She bit her lip nervously.

"I've been following this exposé you're doing. Mayor Schmitz and his crony Abe Ruef have skimmed money from the city coffers long enough to hire very good assassins, my dear. Have you thought about that?"

"Michael reminds me of the dangers every day."

Jefferson noticed that at the mere mention of Michael Trent's name, the furrows in Barbara's brow softened. "You love him," he said matter-of-factly.

"Good thing I'm not an actress," she quipped. "Especially around Peter."

"Frankly, if you're intent on digging in the muck of this city's corrupted developers, having a special agent as a paramour is quite an intelligent move, my dear."

"I didn't plan it that way, Jefferson. It just . . . happened."

Jefferson smiled. "More than a bit handy, I'd say, since the worst offender is Peter Kendrick. You do like taking risks, don't you?"

She folded her arms defensively. "I told you I filed for divorce."

"Yes. And how did Peter take it?"

"He was apathetic. He seems unable to pry himself away from his mistress," she replied without a trace of emotion.

Jefferson placed his hands one over the other on his cane, peering at her. "Well done, child. You really don't care for Peter."

"I never did. You know that," she said, waving her hand to brush the topic aside. "Peter's time is up."

Jefferson dropped his eyes to the valise he'd brought. "Which brings me to the reason for my visit." He took a deep breath, imbuing the room with portent.

Just the way he said it, Barbara knew this was no ordinary social visit. Something was dreadfully wrong, and she didn't like the way he looked away from her rather than at her. Jefferson had always been an incredibly private person, which fueled his legendary status. Everyone wanted to know if the rumors of his affair with her grandmother, Caroline Mansfield, were true. Jefferson never talked about it. Only once in a while he'd open himself up to her, and why he'd chosen Barbara as a confidante puzzled her as much as anyone else. But it was true.

She placed her hand lovingly over his, knowing intuitively that he needed courage. She could feel the arthritic knuckles and saw the numerous liver spots. Unexpected tears welled in her eyes. Foolishly, she'd always believed Jefferson would be there for her; to love her; to give her guidance. She didn't want him to move away from her. . . . move into death. Like other heroes, he was immortal, wasn't he?

Jefferson's eyes scoured her. "I've known you all your life, Barbara. I was there the day you were born. I've cherished our closeness more than you can imagine. I know you feel the same way about me."

"I love you, Jefferson. You know that."

His voice was serious, and the words did not come easily to him as he said, "Then I call upon that love to ask something of you."

"Anything."

His eyes met hers. "Don't be so quick to agree. You may hate me after this."

"What a ridiculous thing to say! I could never hate you. It's not in me to hate anyone. Not even Eugene Schmitz and Abe Ruef. I despise what they do. I hate how they've put in fire hydrants that are not even hooked to the first water main. How they've stolen money meant for concrete to build bridges and roads that will collapse killing hundreds given a mild storm. But I don't hate anyone. You taught me that. Hating is as evil as the evildoer's deed."

"I did teach you that."

"It's served me well. But what has that to do with your visit?"

"I'm going to die, Barbara." He said it dispassionately, as if he were removed from life already. She waited for a choke or quiver in his voice. There was none, nor was there a glint of emotion in his eyes. She saw what she feared most: resolve and acceptance.

Barbara's heart scurried in circles, creating enough friction to ignite and burn into a rage of denial. Her rational mind engulfed her emotions with a wave of logic.

"I know you're ninety-one, but what is it? Your heart? Cancer? Your liver maybe? What did the doctor say?" She rattled off the possibilities like a Gatling gun. Just as quickly, she was ready with cures and causes for each illness. In her heart, she wanted to believe that together they could beat death.

She had to keep him with her a little longer.

"Not a doctor," he replied, looking blankly at the floor.

As his face turned back to her, Barbara noticed an incredible glow to his face, a sense of peace. She choked back a gasp as she realized he'd given up. He was ready to move on.

"I . . . saw my death in a dream," he whispered, as his voice assumed a near spiritual reverence.

"I don't want to hear this," she shivered with cold chills and rubbed her arms.

Jefferson continued. "This kind of dream has happened before. It's hard to explain because I've never told anyone about my dreams. Well, at least no one close. Not for a long time. But the dream is so real. I can touch and see and smell. Have you ever had a dream like that?" He looked at her with wonder-filled eyes, much like a child.

Barbara stared at him in amazement. Suddenly, he looked years younger, his charisma faded and was replaced by naïveté. It was as if she were the teacher and he the student when always it had been the reverse. He needed assurances, and she could provide them.

"Yes, I've had dreams that seem like they're more real than reality. It's as if the truth were unveiled in my dreams. Clear and accessible."

"Precisely. And, because of that, I know that my end is near." He leaned back and sighed, and, with that gesture, was transformed back into the old man again. "What I don't know is if God will take me and punish me for my sins or if I will die a victim of hatred."

Totally unprepared for this comment, Barbara's confusion screwed itself into her forehead, creating a deep crinkle between her brows. "I don't understand any of this. You are the most upstanding man I know. You're practically a paragon. You have enemies, yes, but surely no one would dare kill you."

He laughed. "How little you know. But that's to be expected. I've done a good job of keeping the truth from you."

"I don't understand."

"I know, but you will." He placed his hand lovingly on the leather valise. "I've brought something for you." Slowly he moved his hand across the leather, caressing it as if it were a lover. "This is my legacy to you. Read it carefully, and by that I mean read it with your heart, not your head. My life is contained within these pages. It's odd you know. . . ." His voice trailed off.

"Odd, Jefferson?"

"It is odd to think that one's life is reduced to lines on paper."

"Jefferson, you have a great deal to show for your life. There is the museum, the opera house, the library. . . . "

He cut her off quickly with a sharp wave of his hand. "Toys! Amusements, perhaps, but certainly not my *life!* Never mistake monuments for life. Life is *love.* It's the people you love." His serious tone faded as he looked at her impishly. "My life just has more lines than others do." He handed her the valise. "This is where I wrote those lines."

"Your journals?" She breathed with respect and a heavy feeling of finality. Reflexively, she clutched them possessively.

"To be truthful, they are not all mine. To know truth, one must go to the beginning of the story. Therefore, some are my mother's writings. I call them the "Rachel Papers.""

"Rachel. You've told me about her. She must have been a wonderful woman because you've always spoken of her with such love."

"I hope you still think so after you read this. I have always admired your need to seek out the truth, both in your work here," he gestured with his arm to indicate the newspaper office, "and in your personal life. That takes courage."

"Courage can be painful," Barbara replied ruefully. She looked down at the valise. Surely there could be nothing in these personal reflections that would require courage to read.

"There are many truths, Barbara, and what you read here you may find painful. But it *is* the truth. I want you to read this. I do this selfishly, my dear. I need to know if you see what I see."

"Which is?"

Conspiratorially, he leaned quite close, his voice so low and intent he was nearly inaudible. "See if you draw the same conclusions as I. Specifically, I am speaking of your father's murder."

Barbara choked back her shock. "You *know* who it is?"

"I can never be sure. At least not until the day he comes after me."

"And that is what you saw in your dream? My father's murderer is after you now?"

"I don't know. Perhaps God will intervene as he's done many times in my life and deprive my assailant of the opportunity." Jefferson started to laugh. "The joke would be on my killer, now wouldn't it? I've always believed that God has a bizarre sense of humor. I think I'll ask him about that when I see him."

Barbara tried to shake off the sense of gloom that shrouded her. "Jefferson, I'm honored that you want me to read your journals and those of your mother. But why me?"

Jefferson shook his head in protest. "The answer to that is also contained in those pages." He jabbed his gnarled index finger at the valise. "I've guarded this information all my life. Now, it's yours. Only you can walk this maze."

Suddenly, he stood, teetering only slightly on his cane. Determination shot up his back. His eyes brandished resolution like a mighty saber. "There are many sins in the world, Barbara. Some are not as visible as the theft and corruption you have uncovered in your work. Many sins are invisible, but just as black. I've been ashamed of who I am all my life." His voice faltered suddenly, creaking out the words as they squirmed through barriers of emotion. "I can't explain." His eyes darted about the room, frantically looking for the door, for escape.

She rose to her feet. "There's nothing you can't tell me."

"Oh, but there is." His hand shook as he gripped his cane and moved away from her.

He forgot his customary good-bye hug as he headed for the door. Hunched over his cane, with his back to her, he shuffled away. Barbara had never seen Jefferson Duke frightened, yet now he was truly afraid. What puzzled her most was that he feared her.

He grasped the doorknob and opened it. A rush of cold air swept inside and whirled around Barbara for a long moment. She shivered.

He had almost quit the room when his head jerked around and his eyes pierced through her.

I'll never forget his eyes. It's as if they can see my future.

"Read it, my dear. Then tell me that you still care about me." He paused. "I *dare* you."

He closed the door firmly behind him.

Barbara touched the valise, anxious to begin reading the mysterious journals, when William Melton, the city editor, rushed to her door and poked his head in. "You're late for the meeting. I was sent to get you. Bring your pad. Seems that councilman you accused last week was caught taking a bribe just this morning."

Barbara gasped, "I can't believe it!"

"Believe it, kid. You've got them running for cover," he slapped her good-naturedly on the back.

She looked longingly at the Rachel Papers, knowing they would have to wait.

"Say, was that Jefferson Duke I just saw leaving?" William asked.

"Yes."

"Nice old guy. He got you the job here, didn't he?"

Barbara frowned at William. She didn't like anyone prying into her personal life. And Duke territory was sacred. "You thought I was too young. Not intelligent enough."

"True," he admitted. "Guess I didn't realize how gutsy and stupid you were. Nobody here would take the risks you do."

She smiled to herself as they left her office. "Yes, but I got the story, didn't I?"

Bill laughed. "They'll cast you in bronze."

She rolled her eyes. "I'd rather they cast Ruef and Schmitz into hell."

* * * *

Barbara lay next to Michael, love-spent and naked save for the rope of pearls that glistened only slightly less than the beads of sweat on her face and breasts. She gazed at the handsome brown-haired man whom she loved deeply and without condition. She was amazed at how inexorably he had transformed her world during the past five months.

Barbara rolled over, spooning her body next to his. When they met over four years ago, she'd fallen madly in love with him from the first. Her heart was joy filled and then abruptly he'd left her. It took her years of torment before she discovered the truth about what happened that night in Washington. The truth had been more frightening than she'd believed was possible. Though their lives were filled with danger, she'd found the kind of love she'd only dreamed of in her fantasies. She was twenty-five years old. Only a year ago she'd come to think of her life as over. Michael had given her hope again.

"I love you, Barbara," Michael said, placing his hand on her hip.

"I love you back," she replied, placing her hand over his, caressing the long tapered fingers that loved her and brought her pleasure.

"You're still awake," he stroked her cheek. "I can tell when you're worried, and it's not your job or our investigation, is it?"

"For once I'm not having nightmares about fires breaking out all over the city if that's what you mean."

"It's Jefferson's visit today that's upset you. I could tell earlier during dinner that you were preoccupied."

"It's just so strange, Michael. The way he alluded to mysteries and secrets. And then daring me to read the Rachel Papers as if there was something in them that would hurt me."

"Jefferson loves you as I do. He would never hurt you. I think you should read them and soon."

"I didn't tell you earlier, but he said there's something in that journal about my father's murder."

"Darling, your father *died*. It was an accident. Not a murder."

"You don't know that, Michael. No one's ever proven it."

"I researched the records for you. I checked out old witnesses, and their stories are the same as what the papers reported. It was a hit and run. A runaway carriage on the Barbary Coast. Those brothels are dangerous to anyone—"

"He was not going to a brothel! Lawrence Mansfield was not the type of man who would do such a thing. He didn't drink or gamble either. The whole thing makes no sense."

Michael smoothed a strand of her long brown hair behind her ear. "He didn't love your mother, Barbara. You've told me that. It's all I can do to be civil to Eleanor. Never have I met a more exasperating, selfish woman. How they ever got married in the first place is beyond me."

"Father told me once that she was dazzling when she was young. She was full of life then, and I think in the beginning she might have loved him at least long enough to extract a proposal from him."

"Well, he wouldn't be the first man who fell under a woman's spell," he said, kissing her earlobe. She rolled over to face him and his arms formed a circle around her and drew her in.

"I'm certainly under your spell," she said, kissing him tenderly.

Michael kissed her back with all the love in his heart. "Darling, I wish I could believe you, but the truth of the matter is that, for tonight at least, you're under Jefferson's spell. Why not make some tea and read for a bit? Hmm? Maybe once you've put your demons to rest, you'll feel better."

"You don't mind?"

"Of course not," he replied, tapping his finger to the tip of her nose. "Now scoot."

"Okay." She rose and slipped her arms into a cream-colored satin peignoir.

Moonlight streamed through the lace curtains, casting shadows across the down-filled quilt. She noticed as she left the room that Michael had already drifted off to sleep.

Barbara went to the kitchen stove and put a quarter in the gas meter on the wall, which would give her three hours of gas. She lit the top burner with a wooden match, wondering if the gas lines to her house were safe. So many building contractors had bribed city inspectors to ignore their faulty, cheap work in order to pocket large profits. There wasn't a citizen in the city who was not in danger daily from fire. In fact, the entire city council was on the take. Tomorrow, Michael was going to file his official report to the president of the United States. All of these things she'd written in articles for the newspaper, and in so doing she had placed herself and Michael in mortal danger.

She filled the tea kettle with water, placed it over the flame and put a heaping teaspoon of imported orange pekoe tea she'd bought in Chinatown into a sterling tea caddy.

Barbara loved tea: the brewing of it, the paraphernalia it took to serve proper British tea and the history of it. Every time she made a cup of tea, she remembered Jefferson telling her about his ancestor, Andrew Duke, who worked for the East India Tea Company in the late 1700s. For over a hundred years, the Duke family had been in the importing business, just as her father, Lawrence Mansfield, had been when he was alive.

Barbara was always curious about lives that dovetailed other lives, both past and present. Paths that met and then retreated from one another only to come back together again. Barbara knew that Michael was only trying to ease her mind when he said that her father's death was an accident. But Barbara didn't believe in accidents of any kind. If she couldn't find the man-made answer to mysterious events, she was wise enough to know that every turn of life was a matter of fate. One simply had to look deep enough and far back enough to find the truth.

She poured the tea into a pink floral Haviland cup and then walked to the salon. She turned on the electric Tiffany lamp, eased herself onto the sofa, tucking her feet beneath her. Ordinarily, the aroma of the spicy tea would calm her instantly, but tonight was not one of those times.

The velvet drapes were drawn back over the tall windows framing a magnificent view of San Francisco Bay. Lighted ferry boats, sailboats and shipping barges dotted the water like pirouetting fireflies. She remembered commenting on what a beautiful night it was to her mother earlier when they'd gone to hear Caruso sing, but as usual, Eleanor was so self-involved she noticed neither the beauty of the night nor her daughter's distraction.

Barbara rubbed her forehead. *Are you the only emotional anchor I've ever had, Jefferson? How I will miss you if you leave.*

A pang shot through her. Even though she had Michael in her life now to love her and comfort her, Jefferson had been her mentor, the grandfather she'd never known. She almost didn't want to read his journals. Sometimes living in ignorance brought more happiness than illumination.

"Still," she said touching the valise and pulling out the stunningly old pieces of parchment. "My God," she said with reverence and awe.

Just looking at the yellowed papers and the scrawled penmanship in a woman's hand gave her chills.

"Don't go where angels fear to tread," she reminded herself, but her journalist's innate curiosity took over. That curiosity had guided her through thirteen months of investigating San Francisco's corruption; it had taken her to the knowledge that her husband was sleeping with her best friend and that she'd been married to the devil himself. Barbara couldn't tear her eyes from the ancient pages. Not even the sound of odd-timed church bells ringing or the unusually large number of whinnying horses in the city's liveries alerted her to the dangers around her.

She saw only the words on the pages. She was facing a danger of her own. Mesmerized, she courageously began reading.

Book One

The House of Duke

The House of Duke

Andrew Duke — m: 1776 Brenna York
b: 1736　　　　b: 1756
d: 1814　　　　d: 1814

Ambrose Duke
b: 1781
d: 1862

no issue

Lord Henry Duke — m: 1789 Lady Mary Worthington
b: 1726　　　　b: 1739
d: 1788　　　　d: 1792

William Henry Duke
b: 1765
d: 1788

Charlotte Duke
b: 1768
d: 1800

Sarah Duke
b: 1769
d: 1795

Yuala
b: 1765
d: 1791

Rachel - - - - - Richard Harrison
b: 1781　　　　b: 1769
d: 1835　　　　d: 1835

Jefferson - - - - - Caroline Potter Mansfield — m: 1837 William Mansfield
b: 1815　　　　b: 1817　　　　b: 1814
d: 1906　　　　d: 1882　　　　d: 1881

Lawrence Mansfield — m: 1881 Eleanor Baresfield
b: 1842　　　　b: 1862
d: 1892

Barbara Mansfield Kendrick — m: 1906 Michael Trent
b: 1881　　　　b: 1873

two

*Some say, the earth
Was feverous and did shake.*

—WILLIAM SHAKESPEARE
MACBETH, II, III, L.74–75

Montego Bay, Jamaica—1774

Yuala broke through a cluster of banyan trees, pushing aside the flat, wide-webbed arms of banana trees as she ran through the jungle. Beneath her nine-year-old feet, flower pods erupted and spewed forth millions of vanilla orchid seeds. They mingled with the spores of now-crushed ferns and formed tiny yellow-green mushroom-shaped clouds. Though these clouds were nearly invisible to most human invaders to the jungle, Yuala knew of the presence of the little clouds because she could feel their life potential. Normally, she took great care never to disturb anything in the jungle, but today she was in a hurry and so asked pardon of the life-forms around her for the disharmony she caused.

Yuala's reverence for the rain forest and all its living creatures was deep in the marrow in her bones. It was part of her soul. She would never desecrate the flamboyant flowers by cutting them down and placing them in the porcelain vases the way the mem'saab did. Yuala would pick the frangipani, orchids or canna lilies that needed pruning and then place the withered blossoms gently on the ground where they would decay, feed the plants and begin the life cycle anew. Yuala could feel the life spirit in every rain tree; every tussock of tall grass; every bird, animal, limestone and bauxite rock; every ray of hot sun and dewdrop. She collected the seeds of nutmeg,

15

arrowroot, lemons, limes, pineapples and cocoa from the big house kitchens. Knowing their regenerative powers, she planted them behind her hut in the fertile soil she'd created through her innate knowledge of vegetation and living matter.

Her compost had taken over twenty full-moon passings to compile. She stole vegetable scraps from the table of the master, Lord Henry Duke, and mixed them with dead leaves, blossoms and withered sugar cane stalks from the mill. Carefully and lovingly, she mixed them with a long cane pole, then allowed them to decompose and create a new energy on which her seeds would thrive.

Each herb and plant she grew was a child of the jungle, just as Yuala herself was.

She was born on this plantation nine years ago. She was the daughter of Ona, a slave owned by the previous master, Lord Halpern. Lord Halpern had sold the sugarcane plantation to Lord Henry Duke the year Yuala was born. Ona had died giving Yuala birth near the waterfall, high above the plantation. Yuala always thought of the waterfall as her life source. It was to the waterfall she returned today.

Before the orange face of the sun had smiled on her, while the earth was dark in sleep, Yuala had heard the voice of the waterfall calling to her. Growling like tropical thunder, the voice spoke her name as if the voice itself had come from the belly of God. She had crept silently from her bed without hesitation, leaving her mud-and-grass–thatched hut behind. Yuala knew only to follow the voice.

Yuala felt she was racing against time. She didn't look behind her as she jumped over black mangrove roots and dodged a long silver snake. Yuala had never felt such urgency.

Because it was the place where her birth cry had mingled with the death cry of her mother, Yuala believed the waterfall was a sacred, haunted place. Like the powerful energy she'd felt when she'd played with Lord Duke's magnet when it met steel, the waterfall's force both attracted and repelled her. But never before had the factions of life and death, negative and positive transformed into a voice capable of calling her name.

Yuala pressed forward to meet it without fear, without reservation.

Suspended from a leather thong around her neck was a huge wooden crucifix that banged against Yuala's bony chest as she ran. Mistress Mary, the mem'saab of the plantation, had given Yuala the crucifix for correctly answering all the religious questions posed to her by the visiting Anglican bishop last year. The crucifix was nearly as powerful as her woven chain of arrowroot when it came to dispelling the evil spirits of the night. Yuala took great pride in the cross for it was her first talisman from the white man exalting her special powers. Her people already referred to her as the obeahman: the shaman who could cure the sick, speak to the spirits of the forest, commune with the dead and summon the "loa." Though she was a child, Yuala felt very, very old.

Yuala did not see the coneys scurrying from her path, nor the bats that hung in the low-lying thickly woven masses of vines and fungus. She did not hear the tree frogs, parrots and toucans cawing at each other. Yuala did not use the limited organs of her body to see and hear the rain forest. Yuala used her mind.

Huge coconut palms, red mangroves and hardwood trees concealed the waterfall from view. None of the whites knew of this place and, Yuala vowed, they never would. Her mother's midwife was the only other person besides Yuala who knew of this place.

Brilliant pink and gold metamorphic rocks had arranged themselves in a pyramid of symmetrical beauty. The clearest water in all of Jamaica rushed over this formation. Yuala paused on the edge of the lagoon, mesmerized as always by the beauty and power of the waterfall.

Beams of sunlight pierced the thick tropical canopy overhead and illuminated the heavy mist that danced above the water's spray. Crystal sheets of water shattered into brilliant jewels. The union of water crystals and sun rays birthed a million prisms of light. Gold, silver, purple, blue, green, yellow and red shimmered around the lagoon, bouncing off the rocks, refracting themselves over and over until the colors and the lights looked like falling night stars.

Awestricken, Yuala stared trance like at the incredible crystal ballet.

Suddenly, in the midst of the rainbow a beautiful white woman appeared. She had crystal blue eyes, brighter than the water droplets. Her hair was dark brown, not black like Yuala's, with gold and copper streaks that seemed to form a halo around her face. Her smile was the most caring Yuala had ever seen. She wore a slim-fitting white dress with none of the bustles and hip pads of the mem'saab's dresses. On her feet, strange leather shoes buttoned over her ankle and which were nothing like the kid shoes or satin slippers she'd seen in the master's house.

Yuala sank to her knees. "'Tis the mother of Christ," she gasped, remembering the Christmas story the Anglican bishop had related to the island children.

A tinkling melody rose out of the water, as Yuala had noted many times in the past, but this time the sonorous tones came from the mouth of the apparition.

"My name is Barbara. I've brought you a gift."

The apparition gestured to the ground at Yuala's feet. Nestled between the ferns and mosses was a tiny baby girl. Her eyes were green like the precious pieces of jade Yuala had seen in the big house. Her hair was curly and burnished with an unusual tint of gold and copper. Her skin was much lighter than Yuala's black. Yuala's young arms ached to hold the child. She scooped up the baby, rocking her gently. The child was not real, Yuala knew. She was formed of light and song and the mists of the rain forest. Nothing about her was flesh and bone.

"Her name is Rachel. She's your daughter," the light-timbered voice of the waterfall apparition said.

Yuala's eyes were still dreamlike as they stared at Barbara. "She can't be mine. She's not African. I'm to be the obeahman. I'm to marry a black man and keep the race pure for my people. There are Creoles about, Conchy Joes and mulattoes. I will lose my powers."

"The child is your destiny. Just as her son will be. Just as I am. Remember that her name is Rachel. She is my great-grandmother. You are my great-great-grandmother."

Her mind spinning at a pace she'd never experienced, Yuala reasoned, "But that would mean you are from the future."

"I am of the now. What mankind does not understand is that there is no past, no future—only the present . . . the now. Mankind does not understand, as you do, that all living things are connected. Are all one."

"If I do this . . . mate with my master . . . I shall surely lose my powers."

Water crashed around the apparition, assaulting Yuala's ears. It was as if the water spirits were angry with her. She heard their frustration in their dying cries as they flew into the air and dashed themselves on the rocks.

Anger transformed into serenity as the apparition replied, "You show your prejudice just as much as the white man, Yuala. You, above all others, should understand that the ill feelings of bias, greed and jealousy divide the natural powers of the earth. Storms and earthquakes begin in the hearts of men. Shutting their minds to the voices, vibrations and harmony of the universe and to each other can bring only disaster.

"Take this child, Yuala. Her destiny matters a great deal. Through you, then through Rachel and her son, whom she will call Jefferson, a new city will be founded. It will be the most beautiful city in the New World, set among seven hills. It holds the greatest promise for the greatest good, if the vibrations are positive. You must teach her all you know, the harmonies contained within every living creature and plant, the melodies to be found in the light of the sun, moon and stars. Teach her how to speak with her mind and not with her tongue. Rachel must record your philosophies and skills. She will teach these things to Jefferson. In the generations beyond even myself, so much of the spiritual world will be lost. You must help me save it for my grandchildren and their children's children of the twenty-first century.

"It's my wish that God will look with pride upon the city that Jefferson builds. However, I can tell you that even now in your time, evil men are setting the course of their fate to destroy it. I'm to be part of that new city, and my destiny is to fight their evil. I want you to understand that you are part of my destiny now, in your time and space, and in my future world. Without you and Rachel, my destiny will not come to pass."

Yuala's very old soul took the words the specter spoke and recorded them in her heart. "I will not forget," she sighed and gathered her courage again. "'Tis true then, Lord Duke is to be Rachel's father?"

"Don't be afraid. Fear will rob you of your powers. He will love you, Yuala, as you should be loved. And you will love him with all your heart. There will never be room in your heart for fear when love abides. Lord Duke's lineage will be important to Rachel, Jefferson and to myself."

Pausing, then turning to the right, the apparition motioned for Yuala to look into the glittering bubble of water that formed a translucent mirror beneath her extended arm. "In a few years in earth time, you will learn more fully the lesson of mankind's connectedness. Witness this man, whom you will know as Andrew Duke."

Yuala easily saw a man who looked remarkably like Lord Henry Duke, though younger, surrounded by exotic-looking people with golden skin, slanted dark eyes and lustrous, thick black hair.

The apparition continued. "His destiny is to be the catalyst that strikes a chord passing through time and will touch my life and Jefferson's. His choices and actions could cause my death many years later."

"How can this man affect you?"

"In the days to come, you will hear with your own ears that everything I am saying is true. Stay close to the Dukes and listen to Andrew. His words will be your sign that I speak the truth."

Blanketed with chills and fighting her fears, Yuala said, "I promise I will listen. I will give all my knowledge to my daughter."

Barbara's eyes overflowed with love. "You're still disappointed that I am of another race. Remember this, Yuala, we are all one in the eyes of God."

Barbara smiled at Yuala, and when she did, Yuala believed that never in her life had anyone graced her with so much joy, love and peace. Suddenly, the water seemed to rush over the peak of the rockfall at twice its speed and a thousand times its volume. The prisms of color intensified and multiplied. Yuala's eyes, ears and mind were bombarded with the sheer magnitude of power within the light and water. The water roared and thundered as it crashed on the rocks. Suddenly, Barbara splintered into fragments and became one with the colors. The colors shot into the air, burst wildly anew, and then vanished.

The last, dying silver shards of light pierced Yuala's dark eyes, a reminder of the internal illumination she'd experienced this day.

Yuala continued kneeling as the waterfall returned to its familiar melodious hum and the sunbeams went back to chasing the mists amongst the banyan trees. Yuala was unaware that she still rocked her arms from side to side. When she looked down into the crook of her arms, she found the illusion had vanished, but the love she felt for Rachel remained.

At the center of Yuala's consciousness, like that of most of her people, were spiritual matters. Her ancestors came from Africa, but she knew little else about them. Her father had been sold to an adjoining plantation months before her birth. She knew nothing about him. It was as if Yuala had come into being through spontaneous combustion. If Yuala were to bear Rachel, she wanted her child to know everything about Lord Henry Duke and his ancestral lines that Yuala could glean from her days in the big house.

The master, his family and his house had never meant much to her, other than the scraps of herbs, food and garbage she'd stolen from the kitchens. She belonged to Lord Duke, but she was only nine years old and not worthy of selling yet. This allowed Yuala to make her life in the forest. She was not concerned with the entities of ambition, empire building and material gains as whites were. The apparition spoke of many concepts she'd not heard before, though in her heart she could feel their worth.

Yuala had witnessed a miracle today. Wisdom told her to accept the message. It never occurred to her to question anything.

As she left the waterfall and forest behind, she promised herself she would remember the majesty of the vision and embrace her future willingly. Most important, the awesome words she'd heard were branded in her mind.

three

The earth that opens wide her mouth to swallow men and his words is the redeemer of our souls from bondage to our bodies.

—KAHLIL GIBRAN
"THE WONDER OF THE MASTER"

Montego Bay, Jamaica—October 1781

The trade winds rushed across the island, cooling sand, flora, animals and humans. Startled out of her dream, Yuala pushed away the familiar omen of the brilliant-colored phoenix that burst into her nocturnal wanderings. For months the phoenix had been forewarning her that changes, destiny-making alterations on the plantation, were afoot. As in any birth, there would be a great deal of pain; for Lady Mary, for the Duke children, for Lord Henry and even for Yuala.

At the age of sixteen, Yuala keenly recognized shifts in the earth's vibrations and the correction of energy patterns around the island. For nearly a year, her nights had been invaded by visiting specters and earth gods who came to instruct her not to resist destiny's path.

"Your brother is coming to visit us from China," Mary announced after reading Lord Andrew's letter aloud to the family at breakfast.

Henry leaned back with a bright smile as Yuala served a bowl of fruit. He barely noticed her as she moved silently from plate to plate. She saw William's spine stiffen defensively. Though she and William were the same age, she was invisible to him. Charlotte, at thirteen, at least smiled blandly as Yuala filled the blue-and-white china bowl. Sarah was only twelve, and her enormous yellow-green eyes reminded Yuala of sponges soaking up everything but discerning little.

Intuitively, Yuala knew every word she heard today would matter a great deal to her in the hours and weeks to come.

"Don't stop there, Mary. Continue."

"He states here that Brenna has just given birth. A boy. And they named him after you, Henry. Ambrose Henry Duke." Her hand fell to her lap. "I had no idea Andrew wanted a family. He waited so long to marry. What is he now? Forty-five?"

"A son?" Henry asked exuberantly. "My namesake! By God this calls for a celebration!" He slammed his hand on the table making the silver jump.

"But Father, how can Ambrose be your namesake when I'm your son?" sixteen-year-old William asked.

"Your mother insisted on calling you William," Henry glared at Mary.

Her eyes frosted as she returned his stare.

William adjusted the new, gold-silk brocade vest his mother had commissioned to accompany his tan breeches. He feigned a charming smile for his father. "Perhaps you should have pressed harder, Father."

Henry shoved the barb aside. "What's done is done. But this is the future! Think of it! Andrew here! I didn't think wild horses could get him out of Canton."

Mary glanced back at the letter. "Apparently, Brenna was more persuasive than a horse. They've been in London for nearly a year. She had a favorite doctor there it seems."

"That's reasonable," Henry said.

Mary's eyes flew open. "When I asked the same of you, you said we couldn't afford it."

Henry cranked his neck uncomfortably as if a noose were tightening. "We couldn't back then. Andrew is incredibly rich, Mary. He has been since he first set foot in China. However, I'll wager that we'd go toe to toe these days."

"Just how rich is he?" William asked, tracing his delicate fingers down the handle of a sterling spoon.

"Rich enough to sail to see us for a visit! We'll kill a fatted pig. Invite our neighbors for a party. A round of parties!"

"Henry, don't be ridiculous," Mary chided. "What if he doesn't come? He says nothing here about departure times or arrivals."

"Must you always be pessimistic?"

"I'm being practical. And since when does Andrew want to share anything with us including his precious time? Isn't he too busy making fortunes to tend to family?"

"Mary, just because my brother is successful, and I'd rather enjoy my life than waste it counting figures in a crumbling castle in England as you would have me do, does not make one better than the other." Henry rose with a frown, tossing his napkin down. "Must you kill every idea I have, Mary? Andrew said he's coming. He'll be here, and I'll be ready!" Henry stormed out of the dining room.

Yuala dropped her eyes and stepped through the doorway back to the kitchen. Holding the door slightly ajar, she did something she'd never done. She eavesdropped.

All three children looked tenuously at their mother.

"Perhaps an apology is in order," William offered sourly, revealing a bit too much disdain for his mother.

"You're excused," she said curtly.

William did not back down. He'd come to enjoy making his mother feel uncomfortable. His game made up for his insecurity with his father. William sensed that for some reason he would never be good enough to please his father. "Father is quite excited about Andrew's visit. You are forever wanting more parties. This seems the perfect excuse to me."

"What I want are parties in London, William. Will you get that straight? Your father is being ridiculous about this. Andrew will never show up. I can't tell you how many times this has happened in the past. We get a letter from Andrew stating he will visit on his trip back to London. Months go by. Years. And he never writes to cancel. No explanation. This time will be no different. You'll see," Mary replied, finally putting the letter aside.

Sarah toyed with her fork and did not look up when she asked meekly, "Why must you and Father always argue?"

The truth struck Mary like a lance to a long-festering boil. "Because I hate it here. I want to go back to England. To my rose garden, London parties and early morning rides with my friends. I want you children to be schooled properly. None of you have made the kind of social connections one needs to survive this life in England. But your father doesn't see it like that. He thinks life among these savages and his precious sugarcane is all there is."

William tapped his finger against the table's edge. "Is it true you were more wealthy than Father?"

Mary exhaled the building steam inside her and sniffed pompously. "For the first four years of our marriage he lived off my money. We moved to Charleston from London so that he could make his fortune in indigo, which he did. But when Henry heard about the profits in sugarcane, he never so much as asked my permission to move. He began dismantling the house while I was in town shopping. I don't think I'll ever forget coming home and seeing those barges lined up on the Ashley River not to take our crop to market but to load the bricks from the walls of our house!"

"I don't remember," Sarah said, looking at her sister.

"But we have everything here you love, Mother. Even the pecan and peach trees," Charlotte said, wanting to defend her father.

"Charlotte, you've never made it a secret that you like the beach and tropical flowers. I see you talking with Yuala in the herb garden after I've warned you not to associate yourself with the slaves."

"But she's interesting, Mother."

"Charlotte! Do not defy me again or you'll regret it!"

Charlotte sank down in her chair. "Yes, Mother."

"This is precisely what I'm talking about. How can I blame you? You've never been to England. You don't know what you're missing. And it's all your father's fault."

"Well, I do know what I'm missing," William chimed in. "I read the books and papers sent from England. I would give my eyeteeth to attend Oxford and learn to hunt in Surrey," William said rhapsodically.

"And for your information, Sarah, the only reason we have nice things here was because I insisted every vase, teapot and French mirror be packed with care when we left South Carolina," she replied, looking down at the Italian tiles in the dining floor that had once composed the foyer flooring in their mansion in Charleston.

"Is Father so very rich now like he said?" William asked.

Yuala shook her head and whispered to herself, "Can't they see how poor in spirit they are?" She realized the only joyous person was Lord Duke. She pushed the door open a bit wider so as not to miss a single word.

"He's been distilling his own rum for five years. He's rich enough that he could let us go back to England," Mary said.

Yuala had to agree with her mistress. Lord Duke had just added a new colonnade to the front of the house overlooking Montego Bay. The jungle behind and around the manor house had been cleared away where crops thrived on the hill slopes. Lord Duke had even built a private roadway that he paved with crushed shells and sand. Yuala had been told by the overseer that Lord Duke owned over a thousand acres, producing enough sugarcane to make Lord Henry the wealthiest Duke in history.

In accordance, Lord Henry had ordered the finest Oriental furnishings, ceramics and carpets from Andrew and the East India Company. There was no luxury that Lady Mary lacked.

Except happiness.

Yuala wondered if it had ever occurred to her mistress that it was her responsibility to make herself happy.

"Then why don't you persuade him to make us happy?" Charlotte asked.

Mary glared at her daughter. "Mind your manners. It's not proper to speak of such feelings."

"I want to know," Charlotte insisted.

Mary sighed. "It's my fault, I suppose, that you are all too outspoken. Out of loneliness, I've been too open with you. If I'd had women friends like I did in England, I'd be confiding in them."

"Well, we don't have anyone else but each other, now do we, Mother?" William snarled.

Yuala sucked in her breath knowing she'd never been as disrespectful to another soul as much as William was sometimes to his own mother.

Mary ground her jaw, dispelling her anger. She ignored William's comment.

Mary continued, "I've never had much influence over the workings of your father's mind. Andrew, on the other hand, has had a great deal of impact. Because of Andrew's tall tales of the Orient and India and the money he's made, your father has always been in competition with his brother. I'm afraid Andrew will encourage your father to invest in more foreign trade, which will keep us here longer. He might persuade him to go to China. I can think of nothing worse."

"You mean Father might even be thinking about it?" Charlotte asked eagerly. "How exotic! How exciting."

"Charlotte! For pity's sake, don't let me ever hear you say such a thing!"

Charlotte hung her head, regretting her outburst.

"If we get on a ship, it will be to go back to England. Remember that. I have worked towards no other goal for the past fifteen years. It's his fault that you children have no social skills. No friends. I was a fool myself to let him talk me into raising you children in this godless country." She ground her teeth, rage seething inside. Her eyes shot around the table to the faces of each of her children.

They cowered visibly beneath her scalding gaze.

"You are excused, I said."

Silently, they rose in unison and hurried away from their mother's hot anger.

Mary dropped her face in her hands. "I hate it here. And I hate Henry Duke for bringing me here."

* * * * *

For weeks the house servants including Yuala waxed furniture and floors and polished silver. The guest rooms were covered with a new coat of paint. The plantation seamstresses cut and sewed new gowns for Lady Mary and dresses for Charlotte and Sarah.

Scores of beeswax candles were dipped and dried to fill sconces and French gilt chandeliers in the dining room, salon and vestibule.

Thinking about Lady Mary made Yuala's lips burn, indicating that her mistress's resentment toward Jamaica would turn to jealous acid; an acid so powerful it would destroy her and possibly those around her.

Yuala's magical powers would have no strength if she attempted to wield them against fate, even her own. All she could do was step aside and reap the harvest the gods had ordered for her.

At dawn, the day of Lord Andrew's arrival, Yuala intended to be in the kitchens before the cooks awakened. She was just as anxious to make everything perfect for their guests as her mistress.

Yuala was surprised to find Lady Mary fully dressed in a new shimmering peach-colored, summer-silk gown counting sugar-cured hams, papaya and honey-glazed roast pork, thick slabs of bacon, racks of ribs and the quartered sections of beef to be roasted that day.

The pale Lady Mary's face bore deep penetrations of a lifetime of unhappiness.

"Mem'saab," Yuala quietly addressed her.

Lady Mary jumped slightly, her concentration broken. "Good heaven's, Yuala, don't sneak up on me like that!"

Yuala kept her eyes down as she donned her special burlap apron with twelve pockets she'd hand-sewn years ago. In each pocket, she'd carefully placed spices and herbs she'd grown and dried herself. Blending the island flavors of lime, coconut, sugar and papaya with English cooking methods, Yuala had created dining fare with a reputation for being the finest, most adventurous on the island. "I will do," Yuala said, referring to the kitchen matters.

Wringing her hands, Lady Mary's eyes flitted across the thick wooden table her four African cooks used for butchering. "I can't believe Andrew has docked. I want everything right, Yuala. It's very, very important," she sighed, still dreaming of sailing back to England.

Always attuned to the fourth dimension, Yuala could see dark leaden mists of fear burst from her mistress's lungs when she spoke. Lady Mary had never learned to rejoice in her children, her husband or the beauty of Jamaica. Her only solace rested in her continual ability to complain.

How sad the mem'saab does not understand that her fearful thoughts draw more fear.

"Yes, mem'saab," Yuala whispered. Catching the distant look in her mistress's eyes, Yuala prepared herself for what she knew would be long moments of prattle. Yuala pitied her mistress. Lady Mary had few white friends on the island, save for the "common" wives of the other planters whom she saw only at harvest time and on holidays. Lady Mary's life was not rich and full like Yuala's, who constantly ministered to the sick and those of her race who wished to learn the wisdom to "see" other planes of existence. Lady Mary was lonely, and Yuala knew there was no hope for it.

"Ugh! Sometimes I don't know why I bother trying to teach you heathens anything. There are certain 'ways' things should be done. Proper ways. English ways. Lady Brenna is much younger than her husband, and despite the fact that she has a streak of Scots blood in her, she's a Tudor through and through. God! What I would have given to be able to say that myself in court!" Lady Mary patted her ample skirt, feeling the incredible lush French silk. "Take this gown, for instance. I have no way of knowing what the court fashions are because Henry won't take me back to England. Of course, Lady Brenna has been in England nearly a year, and she'll be wearing the latest rages." Placing the back of her hand against her damp forehead, Lady Mary pulled her hand away and inspected it.

"Merciful Lord! How I hate Jamaica. It's barely dawn and already the heat is too much for me."

"Yes, mem'saab," Yuala replied meekly as was expected of her. She went about her business of rubbing rosemary, olive oil and pungent, finely minced garlic onto thickly cut veal chops. She knew Lady Mary's tiny droplets of anxious perspiration were manifestations of her envious thoughts and had nothing to do with the moderate climate that day.

"Yuala, you *will* see to the kitchens today. Make those addle-brained cooks prepare each meal on time. I want the hot dishes hot and the wines. Oh, Lord! I forgot the wines. Henry will be mortified!" Lady Mary's eyes rolled in her head and her pallid cheeks flushed as she spun herself into a greater state of apoplexy.

Yuala's arm shot out across Lady Mary's path and then just as quickly, she retracted it. This was a method she'd used numerous times with her mistress to quiet and console her without stepping across the line of forbidden social familiarity that slaves never dared cross. "No worry, mem'saab. I see that all is in order."

Having heard bizarre tales of Yuala's strange voodoo powers, Lady Mary had purposefully kept her distance from the increasingly beautiful slave girl. The distance was at odds with Lady Mary's inner need for human caring and attention. At times, she thought Yuala listened to her discourse with deep attentiveness, something she'd wanted from her husband but seldom received.

"Everything?" Lady Mary asked.

"Yes, mem'saab," Yuala gave her consistent and expected response. Then she lifted her face and, looking off to the distance, she said in perfect English, "Go to the front colonnade. Your guests have arrived. They are as anxious as you." Then Yuala dropped her eyes and continued chopping bits of tomato she'd dried in the sun. She kneaded them along with basil and garlic into mounds of risen bread dough.

The hairs on the back of Lady Mary's neck stood on end when Yuala spoke in the low hushed tones of a stranger. She'd been privy to such instances before when Yuala suddenly switched to a commanding English resonance Lady Mary didn't dare question.

"Yes. Yes, I will," Lady Mary replied. Hastily she dashed out of the kitchen and across the red brick pathway that led through the vegetable and herb gardens she'd planted with Yuala's help. She continued past the rows of hybrid English roses she fought so valiantly to sustain. When she succeeded, the plantation house smelled sweetly of roses, that peaceful aroma that took her mind back to the serenity of her youth.

The sound of horses' hooves and carriage wheels on the crushed seashell drive resounded through the open windows like no trumpet blast ever could.

"They're here!" Henry's voice shouted from the top of the stairs as he wiped shaving soap from his clean-shaven face with a linen towel. "Hell's teeth! I cannot believe the day is underway so quickly. William! Where the devil are you, Son?"

"Here," William answered dispassionately. William tried not to show his disdain for his parents and sisters, but the fact was he didn't give a damn about them. However, he was more likely to leave this purgatory his father loved if he continued to support his mother's sentiments for England and the courtly life he desired with every breath in his body. William had even promised himself that upon his maturation, if he had not been to England by that time, he'd swim. Sharks and sea monsters be damned.

Henry glanced at his son. "I think you've grown taller since breakfast," he said, scowling at William's long, slender body that too closely resembled the fops he'd known in Europe. Henry couldn't help secretly wishing his son had taken after his more brawny side of the family rather than Mary's frail royal ancestors.

"You are displeased with my appearance," William jousted boldly and leveled his somber blue eyes on his father.

"Your breeches are too tight, William. See that your mother has them refitted."

"Yes, sir," William replied and walked past him, then took the stairs quickly to escape his father's overwhelming censure.

The carriage and four pulled to a clattering stop.

"Henry! You old devil!" Lord Andrew Duke waved from the open carriage window.

Hopping down from his perch, the driver whisked the door open.

Andrew, a decade younger than Henry's fifty-five years, looked to be another decade younger still. Andrew's blond hair had begun to thin as had Henry's, and their stature was nearly identical. But it was the fire in Andrew's eyes that made his smile radiate and his skin glow.

Andrew clasped his strong arms around Henry, giving him an affectionate bear hug. "God's blood, Henry, you're fit as a fiddle! You haven't changed a hair since you left England. It's grand to see you, brother," Andrew said.

Yuala slipped silently down the main hall to the vestibule. She was joined by several of the housemaids who were as curious as she about the kind of man whom the master admired so vocally.

"Lo, de younger lawd ess bery fine mahn," Ceena, the elderly cook whispered to Yuala.

"Yes." Yuala smiled down at the woman made small with age. Just as Yuala lifted her eyes to the collection of Dukes on the front steps, she felt a chill wind rush across the porch and into the house. The brightly colored cotton-print scarf she wore to cover her hair during meal preparations fluttered lightly against the back of her neck. Humming through the marrow of her bones, her intuition came alive. Her eyes went to the carriage, waiting impatiently for the omen, the catalyst that would alter all their futures. The vision that the shape-changer Barbara, the ghost, had foretold.

Lady Brenna appeared in the doorway holding Henry's four-month-old namesake.

Yuala gasped as she looked into the expectant, intelligent silver blue eyes heavily veiled with fear. She watched as the beautiful Brenna's arms clutched her child closer to her chest. "She has a secret," Yuala said to Ceena.

"What kind of secret?"

Yuala felt her own mind link with Brenna's much in the same way that Yuala could read Lord Henry's thoughts without looking at his face. "She's afraid of dying. But she's not sick. Can't you see it, Ceena? Death. I see death around her and her child."

Ceena only had eyes for Lady Brenna's magnificent ensemble.

"Brenna, how well you look after such a long, tedious voyage," Mary said, rushing toward the coach.

"Thank you, Lady Mary." Brenna's melodious voice wafted atop the tropical breeze.

Andrew helped his wife out of the carriage. He took his cooing son from Brenna's arms and held him up proudly. "He's a scrapper, Henry. Strong as an ox."

Henry took the strawberry-blond baby and beamed at him. Baby Ambrose slapped his uncle square on the nose.

Andrew burst into laugher. "I told you!"

"And you're right! He's an adventurer just like you and me! A Duke through and through!"

Lady Mary signaled for Yuala who responded immediately. "Yuala will help with the child and unpack your things."

"Thank you again, Lady Mary," Brenna said sweetly, her eyes sweeping suspiciously across Yuala's beautiful face. "But I don't allow savages with my child. My nanny is following with the baggage in the next carriage."

Mary stiffened. "Unfortunately, Lord Henry has never felt it necessary for me to import a proper English nanny or tutors for the children."

"I don't know how you could stand it, Lady Mary. Living in Canton and traveling through China and Tibet as Andrew loves to do, I learned that life is cheap to the savages."

Lady Mary took Lady Brenna's arm. "I couldn't agree with you more. Frankly, my dear, I don't know how you've managed in the Orient so long. I can't wait to hear about it."

"Daily, I pray we will live through the experience. It's harrowing."

Lady Mary's ears piqued. She was used to dull routine. Inconvenience. Loneliness. But *harrowing*. What kind of life was Andrew providing for his family for the sake of money?

"Come, let's get out of the sun," Lady Mary, said ushering them inside.

The housemaids came pattering down the brick steps with bare feet, easily crossing the sharp-shelled gravel, and took tapestry bags and leather trunks from the open cart sent from the ship. Lady Brenna's nanny, Molly Smythe, alighted the cart, took baby Ambrose from Lord Henry's arms and disappeared efficiently inside the manor house.

* * * *

Henry and Andrew sat in white rockers on the colonnaded front porch, sipping tall lemon-flavored drinks. Neither of them noticed William crouching below them in thickly planted red and yellow crotons. William intended to learn all he could about his father's newest fancy, Ambrose Duke.

Yuala saw William spying on his father as she refilled Lord Henry's glass. *This is not good for you, William. You will not like what you hear. Please leave before it's too late.*

But William stayed.

Yuala hovered just inside the French doors, hidden by the white cotton curtains. Not once did she believe that what she would hear would affect her as much as William.

"This is truly paradise, Henry."

"I couldn't agree more. I only wish Mary thought so. It must be wonderful to have a wife who's interested in the same things you are."

Andrew's thick blond eyebrows knitted. "Brenna loves me, Henry, and I her. I would do anything for her. I do everything I can to waylay her misgivings about living in Canton. But if Brenna really pressed it, I would leave."

"Come now, man. You make a bloody fortune over there."

"There's tedium to it as well, Brother. But on days when I ride my Arabian among the foothills of the Tibetan mountains searching for jade and sculptures or, even better, an ancient relic, I know I've made the right choice for myself. And for my son," he said. "The East India Company is a greater power in China than the British government, Henry. Mind-boggling is the word for it. But I never thought it would be so hard. So . . . dangerous," he said, looking to the distance. Remembering himself, his eyes shot back to Henry's confused face. "By God, I fully intend for my son to inherit not only my wealth, but my business connections," Andrew said with forced bravado.

"Dangerous? What are you talking about?"

Andrew snorted. "If you think China is a placid land like this, Henry, you're a fool. There's not a day that goes by that I'm not threatened by one of the mandarins. They call *us* the barbarians! Can you imagine? They hate us. Hate our power . . . the East India Company, I mean. They've tried to run me out for years. I've shelled out more pounds in bribes than I've accumulated for myself. And it's never enough. I can't tell you the things I've done to make enough money to buy back our family's land in England."

"What . . . kind of things?"

Andrew lowered his eyes and raised his glass. "Don't ask questions you don't want the answers to, Henry."

The hairs on the back of Henry's neck stood on end. "There's a reason for this visit isn't there, Andrew?"

"Henry, you should know by now, I have a reason for everything I do," Andrew said icily.

"Go on."

"I want to ask if I could leave Brenna and the baby here for six months or so. Just until I get back to Canton and straighten out a few things."

"I don't understand. Why didn't she stay in England? Mary would give anything to be back there. . . ."

"You are a fool, Henry!" Andrew laughed. "Brenna is the most beautiful woman I've ever seen. I saw your face when you met her. You were taken with her. So was your son."

"Andrew, I would never—"

"That's not what I'm saying. You appreciate beauty. So do I. So does any man with blood in his veins. My trips to China last years, Henry. Not months. Brenna would get lonely. It wouldn't take much for a younger man to steal her from me. But here, she would be safe. Jamaica is so remote they wouldn't find us here."

Cold chills covered Henry's back. "They?"

Andrew exhaled deeply, an air of defeat about him. "All right. I guess I'd better come clean. The Su family. It doesn't matter which one. They're all savages. Probably like your slaves."

Henry shook his head. "My slaves are not savages. They're. . . ." He looked out over the hills of cane wafting in the breeze. "They're childlike, really. I take care of them. Some are even like family. I have no overseer here. I do that. It doesn't take a large plantation to make money here, so I don't need all that many. But, Andrew, I'm not in danger from them. In fact, I feel as if I'm their protector."

Andrew searched his brother's face. "You always were a dreamer, Henry. You should have been a poet. You've always thought man could build heaven on earth."

"Yes, Utopia."

Andrew raked his hair. "Well, you succeeded. I, on the other hand, live in hell."

"Then get out," Henry said pragmatically.

"I tried. But somehow one of the Su family followed me to England. They broke into our house. They didn't take anything. That wasn't the point. They wanted me to know that they could come any time, day or night, and kill me. I kept it from Brenna as long as I could. Then one morning she found a dead nightingale in the baby's crib."

"My God, Andrew! What did you do to this Su family?"

"Sold them opium. It flows through China like a river from India. I knew that if I were caught, the Chinese would execute the trader on the spot. But the profits are enormous. I intended to trade only once. That's all it took. I made one transaction to the Su family. Nan-Kang, that was his name."

"And for that they want to kill you?"

"Nan-Kang killed himself, his wife and son during an opium dream. The rest of the Su family have vowed vengeance on me ever since."

"That's why you didn't put a departure date or arrival date in your letter?"

"Precisely. The Su had followed me around the world as it was. I have to protect my son, Henry. I need you to help me."

"Of course, I'll do everything I can. But, Andrew, what can you accomplish by going back?"

Andrew's blue eyes narrowed to chilling slits. "Finish what I started."

Henry grabbed his arm. "Don't do this, Andrew. Killing won't end anything for anyone. It never does. Such deeds live on past us."

"Henry, don't give me platitudes when I'm fighting for my life."

Just as Henry was about to reply, they heard a blood-curdling scream from the bedroom above.

"Brenna!" Andrew dropped his glass and it shattered on the porch floor. He raced inside the house with Henry fast on his heels.

Together they bounded up the stairs.

"Brenna!" Andrew rushed into the bedroom.

Henry saw two maids wide-eyed with fear holding each other in the corner. Tapestry bags were opened and clothes stacked across the bed. Everything looked normal.

Brenna rushed into Andrew's arms. "They know!" she sobbed and hid her face in her husband's shoulder.

"Lady Brenna, tell me what's wrong," Henry said.

Riddled with fear, Brenna couldn't speak, she only pointed to the stacks of lacy white cotton infant gowns. There on the top of the heap lay a dead bird.

"Nightingale?" Henry asked Andrew.

Andrew nodded solemnly. "I fear I've brought hell to your Utopia, Henry."

four

Like our shadows
Our wishes lengthen as our sun declines.

—EDWARD YOUNG
"LOVE OF FAME"

"Did you see it, Yuala?" Charlotte asked as Yuala placed hot curling irons in her mistress's blond hair.

Yuala pretended ignorance though she knew exactly what Charlotte was thinking. She wasn't mind reading this time; the younger girl was transparent. "See what?"

"The dead bird, silly. Father wouldn't let any of us in the room. Mother said it was disgusting and just like the heathens to try to frighten Lady Brenna. Is that what heathens do, Yuala?"

"Only those who are afraid themselves must inflict fear," she answered.

Just as Yuala spoke, Henry passed by Charlotte's door on his way down to dinner. The door was only half-closed and so he could not help but listen. For the most part Henry seldom paid attention to his young daughters' prattle. Tonight was different. Everything about the house seemed unusual to him.

At first, he blamed the feeling on Andrew's presence. Then he thought it was because Andrew had revealed wicked truths about himself. Henry no longer idolized his younger brother. Instead, he pitied him.

The tone of Yuala's voice stopped Henry in his tracks as much as the words she spoke. In all the sixteen years he'd known her, owned her, he'd only heard monosyllables and mumbled responses to orders.

He crept closer to the door and watched Yuala coif his daughter's hair.

"William said that Lord Andrew hates the Chinese as much as he hates the slaves."

"That is sad for William. Thoughts are things. Emotions are things. Hate always comes back to the one who sends it out."

"How do you know that?"

"I watch humans."

Charlotte pondered Yuala's words but did not understand them. "William said that Father dressed Andrew down for his prejudices."

"My master is a wise man," Yuala said, pulling a brush through Charlotte's hair.

Henry had heard all he needed. He pushed the door open slowly and entered the room. Yuala did not turn or acknowledge him. She had sensed his presence at the door.

"Father!" Charlotte squealed, pulling her ruffled duster around her shoulders. "You didn't knock. You always knock," she said with more curiosity than reprimand.

Henry nodded but did not take his eyes off Yuala. "And if I had, you would have stopped your conversation and that would have been a pity. I had no idea your thoughts ran so deep. I've been remiss in not taking the time to explore more worldly subjects with you," he said still staring at Yuala.

Charlotte watched his reflection in her vanity mirror. "I thought you saved them for William. That's what he's always told me."

Henry clasped his hands behind his back, still observing Yuala style Charlotte's hair. "You're quite an artist with my daughter's coiffure," he said. "What else is it you can do, Yuala?"

"Oh, she can do anything, Father. Yuala is a priestess, you know."

Yuala's hands froze. She held her breath.

"Is this so?" Henry asked.

"My people need tending in mind, spirit and body. I've been trained to care for them."

"By whom?"

Yuala felt trapped. If she answered truthfully, he would never understand. How does one explain a thousand lifetimes of knowing in a single word or sentence? If she didn't answer, he would keep pressing her. Perhaps that was where she was destined to go. "What is it you want from me, Master?"

"Yuala, I have paid to have the best tutors in Jamaica to teach my children and those among your people to read, write and cipher. I believe education is the only path to a better world. And you're saying you have not availed yourself of my generosity?"

"I know some things. I spent time learning your speech patterns, but I was too busy learning about healing people. Herbs. Medicines. My reading is lacking."

"Then I order you to take lessons when the tutors come back next month."

"You are most generous, Master."

"Fine. Now answer my question. How do you know such things if you didn't read about them from my library books?"

Yuala hesitated.

"Don't stammer about it. A simple answer will do."

For the first time in her life, Yuala raised her eyes to look directly into her master's face. She did not mean to defy him, only to meet him as an equal. But even she wasn't prepared for the electricity that shot between them. It raced through her like lightning. Never in her life had she felt this connected to another, as if she had found a missing part of herself. Her fingers itched to touch him, but she dared not.

It seemed like an eternity before her thoughts assembled into words. "Simple answers I have, but you would not understand them."

Henry sucked in his breath. He felt as if he'd been hit with an anvil. He wasn't certain what it was exactly that caused his blood to freeze. Yuala's beauty. The power in her strong cheekbones. The silvery gleam of under-standing, caring and warmth in her dark eyes. He had the feeling of being the student coming to the master. He was responding to her sexually like no other woman he'd met. Yet, the connection he felt with her was mental and something more. Something from his soul began to sing. He felt as if he were standing on the precipice of time and that nothing in the future would resemble the past. His mouth was dry. He licked his lips but failed to wet them. "Try me," he stammered.

"Ghosts."

"Pardon me?"

"I've been taught the truths of the universe from ghosts from the past. Ghosts from the future. They are one and the same, really."

Henry had to shake his head to clear the cobwebs his servant had clearly put there by some kind of spell. "Have you heard this before, Charlotte?"

"Why, no, Father."

"Good."

Yuala stood her ground. "Are you prejudiced against me now, Master?"

"You know I don't believe in prejudice, Yuala. How many times have you heard me say that as long as one human being holds prejudice in his heart we are all slaves?"

"Often, Master," she replied. "But those words deal with the earth. My work is with all the worlds."

He leaned forward. "Is that what your voodoo is about?"

She shook her head. "No. It's what unconditional love is about. All God's creatures big and small." Yuala put down the brush. "I'm finished here. May I go?"

"No. Yes, I mean, of course." He stood aside reluctantly. Yuala left the room leaving the door open behind her.

Henry watched her leave, watched the grace of her movements and the silent pad of her bare feet across the Aubusson carpet and onto the wood floor. He noticed she smelled of vanilla and not rose like Mary.

"Father, if you'll excuse me, I need to dress for supper."

Startled out of his reverie he said, "Yes. Yes. I'm sorry, Charlotte. I'll see you downstairs." He bent and kissed the top of her head.

He shut the bedroom door behind him and did not notice Charlotte's stunned look.

Father has never kissed me with that much affection in his life. I wonder what's come over him.

The next day Henry was as electrified as he'd been in that moment when Yuala looked at him. He had not slept all night. He went riding instead of sharing breakfast with his family. He had to be alone to think, he told himself. The coming rainstorm forced him to return before he'd managed to come to grips with the powerful attraction he felt for Yuala.

When he galloped into the drive he noticed Yuala as she tended the bougainvillea in the front garden, her hair wrapped in a white turban. She wore a gauzy white cotton tunic that she'd wrapped in the African fashion around her body and over her shoulders. Her movements were graceful as she bent and clipped dead foliage from the low-growing plants, and then like a ballerina she reached up on tiptoes to pluck a fuchsia-colored blossom from a long vine growing up the garden wall.

Henry thought she looked like an exotic goddess from one of his long-ago dreams of the Ivory Coast. "Is she real?" He rubbed his eyes to clear them. "How could her beauty have escaped me all this time?"

Yuala plucked a second blossom and dropped it in the woven basket at her feet.

Henry frowned at his inability to discern between reality and fantasy. He wished with all his strength he could stop his long legs from closing the distance between them. It was as if she were a magnet pulling him to her. He wanted to turn away, but couldn't.

"Yuala!" He boomed as he marched over to her.

She paused, unbent herself at the waist, but did not turn. She kept her eyes straight ahead on the flowers, but not on the ground as she'd been taught. She knew what was about to happen.

Today is the beginning of my destiny.

She was ready.

"Why aren't you wearing the new black uniforms that arrived from Liverpool? Why are you not following my orders?" Wanting to touch her, he clasped his hands behind his back so they would not betray him.

"The black is too hot and smells of strange dyes," she said. "I found it unpleasant."

Henry's jaw dropped in outrage. "Insolence? From you, Yuala?"

Slowly, Yuala turned and faced him. She lifted her eyes to meet his and just like the night before, they both felt an awesome power shoot between them.

"Yuala," he said breathlessly as a humid breeze slapped the cotton gauze against Yuala's young, lithe body outlining her full breasts, tiny waist and narrow hips. Elongated thighs strained against the tight wrapping and tapered to her shapely knees. She was barefoot save for leather thongs she'd laced around her feet and decorated with brightly colored feathers. Henry could see the outline of her dark nipples as clearly as if she'd been nude.

He held his breath and felt his body responding.

"My Lord," she said as if she was his equal. His paramour.

Brilliant silver lights shimmered in her jet-black eyes like starshine. Her sensuous mouth turned up in a faint, kindly smile, only allowing him to guess at the full power of its beauty. Juxtaposed against the brilliant red and yellow hibiscus and fuchsia bougainvillea, she looked like a young queen from ancient Babylon.

He moved closer, staring at her lips. "We shouldn't be looking at each other like this."

"I know what is in your heart, my Lord. I can read your mind. You wanted to touch me last night." She lifted her hand. "Here. Touch me."

Henry's graying blond hair blew in the wind. He heard the fisherman in the cay talking about the tropical storm that was heading toward Jamaica. The palm fronds banged at each other as the wind grew more intense and raced through the foliage. The long, sinewy arms of bougainvillea waved at Henry. Yuala stood before him, her body like a young willow, bending to the wind, swaying slightly now and then.

Henry reminded himself that she was a slave, yet she was as poised as a queen. She regarded him as her equal, or perhaps not quite her equal. He saw no evidence of fear that normally roots one to the ground; instead she seemed to defy gravity, as if she were lifted from the earth and its concerns. How could he have owned her all these years and never seen this side of her?

"That's not all I want," he said.

"I know," she said, placing his hand over her breast. "You want my body, my Lord. But I want your love. You've never given it to anyone, and I must know that I have it."

His fingers pressed into her soft flesh. "I could love you. I feel it inside me."

"We are all meant to give love, my Lord. If we fail, we die."

Henry forced himself to tear his eyes from her breast and peer into her eyes. The shock of the love he saw there filled him with the courage he needed to break through the last of his misgivings. The last of his prejudices.

He pressed his mouth over hers and found paradise. His hands shook as he pulled her into him. He felt his erection strain against his camel-colored breeches. His flesh was hot and sweat-streaked already. What kind of power did this child have over him?

His every muscle tensed. His nerves ignited with desire, forcing his erection to become harder. Harder still.

He could feel her body beating out sexual signals like a tribal drum. He felt the wind, sun and rain rushing over and around them. It was as if she had commanded all the powers of the earth and sky to force this union.

Yuala felt herself become moist between her legs and so she parted them ever so slightly. She dropped her eyes and stared at Henry's enormous erection. The spreading of her legs caused a raging fever in Henry's blood that she felt without even touching him.

All of this was planned. She could feel the life force between them. All the facets of nature were spurring them on, moving heaven and earth toward the culmination of their union.

The wind grew heavier as the rains neared the shore. The shutters on the house banged back and forth until a servant within the house secured them with a bolt.

Lightning shot through the sky, jolted the earth and sent shock waves under the earth and then up through their bodies, heightening the intensity of their desires.

Yuala continued to gaze into Henry's green eyes, nearly mesmerizing herself. "Love me, my Lord." She felt her own tears mingle with the rain. "I know God put me on earth to make love with you this day, and you will give me a daughter. But I ask you, plead with you, to give me your love, I need it so desperately."

"Oh, my God, Yuala," he said huskily, clutching her to his chest. "I swear to you, I've never heard those words from a single human being. I never knew I needed to hear them until now."

"My Lord," she replied, gazing into his eyes as he held her face in his hands. "Our child will have your eyes. In your eyes, I can see the generations that go back to the kings of England. I, too, am descended from kings, African kings. Royal blood will flow in her veins. The rest of her will be a blend of the best of us. You and me, but one heart. One soul."

The whirl of their histories created a vortex in Yuala's mind, destroying the last of her thoughts, allowing desire full command.

Henry took her mouth again. Never had he experienced a woman so pliant, so willing to mold herself, spirit and body, to his wishes and needs.

He wanted to squelch this desire, stamp out this heat, but her velvety tongue caressed him lovingly in a way he had never been touched before. Less than half a minute, a hairsbreadth span of time, had elapsed, and Yuala had become master and Henry the slave.

"What have you done to me, Yuala?" His words caught in his sharp intake of breath.

"Only God has the answer," Yuala said and placed her hand on his cheek, forcing him to take her mouth again.

Without taking his mouth from hers, Henry tore at the gauze tunic that separated Yuala's body from his touch. He pulled at it and stripped it from her shoulders, bared her breasts, then her belly, her sex, and finally it fell in a clump at her feet. Just as the diaphanous fabric hit the ground, the tropical storm moved over them and pelted the earth with torrents of rain.

The rain stung his skin as Henry yanked off his waistcoat, white linen shirt and breeches. They stood naked in the garden, hidden from the house by the flapping arms of palms, bougainvillea and stalks of hibiscus. Rainsoaked, their skin slid against each other, lubricating every inch, every hollow.

Yuala's mind screamed for penetration, for the climax to her destiny, but her heart wanted more. Yuala wanted Henry's love.

Henry filled his hands with Yuala's full breasts. He slid his hands over her back, ribs, hips, thighs and calves, thinking her skin as smooth as marble. Yet it was too hot for stone. Even with the cooling rains beating at them, Yuala's skin emanted warmth, pulsating from the rapid beating of her heart. She caressed him gently, expertly, as if he were a treasure. She cupped his testicles in her hands and kneaded them. Henry trembled as Yuala took his mouth with hers. This time her tongue was the aggressor.

Shaking and weak he sank to his knees like a penitent man before his god. He wanted to beg for mercy, but he was too selfish.

Pressing her hands into his shoulders she forced him onto the ground and straddled him. Plunging him as deeply inside her as she could, she controlled the breaking of her own maidenhead. The pain shot through her like an arrow, but as Henry's mouth clamped down on her breast she felt desire wash over her in unison with the pelting rain. Yuala only knew that she wanted more of him.

She danced on his penis, gyrating her hips and thighs in circular motions.

An animal groan filled with desire escaped his lips, and Yuala knew he was about to deposit his seed inside her.

Suddenly, she leapt away from him, leaving him stunned.

"What are you doing?" he asked breathlessly, with huge, shocked green eyes.

"This is your land, not mine. I will not conceive my child here. We must go to the holy place."

Henry's mind was befuddled with desire and so much passion that he didn't comprehend the implication of her words. All he saw was a radiance that sprang from her smile, mingled with the rain and seemed to ignite in the air. He would have followed her into hell if she'd only asked. "Show me," he said willingly.

Yuala picked up their clothes. "Follow me."

Naked, she raced through the rain to the edge of his cleared lawns, past the rows of slave quarters, further behind to her thatched hut and further still to the edge of the rainforest.

Henry gave no thought to anyone watching them from the house, to the whereabouts of his children or the slaves. Nearly blinded by the rain, Henry's desire for Yuala had destroyed all his logic and rational thought processes. He told himself that after he satiated himself with her, he would be done with her and his mind would return. But his heart knew differently. He couldn't leave her. Not today. Not ever. He believed her when she told him they were to share a destiny. Share a child. He was not afraid.

They crashed through the banana fronds to the glen near the lagoon. Here, the pelting rains were dissipated by the thick canopy of greenery over-head. The waterfall splashed over the rocks, singing its eternal melody. Yuala smiled at the familiar sound and drew strength from it. She closed her eyes and imagined the golden rays of the sun whirling about them, cocoon-ing them in warmth. When she opened her eyes, she looked at Henry and realized that he could see the golden circle, too.

"It is a holy place," he said in an awestricken whisper.

"I was born here. I have saved this place for you and I to become lovers."

"Our mating was preordained."

"Yes, my Lord."

"It's not voodoo or witchcraft?"

"No, my Lord."

As he looked into her eyes now, Henry realized that they were slightly almond-shaped, revealing a trace of Egyptian blood that must have had its origins near the beginning of time. Fleetingly, he thought of Marc Antony being captivated by Cleopatra. But Yuala was more than an earthly goddess; she glowed in a way Henry could not describe, though "angelic" came to mind.

"Lie here," she commanded, with a voice filled with desire and potent sexuality.

Henry sank to the soft ferns and grasses, thinking that after so much exertion coupled with his age he would never become hard again. Barely had he thought this, when Yuala bent over him and took him in her mouth. She used her tongue to massage every inch of his manhood. Henry cried out in delicious agony.

Again, Yuala sat on top of him, gyrating again with a rhythm he guessed was some ancient mystical African instinct, because Yuala had been a virgin until fifteen minutes before.

Her dark hair pranced across his chest as she flung her head forward and then back like a lion would throw his mane. She splayed her fingers across his chest, holding them over his heart protectively. "I will always care for you, my Lord."

Henry raised his hips to penetrate her further. Again and again, he pressed himself into her. She could read his mind as easily as she could predict the future, heal the sick or mend a broken heart. Henry was hers.

Just as Henry was about to explode within her, she saw his eyes open in wonder; shining ribbons of blue- and peach-colored light emanated from their depths. Yuala knew by this sign he had given her his heart. But what surprised her the most was that she also saw the same colored lights spill from her own eyes, mingle with his and circle them both.

"I love you," he said.

"And I you, my Lord," she whispered to him and to the universe as she climaxed.

Henry exploded with a groan of sexual pleasure.

Yuala sighed. "I have my child. Her name will be Rachel."

* * * *

Yuala was right. Henry became obsessed with her, and each day he loved her more. He cared nothing about anything in his life except Yuala and the child they had conceived.

"You have made me happy for the first time in my life," he said holding her on a Sunday afternoon in the glen. "I wonder what my life would have been like had I known you first."

Yuala shook her head, her long spiral curls dancing about her face. "It was meant to happen as it did."

"But all I've done is amass riches and build this plantation as a legacy for my children. A long time ago, I dreamed about a love like this, but I didn't think it would ever come to me."

"Your accomplishments will be important for your children. Our child's destiny will be different, but important all the same," she assured him as she sprinkled tiny kisses on his bare chest.

"How can that be?"

Yuala's eyes grew dark and pensive. "You have little illumination in your life, Henry. I see that I must change that."

Henry propped himself up on his elbows, crushing a wild orchid beneath him. "I studied at Oxford. . . ."

Yuala put her finger over his lips. "That is not what I mean. I will teach you what I know and you will teach me what you learned at Oxford. These things I must teach our child."

He kissed her cheek. "You are a more willing pupil than I."

"Learning to read and cipher are simple. My lessons will be difficult for you because the white man sees only with his eyes."

"Ha! And you don't?" He pulled her playfully to him. Henry looked deep into her eyes and followed the silver lights to the edge of her soul. The light was blinding, almost painfully so. Here was purity and goodness carefully harvested and poised, ready to feed all who were drawn to it.

He could see every color of the spectrum dancing and spinning about each other, creating a power he knew could defy gravity, raise mountains, cure diseases and conquer evil. Henry was overwhelmed with the love he found there.

"I do have so very much to learn," he said.

* * * *

"How could he do this to me? A slave for a mistress! It's a blasphemy against God!" Mary rammed her fist into her palm.

Andrew was aghast as he watched Mary pace the room. "I wouldn't believe it if I hadn't seen him with her myself. I'm afraid, Mary, this forces me to take Brenna and the baby away from here."

Mary's mind ached, it was so filled with condemnation and anger. "Brenna. Does she know?"

"I haven't told her, and I don't want her to know what my own brother . . . that he could . . ."

Mary put up her hand. "Don't say it. I don't think I can stand any more."

"How will you keep it from the children?"

"Believe me, Andrew, there are days when I wish they knew. They would hate him more than I."

Andrew recoiled from Mary, though he'd chosen to take her side. "I've booked passage on the Friday morning ship. I've told Brenna we're leaving, and frankly she's confused. One day I was telling her I would never again subject her to the dangers in China, and the next we set sail."

Mary stopped at the window and pulled back the curtain. She could see Henry walking toward the house. Not far beyond she saw Yuala standing in the garden. Yuala looked up at her and their eyes met. Instantly, she dropped the lace. "You'll have to tell her the truth. Otherwise, she won't leave. I don't want her here to witness this. It's one thing to hear it. It's another to watch it. Yuala has Henry completely under her spell."

"Gads, this is revolting," Andrew replied sanctimoniously. Mary turned to face him. "Don't worry, Andrew, I'll make certain Henry meets his retribution."

"I'd better see to our packing," he said, pulling on his collar as if the room had become uncomfortable.

* * * *

Mary's heart was dying. She never realized how much emotion she'd withheld from Henry and now that it had come spewing forth, she was shocked at the intensity of the eruption. Her love had turned to hate.

The morning after Andrew and Brenna left Jamaica, Mary learned from the servants that Yuala held pagan rituals in a glen not far from the slave quarters. She bribed Henry's boot boy to inform the master of the ritual that was planned for that night.

"Once he knows Yuala is taking part in blood sacrifices and fertility rites, then he will stop this affair and come back to his family," she said aloud to her reflection in the mirror.

Henry sat on the long, damask-covered bench at the end of his bed. He stuck his sandy boot up in the air and waited for the boot boy to turn his back on him and yank off his boot. Henry placed his stockinged left foot on the boy's back and pushed.

The boy stumbled, fell down and then looked up at Henry.

An anger born of racism gave him the courage to carry out his mistress's bidding. "Tonight, Yuala make magic at the waterfall."

"What? What is that you're saying, boy?"

"Yuala calls the demons. Ya, mahn. She make spells. She bad one."

"Lies! Who told you to tell me these things?" Henry grabbed the boy by his voluminous white shirt sleeves.

"It's da truth!"

Henry's mind raced. Yuala told him how special the waterfall clearing was to her. This was where she was born and their child conceived. This was their love place. Not a harbor for devils and black magic. "I don't believe it! I know Yuala. There is nothing evil about her!"

Henry shot to his feet. For years there had been faint whispers of stories about Yuala and voodoo, but even self-righteous Mary had never been able to prove the rumors were true, though she'd tried.

Henry stalked out of the room. Perhaps Mary didn't know enough about Yuala and her ways to know how to go about finding the truth.

Henry burst into Mary's room, looking for Yuala. "Where is your maid?"

Mary's smile was victorious. She knew the boot boy had done his job well. "She's down the hall, getting my linens. Why?"

Henry didn't answer, but marched down the Persian-carpeted hall. He flung open the door to the eleven-foot-long linen room where Yuala stood lifting a stack of expensive Belgian towels off the shelf. She tilted her head toward him. When she did, the morning sunlight shot through the round stained-glass window behind her, casting a green-and-blue aura around her, bathing her in light like an Arabian princess at morning prayers in a mosque. Her face lit up when she saw him, and her intake of her breath caused her breasts to rise and taunt him in his anger.

"My love," she breathed with all the love her heart could hold.

Henry melted. He had never met anyone who could harness his emotions and bend them to her will the way that Yuala did. At that moment, he was afraid that what was said about her was true. She was a witch and the magic she practiced was on him.

"You are angry because you have heard of the ceremony tonight."

He was stunned. "How could you know that?"

She laughed lightly, a sprite's kind of tinkling chuckle that came from a happy soul. "I hear this, Henry, in here," she touched her temple, "and in here," she touched her heart.

Henry looked at her hand, curving over the swell of her breast. He held out his hand and walked toward her.

"Yes, Henry, come feel the words in my heart." She smiled and cupped her breast in her hand, offering it to him like benediction.

He sank to his knees and buried his face in her belly. "God, I fear I am possessed by you."

Her face went dark. "Never say this! I am not a demon. I am flesh and blood, and I carry our child!" She clamped her hands on either side of his face and forced him to look at her. "For you to be possessed, my spirit would have to be inside you. I am here, Henry. Here to love you."

"And I love you."

She placed her lips on the top of his head, and he wondered if she were again reading his mind.

five

The actual race of man is not the first, for there was a previous one, all the members of which perished. We belong to a second race, descended from Deucalion. As to the former men, they are said to have been full of insolence and pride, committing many crimes. . . . They were punished by an immense disaster. All of a sudden enormous volumes of water issued from the earth.

—"ON THE SYRIAN GODDESS"
AS NARRATED IN THE ANCIENT SANCTUARY OF HIEROPOLIS OF ARAMEA

Rachel was born October 22, 1781, and from her first breath, she was very ill. High fevers, distended belly and hard stools like burnt-out coals promised the tiny golden-haired baby would not live long.

"The doctor from Montego Bay says she can't possibly live another two weeks," Henry said morosely.

"I'm not afraid, my love. I will cure our child by driving out the demons who have wrongly sought to weaken my powers by taking over our child."

"Yuala, please. Maybe my doctor isn't as knowledgeable as he should be. Let me take her to the hospital in San Juan. If I leave today . . ." Henry was desperate to save his tiny daughter.

Yuala placed her hand on Henry's cheek. "She will be fine. It is not her destiny to die."

The water shooting over the rocky fall was nearly transparent. A full silver moon hung above a tall palm tree, casting a brilliant light on the flower-bedecked glen below. There were no shadows this night. No places for fear to hide. Thick three-inch-wide beeswax candles were lighted and formed a ring around Yuala and her two-month-old baby, Rachel.

Yuala showed Henry where to hide behind the japonica and crotons. "It is important none of my followers see you. You are not a *houngan*," she said, meaning a male member of the cult. "But I am the Mambo, the female healer, priest and counselor who will perform the ceremony."

"Very well," Henry acquiesced.

Yuala brought Rachel into the circle of light and began praying ancient African prayers Henry did not understand.

She wore necklaces of shells and a tightly tied white turban. A long, snowy white dress with white embroidery hung loosely on her body and its billowy sleeves reminded him of a Catholic priest's vestments. The rest of the cult surrounded the circle and sat outside the light.

Yuala lifted Rachel to the moon, and the baby screamed. She continued wailing and screaming, piercing the silent night with such pain and anguish that Henry was nearly ready to believe the child *was* possessed.

Yuala stripped Rachel of her clothes, and again, Henry saw the horridly distended belly. Rachel's cheeks were inflamed with fever. On each intake of breath the baby stopped screaming, opened her glassy green eyes, sucked in another lung full of air and then began wailing again.

Fascinated, he watched as Yuala led her "congregation" in a hauntingly lovely African song. She laid Rachel on the straw mat and then placed her hands on Rachel's belly.

Yuala silently said a prayer and then began her chant aloud. "Lord, Lord," she boomed to the night sky and glittering stars above. "Save this child from hell, Lord Jesus Christ, mightiest of all the gods that roam the earth and sky. Save this child! Take the heat from her body, heart and soul. Save this child and let her walk among the palms."

As Yuala prayed, her head bobbed back and forth on her shoulders as if disconnected. Her voice grew louder and louder. Henry had never seen her like this; she'd always spoken in soft, melodious tones to him. But this was nearly the voice of a man. This voice had power.

Henry noticed that the continual nodding of Yuala's head had forced her turban undone. It fell in a shimmering white cascade to the ground, and then her hair—the wild, curly waterfall of dark silken hair that he adored—fell down her back and nearly covered Rachel. As the ends of her hair touched Rachel, Henry saw the distended belly begin to deflate.

"God in heaven!" he said a bit too loudly. He suddenly remembered himself and ducked below the japonica bush. He blinked his eyes and then rubbed them to be sure he wasn't seeing things.

Yuala continued praying, her eyes shut, her face toward the heavens. Her hands laid gingerly upon her baby.

"The angels and saints of the Lord have come to save this child from evil!" Yuala cried, still keeping her eyes on heaven.

Henry's eyes swooped back to Rachel. "This is a miracle."

Rachel abruptly stopped crying and her breathing returned to normal. The flame in her cheeks was gone; the green eyes were cool.

Yuala came into the circle of light. She unfastened a hook at her shoulder and peeled off her bodice to reveal a milk-filled breast. Rachel suckled voraciously as the cult silently turned and left her in peace.

Henry was dumbfounded. He waited until everyone was gone. With tears in his eyes, he walked up to Yuala and Rachel and embraced them both.

* * * *

For five years, Henry lived in a dream world filled with love, goodness and the magical healing that Yuala performed on the ailing members of her cult. He never questioned her pots, brews or prayers. They healed because she believed they would heal and so did her patients. Because he allowed Yuala to perform her ministrations as she saw fit, his plantation had the lowest tallies when the tropical and swamp fevers swarmed over the island like invisible locust clouds.

During this time, Henry built a stone house for Yuala and Rachel and furnished it as resplendently as he had his mansion.

He took nothing from the manor house, instead ordering new tables, chairs and beds. Once Mary had discovered Henry's affair, she banished Yuala from the house. Mary told Henry she never wanted to see him except for propriety's sake when visitors came to call.

In essence, Henry lived with Yuala, slept with her and ate with her. Once a week, Henry arranged visits with his children, though only Charlotte bothered to come. William and Sarah had sided with Mary. As far as they were concerned, their father had been corrupted by the devil. They prayed for his salvation every night.

Henry looked back on his life with Mary and the world he built as if it had happened to a stranger. Never had he been at such peace as he was with Yuala. Never had he been as mentally and spiritually challenged.

"Now that you have all these shelves, you can put your potions next to my books."

Yuala handed him one of her ivory statues of St. Anne. "Now I shall be able to see Jesus and Mary wherever I go in this room."

Henry kissed her cheek. "You have the oddest mixture of truths running through your brain, Yuala. But who am I to question your simple logic and profound wisdom?"

But of all the things Henry gave Yuala and Rachel, the ability to read and write English was the most valuable. Just as Yuala had promised him, learning for her was easy.

She read Rousseau's *The Social Contract* and learned about new scientists and archeologists who uncovered ruins at Pompeii and Herculaneum. She learned that the colonies in America had fought a war to set men free and heralded the fact that "all men were created equal," though she wondered how they justified the ownership of slaves.

Yuala read daily and became more confused than the day before about the world she lived in. She found comfort in knowing that men all over the world, no matter their penchant for scientific facts or quests for knowledge beneath the earth, were learning what she had always known. . . . Man was a tiny thing in the cosmos. He was only what God intended he be, simply his breath, a small but equally awesome and unique entity.

* * * *

When Rachel was three, Henry began teaching her to read.

"I want you to speak pure English, Rachel, and not this 'Island Carib' that the slaves speak."

It bothers me to no end to hear that garbled mess of Mayan, Tupe-Guarani, and that horrid bastardization of Spanish, French and English.

"Rachel, child, you have a brilliant mind. It is my wish that you communicate that fact to others all your life."

"Very well, Papa. I shall do as you say." But, too often, Rachel slipped into the dialect of her playmates on the plantation.

Rachel was a dutiful daughter and extremely intelligent, Henry found. In fact, of all his children, Rachel was the smartest. Henry watched as Rachel learned Yuala's unwritten formulas and special healing potions and salves as if they were second nature to her.

One day when Rachel was five, Henry stood in the doorway to the stone house with the sun at his back.

Rachel was working away at the large wooden trestle table in the back of the house, which Yuala called her "creating space."

"What are you making, Rachel?" He asked simply.

Rachel looked up at him with a smile so radiant and happy to see him the force of it hummed in his ears. "A poultice for gout, Father. Mother is gathering the roots we need." She motioned with her tiny hand to the sturdy straight-back chair with rush seat that he always occupied.

The perfume of dried flowers, lemon and lime rinds mingled with the pungent aromas emanating from the herbs Rachel was assaulting. It was an intoxicating and calming odor that Henry not only liked but craved, nearly as much as his time with Yuala and Rachel. These days, nearly every sight, sound, smell and texture reminded him of Yuala. Incredibly, his feelings were more intense now than they were that first stormy afternoon by the waterfall.

Rachel went to her father and kissed him squarely, impudently on the mouth and sat in his lap. "What shall we talk about today, Father?"

Sunbeams jumped merrily into Rachel's abundant coppery curls. Her hair was nearly as legendary as her mother's. Small-boned and framed as she was, Rachel's head was oddly larger than her body. Coupled with a thick mass of curly, coppery blond hair, Rachel's head resembled a pumpkin plopped on top of her shoulders. Henry feared she would never be a pretty girl, but born on the edge of two worlds as she was, beauty would never be a concern. Life would always be difficult for her. She would never fit in.

He pulled a particularly errant corkscrew curl. Tears misted in his eyes.

She placed her little arms around his neck and smiled at him with a heart filled with nothing but love.

At that moment, Henry's head reverberated with Mary's blistering accusations that their children would never know a "normal" life in England. Henry's selfishness and need for adventure had made them all outcasts on this island. His daughters would grow up to be spinsters and never fulfill their dreams of having children of their own. William was becoming hard-hearted and resigned to a life that offered him no opportunities to prove his own worth to the world.

Suddenly, Henry realized that Rachel would grow to womanhood without him. What would life be like for her, a half-breed? A mulatto? Hated by both worlds. Not quite a slave, but not truly free, either.

"How I would like to take you to London and give you a proper education."

Rachel's jade eyes flashed humorously at him. "Mother says I will never go to London. It's not my destiny." She put her little hands on his cheeks and kissed his mouth. "I just want to play with you and make the poultice for Mother. I love you, Father."

Henry's throat constricted as Rachel hugged him with all her might.

How is it that I've sired three other children and not one of them has ever told me they love me?

They respected him and revered him, but that was all. Rachel wanted nothing from him except his love.

Yuala stood in the doorway long enough to record the memory of Rachel and Henry's embrace.

"You could change the way your children feel about you, Henry. They must *feel* your love. Only you can work this miracle. I advise you to begin soon."

Rachel's head spun around. "You have been to the waterfall!" Rachel scrambled out of Henry's arms and went to her mother.

Henry sensed foreboding in both their voices. Yuala had been given a vision. He knew from the tiny shadows of sadness in her eyes that the truth would be painful.

"Don't be afraid, my love," he said to Yuala. "You can tell me."

Torrents of tears cascaded over the edges of Yuala's eyes as she rushed to him and held him. "I saw your death."

"Oh, God." Henry tried to breathe. His heart stopped for a moment. He hadn't thought the truth to be this dire. "I was wrong. I am afraid." He clung to Yuala, and they cried together.

Emotions rushed through the room, battering the walls like a tropical hurricane. Metaphysical questions bombarded each other as Yuala read his thoughts, and Rachel read those of her mother. Answers to questions swarmed about them like bumblebees, the makers of sweet honey yet the carriers of the sting of fear. As gifted as she was in the knowledge of the heart and mind, Yuala knew nothing of the armor one wears when facing earthly death.

"I had not thought it would hurt me so," she sobbed. "To not touch you . . . Henry . . . ever again." Her tears rolled unabated down her beautiful cheeks, like the waterfall she loved. But there was no song to sing, no joy in their flow.

The little trinity they had been, living in bliss and love, was coming to an end. Yuala felt the blood drain from her body. Her skin turned icy cold and matched the temperature drop of both her daughter and lover.

"Perhaps there has been a mistake," Henry said, wringing his hands in his usual fashion. "You could be wrong," he protested.

Yuala was silent as Rachel looked at her mother and then sadly at her father.

"I'm young and healthy! I have every reason to live now that I have you and Rachel!" His eyes were frantic as he watched resolve take residence in Yuala's eyes. Henry was more frightened than he had ever been in his life. Suddenly, he realized he was afraid because Yuala was never wrong about her visions.

He grabbed them both and held them as tightly as he could. Slowly the initial shock retreated to the shadows and was replaced by an uncommon resolve. Suddenly, everything that Yuala had taught him, the meaning of his destiny on earth, his role in her life and hers in his, made sense. He was surprised at how unafraid he was. He looked upon this not as a curse, but as fortune. He had time yet. That he could feel in his own heart without asking. He could right his wrongs with his children. He could make amends and set his house in order.

This time, it was Henry whose smile and loving caresses gave Yuala courage. "We'll make the best of it, you and I," he said, wiping her tears with his palm. He gazed into the silvery depths of her eyes, and once again he saw her shining soul. His strength abrogated her fear, and she smiled.

"You must wait for me on the other side of the door, Henry."

"What door?"

"The door to eternity where our souls will always be together. But I must tell you this: I will remain between worlds for a time."

Henry was unable to comprehend what she was saying, but he listened intently as his intuition told him that soon he *would* understand.

"You mean you will live a long time here?"

"No. I mean that it is my destiny to remain with Rachel until she dies, but I will not be on earth. She and I have much work to do for our grandchildren and their children."

"You mean you'll be a ghost? You're planning for this? This is preposterous. There is a heaven and a hell, and that's all there is to it!"

Yuala chuckled and even Rachel covered her mouth with her hand to stifle a giggle at his naïveté. "You are too English. That, too, is good. Time will be nothing to you, Henry, so you will hardly know that I am not with you. It is only the earth that moves so slowly."

Time, Henry thought. *Time needed to move slowly in order for him to atone for his sins*, he thought guiltily. If God did love him, then Henry would have just enough time.

* * * *

In September 1788, the height of the hurricane season, Henry chose to ride with William to the newly acquired land east of their plantation. This would give them time together, Henry hoped. Time to ease his own conscience.

This particular area was the thickest and densest part of the jungle, the ground so overgrown with foliage and flowers that Henry was surprised the plants hadn't all died from fighting each other for sunlight.

The humid air clung to their backs and necks like clammy hands. Their linen shirts were drenched with sweat as they rode. They would be silent for a while, the heat so oppressive it tired Henry just to speak. He had so much to say to his son, so much he wanted to tell him and explain to him about the way of the world.

William was more handsome than Henry ever thought a Duke could be. The life in Jamaica had been good for him in that respect, tanning his skin, bleaching his blond hair almost white. His green eyes reflected the green of the jungle. The hard work and long days on horseback had strengthened his body and toned his muscles. Henry couldn't understand why women hadn't thrown themselves at William's feet. Henry remembered lots of young girls and their crushes on him when he was William's age of twenty-two.

But that was England, Henry thought to himself. This was Jamaica. There weren't the parties, balls and teas to give young people interaction like there were in England or Charleston. Mary had been right about that. Truly,

William had little to choose from in the Caribbean in the way of a wife. It was sad. William might very well be the end of the Duke lineage.

"I want you to give me a grandson," Henry said aloud without realizing he had said the words.

William laughed. "Don't you think acquiring a wife would be a more appropriate first step?" Then William's handsome face soured. "On second thought, I guess you wouldn't find that important," William said bitterly.

"I've made mistakes. I admit them. Bringing the family here was one of them. I have deprived you of the kind of social life you were born to. You are a Duke."

William slowed his horse from a trot to a walk. He eased the reins to the left and guided his horse around a tree stump. He paid no attention to the wind that had suddenly kicked up.

"Being a Duke isn't all it should be anymore, Father."

"That, too, is my fault," Henry replied wearily. He reined his horse around the stump and ducked low so as not to hit his face on a low-hanging tree branch. He felt a sharp pain in his left arm, but he attributed it to the quick rein he had maneuvered.

William's eyes were narrow as he spoke, not looking at his father, not looking at the jungle ahead. "How could you love a black-skinned woman, Father? A slave? Why, everyone knows they are nothing more than animals."

"Silence!" Henry boomed at his son. But the outburst sent a searing jab through his chest. "Never . . . speak of her like that." He struggled to keep the pain out of his voice and off his face.

"They say she has tricked you with love potions and put you under a spell. She has used voodoo on you."

"Perhaps," he said softly with a rush of breath.

The palms above began slapping each other as the wind sailed through the fronds. Neither Henry nor William looked to the sky to see the broad tail of cirrus clouds that had been forming for days. The storm that hovered just to the east of the Dukes as they rode into the jungle that day only hinted at its strength. Omnipotently, the storm raged its fists and the onslaught began.

The horses reared their heads, whinnied and tried to buck their riders, but Henry and William were superior horsemen and both knew precisely how to calm them. The horses bowed to their masters.

"You admit it, then," William parried.

"I admit I love her, and I don't know why." He clutched his chest but did not crumble in the saddle. Perhaps he should have eaten breakfast this morning, he thought.

William snapped, "I think it is a disgusting thing to bed a black woman. Even though her child is nearly as white as you or I, there is something not right in all this, Father. That child will never have a normal life. She is a slave, you know."

"I've thought of that. Thought of perhaps changing my will . . . providing for her. . . ." Henry felt another charge of stinging heat jolt him. This time he knew it was his heart. He gasped for breath.

"Your will . . . ?" William was shocked and suddenly turned to face his father.

That was when he saw it. Death.

Henry's face was a ghastly white, as if he had already died and didn't know it.

"Father! Father!" William reined in his horse, jumped to the ground and rushed to Henry, taking his father in his arms. "Father, don't die. We have so much to say, you and I!"

"William, I'm so sorry about it all. . . ."

"Don't talk," William cried as he laid his father on the ground. He didn't know why he was crying, only that once again things would change, and William didn't like change. William was the kind of man who reveled in congruency. Just when William believed he was learning the rules of the game of life, someone switched the players, shortened the game or altered the winnings. William didn't like this particular change at all.

"Father!" William thought Henry was dead. But then Henry's eyelids fluttered.

All his life, his father had been there. Henry wasn't a loving man, nor a happy man, but he had been a man William could depend upon. When Henry and Andrew Duke had toasted Ambrose Duke's birth and proclaimed him their shining star, William knew he could depend upon his father to continue believing in Ambrose's future more than William's. Even when the lunacy of his affair with Yuala began, Henry never dropped his obsession with her. William knew he could depend on that, too.

Frantically, William unbuttoned his father's shirt and was oddly struck at how muscular his father still was. Any woman would have been overjoyed to bed him, for his body was as fit as William's own. It was his insides that had crumbled.

"Fight it, Father. For me," he wept.

"I hope God has forgiven me for loving Yuala."

"I forgive you, Father."

Henry clutched at William's shirt. "But will you forgive me for not giving you all the love I should have?"

William was shocked for the second time. "You know I felt neglected? All these years?"

"Yuala gave me that revelation, Son."

"Then I bless her," William said through his tears. "Just don't die!"

Henry put his hand to William's cheek. "You may have just saved my soul."

Henry died with his eyes closed.

Two hours passed before William could even move. He kept holding his father, looking into his face and crying. He prayed for his father. He prayed for himself even more.

The wind that had spiraled through Windward Passage between Haiti and Puerto Rico, wreaking havoc on natives, planters and ships in the harbor, was now headed for Montego Bay. There had been no word of any devastation from Kingston on the other side of the island because the storm had skimmed just north of the city. It seemed as if its target was the Duke Plantation.

It was the horses that told William that Lord Henry Duke would not be the only Jamaican to die today. They bucked, whinnied and tried to warn William of his folly in remaining in the jungle. Their snorts and cries finally rousted William from his anguish.

William raised his eyes. The heavens opened and deluged the land. Emotionally drained, William was listless and barely had the energy to ride back on his own, much less hoist his father's body on his stallion to take him home. Rain-soaked, William dragged his father's leaden body to the horse. The rain came in battering sheets that nearly forced William off his horse. Twice he had to stop, and when the eye of the hurricane passed overhead, he was able to get nearly out of the jungle. Only one treacherous mountainside remained to traverse, and then he would be home free.

Jutting out of the side of the mountain like trolls with long grasping fingers, the sharp rock formation tripped William's horse. The horse broke his stride and William hit the ground with a thud. It was a second formation that pierced William's skull just as the eye of the storm passed overhead. The next round of ninety-mile-an-hour winds and pelting rain washed away William's blood before swirling across the jungle, sugarcane fields and finally back out to sea, leaving in its wake death and destruction, and forever changing the lives of those on the Duke plantation.

six

*When nature removes a great man, people explore
the horizon for a successor; but none comes,
and none will. His class is extinguished with him.
In some other and quite different field,
the next man will appear.*

—RALPH WALDO EMERSON
"REPRESENTATIVE MEN: THE USES OF GREAT MEN"

In the throes of her first nightmare, Rachel thrashed about her bed as the tropical storm moved across Jamaica. Even in her dream, she knew the pain she was feeling would only be worse if she awakened. It would be real.

"Mother!" She screamed and bolted upright. Sweat-soaked and terrified, she didn't understand why such horrid images had invaded her sleep. "Mother!" Tossing the quilt aside, she slipped her legs over the edge of the soft mattress. "Where are you?"

The stone house suddenly seemed enormous as Rachel raced from her room to the large open room where she, her father and mother cooked, ate and conversed. The doorway was open as always, despite the sheets of rain that blew across the threshold. "Mother!" Rachel called again as she went to the open door and looked out at the storm. Palm fronds whipped about in the wind like frantic banshees. The rain trampled the herb garden and smashed jasmine blossoms into the muddy bauxite earth. The curtain of rain obscured Rachel's vision, forcing her to use her mind's eye to find her mother. Suddenly, Rachel knew where to find her.

Rachel dashed from the cabin and raced away from the glen and singing waterfall, through the long paths they'd made in the jungle that would eventually lead them to the big house. The winds tried to push her back and the slippery grasses tripped her twice. It was as if nature were trying to warn her, or protect her.

"Mother! Mother!" Rachel screamed at the top of her six-year-old lungs. She cleared the jungle and saw the old grass-and-mud–roofed hut Yuala had once called home.

Rachel found Yuala on her knees bent over and clutching her heart. Rachel sank to her knees and put her arms around her mother's head. "Mother . . . I was so frightened when I could not find you."

Yuala looked up at her daughter, her eyes filled with tears and pain.

"What is it?" Rachel asked.

"My love has left me. I feel it here," she placed her hand over her heart. She looked at Rachel. "Henry is dead," she groaned.

"I know," Rachel finally admitted to herself. "I saw it in a dream. A woman came to me and told me to find you and care for you now in your grief."

Yuala's shattered mind barely heard her daughter, but deep in its labyrinths a connecting spark ignited. "The woman with brown hair and eyes as blue as the sea?"

"Yes," Rachel breathed in awe. "She told me her name is Barbara. You have seen her, too?"

"She told me of my destiny . . . of you and Henry. Now she comes to you. I was nine before I was given the vision."

"What does it all mean?"

Fear stemmed Yuala's tears. "Perhaps it means my powers have left me."

"La!" Rachel's green eyes widened. "Is that true? Can't you see things? Or feel them anymore?"

Yuala clutched her stomach. "I feel only loss and grief."

"What shall we do?"

Yuala had to think of her daughter and her future. In the days to come, Yuala's loss of Henry would render both her and Rachel vulnerable to enemies. Yuala had always known who her enemy was and had felt her power. Her enemy was Mary. Yuala needed help in her time of vulnerability and grief.

Yuala's black eyes, still inflamed with panic, suddenly eased like a tiny boat sailing out of a storm into calm waters. "We go to the obeahman."

As they made their trek to the hills, Yuala explained to Rachel who and what the obeahman was.

The obeahman was a pure-bred African who had never intermarried, one who had kept his blood clean so that he could practice the highest order of magic, which was his life's purpose. The obeahman lived among the Maroons in the hills and mountains a day's walk from the plantation. Taking their name from the Spanish word *cimarron,* meaning "wild" or "untamed," these escaped slaves or, in some cases, the descendants of formerly freed slaves between the changeover from Spanish rule to British rule in 1655, had founded colonies of their own in the thick woods over a hundred years ago. Here, in isolation, they lived off the land, cultivating a few crops as were necessary for survival and procreating without formal marriages, since most of the Maroons cohabitated by virtue of serial monogamy rather than polygamy and, thus, went from one mate to another over a period of a lifetime.

The Maroons were most noted for their continual warfare-like harassment of the British for the past hundred years. They were encouraged by the Spanish to do this since the Spanish were busy fighting buccaneers and privateers. Their presence and hiding places were known to most of the slaves on the island. No white man had ever caught them, their methods of becoming "one with the forest" were so clever and cunning.

The news of Lord Henry's death and that of William, his only son, was first transmitted by African drum beaters. Slaves from Kingston to St. Elizabeth knew of the search party that had found William's body, nearly bloodless from the puncture in his skull, before their British owners had even guessed at the tragedy. The Creoles, Africans, Spanish and aboriginal Arawak Indians mourned for Yuala and prayed for her because her prayers and healing potions had saved many bodies and souls.

While the Britishers came from all over the island to pay homage to a man who was always respected, many of the slaves prayed for the death of their own "mastahs." Too many of the slaves and runaways interpreted Lord Henry's death as a sign from Jesus himself that the end of slavery was near. Many among the Maroons did not understand Yuala's love for a man who owned her. She was not entirely welcomed to their camp when she seemed to appear like a vision in front of an enormous yellow and orange hibiscus.

"Tell the obeahman that Yuala has come," she instructed a timid-looking woman who wore only a cotton muslin sarong around her waist and badly executed turban on her head.

She stared blankly at Yuala.

"The *obeahman*!" Yuala boomed at the woman.

The woman jumped a half-foot off the ground in fright and tore off to a mud and grass hut with its familiar domed roof.

In seconds, the obeahman emerged.

Yuala held Rachel's hand as she stood before the obeahman who was draped in brilliant feathers, flowers and dyed beads worn around his neck, waist, wrists and ankles. He was a fascinating and frightening monstrosity to behold, but Yuala and Rachel both knew this was all for show.

Yuala had always thought it strange that the Africans as a group revered their own fears rather than their own powers. Such tendencies allowed for persons such as herself and the obeahman to elevate themselves in their cults. It was a transitory thought, but Yuala promised herself that she would pray on this observation.

They sat opposite each other over a flaming fire, the obeahman on the north side, Yuala and Rachel on the south. Yuala thought that Rachel looked like one of the angels in her Bible book, as the fire created a golden haze around her coppery blond curly hair.

The obeahman stared into the fire and as he began speaking about the future, Yuala was quick to notice that as the words came and went out of his mouth, his pupils dilated, thus letting out the truth, blocking out falsehood. The fire kept a steady flame, never ebbing nor igniting enough to cause the pupils to change their size. She knew this man spoke the truth.

"You will become a prisoner of the mem'saab. You and your child will travel across the sea where you will live for twenty passings of the seasons. Teach your child well. She will bear a son who will have the potential to be as great as his father. It is for this grandson that you must live in the great land to the north. His destiny is in the great city by the sea."

"The Golden City." Yuala was covered in chills from the crown of her head to the ends of her toes. "It is truth! La! I don't want to leave this island. It is my home."

"The choice is not yours."

The obeahman gazed blankly at her, he was still in trance. "You will be buried anonymously, no marker, save a cross that your daughter makes for you."

Rachel clutched her mother's arm in fear. Her eyes were wide. She, too, knew this would come to pass.

"Your daughter must cut your hair and save it. There is great power in the hair of one so gifted from the gods. Had you not been afraid at this time, Yuala, you could have seen all these things yourself."

Rachel looked at her mother. "You? Afraid?" Rachel had never thought her mother knew anything about fright. Rachel had feared many things, the steamertail hummingbird that flitted around her head threatening to poke her eyes out; the coney, that overly large rat that scurried beneath the flooring in their stone house; and, of course, the demons that her mother had cast out of the sick people who came to see her. Rachel couldn't help but think that all those demons had to go somewhere when they escaped from possessed bodies. Did they simply hide in the woods? Waiting to jump into Rachel? Why hadn't her mother really used her powers and destroyed them?

"In America where Rachel and I must go, I will not have my cult," she said sadly, nearly choking on the loss.

"Your only power is to invest your knowledge in your child. Your grandson will be as fair as your daughter. I can see his face clearly before me. He is a good person, but he will bear much pain. I can see his heart breaking many times, just as yours does now. Rachel, too, will suffer pangs of the heart."

Yuala's eyes inflated in her face, then instantly suspicion snapped them into narrow, discerning slits. "Why should this be? Why must we suffer so much? Our hearts are loving hearts. We wish no harm to anyone."

"Out of pain is born greatness that will enhance the soul into the next lifetime and, if one so chooses, will create extraordinary benefits for the world should the soul come back to this world in a future life. You must understand that through your grandson and his heirs, a great wrong will be righted.

"Before our births, we all choose our own destiny. It is God's gift, this right of choice. Your grandson has chosen in his next lifetime to pay for the sins his ancestors have now committed. He has chosen to be their savior. Your daughter must warn him to be wary of the men with golden skins and almond eyes. He cannot avoid his destiny, but if he is forewarned, if he is knowledgeable, he will wash away the wake of old sins committed by his father's brother. His descendants will be spared. We are all the summation of all that has gone before us. In the wake of our spirits is the spawn of the future. We live not for ourselves, but for the next generation to come."

"This I know," Yuala replied. "My daughter has the blood of kings. My wish is that my grandson become the king of America and fulfill his destiny. I will remain with him as his guide."

The obeahman rose abruptly, scooped up a handful of dirt and tossed it on the flames, extinguishing them. "I mark your words. Granted. Done." He spun, haughtily flinging his elaborate robe of feathers around his shoulders, and walked away.

Yuala realized that her entreaty to him had elevated his stature in his community. For years to come, they would all speak of the day when Yuala had lowered herself because of her fear and had come to the obeahman.

* * * *

One week after Mary Worthington Duke buried her husband and son side by side on the family plantation, she wrote to an old friend in South Carolina inquiring if he knew of anyone who was willing to purchase a personal maid and her mulatto child for two hundred pounds.

The reply came in three weeks with an affirmative answer and a bank draft for the purchase from a young plantation owner, Richard Harrison.

Mary saw to it that Yuala and Rachel were escorted in shackles to the boat in Kingston, which shipped them to Charleston.

Once the ship sailed and Mary was satisfied that Yuala was out of her life forever, Mary announced to her daughters, "No one on this plantation is ever to speak Yuala's name again. Both her name and that of her bastard will be stricken from the slave records."

Charleston, South Carolina—1790

Yuala and Rachel were sold to twenty-one-year-old Richard Harrison, a cotton planter who lived seventy-five miles from Charleston. Yuala was an obedient and docile servant for her new master and wisely used the time to teach Rachel everything she knew.

Not a day passed that she did not speak of Henry. Yuala knew that he was waiting for her and so she prayed for the end of her miserable days on earth.

Time passed and life for Yuala and Rachel was tiresome and filled with little joy and a great deal of work. By the time Rachel celebrated her tenth birthday, she was an accomplished laundress. No one in the big house seemed to realize she was only a child. The only thing that set her birthday apart from any other day was the fact that a large party the master had given the night before had produced extra washing. There were no cakes like her father provided when he'd been alive. No one picked her flowers, no one hugged her and kissed her for luck like he used to do. Rachel missed her father more than she'd ever thought was humanly possible.

On her birthday night, just before they went to sleep, Yuala knelt by Rachel's pallet holding a flickering candle stub. She touched her daughter's waist-long hair and caressed her cheek. "I said prayers all day for you."

Rachel touched Yuala's haggard face. "You miss him as much as I."

"More."

"I love you, Mother. I've said prayers for you that you receive your wish." A tear fell down her cheek. "But that means you will die and leave me. I don't want to be alone. Not here," she sobbed uncontrollably.

"I will never leave you, Rachel. You have the sight. You are a doorway to the other world beyond this earth. You will see me."

"But it won't be the same."

"You must be strong."

"Hold me tonight, Mother. Let me hold you while you go."

Rachel hugged her mother tightly, but just after midnight she felt a rush of icy wind sweep across her body. "Oh, no!" she cried, rocking her mother's body, holding her still warm fingers. "I am not afraid. I know you will come to me on angel's wings when I need you."

"I promise I will," Yuala's voice echoed from another dimension.

* * * * *

Rachel stood in the barren slave cabin as two house slaves came to take her mother's body to the burial ground the following morning. All slaves on the Harrison plantation were buried the same, with no marker and no service, just as the obeahman predicted. Rachel knew there would be many prayers for Yuala, she would see to that.

Rachel fingered Yuala's wooden crucifix that hung around her neck. It was the only possession they'd been allowed to take with them out of Jamaica.

As was his practice, Richard Harrison visited the families of departed slaves. It was a good business gesture. He was uncomfortable standing in the minuscule cabin that reeked of mold and wood rot. Rachel was scrawny and malnourished. He was surprised that her torn and faded cotton dress had obviously been one of her mother's which she'd belted around her middle with a piece of twine.

"Why aren't you wearing one of the dresses I provide for the other slave children?"

"I'm not like them. I'm different."

He looked at her, puzzling over her strange and articulate answer. Rachel *was* different. Clouds of coppery blond hair overpowered her face and nearly covered her body, as if all her energy went into growing her hair. He noticed that she had a habit of hanging her head and then suddenly, flicking her eyes up at him, then just as suddenly dropping her gaze again. He couldn't tell if she were openly defying him, since slaves were not allowed to look upon their masters or if she was just curious about him. She was only a child after all.

What unnerved him was that her movement was enough for him to catch the flash of blazing emerald eyes unlike any he'd ever seen.

Richard Harrison was the most conventional man he knew. He believed that everything in this world was right or wrong, good or evil, black or white. He did not understand how any white man, including the respected Henry Duke, could bed a black woman. It rattled the walls of decency.

"I'm sorry about her passing. You'll be given a day off from your duties, as is customary with all the slaves at times like this."

Rachel barely heard his rehearsed condolences.

"Lonesomeness. That's what killed her," Rachel said.

She fought every tear that threatened her eyes because she did not want him to see her pain. She'd told her mother she was not afraid, but why was it so hard to live up to her own words?

"But she had you," he suddenly responded, reacting to her grief.

"She missed my father too much. Life was never the same for her after he died. I'm glad they are together now." Rachel looked past him to the willow tree that swayed in the breeze. She didn't want him to know how much her heart was breaking. She was more alone than anyone could be. No one understood her heart and mind the way Yuala did. How could she tell Samuel, the coachman, that she could look into the waters of the pond and see another man's soul? How could she explain to Crystal, the cook, that she knew how to mend a broken heart or shatter a cloud with her thoughts? How could she discuss the political theories of Voltaire and Rousseau with the twelve-year-old girl from Barbados who plucked chickens ten hours a day because she wasn't smart enough to do anything else? Rachel was not afraid of beatings or whippings like the other slaves. Rachel was afraid of wasting her mind.

"I have spoken with my wife about this matter, Rachel, and we think it would be more appropriate for you to stay in the cook's quarters and perhaps aid with my daughter, Maureen, now that she is four. She has no playmates and you being older could help keep a watch out for her."

Rachel looked at him with huge luminous eyes and lowered her thick blond eyelashes. She knew precisely what he was thinking.

He knows I'm African, but I look white to him.

She nearly chuckled at his stupidity. "I will help you with your daughter," she said politely, in perfect English, just like her father had taught her.

Richard started to leave, but turned back to her as he was halfway out the door. "Rachel?"

"Yes, Master?"

"Is it true your mother could read?"

"Yes, sir. So can I. I speak seven languages now including French which I added to my accomplishments this past year."

He was incredulous. "How can this be? Slaves are incapable of learning."

She looked him dead in the eye. "I stole the information out of your library when the family went to Charleston to shop."

"You stole it?"

She smiled wanly, still not wanting to push over the barrier that separated master and slave. "Yes. But you can't steal it back." She tapped her temple. "What is in here is mine."

Chills coursed Richard's spine as he gazed in amazement at her. "What a strange child you are."

"Yes, sir. More than you know. But you needn't worry. I will do nothing to upset your balance of power here."

"My *what?*"

She took a step nearer him, though keeping her gaze demure. "My father, Lord Henry, often spoke of his fear of a slave uprising in Jamaica. He said it was like an ever-present guillotine, ready to fall at any moment. I have never informed any of the slaves of my talents. You needn't be afraid of me."

"How . . . ?" Richard stuttered. It was as if she could read his mind. The idea was vastly unsettling. And yet, he believed her. Rachel would not cause him problems. "Tomorrow, report to the kitchens at breakfast."

"I will."

Rachel went to the doorway of the whitewashed cabin and watched him walk back to the huge red-brick mansion. He was a good man, an honest man, but he was greatly limited in his thinking. She liked him and she never blamed him for the fact that she and her mother had been forced to leave Jamaica. For that she blamed Lady Mary Duke.

seven

*We are ne'er like angels
till our passion dies.*

—THOMAS DEKKER AND THOMAS MIDDLETON
THE HONEST WHORE, PT. II, I, II

Charleston, South Carolina—1813

Amelia Harrison lay in her bed, exhausted after another still-born daughter was taken from her. Rachel was the only person in attendance because Amelia trusted her. "Richard will be disappointed. He wanted a son."

Devoted to her mistress, Rachel was pained by seeing Amelia forcing herself to bear children that were clearly not her destiny. "Rest, Milady. You are particularly weak this time. With the swamp fever at the Burke's plantation, we can't take any chances."

"You sound like Richard."

"Yes," Rachel said, piling the dirty linens in a corner for washing.

Amelia lifted one eyelid. "I've heard gossip again about you, Rachel."

"Idle minds have always been a puzzle to me."

"You told Crystal this baby would not live. You told her there would be four, then no more. Only Maureen survives."

"That's true."

"Why didn't you tell me? I had such hopes." A tear trickled down her cheek.

"You didn't ask me."

"I was afraid."

"I know that. That's why I said nothing. My knowledge is not for myself but for others. It takes courage to want to know the future."

Amelia's fingers trembled. "I'm cold."

Rachel covered her with soft blankets and tucked them tightly around her. "You are thinking now you should ask me things. You are thinking if I have seen your death."

"My God," Amelia replied weakly. "You are strange."

"But not evil. You are thinking that. I have a gift. For instance, I have an uncle who lives in China. Often I have forced myself to see Lord Andrew, but he does not come to my dreams. I know that he is alive, I can feel that."

"Did you think he would not be?"

"Yes. My mother told me of some hate-filled men who vowed to kill him and even his child. But he is safe."

Amelia's energy was dissipating quickly, but in all the years Rachel had been a companion and maid to Maureen, she'd always wondered about this educated and unusual girl. "Magic. Is that what it is?"

"The only magic is love, and that is not to be feared."

"But the slaves, they come to you when they are sick. Richard told me that often he's brought the doctor to the cabins and they have been puzzled at the quick cures you have magically created. How is that?"

"My mother was a healer. I studied from her just as Maureen studied from a tutor. The others only come to me when they have no hope. I'm not accepted by them because my father was white. They believe I'm an outcast. But this material world is not my life. It's a passageway back to my true self."

"In heaven?"

"Yes," Rachel replied to comfort Amelia. "You will discover that when you return."

Amelia laid her hand on Rachel's arm. "Am I going there soon?"

Rachel peered deeply into Amelia's thin face. "Are you so very certain you want the answer?"

"I'm afraid of dying. But, yes. I want to know."

Rachel nodded her head. "You will not have any more pain."

Tears slipped out from the corners of Amelia's eyes. "Richard . . . I love him so. How will he be? I will miss him."

Rachel smoothed a limp strand of hair from Amelia's brow. "You aren't leaving him. You will still see him from heaven. And pray for him."

Amelia closed her eyes. "I have felt so tired this time. This child took so much from me. I'm so very tired. . . ."

"Rest now. I will call the Master to come to you."

"Thank you, Rachel, for everything."

Richard was waiting just outside the door. "I heard you talking, I didn't want to interrupt." His eyes were red from crying. He'd been up all night waiting for the birth. He'd known Amelia was in trouble from the outset of her pregnancy. She'd been incredibly fragile all her life and this fifth pregnancy was too much for her. She'd been bedridden nearly the full nine months. How she hadn't lost the child before this was a miracle. A false miracle that had given him false hope.

He felt adrift. His only anchor was Amelia and now he was losing her.

"How is she?"

"Weak. But she needs you."

He put his hand on Rachel's shoulder. "No, I need her."

"I understand."

Richard went inside the bedroom and when Rachel turned around, Maureen stepped out from the shadows.

"What did you do to my mother?" she demanded. "Why is Father crying?"

Rachel knew she sensed danger and loss. She wore her fears on her face. "I have comforted her is all."

"I've heard about you. Voodoo and black magic! I don't want you in my house anymore. My mother is going to die, isn't she?"

"Miss Maureen, it's not my place to . . ."

"Shut up!" Maureen pushed her aside and trounced down the hall. "I'm holding you to blame for this."

Rachel watched her disappear down the hall, and in that instant she felt the past come back to haunt her. Suddenly, she was back in Jamaica, and she was a little girl standing beside her mother as they were sent away.

Rachel knew that with Amelia's death, life on the Harrison plantation would never be the same.

Richard went into a deep mourning for over six months after his wife's death. He ate very little and seldom went out of doors except to visit Amelia's grave or to exercise his horse. He had no interest in the business of his plantation and Maureen could see the plantation sliding into depression just as Richard was. She had to do something quickly.

"You're overtaxed with all these details, Father. Let me help you."

Richard started to wave her away. "Women don't know how to run a business."

"I do. I've helped with the accounting books. I'm good at figures. I've traveled with you to Charleston to watch you make the deals with the cotton buyers. Since I'm very certain you will be feeling better very soon, let me help you for a few weeks," she said.

Richard sighed with relief. "It's true. I have no mind for it anymore. No desire." His eyes filled with grieving tears and he pinched the bridge of his nose with his thumb and forefinger.

Maureen looked away. God! How she hated these maudlin scenes. "I think you'll be surprised at what I can accomplish for you. You said it yourself, I'm all you have here."

Richard's blue eyes were gray and lifeless. "Very well, but just until I feel better." He looked out the window to the gardens and beyond to Amelia's grave. His shoulders quivered. He wished he were dead.

Maureen put her hand on his forearm. It was the most intimate gesture she'd used on a human being since she was a child. "Don't worry about a thing, Father. I'll take care of everything."

* * * *

Rachel was a beautiful woman at thirty-one, but she never wanted to draw attention to herself from anyone, white or slave. Yuala had told her that her destiny was to love and be loved by Richard someday. She believed she was saving herself for him. Therefore, she worked aggressively at being dowdy until the day she would know that Richard was to be hers.

She made her clothes large and ill-fitting, choosing dingy cast-offs from the other slaves. Her shoes and boots were riddled with holes and barely had enough leather to retain a color much less a shine. She kept her coppery blond hair wrapped in a faded handkerchief, but no matter how hard she tried, she could not hide the intelligence in her green eyes or the beauty of her soul.

Life for Rachel was almost perfect. Every day upon rising, She counted her blessings. She lived in a fine, beautiful home and was allowed to spend her days caring for Richard and the ever increasingly bitter Maureen.

Rachel had long witnessed Maureen's childish selfishness turn to self-centeredness and then to greed. Her insecurities spawned jealousies that kept her from having real friends or the attention of beaux like most young women in the county.

Though Richard had showed her a great deal of attention, it was never enough. For Maureen there must always be more. Rachel believed that Maureen had a hole in her heart that could never be filled until she learned to love herself.

"Father, I want you to make it official to the servants that I am the mistress of this house," Maureen demanded as she spread her taffeta skirts over her dainty feet.

"That goes without saying," Richard said, striking a match and lighting his pipe. "Why such formality?"

"I'm receiving a great deal of insolence from the servants, and they should show me respect. I thought that if you announced it to them it would make a difference."

"Precisely what kind of insolence are we talking about?"

"It's Rachel, actually, Father."'

"Rachel? Good heavens!" He laughed. "I find that hard to believe."

Maureen tilted her chin. "Are you accusing me of lying?"

"Don't be so defensive. It's just that Rachel—"

"Can do no wrong in your eyes," Maureen replied bitterly. "She's too old to be living in the third-floor room anymore, Father. I'm a grown woman, not a child. She doesn't need to minister to me anymore as if she were still my companion."

"Why, I can't remember a time when Rachel hasn't been a part of this house."

"Then this change is long overdue. She needs to take a husband and live in the cabins. Mate her with someone."

"Maureen! Have you any idea how crass you sound? She's not an animal. She's . . . well, Rachel. She was with your mother when she died."

Maureen bit her lip and slid her eyes frantically around the room, looking for the words she needed to manipulate her father to her desires. "People are talking, Father."

"People."

"In Charleston. The Burkes mentioned it at the barbecue last weekend. Rachel goes everywhere with us."

"Well, that's true."

"It's unseemly."

He drew long on his pipe. "Why is that?"

"Rachel is, well, a reminder that her father was white and her mother a slave. It was one thing when I was a child . . . and Mother was alive. It's quite another thing now that Rachel is mature."

"And beautiful," Richard added absent-mindedly.

Maureen caught her breath. "You think she's beautiful? You never told me I was beautiful."

He stopped himself before he fell into what he recognized as a trap. It stunned him that his daughter was the hunter and went so far as to consider him the prey. "I've told you that quite often."

"Pretty. You said I was pretty. Never beautiful. And this is what I'm saying. If you think that, don't the Burke boys think Rachel is beautiful, too?"

Richard saw through his daughter's transparent motives and the clarity pierced his heart. "I see. You think having Rachel around keeps the men from asking for your hand?"

Confused, Maureen didn't understand the question at first. "Suitors? What would I do with them? I don't want another man in my life. I have you. I want to be mistress of this plantation. Just as mother was."

"That's silly. You have your own life to live, Maureen."

"This plantation is my life."

Maureen's true nature hit Richard like a shock wave. He'd never neglected his daughter, yet somehow, by some twisted mechanism in her brain and soul, she'd become hard-hearted.

It's no wonder the young men don't come to call. They have seen what I have ignored.

For the first time Richard saw the hard glint in Maureen's eyes. He saw the narrowness of her mouth. He saw her intractability.

She stared at him incredulously. "Haven't you always told me that? This plantation is your life?"

"Of that, I am guilty. However, you didn't understand. I loved your mother. Amelia and I, we built every inch of this house with our hearts and bodies. It is our creation. But it is . . . was . . . not our life."

Maureen rose and smoothed the wrinkle in her skirt as if she were brushing off his insights like so much trash. "I deserve this plantation. I've dreamed of nothing else. And I don't want Rachel to accompany me anywhere. Ever." She trounced out of the room not allowing Richard a response.

Shifting his gaze to the windows, he felt a wave of overwhelming sadness. *What a disappointment you are, Maureen.*

* * * *

The following morning, Richard, clad in tan riding breeches, brown shiny hunting boots and a velvet trimmed waistcoat, assembled the servants.

Rachel stood with the others at the entrance to the glass-windowed breakfast room, a small rotunda of light and plants that had always cheered Richard, but was also Rachel's favorite. Outside the wall of windows the autumn leaves had turned to gold, amber and flame and seemed to shoot reflective orange light around the room.

"Good morning, all. I've brought you together to announce that from this day forward you will take your direction from Miss Maureen. With Mistress Amelia's passing, I have been remiss in keeping informed of your duties and chores. Miss Maureen tells me she would like to update some of the draperies and upholsteries. You will assist her with those. Am I understood?"

"Yes, sir," they replied in unison.

"Very good." He turned to Rachel. "I'd like to speak with you in private."

"Yes, sir," she replied, not realizing she was smiling at him as she followed him into the breakfast room. Silver servers were filled with sausages and biscuits. China platters overflowed with fresh fruits, but Richard's mind was not on food. "I had my eyes opened yesterday."

"You have grieved a long time."

He shook his head. "It wasn't grief that kept me ignorant of some very damning facts this long. In the process of running my plantation and being so in love with my wife, I've distorted my daughter."

Rachel hung her head.

"You know this, don't you?"

"Sir?"

"That Maureen is jealous of you."

Rachel's head snapped back. "Of me? No, I did not. I know that she has a heart filled with bitterness, but I didn't know she singled me out. For what reason?"

Richard took a step closer. "At first, I couldn't figure it out. I thought her demands unreasonable. Childish. I was awake all night contemplating her requests. The manner in which she spoke. I knew she had underlying reasons for her actions. Then I put some elements together and came to the conclusion."

Rachel felt the hairs on the back of her neck stand on end. She trembled and held her hands to steady them. "Which is?"

"You're in love with me." He said it as a challenge. There was even a bit of mockery in his voice. Because there was thirteen years' difference in their ages, Richard looked upon Rachel as nearly a child, though she was not. He knew she was wise in ways he didn't even want to understand. But he'd kept her on another plane, lumped in with all the servants.

Rachel sensed that the time of her destiny had come. She'd been in love with Richard all her adult life. She'd done everything to hide it, including dressing shabbily so that he would not be attracted to her while Amelia was alive. He was the reason she was born. She knew it.

If she failed to be bold, the moment would be lost forever and she with it.

She lifted her face to him and for the first time in her life, she allowed Richard to see the intensity of her love. She opened her heart willingly and unconditionally.

"It's true," she said in a near-whisper.

Richard stumbled back a step, so struck was he with her admission. He'd planned to explain to her how theirs could never be a union like her mother's and father's. He'd planned to point out that he was different. This was America, not Jamaica. He was not desperate for companionship the way Lord Henry might well have been living in such a remote part of the world. He'd planned to tell her that Maureen was right in wanting Rachel to move on with her life and strike a union with another slave.

Instead he stood dumbfounded as Rachel rushed on.

"I wasn't certain when my time would come to reveal these things to you, but I knew it wouldn't be much longer. Like my mother, I am to have a child. A son. His name will be Jefferson. You were chosen by God to give him to me. I have loved you for such a very long time. But I never would betray Mistress Amelia and the love you shared. Your life with her was sacred and meant to be, just as your life with me was destined." Rachel moved close to him so that he could feel the energies between them.

"This is preposterous! I'm middle-aged. I'm nearly at the end of my life. I could never have a . . . son," the word ached in his throat the way truth pains the heart when it's kept too long and not realized.

"Richard," she breathed his name for the first time in her life. "Please allow me to say your name." She reached up to touch his cheek.

He grabbed her hand as if to stop her, but when he did, he looked at the creamy skin, felt her warmth and pressed his lips to her palm. "My God, is it possible I am not meant to be alone?"

Tears filled Rachel's eyes. "Oh, Richard, none of us are meant to suffer the torture of loneliness. There are so many of us, but so often we see only with our eyes and minds and not with our hearts. If you close your eyes, you'll see that I'm just a woman, not a slave. And I love you with all my soul."

A tidal wave of emotion washed over Richard. He felt weak and strong at the same instant.

Suddenly the room was filled with a golden haze that Richard was certain emanated from the yellow-haired woman before him and not the autumn-tinged scrub oaks outside the windows.

"Richard, yours is the most loving heart I've known and you must realize that it could never be shut down. Not even by death. The love you had for Mistress Amelia must be given to someone else in order for you to be the man you are. Loving is the basis of your being."

"Then how is it that my daughter does not understand that about me?"

"She has much to learn and she chooses difficult paths. But it is her choice, not yours."

He pressed her hand to his cheek and let her hold his face as he peered into her eyes. "I envy you your wisdom."

"We have all our lives to share these things with each other, Richard." Impulsively, she stood on tiptoe and pressed her lips to his. It was a tentative kiss, one she'd give a child she'd healed. She wasn't prepared for Richard's forceful response when she pulled away and looked up at him.

"Rachel," he whispered sensually. His hand clamped her waist and pulled her to him. Still looking in her eyes, he was mesmerized by the love and surrender he saw. It overwhelmed him and inflamed him at the same time. "I'm feeling things . . . emotions . . . I haven't felt in years."

"Kiss me, Richard," she replied demandingly.

It was more an explosion than a kiss. It took her breath away and made her unsteady on her feet. Richard was panting as if he'd been struck in the chest. Rachel had never felt this much passion. She'd never known it existed. She was shocked and a bit afraid. She'd instigated this exchange. Now she was a victim of it.

"My God, Rachel," he moaned, clamping his mouth over hers again and invading her with his tongue. Desire mounted to a fever pitch, opening his mind and heart. Suddenly, it was as if he saw his life in its simplest forms.

Dragging his lips from hers, he said, "Everything you say is true. I can feel it."

"Oh, Richard, you have made me so happy."

He closed his eyes, feeling the sting of tears. "One thing I have learned is that life can be cut short. I don't want to waste any more of it."

"Nor do I," she replied, kissing him again.

Richard swept Rachel up in his arms. "You love me?"

"Yes."

"All these years?"

"Since the day I arrived. I always will," she said.

"That's all I ask," he said.

Rachel had prayed all her life for this moment. She would take it for she deserved all its joy for as long as it lasted, an hour, a day, a week. For this moment, Richard was hers. All she could hope was that one day he would come to love her back.

Richard kissed her as he carried her up the staircase to his bedroom. Neither of them saw Maureen lurking behind the library doors.

"Slut! Voodoo whore!" Maureen snarled to herself watching them. Still dressed in her morning riding clothes, she whacked the riding crop against the back of the dark-brown tufted sofa and slit the leather.

"The bitch!" She stormed across the room to the portrait of her mother that hung over the mantle.

She was angry at herself for not breaking up their tryst. She felt betrayed not only by her father, who had always told her that copulating with a black was akin to eternal damnation, but by the trust she and Rachel, her companion since she was four years old, had once shared.

However, Maureen had become caught in the interplay between her father and Rachel and had been as fascinated at what was happening nearly as much as the two participants.

Pressing her palms against her temples, she said, "This is no ordinary affair, Mother." She looked up at Amelia's portrait.

Her eyes darted about the room as scenes from the past whirled across her vision. "No. This has been coming on for years. Many years. I remember Rachel telling me stories about her mother, Yuala, and her father, Henry Duke. My God! At the time I had been disgusted by all of it, but now I can see that Rachel was giving me a warning." She flung the riding crop down on the console.

"Now I see this picture more clearly, Mother. Rachel has wanted father practically since she came here! My God, we've been blind to that slut! Thank God you're not alive to see this, Mother."

Maureen's mind strung the clues together like worry beads. Because Rachel was so light-skinned, green-eyed with coppery blonde hair, Maureen believed that Rachel wanted to be white. Yes. That had to be the reason Rachel set this subconscious trap for her father all this time. As long as Amelia was alive, Rachel didn't stand a chance. Now, of course, everything was different.

Maureen didn't care if her father and Rachel rutted together every morning and evening. In fact, she rather liked the idea. "This could be a good thing," she said aloud. "If father continues to be besotted by Rachel, he'll never think of marrying again. A Johnny-come-lately son could drastically alter my inheritance if he were to marry. As long as he's sleeping with a slave, her children will be bastards and slaves, to boot!"

Maureen clapped her hands together and then rubbed them gleefully. Since she was the firstborn, she believed that the mansion, plantation and all the slaves would be hers since she had purposefully *not* married in order to take possession of what she felt was rightfully hers.

Maureen didn't need a husband. Maureen was smart. She planned for her future. And her future was this plantation.

Maureen looked over to the French doors that opened to the gardens beyond. In front of the windows sat the newest addition to the house furnishings, a new piano her father had imported from Austria, his birthday gift to her last month.

This was an experimental piano reflecting the changes that Beethoven had wrought in the instrument. There was better tonality and greater percussion. It was made by Anton Walter, the Viennese piano maker who worked closely with Mozart and now with Mozart's prized pupil, Beethoven.

In these pianos, the hammer pointed downward rather than away from the player and instead of being hinged to a rail passing over all the keys, they were attached individually to their respective keys. As the front of the key was depressed, the back rose and carried the hammer with it. A projecting point at the rear of the hammer shank caught on an individually hinged and sprung piece for each key. As the back of the key reached its highest point, this piece, the fabulous form that allowed for *escapement* that Mozart had sought for so many years, now tilted backward on its hinges and reached the point at the back of the hammer shank. The hammer was now free to fall back to the rest position when the key was still depressed.

Maureen went to the piano, sat and placed her hands on the keys. Her hands sounded like tiny white doves flitting over the ivory keys, gifting them with song.

As music filled the room, Maureen smiled victoriously to herself. This piano told her all she needed to know about her future. She needn't worry about her father and Rachel. Maureen was still first in her father's heart and first in his will.

eight

Of ancient race by birth, but nobler yet
In his own worth.

—JOHN DRYDEN
"ABSALOM AND ACHITOPHEL"

Jefferson Duke was born on January 22, 1815, just two weeks after the Battle of New Orleans, a fiasco on all counts since the Treaty of Ghent in Belgium, signed on December 24, 1814, a full fortnight before the battle, had already declared the war over.

Maureen declared a war of her own.

Watching Richard hold Jefferson in his arms beneath a spreading oak tree, Maureen seethed.

He acts like this baby is the Messiah! Worse, he hasn't paid attention to me in weeks.

Maureen gasped as Richard bent over and kissed Rachel on the lips. "He's insane. Kissing her in full view of the servants. This has to stop!"

Maureen purposefully spread the gossip about Richard's affair with Rachel and the birth of her bastard. She knew if she had enough support from friends, she could make her father give up Rachel. Then she'd be free to do as she pleased with the plantation.

First, she needed to create anarchy within. She enlisted the support of the slaves in the house.

"Yes ma'am, she's a Jezebel," Jedediah, the butler, said to Maureen.

"Contaminatin' this house with her bastard, dat what she done," Zeke the gardener agreed with Maureen.

At Sunday services, the matrons of the county whirled their black bombazine skirts around Maureen in a circle of confidence.

"How can you let your father be led astray like this, Maureen? You must speak with him. Doesn't he know he's condemning his soul to everlasting hell?" Mrs. Whatlin said.

"That's right, Maureen, it is your duty to bring him back to his senses and to the fold," Julie Carson agreed.

Maureen shook her head. "I've done everything. But now he has a son. And that son is as white as I am."

"Spawn of the devil, that's what he is," Mrs. Whatlin said.

"You must get out of that evil house, Maureen. She could poison your mind, too."

"She wouldn't dare," Maureen said confidently.

"Nevertheless, the devil uses weak souls to do his bidding. You must be on guard at all times." Julie clamped her hand over Maureen's pleadingly. "Come to town, Maureen. You'll be safe here until this evil time has passed."

But Maureen didn't want to move. Possession was nine-tenths of the law. She wanted to be rid of Rachel and her baby.

"What I need is a plan," she said to them. "I must save my father." *And save my inheritance.*

But matters only got worse for Maureen.

One by one, Richard resumed all his duties as head of the plantation. Maureen had little left to do other than the bookkeeping.

"I'll be taking over the books again, Maureen. And now that Rachel is feeling better after such a difficult birth, I've decided that she can help you with the servants."

Maureen was aghast. "You're stripping me of the last of my duties as mistress of this house! Why don't you come right out and say it, Father? You want Rachel to take my place."

Richard pondered this. In his mind, there was no one in his life now except Rachel and Jefferson. Maureen was his daughter, but she was old enough to have a life of her own. Suddenly, he looked at her and wondered why this pretty and intelligent woman wanted to spend her life as a spinster. "I think it time you made a life of your own, Maureen."

Maureen's eyes turned stormy with rage. "This plantation is my life. You know that. I've watched and studied all you do so that someday I could run this plantation with you!" She threw her arms in the air frantically. "You rut with a black woman and think that I, your flesh and blood, will stand for this degradation?" Spittle rained from her mouth. "Now that you have a bastard son you want to change everything in my life, too?"

"Maureen . . ."

"You think you're God!"

"I think nothing of the sort."

Maureen picked up a Limoges porcelain vase and flung it at the wall. She picked up a leather-bound book and hurled it at the fireplace. "You treat me like I'm nothing to you anymore! Yet you shame all of us!"

Richard's ire boiled. "You make me ashamed," he blasted her back. "You are not only spoiled and selfish, but an unloving woman. At least God has the wisdom not to give you a husband or children. Is there no warmth in your blood?"

"How can you say this to me? Ask your friends what they think."

"You're cruel and heartless, Maureen."

Maureen couldn't believe her ears. To her mind she'd done nothing all her life but live for her father's love. "I will not remain in this house if you make Rachel the mistress."

Richard didn't want this kind of alienation between himself and his daughter. His heart was breaking as he realized how callous Maureen had become. What had he done to her that had warped her mind? Where had he gone wrong? How could he have changed things? "You must make that choice for yourself."

Maureen's anger quickly died. She realized she'd put herself in an untenable position. Wisdom told her that situations always changed. Rachel would be mistress now and she could flaunt her bastard all she wanted, but one day, Maureen would be back. Then, she would make Rachel pay for this indignity. Maureen looked soulfully at her father. "Then I'll go."

As she packed her belongings, Maureen heard the slaves grumble amongst themselves that she was "abandoning" them, but she didn't care. The house servants were in an uproar over this upset in the balance of power. They'd never known a slave to become the master. They were afraid, and it was all Maureen could do to keep them calm. They began having nightmares that Rachel's voodoo was stealing their minds. The older slaves crept surreptitiously from room to room as they carried out their chores, and they told Maureen they were praying that the "loa" would make them invisible to evil spirits.

Maureen was pleased at the way the slaves backed up her position.

However, the slaves had no choices in their lives. They could complain all they wanted, but they were powerless to change their fate. Maureen, on the other hand, believed in being the master of one's destiny. She was hoping to devise a new plan of attack once she was removed from the plantation.

On the day she left, Richard looked at her. "I wish you could understand how I feel," he said as the servants carried out four trunks loaded with gowns, dresses, hats, shoes and coats.

"I understand that you've temporarily lost your mind, Father," Maureen said, adjusting a pert royal-blue hat. "However, I love you. I have always loved you, and I always will. When this insanity is over, I'll be waiting in Charleston." She shoved her hands into a pair of lace gloves as the coachman held the carriage door. "Now, Father," she looked at him with committed eyes. "Will you be coming into town for dinner on Sunday? I'll have a lovely goose cooked for us."

"Goose?" he laughed.

"You know about cooked goose, don't you, Father?" She asked sarcastically.

"Obviously, you think I do."

Maureen stepped into the coach. The coachman shut the door and climbed up to his perch.

"Don't bother about the dinner, Maureen. I'm staying here."

Maureen stuck her nose in the air. "You will write, then?"

"Yes."

The coach rode away.

Rachel had remained in the house during Maureen's departure. She knew Maureen was bitter and resentful of the change in Richard's life. Rachel also knew that Maureen was selfish, mean and vindictive.

Frankly, she was glad Maureen's angry vibrations would no longer be in the house. Just being under the same roof with the woman was unsettling.

Rachel busied herself with the evening meal. She set the table and helped Crystal dish out the potatoes and peas.

She waited for Richard in the dining room. When he didn't return for quite some time, she picked up the newspaper and began reading about the war that January.

England, Austria and France had met and formed a secret treaty to resist the demands of Prussia and Russia. The rumors of war between the allies had upset everyone in the United States, for their economic life had been cast with the French during their battle with Britain.

The only news that Rachel paid much attention to was that the French intended to prohibit slave trade that year. As she thought about her green-eyed, golden-haired son, she prayed that the United States would not be far behind. She was sure that somehow Jefferson would not live his life in bondage.

To Rachel, it seemed the whole world was war weary. Most of the actual fighting had been centered in the Great Lakes area, Lake Champlain, Lake Erie, the Battle at Lundy's Lane on Canadian soil a mile from Niagara Falls, Queenston Heights again near the Falls and, of course, the Battle of New Orleans. The war itself had been more of a nuisance than an actual threat to their lives in Charleston. The British were too busy fighting Napoleon to spend money on rousting out Americans again. The Americans were fighting mainly because of the British impressment of sailors, occurrences directly related to the great amounts of goods being shipped between the two countries.

During the war, the Americans depended upon their own abilities to produce their own goods, and manufacturing took a decided upswing, Rachel read in the Charleston newspapers that were delivered to the plantation by courier twice a month.

Richard returned to the house and marched into the dining room. He sat down and rang for his food without saying a word to Rachel.

Crystal came into the dining room with a platter of sliced ham. "Is there anythin' else, sir?"

"No, Crystal, this is just fine. Some coffee maybe."

"Yes, sir," Crystal replied and took a silver coffee pot from the hunt board and poured him a cup. She glanced at Rachel as she quickly left the room.

They ate in silence.

Rachel didn't want to discuss Maureen, yet she thought it would be best for Richard to say what he felt.

Suddenly, he looked up at her. "Best thing for everybody, her leaving." He put his head down and continued eating. Then he looked up again. "Do you think I'm a man of vision, Rachel?"

Most people would think that the two thoughts were not connected, but Rachel knew Richard better than most people. "What did she say?"

"That I was backward and uncivilized. I told her I was a man of vision, and she laughed at me. Laughed!"

"I would definitely say you're a visionary, Richard. However, a man who is out of sync with time cannot expect to be accepted. Hundreds of years from now, people will think more like you than like Maureen."

"Thank you for the flattery."

"I was being honest. It can be no other way. You're the kind of man who will lead others to the future, Richard. You must know that about yourself. You're always talking about 'the new wave of industrialization' that's coming."

He smiled for the first time that evening. "I do, don't I?"

"Yes, my love."

"Then I won't allow myself to dwell on Maureen's tantrums."

"It will only upset you," Rachel said.

Rachel tapped her finger thoughtfully against the handle of the Sheffield knife. "I was thinking how wonderful it would be, Richard, if we could be like Adam and Eve. Creating a new order of man . . . a new world. I'd like to think that Jefferson is the best of both our worlds, that there will come a time when there are no slaves, no servants, just people helping other people. Order would be maintained by each person doing his or her part in life. The world will be a place where people love each other for who they are."

"Isn't that what we have? Utopia?" He smiled at her.

Rachel looked around the room she used to spend hours cleaning. Her days used to be filled with work. Now the days seemed to drag by. "I cannot spend my life being so idle, my love. You expect me to act like something I'm not, just because you've moved me into your bedroom."

"I told you before, your only duties now are to me and the baby."

"Jefferson is sound asleep after his last feeding. However, it seems to me that you require more nurturing than our infant," she teased as she went to him.

He put his coffee cup down and slipped his arm around her waist. He laid his head on her soft abdomen. "I want you to have many more babies as beautiful as my son."

She smoothed a lock of graying blond hair from his forehead. "No, there will only be one."

"It's so amazing to me to finally have a son. I have an entirely new perspective on my future. His future."

Rachel looked away. "Jefferson is a slave."

Richard waved his hand as if batting her objections aside.

"A mere matter of paperwork. I'll contact my solicitor. Then Jefferson will be free and so will you. Now," Richard stood and took Rachel's hand, "Come with me to the library so I can tell you about my plans."

Richard was filled with a youthful vigor that showed in the bounce he had added to his walk. His affair with Rachel, the exploration of body, soul and mind that he indulged himself in through her, expanded his life and his vision of the future.

He sat on the leather sofa with Rachel next to him. "It will take nearly a year to accomplish all this, but I've ordered a chain-stitch loom and the new circular loom from France which can make tube stockings without a seam."

"That is amazing!" Rachel was awed at these new inventions. "This plantation grows an enormous amount of cotton."

"Precisely! Instead of shipping the raw product to England, we will make our own fabrics and eventually our own clothes for market."

"How did you get this idea?"

Richard smiled mischievously and then planted a sound kiss on Rachel's soft lips. "I watched you sewing baby clothes, and I thought about the fact that it had taken us six weeks to get these soft flannels from England. If we could make our own cotton flannels, you wouldn't have to wait so long. I kept thinking that the baby was going to be born before the flannel arrived."

Rachel smiled broadly. "I inspired you?"

He laughed. "To say the very least, Rachel, you have inspired me."

* * * *

The looms were installed in a warehouse section in Charleston where Richard bought the land for four thousand dollars from the heirs of the owner, who were more greedy than they were smart.

Rachel had only been there once when Richard was in the bloom of his naïveté regarding their affair, treating her as almost his equal in public. She had noticed the shocked looks on some of the women's faces and the envy and even lust in the eyes of his gentlemen friends. Richard was oblivious to it all. He was in love with Rachel. That was all he cared about.

They arrived at dawn when the sun was just beginning to burnish the tips of the masts that bobbed in the Bay. Rachel could hear the blasts of low, nearly mournful sounds through conch shells that reminded her of Jamaica.

Before a vision of her mother and father congealed in her mind, she heard the clanging of brass bells from the larger merchant boats as they steered their way around the smaller fishing boats. At dawn, the marketplace burst into activity. Merchants and seamen lowered baskets of oysters and crabs from the Atlantic, vegetables from New England, fruits from South America and flowers from the West Indies, down to the peddlers who hawked their wares up and down the residential streets of Church, Broad, Charlotte and Calhoun.

Rachel loved Charleston, its beauty and activity, and she often wondered what it would be like to live here and be free. She allowed the thought only a scant amount of time to dwell in her heart.

Rachel was a realist and her yearning to be free could also bring a separation from Richard. She loved him more than she ever thought possible. She was happy with Richard, but her joy was dulled each day when she looked out at the fields being tended by her fellow slaves. In her mind, she knew she would convince Richard not only to free herself, but to free all his slaves.

I will convince him that he can change the world one life at a time.

"Richard, you know I love this city, and I'm grateful for our visit, but it seems a bit capricious on our part just to find a riding instructor for Jefferson."

"Rachel, the boy has been riding since two. Bareback since three. I want him to learn dressage. Jumping. He'll be an excellent horseman when he's grown." He rubbed his chin thoughtfully. "I was also thinking to find a fencing master and bring one to the plantation as well."

"I agree that Jefferson is bright and eager to learn. But his penchant for daring produces too many bruises and bumps on his head."

"I'll find a piano instructor. Would that suit you?"

"More than the fencing? Yes."

"He'll have all three," he kissed her soundly. "I'd do anything to make you happy."

"Anything, Richard?"

"Yes, my love," he smiled.

Rachel looked at him solemnly. "Then I want you to free all the slaves."

Richard stared back. "I'll consider this request," he said.

"You will?"

He nodded. "Understand that such a move would upset the equilibrium of the plantation owners in this state. Such a move could cost us to be ostracized financially. The buyers wouldn't buy our crops. It could be disastrous."

"Does anyone have to know?" Rachel asked.

"How could they not when all the slaves take off?"

"Who said anything about leaving? Where would they go? Where would they work? Life on your plantation is not any more difficult than life somewhere else. The bondage in our hearts cannot continue. It depletes our mental and spiritual energies."

Richard looked at her curiously. "I try to understand what you say, Rachel. But sometimes your riddles are too much for me. Be patient with me."

She smiled. "I have all the time in the world."

"Good, now let's be about our business and get back to our son," he said.

* * * *

Jefferson liked the way his father encouraged him to try just about anything he wanted to do. He asked his father to read stories to him, but Jefferson was so full of questions that Richard taught him to read by the time he was four.

"Now you can find your own answers to all these questions you pose, Jefferson."

"I ask too many?" Jefferson inquired.

"Not of me, Son. Never of me," Richard hugged him.

When Jefferson was seven years old, he was learning to play chess with Richard on the front lawn beneath an enormous oak tree. They sat in white-painted wooden chairs at a games table Richard had imported from England a decade before. The summer breeze wafted through the leaves of the oak tree.

Richard had just returned from yet another buying trip to France. His business was growing at breakneck speed. He didn't know how he was going to fulfill all the orders for cloth he had sold.

Dark circles had formed under Richard's eyes, a nervous twitch developed at the corner of his right eye and a broken blood vessel appeared at the bottom of his left eye. He was weary, but he wanted to spend time with Jefferson.

"I really enjoy your company, Jefferson," Richard said. "In fact, I think the next time I go to France, I'll take you with me."

Jefferson was beside himself with excitement. "You mean I could sail with you? Across the Atlantic?"

"Of course," Richard tried to smile, but the effort was too great.

Jefferson saw an odd look cross his father's face. Then Richard's face turned pasty white. "What is it, Father?"

Suddenly, Richard's face froze, then fell. His eyes rolled back in his head and he sagged back in his chair.

Jefferson jumped out of his chair, knocking down pawns and kings. "Father! Father!" He screamed frantically and tried to awaken Richard.

Richard didn't move.

Jefferson ran for the big house. "Mother! Come quick! Hurry!" Jefferson's shoes clomped across the wooden foyer and into the salon, but he couldn't find his mother. He called up the stairs. "Mother!"

Rachel came racing out of the master bedroom. She nearly flew down the staircase. "It's all right, Jefferson." She rushed out the front door with her son.

"No, it's not, Mother. He's dead! I just know it!"

"He's not dead, Jefferson. I would know if my love were dead."

Rachel tried to lift Richard, but he was too heavy. She called for the other servants to move him into the house.

When Doctor Dessault arrived, he told Rachel that Richard had suffered a stroke. He was alive, but his mind was gone. Doctor Dessault was one of Maureen's strongest supporters. He not only didn't think it was right that Richard carry on with Rachel the way he did, but now believed that God was proving Doctor Dessault accurate in his judgment.

Doctor Dessault immediately contacted Maureen in Charleston and told her about her father's illness. "It's your duty to return home and care for your father," he told Maureen.

"I certainly will," she said firmly. "I'll pack right away."

Maureen was well received by the house slaves who thought Rachel had gotten "uppity" during the past seven years. None of them would admit that Rachel was a better mistress than Maureen, but their universe had been set out of balance. They needed to make things right again.

Maureen instantly ordered Rachel and Jefferson back to the slave cabins. Maureen looked directly at Rachel with eyes so hard they had calluses,

Rachel thought. "I have held my tongue because I love Father and didn't want to upset him. Since he is incapacitated now, I will run this house the way my mother would have wanted it run. God rest her soul."

Jefferson didn't know why Maureen was calling upon God. He didn't listen to cold-hearted prayers. He also noticed that she put great emphasis on the words, "my mother," and he wondered what she had been like. He had always thought of Maureen as much like himself. The notion of being "half" of someone's blood relative had never registered in his young brain.

By the end of that hot, cholera-ridden summer, Jefferson was to learn many things about himself, his mother and life as it was going to be under Maureen's regime.

nine

Make no little plans; they have no magic to stir men's blood.

—Daniel Hudson Burnham

Maureen lost no time her first days back on the plantation setting straight every wrong, imagined or real, against her. She ordered the house slaves to tend to Richard's physical needs, but she would spoon-feed him at mealtime. He was to have no visitors without her prior approval, including his attorney and his doctor.

On her third morning home, she found Richard's desk drawer was locked.

"Who has been in this room, Jedediah?" Maureen demanded.

"Only Rachel and the boy."

"I want every piece of furniture scrubbed and rewaxed. The books dusted and the rugs beaten. I want everything whistle clean."

"Yes, ma'am."

Maureen tugged on the locked drawer. Dismissing Jedediah, Maureen waited until the servant was out of the room. She crossed to Richard's smoking table and pulled out the center drawer where he kept his matches. She emptied the drawer, turned it over and slid back the false bottom revealing a brass key.

She smiled. "How I love a man of habit."

Taking the key she unlocked the desk drawer. "I knew he was keeping secrets," she mumbled to herself as she broke the seals on the legal documents. Eyes widening, Maureen read the papers that meant freedom to her foes.

"Never!" She ranted and tore the sheets into tiny pieces. "Not in a million

95

years will I let that bitch get away with this!"

Then she read the final document that would have freed Jedediah and the others. "No wonder he had a stroke. He lost his mind weeks ago. Thank God I found this before it was too late."

She continued shredding the papers. Then she placed the pieces in the fireplace and set them on fire. Staring at the ashes, she vowed, "No one will rule this land but me. It's mine. Only mine."

* * * *

Maureen put Rachel and Jefferson to work in the fields. Jefferson was young, but he picked twice as fast as the rest of the slaves and when he had filled his quota for the day, he went back and helped his mother fill her gunnysack to the brim.

Because they kept to themselves and assumed a more than detached demeanor, no one spoke to them and the overseer found no fault with them. But as they stood in the food lines at night after the hot sun had gone down, Rachel felt the eyes of the other slaves reach inside her, past her now-sunburned white skin, past her copper hair, and clamp their jealousy across her heart like iron bands.

Though she'd always worked hard in the manor house, Rachel had never worked in the fields. Her hands had never worn calluses and her skin had never peeled from the sun. Her back ached from morning through the night. She was not used to merely beans, rice and salt pork as her daily diet. She longed for a freshly washed strawberry and a hunk of Crystal's fluffy biscuits with honey dripping out of the comb. She remembered the taste of champagne she'd shared with Richard. But most of all, she remembered talking with Richard, and his smiles, his dreams, his plans for the future and the smell of his sweat after they'd made love. She wished she could hold his hand tenderly the way she once had.

They'd been fools to live the idyll they had, but it had lasted for almost eight years. They had a wonderful, bright son to show for their love, and for the courage they'd both had in risking their hearts. The days of Camelot were over.

Rachel turned to her son. "Tonight we begin a new kind of education for you, Jefferson," she said with a mysterious tone, born of finality.

"What kind of education?"

"I'm going to teach you about the obeahman and your grandmother, the Mambo."

* * * *

Richard never recovered from his stroke. He never learned to walk, talk or laugh again, but through sheer strength of will, he stayed alive until 1835, when Jefferson was twenty years old.

Rachel had degenerated over the years along with Richard. It was as if she'd had a stroke that affected only her will to live. Maureen made certain Rachel was never allowed back in the house, but Rachel found ways around her.

The two played an elaborate cat-and-mouse game. Rachel sent messages to Richard in her thoughts and prayer asking him to come to the big window in his bedroom where she could see him at an appointed time and day.

Through finger pointing and garbled mumbling, Richard's nurse realized that he liked to sit at the window. She thought he liked to watch the wind through the trees.

By requesting to be the laundress, Rachel carried piles of clean linens from the backyard behind the smokehouse to the main house where she could watch Richard at his window.

"My eyes aren't as strong as they once were," she said to Jefferson. "But I can tell he's smiling at me."

"But his face is paralyzed, Mother," Jefferson said.

A crooked, cagey smile cracked Rachel's lips.

"That's what he wants *her* to think. He may not be able to talk, but he can smile. I know what he is thinking." She nodded, eyes sparkling.

Jefferson was as tall as Richard, which caused his feet to dangle a full six inches off the end of his pallet. His shoulders and biceps burst the seams of his cotton shirts on a regular basis. "You honestly think that he can read your mind?"

"I know it. Someday, if you practice the things I've taught you, you will find that it can be done."

"I don't believe in magic anymore, Mother," he said bitterly. "For the first seven years of my life, I had tutors and piano lessons. I learned that I'm an intelligent person. For the past twelve years, all I've learned is how far I can push my body to pick cotton one more hour without my back feeling as if it will break in two. I'm wasting my life, Mother. Wasting my brain. And why? Because of one petty woman's jealousies! I don't believe in dreams anymore."

Rachel took his hand. "Don't ever say that! Dreams are all we have!"

He shook his head and walked away from her, leaning his over-six-foot frame against the cabin's doorjamb. Gazing out at the Carolina sunset glittering over the cotton fields and marshes, he said, "I see skies like that and I know I can paint them. I have talent. My art tutor told me he'd never seen a child as gifted as I am. And what good is it if I'm not allowed paints and a canvas?"

Feeling all his frustrations, Rachel sighed. "Do what I do. Use your mind as the canvas for now. Someday soon your life will be different and you will paint the places you love. The people you love. I can see it in my mind's eye."

Jefferson couldn't help but laugh. "You never give up, do you, Mother?"

"Never. And neither should you." She stood next to him. "I'm getting old, Jefferson. I need to write in a journal for you my visions and the old ways that my mother taught me. You may not think you need them now, but someday they will be great comfort to you."

"Write? With what? We have no quills or ink. Certainly no parchment."

"I'll find a way."

* * * *

Rachel had learned many ways around Maureen Harrison. Crystal, the cook, was old, and though it was her exacting and talented eye that produced the gourmet meals Maureen enjoyed, she actually did little work in the kitchen. Crystal had a great deal of free time.

A young slave boy, Joshua, born with a clubfoot, was utilized as a messenger from the manor house to the overseer's cabin, and from the main kitchen to the slaves' kitchen. Through Joshua, Rachel was able to procure certain items that she felt were necessary to her.

Joshua's huge black eyes looked at Rachel as she stood next to the boiling cauldron of white linens behind the smokehouse. The smokehouse was located the furthest from the manor house so that the smoke and odor would not permeate the house. Formerly, the black iron laundry pots had been located next to the main kitchens, which were built closer to the manor house, but were not located inside the manor house proper.

Maureen had moved the laundry center further away so that she would never be exposed to even a passing glimpse of her nemesis, Rachel.

A wooden board, narrowed and rounded at the end, sat atop two sawhorses. It was covered with a thick pad of cotton with a muslin cover that was decorated with scorch marks from the heavy black irons. There were two rows of seven irons in various stages of temperature, because Rachel was quick at her work.

"You sure you want me to do this, Miz Rachel?" the nine-year-old Joshua asked.

"Yes."

"You could get a whippin' if Master Watkins finds out."

"I'll risk it," she said, thinking of the black-whiskered overseer Watkins. She looked over her shoulder to make sure they were still alone. "You just tell Crystal what I said and I'll take care of the rest."

Joshua took the neatly ironed stack of towels and napkins back to the manor house and entered the butler's pantry where Crystal was counting silverware and china.

"I have a message from Miz Rachel."

Crystal's glaucomic eyes moved slowly from her count of twenty-five butter knives over to the child. "What?"

"She wants you to get her some writin' paper, a quill and ink."

Crystal's smile cracked across her narrow face forcing the fine webbing of lines up into a curve in her cheeks. "Is that so?"

"Yes'm."

"And I 'spoze she wants a sanding box, too?"

Joshua grinned. "Yes'm."

Crystal's face collapsed. "Keep quiet about this. Take that bag of Miz Maureen's underthings to Rachel. Tell her that I'll be *glad* to do this for her."

Joshua's surprise puffed his eyes open. "I'll tell her."

Crystal had no family anymore. Her only love, Benjamin, had been sold to a plantation in Virginia for an incredible sum of money when she was twenty-four and he was twenty-five. Her baby daughter had died of cholera. Crystal kept her thoughts to herself and her heart slammed shut, and tried to stay as aloof from this world as possible. The only link she allowed in her life that kept her earthbound was Rachel and her boy, Jefferson.

Crystal had loved Rachel the first day she'd come to the plantation. She'd watched her fall in love with the master when Rachel was only seven years old, though Rachel didn't know it until she was ten or eleven. Crystal only allowed herself one other emotion in life and that was her hate for Maureen Harrison.

Crystal put the butter knives in the drawer and locked it with the key she wore around her neck. She placed the key inside the black-and-white-striped cotton dress, the uniform Maureen insisted she wear. She walked down the hall to the library. Knowing Maureen was still in her chambers, she crossed to Richard's desk.

She chose three quills from the crystal tumbler that held over a dozen. She took the double-china inkwell that had been imported from Portugal, the leather sanding box which contained the globose seed capsules of the round-crowned, high-branched sandbox tree used to blot ink, and a very large stack of writing paper.

Without checking the hallway or curving staircase for other servants, she went straightaway back to the butler's pantry. From the staples closet where she kept the more readily used household items—candles, wicks, whale oil and matches— she took a large container of blackest India ink and using the funnel that hung on the wall above her, she emptied a goodly amount into a glass jar. She then melted a wax seal on the jar, placed a lid on it and hid all the items in the locked china cabinet. No one in the house had a key to the china cabinet except Crystal. It had been given to her by Master Harrison on the day of Amelia's death, and since then, no one had ever asked for it back. Crystal had overheard Maureen say to her father, "You don't expect me to count china like a servant, do you?"

The items were delivered to Rachel via Joshua the following Saturday in the bottom of one of the laundry baskets. Rachel hid the items in the pockets of an apron she wore beneath her skirts when she walked back to the cabin she shared with Jefferson.

"I knew Crystal wouldn't fail me," Rachel said to herself as she put the instruments in a hole she dug in the earth beneath her pallet and which she'd lined with bricks and rocks she'd found on the plantation. They would be kept dry and safe until she needed them to exact her revenge.

It was two weeks before Maureen detected the absence of the writing tools. She immediately summoned Crystal.

"You're the housekeeper! What could have happened to them?"

Crystal kept her eyes lowered and shrugged her shoulders. "Maybe a thief."

Exasperated, Maureen threw her hands in the air. "You're all alike! Not good for a damn thing! Those were my father's things. It will upset him greatly when he hears of this. Fortunately, I have my own writing utensils in my room so I won't be inconvenienced by all this." She turned back to the desk, amazed at the audacity of the thief. "What could anyone do with them? No one here can write."

"Yes'm. The Master, he don't need them no more."

Maureen turned around, pondered Crystal's words, and as she did, her tightly drawn lips relaxed as her mind already began dismissing the matter. "I suppose you are right. The thief probably thinks he can *sell* them. Hmmm. Who knows?" She started out of the room. "Send someone to fetch my blue silk from the laundress. I'll wear that for dinner this evening with the Kanes."

"Yes'm." Crystal replied noting that Maureen always referred to Rachel as "the laundress."

Word about the missing writing utensils spread quickly through the manor house. The downstairs maid, who knew Crystal was the thief, told the upstairs maid, who told Richard Harrison's nurse of the incident and who happened to repeat the entire scenario to Richard, thinking that his mind was as numb as his body.

The two-hundred-pound woman, with the aid of the upstairs maid, had just settled Richard back into bed after his bath.

"Now why would she take them things?" The nurse mused aloud.

Just then, Richard began his facial quirks and minuscule gyrations that he was able to attempt with his upper lip when he wanted something. He lifted his good arm, and it flopped back on the bed. He pointed toward the window.

"We know what that means," the nurse said with a heavy sigh.

"He sure is a lot of work," the upstairs maid said.

With great effort they heaved Richard, a bit unceremoniously, into his wheelchair and took him to the window. The maid pulled back the heavy blue velvet drapes with the four-inch-long gold silk fringe and tied them back.

Richard began mumbling again and making signals that meant that he wanted the window raised. The nurses raised the window.

He leaned forward so that his head stuck out the window. He could move his neck from side to side, and he scanned the yard for any sign of Rachel.

He held his breath as she came into view.

She was carrying a huge woven basket on her head. She wore a bandana around her hair, a soiled apron and leather shoes that were tied around the insteps with hemp. Her back was bent, looking as if she carried the sorrows of the world.

My heart is breaking inside, Rachel. I had wanted you to be free. I had wanted you all to be free.

What has Maureen done to you?

What have I done to you?

A wrenching pain from his solar plexus shot through his insides. Still, he remained unable to move. The pain served only to remind him of his impotence. Once he'd had the power to make changes. With the stroke of his pen he could have freed Rachel.

I could have married her.

But I was afraid.

Now, I'm cursed with never being able to touch her again.

God forgive me.

His glimpses of her were so rare he couldn't take his eyes off her. "See me, Rachel," he called to her in his mind. "I know it was you who took the pens and ink."

It was a daring thing she did, but Rachel stopped dead in her tracks, put the basket down, and in broad daylight, she lifted her eyes to him and slowly pulled the kerchief from her hair. A summer breeze blew her long, copper curls about her face, and for the first time in twelve years, she allowed her love to shine in her eyes as bright as the sun. At that moment, Rachel didn't care if Maureen saw her. She didn't care if she was punished at the end of a whip. Rachel didn't give a damn about anything except Richard.

"I love you," she mouthed.

Her eyes, not young anymore, had a tendency to blur the world, until today. She *clearly* saw Richard smile at her. It was not a half-crack that she'd seen before, but a full parting of his lips, showing his white, even teeth, showing his joy once again.

"I forgive you," she said aloud.

A tear slipped out of his eye showing her that he felt her words. *I will love you forever.*

"I will love you back," she answered his thoughts with spoken words.

Slowly, she covered her hair with her bandana and replaced her laundry basket atop her head and reluctantly walked away.

* * * *

Jefferson watched his mother as she sat in the candlelight writing with the quill pen. "What are you writing?"

"A love story."

"May I read it?"

"Yes. It's for you. I've chronicled everything about my life with your father that I can remember. And I do remember it all.

I have also put down my memories of my mother and father and their life together along with Mother's potions, incantations, prayers and words of wisdom and truth about the worlds."

"You mean 'world.'"

"Worlds. This one and the one beyond." She touched his hand. "I am getting old, Jefferson. You'll be leaving this plantation soon. I've seen it in my dreams. I'll be going to live in another world. An unseen place from this world. But I will be with you always. Promise me you will remember that."

"I don't want to talk of dying or voodoo ghosts." Jefferson looked away.

She put her hands on his cheeks and turned his face back to her. "In your future you will see me and think I'm a ghost. But I will be real. Shortly, things will change for you and me. Now promise me."

Jefferson's eyes probed his mother's deep-green pools. "I promise." Then he looked away. He didn't believe anything would change for him. He was a slave and that was his destiny.

* * * *

Jefferson's twentieth birthday came and went like any other day on the plantation. He awoke in the morning to the sound of the predawn overseer's bell. Jefferson and Rachel rose from their pallets, rinsed their faces from a chipped, brown pottery jug and walked out of their cabin, he with his gunnysack in hand. She went to the laundry tubs.

Every morning, Jefferson felt Maureen's eyes on his back, and like cat claws they raked his skin, drawing blood from his youth and diminishing his dreams until there was nothing left but ashes.

He wished he could pray for his enemies the way his mother taught him, but he couldn't. He had too much hate in his heart.

"Someday, I will get away from you, bitch," Jefferson promised himself every night. But every day his routine was the same, unaltered by God or time.

ten

Which if not victory is yet revenge.

—JOHN MILTON
PARADISE LOST BK. II., L. 105

In her dream, Rachel stood on a windy hillside where skies unfurled like bolts of china-blue silk. Wildflowers beckoned to her as she walked past them, not seeing their beauty. She was mesmerized by the silver river water.

"But it's not water, it's mercury, like in the thermometer Richard showed me in his library." She paused and waited for the whirlwind of golden sparks to appear as had happened so many times before in her dreams.

"Mother," Rachel said in a hush as Yuala appeared in her gown of crushed pearl and gold.

"You must be strong, Rachel. Stronger than you've ever thought you'd need to be."

"But why?" She felt a chill.

"Richard is coming to join me, Rachel, on this side. Two weeks after he goes through the door to this side of existence, you will come back to me."

Rachel felt the incomparable peace she always experienced at these times when she spoke to her mother. "Thank God, Richard's suffering is over. And mine," she began to cry. "Mother, I have missed you so very much."

"And I've missed you, child. It's Jefferson's turn to seek his destiny. Your presence on earth only holds him back."

Yuala's smile lightened the atmosphere around Rachel as if it had been shot with silver moonbeams. Again Rachel was comforted.

"I understand . . ." Rachel hesitated. "But I must ask. Does it hurt as much

105

over there not to hold him in my arms?"

"No, because you hold him in your heart. It's better."

"I see."

Yuala's voice was filled with concern. "You worry over him."

Rachel nodded. "I do. He's not as open as you and I were at his age. He sees so little and understands only his anger and pain. I'm frightened for him."

"He'll learn in time, and you will help him from this side more than you could in his world."

The golden haze burnished itself, forming flames that shot to the sky. Yuala vanished and Rachel returned through the door to reality.

* * * *

Jefferson shoved a raw turnip into his mouth as he sat listening to his mother's description not only of his father's death but hers, too. He almost choked on the turnip.

"This is ridiculous!" He bolted to his feet. "I can't imagine life without you. You're all I have! We're family! You can't just leave me here alone." He turned away pretending not to feel his own tears.

"I don't want to talk about this nonsense. It was just a dream, Mother."

Pitching his dull knife onto the floor, he went to the doorway. He looked out on the blazing sunset and then over to the mansion where Richard indeed lay dying. "Maureen has called for the doctors, the whole plantation's talking about it. According to the house slaves, Richard refuses food." Jefferson angrily bit his lip. "It's as if my father wants to die. I understand that. But not you, Mother, you're in perfect health. I won't hear any more about how you're planning your own death."

"I'm not planning this. My heart aches to think of you alone. But it's my destiny. Your destiny. Never question my dreams. And never question God's will."

He spun around and peered through the twilight darkness in the cabin. "This has nothing to do with God. Voodoo, maybe, but not God. You're going to will yourself to death. That's what you're doing." Jefferson thought of a thousand more blasts to deliver, but his stomach lurched and he felt his heart shatter.

Jefferson was afraid. His brain was awash with tales of voodoo, the story of the faith healing Yuala had performed on his mother, of the fact that Yuala had predicted Henry's death and her own. He thought of the way his mother and Richard silently communicated with each other as if they indeed could read each other's minds. He thought of the thick packet of papers of wisdom she'd compiled with a near vengeance this past year. It was her "legacy" to him, she'd said. He was a grown man and yet he was as fear-filled as a child.

"How can you leave me? Don't you love me?" He rushed to her and though he was twice her size, he slumped to his knees and buried his head in her bosom. "What will I do without you?"

"You're leaving here," she said, caressing his thick blond hair.

His eyes shot wide open as his head jerked back to look in her face. "Am I to die as well?"

"No. You will journey in a ship across the sea as the obeahman told my mother and me long ago. You will go to California."

"California? Why, that's on the other side of the world. Did you forget I'm a slave?"

"Everyone will think you are a free white man."

Jefferson's mind was filled with reports he'd heard from other slaves who'd tried to escape. There were man-eating dogs, the tongue of the lash that would shred his back once he was caught. And he *would* be caught. He *knew* Watkins. The Harrison overseer had never lost a slave to the Carolina marshes nor the thickly forested and grassy banks of the Ashley River.

"Impossible."

She shook her head. "No, it's not. I have heard of the whites helping slaves escape. There is a network of them all the way to Boston. The first one you get to is the Tremont plantation to the north of here. You've seen it when we went into Charleston with Richard."

"I remember."

"There's a woman who works in the kitchens, Sally. She's white and works for hire. She will hide you. Then she will tell you of the next stop on your journey and give you their name and location. Each house, farm and family will tell you of the next stop. You will travel by night until you are far enough north when you can walk the roads safely in the daylight."

"And the dogs?"

"Richard got rid of them, remember?"

"I did forget. But still . . ."

Rachel felt his misgivings and fear as they coursed through his body. She straightened her back and clenched her jaw. "Listen well, Jefferson, it might be too dangerous to explain all this more than once. Your travel will not be as hazardous as you think because you look white. Once in Boston, you'll go to the harbor and find a ship that sails for California."

"Ships cost money, Mother."

"I've saved a bit of money that Richard gave me long ago. It will help a great deal. However, I've heard that you can exchange work for your passage to California."

"It still sounds like slavery," he frowned. "Where do I go once I get to California?"

"I don't know. But you will. The moment your eyes see it, you will know your future home. Don't depend on logic to tell you this. Richard told me once that most of the ships going around Cape Horn and on to California set sail from Boston."

"Mother, I'll never get to Boston. Maureen will have Watkins combing every blade of grass for me."

Rachel's eyes were stern and deliberate. "Don't worry over Maureen. I will take care of her."

"How can you? You said you would be dead."

Rachel's eyes shot to the open door to their cabin and to the flickering light in the upstairs room where Maureen was sleeping. "She will die before me." She looked down at Jefferson. "There will be no one on the plantation to stop any of the slaves from escaping."

Jefferson's face beamed with hope again. "Then you could come with me."

"No, Jefferson. This is my home. In death, Richard and I will be together. Crystal will see that I am buried not far from him. It will take a week for the authorities to make their move. By that time, you'll be long gone, and Richard and I will be together."

Jefferson was dumbfounded by all she told him. He wasn't accustomed to leaps of faith. He didn't know how she was going to do it, but his years with his mother had taught him that she had *never* been wrong.

Richard died on Sunday, June 27 at 2:22 in the afternoon. Rachel knew he'd chosen the Lord's day because it was the most spiritual day of the week. Rachel chose the same day to deposit a voodoo doll in Maureen's likeness in the top drawer desk in Richard's library, by way of Joshua who hid the doll in between the linen sheets he handed to Crystal, who then nonchalantly placed the doll according to Rachel's instructions.

The doll's hair was Maureen's hair taken from her clothing that Rachel had painstakingly laundered for years. It wore a scrap of lace from Maureen's camisole, a button from her blue silk gown and a hook from her corselette.

The night of Richard's death, as all the plantation slaves sang mournful hymns, Rachel packed a gunnysack with a new suit of clothing, underwear and shoes—all Richard's, of course—the money she'd promised Jefferson and her completed "Rachel Papers."

"How will I know when to leave?" Jefferson asked.

"There will be a sign from God that no one will mistake. Your instructions and the list of those in the underground who will give you safe journey are inside the sack. Each day when you go to the field, watch the house for the sign. I will put the sack near the whipping tree, under the earth where the soil is loose. There will be a rock to mark its place."

"What about Watkins?" Jefferson asked.

"When the sign comes, he and all his hands will leave the fields. That's when you make your break."

Rachel kissed Jefferson. It was a final kiss and he knew it. His eyes were filled with tears when he opened them. "Mama."

Her smile quivered. "Be strong for me. I want you to promise me that every day of your life you will say a prayer for me. What I am about to do will not please the Lord. You will have to save my soul for me, Jefferson."

"My God! Mother! Then don't do it!"

"To save you and my grandchildren, I must make this sacrifice. I have courage. So must you."

That night Rachel went to her knees and began her prayers aloud. Jefferson watched her until his eyes were weary and he fell asleep. In the morning when the call came to go to the fields, Rachel was still on her knees, hands clenched so tightly they were nearly white. But now her words were in a dialect he barely understood. He knew then she was calling on the "loa." She was deep in her voodoo.

"Where's your mother, Jefferson?" Watkins demanded.

"She didn't finish the laundry because of the master's funeral. It's a powerful lot o' linen."

"Yes, well. See that she finishes soon. I want her in the fields again. We're shorthanded."

"Yes, sir."

Rachel remained on her knees all that day, taking nothing to eat or drink. By the time Jefferson returned, she looked ten years older. It was as if her praying not only sapped her energy, but the very life out of her.

"Please stop this, Mama."

But Rachel was in trance and couldn't hear him.

Through the night Rachel continued to pray aloud, whispering the words that would free her son and bring her revenge.

The next morning was Tuesday, and the house slaves bathed outdoors on this morning. None of the family or friends had arrived yet for the memorial service, and indeed, few had even a chance to receive the news, because the plantations were spread so far apart.

Richard's body was laid in rest in the front salon as was the Southern custom. Maureen was asleep in her room. Rachel was still on her knees in prayer.

"I'm going to the fields, Mama," Jefferson said, kissing the top of her head. She did not respond. He picked up his gunnysack. "Mama?"

Silence.

Jefferson shook his head sadly and left.

Watkins again inquired about Rachel's whereabouts.

"She's sick today, sir. She's pale and weak and cannot eat or drink," Jefferson told the man who sat astride his horse, with his hat pulled low over his forehead to block the strong morning sun.

"You'd better be telling the truth."

"I do not lie."

Watkins eyed him suspiciously but only for a second. "That's the truth of it, Jefferson. I believe you."

Jefferson walked away as Watkins turned his face toward the manor house.

"God in heaven!" Watkins whacked his horse's hind end. "The manor house is on fire!"

The fire raged all morning.

Later everyone would claim they didn't know how it started.

"Someone must have forgotten an oil lamp," Watkins told the authorities. "Wind could have knocked it over."

But there were others, like Crystal and Joshua, who knew the fire started with a voodoo doll.

The blaze started in the desk drawer in Richard's library, which was located directly beneath Maureen's bedroom.

The silk draperies were sucked up in long fingers of fire in seconds. The furniture was old, and made of very dry wood. The fire annihilated the rugs, the upholstery, the oil painting of Amelia, the Spanish globe and the reams of paper upon which all the classic novels and thoughts of man had been printed. All of Richard's personal possessions, his tobacco jar, his pipes, pistols and fencing swords were destroyed in the inferno. The satinwood desk was reduced to ashes.

Oddly, none of the library walls succumbed to the fire as quickly as the library ceiling. It was as if the fire shot rockets of flame through the floorboards straight up to Maureen's bed.

The smoke dulled her senses and caused her to sleep even more deeply that morning. She barely rolled to her side as a wall of fire rose up like a demon and possessed the white lace bedhangings and the posts of her carved wood bed. The gold damask spread, which she'd newly purchased that year in Charleston at an outrageously expensive linen shop off Meeting Street, exploded in a vortex of heat and flame, sucking Maureen across the dimensions from life to death.

There were no servants in the house to save Maureen, since they had been ordered to take their baths.

They formed a bucket brigade and began dousing the library with water upon the first signs of smoke and flame. None of the house slaves would venture into the house to save anything or any person, too superstitious over the fact that the master was already dead and lying in the salon.

None of the servants would admit they were pleased with the reckoning Maureen had met that day. The house slaves and some of the field slaves, though not many of the latter, mourned the death of one of their own kind.

Crystal found Rachel dead and in a crumbled heap in her cabin the afternoon of the fire.

When Jefferson heard Watkins yelling about the fire, he instinctively started to run after him and help form the bucket brigade.

Suddenly, he heard his mother's voice, "Run, Jefferson. Run, now!"

Still, Jefferson dashed toward the house yelling, "Fire! Fire!"

His words spurred the slaves to action, but their buckets were impotent against the mighty inferno.

As Jefferson neared the oak tree, he hung back from the rest, letting all the slaves overtake him. He watched as they moved a like a wave toward the manor house whose second floor was now engulfed in flames. He doubled back, went to the tree and found the rock. He peeled up a piece of sod, dug under the dirt and found the sack his mother must have buried during the night.

"Run, Jefferson!" He heard his mother's voice again.

Jefferson turned to the north, said a prayer and ran for his life.

eleven

The Mount of olives shall cleave in the midst thereof toward the east and toward the west, and there shall be a very great valley; and half of the mountain shall remove toward the north and half of it toward the south.

—Zech. 14:4

San Francisco Harbor—December 20, 1835

Jefferson gazed at the curling winter fog as it pulled itself from the tops of seven hills that loomed over the San Francisco Bay. Sylvan valleys were infused with the breath of future Babylonian splendor his mother had foretold, and for the first time, he realized the enormity of his purpose.

"It's everything you said it would be," he said with a smile.

"What's that you say?" one of the crew asked as he passed by.

"It's colder than I'd thought," Jefferson replied, pulling his wool cap over his sandy hair and covering his ears. He'd never asked the man his name. He knew only a select few of the crew by name. It was best that way.

"Aye. 'Tis that. You're not used to the cold then, Jefferson?"

He folded his arms across his chest. "Just need a new coat is all."

"Ah," the man nodded. "Carry on."

"Aye, sir." Jefferson waited while the man moved on. He'd made a practice on this trip not to reveal anything about himself or his past. Even the slightest morsel of information could lead to his doom.

He glanced longingly over the ship's side. *I'd give anything to swim to shore right now. Freedom. I wonder . . . what will it be like?*

Patience, Jefferson. You can wait one more day.

He hung back, steadying the disinterested attitude he'd been noted for on this trip. As far as the rest of the crew was concerned, Jefferson had signed on for a normal tour of sail, which included the trip around the Horn and back again to Boston. Now that he had reached California, Jefferson asked the captain to be let out of his contract. The captain had agreed that though Jefferson worked hard, he was not cut out to be a sailor.

Jefferson spoke only when spoken to and grunted single syllable responses. He diverted conversations around his background back to the questioner with the delicate ease and grace of a skilled swordsman. Jefferson was a mystery to his fellow deckhands, just as they were to him. Jefferson was different. He was fighting for his life.

The brig *Pilgrim*, upon which he'd made his home since August 20, had been an alien ship, a foreign environment for a man who'd never felt the sea beneath him. As unsteadying as the idea was that water was his terra firma, even more unsettling was the reality he could never see his mother again. There was no returning home.

He wondered if his grandfather, Henry Duke, felt like this the first time he'd leaned over the live-oak-and-redwood side of the triple-masted schooner, the *Magellan*, and seen South Carolina.

Jefferson found it hard to believe that the palmetto trees, jasmine and scrub pines of Charleston could have been more impressive than the beauty of San Francisco Bay. His clear eyes narrowed as he thought, "That was 1760 and grandfather had the advantages of royal blood and wealth to help him make a future."

Rachel's voice haunted him. "All that he accomplished was for you to have this moment in time," she said.

Smiling to himself, Jefferson saw a vision of Rachel standing beside him. It was almost real. He reached out to her.

She raised her hand to his. "Have courage, Jefferson. I'm here."

As she faded away, courage lined the edges of his soul and gave him the strength he needed. Even though his only possessions were the clothes on his back, he knew he was doing the right thing. His mother had died to give him this chance at a new life. He felt ambition and desire ignite deep in his heart. "I'll build your vision for you, Mother. San Francisco will be a city of equality and the unconditional love you had for me."

Jefferson was amazed at the emotions he felt just looking at the bay. Gone was his hatred and bitterness toward Maureen. She was dead. That part of his life was over. Often Rachel had said that negative thoughts would destroy him. Now he knew that to be true. His heart was lighter, just being away from Maureen. His future seemed bright and hopeful.

As he gazed at the inlets, coves and tributaries of San Francisco Bay, he was aware he was living out Yuala's prediction for him. The forces of fate had contrived his escape from the plantation and arranged his passage on the ship. He knew he'd certainly planned none of it. It simply happened. Jefferson was flying on the wings of destiny. His only choice had been acceptance.

The ship sailed through the narrow pathway of water bordered by the mainland on either side.

Through the foggy mist Jefferson saw a rock island.

"Is that Alcatraz?" He asked Simpson, who stood next to him.

"'Tis," he said in his clipped New England dialect.

"I've read about it," Jefferson said.

"So have I," Simpson said. "It was discovered by Don Juan Manuel de Ayala in 1775, of Portola's command. When he anchored, it caused such a fluttering from the thousands of pelicans who were feeding nearby that he named it 'Pelican Island.'"

"Yes," Jefferson grunted.

Simpson nodded and pulled out his wood pipe.

Two points jutted into the Bay, still unnamed, but the little cove was called Yerba Buena. Off to the left was the enormous and densely forested Angel Island, which Jefferson knew they would scavenge and harvest for the ship's year's supply of firewood. This time of year, the so'easter wind was the bane of California, rolling into shore with such a ferocity that vessels were never safe from rains and winds. Except for the ports of San Francisco and San Diego, most ships were forced to lie anchor three miles out from shore with slip-ropes on their cables in order to pull anchor and head back out to sea as expeditiously as possible. The force and swell of the entire Pacific rolled toward land with breaks so heavy that entire ships had been lost. But once the four sails of the *Pilgrim* had passed through the Golden Gate, she was no longer in danger from the so'easter.

Jefferson sucked cool morning mist into his lungs. He wanted to remember this taste, its weight and texture this first time.

This is my chance to erase the past and put Mother's soul to rest.

The ship dropped anchor, cast off the yard and gaskets from the sails, and stopped them all with rope-yarns. Deckhands lowered the ketches over the side to take the first parties to shore.

Jefferson watched as Captain Thompson, puffing on his customary cigar, paced back and forth on the quarterdeck as he issued orders. "Heave ho, there!" he shouted impatiently.

Jefferson quickly turned away from the Captain's eye and swabbed the deck, which was an even more tedious, backbreaking job than picking cotton. Last night he'd stood "anchor watch" from twelve until two, taking the larboard side, and his watchmate, John, taking the starboard side. Bells were struck every half hour as they did when at sea, and the second mate stood watch until eight when breakfast began after the regular morning chores.

The captain, as had been his routine on this voyage once port was set, would then disembark and spend most of his time ashore, arranging for the sale of goods aboard ship while the chief mate took over the captain's duties on ship.

Jefferson shoved his rag mop across the wood deck, hoping his near glee over the captain's departure didn't show.

Naively, Jefferson had believed that once he left South Carolina, he would leave racial prejudice behind. During the fifty-eight days of his northward journey, he met whites who were good and courageous and who risked their lives for himself and other slaves. He would never forget their dedication.

His mother had been correct that his trip north would not be difficult because he so easily passed for white. Twice, once in Virginia and once in Delaware, he'd almost been refused aid because his contact did not believe he was a slave.

With his hair, features and physique, and Richard's clothing, he looked more the lord of the manor than Richard. Jefferson had always been accused of proud bearing. Once he left the marshes of South Carolina, he reveled in his ability to look every man in the eye. It was no longer necessary to lower his gaze, nor stoop his shoulders. For the first time in his life, he felt like a man. But all that was short-lived once he met Captain Thompson.

The flogging of one of his crewmates was the first incident of such cruelty that the new deckhands had ever seen. When it was over, Jefferson had asked a few questions of his shipmates. He discovered that most ship captains rule with a heavy hand, as it is necessary to maintain discipline. The world at sea, by its very nature, was an easy prey for anarchy.

Jefferson had seen Watkins lash a field hand once while still on horseback with his horse whip, but he'd never seen anything like the spectacle of near-insanity and torture as he had witnessed on the sea.

Jefferson had been up in the top gallant when the scuffle between the captain, John, the Swede, and Sam, a tall, intelligent-looking African, broke out in the cargo hold. Because the topmast studding-sail boom had buckled, sprung out and then broke off the boom-iron, Jefferson had to take the main top gallant studding-sail.

"Lay loft, there! Furl that main-royal!" The chief mate yelled at Jefferson.

Jefferson left the studding-sail and went across the crosstrees. The hands below had been working to help get the necessary ropes taut. As Jefferson glanced down, he saw the captain bring Sam on deck.

The captain was shouting something to the first mate and then Jefferson saw Sam being tied to the shrouds by his wrists. His jacket was off and his back was bare. The captain held a thick rope in his hand, splayed at the ends to bring about the ripping of flesh Jefferson had feared all his life in South Carolina. All hands watched as the captain railed at Sam with every sling of the rope.

Rage shot through Jefferson's mind. He wanted to shimmy down the mast and put his hands around the captain's neck and watch his cruel, inhumane eyes bug out of his head. But Jefferson didn't do that. He remained high above the scene where he could almost pretend he wasn't part of it. He saw the others below, saw their faces turn ashen as the whip hit Sam's back six times. Jefferson gripped the mast with such ferocity, his fingernails left imprints. He shut his eyes, foolishly thinking he could blunt out the sound of the hemp slaking Sam's skin off his back.

Sam shook, writhed and cringed from the pain, but he never said a word. There were no screams, no pleas for mercy. Three more times the rope swung at Sam before the captain ordered him to be cut down.

Jefferson could not hear the words below, but he watched as John, the Swede, was brought up, but he threw off the second mate, then the third mate, before walking directly up to the captain with his wrists thrust forward.

Captain Thompson was in a rage, pacing back and forth, flinging his bloody rope about. There were words between the men, and then John was tied to the foresail. The captain cursed John and then began the whipping.

Jefferson nearly vomited his disgust when John screamed in agony. Finally, the man crumbled, was cut down by the mate and walked slowly of his own volition into the forecastle.

Captain Thompson was a monster full of rage screaming at the hands. He likened himself to God and claimed that he was the "slave-driver" of this ship and that Sam was an "African slave."

Jefferson's blood went cold at the words. He'd boarded this ship to earn passage to California, and they'd been putting in at trading posts all along the coast. At that moment, Jefferson believed that he would have to leave the ship at the very next anchor. What happened to Sam could happen to him, and Jefferson wasn't so sure he would be as courageous and noble as Sam.

The captain went below and the hands broke apart and went back to work. Jefferson realized he had been right to keep quiet and aloof from the men. Sam had never been a slave, but Jefferson had. It was Jefferson who should have been on the other end of that rope, not Sam. He wondered if there would ever come a time when he would not think of himself as a fugitive.

twelve

Where we love is home,
Home that our feet may leave,
but not our hearts.

—OLIVER WENDELL HOLMES
"HOMESICK IN HEAVEN"

The process of exchanging goods in California fascinated Jefferson, and from this observation he formulated his plan for the future. The *Pilgrim* was stocked with all manner of goods from Boston. The trade room aboard ship was in the steerage, and here the lighter goods such as tin-ware, boots and shoes from Lynn, calicos and cottons from Lowell, crepes, silks, shawls, scarves, necklaces, bracelets and hair combs were laid out for the buyers to peruse and purchase. The furniture was from China and England. The larger items like casks of spirits, wine, coffees, teas, sugar, spices, raisins and molasses were sold sight unseen and delivered from the cargo hold later.

For a week to ten days, the ships lay in harbor as the Spanish dons and their ladies from Monterey, Santa Barbara, San Diego and San Francisco rowed out in small boats to shop.

As Jefferson studied all the commerce taking place, what impressed him most was the incredible amount of money to be made as a trapper in California.

Wolf, elk, fox, coyote and mountain lion hides were unlimited. He witnessed trappers coming aboard and trading over two thousand hides caught by a single individual. There seemed to be no limit the exorbitant amounts of money the dons spent.

The entire scene assaulted Jefferson. He'd been taught by his mother to respect the earth and its creatures. Yet, he heard these men talking about the overabundance of wildlife that threatened the domesticated cattle and the rancheros. It was the first time Jefferson came to terms with the balances that must exist between man and beast. Having always grown up in warm climates, it wasn't until Jefferson went around the tip of South America and nearly froze to death for lack of warm clothing that he truly understood the need for life-saving furs that would keep Easterners cold during their harsh winters.

"But these people have more money than sense," Jefferson observed as he watched the wealthy Californians spend money freely.

Think of the lives I could buy out of captivity with that kind of money. If only the laws were different. If only the world were different.

Suddenly, Jefferson heard his mother speak to him though she did not appear. "The world is what it is. It is not heaven. It is material. It is the space you must work within. Make the best of what you have been given. God asks no more."

Looking around the ship at the Sangre-azul women, pure Castilian blue-blooded beauties, with their raven hair and skin so white the blue veins showed through, his breath caught in his throat.

The most elaborately dressed was a young woman he heard the captain greet as Señorita Dolores Sanchez. He watched her as she flitted from cask to trunk inspecting brocades and satin shoes with spangles and jewels, choosing only the best.

Jefferson had only read about the splendor of the Spanish court in *Don Quixote*. To him, Dolores Sanchez was the epitome of exotic beauty. Beneath the shadow of her lace mantilla, which was raised high on her head by tall, jeweled combs, she inspected every necklace with exacting eyes. She held her head pridefully and never cast her eyes at the men on the ship as some of the other women had. He watched as she opened the velvet drawstrings of her reticule and extracted handfuls of silver coins to pay for her purchases.

"I've never seen so much silver," Jefferson gasped to himself. "It must be a king's ransom."

He remembered hearing that there were no banks in California, no credit system or bank notes. Only silver coins and hides were used for barter, and the Californians were willing to spend it all.

They didn't care that they paid three times the value of goods. Because they were at the mercy of the few ships that sailed around the Horn to sell to them, their only concern was availability of merchandise.

Jefferson infused these observations in his head and calculated them with his own knowledge of hunting squirrel, possum and racoon. Trapping larger game would take time, but to build a city, he would need to live, work and trade in the white man's world. With each animal life he took, he would bless it and bless the life his hides would save from cold.

Once I've learned to trap, I'll open my own trading post with my profits. Then I will buy goods and re-sell them. If I make good profits, I won't have to hunt and trap more than a year or so.

Jefferson would build his empire just as his grandfather had, but his would be in the retail trade.

The second mate came up from behind him. "Jefferson, you'll take the second crew in."

"Yes, sir," Jefferson kept his eyes lowered to the knot he was tying.

"Cap'n says you're leavin'. Pack yer gear," he said simply and handed him a small cloth bag that held silver coins to represent the $110 he had earned for four months at sea.

"Yes, sir." Jefferson took the money and shoved it quickly into his trouser pocket. He finished the knot and looked at the hill above Yerba Buena Cove.

The hill was now alive with people coming down from the Presidio and the Mission and the surrounding ranchos to greet the ketch. The natives to this land were called Indians, he was told, and they were the slowest for they had the least amount of money to spend. From the sandy trail that circled around the crescent-shaped beach came a pair of galloping palominos both bearing Spanish dons and behind them an ox-cart piled high with hides and furs. Jefferson watched as Captain Thompson and the first party climbed out of the boat and were met by many smiling faces.

Four hours later, Jefferson had packed his worldly belongings, rowed away from the *Pilgrim*, and stepped onto the golden shores of San Francisco. The first party from the ship was being escorted up to the Presidio, now that the major portion of business had been conducted. Confidently, he walked directly to the shanty owned by William Richardson, who since his marriage to Maria Antonia, daughter of Lieutenant Ignacio Martinez of the Presidio, had been known as Don William Antonio Richardson. Jefferson spoke directly to the don himself.

"How do you do, Don Richardson?" Jefferson offered his hand, and the man took it. "My name is Jefferson Duke," he said, thinking that no one would ever know about him this far from South Carolina. In his mind, Jefferson was free. He would never think of himself as a runaway again. Such thoughts were negative and cast a pall on his future. "I have a business proposition for you."

Richardson, who looked a bit weary and who'd been directing a half-dozen Indians loading hides for shipment to the *Pilgrim*, never looked at Jefferson and kept about his business. "I'll bet you do."

Undaunted by the man's abrupt manner, Jefferson pressed on. "I'd like to purchase a rifle, some ammunition and discuss the purchase of a horse."

Richardson stopped and surveyed the young Jefferson. "You ever hunt before?"

"A little."

"You're off the ship, aren't you?"

"Yes, sir."

"You're not from Boston?"

"No, sir. South Carolina. Jefferson Duke from South Carolina."

Richardson leaned on his hands and the rickety counter groaned under the pressure. "What you want is to purchase my goods, son. What kind of business are you talkin' about?"

Jefferson's heart was in his throat. He needed this man to help him or he would end up a trapper all his life. "I haven't got enough money to pay cash for all these things. I want to be your business partner."

"My *what?*"

Jefferson swallowed. "Partner."

"That's what I thought you said."

Jefferson's eyes locked on Richardson and didn't waver. "I don't want a grub stake. I'll pay you half the cost of the goods and horse. Winter is here and you know that in three months I can deliver approximately a thousand hides."

"How do I know that? You're from South Carolina. That ain't trappin' country."

"I'll do it," Jefferson assured him.

"And if you don't?"

"I'll give you back everything but the ammunition, plus all the hides I've collected."

Richardson was incredulous. He pulled on his long mustache hairs that were badly in need of a clipping. "I got trappers that bring in that much, maybe three fellas together and they split it up. But you'd have to work night and day to bring in that number."

"I realize that."

Richardson exhaled and came around the counter. He put his hand on Jefferson's shoulder. "Son, you're either very good or real damn stupid. But I'm gonna take your proposition, because I'm gonna win either way. And when spring comes, you're gonna learn a valuable lesson."

"What's that?"

"Know your limits." Richardson's eyes bore into Jefferson with concern. "There ain't no way, son. No way."

Jefferson's lips parted in a broad, nearly cocky smile. "Could I buy that palomino you've got out back?"

* * * *

The San Francisco Bay was ringed by large, lavish ranchos owned by Spanish dons who snapped up large tracts of land in 1822 when Mexico gained independence from Spain. Then in 1833, the secularization of the missions changed the economic, political and social aspect of much of California. The padres lost their control and the great cattle ranchos, which had belonged to the missions, were opened to private grant. Several of the old Santa Barbara and Monterey families moved up the coast and took possession.

General Vallejo's ranch was located at the northeast end of San Pablo Bay, with Lieutenant Martinez's Rancho Pinole with its eight thousand cattle and one thousand horses just south of it. From just south of Point Richmond to south of Lake Chalbot was the Peralta Rancho and behind it in the hills was the Moraga Rancho. The tracts of Castro, Soto, Amador, Pacheco, Alviso and Estudillo all lay along the southeastern regions of the Bay. Around and up the Peninsula was the Arguello Rancho, which was Don Richardson's father-in-law's estate; the vast Buri Buri Rancho; La Visitacion Rancho; the properties of Bernal, Noe, Valencia, Nunez and other smaller tracts. On the ocean side of the Peninsula were the ranches of Diaz, Guerro, De Haro and the San Miguel Rancho.

Jefferson thought it interesting that the few Anglo-Saxons who had come here as he had, off sailing vessels or down from the mountains to the east for the hide trade, had all settled in the Yerba Buena Cove area as had Don Richardson.

As he mounted the golden palomino and headed south toward thick forests and the Montara Mountains, Jefferson knew that when he came back to settle, it wouldn't be across the bay at San Pablo with the Spanish, but right there, next to Don Richardson—an Anglo-Saxon.

For the first time in his life, Jefferson would fit in.

* * * *

Camp consisted of a used whaling tarpaulin stretched out across four red-wood poles that Jefferson had fashioned out of young trees. Richardson had told him that he'd built this type of structure as his first trading post. It kept the rain off his head and hides, and that was all that was necessary.

Along the banks of the San Andreas Lake, he set iron single-spring traps for muskrats under the water to hide human scent. When they came to feed on water lily roots and water-grass roots, the trap clamped down and drowned the animal. His mother had told him once that drowning was a near painless death. He blessed the muskrats in his prayers. He believed they blessed him in return.

The trap was chained to a stake placed a few feet out from the bank in deeper water. In the forests, he set double-spring traps along the wooded ridges for fox and wolves. He fastened the traps to a stake so that the animal could not carry the costly traps away.

Bobcats were caught in traps concealed in logs as they crossed streams and tiny creeks. Beavers also were caught much like the muskrats, except that near beaver dams, he placed the traps a bit deeper in the water and double secured the stakes, since beavers were known to "twist off" their own leg to escape the trap.

For larger animals, like deer and bear, he used the Pennsylvania rifle, even though people were already referring to them as Kentucky rifles, ever since the Battle of New Orleans, which immortalized Andrew Jackson's "Kentucky Mountain Men" in a ballad. The Pennsylvania rifle's accuracy was legendary. This fact Jefferson proved himself by putting eight consecutive shots into a five-by-seven-inch target at sixty yards' range.

Richardson had told Jefferson that the British claimed the Americans were able to hit a man in the head at a distance of two hundred yards. "A buck or elk oughta be no problem," he'd said.

Jefferson practiced for days to make certain his shots were accurate and that his prey were killed instantly.

The only drawback to the rifle was that it took a great deal of time to reload. The patch had to be put across the muzzle and the ball started truly down the bore and rammed.

Jefferson's morning started two hours before dawn. He checked his traps, removed his catch, which he stored in huge sacks on either side of his horse, and then reloaded the traps. He then had another round of traps filled before dawn when the animals came out for morning feeding.

Each morning he hunted deer as they fed. He skinned the deer, taking what meat was necessary for survival and burying the carcasses. When his horse was loaded down, he rode back to camp, skinned the smaller animals for their fur and hung them to dry.

The woods and mountains were teeming with so many animals that his time stalking an animal was almost nonexistent. He barely had to hide among the scrubs, pines and redwoods except when he set his sights on larger game such as a bear or lion. Compared to working on the ship and breaking his back under the blazing Carolina sun, his life as a trapper was bliss. His father had taught him to use his brain at all times. From his days living in fear as he made his escape from Carolina, he'd learned to *think* like an animal.

Jefferson was unaware that his desire for success had altered his perspective. He never wanted to return to his former life. These days, his life was framed only by freedom. He could work as late or as long as he wanted. He could say, do, think and feel anything he wanted. He used his time of skinning, drying and tanning his hides to formulate his plans. His sense of concentration became keen, and he learned to focus his thoughts.

"Thoughts are things," his mother had said.

Not once, as he slept under the cold stars and silver moon, did he think negatively. "Mother was right. In this land, anything is possible! I can do anything!" He shouted until his voice echoed through the night.

On April 3, 1836, Jefferson brought down his hides from the mountains.

He'd gone to Yerba Buena Cove and found changes had occurred over the winter.

In 1834, Governor Alvarado commissioned Don Francisco de Haro to make a plan for the Yerba Buena section that would include a public plaza. A Swiss surveyor, Captain Jean Vioget, centered the plaza where Candelario Miramontes had been cultivating a potato garden for years and then laid out three streets radiating from the square. These would later be named Stockton, Pacific and Pine.

By the time Jefferson came to the cove, Don Richardson had started building a wooden-frame house for himself on the muddy Calle della Fondacion on a square of land 275 feet by 275 feet, which he had bought as a grant from the Alcalde and Governor Chico for twenty-five dollars.

Jefferson flopped a pelt of lush beaver skin on the counter. "You must have been counting on my skins."

"How's that?" Richardson ran his hand through the brown, sable and black fur.

"Building a new house takes a lot of money."

"I know. But it was a good winter for trading."

Jefferson beamed. "It was a good winter for trapping."

Richardson was skeptical. "How many?"

"My quota."

"That's impossible! You would've had to work day and night! Only a seasoned man could do that well. How do you know so much about hunting?"

"I read about it in a book," he leaned over the counter. "Let's add this up," Jefferson suggested, chuckling.

There were sixteen hundred skins all together, but Jefferson only sold the first thousand to Richardson, to keep his bargain, and kept the rest for himself. He had plans for the last six hundred skins.

Jefferson then went to the Alcalde, whom he found at the Presidio, and bought two lots, just as Nathan Spear and Jacob P. Leese of Ohio were doing that very same day. Though the ten-foot-high wood door to the Alcalde's room was shut, Jefferson heard the conversation.

"I intend to build a sixty-by-twenty-five-foot house with a real piazza," Leese said.

"Is it true that Captain Hinkley is building, also?" a second voice asked.

"The Adobe Custom-House will break ground next week," the Alcalde said.

Jefferson watched the two Americans depart before he was ushered in by a silent, half-stooped Indian.

Jefferson shook hands with the Alcalde. "I'd like two of those lots. One on Calle della Fondacion and one on North Beach."

Surprise riddled the Alcalde's face. "Why two?"

"The first will be for my home. The second I intend to use as a place of business, it being so close to the water."

"What kind of business?"

"A trading post. Initially."

The Alcalde looked at Jefferson appreciatively.

"You're the one from the *Pilgrim*."

"I am."

The Alcalde's hearty laugh bounced against the white-washed adobe walls. "You made the ridiculous bargain with Richardson. So tell me. How many hides did you get?"

"Sixteen hundred."

The Alcalde's jaw dropped.

"That's why I want two lots. Six hundred hides I intend to sell myself and keep the profit. You'll find that I am not an ordinary man to do business with."

The Alcalde harrumphed. "You're young. And impudent. You cannot have the lots. Impossible. Now go away."

Jefferson nearly fell back in shock. "Why not?"

"You must first be a citizen of the New Republic of Mexico as have the others."

"And how do I do that?"

The Alcalde pulled out a drawer, which banged against his potbelly. He withdrew a piece of parchment. "Sign here," he said, handing Jefferson a quill.

Jefferson smiled politely. He supposed for some, giving up their citizenship to America was an important decision. But Jefferson had no country. Technically, he was still a slave, not entitled to land ownership. Not entitled to anything. This man was handing him a shortcut to his dream. He couldn't believe it. He wondered if it was possible to contain this much joy. Jefferson's hand shook as he took the quill and signed his name with a flourish.

"Is there anything else I should do to become a proper citizen?"

The Alcalde blotted the ink. "Joining the church wouldn't hurt."

"Of course," Jefferson replied. "Would Sunday be too soon?"

The Alcalde took out the map of the three hundred square vara lots. There were two newly inked Xs on the lots purchased that morning. "Sunday would be fine. Now, which lots were those again?"

Jefferson's eyes gleamed with joy. He could almost feel the roots growing out of his toes and down into the sand of Yerba Buena.

thirteen

*It takes a great deal of Christianity to wipe out
uncivilized Eastern instincts,
such as falling in love at first sight.*

—RUDYARD KIPLING
"PLAIN TALES FROM THE HILLS"

San Francisco—1836

They were called "The Beautiful Days" by the wealthy dons whose lives were filled with festivals and visiting other wealthy families up and down the coast of California.

Dolores Sanchez exemplified every aspect of these continual horse races and *meriendas*. Many was the month she rode in her father's resplendent carriage three hundred miles down the coast with her duenna to Santa Barbara visiting five or six ranchos clearly intent upon breaking the hearts of the young dons she'd known since childhood.

It was all a game to Dolores. Though she was high-spirited, insisting that she help herd and brand cattle with her brothers, she was a prisoner of Castilian mores. Spanish dons were hospitable to the Yankee invaders but only to a point. They might share meals in their homes with them but they never shared their daughters. Every night after vespers, Dolores was locked in her room by her father.

Initially, Dolores thought nothing of the imprisonment. She believed her father loved her and wanted the best for her. She didn't know he meant only

129

to protect the Castilian blue blood in her veins. All her life, Dolores's every wish had been met. Her beauty was like a magic wand. She had everything she wanted.

Until she met Jefferson Duke.

Dolores wore a pale-yellow silk dress overlaid with elaborate white lace, with six petticoats underneath, to the Fourth of July celebration. The Sanchez family had been fetched in by the Richardson launch along with other families from the area who arrived in boats provided by Captain Hinkley's ship, the *Don Quixote*, which was anchored in the bay.

Carrying a white lace parasol to shade her alabaster skin from the sun, she was hoisted from the launch by a young American naval officer.

"You needn't carry me all the way, Señor," Dolores said, looking the man boldly in the eye.

"It's my job to protect your exquisite gown."

"Really. And who hired you?"

"Your father," he replied, carrying her a full sixty paces further than was necessary.

Dolores glanced back at her scowling duenna and chuckled to herself. "You may kiss my hand, Señor." She extended her lace-gloved hand to him, dazzling him with a smile.

"I pity the men who dance with you tonight, Señorita."

"And you won't be among them?"

"Certainly not. Your father would never approve."

Dolores dropped her smile as her duenna and her mother walked up, followed by her three brothers and lastly her father.

"Come, the wagons are here to take us to the Leeses' house," Don Miguel Sanchez said to her.

Dolores spotted the newly painted frame house first. "Look, father, they are flying the Mexican flag right next to the American flag," she said, pointedly thinking of the young officer who'd just held her in his arms.

Fernando, her brother, lifted Dolores from the wagon, deposited her a bit unceremoniously on the ground, and took off toward the series of small tents erected to accommodate the guests during their three-day stay. A huge canvas tent was stretched out under hundred-year-old trees. A banquet at five o'clock would be served on long tables under the tent.

Everyone marveled at the very large interior room of the house where already the Leeses had planned a new English china cabinet. The room was decorated with bunting from the *Don Quixote*, and outside a band, comprised of a clarinet, violin, flute, drum, fife and bugle, was assembled from the ship's sailors.

Once all the guests had arrived, two six-pounders from the ship blasted their salute to America's independence. Toasts and speeches lasted until dinnertime, and the dancing continued for five hours.

Dolores danced with all the young grandees she'd known since childhood; the Castros, Haros, Estudillos, Martinezes and Guerreros. Though the boys tried to woo her, extolling her beauty, Dolores remained uninterested.

Intuition told Dolores that something wondrous was going to happen to her tonight.

Jefferson told himself he didn't have time for fun and so he declined the Leeses' invitation to their party. "I have to work," he said.

"All work and no play," Mr. Leese replied with a shrug.

"Will make me rich," Jefferson said.

"Jefferson, with the increasing number of ships coming to the bay, there's so much money flowing through your hands from the landowners and trappers then out to the ships. You and Don Richardson must be rich already."

"I can never be too rich. Wealth gives a man freedom."

"Really, Jefferson? I thought it was happiness that made us free. Says so in the Declaration of Independence."

Jefferson's brows knitted as he thought of cotton fields and his old life. "Not for me."

"Have it your way."

Jefferson could hear the music as it wafted through the night air from the Leeses' house, only five lots away, but he paid it no attention. He had his eye on the Mexican brig that had just anchored. Jefferson's tarp structure was situated closer to the beach than Richardson's post, giving him first shot at potential customers as they came off the ship. In three months, Jefferson had traded his own hides for money and goods. These goods he'd turned into more money, then he turned around and bought more goods to retail. This past June, a record number of ships had come into the bay. Also growing in this short length of time was the number of Bostonians who wanted to build houses on the twenty-five-dollar lots. Already he'd heard the Alcalde had sold lots to Jean Vioget, the Swiss, and John Calvert Davis, Bob Ridley and Juan Fuller, all from England. Yesterday brought the newcomer William Alexander Leidesdorff, who was half-Danish.

The sun had been set over an hour when Jefferson padlocked the crates and barrels that held his goods. He threw tarps over the entire stock. Then he tied them down with heavy rope. He saddled his horse, adjusted the makeshift log-carrying rig he'd fashioned Indian-style and headed for the woods as he did every night.

Once he was in the woods, he began felling trees, trimmed their branches with a small, razor-sharp hatchet, then hauled the logs back to his lot on North Beach. While everyone else was paying exorbitant prices for framing boards and lumber that he sold out of his lean-to, Jefferson intended to build a log-and-mud cabin that cost him nothing for his building materials. Someday, when his profits were large enough, he would build a proper house, with wooden floors, glass windows and even a marble fireplace. Until then, he would keep a tight rein on his finances.

When Jefferson returned with his load of wood, the band at the Leeses' house was still playing. He stacked the logs next to the half-finished wall he'd erected last week, wiped the sweat from his brow and stopped to rest for the first time that day.

The loud dance music had suddenly stopped and a single violin played a familiar song that reminded Jefferson of his mother.

"That's Mozart they're playing. I haven't heard the Symphony in G Minor since I was a child," he said aloud, listening to the stormy strains. He remembered his music tutor saying, "Jefferson, this music is a radical departure for Mozart. He's being influenced by the new Sturm und Drang movement begun by Haydn."

"Whatever it is, I like it," Jefferson had said, enthusiastically pounding the keys of Maureen's piano.

Thinking back on those days, he felt a pang of grief. He not only missed his mother. He missed his father who had given him cultural advantages, opened his mind and let his talents for art and music be realized. For so long, Jefferson had blamed the stroke that impaired Richard and made his mother a slave again. He didn't care so much for himself; he had been young. But for her, he had hated Richard's infirmity because it had given Maureen power.

Even in his illness, however, Richard had been strong. He'd never stopped loving Rachel or Jefferson. Though Jefferson's parents may have seemed mismatched to the rest of the world, they were family. They were the people he loved still.

The music continued filling the air.

His shirt sweat-soaked, his pants filthy with tree sap and sand, his hair uncombed and his face unshaven, he walked toward the Leeses' house as if mesmerized by a siren's call.

Dolores banged her white lace fan against a pale-yellow silk rosette on the left side of her skirt. "Can you feel it, Angelica?"

"What?" Angelica Martinez asked as she glanced at her drowsy duenna, who sat in a crude rocker under the porch roof.

"I don't know. But it's something. I feel as if I'm about to jump out of my skin, I'm so restless."

"It's the weather."

Dolores frowned.

Angelica lived on the north side of the bay. Her father's ranch was not as large or as industrious as the Sanchez rancho. Angelica's mother had died three years ago, leaving all the household duties to her. She did not roam the hills the way Dolores did, nor break horses nor do anything that was exciting. Angelica was content to cook and sew all day.

"I'm bored," Dolores said. "Angry . . . tired. I don't know. Maybe I need . . ." Dolores held her breath as she watched Jefferson walking into the lamplight, "a man," she said huskily.

"Dolores Sanchez!" Angelica's eyes nearly popped out of her head. "How can you be so bold?"

"I'm just being honest," she retorted and snapped her fan out and shoved it next to her cheek to hide her earnestness. "That's what you're here for, too, isn't it? To finally snare Fernando into a proposal?" Dolores asked, not taking her eyes off Jefferson.

Angelica's mouth dropped open. "Must you be so crass about it?"

Dolores laughed and her beautiful face mellowed. But she kept watching Jefferson. "I'm sorry. I don't know why I do that."

"Of course, you do. You've always been haughty and you've never cared about anyone's feelings but your own."

"That's not true!"

"It is, too. Just because you're a Castilian, you've lorded it over the rest of us forever. I may be Andalusian, but I'm just as good a person as you are."

Dolores's foot tapped on the saultillo-tiled porch floor. "And I suppose you don't consider yourself better than a Mexican-born Spaniard or a

California-born Spaniard? What about a Mexican or even an Indian? You're all the same?"

"Of course," Angelica replied with a pout.

"Then why did you turn down José Mateo's proposal? Hmmm?"

"He's too . . ." Angelica searched for an explanation. She'd forgotten all about José.

"Your father told my father that he wouldn't have his daughter marrying beneath her. He's trying to match you with my brother, Fernando, that's what he's doing."

Angelica's face turned crimson. "I love Fernando."

"You do not. He's obnoxious, self-centered and spoiled by my father. None of the Castilian girls will have anything to do with him. But a marriage with him would bring you up into our class, wouldn't it?"

Unused to speaking out for herself, Angelica fought her anger. She looked like a steam kettle sputtering and spitting, fighting to contain herself. Finally, she blew.

"Dolores Sanchez, someday your precious Castilian vanity will be your undoing, and I hope I'm there to watch it."

Angelica stormed into the house.

Dolores didn't have time to waste comforting her friend. She was too curious about the tall, broad-shouldered stranger.

Jefferson walked up the porch steps. In the half-light, she couldn't see his face, but she liked his long, purposeful strides. He strode past her, never looking to the right or left, but toward the band, as if he were in a trance. He looked as if he'd just walked in from the range, not taking the time to bathe or dress as the other men had.

He was enraptured by the music, she could tell from the expression on his face. He seemed not to notice anyone, not even her.

Not having come to Yerba Buena in three, maybe four months, Dolores knew nothing about him. She didn't have to turn around to know that her mother's eyes were on her every move. Dolores didn't care. She followed him as he circled around the dancers, stopped in front of the band, placed his foot on a wooden keg and simply listened to the violinist.

"Would you care to dance?" Dolores asked.

She could see her mother coming quickly toward her, her arm outstretched, ready to snatch her away from the blond god who'd been sent to cure Dolores's boredom.

Jefferson looked at her then. She was beautiful, fine-boned and obviously aristocratic. "You're the princess I saw on the ship I sailed in on."

Dolores thought her heart would melt. "Princess?"

"Well, you spent so much silver that day, I thought you must be a princess."

Dolores took his arm. "Dance with me."

"It's been a while," he lied, for he'd never danced with a woman in his life.

She held out her arms as he slid his hand around her waist, and just as her mother was about to seize her brash young daughter, Jefferson whirled her around escaping capture.

Once Dolores was engaged in a waltz, there were no restrictions upon her. She could say anything she pleased. "Señor, you've rescued me from a fate worse than death."

"And that is?"

"My parents." She raised her eyes to his. "And the equally horrid pastime of listening to the same polite conversations I've had with everyone here all my life."

"You were born here, then?" he asked, glancing at the other dancers, taking his step cues from them.

"Yes. I'm Dolores Sanchez. Don Miguel Sanchez is my father. And you are . . . ?"

He looked into her dark, smoky eyes. "Jefferson Duke. And you, Señorita Sanchez, will probably be thrashed by your duenna when this dance is done."

"I don't care."

"Well, I do." His eyes darted to the side where he saw the fuming, short, middle-aged woman watching them with hawklike eyes. "Is that her?"

"My mother," Dolores smiled coyly.

"Do you enjoy upsetting her?"

"Sometimes. But I think you don't much care about what people think of you, either."

"Why do you say that?"

She looked at his sweaty shirt. "You aren't exactly dressed for the ball, are you?"

He chuckled. "I hadn't planned to attend. It was the music that drew me. My mother loved this piece."

Dolores's eyes filled with genuine compassion. "She's dead?"

"Yes," he looked away for a moment.

"I'm sorry," she said softly. ". . . And you live here now?"

"Yes. I've opened a new post on North Beach. I'm the newest merchantman of Yerba Buena."

"I'm pleased to meet you, Jefferson Duke."

Just then the music stopped, but while the other dancers applauded, Jefferson took Dolores's hand and pulled her through the clusters of dancers toward the porch where her parents now stood.

He bowed slightly and pulled Dolores up beside him as if she were precious bounty, then abruptly dropped her hand.

"Señor. Señora. I regret that I have taken liberties with your daughter for this dance without proper introduction. I don't wish to cause you embarrassment, nor suffering because of my actions. Allow me to introduce myself. I am Jefferson Duke, late of Charleston, South Carolina. I arrived here aboard the *Pilgrim* and am now happy to regard California as my home. I am engaged in merchandising on North Beach. I have recently purchased a site for my new home not far from our host. Please forgive my indiscretion. It won't happen again." Jefferson bowed, took Señora Sanchez's lace-gloved hand and faintly brushed his lips over the top of the lace. He bowed again to Dolores's father and left immediately.

It all happened so fast Dolores couldn't remember breathing. One minute, he was standing next to her, and the next, he'd vanished. She looked at her mother, who was equally aghast.

It was her father who spoke first. "I should have dressed him down."

Dolores was smiling. "No, Father. It was my fault, not his. I asked him to dance. I didn't give him time for proper introductions."

"*Sancta Maria!*" He hissed.

"You can punish me if you like, Father. I don't care. It was worth it. I've never met anyone like him before."

Dolores's mother was shocked as she looked at the dreamy expression on Dolores's passionate, spirited face. "And you will never meet with him again. He's a Yankee. He's not Castilian!"

Dolores glanced at the implacable look on her mother's face. Suddenly, Dolores's perspective of the world altered. Angelica's words came back to her. Her vanity, her haughtiness over her blue blood, was beginning to boomerang.

Dolores had fallen in love with a man she could never have.

Book Two

The House of
Mansfield

fourteen

No one is so accursed by fate,
No one so utterly desolate,
But some heart, though unknown,
Responds unto his own.

—HENRY WADSWORTH LONGFELLOW
"ENDYMION"

San Francisco—1838

Caroline Potter Mansfield stood next to her husband, William Mansfield, as they awaited the lowering of the launch that would carry them the last mile to their new home on San Francisco Bay. "It's nothing like I expected. It's breathtaking." She rubbed her arms to divert the chills she felt.

"I told you it would be beautiful, but you wouldn't listen."

"I'll make no secret about the fact that I'd just have soon sailed back to Boston." She looked out on the lush hills around the bay. The noonday sun had come out and lit the spring grasses and flowers. *Something is different about this place. How could I have been so wrong?*

"I can almost see the gold right now!" William exclaimed.

Caroline rolled her blue eyes and sighed. "All my objections are coming back to me, William. Eight hundred ounces of gold in an entire year is *not* a great deal of gold. I've been telling you this ever since you read that report from the United States Mint. You're overreacting because things are so

138

difficult at home. We could have made it. Your emporium would have pulled through."

Tall and severely thin, holding onto his top hat in the gusting wind, William looked like an undernourished sapling. His bland features came to life only when he was angry. "I don't know why I even speak to you . . . a woman. What do you know about enterprise, anyway?"

"Find another barb, William. That one lost its sting a long time ago."

"You try my patience, Caroline."

"And you, mine," she replied coyly. The truth of the matter was that Caroline *did* know more about business than William.

"And I don't want to hear anything about your superior intelligence, either," he said.

"Why, William, I've never said that."

"You didn't have to. Your father did on all too numerous occasions."

"So you think that now that he's dead, you're free to belittle me."

He looked off to the harbor. "Something like that."

Caroline wanted to hit him. On second thought, she'd probably hurt him. Badly. "You forget. If it weren't for my father insisting we marry, I wouldn't be here with you today."

"Believe me. I haven't forgotten."

Caroline looked off to the bay, feeling grief bite her eyes more than the wind. Her mother had died when she was fifteen, and three years later her father was gravely ill. Though they owned their home, his income was nonexistent and so it fell to Caroline to support them on her salary as a literature and poetry tutor. Living amid the rich literary culture in Boston, the only respite Caroline had from caring for her father and dodging their bill collectors was her own writing.

Caroline was resourceful. When she heard that Sarah Josepha Hale, the editor of *Lady's Magazine,* was paying fifteen dollars per poem, Caroline rushed to her office and sold four poems in the first month. By 1838 she was being paid top wage of twenty-five dollars per poem.

She'd heard that Nathaniel Hawthorne's "Wakefield," "The Gray Champion," and "Young Goodman Brown," all written three years earlier, were of the same pay scale. Caroline was ecstatic that she was ranked amid such illustrious company. Even Edgar Allan Poe's "A Dream Within a Dream" hadn't received any more money. Caroline had genius gift, a man's pay, but none of the recognition she desperately desired. Because she was a

woman, and too often her work was lumped in with the mediocre poems
Sarah Hale produced, Caroline's frustration nearly swallowed her.

She wanted to change the world and did everything in her power to
accomplish her goals. She espoused much of the credo of her mentor Sarah
Hale by writing articles about wives being "help-mates" to their husbands
rather than household drudges. She supported civic involvement and joined
the "committees of correspondence," which were composed of Boston society women who raised over three thousand dollars for the Bunker Hill
Monument, a feat the male Boston population had failed to do.

In the summer of Caroline's twentieth year, her father took a turn for the
worse. With death shadowing his eyes, Cyril Potter panicked.

"Caroline, you must stop arguing with me and marry soon. You're nearly
an old maid. I don't have much time left," he said in a craggy, cracking
voice.

"Papa, I can take care of myself. Haven't I done well with my writing and
teaching?"

"Men's work," he said and flopped his thin, saggy-skinned arm at her. His
glaucomic eyes tried to focus on her, but the effort was tiring. He closed his
eyes and water seeped out the sides and into the deep webs of his face. "You
should have a child. Children are blessings."

"I will," she said.

"No, do it now. Before I'm dead. Promise me."

"Papa," she started to plead.

"Promise."

"I will," she finally promised, knowing that if she didn't they would go
through the same routine conversation every night until she relented.
"Sometimes I think the only thing keeping you alive, Papa, is to make sure
I get married."

Caroline chose William Mansfield for a husband because he fit the majority of the desirable characteristics she'd listed in her diary. First was that
he be Boston-based. She had no use for a seaman who was gone all the time.
She wanted a man whose schedule was on a par with hers.

Her second requirement was that he be completely manipulable. Most
men would not allow their wives to work, and Caroline wanted to work.
Therefore, her husband would have to agree with her ideas, *all* of them, or
else. For Caroline, all other attributes—charm, looks, social graces, background, kindness, sense of humor—paled in comparison to the first two. She

was marrying only to please her father, and she believed somewhere in the deep recesses of her High Church Episcopalian upbringing that to refuse her father's dying wish would doom her to hell. It seemed a small enough request, and so she chose to grant it.

William Mansfield was one of two sons of John Mansfield of Liverpool and Elizabeth Carey Mansfield of Boston. The Mansfields established and owned the emporium on Washington Street. David Mansfield, William's older brother by five years, was the energy, brains and force behind the business. William was a competent enough clerk and bookkeeper, but it was David's creativity that brought the public to his store to shop. Caroline believed that William wouldn't know creativity if he fell over it.

William, therefore, was the dull, stable, dependable man she'd dreamed of. And as luck would have it, William was infatuated with Caroline.

He met her coming out of Sarah Hale's office at the magazine. He had been there to drop off fashion plates that he was paying to have published in the magazine for his store. Caroline was submitting her newest article on the progress of "Seaman's Aid," a charity founded by Sarah Hale herself that was still the most successful of its kind in Boston.

William was speechless in Caroline's presence, a fact that Sarah Hale didn't miss. "William put your tongue back in your head. Meet Caroline Potter, my favorite poet."

"Howdyado?" he said, taking off his beaver hat and looking for an escape from his embarrassment.

"I'm pleased to meet you, Mr. Mansfield."

"You're a poet? Why, I always thought of poets as wearing glasses, thin-lipped and pale from all those hours indoors. You are, well, quite beautiful," he gushed.

Caroline couldn't help but think his description of a poet fit himself perfectly, but she had the good sense not to say so. "I adhere to Mrs. Hale's tenet of being hearty and I take my exercise outdoors whenever possible."

"That's why your cheeks have such a bloom to them," William said with such a sweet and syrupy intonation, Caroline nearly cringed.

"I really must be going, Mr. Mansfield. Perhaps I'll see you again soon."

"I do hope so, Miss Potter. I do so very much hope so."

Sarah and Caroline couldn't help but to laugh once he was gone. Had she known that William Mansfield would be the man who would fulfill her father's dying wish, she wouldn't have laughed.

When Caroline married William, she had not counted on *his* father dying of a sudden stroke. Nor had she counted on David inheriting the majority of the business, nor had she ever seen the first inkling of William's jealousy toward David. And especially she had not seen the streak of adventurism that formed the marrow of William's bones. Caroline realized she had done a poor job of fitting a husband to her requirements list.

"There's nothing to keep us here, Caroline. Your father is dead and now with David running everything, I'll never get a chance to prove myself."

"Prove yourself?"

"Yes,'" he said meekly. "I do have dreams and goals. I'm just as good at merchandising as my brother."

Caroline continued piling her luxuriously thick silver-blond hair atop her head. She placed a lace-edged nightcap over it. She looked at William's reflection in the mirror, saw him pacing back and forth in his flannel night-shirt, his nightcap askew upon his unruly curly brown hair.

"William, how is it possible we've been married over two years and I don't know you at all?"

"You weren't paying attention," he said bitterly.

"William, you never said anything like this."

"Actually, I haven't. But I thought it."

"Are you saying you want to leave Boston?" *My source of income?*

"Yes."

"And where would we go?"

"San Francisco," he said boldly. "I've taken all my savings, all my inheri-tance and bought every bit of goods that we'll need for a year. I've applied with Governor Chico, I think his name was, for two lots across from the town square on which to build my emporium." He looked at Caroline who had turned white. "Did you hear me?"

"Yes. Every word."

"We can't lose. The retail market in Boston will be off for another three years here. I've heard some investors and bankers saying that it won't turn around till 'forty-one or 'forty-two. I can't wait that long! I've waited too long for father to die—" He stopped immediately and put his hand sheep-ishly to his thin lips. "I didn't mean that the way it sounded."

"I can't go," Caroline said, feeling as if her life were slipping away from her.

He rammed his fist into his palm. "I've made up my mind." He stared at her waiting for her response.

"Go ahead. But I'm not going with you."

"Oh, yes you are."

Caroline cleared her throat for emphasis. "I am *not* going halfway around the globe on a whim to build a retail store simply because the *Alert* has put into harbor with a pinch of gold dust from some Indian."

"If the Indian could find it, so will others."

"I'm not going."

William rocked back on his heels and confidently clasped his hands behind his back. "And just where do you think you're going to live?"

"I'll give notice to my boarders and move back into my parents' house."

He shook his head vigorously, but it was the smirk on his mouth that gave Caroline chills. "I sold it. I used the money to buy the Sheffield silver that arrived last week."

"You what?" She bolted to her feet and threw her silver hairbrush at the wall. She felt like Napoleon at Waterloo. This could be her last stand. Courage ripped through her body. She wouldn't go down without a fight.

Suddenly, William lost his courage. "I sold it."

"You had no right!"

"You're my wife. You can't own property. Actually, you have no rights at all." He kept backing up as she moved closer, her fists clenched at her sides.

William had never seen Caroline so angry. Upset, yes. Determined, yes. But out-and-out anger was foreign to her personality. Or so he thought.

"You make me want to kill you, William, you really do," she growled. She whirled on her heel and began tearing the bed linens apart.

"What are you doing?" His eyes protruded out of his pasty face like two overblown grapes.

"I'll never forgive you for this! Never! And I'm never sleeping with you again!" She faced him. "So help me God, William Mansfield." She could barely catch her breath, she was so enraged. "I'll pay you back for this, and if I don't, God will. I'd watch my back if I were you!" She threw the counterpane and two pillows at him. "You sleep downstairs by the fire with the dog, but not in my bed!"

He was aghast. "This is *my* house."

Caroline clenched her fist and pulled it back. "Not anymore it's not! You sold my house? Fine. I'm taking this one in exchange."

Caroline was a fury from hell, and William had never witnessed anything like it. He took the pillows and blanket and stumbled out of the room, never taking his eyes from her fist, which he knew she would use on him.

* * * *

Caroline's first steps on the shores of Yerba Buena were lost in the fog of her past memories. She barely remembered the wagon ride to the Presidio to meet the Alcalde, nor the return trip to inspect the site of the emporium on Dupont Street. Caroline only knew that the life of her own she'd dreamed about, and held so dear, was now over. She'd never planned on this kind of tumultuous change in life. There had been nothing in her philosophy books or history books that explained *how* it was that a human was supposed to mentally cope with these situations. Caroline found she was a victim of her own folly.

It took fourteen ox-driven wagon-loads to deposit the Mansfield worldly goods on their building site. William had not bothered to tell Caroline there were no hotels in Yerba Buena, no restaurants or boarding houses; there was nothing. One man, Captain William Hinkley, was using the old poop cabin from his ship as a house. Caroline found herself dependent on other people for the first time in her life, and she blamed William for it.

"Where are we supposed to sleep? And eat, bathe and dress?"

"Uh . . . in a tent?"

She glared at him. "Is that so?" She looked around. "Why is it that you didn't think of these things, William?"

"I thought it would be like Boston."

Caroline was fuming. "You thought there would be towers of gold waiting for you. William, you're more naive than I'd thought." She looked away and muttered to herself. "And a thousand times more stupid."

She dropped her arms, now resigned to the fact that, as usual, she had someone *she* was responsible for. It was obvious that she was going to have to not only take care of William, but that if she allowed him to make the decisions, they would both live in poverty for the rest of their lives. She'd always wanted to change the world. She realized she would have to start with William.

"Very well. You pitch the tent." She started to walk away.

"Where are you going?" he asked sheepishly.

"To make a friend."

"You don't know anyone. You don't need anyone. We have everything we need."

"You're wrong, William. Dead wrong."

At Clay and Dupont Street Caroline found the pretty frame house of the Leeses. Caroline knocked on the door, and it was answered by an eight-year-old Indian girl.

"Is the master of the house in?" Caroline asked, peeking behind the child to see two men seated at a trestle table and two pine benches. Next to the wall was a beautiful china cabinet, and on the table were prettily painted china plates. "Mecca," she whispered to herself with a smile.

The older man with the dark beard and hair rose. "I'm Jacob Primer Leese," he said. "Won't you come in, please?"

Caroline stepped onto the wooden floor not knowing it was one of a very few wooden floors in Yerba Buena. "My name is Caroline Mansfield. I just arrived on the *Alert* and my husband and I—"

"Are my competition," Jefferson said, rising from the table. He wiped his mouth with a snowy linen napkin. Stepping around the bench, he strode over to her. He seemed to dwarf the room and when he loomed over her, she felt suddenly protected.

He peered into her eyes, still smiling.

She smiled back.

Why am I trusting this man so easily? I don't know him. But he looks at me as if he knows me. How is that possible?

He beguiled her with his presence. She had to drag her eyes away from his face in order to form clear thoughts.

For years I've looked at people, fat ones, old ones, young ones and they've all seemed the same. But as to degrees of their personality showing on the outskirts of their faces for all the world to see, I've never seen it.

Caroline was used to the closed-in, heavily guarded looks of proper Bostonians. This man literally beamed at her and not like some star-struck swain. His force of energy drew her to him like a magnet, powerful, and she didn't know what to make of it, except she was intrigued.

She understood nothing about her reactions to him.

"My . . . my competition?" she asked.

"I own the trading post on North Beach. It was to your right when your party came ashore this morning. It's that log structure you see. Right now, I'm building a proper house on Montgomery Street not far from here. I'm

Jefferson Duke." He gave her a half-bow, keeping his eyes on her all the time.

"I'm pleased to know you," she managed to say without stumbling. Caroline extended her hand, and, when he kissed it, she was keenly aware of the fact that she was married.

It was an odd and unsettling thought.

What am I doing wanting this man to kiss my hand?

"We haven't many American women in the settlement and certainly none as beautiful as you."

Her mouth went dry. Nervously, she replied, "Thank you, sir. You're far too gracious."

Jefferson smiled. "Grace has nothing to do with it. I was being honest."

God, he's bold. But then so am I, feeling this attraction. She glanced out the corner of her eye and saw that Jacob Leese was taking all this in. She didn't want to be the subject of a scandal her first day in port.

"Mr. Leese, I was wondering if there was anyone in the settlement from whom I might obtain room and board for myself?"

Jacob's bushy eyebrows shot up. "Just yourself?"

"Why, yes."

"Not your husband, too?"

"No, he intends to stay with our provisions until the store is built. He didn't tell me when we left Boston that he'd intended for us to live in a tent."

"Otherwise you wouldn't have come?" Jefferson asked.

"No."

"Then I'm glad he kept his mouth shut," Jefferson said.

Caroline gasped and fought the tingle of pleasure shooting through her limbs. She licked her dry lips. Jacob was biting his tongue not to smile at Jefferson's flirtations.

Jefferson shot her a dazzling smile. "Tents aren't all that bad. I've spent many a night in the open myself."

Finally, Caroline decided the only way to escape Jefferson's powerful charisma was to fight back. Turning on an equal measure of charm, she flashed her eyes at him and said, "It's not the tent I object to, nor even subjecting myself to harm from the bears and mountain lions I'm told creep down from the hills from time to time. It's simply that I don't wish to sleep with my husband."

Two shocked jaws gaped at Caroline. Then suddenly both men howled with laughter.

"Beg pardon?" Jefferson asked, bursting into laughter.

Jacob howled with him.

"Oooph! You're infuriating! The both of you!"

They stifled their laughter.

Jefferson wiped a tear off his cheek.

"I'll pay you," she said to Jacob.

Instantly his face was serious. "How much?"

"A dollar a night for the bed only."

"Make it two dollars a night."

"I want breakfast included. I'll make my own supper."

Jacob scrutinized her for a moment as he pulled on his whiskers. "Done," he said and thrust out his hand to seal the bargain.

Jefferson could only stare at them. "What if I make you a better price?"

Caroline couldn't stop the smirk that crept to the edge of her mouth. "Johnny-come-latelys must have been fashioned after men like you, Mr. Duke. I find it interesting that there is no such thing as a Janice-come-lately."

Caroline picked up her voluminous blue-cotton skirts, crossed to the door and opened it. "I'll come back shortly with my things, Mr. Leese. It's been a pleasure doing business with you."

When she closed the door behind her, a rush of wind swept in.

"God Almighty!" Jefferson breathed. "I've never met a woman like that before. Half angel and half bobcat."

"That, my dear boy, was a tsunami."

"I didn't know they had tidal waves in San Francisco."

"They do now," Jacob smiled and slapped Jefferson on the back.

fifteen

A week after their arrival, Caroline and William were invited to their first *merienda,* a large picnic on Rincon Hill. On that day Caroline realized her attraction to Jefferson was the most real thing in her life. It was her marriage to William that was a lie.

Being introduced to their new neighbors in town, Caroline surreptitiously watched Jefferson as he greeted his friends and pretended not to notice her.

Each chance she got, she stole a glimpse of Jefferson.

And he did the same with her.

"I'm so pleased to meet you, Mrs. Mansfield," Don Alejandro said.

"The pleasure is mine," Caroline replied, dragging her eyes off Jefferson and onto the young man speaking to her.

"I've heard that you were beautiful, but I was quite unprepared for the impact of your loveliness," he said.

"You are too kind."

"Not in the least, I assure you," he said, moving a step closer.

Caroline looked for William, who was conversing with Jacob Leese. "My husband," she started.

"Needs to guard his treasures more carefully," Don Alejandro said with a mischievous smile.

"Not at all, sir. I can take care of myself," she said proudly.

Don Alejandro chuckled. "Yes, I've heard that much. Now if you would permit me, I would like to introduce you to the young ladies of the rancheros."

"Thank you," she said graciously. "I would like that."

In the next instant, Caroline met Dolores Sanchez among several other young Spanish ladies.

Caroline didn't realize at the time that she was hiding behind the masque that her marriage to William created for her, but she was. To all present, Caroline was a married woman. When others spoke to her, their guard was down. Even Dolores did not realize that Caroline was falling in love with Jefferson.

"I'm so happy to meet you," Dolores gushed. "We want to hear everything about Boston. It's fascinating to us that you come here from so far away."

"Really? Boston didn't seem 'fascinating' to me when I lived there. But I do understand what you mean."

Dolores was wearing an incredibly delicate, white lace mantilla shot with silver threads that spun around her head and shoulders like an ethereal web.

"What a gorgeous gown, Dolores. I remember seeing one much like it in New York. The fabric is from Lyons, France, is it not?"

"Why, yes," Dolores answered with only a trace of accent. "I saw a picture of it in the *Lady's Magazine*. I told my Papa no other dress would do."

"I used to work for that magazine," Caroline nodded happily at Dolores's surprise. "I knew Sarah Hale personally."

"This is wonderful! How I have wanted to talk about these beautiful things she writes about. When the *Loriotte* dropped anchor, there were only six copies of the magazine. We all fought over them like cats and dogs. I got one of them," she said proudly.

"Now," she said, ushering Caroline to a blanket on the grass. "Sit with me and tell me about Boston. Did you have one of those beautiful houses like I see in the magazine? Or one of those dressing tables? What beautiful lace they have . . . even more lovely than my best gowns!"

Caroline was delighted to have such an attentive audience as Dolores. As Dolores's friends stopped by to chat, one by one they sat with them, and while Dolores translated as best she could, they all listened as Caroline explained the newest fashions and, even more importantly, the newest thinking about women popular on the East Coast.

Caroline had just embarked upon a discussion about calisthenics and gymnastics and their importance to the female form when out of the corner of her eye, she saw Jefferson talking with Don Richardson and Jacob Leese.

"Mrs. Hale believes that archery is suitable for women as a path to good health. Of course," Caroline caught her breath when Jefferson looked right at her, "the odds-on favorite is horseback riding."

It was Angelica who giggled first, grabbed Dolores's arm and said, "Dolores, he's looking right at you."

"Don't stare, Angelica!" Dolores said as she unabashedly stared right back at Jefferson.

Caroline followed Dolores's gaze. Instantly, her back froze.

Dolores and Jefferson?

Caroline kept her eyes locked on Dolores and didn't dare look at Jefferson.

My God, I've been a fool. Of course he would find Dolores irresistible. Who wouldn't? I wonder if they're lovers?

Caroline watched Dolores intently. The beautiful Castilian didn't hide behind her fan as Caroline had seen the other girls do. She boldly let Jefferson and the rest of her entourage on the picnic blanket know precisely what was on her mind. "Have you met Señor Duke?" Dolores asked Caroline without moving her eyes from him.

"Yes," Caroline replied flatly.

"Is he not beautiful?"

"I suppose."

Angelica giggled again. "Dolores has talked of no one else since the day she met him. Her father would whip her if he knew how much he is in her thoughts."

Caroline was stunned. "Why?"

Dolores cocked her head and reluctantly moved her dark eyes to Caroline. "Jefferson is not blue blood. I am," she said haughtily.

The other four girls nodded their heads solemnly. They looked back to a group of half a dozen young men all dressed in tight black pants and bolero jackets with expensively embroidered, white-ruffled shirts. Their flat-crowned, broad-brimmed black felt hats sat seductively on their heads. Like their female counterparts, they held themselves erect with dignity and walked like gliding swans. More often than not, Caroline could tell, their blue blood was regal.

"Those are the men our fathers intend for us to marry," Dolores said.

"Except for me. I will marry Jefferson Duke."

Caroline couldn't decipher if Dolores truly loved Jefferson or only wanted him because her father had deemed him taboo.

The gaiety of the picnic turned sour in Caroline's mouth. Returning home that night and for the days that followed, she was overcome with melancholy.

The more she forced herself not to think about Jefferson, the more she did. At night she lied awake wondering what it would be like to taste Jefferson's kisses, to feel his hands explore the most intimate parts of her body. Then suddenly she would see Dolores's face, and she wished she'd never befriended the girl.

Caroline could no more stop her heart from wanting Jefferson than she could stop breathing.

She saw him day after day, working on his house. He made excuses to stop by and say hello. She made excuses about things she needed for the emporium she was building in order to see him.

She knew she looked in his eyes too long and that she lingered far longer than it took to place her orders. She felt alive just being with him.

Her emotions grew by the minute until she thought she would explode. But she didn't.

Caroline also realized she felt no guilt or shame wanting Jefferson. She was married, but she'd never loved William. He was her father's wish for her. Not her soul's wish. She could never forgive him for stealing her house out from under her. William was lucky she was with him.

But when Caroline saw the need, desire and pain in Dolores's eyes when she looked at Jefferson, she knew exactly how the pampered, beautiful and spirited Spanish girl felt, because she felt the same. The difference was that Dolores was entitled to Jefferson, and Caroline was not.

I've never been this miserable in my life.

She'd fallen in love and her heart was breaking.

* * * *

"It's the finest building in Yerba Buena," Jefferson said, coming up from behind Caroline as she stood with her hand over her eyes shielding them from the bright sun as she watched the Indians pound shingles onto the roof.

Caroline stood stock still. For two weeks Jefferson had been trapping, and they hadn't seen each other. Now he was back.

Caroline felt Jefferson all around her. His presence enveloped her. When she closed her eyes, she felt her passion ignite. She wanted desperately to lie in his arms. She imagined him sliding his hand around her waist, then cupping her breast and pulling her to his strong chest. She envisioned the feel of his lips against the nape of her neck, that place she *knew* was sensitive, but which William had never discovered. She could almost feel Jefferson's powerful fingers move up to her temples and then slide easily into her hair. He would hold her closer, tighter—

"You've done a marvelous job with it all, Mrs. Mansfield," Jefferson said.

She didn't know how she did it, but she found her voice. "My husband," she placed a great emphasis on the word, "will be pleased to hear that."

"Everyone knows that you're the mastermind behind the emporium," Jefferson said.

She could see their shadows on the ground. They fit into each other as if they were meant to be.

This is impossible! Please go away, Jefferson. Don't make me think these thoughts. I don't want to feel this need. This pain.

She needed to be calm. She was anything but calm. She turned and faced him. He took her breath away.

"Do you trap often, Mr. Duke?"

Jefferson was sinking into her piercing blue eyes. He didn't know his head moved closer to her with every word he spoke. He hadn't wanted to come here, he had fought it for days. To him, her lips were begging to be kissed. "I haven't hunted for months. I had to get away."

"Really? Why's that?" Caroline asked. *You're married, Caroline. Remember that.*

"I made enough money off the last ship; I deserved a holiday," he lied.

He was keeping his distance, she knew, and it stung her pride.

She took a step back. "Mansfield's Emporium will put you out of business, Mr. Duke."

"The hell it will!" he straightened. Jefferson was nearly consumed with his need for her. It took every ounce of his strength to keep his arms at his sides and not put them around her.

Doesn't she know I should be holding her close to my heart? Doesn't she know we were meant to be together?

Every time he thought he had control of his passion, his body, his heart and mind bent to her will. How was it possible for her to keep doing this to him? How could he, Jefferson Duke, a man with the royal blood of kings in his veins, become this obsessed with a woman? He was enslaved again. And this time, running away would not free him.

All he could do was follow her suit.

"You know nothing about these people, this place, this land. You come here from Boston and—," he searched for the right words but only the wrong ones came to mind. "You won't even sleep in a goddamned tent!"

Caroline glared at him. Why did he attack her like this? And especially when all she wanted was to make love to him. Her temper flared like brush-fire. "You just watch me, Mr. Duke. We'll see who owns the emporium and who puts who out of business!"

"We'll see about that."

They were evenly matched. Fire for fire. "I have just as much right here as anyone! Just because I'm a woman, you ignorant, stupid men think we can't do anything! You just wait and see who has the last laugh, Mr. Duke."

Caroline whirled around and stormed inside the two-story emporium building. When the door slammed, the Indians who were on the roof all laughed uproariously. They didn't understand all the words, but they knew a lover's spat when they saw one.

September 4, 1838

The wedding fiesta of Fernando Sanchez to Angelica Peralta drew over one hundred guests from the settlement and the surrounding ranchos.

Gaiety strung the seven days of festivities together with colorful ribbons of happiness. There were picnics in the late mornings, bullfights and contests of equestrian skills in the corrals in the afternoons. During one of the contests, the bridegroom astounded all the guests by demonstrating that he could pick up a small gold coin off the ground, while rushing by on horseback, not losing speed for a single second.

The guests danced every night until dawn and only from seven until ten in the morning did anyone sleep.

Caroline had never experienced anything like it. It seemed the Spanish had nothing more important in their lives than to be happy. While the dons and their ladies were eating, drinking and playing, Caroline was observing. Even amidst the festivities, she couldn't take her mind off business.

She noticed the women came to the hacienda with trunks filled with clothes. Had they been in a large city like New York, she could have understood the competition for the limelight. It was incongruous that these women living in the middle of nowhere should not only possess such fabulous brocades, jewels, ornate combs and fans, but that their need for even more was insatiable.

It was at the Sanchez wedding that Caroline's path for the future took a turn in two ways.

Until now, she'd wanted the emporium built so she had a roof over her head. Now, she saw her first visions of the kind of merchandise she would sell. Because she was thrilled with this great self-discovery, Caroline allowed her defenses against Jefferson to weaken. She was exhausted from fighting the attraction. She laid down her armor.

Jefferson was wearing tan breeches, brown boots and an open-neck white shirt as he walked up the hill toward her. He appeared as he always did, like a desert mirage taking form out of the rising mist. His golden hair refracted the late-afternoon sunlight, absorbed the rays, and then shot them back out in tiny spectrums of color nearly invisible to the eye, but clearly seen by her heart.

Caroline was bewitched, and today she didn't care.

The guests were watching the bullfight, the young matador slinging his red cape first to the left and then to the right, employing ancient rhythms man had always used against beast. Cheers went up from the crowd. Wildflowers were tossed into the ring.

Jefferson picked up a larkspur which had landed at Caroline's feet.

"You're more beautiful than the bride," he said, wishing he could touch the spun-silver tendril of hair that brushed her cheek. He wondered if she knew the power she held in her eyes.

"Thank you," she said, dropping her gaze, then looking back to the ring. "Is William here?"

"No. He's not feeling well. The heat is too much for him."

Jefferson didn't hesitate a second. "Then come with me," he said, taking her hand.

"Where are we going?"

His eyes delved into hers. "Does it matter?"

Caroline's breath caught in her throat. "No," she replied. And for the second time that day her life took a turn.

Jefferson walked her down the hill to where his horse was tethered. He pulled her onto his horse behind him where she would have to lean against him for support. She put her arms around his waist and leaned into him, feeling the sinewy muscles in his back. She wanted to rest her face against that strong plain between his shoulders, but she held her head erect. She could smell the spicy rum-scented soap he used.

This is crazy. I shouldn't be doing this. I'm going to regret this decision. Won't I?

Or will I regret it if I let this moment pass me by?

At that moment, Jefferson lovingly placed his hand over her hand and pressed it into his stomach. Caroline felt her heart bang against her rib cage.

"Hang on tight," he said.

"I am," she breathed and rested her head on the back of his neck as they rode off to the woods.

Jefferson tethered the horse to a huge redwood tree, his outline against the forest thrown into relief by the brilliant sun that was sinking quickly behind the hills. Overhead the full moon rose above, casting an eerie kind of silver light that mingles with the golden rose of twilight. Then the sun sank. The moon rose.

Jefferson had dreamed of this moment every night since the day he first laid eyes on Caroline. Now that it was here, he vowed to savor every nuance of it.

Jefferson had never been with a woman in his life. He was not practiced, but his body and his heart guided him.

His hand shook as he touched her tiny waist to lift her down. Even through the fabric of her gown, he could feel the heat of her skin. She was trembling like a frightened child.

"Maybe we shouldn't . . . ," she said, backing away from him a half-step as she was caught in the same moral agony he had been drowning in for months.

"Please, Caroline. I've never loved a woman."

"Never?" She was incredulous.

"No, never," his green eyes were filled with sincerity. "I've always believed the woman I would love . . . make love to . . . would be very special. The first day I saw you, I knew you were that woman."

She touched his cheek. "I had no idea."

His eyes rested on her sensuous mouth. He had memorized its outline long ago. He'd thought of kissing her so many times, it nearly seemed a fait accompli. He raised his finger to touch her cheek. When his skin met hers, he felt the melding of their vibrations.

For the first time in his life, he knew what his mother had felt for Richard and the kind of quickening Yuala had experienced with Henry Duke. This was their legacy to him: this love that was his for eternity.

Nearly in a trance, Jefferson watched his fingers slowly cup the edge of her jaw, gently, tentatively, nearly frightened to learn any more terrain. Her skin was smooth and warm, like the sun-gilded rose petal that grew on the east side of his father's mansion back in South Carolina. He cupped her cheek. She leaned her face into his palm, then raised her hand and covered his. She slowly moved her lips to graze the ends of his fingertips. She kissed them one by one.

Scorching sparks of passion raced through his hands down his arms and shot into his heart as Caroline branded him with the light from her soul. He felt it, this electricity his mother had tried to explain to him a thousand times that permeated every living thing on earth. She'd told him that the most powerful, most elevated of all energies was that of love. It had taken Jefferson twenty-three years, but finally he believed.

"Jefferson, my love," she breathed softly. The sound of her voice fluttered across the space between them and recorded itself in his brain for all time. Suddenly, Jefferson realized that her voice had always been more than comfortable, more than seductive, it had been familiar. It was as though he had carried the remembrance of it in his subconscious. Or perhaps this was a sign from God. Though his mother had never quite been able to explain precisely the tonality of Yuala's voice, somehow, he knew that the pure crystal resonances he just heard were much like his grandmother's.

Caroline moved his hand to her long, white throat, then lower to its base where he could feel the rhythm of her heart. Fever blazing from within heated her skin. He curled his fingers around her neck and tilted her face up to his. He could stand the ache of wanting no longer. His lips loomed over hers matching heart for heart, desire for desire.

He dragged his eyes from her mouth and gazed into her eyes. For a long moment, he allowed himself to stand on the precipice before plunging himself over the edge. In that split-second of hesitation, the torture of their forbidden love flung its shackles about Jefferson's intellect.

"God forgive me," he moaned.

A tear crept over the corner of Caroline's eye and fell off her lash. "Please, Jefferson, if you have regrets walk away from me now."

He felt his heart rend in half as the thought flitted across his mind. "You don't think what we're doing is wrong?"

"If I had any doubts, I no longer do," she said, allowing her eyes to peer deeper into his. Then it happened, just as Rachel told him it would. The light from Caroline's soul gleamed in her eyes and as he banished the final shadows of his fear and succumbed to her, his own light mingled with hers creating a force so strong, so powerful, it rocked his body. He saw spirals of gold, silver, blue and purple stream from her eyes like tiny pinwheels and envelope the two of them in a whirling haze of magic, of love.

He cupped her face with both his hands, feeling the power of his emotions. "I love you, Caroline. I'll never love another."

Caroline no longer felt the earth beneath her feet. She'd been transported to some celestial sphere where time knew no place and only she and Jefferson existed. She, Caroline, of the logical brain, saw and felt things that had no explanation, no reason, but they existed more tangibly than the entire accumulation of knowledge and experience she'd stored in her mind.

She, too, saw the shimmering golden haze that surrounded and protected them. She looked into Jefferson's eyes and knew they belonged together. She felt, but could not hear, words in her mind like the divine utterances of some ancient oracle that her life's purpose was this moment with Jefferson. Nothing in Caroline's strict New England upbringing nor her newly found egalitarian philosophies had ever prepared her for the thoughts she now felt in her heart. Caroline had always believed in controlling her own fate, but now she knew that humans controlled very little. Control was God's domain. They were floating on the wings of destiny.

"I love you, Jefferson . . . for eternity." Caroline closed her eyes and gave herself over to the power of love.

Jefferson brushed his lips against Caroline's mouth with such adoration and reverence that a new wave of tears washed against her eyelids. His mouth covered hers, finally ending the agony of loneliness they'd both known. She met his passion and pressed her lips against his.

A whorl of need exploded within Jefferson as he ringed the edge of Caroline's mouth with his tongue, engraving its design in his mind. He tasted the sweet interior as rushes of searing want engulfed him. Eagerly her tongue bombarded his nerves with a sensuous assault. He wanted more.

His hands glided across the slope of her shoulders and down her arms. He lifted them slowly and placed them around his neck.

"Feel me, Caroline. Pull me next to you."

His words, even more than his touch, caused passion to groan deep in the recesses of her throat.

He touched the back of her neck with his blazing fingertips and un-buttoned the diaphanous organza collar that kept her skin from his touch but not from his sight. The fabric shimmered in the moonlight like angels' wings, as he peeled it away from her. He unhooked the bodice of her gown and sent her breasts spilling into his hands. With torrents of desire raging through his blood, Jefferson tried to be gentle, but instead, he crushed the pearly skin into his hand. He felt Caroline grow weak in his arms. She moaned again.

"You make me weak."

His lips crushed hers again. He dragged his lips across the precipice of her jaw, down the ivory column of her throat then stopped instinctively near, but just above, the base and suckled there for a long moment.

"Oh, God," she groaned and slid her hands to his buttocks and pressed his hips into her pelvis.

With his tongue he caressed the spot, languishing in the pleasure he was giving her. In a torturously slow crawl, Jefferson blazed a path with his tongue to Caroline's breast. When his mouth came to rest, he pulled the hardened nipple between his teeth causing new tremors of desire to rupture the last of her strength.

Caroline's knees gave way beneath her as she sank to the ground. The soft grasses sighed and then bent beneath her. A chilled night breeze fluttered through the leaves and tickled the pine needles above. The pungent odor of eucalyptus and pine wafted downward, marking itself on this memory. She looked up at Jefferson and saw the moonlight as it pirouetted around the sil-houette of his huge muscular frame. She watched as he pulled off his boots, shirt and trousers. *No Adonis in Greek lore could ever have been as hand-some*, she thought to herself as he knelt beside her. She lifted her arms to him, and as she did, moonbeams skittered across her white skin then hid in the silver tendrils of her hair. Jefferson unbuttoned her gown and lifted it over her head. She started to take off her pantaloons, but he stopped her.

His eyes were smoky emeralds. "I want to do this," he said in a voice like thick velvet rubbing against itself.

He lowered his eyes and watched as the curve of her waist came into view, then the rounded swell of her abdomen, the dip of her pelvis, and finally the soft blond down that covered her sex. He laid his hand over the down, marking it as his own property as he finished peeling off her garters and stockings. Her legs were long and curved delicately at the knees and ankles.

"Now, my love," she said and opened her thighs completely to him.

He sank himself into Caroline, feeling tiny muscles in her soft walls beating against him like hummingbird wings. Perspiration slaked down his bare back and buttocks as he thrust himself deeper and deeper. He slid his hands under her buttocks and tilted her hips nearly straight up. She hugged her creamy legs around his waist and put her hands on his shoulders. He felt her nails burrowing into his skin as he brought her to a climax.

Cataclysmic seizures ripped through Caroline, breaking through her heart and creating an eternal open fissure in her soul. She waited at its entrance for Jefferson.

His breath rushed out of his chest like an animal panting. His heart raced so wildly he was certain he would die. Though he savored the press of her skin against his rigid shaft by pulling himself almost completely out of her each time, he was aware of something even more pleasurable to come.

He sank deeper into her with each penetration knowing there must be a physical path to her soul. He would touch her somehow the way she had touched him. He pressed deeper in his quest, no longer able to hear the wet slapping sound of their fevered skins, no longer able to see her face. Finally, he reached the tabernacle he sought. It was as golden, loving and powerful as he had always known it would be, and it welcomed him with a glorious, magnetic force he knew he would never escape. There at her altar, Jefferson laid the gift of his seed and all the love in his heart.

Jefferson stayed inside her as he rolled onto his back, pulling her with him. He dared not speak nor open his eyes. He listened only to the rhythms of their hearts beating. He pressed his forehead to hers wishing he could fuse their minds. He wondered if Yuala's kind of thought transference was possible between himself and Caroline.

When he looked at her, he felt his insides rip apart. "Will you ever be mine?"

"You've made me yours."

He kissed her sweetly. "No, I meant . . ."

"I know what you meant," she said, tears filling her eyes. She closed them, and, when she did, he kissed her lids, one at a time.

"Oh, Caroline." He held her tightly. *It's going to take all the forces of heaven and earth to make something good come of the mess I've just made of our lives.*

sixteen

O! Many a shaft at random sent
Finds the mark the archer little meant!
And many a word, at random spoken,
May soothe or wound a heart that's broken!

—SIR WALTER SCOTT
THE LORD OF THE ISLES, CANTO V, ST. XVIII

Dolores Sanchez's bloodshot eyes filled again with a new wave of tears. Sinking her face in her pillow, she tried to muffle her sobs. The walls of the Leeses' canvas tent did not absorb sorrow, and only allowed for its transmittance to the outside.

"Dolores?"

"Father?" She felt as if her pain would strangle her.

"What's wrong?"

"I . . . I . . ." Her round eyes were filled with sadness. "I love Jefferson. But he doesn't want me. He wants the Mansfield woman."

"Duke? And the Mansfield woman? She's married! This is preposterous!"

"She's an adulteress!" Dolores spat out the words, but throwing accusations didn't stop the pain in her heart.

"Don't fret! He's forbidden to you. His blood would taint the purity of our line. We're registered in Mexico in the Corte de Purismo de Sangre, are we not? Where's your pride?"

"Pride? What good is pride when I love him so?"

"Forget him!" Don Sanchez demanded angrily.

161

"I won't! I must have him. I'll figure out a way to rid his heart of her. Then he'll be mine."

"Never let anyone hear you say these things! You're a Sanchez. I will choose your husband for you, and you'll make a good marriage. No daughter of mine will marry an American. Never!" He stormed away.

"I can't let him go without a fight." Dolores wiped blistering tears from her cheeks, resolve giving her courage. "No one is going to stand in my way. Not even you, Papa."

* * * *

Jefferson Duke envied William Mansfield for two reasons: Caroline and the emporium. Actually, in Jefferson's mind they were one and the same. She was the mastermind behind everything the emporium was. She bartered for hides as well as Jefferson could. She bought goods off the ships at slightly better prices than he did. He was certain her beauty combined with the sea captains' long and lonely journeys to California had a bit to do with Caroline's negotiating power.

Jefferson's trading post was doing well, but with the competition from Richardson, whom most of the residents had known longer, and the Mansfield establishment, all three of them had to work more diligently for every dollar.

If Caroline and I were married, there would be no limit to what our minds and ambitions could accomplish. No limit to our happiness.

"Lord knows, everything else about us is on fire," he said to himself as he lugged sacks of flour into place in front of his crude counter. He checked the barrels of various sized nails, the new sets of tools and saws that had arrived and the new bolts of calico and cottons.

He stopped abruptly as he looked at the fabric and thought, *Cornflower blue . . . the color of your eyes. My God, must everything remind me of you, Caroline?*

He realized it didn't matter what he did or saw, she was perpetually on his mind. What a fool he'd been to think that once he'd tasted her body, his love would be quelled and the fire stamped out. Instead, a taste only whetted his desire for more of her. It was nearly impossible for them to be alone, but they had managed it three times. It was dangerous, this life they were leading, loving in the shadows and beneath the night cloak in the forest. But

Jefferson was a victim of his own passions. He found he was strong for a day, maybe two, but never any longer. He'd make an excuse, no matter how flimsy, just to see her.

Because of Caroline, Jefferson began building his "proper" house long before he was financially able. His lot was located not far from the emporium and the construction gave him a reason to ride past her store every day.

Some days she almost ignored him completely and he was forced to talk to William, a difficult task since William wasn't given to small talk. Other days, the look in her eyes was so intense that he was afraid she'd thrown too much caution to the wind and William would learn the truth.

William never did.

For months, Jefferson and Caroline lived and breathed each other. It was heaven. It was hell. They both knew it would have to come to an end, and it did.

It was through Dolores Sanchez that Jefferson was able to garner extra business. Because the Sanchezes were so rich and hospitable, many of the Spanish from Monterey and Santa Barbara received invitations to visit the Sanchez ranch nearly every week. This made a stop at the North Beach area necessary, for it was here they boarded a launch that took them across the Golden Gate to the opposite side of the bay where Dolores lived. During the transfer from coach to launch, the Spanish men and women perused Jefferson's shop and placed orders for building goods and household items. Several times Jefferson expressed his thanks to the Sanchez family through a note.

Dolores kept the notes after her father had discarded them without much thought. She took it as a sign of Jefferson's affections. She arranged for a stop at Yerba Buena on her way to visit friends in Monterey.

Dolores swooped into Jefferson's trading post, her full skirts barely making it through the doorway without being crushed. She was followed by her diminutive, weathered-looking duenna, Maria Valleje Sanchez, who was her great-aunt on her father's side.

"Señorita," Jefferson smiled and bowed to her. He took her hand and kissed it as was expected of him. "How lovely you look . . . ," he peered over his shoulder, "and your aunt, too."

Thrilled simply to stand next to him, much less touch him, Dolores lost her train of thought for a moment. "I received, I mean my father received your letters. We're pleased that you have helped our friends. They all speak kindly of you."

"You've helped my business, and it's needed all the help it can get," he chuckled.

While Dolores gazed longingly at Jefferson, following him around from counter to shelves, he carried on a light banter of conversation. Neither of them saw Caroline and William Mansfield pull up in an ox-driven wagon. William assisted Caroline down from the perch. She reached back under the seat and withdrew a bag of silver coins they would use to purchase extra building material for the interior of their store.

Inside the post, Dolores was in a world of her own where only she and Jefferson existed. He turned to her after asking her a question. He paused, smiled and waited for her reply. Wafted out of reality on a cloud of romantic fantasy, Dolores suddenly threw her arms around Jefferson's neck, leaned into his body and kissed him with all the passion she'd saved for him over the past year.

Dolores's duenna was so stunned, so shocked, she could only gape at her outrageously immoral grandniece. "Hieeey!" she breathed finally.

Just then, Caroline entered the doorway and saw Jefferson and Dolores embracing. At first, she couldn't believe her eyes. She had to blink them twice. Jefferson's hands were resting on Dolores's tiny waist, and he seemed to be enjoying this kiss as much as Dolores. Pain screamed across Caroline's mind, howling, *Fool. Fool.*

I wish to heaven I could faint. I don't want to see this.

She felt the blood siphon from her body. Her face paled. A sharp pang shot through her heart. Beneath her voluminous skirts, her knees shook. She tried to tell herself this was one of those earth tremors she'd heard hit the bay area from time to time. There had to be a logical explanation for this. Didn't there?

"Excuse us, Jefferson," William said. "We came for paint and finishing nails. Perhaps we should come back later?"

To Caroline, it was an eternity before Dolores extracted her lips from Jefferson's mouth.

He had a dazed and stupefied look on his face as if he had been so immersed in the kiss, he hadn't realized it ended.

Caroline could actually hear her heart ripping to shreds.

Dolores's eyes held a triumphant gleam, and her lips were still red with desire. Instantly, her duenna grabbed Dolores's hand and jerked her toward the door muttering a string of berating words in Spanish.

"*Vámonos*, Dolores," Maria Vallejo Sanchez yelled, then hissed at her grandniece. She literally pushed the girl out the door. Dolores kept her eyes on Jefferson and waved daintily to him as she was being shoved outside.

"Good-bye, Jefferson," she breathed sensuously.

Jefferson saw the panic in Caroline's eyes. "Good-bye."

"Do I hear wedding bells, Jefferson?" William teased.

"Huh? Of course not. I don't know what got into her. She just up and kissed me," he said, looking at Caroline. "It was the damndest thing."

"I'm sure it was," William smiled cockily. "Looks to me like she's going to have a bit of trouble on the rancho tonight. Don't be surprised if her Papa demands restitution."

Jefferson's eyes shot to William. "Dueling?"

"I hear the Spanish like it more than the Creoles in New Orleans."

Jefferson swallowed the lump in his throat. "I wouldn't want to get killed for something I don't want," he said pointedly, as he looked at Caroline who was on the verge of tears.

"Are you sure about that?" Caroline asked.

"Absolutely," his eyes bore into hers earnestly.

William tapped his toe on the dirt floor. "Well, Jefferson, I need those nails. I have workmen waiting."

"Yes," Jefferson said, taking his eyes off Caroline and smiling at William. "When your servant brought the message, I assembled everything around back. I'll load it for you."

Jefferson went out the door while Caroline dug in her bag for the silver to pay their invoice. Her hands shook as she counted the coins and laid them on the counter. She went outside and climbed onto the perch on the wagon and waited for William to join her.

She couldn't look at Jefferson when he finished loading the wagon. "I left the payment on the counter."

Jefferson shook William's hand. "Good doing business with you."

As they rode away up the hill, Caroline knew that she'd made another turn in the road to her destiny that day. She was in love with Jefferson, and though she'd tried to fool herself into thinking they could go on as they were, she now realized that her romance had reached its end. She might never be sure if Jefferson was attracted to Dolores or not. Even if he were, she couldn't blame him. He was free and Caroline was not. That fact alone kept her trapped in a private hell for the rest of her life.

Caroline couldn't leave William for both financial and moral reasons. Every nickel she had in the world was sunk into their business. She had no family back East, only this partnership with William. If she left him, she would have nothing. Not even passage back to Boston or her old job. The idea of spending the rest of her life as governess to someone else's children and never seeing Jefferson again was more than she could tolerate. And, too, she believed that once married, always married.

Her intellectual mind was a myriad of philosophies that condoned her adulterous affair with Jefferson, but she could not condone causing William pain by divorcing him. She knew she was William's strength. Without her, he was a lost soul. Jefferson was strong. She was strong. William was weak. Caroline made a sacred pact the day she married William at the high service.

Caroline's wedding vows had sealed her fate once, and today they sealed it again. Tonight she would sleep in William's bed, and she would allow him to make love to her as he had wanted to do since they left Boston. From this day forward, she would be a wife to her husband. It was the best thing, she thought, for herself, for William, for Jefferson and especially for the child growing inside her.

seventeen

After the wind, an earthquake;
but the Lord was not in the earthquake!
And after the earthquake, a fire;
but the Lord was not in the fire;
and after the fire a still small voice.

—1 KINGS 19:11

C*rack!*
The physician smacked the baby's buttocks, but it lay still. *Crack!* Again, Caroline heard the sound of flesh meeting flesh, the muttering sound of prayers being uttered, a man's curse, but no sound of life.

She couldn't see them, any of them, those medical ghosts in white cotton smocks who attended her. She could smell blood and medicines, but they, too, were a haze.

"God, please. Let me die. Save my child . . . ," she mumbled as she had all through the long and painful night.

Suddenly, there it was. A small voice, not a wail or angry cry, but a struggling sound as life entered the body of her baby.

Smack! She heard the doctor hit the baby's back.

This time the wail was loud, clear and very much alive.

"My baby!" She stretched out her weary arms, but she could barely focus on the nurse who held the baby up for her to see. "A boy. . . . I always knew it was a boy."

Caroline smiled through swollen lips. Her breech delivery had been so painful, she'd bitten her lips in over a dozen places. Her eyes were nearly swollen shut as well from the tremendous amount of straining. "Lawrence. His name is Lawrence."

The nurse nodded and took the baby away. Caroline felt the doctor's cool hand as he wiped the sweat from her brow.

"I don't know if being in Boston to have your baby was a gift or a curse, Caroline. The trip around the Horn in your early months did you no good, but I also doubt seriously either of you would have survived the delivery had you not had proper care. There aren't many hospitals in California."

"There are none." Caroline's mind began to fog over again. "There're only two wooden floors, and mine is one of them."

"I want you to rest."

Caroline tried to prop herself up on her elbows but she was so weak she could barely lift her head off the pillow. "I must write my husband."

"Tomorrow, Caroline. You have all the time in the world."

"Yes," she said, giving in to the anesthetizing fog that rolled over her much like the green-silver morning fog that funneled through the Golden Gate. "Time." Caroline passed into oblivion.

Lawrence William Mansfield was a small baby, though not as sickly as the doctors had initially feared. Because his birth-weight was low, Caroline was advised not to return to California until Lawrence was six months old. She argued that she needed to help William with the business. Only she knew how she wanted her new house to be built, and only she understood the focus of retailing they needed to take. She'd left California so abruptly, she hadn't had time to educate William about the pampered Spanish girls and their tastes in finery and household goods.

Caroline did the next best thing. She wrote to William informing him of the doctor's decision and news of the baby, his brother and the family's Boston store. She also told him she would buy their inventory and then ship the goods to him. She had used this same excuse of a buying trip to convince William that she needed to return to Boston.

What she didn't want him to know were the details of the baby's birth. Had Lawrence been full sized, there might have been skepticism. Caroline simply told William's family that the baby was premature. Lawrence was so scrawny and pale with white tufts of hair shooting out from his skull and such pale blue eyes, they were the first to agree that this odd-looking, though not ugly, baby was definitely not fully formed.

* * * *

Caroline lived in the elaborate Beacon Hill Federal-style home of her brother-in-law, David, and his wife, Cassandra. She shared a nanny with David's two children. For the most part, Caroline could come and go as she pleased.

She went back to the *Lady's Magazine* and visited with Sarah Hale and discovered that Sarah had fallen on desperate times with all the economic upheaval of the mid-1830s. In 1837, Sarah had combined forces with Louis Antoine Godey, the publisher of *The Lady's Book,* and together they were now publishing *Godey's Lady's Book* and *American Ladies' Magazine*, which was already being called *Godey's Ladies' Book* by everyone on the streets.

Caroline was filled with new excitement about the trends coming as they headed into the new decade. The new magazine refused to borrow from the English and French. There was a new emphasis on American fashions, American writers and poets.

Caroline took this news with her when she bought American-made hats, which had less frippery ornamentation than French hats. Though there was no opera in San Francisco, it did not stop her from buying knitted opera caps, which would keep a woman warm on a chilling foggy morning.

Caroline found the best seamstresses along the Charles River waterfront. In these small, close rooms she found the older women who were too blind, sick or just plain too tired to work in the sweatshops any longer. Instead of working the looms that made bolts of fabric, they knitted, embroidered and hand-stitched fabulous dresses together.

Caroline passed over the bland cream silks and taupe cottons in favor of blue taffetas, palest yellow fichu, emerald silks, burgundy satins and forest-green crepe. She ordered the latest style changes of bateau necklines, huge, nearly overwhelming balloon sleeves and the new French gigot sleeves trimmed in thick banding and laces. She ordered linen handkerchiefs edged in a narrower lace, not more than one-and-a-half inches. She bought drop earrings, parasols, poke bonnets, satin hair ribbons, walking sticks for the men, boots, stevedore hats, flared-bottom waistcoats and tassels for everything from a drawer pull to a cane.

For six months, Lawrence grew strong and healthy while Caroline forced her heart to grow away from Jefferson. There was no sign yet of Jefferson in Lawrence's features; he looked so much like Caroline.

She kept her mind on business and finally, by the time she was to return, she had accomplished the amazing feat of being able to go nearly one hour without thinking of Jefferson.

She was sitting by the fire one night reading the Bible when David walked in.

"I hate to disturb your worship," he said. "I have a letter from William."

Before she even touched the envelope, Caroline heard gale winds blowing again. Something was in the letter she didn't want to read. A terrible foreboding hovered over her, and she shrank back in the chair.

"Whatever is the matter?" David asked. "You're as pale as a sheet. I'll get you some brandy while you read your letter."

"Thank you," she said and took the letter. She broke the wax seal. Her eyes skimmed the page quickly and found the usual chatter about the weather, the low inventory, the increasing number of ships pulling into the harbor, William's questions about her and the baby. And then she saw it. Her hands turned to ice.

"Jefferson," she whispered to herself as she read William's letter. Pangs of loneliness threatened to rip her apart. No matter how hard she worked, how she occupied her mind, she was inexorably in love with him.

She could think of no way to stop the torture.

She continued reading the letter.

Of course I had not mentioned your pregnancy to anyone, my dear. Not that I was being pessimistic, but our early reports from the doctor did not bode well. That's all behind us now, is it not? Now that I know I am the father of a son, I had a small celebration here at the emporium. I broke out my best keg of rum and issued cigars to Don Richardson and Jacob Leese, Jefferson Duke and the newcomer Nathan Spear. I'm afraid most of us got a bit ripped that night. Jefferson Duke made it a double celebration by stating that he intended to ask Dolores Sanchez to be his wife. We all laughed, of course, poor fellow, because her father would never allow it. However, he just might pull it off, she being so enthralled by him and he by her, I think. We all teased him that she was one of the best shots in the district and not to cross that hot-tempered lady. Even if I were her father, I would not attempt it.

I hope you are well and I cannot wait to see you and my son.

Your husband,
William

Caroline dropped her hand to her lap.

Even William had deduced that whatever Dolores wanted she would get . . . ultimately. She also realized from the letter that Jefferson had no intention of marrying Dolores until he knew about Lawrence. She wondered why he had waited so long. She left California almost a year ago. Perhaps Dolores's battle with her father had proved too strenuous. Jefferson seemed all too eager to have Dolores that day in his store. Had she been wrong to leave?

She shook her head. *I had to leave. . . . I was two months along.*

Suddenly, she realized David was standing next to her with the brandy.

"What did you say? You're leaving in two months?"

"I would like to," she replied, sheepishly taking the brandy.

"Caroline," he said in that overprotective, egotistical manner she detested. David was a generous man, but his patronization of her was nauseating at times. "The doctors have told you that you must stay for the baby's sake. You're just reacting to William's letter. I understand that you miss him, but when he wrote that, I'm sure it was when he'd first received news of his son."

Caroline looked at him. *Heaven! But this man is unnerving. He talks to me as if I'm a child. He talks to all women like that. No wonder women are still subservient with male attitudes the way they are.*

"You're right," she said, stroking his male ego. "I just missed William was all."

"Understandable, my dear," he said, lighting a match to his clay pipe. Then he gave her one of his sappy, overly sweet grins which he thought looked compassionate. She thought it looked idiotic.

San Francisco—1842

Jefferson slit the throat of a deer he would skin, then preserve the meat to feed himself for the next several months. A stream of blood gushed out, covering his hands with warm sticky red goo. He remembered his difficult days of trapping when his furs established him in his business. Now he no longer needed to hunt except for his food.

Back then he had blessed the animals the way his mother had taught him. As long as there was an exchange of prayer between man and beast the two would always be able to exist on the earth in harmony. He remembered thinking at times he could hear Rachel whispering to him. At the time, he'd thought it was just his memories playing tricks on him.

Now he knew better.

The more he missed Caroline, the more he poured out his love for her, the more often he heard his mother.

At first, she came to him just as he was falling asleep or waking up. He told himself the visions he saw were his imagination or part of his dream.

But as the visits became more frequent, he realized that his mother was truly with him. Just as Yuala had never left Rachel alone on earth, his mother was there with him to guide him.

Jefferson was glad he no longer had to trap for a living. These days when he came to the mountains it was to pray. Here he allowed himself the luxury of hours of meditation.

The sky was an indigo shawl studded with a billion glittering stars, reminding him how vast was the universe and how alone he was.

Sinking back on his heels, Jefferson felt tears fill his eyes. "Mother, it's been a long time since you've come to me. Tell me what is to be my fate? Am I to love Caroline so much it aches with every breath? To never see her again? What purpose has my life served if all I'm to have is pain?"

He opened his arms wide, "Teach me to die, Mother, like you did. If you love me, then let me leave this place. I can't bear it a moment longer."

He heard the wind howl.

I've done everything to get you out of my mind, Caroline. I even thought I could replace you with another woman.

It was the night at the emporium when William had thrown a party. Caroline was in Boston, and so, Jefferson had thought it would be safe to go to the party. Hopefully, he wouldn't give himself away. However, there'd been whiskey at the party. Too much whiskey. And Jefferson got blinding drunk. He'd had a good time, too, until William began bragging.

"Can you believe it?" William shouted to everyone, standing on a pickle barrel. "I have a son! Caroline has made me so happy."

Everyone congratulated William by pounding him on the back and offering more toasts.

Memories of Caroline—the sound of her voice, the feel of her skin, the taste of her—rushed over Jefferson like the wind. He thought he would implode from the pain.

Surmising that the only way to crush Caroline out of his soul was to replace her with another woman, Jefferson tottered on numb legs, raised his tankard in the air and said, "Hear, hear! I want everyone to know that I intend to marry Dolores Sanchez!"

At first he heard a guffaw and then a howl of "Attaboy!" Then there was only silence.

His eyes half-hooded, he gazed around the room. "Sho ya don't thin sssshe'll acshept?" He swayed to the left, spinning clumsily on his heel, and faced Jacob Leese.

"Her father will never allow it. You're not blue blood," Jacob said. "And if he gets wind of your intentions, you may find your backside full of buckshot."

"Realwy?"

"'Fraid so."

Jefferson didn't remember anything after that. He'd passed out.

A swift meeting with Don Sanchez to render his formal apology for his disrespect was accepted. That same day, Don Sanchez arranged for Dolores's marriage to his cousin's son in Monterey. He told Jefferson that he was embarrassed by his daughter's inappropriate behavior and that he knew he was the only person who could put an end to her indiscretions.

Jefferson assured him that nothing had "transpired" between them. Don Sanchez believed him.

I wonder what Don Sanchez would think if he knew Yuala was my grandmother?

Bitter tears sprang to his eyes. "I feel as helpless as when Richard suffered his stroke and Maureen banished Mother and me to the slave cabins."

Entwining his fingers around each other to keep his energy from escaping into the cosmos, Jefferson prayed again.

"Mother, how I miss you and your wisdom. I've disappointed you. I know I have. I've made a mess of Yuala's dream. But I love Caroline so very much. What is the answer for us?"

Suddenly, a shooting star sped across the galaxy, spewing light and sparks in a long tail. It climbed over the night sky, showing the world there were miracles yet to be discovered.

Fifty yards in front of him, he saw a vapor, white, pure and clean, take form and hover just above the ground. He didn't dare look away, knowing it would disappear. He couldn't see a face or body, so he knew it wasn't human. Some might have thought it was the night air trapped between the trees. Some might have thought their eyes were playing tricks on them. Some might have believed it was a reflection of moonlight. Jefferson knew better.

"Mother?"

He believed that what he saw was more of a reality inside his mind than outside. He looked with his mind's eye. He listened not with his ears, but with his heart.

"My son, don't be afraid."

Chills blanketed his body and crawled across his scalp. "Never. Please help me, Mother."

Rachel smiled at him with a greater radiance than she'd had on earth. "You've done nothing wrong, Jefferson. She is married, yes, but not in her heart. I was never married legally but was in my heart. Only you can take this burden of guilt from your shoulders. It weighs you down, and you have a great deal to accomplish with your life."

"What is the purpose of my life? I feel nothing but sorrow."

"Out of your dreams and efforts, this city will grow. You were meant to be one of its leaders. You have a pure heart, Jefferson. Show others the things I have taught you. Make this city a paradise for your son."

"My what?"

"Your son. His name is Lawrence. It's important you do not press Caroline to leave her husband. Your son must be legitimate, Jefferson. For your granddaughter's sake."

"My granddaughter?"

"Yes, Barbara. She's the one who came to my mother in a vision. The destiny of your city lies in your hands, and in her lifetime, in hers. She will battle evil, just as you battle bigotry and prejudice today.

"But I come tonight to warn you of other dangers."

"Other dangers?"

"In the east, there exists hatred in a man's heart for all who bear the name Duke, as you do. He threatened your great-uncle, Andrew Duke. Now he threatens his son, Ambrose. But he will leave his own country. The leaders there can see his evil. In the days to come, you will be challenged. In the years to come, you must be cautious. This man who comes across the water has a black heart. He is blinded by hatred and will try to kill you. He will inflict great pain."

"How can I stop him?"

"Always remember that thoughts are things. You cannot change him until his eyes are opened to the foul of his soul. But you can protect yourself and your family from his wrath by keeping your heart filled with love. Your soul filled with good intentions.

"Surround yourself, Caroline and your son with positive protective thoughts. They will form an armor of silver-white light. Falter and you will perish."

"I'll do it," he promised.

"It's important, Jefferson, because someday you and Barbara will conquer many evils together. If you fail the city will be destroyed."

Suddenly, Jefferson was overcome with fear as he realized the full impact of her words. "How will it happen?"

"A great earthquake and then a fire. I have seen it many times in visions."

"But I'm only one man. How could I make a difference?"

Rachel raised her arm and as she did, he saw a shower of silver light appear. "What a poor teacher I am," she sighed. "Every man matters, Jefferson. Otherwise, you wouldn't have come to earth." The silver shower circled around her and increased in intensity. "You and Caroline will have many moments together. Your child comes to you now, Jefferson. His name is Lawrence."

The moon went behind a cloud as the last spark of the comet's tail died in the sky. The mist between the trees evaporated, and Rachel went with it.

Stunned that he was awake and not dreaming, Jefferson scanned the area for tangible evidence of his mother's visitation. He found nothing. For a moment he thought he had lost his mind.

Then the truth hit him like a javelin. He sank back on his heels. "Caroline's child is named Lawrence. Her child is mine!"

It all made sense. She hadn't run away because of Dolores, but because she was pregnant. At once, he was filled with joy and sadness. His son was of Caroline's body, but he would never be able to call his son his own.

He had come all this way, through the South Carolina marshes, through the city streets of Boston, around the Cape and worked nearly every waking hour all these years only to find that he was still a slave.

His fate had kept him from the greatest joy a man could have . . . his own family. The woman who should have been his wife and his only son belonged to another man. Both of them carried another man's name: Mansfield.

Was the lesson he was to learn that freedom was only an illusion? Or was the answer truly to be found in his mother's words?

Pain and confusion clouded Jefferson's mind. Maybe he was insane. He forced himself to concentrate on reality. The *fact* was that he had founded a dynasty.

The illusion was that he had believed it would be named Duke.

Book Three

The House of Su

The House of Su

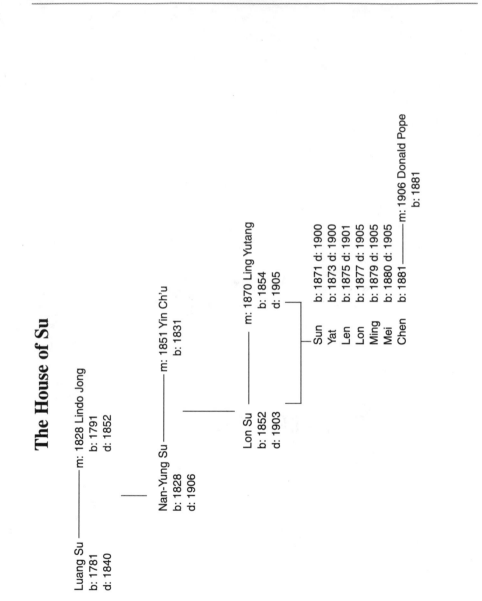

Luang Su ——————— m: 1828 Lindo Jong
b: 1781   b: 1791
d: 1840   d: 1852

Nan-Yung Su ——————— m: 1851 Yin Ch'u
b: 1828   b: 1831
d: 1906

Lon Su ——————— m: 1870 Ling Yutang
b: 1852   b: 1854
d: 1903   d: 1905

Sun   b: 1871 d: 1900
Yat   b: 1873 d: 1900
Len   b: 1875 d: 1901
Lon   b: 1877 d: 1905
Ming   b: 1879 d: 1905
Mei   b: 1880 d: 1905
Chen   b: 1881 ——————— m: 1906 Donald Pope
                                    b: 1881

eighteen

I have Three Treasures.
Guard and keep them safe.
The first is Love.
The second is, Never too much.
The Third is, Never be the first in the world.
Through Love, one will be courageous.
Through not doing too much, one has
amplitude of reserve power.
Through not presuming to be the first in the world,
one can develop one's talent and let it mature.
If one forsakes love and courage,
forsakes restraint and reserve power,
Forsakes following behind and rushes in front,
he is doomed!
For Love is victorious in attack and
invulnerable in defense.
Heaven arms with Love
those who would not see it destroyed.

—LAO-TZU

THE TREASURES, CHAP. 66–67

China—1839

The Manchus were a haughty people occupying the Middle Kingdom, which they knew was the center of the planet Earth. They knew little of the outside world and didn't care. Europe, in their minds, was a group of tiny islands where the outer barbarians lived and owed the same kind of honor and allegiance to the Celestial Empire as did the other satellite countries of Burma, Annam, Korea and Nepal. England was but a vassal of Holland, which was actually a part of France and all were owned by the Portugese, the Manchu thought, because their clothes looked much the same and they drank wine like the Dutch and kept snuff in metallic wire boxes that they carried with them everywhere they went, usually in their silly-looking, tight-fitting clothes. The Dutch and the English were *hungmao fan* or red-haired barbarians. All the barbarians lived by trade, an insignificant pastime that obsessed these men. All barbarians were tall and white, except the dwarfs of the northeast, and they lived on bread, potatoes and fowl, which they seasoned with jams and jellies.

The Chinese were able to distinguish between the various classes of barbarians; at least their caste system was in line with Chinese precepts, because the upper classes used stone for buildings, the middle class used brick and the lower classes used earth. However, in every way, the barbarians were inferior to the Manchu and even inferior to the Chinese civilization as a whole. The *only* reason the Chinese allowed the barbarians any entrance into the country at all was because of the tradition of courtesy.

Confucius had laid down the maxim, "To have friends coming to one from distant parts, is not this great pleasure?"

The Manchu kept their contacts with the barbarians as brief as possible, accepting their tributes to the Celestial Empire and to the Son of Heaven, but at all times they were aware that it was a crime to teach a foreigner the Chinese language. Prolonged contact invited infiltration, and the Manchu guarded their bloodlines viciously.

The Manchu had taste and discernment. They were the ruling class and none among them, unless accused of a crime against the emperor, would ever live in poverty, want or loneliness. Manchus believed in their divine right, the Mandate of Heaven that had ordered their destiny to rule the lowly Chinese, and the great country of China. They kept foreign ideas and innovations barricaded outside the boundaries of their domain, while never admitting that *they* were, in fact, foreigners to China. The Manchus had their own language, a strange linguistic concoction of Finnish, Hungarian and Ural-Altaic that they forced all Chinese officials to learn.

Far too many Manchus were bigoted and strove to reinforce the differences between the two cultures rather than assimilate one into the other. Intermarriage with the Chinese was strictly forbidden in order for the emperor to keep the race pure. Manchu nobles and princes might take a Chinese concubine, but they married only Manchus.

In 1839, there were 400 million Chinese. Only 5 million were Manchu. The Manchu ruled the Middle Kingdom with the same blind apathy and rapacious egotism that had brought down the wrath of heaven against their ancestors. To maintain the balance and symmetry between heaven and earth, the Manchu were given a ticket to retribution.

September 1, 1839

In the Bay of Swatow, east of Canton, Luang Su, a Manchu Prince, with the shaven head and long black queue, wearing his black silk mandarin hat with the coral button denoting that he was a mandarin of the second class, raised a delicately painted porcelain cup to his thin lips and sipped hot tea. The embroidered golden pheasant on his quilted tunic, the *plu tzu*, declared his rank was civilian. If he'd been of the military, his *plu tzu* would have been an embroidered lion. There were nine ranks of mandarin beginning with the ruby buttons of the first class and descending through the coral, sapphire, lapis lazuli, crystal, white jade, gold, worked gold and finally worked silver button. The Imperial yellow color could only be worn by the Son of Heaven, the emperor, Tao-kuang.

Luang Su leaned back in his satin-lined chair beneath a red silk umbrella that blocked the setting sun from his narrow discerning eyes while three servants fanned him with peacock feathers. He plucked a fully ripened peach from a golden platter served to him by an uneducated Chinese and sank his teeth into the juicy pulp as his oarsmen rowed his Chinese man-of-war junk toward the barbarian's ship which they called the *Lily*.

Luang Su was a highly intelligent man, adept at political games and tricks that kept his opponents stepping on their own toes and not his. He brought his own interpreter with him to deal with the British, but the man was a masque to cover the fact that Luang Su understood English very well.

He saw the corpulent, unshaven captain of the *Lily* standing on the wooden deck of his schooner waiting for him. Of all the men that Captain Young would deal with in China, Luang Su was the most important. Only Luang Su was powerful enough to allow Captain Young's opium illegal entry to China. For this privilege, Captain Young paid Luang Su a great deal of money.

The junk pulled up to the large schooner, and with the aid of three servants and two British soldiers, Luang Su lumbered aboard. He allowed the captain to bow to him. Out of courtesy, he returned the bow, but not too deep, not to give too much reverence to the barbarian.

"How good to see you again, Luang Su," the captain said, and immediately a deckhand appeared with a cigar for Luang Su. Then the cook came with a wooden tray bearing a cup of Luang Su's favorite Madeira wine from Portugal.

Luang Su looked disdainfully at the wooden tray, wondering why these immensely rich men did not purchase trays of gold as he'd done. He sipped the wine without smiling, then offered his thanks through his interpreter.

Luang Su raised his eyes to the captain and said, "Why is it that this British ship has anchored here in Namoa when you know that all foreign ships are only allowed to anchor at Canton?"

The interpreter rattled off the words in English.

Captain Young answered immediately. "Ah! We're bound for Canton. But an ill wind has forced us here to Namoa. I was hoping that we might take on supplies and water."

"You shall have all you need."

"Thank you," Captain Young smiled.

Luang Su's long slashes of black eyebrows crept together and formed a suspicious line across the top of his eyes. "Afterward you must depart *immediately*!"

"Of course," Captain Young bowed slightly.

Luang Su leaned down and out of his boot he withdrew a red document which he handed to his interpreter who read aloud: "This is a true copy of the Imperial edict dated Tao-kuang, seventeenth year, sixth moon, fourth sun. As the port of Canton is the only one at which the Outer barbarians are permitted to trade, on no account can they be allowed to wander and visit other places in the Middle Kingdom. His Majesty, however, being ever desirous that his compassion be made manifest even to the least deserving, cannot deny to such as are in distress from lack of food through adverse seas and currents the necessary means of continuing their voyage. When supplied they must not linger but put to sea again immediately."

The interpreter handed the edict back to Luang Su, who put it back in his boot and rose to his feet as a signal that his attendants might now leave him.

Luang Su then turned to the captain and began a conversation that they had discussed many times in the past. Luang Su made certain his intonation was strained, his dialect not pure in order to continue to fool the barbarians as to his fluency of English.

"How many chests of foreign mud have you on board?"

"About two hundred."

"Are they all for Namoa?" Luang Su asked.

"We want to try the market here," Captain Young said.

"You are wise. Further up the coast the officers are uncommonly strict. I am informed that at Amoy smugglers have recently been decapitated."

"We have no intention of going to Amoy," Captain Young said with great reassurance.

"You are wise, I repeat. We can assume then that you are landing your chests here."

"With your Excellency's permission."

"My permission, if I may put it so, depends upon your offer."

Captain Young took Luang Su aside and from his brown woolen waistcoat he withdrew two heavy bags of gold coins. Luang Su shook his head. The captain said nothing, sighed and from the left hand inside pocket of his waistcoat withdrew a third bag.

This was their standard procedure.

Luang Su smiled disapprovingly at the third bag. "Am I to understand you have no information for me from England?"

"About the Duke family?"

"Yes."

Captain Young looked longingly at the third bag of gold. "I'm afraid to say that as much as I want to keep my gold, I have nothing more to report. Just as it was last time, the Duke women from Jamaica are long dead. None left heirs. Your family's search is in vain, Luang Su. I told you before that only Ambrose Duke who still lives in Canton can be found."

Luang Su's eyes filled with zealous indignation. "My seer has told me there exists another, a much younger man. He lives by the water. It must be

England of which you have described to me."

Captain Young shook his head. "May I suggest consulting another fortune-teller?"

Luang Su struggled with the demons churning inside him. His family was doomed if they did not avenge themselves against the Dukes. "My advisor is the best. It is your investigation that lacks accuracy."

"Luang Su, I don't know what to say. It's been seven years since I first began inquiries for you. Perhaps if you ask your . . . advisor to be more specific. What city by the water? Perhaps it's not England."

"No! He told me the people there speak your language."

"English is spoken in many countries. America, for example."

"The new world," Luang Su considered this.

"Ask your advisor if it's possible this Duke could be in America. I have contacts there in New York, New Orleans, San Francisco and many other ports. Please do this for me, Luang Su. I would like to help," he said handing over the third bag of gold.

Luang Su's expression was implacable. "You are not interested in helping me. You want only to keep your gold."

"I'm mercenary like that, yes," Captain Young smiled, then instantly realized his mistake. Manchus were known for their lack of humor. "Give me more information. I'll do the best I can."

"Humph," Luang Su mumbled as he turned away. "Just remember, without my permission for your mud, I can have all of you executed."

"That fact has never left my mind for a second," Captain Young assured him.

Luang Su went to the edge of the schooner, bowed respectfully to the captain, then climbed down the hemp ladder to his junk. Seating himself comfortably against the coral satin of his specially made chair, he never looked back at the British ship as they rowed back toward land.

* * * *

There was nothing mysterious about the opium trade in China. The British East India Company needed a market for the vast quantities of opium produced in India. For years, the Chinese refused to allow trade with the British for their manufactured goods and clothing. The Chinese had no need for these items, the Son of Heaven stated. In the few instances when he did allow trade with the British, the Son of Heaven levied huge import taxes.

However, the Chinese were quick to allow the sale of Chinese tea, silk, rhubarb, nankeen (a cotton fabric from Nanking), porcelain, lacquer ware, Chinese furniture and hand-carved objects. All goods were required to be paid in silver. Thus, chests of silver had been pouring into China for decades, and the imbalance of trade was killing the English.

The English were allowed to trade only through the Hong merchants in Canton, and nearly every transaction involved heavy bribes. Even the Hoppo, the emperor's own financial representative, was deeply involved in the payoffs. Rare was the Hoppo who retired at his end of term at the Board of Revenue without having accumulated vast wealth.

The trading system and the chain of bureaucrats who demanded bribes became more convoluted by the day. Everyone from the customs officials, the interpreters, the pilots who guided the ships up the Pearl River, even the compradors who bought the supplies for the British business-houses were on the take.

Luang Su was simply part of the system.

The British retaliated against the Chinese in the only way they knew: opium. The Chinese were easily susceptible to smoking the drug since even their women had been smoking tobacco for centuries, a habit introduced to them by the Formosans. But it was the Turks and Arabs who brought poppies to China and showed the Chinese how to eat the raw opium for medicinal reasons.

In the 1600s, the Chinese mixed the opium with tobacco and smoked it. Though the emperor issued an edict in 1729 forbidding the sale and the consumption of the drug, the number of smokers increased despite cruel punishments if one were caught. A hundred years later, the eunuchs and even members of the Imperial bodyguard were opium smokers.

The emperor restricted poppy growing inside China, which was a simple task because the Chinese opium was inferior and not satisfying. Only Indian opium would do. By 1835, the opium trade had produced 2 million Chinese addicts; profits for British captains were in excess of a hundred thousand pounds a year. The number of chests of opium had increased to twenty thousand. That number would quadruple in less than five years.

But Luang Su had more interest in the opium trade than most. It was because of opium that his father killed his wife and committed suicide. Luang Su's newly married uncle lived next door and he rescued the one-year-old baby before the authorities arrived. He told the officials that he had already buried a strangled baby, thus Luang Su's death was reported falsely. His uncle, aunt and Luang Su moved to Peking and told people Luang Su was their son, but because they were all Sus the whispers of scandal followed them.

Daily, Luang Su's uncle and aunt reminded him of the dangers of the opium his father had bought from a barbarian named Andrew Duke. They never let him forget his real parents and the evil done to them. They told him it was his heritage to avenge his family. They told him he must search the world over and eliminate the Dukes.

* * * *

Luang Su's oarsmen pulled up to the wharf where he docked his boat. His was the wide slip at the end of the pier where none of the locals could bother him, nor impinge upon his territory. He liked being able to dock without a hundred eyes watching his every move or scrutinizing his fat pockets.

With his servants fluttering around him, Luang Su passed the tents of the vegetable merchants, the doughnut maker and the mat-shed where three young girls cooked rice cakes, diverting his gaze from the familiar faces of the opium dealers who rode out to the British ship. They pretended not to know each other.

The Bay of Swatow was small and the village was nothing like Canton with its foreign section of warehouses and factories built by the British and Americans. Luang hated being here when he'd actually once lived in the great Imperial City, Peking.

He missed the high purple-stained walls that hid the city and deeper into its core, the Forbidden City itself, where he'd once been summoned to the emperor's court for a reward for his meritorious work for the empire. He'd been only twenty then and full of ideals. It was better now to be fifty-eight and full of money.

The few nice homes in the district showed blank-painted walls to the muddy street. Once behind the iron and wood gates, Luang Su's home was as near to perfection as he could make it.

Willow trees swept long green fingers to the ground which was covered in carpets of flowers. Lotus blossoms popped out of the pool whose water was so clear, the huge gold fish with telescope eyes could be seen from a distance. Delicately pruned trees were overladen with pears, apples, apricots, filberts and walnuts depending on the season. Next to the entrance of his house sat two brightly painted porcelain dragons and a tiny iron pagoda in which sat a flickering candle. Under the fruit trees a stone bench offered a peaceful place for Luang Su to sit.

Luang Su entered his garden and heard the familiar brass gong sound softly as one of his servants who trailed behind him was required to do each night. There was a muttering of female sounds coming from the house. A red silk pad was placed on the stone bench as he sat. A tiny footstool embroidered in black, gold and orange was placed under his satin-slippered feet.

"Tell my wife to bring Nan-Yung to me," he said to the servant who was half-bent at his feet.

"Yes." The middle-aged man shuffled off to the house.

Luang Su looked up at the early September sky. Soon the rains would be upon them. Then winter. He didn't like the winter, for the barbarians were forced by edict to close their warehouses and trading houses in Canton. They were not allowed to live inside the city, but outside on a tiny island. The smooth-flowing river of silver and gold that had found its way into his pockets would dry up. He frowned.

Though he was the magistrate of this area, he was not a viceroy of a province as he'd hoped he would be someday. But Luang Su had altered his life plan over ten years ago when he'd been convicted of dealing in opium.

He was not stripped of his rank, but he was relieved of the large territory of Canton over which he reigned at the time. His son had just been born. Now, Nan-Yung was eleven. Time was escaping Luang Su. Even more importantly, his chance at immortality was vanishing before his eyes.

Lindo Jong, his wife, had conceived only once. Had Luang Su not been convicted of his crimes, brought shame on his family and been publicly humiliated by the emperor himself, he would have taken another wife. But no Manchu woman would have him.

He smashed his fist to his palm. "Again my demise is due to the Dukes. Ambrose Duke," he breathed his enemy's name with venom.

Never would Luang Su admit his own folly. He was a man used to blaming others for his mistakes. His lack of success. He was blind to his own greed. His need to fabricate facts out of lies.

Perspiration erupted on his upper lip. "I will rid the world of the Dukes!"

Suddenly, his heart fluttered. Anxiety riddled him. He put his hand to his heart.

I am getting old. I have failed in my most important duty. My only chance to redeem myself and my father is through my son. Yes, Nan-Yung will be the torchbearer.

"My Lord," Lindo said as she approached, dressed in beautiful white satin robes, her hair elaborately coiffured and decorated with long hair pins to which crystal prisms were attached, looking much like the chandeliers that hung in the Forgotten City. Her face was thickly powdered with snowy white rice powder to cover the smallpox scars that marred her beauty when she was twenty-five. Her lips were painted deepest burgundy in a tiny round ball and her eyes were outlined in kohl. She wore flat-soled, golden slippers with no heel on her feet, for Manchu women did not bind their toes back and force the heel to elongate into the hollow heel of their shoes. Manchu women did not cripple themselves as the Chinese women did, because they were born with fashionably small feet and their "Lily Walk" was natural, not artificially produced. Manchu men did not worry about their wives running away from them, because they provided well for their women, something the Chinese found more difficult to do.

He saw her concern sitting on her face. "I'm fine."

She bowed deeply, but Luang Su took no more note of her. His eyes were on Nan-Yung who followed after her.

"Come," Luang Su motioned with his four-inch long fingernail which was covered in a sheath of green jade. "Tell me what you did today."

"I read," Nan-Yung was exquisitely dressed, which pleased his father. He wore a satin tunic over black silk pants and a tiny replica of his father's mandarin hat.

"And what did you read today?" A half-smile parted his lips, but there was no sparkle in his eyes.

"Passages from the *Tao Te Ching*."

"Such as?" Luang Su interrupted.

Nan-Yung knew this recital was coming. He was prepared. "Soldiers are weapons of evil. They are not the weapons of gentlemen. Even in victory there is no beauty. And who calls it beautiful is one who delights in slaughter. Repay evil with good."

"Enough!" Luang Su ordered and rose as if he'd been shot out of his seat by a rocket. His eyes went to Lindo. "Did you choose his readings?"

She bowed her head, happy not to look at him. "How could I, since I do not read?"

"I chose them myself, Father. I thought it would please you. You being an honorable man. A gentleman." His sincere eyes showing no sign of remorse nor emotional tears that Luang Su detested.

"Ah," he said and sat again. "Perhaps the time has come in our history again for us to put down the book of Tao. Soon, there will come a war."

"A war, Father?" Nan-Yung was incredulous. "With the Chinese rabble who threaten to dislodge us from our home because they are jealous of our standing so close to Heaven?" He repeated his father's sentiment.

"No. With the British. Though the Son of Heaven was once mighty, he's lost power. The damage from the flooding of the Yangtze when you were a small child has never been recouped. His refusal to allow the British to trade openly has brought the siphoning of silver from the government's treasure chests. It's the emperor who's guilty for the great opium trade. He's a stupid man."

"A man of short vision," Nan-Yung said.

"Precisely," he sighed. "Famine and drought, rebellion in the north, uprisings in Formosa and Canton. And now the barbarians have challenged him. His power is nothing compared to their great ships. I've seen their cannon power. I've seen the determination in their faces that the opium money continue making profits." He slammed his fist against the stone bench. "Can't the emperor see that heaven is unhappy with him?

Nan-Yung shook his small head. "Blind."

Luang Su looked intently at his son, at his bid for immortality. "The barbarian cannons will fire soon. Then we'll leave."

"Leave our home?" Nan-Yung's eyes shot to his mother who suddenly wasn't so demure as she took an aggressive step forward.

"Fear nothing. We have money. We'll go to the Celestial City itself. I'll demand an audience with the Son of Heaven, because soon the barbarians will sail right up the Yangtze, up the Grand Canal and right to the walled city. When they do, I, Luang Su, will be there."

Nan-Yung quickly stepped back and bowed as his imperious father rose and stalked into the house, his three servants fluttering behind him like a bevy of quail.

On September 4, 1839, the British fired the first shots at Kowloon. The Opium War had begun.

nineteen

*Man is free and must choose either
the Wise Lord and his rule or Ahriman, the Lie.*

—ZOROASTER

The Su family took the Grand Canal, the world's longest artificial waterway, which stretched from the Mongolian Plateau in the north where the Great Wall of China separates east from west down to the East China Sea. It passes through the river basins of the Hai Ho, Huai Ho, Yangtze and Chlien-tlang Chiang and connects Peking in the north with Hangchow in the south on the sea.

The actual construction of the canal began in the early fifth century and was not completed until the end of the thirteenth century. For 1179 years, Chinese laborers believed in an end product that would facilitate communication and transportation of goods and passengers, and increase the economy and elevate the physical well-being of the people. Since the Chinese were oriented in these days to pay glory to the accomplishments of man, the Grand Canal stood for centuries as man's triumph over nature.

It took political corruption, mismanagement and greed to block the canal. Silt began to fill up the waterway and stop the commerce of the hundreds of thousands of people who lived along the inlets, coves and the crowded three-story ramshackle houses that clustered along the waterways up and down the Yangtze River. The government was called upon to appropriate funds to keep the canal moving, but by the middle of the nineteenth century, the government was an imperiled entity. It had lost its strength, courage and the respect of its people.

Luang Su looked angrily at his oarsmen who were fighting against the low waters of the Grand Canal. He turned to the tall, fat Chinese man who wore no shirt, only a thick leather belt around his potbelly and black pants.

"Make them row faster!"

The man took out a whip and cracked the frayed edges above their heads. "The next strike will land on your backs!"

The oarsmen leaned into their work, their thin arms beneath the black nankeen shirts they wore nearly trembled from the strain. Suddenly, however, the boat began to move.

"Ill wind." *That's what it was,* Nan-Yung thought to himself as he watched the other junks trying to make it up the canal. If only a breeze arose, then they could unfurl the bright red sail he loved so much and move swiftly to the Imperial City.

Luang Su looked down into the murky waters. "No money from the government coffers to clean the silt from the waterways. It's the end of the Empire." He shook his head sadly.

Nan-Yung was glad his father could not see him as he snarled at his pompous back. No money. Ha! There would be plenty of money for all China's needs if men like his father were not draining the life from this beautiful country. Nan-Yung would spit on his father's lies and self-deceit if he thought he could gain control of the situation by the act. But he was only a boy. Eleven years old. His entire fate was still being determined by his father's ego.

Purple-stained stone walls rose up in a series of mazes winding around the innermost private world of the Forbidden City hidden from the world. Kublai Khan's vision of a Celestial city known as Khanbalic remained only in the checkerboard layout of Peking. A sixty-foot-wide street shot out in front of Nan-Yung as their boat docked at the edge of the canal. Two of the boatmen jumped onto the mildew-covered stone-walled edge of the canal and tied the hemp to a stone post.

As Nan-Yung stood looking at the bright yellow pagoda roofs of the gatehouses, which were the only structures to soar above the walls, he was dumbstruck beholding architectural splendor beyond all his dreams. There were no towers shooting into the sky as he'd thought he would find, because, as his father had told him, respect for the emperor and for the *feng shui*, the spirits of the water and wind, nothing could be built higher than the Emperor's dwelling. But the sheer magnitude of it all held him dumbstruck.

The day was clear, with no sandstorms from the Gobi Desert sweeping over the groves of white pines, no rising mist from the grassy hills that seemed to lap over each other like ocean waves. Nan-Yung could see the full height of Prospect Hill and down the slopes to the city that was buzzing with life. He couldn't wait to see the multitudes of mansions and palaces, crammed beside each other, hiding the intrigues he'd heard about.

They entered the city on foot at the south gate of the Outer City. On either side of the raised causeway, Nan-Yung saw the 640 acres of the Temple of Heaven and the 320 acres of the Temple of Agriculture on either side of them. Bony sheep, their hooves stuck in mud, grazed on thin scruffs of grass. He saw black crows swoop malevolently overhead, then shoot into the craggy trees. Nan-Yung shivered as he looked at the foreboding landscape. He wondered if this was an omen.

Just inside the gates, it was as if every stone, every board, every piece of mortar were alive. "Father, I've never seen so many people crammed into one place."

"It's more crowded than I remember," Luang Su replied.

Mat-shed booths and rickety shops rubbed shoulders looking for mutual support. Brightly colored flags announced the kind and type of wares being sold. Nan-Yung saw rope dancers and peddlers taunting his appetite with sweets, figs and dates. There were diviners telling fortunes with a toss of the *I Ching* sticks, barbers, puppeteers, storytellers and chiropodists. He smelled a thousand scents from the roast monkey, garlic-studded mutton, pig and fowl, ginseng, soy and tobacco to the stench of human and animal dung that the night-soil merchants collected in glass and pottery jars and then sold to the farmers in the country.

Luang Su looked down the street. "Where's the sedan I ordered? I was told one would be waiting for me," he said, seeing no coral-satin–lined sedan with coral and black silk fringe on the canopy denoting his second-class mandarin status. In fact, he saw no rickshaws, no chairs, nothing.

"How can this be?" he bellowed indignantly.

Nan-Yung wanted to smile to himself. He wondered if his father was having a bit of comeuppance.

"We'll have to rent a Peking cart," he said to Lindo and Nan-Yung as he left them to negotiate the price of one of the wheelbarrow type carts which was pulled by two scrawny men. One of the men argued with Luang Su, but he finally gave in to him.

Luang Su, Nan-Yung and Lindo fitted uncomfortably into the cart. As they moved through the streets, Nan-Yung watched as, because of the Su's mandarin status, they were given deference by the throngs of lowly Chinese.

Luang Su's boatmen went ahead of the cart, flicking the onlookers away with thin bamboo rods. Squalid, ragged children jeered and pointed to the Peking cart, but they quickly darted away from the sweep of the stinging bamboo rods, keeping their heads down but their eyes riveted on Nan-Yung.

Nan-Yung was fascinated by their crippled and diseased bodies, their pockmarked and lesion-infested faces. He wondered why Peking had more disease than his own town, especially since this was the Kingdom of the Emperor, the Celestial City.

I thought this was the closest I could come to the divine. Why, there's no perfection here. How could I have been fooled?

Riding through the narrow, noisy streets, the hideousness of the children seemed to increase. "Father, have you noticed how the children seem to rise up out of nowhere and vanish into the muddy street or slip through a stone wall? And why do I feel their jealousy and hate so keenly?"

"Don't look at them, Nan-Yung. I never do."

The sights grew more distorted to Nan-Yung. He saw city officials walking about in soiled garments. The night gatekeepers were dressed in tatters and carried only their lanterns and a large rattle. He saw a high official wearing the green color of mandarin first class stop a man in his entourage, pick lice off his neck and then deposit the lice in his own mouth, savoring it as lice was considered a delicacy in Peking City, but not in the provinces.

The streets were watered every night for sewage disposal, which then ran down into the moat that surrounded the city. There was mud, dirt and grime everywhere. The houses and shops made of frame and brick were dilapidated from too many rains and floods.

"Father, I see no pride here. Only a cesspool. Let's go back home."

"Not with war coming. Your questions make my head pound. Be quiet!"

Nan-Yung hid his anger. *Who cares about war? Anything would be better than this.*

The cart turned down Hsi-la-hu-tung, or Pewter Lane, a fairly wide side street in the Tartar City east of the canal.

The Su family climbed out of the Peking cart. As his father paid the cart man, Nan-Yung looked about and realized that the canal ran parallel to the high purple walls of the Imperial City.

"Father, are we finally at the Forbidden City?"

"Of course not," Luang Su replied tersely. "We're to rest here until the Emperor summons me."

As with most of the houses in Peking, this one had dingy, rickety walls on the outside, but once inside the gates, a rather picturesque garden awaited their pleasure. It was not as large nor as meticulously groomed as their garden at home, but peonies were in full bloom, along with lotus, almond trees, plum and pomegranate trees. The cesspool contained abundance after all, Nan-Yung thought.

Luang Su sent his boatmen to bring his bundles of clothing to the house. He was terse with his commands, so Nan-Yung knew his father was not happy with the accommodations.

Once inside the pavilioned house, matters continued to worsen.

"Why are there only two servants on hand?" Luang Su asked. "This is a direct insult to me! Everyone knows that a minimum of six servants is required by my station."

Nan-Yung followed his father throughout the house as they conducted an inspection. "The rooms are small, Father."

"And there are no embroidered hangings. And where are the fresh flowers?"

Something was terribly wrong.

Luang Su grew more worried as he looked out the window at the house next door. The roof of the house just above theirs was carved with feng, the phoenix and crested pheasants. There were carved cranes on the rafters that signified longevity and flying bats, the emblems of happiness. But the house the Su family occupied had none of these.

"Worst of all, there are no gargoyles or ugly lion dogs to ward off evil spirits, Father."

Luang Su nodded at his son. "This is more than a bad omen. It's a disaster."

Luang Su could not look into the teary eyes of his wife. He brusquely pushed past Nan-Yung and disappeared down the hall toward his bedchamber. "I'm not coming out until the emperor himself sends for me," he said and closed the door.

Nan-Yung's naive eyes wizened. He looked up at his mother who trembled with fear. "The emperor is not pleased with my father."

"I fear not," she answered.

"What can I do?" Nan-Yung asked.

She lifted her long, swan-like neck with dignity. "We'll burn incense in the cloisonné and bronze burner. It's the finest vessel in this miserable house. We'll ask heaven to protect us."

Nan-Yung marveled at his mother's strength, wondering why his father had none when it came so easily to her, a mere woman.

It was not until the spring of 1840 that Emperor Tao-kuang sent for Luang Su. For eight long, exceedingly cold and icy months, the Su family had withstood the lack of firewood for their home, meager meals, lack of proper household staff and the humiliation of living with the lower classes of Peking. While Luang Su retreated into depression, Nan-Yung explored the new world of Peking. Most of his ventures outside the house and garden were short both in distance and time, for each day his father said to him: "Don't be gone too long. The summons will surely come today."

Nan-Yung would wave and be off to purchase their foods and supplies. He learned much about the city from the vendors. By the warming month of April, he knew that the most auspicious of the city gates was T'ien An Men or the Gate of Heavenly Peace. It was important because every day the Emperor faced the south from which all his power came. South was the source of celestial energy.

Nan-Yung even tried saying his prayers to the south every day for over a month, but he didn't see much difference. He received no miracles whether he faced north or south. Nan-Yung hated living in suspension, as he and his family were doing, wondering what the emperor wanted with them.

He wondered what kind of reward his father was going to receive. He even tried facing the north when he sacrificed as he'd discovered the emperor did at the Altar of Heaven when he was the worshiper and not the object of worship.

Very early one morning, on one of his escapades, Nan-Yung ventured as far as the Wu Men or the Gate of Zenith, which was the actual entrance to the Forbidden City itself. But he was not allowed to enter. Only the young girls being considered for harem entered these gates, and of course, mandarins and officials like his father. But never a young boy like himself.

Just then Nan-Yung heard the familiar swishing swatting sound of thin bamboo rods and the scuffle of weary, slippered feet and knew that a mandarin was approaching the Forbidden City.

Nan-Yung moved back away from the imperial gates as the green satin sedan of the mandarin moved into view. Nan-Yung thought that this must have been an illustrious man, because the fringe on the canopy was longer than most and the top of the braid was studded with pearls and colored stones. There were six servants in the entourage and behind were two more sedans, both in green brocade. The second sedan was completely shut with opaque curtains. Nan-Yung assumed this sedan must be carrying the wife.

But in the last sedan, he saw the curtains part and a young face peek out at him. Tiny fingers curled around the edge of the bordered brocade as a young girl boldly moved the curtain back to reveal her face in full. This was shocking behavior for a Manchu of her class, especially before seeing the emperor.

She was only about six years old, he guessed. Her skin was the color of luminescent alabaster and seemed to cast a white glow around her. Her eyes were dark almond pools and her hair hung in a thick unadorned sheet down her back and onto the white satin pillow beneath her. She was dressed regally in pale sea-green robes studded with many jewels.

Nan-Yung dropped back another step. "Lo, I've never seen such a light in a human face. She looks like the sun."

Suddenly, she smiled at him. It was not a timid smile in the least, but a broad happy, free smile that burst across her face like dawn. Then he realized that she was laughing at him, but he didn't know for what reason. He glanced down at his clothes, thinking perhaps he was dirty or perhaps he was dressed inappropriately to be at the entrance to the home of the Son of Heaven.

Nan-Yung frowned. "Don't laugh at me," he said, but not too loudly.

The girl hugged her stomach as if he were some incredible joke.

Still, he could not take his eyes off her. "So beautiful."

Her laughter halted. She reached into her pocket and pulled out an odd-shaped stone or jewel of some kind. She held it in both hands, touched the stone to her forehead, closed her eyes for a moment, then quickly pitched the stone at him.

Nan-Yung's right hand shot into the air reflexively as if of its own volition and retrieved the stone. He'd wanted to ignore this outrageous child who was poking fun at him. Instead, he realized he was more than intrigued. He was mesmerized.

She's cast a spell on me with her stone.

"Open the gates!" The head bearer shouted to the gatekeeper.

The gates opened and the entourage entered the Forbidden City.

The little girl stopped smiling and looked forlornly at the magnificent city within the city. Her eyes darted back to Nan-Yung.

What's wrong? What do you see, little girl? What causes you such pain?
She looked at him one last time. She snapped the curtains shut.

Nan-Yung watched as the entourage disappeared into the maze of pagodas, temples, living quarters and magical-looking gardens. Nan-Yung looked around and realized he'd lost track of time. He'd be reprimanded for coming home too late. But he didn't care.

Something had happened to him that morning, though he wasn't quite sure what it was. There was something mysterious about that little girl, barely more than a baby. Perhaps she was being sold in the harem and would never come out again. He knew that many of the harem women were never taken to wife, and once inside the walls of the Forbidden City, they were never allowed to leave and marry another. They were doomed spirits these tiny children and yet, for some reason, he knew that something . . . fate? her courage? He wasn't sure what it would be that would keep her from the clutches of the emperor.

Nan-Yung walked back down the graduated levels of the terraces to his temporary home holding the smooth, clear stone in his hand, wondering about the young girl and her fate, knowing that he could never forget her.

It was after the Hour of the Snake, nine in the morning, when Nan-Yung reached his house and found the servants bustling. In front of the dingy gate he saw a magnificent sedan, six bearers and seven bare-chested, golden-belted eunuchs who could not have been sent by anyone other than the emperor himself.

Just inside the garden he found his mother dressed in her finest robes, her hair coiffured and adorned with elaborate flowers and tinkling crystal prisms hanging over her ears.

"Nan-Yung!" Luang Su shouted across the dusty tiled terrace. "Where have you been?"

Taken aback by his father's booming voice, Nan-Yung slipped up and told the truth. "At the gate of Heavenly Peace."

"You should have stayed," his father replied restlessly as he fidgeted with his coral-buttoned cap. "We're due at the Forbidden City before noon."

"All of us? Why would the emperor want to see Mother and me?"

"I have no idea," his father said pompously and a bit put out. "But that is the command. I can only assume from this unorthodox order that the Son of

Heaven wishes to commend me for my duties and wishes to bestow a great honor upon me. Therefore, it is appropriate that all of my family should be witness to the glory I have brought to the Su name."

Luang Su turned to a servant who held a black-lacquered jewelry box lined in red satin open for his inspection. He withdrew a huge emerald ring, an heirloom from his father's father. He jammed it angrily on his index finger. "Go outside the gate and see if the second sedan has arrived," he commanded the servant.

The servant bowed and scurried away. He returned in an instant with an affirmative nod of his head.

"We must leave," Luang Su barked at his family then nearly flew past them in his haste to begin his journey to the Forbidden City.

Nan-Yung and his mother were assisted into their less elaborate but just as large sedan and the curtains were closed around them. Nan-Yung had to smile to himself as they set out wondering if the beautiful, shining girl would laugh at him now that he, too, was going to be accepted into the presence of the Son of Heaven.

Like the shining girl, Nan-Yung could not resist a peek through the curtains at the incredible sights of the Forbidden City once they were inside the smaller side gate to the right of the Gate of Heavenly Peace. Nan-Yung noted that his father must not have been as important as the father of the shining girl for she had gone through the Gate of Heavenly Peace.

Inside the walls, Nan-Yung said to his mother, "It's truly like heaven."

The buildings were wreathed in raised terraces, each bordered by white marble balustrades. "The Ming Emperors brought the marble from far-away Yunnan," Lindo explained to her son.

In a huge courtyard, the sedans were lowered and the Su family alighted, then proceeded on foot up a white marble staircase that seemed to float in the air, suspended by exquisitely carved five-clawed dragons, the Imperial dragon of the emperor. On both the left and right were the Vermillion, uptilted temples to the Tutelary Gods and the Imperial Ancestors, where it was law that the emperor sacrifice on the anniversaries of both the birth and death of his predecessor. Here were the adornments and carvings of the cranes and feng that warded off evil spirits which Luang Su had looked for in his temporary house and had not found.

Nan-Yung stole a glance at his father. *Lo! There is fear in his eyes. But why?*

Like the sound of a warning brass gong, Nan-Yung's intuition hit him. He was a young boy, but he was smart, wary and astute. Something was terribly amiss in their long wait for the emperor.

Nan-Yung had paid attention to the politics he'd heard in the streets of the Celestial City over the past year and a half. He knew all about the Opium Wars. He knew about his father's association with the British.

Suddenly, Nan-Yung understood why he was with his father today.

He remembered the royal decree handed down by Emperor Tao-kuang last year that would rid his court of turbulent concubines and comedians and the most threatening of the power-mad eunuchs, but above all this, the emperor intended to rid China of evil opium.

The emperor had decreed that he would execute several dozen British leaders and a few of their Chinese collaborators. The emperor intended to bring the barbarians to their knees. He wanted a promise from the British that they would stop the opium trade. He stated that not even the mandarins would escape his wrath. He would "behead convicted wholesale brokers," order the "strangulation of opium-den keepers, and officials who had taken bribes."

Nan-Yung realized that today his father would die.

As they crossed the Golden Water River by way of one of the five floating marble and stone bridges which stood for the five canons of Confucianism, Luang Su fell back and marveled to his son. "I have such feelings of majesty here. I forgive the emperor for making us live in a hovel this winter. For now I can truly appreciate all this beauty. He must think highly of me to allow me this audience. Perhaps he will favor me as he did General Lin Tse-hsu and give *me* the privilege of riding a horse in the Forbidden City."

What a pompous ass he is! I could die because of his self-centeredness.

"Father, are you certain your hopes are not lofty ones?"

Luang Su snarled at his son. "I was wrong to take you into my confidence." Then he burst forward with angry energy and passed through the Gate of Correct Conduct which was to the west of the T'ai Ho Men or Gate of Supreme Harmony. Nan-Yung looked down at the Dragon Pavement Terrace, not looking up at the massive, multi-tiered roofs that soared above them, opening to the brilliant blue sky. He nearly stubbed his toe on the triple flight of white marble steps ahead of him. Nan-Yung had to be careful not to let his father see his anger.

He's leaving Mother and me with no protection for the rest of our lives.

Without him we have no income, no home, no future. Worst of all, we'll have
no respect! Our name will be worse than mud. It will be excrement!

Ha! Respect. All he's ever preached is avenging our good name against
some faceless barbarians like the Dukes. What do I care about some ghosts?
It's my own father who has brought our family down, and I will never for-
give him for it.

They entered the Throne Hall of Supreme Harmony. Hundreds of
eunuchs with their prematurely aging faces, flaccid stomachs and bald heads
bore testimony to their pre-adolescent castrations. They were dressed in fine
satins and silks, with golden girdles and jewel-encrusted robes. Nan-Yung
had heard about these oddities of court from the street people.

There were three thousand eunuchs at court and three thousand women.
The eunuchs controlled all the departmental supervision and their various
duties included responsibility for the furs, silks, porcelains and tea; tending
the vaults of silver and gold bullion; others maintained the stores of food-
stuffs. Some eunuchs collected rents from bannermen. Others programmed
court theatricals and plays. Some were in charge of the kennels and the
breeding of Pekingese dogs. Some were charged with maintaining the court
grounds, gardening and housekeeping. Under these headings were sub-
sidiary posts such as the palace stud, imperial buttery, imperial armory,
imperial weaving and dyeing office, library, boatmen, laundry and so on.

The palace intrigues, the pitting of one woman and her cohorts against
another more powerful woman or potentially more powerful woman, always
managed to be the top priority at court. Eunuchs and their loyalties were
bought and traded every day. Everyone inside and outside the Forbidden
City knew that a eunuch was incapable of integrity.

Nan-Yung's theory was that any man who agreed to bodily mutilation
knowing that according to Confucian doctrine this reflected the imperfec-
tion of the spirit and without perfect spirit, the eternal life was in jeopardy,
was a fool, an idiot or both.

Perhaps that fear explained why so many eunuchs kept their testicles
carefully safeguarded in glass jars so they could be buried with them at
death. The operation cost only six taels and once a year there was an inspection by the Chief Eunuch who demanded that each eunuch produce the
amputated private parts, correctly labeled, in order that he ferret out
imposters.

In most cases, the palace offered a eunuch a place to live, ten taels a month and daily rice, plus a cut of all the money that passed through his hands whether in the form of furs, jewels, figs, meats, antiques or silks. Tribute for loyalty was generously bestowed on eunuchs by the emperor. Thus, for a man faced with life in the streets as a beggar, the palace life looked sweet.

Nan-Yung thought it a humiliating life. Everywhere the emperor went, so did a eunuch who perpetually carried a yellow satin bag of birch wands. If the emperor found a eunuch committing an offense, he was beaten once. When the scabs formed, a second beating was ordered, and if he tried to run away, he was put in the cangue for two months. When Nan-Yung thought of wearing the dreaded wooden collar with his hands shackled to his neck, his brain went into a panic.

I have to find a way to get out of here. What if the emperor throws me in prison? I won't be able to stand it.

Passing into the Throne Hall itself, he thought, *What if the emperor wants to make me a eunuch?*

Castration will be torture.

I have my father to blame. Lo! I will never be weak like him.

They stood before the aging emperor who sat in a low-backed, intricately carved, dark wood chair. Behind him hung an incredible silk tapestry of thousands of clusters of bamboo, water, sky and terrain. It was the loveliest landscape Nan-Yung had ever seen.

Eunuchs, officials and bannermen were everywhere.

Nan-Yung saw armed members of the army against the walls wearing their quilted breast jackets, black loose-fitting pants and silver- and gold-engraved scabbards which he knew held razor sharp scimitars. Nan-Yung also noticed the three barbarians neatly dressed but not in the finery the Chinese wore. Of the three, one man stood out.

He looked old to Nan-Yung, possibly over sixty, but his eyes were the color of jade and they sparkled brighter than polished stone. His hair was nearly gold as the sun, and his skin was white like the moon. He was taller than anyone in the room, and he was powerfully built. He had a majesty about himself that rivaled the power of the emperor.

"No barbarian is allowed at court," Nan-Yung said to his father.

But Luang Su was not listening. His eyes were focused on the Englishman.

"Duke."

"The barbarian is Ambrose Duke," one of the court members whispered to another behind Nan-Yung.

Nan-Yung felt the hairs on the back of his neck stand on end. "Our enemy?"

"Yes, my son."

Nan-Yung swallowed hard.

"Their heads will roll," one man whispered.

"They say the man who calls himself 'Duke' works for the British East India Company. Everyone in the Middle Kingdom knows they import opium to China."

"Duke is the reason the Middle Kingdom has been fouled."

"The emperor is right to make him kowtow. What a fool that he will not do the emperor's bidding," another man said.

Nan-Yung's eyes flew to the powerful Englishman whose jade eyes held too much defiance for his own good. "Duke," he breathed the foul name.

Then the emperor's voice filled the air. "Ambrose Duke, you will pay homage to the Son of Heaven or I will have your head!"

Ambrose Duke turned to his two companions. "I don't understand what he is saying! Charles, can you interpret for me?"

The young, red-haired Charles whispered to Ambrose. "He wants you to bow to him or he will kill us."

Ambrose peered into the emotionless black eyes of the old emperor. "This is not a man of mercy. My bowing to him will not save our necks."

Ambrose couldn't believe this was happening to him. For three generations, the Duke family had been involved with the East India Company, making millions of pounds a year, discovering the finest antiquities for English homes, even his uncle Lord Henry Duke's home in Jamaica. God rest his soul. Now it looked like Ambrose was going to join his father and uncle.

"My God, Charles, they're going to try me for my father's crime of opium trading. I've never sold the first gram of the stuff."

"I know that. But they don't know that."

"First we were shanghaied to the interior of this Celestial City. Now, I'm on the verge of death because of an idiotic war that is none of my doing."

Charles leaned over. "Maybe you should try explaining to them that if they would sell their porcelains and goods to England, there would be no war."

"Do you think they'd listen?"

"What other chances do we have?" Charles asked earnestly.

"Good point," Ambrose drew a deep breath and stepped directly in front of the emperor.

"You've kidnapped me from my place of business. My family knows nothing of my whereabouts, or even that I'm alive. The British East India Company, with whom I'm affiliated, may indeed be involved in this opium trade, but I am not. I buy antiques and furnishings. If you have a problem with opium, your Highness, look to the problems you have with your people. Look within your mighty kingdom. I promise you this, there would be no opium trade, no smuggling, no bribery, no Opium War, if it were not for you, sir, illustrious Son of Heaven. You are unable to control your ministers and your commoners who are buying the opium. England wishes to trade furnishings with you. Trade your porcelains for our porcelains and end the war."

The emperor allowed the translator to finish.

Nan-Yung strained to hear the translation. "Father, I've never heard such insolence. The fool, Duke, is a dead man."

"That he is, my son," Luang Su replied, wiping revenge off his bottom lip.

The emperor spoke. "I will rid the Middle Kingdom of this vice. I'll strike dead all who deal in this evil. I have brought you here, Duke, to be a witness, to go back to the barbarians and tell them of the power of the Son of Heaven."

Ambrose was puzzled. "Witness?"

Just then four members of the guard swooped up from behind Luang Su and yanked him to the foot of the emperor where he kowtowed immediately, prostrating himself, lower than the emperor, flat against the smooth marble floor, showing his dedication to the mighty Imperial One.

"I am at your service, Son of Heaven," Luang Su kept his face toward the floor and his eyes riveted on the marble.

The emperor did not look at Luang Su but at Ambrose Duke. "I have brought the House of Su here for the barbarian's view. You will remember my edict. What the Son of Heaven has decreed is law."

The emperor waved his hand. Ambrose Duke watched horrified as his two companions, Charles and Edward, were hauled to the feet of the emperor. Terror-stricken, they kowtowed to the emperor.

"Luang Su, you have taken bribes from the barbarians. Because of you and other Manchu like you, who believe that your power is greater than that of the Son of Heaven, the Middle Kingdom is at war. I have brought your family here so that they may share in your humiliation, your fall from grace. All in China knew of your betrayal to the Middle Kingdom. No longer will the name of Su command respect. Your family will curse your body. You will never have the prayers of your children or their children, for this day I declare that eternal life will be denied to you."

The emperor's black eyes flashed with anger as he surveyed the rest of the court.

Nan-Yung watched Ambrose Duke and saw that his fists were clenched into white knots. Duke could keep his anger under control. For a barbarian, Ambrose Duke was powerful. Not weak like his own father.

Nan-Yung was impressed.

"Off with their heads!" the Emperor declared.

Suddenly, three scimitars flashed into the air above them, their silver reflecting the sunlight that slipped through the latticed windows. The faces of the Manchu henchmen were stone.

Fffffttt. Fffffttt. Fffffttt.

The heads of Charles, Edward and Luang Su rolled on the floor. Blood flowed over the white marble and stained the satin kneeling cushions.

"God Almighty!" Ambrose said to himself, then bit his tongue knowing to speak would cause his own head to roll.

Nan-Yung felt his stomach lurch and the energy seep out of his body. But he remained silent. He was stronger than his father.

He was stronger than Ambrose Duke.

In that flash of a second, Nan-Yung was suspended between life and death. Good and evil.

He chose evil.

His mind rolled over the dark side. He saw the world differently now. A veil of rage, hate and bitterness clouded his thinking.

Nan-Yung believed he saw the world clearly now. His eyes shot to Ambrose Duke, the man responsible for this turn in his life.

My father was right after all. The Dukes have been the bane of our existence.

"You!" the emperor commanded as he pointed at Ambrose Duke.

Nan-Yung jumped in fright at the sound of the emperor's voice.

Two guards swooped down on Ambrose and grabbed him by the arms.

"Take him back to Canton! Speak to your Queen. Tell her of the mercy I have granted you. Tell her to put a stop to the evil opium."

Nan-Yung watched as Ambrose Duke was dragged out of the throne room by a group of half a dozen warriors.

This can't be! Duke is being spared! He should die for his heinous crimes. Die for what his family did to my grandfather! Die for killing my father. Where is justice?

Nan-Yung reasoned that if the barbarians were forced to leave China, there would be no war. His father would be alive, and Nan-Yung's own life assured. Now everything was as if the pins had been taken out of the tapestry of his life. The threads shot in erratic directions.

"You! Son of Su," the emperor commanded.

Nan-Yung did not wait to be hauled to the floor. Instantly he kowtowed and prostrated himself. "Son of Heaven," he muttered.

"Your father's head will not be scwed back to his body. His body will remain mutilated as a sign and warning to others throughout China of my wrath."

"Clemency," Nan-Yung pleaded.

"Denied."

"I obey the wishes of the Son of Heaven."

The emperor's voice softened a bit. "You, the living, will be stripped of the second-rank mandarin. The Son of Heaven is merciful. You will continue to live in the Celestial City in the house provided for you. I will send for you in the future when my needs desire. Until then, leave my sight, Son of Su."

Nan-Yung rose lowly, keeping his back bent down as did his mother. They backed out of the throne room with all the humility required of them. Once their feet hit the Dragon Terrace Pavement, they straightened.

Nan-Yung walked before his mother.

"You walk before me, my son. It's an act of defiance."

"I'm making new rules for my life starting today, Mother. You will not control my life the way my father did. He nearly got us killed. He was a fool. Somehow I will finally avenge us against the Dukes."

"You're a child. What can you do?"

"I will make them pay for making a beggar of me. Even the despised eunuchs are of more stature than we."

"It is true that, because of Ambrose Duke, the line of our ancestry is broken. There's no pride, no lineage to pay homage to now that your father has disgraced us. Worst of all he cannot help us from the other side."

"I had not thought of that, Mother. Thank you for reminding me. Now, I hate him even more."

"Listen to me, Nan-Yung. Only if you avenge us will we find eternal peace. It is up to you, my son. I pray that you have courage."

Nan-Yung stopped dead in his tracks and faced his mother. "It's not courage I need, Mother. It's opportunity. Only then will I create my own destiny."

She walked emotionlessly past him. "See that you do."

twenty

The gods feared that they had made man too perfect, and they breathed a cloud of mist over their vision.

—QUICHE LEGEND OF THE NEW WORLD INDIANS (AZTECS)
BANCROFT'S *NATIVE RACES*, VOL. V

The Emperor Tao-kuang died in 1851 and was succeeded by his son, Hsien-feng, whose name meant "of Universal Plenty" and who was twenty years old. It was the same year Nan-Yung turned twenty.

For eleven years Nan-Yung and his mother had lived in the ugliest section of Peking, bemoaning their fate, taking no responsibility for their lot, and living off the meager "generosity" of the emperor. They had sustained life, but that was all. Nan-Yung found no joy in anything he did because he chose not to. Instead, he blamed the barbarian, Ambrose Duke, who had escaped the emperor's wrath. For years, nightmares haunted Nan-Yung's sleep and caused him to fear any of the Imperial Guard, thinking that surely this time they were coming to behead him.

From the windows of his house he saw the young emperor many times being carried through the streets on his palanquin, with great processions of bannermen and eunuchs around him. It seemed that the opulence of the empire had increased over the years, yet the plight of the lower classes of Manchu, like himself, not to mention the lowly Chinese, had worsened.

None in Peking respected the Su family, for the emperor had posted an edict on the city walls as he said he would. Further, the emperor had cursed him more stating that when Nan-Yung married he would have to give his children the name of Su rather than his own name of Nan-Yung as was

207

custom, to further humiliate the Su and to further make his point to the opium traders and users.

As far as Nan-Yung was concerned, his life in China was a living death. It was the largest kingdom in the world, but he felt constrained, claustrophobic. Nan-Yung sought escape in a mental sense at first, but that was not enough. He knew he would have to leave China altogether. He knew what he wanted. It was the *how* of the matter that stopped him.

* * * *

Yin Ch'u sat immobile before the astrologer, the matchmaker and the fortune-teller who spun the *I Ching* yarrow sticks in his hands waiting his turn at Yin Ch'u's future.

The fortune-teller, Sing-Lu, was an impatient man, too small and fine boned, too much like a woman, Yin thought, which explained his lack of character. She'd heard many tales that he misused the *I Ching* sticks and told only the fortunes that his client wanted to hear. Yin Ch'u was smarter than the fortune-teller because she knew to believe only in herself and her instincts. She would listen to what he had to say, but that was all. She was careful not to let her opinion of him register on the tablet of her face. This was a difficult task for there was little about him at all that was appealing. He could not have weighed seventy pounds. She was taller than this man and had no pockmarks on her face like he did. Because Yin was naturally beautiful and fair, she had escaped many rituals and tortures for beauty. She wore no rice powder laced with lead which might cause rashes, acne or worse, even death. Her hair had always been her vanity, and she needed no extra hairpieces to form the twisted, sleek hair designs desired by the Manchu. Best of all, her hands and feet were so tiny, so utterly perfect that her feet had never been bound. This piqued the envy of nearly all her female companions. She only knew of two other girls with fortune as good, as bountiful as hers. She thanked the gods every day for giving her so many gifts because she feared reprisals, curses and hexes.

Yin Ch'u was a superstitious woman and her experience in life had taught her that it was a good thing to be. When her friends and sisters did not pay attention to the fortune-tellers and oracles and did not listen to the voices in the wind that spoke to man at all times, if only man would choose to listen, they were the ones who suffered, not Yin. In these matters, Yin knew she was a wise woman.

She looked at the fortune-teller. "Since you're are so impatient, Sing-Lu, you may cast your yarrow sticks first. I will hear the others later."

Sing-Lu merely nodded. He took out his little leather-covered book with the two Chinese characters painted on the cover and whose pages were worn from years of consultations and placed it on the ground. Then, from out of his black silk drawstring bag he retrieved a brush, paper, a black stick and a stone tablet with a depression in the center where he would shave the charcoal into the indentation, mix the powder with his saliva and make his ink. Then, as always, he would write down his findings about Yin Ch'u's future.

He scooped up the smooth yarrow sticks and held them in his hands as he closed his eyes and concentrated on his purpose. Suddenly, his eyes popped open and he took out one stick and placed it in front of Yin. Then he placed the entire bundle in the middle ground between the two of them.

Yin divided the group in two. Sing-Lu took one stick out of the pile closest to his right hand, then held it between his fingers in his left hand. The other pile he put into his left hand and began removing groups of four sticks each until there was only one group left. This group he held between the middle and forefinger of his left hand. Then he picked up the other pile from the floor and began removing groups of four sticks until there was only one group left. He laid the last group on the floor along with the other sticks he was holding. He went through the motions quickly, his hands looking like hummingbirds.

Sing-Lu picked up his charcoal and drew a line on the paper. He began his ritual of counting and recounting the little piles of sticks and making lines on the paper until they numbered six lines.

He checked the markings of broken horizontal and vertical lines. He clucked his tongue over them, opened his book and consulted the oracle within, matching up the markings at the top of his drawing to the matching characters inside the book.

"It's as I suspected. You will not be chosen by the emperor. I am sorry to bring such bad news."

Yin Ch'u allowed none of her joy to escape. Rigid as marble, her face and even her normally very expressive eyes revealed nothing. "I shall consult the stars next."

She turned slightly on the opulent, down-filled satin pillow upon which she knelt. "Tell me what the planets say."

The astrologer's books and notations were many and he seemed flustered about trying to bring all his information together. But this was the man she trusted most, for his work seemed more scientific than the polished piles of the *I Ching* sticks, though they'd never been wrong either.

"It is so. As it has always been. You will travel great distances. You are the seventh daughter which gives you 'the sight,' but you will only have one son. His wife will give you seven granddaughters. The seventh will be a very courageous woman. Her destiny and yours are strongly linked. This you must remember. She will be the loving daughter you want and need to fill your heart.

"The man you marry will be a man of means."

"But not the emperor?" she asked for clarification.

"No. It's not your fate. Your Venus is in Capricorn, meaning that you will be more beautiful in the years to come than you are now. You'll be richer the older you get. More intelligent the older you get. It's not good that you were born in 1831, the year of the Sheep. You think you are bold, but you are not. You are not a leader, but a follower, one of the crowd, with little to make you an individual. Tsk," his tongue clacked against the roof of his mouth. "Never have I seen so many conflicting planets. Against a great foe, your strengths are not found in warlike methods. You must conquer by your silence and simply your presence. Your element is metal. Therefore, few will be able to break your will, though they will try. You are stronger than those all around you as long as your intentions in life are well-meaning."

"What else do you see, old wise one?" she asked, looking at the circle that was divided into twelve zodiac houses.

"Sometimes I see things that I choose not to tell."

"Tell them to me," Yin Ch'u replied firmly. "I'm only a child, but I understand a great deal."

"That's true because you've been given the gift of prophecy. You don't use it now, but should begin now to sense its presence. The one who holds your heart will not be your husband. Your love will be in the shadows."

Yin Ch'u's back straightened like a rod. "He's not of our race."

"You can see him?"

"Yes. He's there, like a vapor," she pointed beside Sing-Lu. "I can't see his face."

"You're not supposed to—yet."

"What else do you see?" she asked swallowing hard.

"Your destiny is to be the catalyst for others to make their way in life. Through you a great wrong can be righted. Hatred annulled. Anger quashed. But it is up to others to choose. It is not your decision."

"I don't understand," she said.

"You will in time." He paused. "I can tell you that you will be leaving China within the month."

"This is impossible."

"Nothing on this earth is impossible. Most people think that man cannot accomplish much with his life. They are people of small minds. The mind can create anything it wants. It can heal. It can create wonders of art. It can communicate with the divine. You of all people should know this."

"And how will I know my one true love when I see him?"

"You will know," Sing-Lu replied. "As long as you believe."

"I believe."

"Good," he said. "That's all you need to know." He sat back. "Now you must take your horoscope to the Forbidden City for the emperor's astrologer to study."

* * * *

It was in the mat-shed that Nan-Yung first heard about the gold in San Francisco, which was located across the China Sea, across the Pacific Ocean in the land of America.

"How much gold is there?" he asked the withered old vendor.

"The barbarian seamen in Shanghai report enough to build more palaces than the Forbidden City and to roof them all in gold."

"That's hard to believe," Nan-Yung said.

"It's the truth," the man said, snatching the tael out of Nan-Yung's hand. "But why would it matter to you? It would take a great deal of money to go to America, unless you work as a slave to the barbarian."

"Never!" Nan-Yung threw his head back indignantly.

The vendor turned back to his grill, lifted a two-tined long tin fork and turned the strips of meat, testing their doneness.

Nan-Yung's curiosity grew like a great fire-breathing dragon. He had to know more. "There are ships going to San Francisco?"

"Daily. Out of Shanghai. Many Chinese leave here and go there to dig for gold. I heard the son of my brother is working on the ship going to America to pay his passage."

"I would never do that. I won't owe my life to another."

"Ha! You already owe to the Son of Heaven. Ha! You son of Luang Su!"

Nan-Yung bristled, for hearing his father's name was like hearing a curse. In all of China, he had become a joke. The opium war was over, but the addiction had not died. It simply went underground. Literally. There were more opium dens beneath the earth than ever before, and many Manchu mandarins were getting richer by the day. However, Nan-Yung had learned it was best to keep his silence. His day of retaliation against those who laugh at him now would come.

He started to walk away when, suddenly, heralds banged their tiny brass gongs and beat little drums announcing the passage of a mandarin. As Nan-Yung looked up, he saw scores of eunuchs and not one but a stream of sedan chairs and palanquins being carried out of Pewter Lane.

"What is happening?" he asked the vendor.

"The new emperor has called the maidens so that he may choose for his harem. The word is that there are sixty girls."

As Nan-Yung watched the finely robed and bejeweled young girls pass by him, he recognized Tz'u-hsi and her sister who lived down Pewter Lane from him, though their house was the finest on his street. The procession passed slowly and stopped many times. One particularly lovely girl with the greatest beauty of all the girls stopped and looked at him.

Yin Ch'u cocked her head to one side, then the other, as if inspecting him. What she saw must have pleased her for her face broke into a wide smile.

"The shining girl!" he breathed. "She's as audacious as ever."

"You know her?" The vendor asked.

"No. But I will."

The vendor shook his head, though his eyes remained on the intoxicatingly beautiful girl. "She will surely be chosen. Never have I seen one so delicate."

Nan-Yung kept his eyes on her. He, too, was spellbound. "I'm sure her father will be honored by her marriage to the emperor."

The vendor took in the richness of her palanquin. "I think her father is a very rich man indeed. Her dowry would be considerable to any man. Of course, the emperor does not worry over such things."

"Dowry?" Nan-Yung's mind was racing. He needed money for passage to America. He could already see himself digging for gold and coming across acres of it. He envisioned himself living the life of an emperor in San Francisco, wherever that was. He realized he needed this girl. But it was too late. Or was it?

Suddenly, he scooped up a hunk of delicate roasted duck and put it on a wooden skewer. Then he turned to the flower stall next to him and yanked a handful of apple blossoms out of a glass jar filled with water.

"What are you doing?" demanded the flower merchant, but Nan-Yung had not a second to spare. Soon the entourage would start up again, and he would never see the shining girl again.

He dashed over to Yin Ch'u and boldly presented her with his gifts. "I hope he refuses you."

He paid no attention to the eunuch standing three feet from him whose duty it was to keep onlookers away from his charge.

Yin Ch'u looked down at him, the scent of apple blossoms filling her nostrils, and smiled. "I'll be the first he dismisses."

"Oh, ho! What happiness this gives me to hear this. How do you know this?"

"It's in my horoscope. I'm destined to travel across the seas."

Nan-Yung's breath caught in his throat. *This is too good to be true.*

The eunuch snarled. Then he growled, "Get away from there, boy!"

Nan-Yung ignored him. "You're going to live across the sea?"

"Yes."

"This is incredible. That's my fate as well. You are my destiny."

"Yes," she smiled indulgently as if he were a mongrel puppy or some lesser being. "I know many things, Nan-Yung."

"You know my name?"

"Of course. I always have. I see things. Even names."

"If you know so much, then how is it that you haven't come to me before this?"

"I haven't come to you now. You've come to me," she giggled. "Silly one, the time wasn't right."

Nan-Yung didn't like the tone she used with him, and yet he was still mesmerized by her. Suddenly, the procession began. The slack-skin-faced eunuch was annoyed with Nan-Yung's outrageous behavior. He pushed Nan-Yung away from the sedan.

"Go away!" The eunuch demanded and then turned to the bearers and issued orders. The palanquin moved forward and though Nan-Yung walked alongside of her, Yin Ch'u closed the curtains and refused to talk with him any further.

They came upon the gates to the Forbidden City and Yin Ch'u disappeared with the others of the procession. She was the strangest girl he'd ever seen, and yet he was drawn to her. When the last palanquin had disappeared, he had a sinking feeling that he would never see her again. How strange all this had been. She knew who he was, and he knew nothing of her. Not even her name. But something told him to keep believing in her, in her return, because she was the answer to his dreams. She was his passage out of China.

The sixty Manchu girls were escorted over the Golden Water River and through the Gate of Correct Conduct. Yin Ch'u knew she should be paying attention to every lotus blossom, every embroidered hanging, but she didn't. She was thinking of Nan-Yung. She knew she wouldn't remain a virgin inside the Forbidden City, untouched by the emperor simply because her planets were not aligned correctly. She felt sorry for the other girls who would undoubtedly be subjected to a life without any man or children.

Inside the Nei Wu Fu, the offices of the Imperial Household Department, the chief astrologer awaited the entourage. Yin Ch'u waited patiently as each girl was brought forward. One by one, they were accepted or dismissed immediately. In all, twenty-eight girls were elected, Yin heard later, but her dismissal came as quickly as she knew it would.

Borne out of the palace with a smile on her face, Yin knew that she must not allow even one passing of the moon to keep her from seeing Nan-Yung.

Yin Ch'u sent Nan-Yung a note by messenger, an ally she'd had within the walls of her father's house. She arranged a meeting with him for the following day at the stalls in the Inner City. At that time of day, she knew no one would interrupt them, no one would call her back to her house. There were a few ways that a young Chinese Manchu girl could get around her father's guards and eunuchs, and shopping for hair ornaments, silks and jewels was one of them.

* * * *

The next day when Nan-Yung saw Yin approaching on the palanquin he knew his life was finally set in order.

With the help of her youngest eunuch, she alighted the palanquin. Nan-Yung stood back, again surprised at the light that seemed to emanate from this girl. Rather than look at him, she went straight to the stall and waited while her eunuch circled behind the palanquin to sneak his opium pipe from his black trousers.

Nan-Yung went up to her. "I don't know what to say."

"You should say nothing at all, for it is I who will do the talking. You are to marry me, Nan-Yung, it is written in my stars. We must leave China once I escape from my father's house."

He grinned.

Yin didn't see the malevolent light at the bottom of his eyes.

"We'll go to San Francisco," he announced.

"I've never heard of that place."

"I intend to be a rich man, and then I will make good the name of Su. No longer will the Chinese look upon my house, or my children, with disdain. Once I'm rich, I'll repay the barbarian for the evil that he's done to my family."

"What barbarian?"

"The man who was responsible for my father's execution. The man with the name Duke."

Yin Ch'u nearly fell back from the heat of his intense hatred. It encircled him like an evil web. She wondered casually what potion or hex she could put upon him to dissipate the force of his emotion. "You carry your revenge with you always?"

He eyed her quickly and looked away. "I'm only ambitious. Not vengeful."

"Do not lie to me."

Deep-felt pain blazed below the haze of hatred in his eyes. "Sometimes revenge is a necessary part of life."

"Be wise, Nan-Yung. Let it go." She turned her face from him.

"You're afraid of me," he surmised.

"I'm not. You are my destiny. But I can see that you must shift the poles that form the axis of your spirit. I tell you this for your own good."

"I will think about this."

She smiled. "That's good."

Nan-Yung took her hand and when he did, Yin felt an electricity between them. It was the first time she ever wanted a man. She knew they had the capability of founding a strong family.

"I don't have passage to America," he said. "It will take a great deal of money."

"I'll steal it for you. I have many jewels."

Nan-Yung's hopes soared. "When will you do this?"

"Next week we leave," she said seeing the future as clearly as if she were already living it. "I'll meet you here in the marketplace, as I have today, at noon when there are many about. We'll disappear into the crowd. You must arrange for a boat to take us down the Grand Canal."

"I will," he said too eagerly.

She felt a rush of excitement, both from the possibilities about her future and from still holding Nan-Yung's strong hand.

She turned from him. She never looked back, never said farewell. They would have no difficulty slipping out of the city on one of the many red-sailed junks that skimmed the waters of the Grand Canal to Shanghai. Booking passage would be an easy matter with her gems. She knew instantly when Nan-Yung spoke of San Francisco that this was the place across the ocean she'd been told about by the fortune-teller. She believed everything was in order. She was moving toward the future, her destiny. She went back to her palanquin for her journey home.

Not once in all her calculations, all her bevy of questions for the sooth-sayers, did Yin ever inquire if her destiny was one of happiness.

She would have been shocked at the answer.

—twenty-one—

*Tell, priests, what is gold
doing in a holy place?*

—PERSIUS (AULUS PERSIUS FLACCUS)
SATIRES, II, L. 69

San Francisco—June 22, 1851

Jefferson watched the flames devour row after row of houses. This was the fifth such fire since he'd come to San Francisco sixteen years ago. He'd foolishly hoped that by now, San Franciscans would have learned their lesson, but they never did. They were too busy keeping their eye on today, on the quick gold, the fast buck and the next con to be pulled, rather than on public safety or quality construction.

There were always some who accused him of making it rich off these fires, which in fact he did, but he didn't relish the idea one bit. When a city was new, there were millions to make without risking human life. But San Francisco bumped along, as it had from the beginning, with haphazard city planning, corrupt politics and the best promoters a city could buy: gold and greed.

Orange and crimson tongues of flame licked the walls of the bank building as invisible arms of heat engulfed it, squeezed it and finally crushed it. Like a wanton lover, the building succumbed to the flames; they became one and then perished save for the tiny offspring of a spark that ignited the building next door.

Jefferson didn't like the ever-hardening shell that continued to build itself

217

around his emotions and sentiments. Though he was loathe to call it cynicism, that was precisely its name. He was thirty-six years old, successful in business and respected in the community. But in Jefferson's mind, maturity and disillusionment had ground away at his psyche bit by bit until even he found it difficult to find his essence and the dregs of his dreams.

He'd barely noticed the passage of the gold rush years with their bawdy glamour and raunchy diversions. Except for the rise and fall of inventories, Jefferson marked the years by the ever-increasing loneliness he felt even when he was in the same room with Caroline. Miraculously, he had found just enough stolen nights in the hills, the gardens behind the Presidio or in his bed with Caroline to keep him from going insane. Upon her return from Boston with their son years before, he'd found a way to see her, and their love was still strong. But still in the shadows.

Too many carriages were rumbling down Powell Street, heading down to the water toward the fire, for Jefferson to hear Caroline approaching from behind.

She couldn't help the sharp intake of breath every time she saw him. "Jefferson . . . my love," she dared to say.

He felt her presence, as he always did when she was near. He'd taught himself not to spin around and greet her with open arms. He waited until she came near and stood beside him. Perpetually cognizant of the whispers of scandal that clustered about them both, he made no gesture that would alert passersby to his true feelings.

"Good day, Mrs. Mansfield," he said politely.

"I knew you'd be here," she said, her eyes grazing his face, leaving indelible paths of possession in their wake. She dragged her eyes off him and looked at the fire. "I've heard the losses far exceed the fire of May 3 and 4. At least the fires haven't been seen clear to Monterey this time."

"Hopefully there won't be any suicides this time."

Tears sprang to Caroline's eyes as she remembered the stories of good friends of hers who, upon hearing of the deaths of their wives and children, had shot themselves with pistols purchased from her emporium. Without thinking, she reached for his arm for comfort and rested it there protectively. "Tell me you'll never do such a thing."

"If anything should happen to you or Lawrence, I don't know what I would do." He touched her small, lace-gloved hand. "I love you."

Her arms ached to hold him, not just in private, but publicly. "I hate this life we lead. I want all the world to know we are one."

"Say the word. Tell me you will leave him."

She turned her eyes back to the fire. "I can't do that. You know that."

"I know. You gave your promise to your father. You let a dead man rule our lives."

She scowled. "Don't judge me. You've told me about the times your mother visits you in your dreams. The dead are living. You said so yourself. You're just feeling possessive."

"You're right. I want you . . . now."

"Then you'll be glad to know that William left last night on the steamer *Tennessee*."

Jefferson wanted to pick her up in his arms and whirl her around, he was so happy. Instead, he secured his mask of calm and pretended to watch the fire. "How long will he be gone?"

"Three months."

Jefferson knew that William had never been gone so long, but he couldn't resist teasing her. "What awful timing he has!" He feigned a scowl.

Caroline's eyes popped open. "What do you mean?"

"I have so much work to do. There's the new warehouse and new supplies to be unloaded." He watched her squirm out of the corner of his eye. He cupped his chin with his fingers. "I was going to work out a new inventory system, but I suppose I can squeeze in some time for you."

Jefferson couldn't suppress his laughter any longer.

Caroline playfully punched his muscular upper arm. "Oh, you!"

Boldly, he gathered her into his arms and quickly kissed the top of her head before releasing her. "Sorry . . . I couldn't resist."

"I suppose I deserve it for all the times I've had to put you off for one reason or another," she said glumly.

"What's important is that we'll have more time together now." Jefferson put his palm to his forehead. "I just had a thought. What about Lawrence? You'll need to be with him at all times when you're not at the emporium."

"I thought of that. I've hired Lydia McGillivray as a nanny. She arrived two weeks ago on the *Antelope* from New York. She has no family and says she was governess and tutor for the Throckmortons."

"Those are illustrious credentials. Do you believe her?"

Caroline laughed. "Frankly, no. But she's got spirit and hasn't already resigned herself to a life on the Barbary Coast, as many of the young girls do when they come here. I give her credit for that. Honestly, through the gold rush years, I was afraid that I'd never again meet a young woman with self-regard. It seems lately that with every incoming steamer there are more wives joining their husbands and more families looking to make a real home here."

"It's a good sign."

Her eyes beamed with love for the land and for Jefferson.

He believed that whenever he looked into her eyes, he saw his own future. He tried to stop the words that catapulted from his heart to his lips, but couldn't. "I dream of the day when we can be a real family. You and Lawrence and I."

He lifted his finger to touch her cheek, but the sudden sound of clattering horses' hooves against the cobblestone street forced his arm back to his side. He turned and smiled at the oncoming carriage.

Caroline lifted an arm and waved to Mrs. Ned Beale who rode proudly in her large barouche, the first private carriage in the city. "I've thought about importing turnouts. I'd like to see chaises and buggies here just as elegant as those in New York and Paris."

Jefferson wasn't fooled a bit as she danced on the neutral territory of sales, inventories, advertising and stocks. He saw the red stain of eagerness and wanting on her cheeks. He noticed the way she chewed on her bottom lip hoping to bite back tears. He'd used the same tools to keep his emotions from toppling the foundation of his life. Jefferson didn't fear exposure for himself as much as he did for Caroline and Lawrence, for ultimately he knew they would suffer more than he ever would. But his greatest fear was that in the blinding pain of naked truth, he would lose Caroline. Jefferson could not live without her.

"When can I see you and where?"

"Tonight. I'll come to you at half after twelve. We'll have hours, Jefferson. Hours."

She smiled at him, but it was only the half-smile one gives a neighbor, allowing no one but Jefferson to see her passion.

Like the fire that raged inside them both, Caroline wanted to consume him and to be consumed. She believed there was no thirst for love greater than hers, except that of Jefferson for her.

He didn't dare touch her as she walked away. But as she left him, he literally felt the air attenuate and become thin as if she had become a shadow slipping into the ethers of space.

* * * *

"Mama! Mama!" Lawrence screamed into the darkness of his room. "Maaaaamaaa!"

Caroline wore a blue silk summer dressing gown as she waited for the hours to pass until she could be with Jefferson. Under the pretense of retiring to bed, she'd immersed herself in her acting role so that Lydia wouldn't suspect anything. Lawrence's screams lanced through the closed mahogany door to her bedroom and jerked Caroline to her feet.

Caroline's door flew open at precisely the same moment as Lydia's door. The young girl raced down the hall tying her cotton wrapper about herself as she nearly flew past Caroline.

"Do' na worry yerself, ma'am. Ye lave meh, now?" Lydia's coppery red hair fell in a long veil down her back, and it swayed to the right and then to the left in a solid curtain as she moved. She rushed into Lawrence's room and immediately lit the oil lamp next to his bed. Before Caroline even reached the door, she heard faint, soothing murmurings in the half-clipped, half sing-song voice that was distinctively Lydia's.

"Shhh. There, there, me darlin'. Ye canna be cryin' now, can ye?"

Lawrence tried to catch his breath, but his sobs were too powerful to be contained within his thin, narrow chest. "It was terrible."

"What was?" Caroline asked, slipping into the room. She sat on the other side of the bed. She put her hand on her son's head and smoothed his blond hair. Everyone said how much he looked like Caroline, but she knew that even the texture and weight of his hair was purely Jefferson. She rubbed his back and waited for his nerves to calm. Lawrence did not wrest himself from Lydia, not wanting to take her authority from her, but slowly reached his hand out and touched his mother's knee. Though just a boy, Lawrence had a knack for understanding human nature.

He had liked Lydia from the first day she arrived. She was his first real playmate, even though she'd told him she was nearly twenty. Most of the other children didn't like Lawrence because he was studious, smart and preferred adult conversation to playing with toys.

Lydia had wonderful stories to tell about Scotland where she was born and about Ireland where she'd lived most of her life. She told him about the terrible potato famine that killed her brothers and sisters. Lydia not only liked Lawrence as much as his mother did, she had time for him, which his mother often did not. Caroline felt guilty about being forced to divide her time between her son and the business. But without Caroline's head for business, William would have gone bankrupt a long time ago. It was Caroline who kept them from starvation and kept a roof over their heads, while William fed his own ego, pretending he was the driving force behind the emporium.

"Tell me, Lawrence, what did you dream? Why was it so terrible?" Caroline asked again.

"I'm afraid. I've never had a dream like this before."

Lydia's clear blue-gray eyes sparkled in the lamplight. "Ye need no be afraid." Then she turned to Caroline and whispered conspiratorially. "'Tis about the shipwreck, he's dreamin'."

Caroline's jaw dropped at the exact same moment that Lawrence's head shot up.

"How did you know?" Lawrence asked.

"Yes," Caroline's eyebrow raised. "How did you know?"

A pixie-like smile danced across Lydia's lips as she looked from mother to son. "Why, I heard him sayin' so, just as I came into the room," she replied innocently.

"Oh. I see," Caroline put her arms around Lawrence. "I understand now. You were worried about your father. Is that it?"

"Yes," Lawrence sighed as he rested his head against her warm bosom. "It truly was awful. I saw the ship being pitched about. The sea was blacker than night. I saw Father clinging to the edge of the ship. Do you think he's all right?"

"Yes, Darling. I'm sure of it. Perhaps it was the fire today that upset you. I'm sure it seems that all the world is about to end when things like this happen. And this is William's first trip away from us. But your father is alive and fine. You're here with me and Lydia. We're all safe."

She kissed Lawrence's cheek and gave him another hug as she tucked him back into bed. She glanced at the clock on the wooden mantle and saw that it was past eleven. She wouldn't be able to meet with Jefferson tonight.

Lydia blew out the oil lamp and went to the door with Caroline.

"Pardon, ma'am," Lydia whispered just as they reached the hallway. "I was wonderin'. . . . Perhaps I should stay with the wee one tonight. That way ye could go 'bout yer business."

"Business?"

"Gettin' some proper rest, ma'am. I wouldna' mind."

Lydia's smile was so pure and well-intentioned and though Caroline searched her face scrupulously, she could find no malice in Lydia. "Perhaps that would be best."

Lydia nodded and quickly went to her room, pulled the counterpane and sheets from the bed and went straight back to Lawrence's room where she erected a makeshift pallet on the floor next to his bed.

Half an hour later, both Lydia and Lawrence were fast asleep and had no knowledge of Caroline's midnight departure from the house.

The summer night was hot with no breezes to sweep away the smoke from the dying flames. Already the excitement from the fire had abated and the city had fallen into an exhausted sleep. Few people were about that night. Even the crickets slumbered and no one, not man or beast, knew that Caroline and Jefferson were weaving dreams.

She sat on the edge of the bed gazing out at the last flickering flames down near the bay. Huge black funnels of smoke coiled into the indigo night sky like striking snakes and blotted out the stars. Jefferson cupped a creamy breast in his hand and then slowly watched in the bright lamplight as each of his fingers curled around the erect nipple. He planted a delicate velvety kiss on her temple. Slowly, her eyes closed, her hand dropped the heavy drapery and she succumbed to him. A trickle of perspiration slipped down the column of Caroline's neck as she leaned back against the dark mahogany headboard. A pleasurable moan rumbled over itself deep in her throat, but did not escape her lips. Gently, she placed her hand over his and pressed the tips of his fingers into the full flesh of her breast. Every inch of her craved him.

"My God, Jefferson, I thought I would never feel you again." She did not rush the moment, wanting to experience every millisecond of pleasure they gave to one another.

She remembered thinking in the first days of their affair if the illicit veiling she wore was the catalyst that fueled their raging passions. Now, after a decade of being forced to slip among night shadows, stepping over truth and romancing this lie, she marveled that their love had not died in its own flames. She loved him more now than ever before. With each passing day, she believed it impossible for her love to grow any more. She found she was always wrong. Caroline's emotions lived in the deepest, most profound wells of her heart. Here, they were hidden to the world, but for her, they were the source of her courage, the only sparks that gave meaning to her life.

Caroline believed she knew everything about Jefferson. His favorite food was steak. He liked huge hunks of pepper in his gravy and demanded his vegetables be crisp. He went to Mass every Sunday at Mission Dolores, but he told Caroline he never actually converted to Catholicism. A crucifix hung in every room of his house. His politics were liberal, but he demanded law and order, which was a holdover from the gold rush days when greed overcame common sense. He loved horses, the High Sierras, warm fires, brandy, hot daily baths, women who spoke their minds and gray suits, never brown. He liked jewels on women but not on men. He was slow to anger, but she'd seen him lift a corrupt politician off the wooden sidewalk on Stockton Street by his neck and nearly choke the man to death. He hated snow, injustice, cruelty and gossip in that order. He liked soft lights on when they made love, unless they indulged themselves for a second time, then he wanted them off. He loved her above his country, but not above his God.

Just when she thought there were few surprises left to Jefferson, he revealed a side she hadn't seen. But always, none of it was out of character, and simply reaffirmed the things she knew and loved about him.

"It's very odd, Jefferson, but I feel that we are more than married. We're of one mind. One spirit."

"I believe that's so," he said.

"Sometimes, I honestly believe I can feel you thinking about me. Sometimes I tell myself I'm being illogical, but in my heart I know I'm right."

He nodded. "We can test your theory."

"How?"

"Tonight at eleven o'clock, you thought about me. You were sad. Why?"

She opened her mouth in shock. "I did! Lawrence had a nightmare. I was afraid I couldn't see you."

He touched her cheek. "My mother told me that lovers who decide to be together in this life are always connected in their minds. That's how we're brought together in the first place. I willed you into my life."

"Sometimes you say the strangest things, Jefferson."

"Do you think I'm strange?" he asked, looking over to the locked door that led to his private study.

"Of course not."

"Maybe if you knew me better you wouldn't say that."

"Jefferson, there's never been a woman on earth who knows a man as well as I know you."

"You don't know everything," he said, glancing at the door again.

Caroline sat erect. "You're doing it again."

"Doing what?" he asked, looking at her.

"Acting mysterious."

"What's wrong with a little mystery?" He forced a chuckle.

"Nothing except that when you get like this you always look off to the study. Why is it that in all these years, I've seen every room in your house except that one? What's in there that you don't want me to see?"

"Why, nothing. My life and my house are open to you," he said.

"No, you're keeping something from me. I can sense it."

Jefferson swallowed hard. In all these years, he'd never had the courage to tell Caroline the truth about himself. About his former life as a slave. Years ago, he'd painted his mother's portrait and hung it in the study. From his encounters with Yuala's ghost, he'd painted what he believed was her likeness and hung it in the study as well.

A million times, he'd wanted to fling open that door and tell Caroline everything. A million times he'd failed, and the reason was simple.

He couldn't bear losing Caroline.

He feared the shock would split them up. He feared his secrecy, especially once Lawrence was born, would anger her. He feared she didn't love him enough to accept the truth.

His vulnerabilities ate away at him, and he didn't have the slightest notion how to stop them.

"Okay, so don't tell me about the even more mysterious study," she teased, kissing his bottom lip.

He kissed her back. "Tell me you love me."

"I love you. I always have and always will," she said, her eyes falling away from him pensively. "Can I ask you something else, then?"

"Sure."

"Sometimes when I am alone reading, I can feel you call my name. It's not a ringing in my ears, but the distinct sound of your voice. Then I can feel you beside me, as if you have escaped your body somehow and come to me. How is that possible?"

Jefferson chuckled. "My mother called it 'soul travel.' The ancient yogis in India do it. It's complicated to explain. But at those times, I am more with you than I am with myself. Just know that I am there."

"I'm a journalist by education, Jefferson. I'm sorry I need facts to substantiate events. Mystical thoughts are difficult for me to grasp, but things are happening to me that I don't understand."

"Just know that you're never alone. I'm always with you. Always."

He placed his lips against hers, savoring the moment. He tried not to think of the future, of any moment beyond this, but Jefferson had always been too demanding both of himself and of fate.

"Marry me, Caroline. . . ."

"Don't, Jefferson. We've already discussed this."

"I know," he said, as an ache spread in his heart. He was a fool to keep this dream, despite his mother's predictions that he and Caroline would never marry.

I'm like an addict drawn to his opium. But I can't live without some kind of hope that I can tempt fate.

Dejectedly, he sat back on the bed and leaned heavily against the head-board. He stretched out his arm and Caroline curled up next to him. She placed her hand protectively over his heart, as if to blunt the blow she inflicted.

"I can't give you what you want, Jefferson. And yet, I know how utterly selfish I'm being. I have a family. You don't. I've taken that chance away from you. Perhaps," she gulped back the white hot lump in her throat and prayed for courage to continue, "perhaps it would be best if you didn't see me anymore. Then you'd be free to love another."

The words were barely out of her mouth when she was overcome with dread. She'd never felt such a rush of icy cold as if death had come to visit. Her heart literally stopped for a painfully long moment. Suddenly, she had no thoughts, no emotions, no awareness of herself. It was as if she didn't exist. Fear shrouded her eyes. She kept her eyes leveled on his chest, not wanting to look in his eyes and see his answer.

What was she saying? She knew she could never go through with it. *But what if he accepted her sacrifice? Could she leave San Francisco?*

She knew he thought she was a strong woman, but she wasn't. She knew she couldn't live in the same town as he did. It would kill her to watch Jefferson create a life without her. Yet, she'd done just that to him.

"I'm the one who is being selfish," he said finally. "I'm sorry, my love. I was wrong to ask you to abandon your principles. Truly, I'm happy just to see you." He lifted her face to him. "You're loving and valiant, and I don't want to change anything about you. It's just that, when I haven't been with you for so long, I get these ideas. . . ."

"Building castles in the air?"

"Something like that. I suppose I ought to stick to building them on earth." He pulled her closer. "You remind me a great deal of my mother."

She laughed. "I'm certain your mother was much more of a lady than I. No one ever called her 'outspoken' or 'independent,' especially in print." Caroline couldn't help thinking about the article in the *Alta California* about her political views.

A vision of Rachel, her copper corkscrew curls fluttering in the wind, came to him. Suddenly, frosty memories of the labels Rachel had worn, like "slave," "mulatto bitch" and "black whore," rang with the tone of Maureen's voice.

Again he was all too aware of his bastardy and that he was not the legal white descendent of the royal Duke line. He desperately wanted to tell Caroline the truth.

"There's something about me you don't know," he began.

"Jefferson, you look so serious. It isn't bad, is it?"

He noticed that she stiffened in his arms. "Bad?"

Fear crept between them. Caroline felt it. She didn't like it one bit. "Are you in trouble? Is it something with the business? The law?"

"The law." Jefferson's mind fought the mire of the past. He was stuck in a tenuous position, most of it of his own making. His throat constricted as if he were being strangled. "No, it's not the law," he lied. *I'm a runaway slave. According to some laws, I'm a fugitive. According to God's law, there's no such thing as a slave.*

"Then what is it?" Caroline swallowed hard.

"My mother," he replied, looking over at the study door.

"Tell me about her."

Jefferson relaxed a bit, pulled the snowy linen sheet over their bodies and stroked Caroline's shoulder. "She wrote things down," he replied, remembering the cache of papers Rachel had diligently inscribed.

"She was a writer, then. How marvelous! You never told me this. Was she published like I was?"

"No. She never finished her story." His voice trailed off, thinking that perhaps if it weren't for him, maybe Rachel would have lived longer. Maybe she would have written a book or poems. A sudden flash of anger darkened his eyes. "She died too young."

Compassion tunneled across Caroline's face. "You miss her a great deal."

"Tremendously. She wanted so much for me, Caroline. Actually, for you and I."

"What?"

"I never told you this, but Mother could see things. Future things. She had visions. She told me that my destiny was special and that I was to come here and build a city. She told me you and I would have a son."

Caroline gasped. "My God, did she really see me?" she asked, wide-eyed with awe and curiosity.

He shook his head. "Not really. But she told me what you would be like. And you are."

Fascinated, Caroline curved around and sat up to face him. Her eyes brimming with wonder, she looked like a child at Christmas. "Did you believe these visions?"

"Not when I was young," he said with a bemused chuckle. "I told myself that I was well-educated and more scientifically aware than Mother, who'd not had the kind of tutors I'd had, though she was quite educated."

"Right," she nodded. "That's because you were a male and she was a female."

No, he thought. *It was because Yuala spent her time teaching Mother about herbs, spells and healing roots. Henry Duke taught Mother to read and cipher, but there had not been tutors.*

"I believe Mother's visions now."

"Why now?"

"Because they've come true."

"Ah . . . the science of observation. I agree that it's most important to possess the facts. I would liked to have known her," Caroline replied, falling against him. "But there's something else you haven't told me. I can sense it."

Jefferson's fear returned. *All I have to do is unlock that door and show her the portraits. She'll understand in a heartbeat. And then what?*

"Tell me, Jefferson. Anything that causes you this much struggle must be important. Please let me help you carry your burden."

He nodded. He was going to do it. He had to. "My mother," he began again, "she was, well, she and my father . . ."

Caroline squeezed his hand to give him courage.

Jefferson raised her fingers to his lips. *How sweet you are. I couldn't go on if you left me, Caroline.* He lost half his heart. Half his courage.

"My parents were never legally married," he said, probing her eyes wondering if half the truth was sufficient.

Caroline blinked. "That's it? That's what you were afraid to tell me?"

"Yes."

"How silly of you, Jefferson. I don't care what your parents did or didn't do. It only matters to me that you love me."

He hugged her tightly. "You must understand. I'm a bastard. Our son is a bastard. That's why I want to marry you, Caroline. I want to legally adopt Lawrence and give him his rightful name."

"Rightful name."

"Yes."

She moved away from him. "Jefferson, I couldn't do that to Lawrence. He's a happy boy right now. His world is centered. He has no concept of what being a bastard is. But you do. It's haunted you and even caused you guilt, caused you to keep this part of yourself from me all these years. What would that do to him? What would we gain if we did that to him?" She shook her head. "I can't be that selfish, Jefferson. Yes, we'd be happier. Incredibly happier, but would the greatest good be served? We have to ask ourselves that."

Jefferson dropped his eyes. "You make me feel ashamed of my own desires."

"I didn't mean it like that. I just meant—"

He put his fingers to her lips to stop her. "I know what you meant and you're right. So very right. I won't bring it up again."

"Thank you for confiding in me, Jefferson. It took a great deal of courage to tell me that," she said, closing her eyes and kissing him.

Jefferson felt his insides turn to ice.

I'm more coward than you know, Caroline. And I'm not your hero.

Moved to the depths of his being, Jefferson derided himself for foolishly wanting the outward trappings of a marriage license. After all, his mother had not taken Richard's last name. She was born a Duke and by his bastardy, Jefferson was given Henry Duke's surname. He would always be enslaved to the Duke name, as would Lawrence should he adopt him. What if there were no rewards to reap by inheriting the Duke name?

Jefferson realized that this love he held in his arms was pure and real, a rare precious treasure he knew few mortals ever found. This night was a new beginning for Caroline and an awakening for him.

No longer would he dream of what could not be. It was time for him to build a new future. This time, his foundation would not be false. He would keep his treasure polished, but hidden, and he would make no decisions that would jeopardize its safety.

As a friend of the family, he saw Lawrence as much as any father, certainly more than William who cared more about his ledgers and inventory books than he did people.

One day, when Lawrence was grown, there was a chance that he could discover the truth. To prepare for that day, Jefferson had a great deal of work to do.

He had an empire to build, a city to support and a mansion to build. Jefferson's thoughts spun wildly as they framed out the future. The house that Lawrence and his children would someday inherit from him would be nothing short of palatial. It was imperative it sit high on a hill with San Francisco at its feet and only heaven above its head. He would fill it with fine antiques, tapestries, rugs and crystal. If it took the rest of his life, he would make certain that no Duke before him had ever lived as grandly. He would live a life that his son and his grandchildren would admire. He would rise to such a position that should validation of his indenture as a slave ever surface, no one would dare believe it. Only Jefferson could protect Lawrence and Caroline from the lashes of that kind of pain.

He would build his castle in the air, for only there could he bring his dream of a life with Caroline out for viewing.

Jefferson leaned over and turned off the oil lamp and then pulled back the drape so that he could see the night sky. As Caroline slept, he watched the horizon for the first sign of dawn's blush. It was the familiar signal to him that Caroline must leave his bed and return home.

Once again, the idyll was over.

twenty-two

All men would be tyrants if they could.

—DANIEL DEFOE
THE KENTISH PETITION

February 1852

His black silk trousers patterned with dried mud and his long tunic smelling of sweat and disappointment, Nan-Yung sauntered beside his slow-moving pack mule. In less than two months of panning and digging in the mountains, river beds and creeks of California, Nan-Yung realized what little gold that remained was requisitioned solely to the white man. Men of the yellow race were discriminated against even more than the few black men he had encountered. The fact that Nan-Yung had more real cash than most American miners did not buy respect nor could it buy a property lease.

Understanding very little English and even less about mines, stakes and properties, Nan-Yung had been thrown off the Twin Mines property and the Lucky Lady mining camps. Naively, he'd believed the tales about America being the land of the free. It seemed that every step he took touched "privately owned" land.

Aimlessly, he wandered further into the hills until he found an unoccupied tract of land with a cold, gushing stream running through the middle of it. After two weeks of backbreaking panning, Nan-Yung awoke one morning to find both his tiny cloth sack of gold dust gone and his long queue tied to a stake which had been thrust into the ground next to his head.

When he twisted his body onto his side, he found his nose against the tip of a sharp knife blade.

"Lookee here, Nate," the greasy-bearded, brown-eyed man snarled at his companion.

Nan-Yung winced as the pungent odor of the man's breath and sweat assaulted his nostrils. Nan-Yung's eyes narrowed. It was a familiar smell. All barbarians smelled like this man. He didn't flinch, and mentally commissioned his body not to show any sign of fear. The particles of perspiration that formed on his forehead quickly disintegrated.

"Shall I cook us up a Chinee?" The smelly man stuck his knife in Nan-Yung's belly, slit the fabric and carved a shallow groove in his skin.

Nan-Yung centered his concentration. He felt nothing . . . except hate rising like a thick bubble deep in the pit of his abdomen.

The man called Nate sauntered up, stood beside his partner and looked down at Nan-Yung. He shook his head. "I got the gold," he said and held up Nan-Yung's tiny sack of gold dust. "Just stick him, and let's go." Nate ground his teeth against the stinky cigar he held in his mouth and nonchalantly walked off.

Nan-Yung didn't understand their words, but he knew what had transpired. He was going to die just like his father. Irreverently, at the hand of the barbarian.

Suddenly, Nan-Yung flung his arms over his head and yanked his queue off the stake. Then he sprang to his feet and contorted his face into the oddest, most gruesome, frightening expressions he could think of. He rattled off Chinese obscenities along with long-forgotten Chinese curses. He flayed his arms about and spun around as if he were possessed by demons. He made animal sounds, dying sounds and high-pitched eerie sounds like those of a banshee he had met once in a childhood dream. He acted like a psychotic.

His ploy worked. The smelly man, obviously half-drunk, plunged his knife at Nan-Yung several times, but he was unable to land a blow. Nan-Yung pirouetted and whirled out of his way. He flung his leg over his head and continued his eerie unhuman sounds and mannerisms.

Nate jumped onto his horse. "What the bejeesus did you do, Charlie? Let's get the hell outta here!"

Charlie, the smelly man, stumbled backward toward his horse, still poking the air with his knife, though Nan-Yung was clearly out of reach.

Charlie's brown eyes bulged out of his head in fear and shock as he watched Nan-Yung jump and whirl into the air, spittle raining from his mouth. Charlie quickly grabbed the reins of his horse, put his knife between his teeth and hauled his heavy body onto the horse's back.

Nate spurred his horse and took off at a gallop into the woods. Charlie was right behind him, though he continued to watch Nan-Yung as he rode away. "I ain't never seen nothin' like that! Nate! You think he got the rabies? Nate! Did you hear me? Goddamn Orientals." Charlie's voice was drowned out by the thick canvas of trees and underbrush.

Nan-Yung fell exhausted to his knees and watched his two assailants disappear. For a long moment, he heard the muffled sound of horses' hooves on pine needles and dried leaves. Then he heard nothing. It was as if they'd never existed. Almost.

Though his hands were still shaking, Nan-Yung's mind was calm as it calculated every nuance of the incident. His assailants could easily have murdered him that night. His gold was gone, and so was his dream. Nan-Yung cursed his would-be-murderer for his lack of courage. Nan-Yung wished he were dead.

He sank back on his heels and flung his shameful face into his hands. Nothing had turned out the way he had dreamed. "How can this be? The fates have arranged for my wife and I to come here, but I own less now than I did in China."

Nan-Yung's shoulders slumped heavily under his grief. He remembered the long trip to America, then slowly he remembered other things. He remembered the look in the barbarian's green eyes when Nan-Yung stood with his father before the emperor.

Resolve and understanding sifted through his mind. He began to comprehend the twist of fate. Like a shining beacon the truth came to him. White men ruled America. White men owned the land, the gold and had the power to eliminate anyone who got in their way. Nan-Yung's foe in America was even more powerful than the emperor had been in China.

Nan-Yung saw his revenge more clearly now. The fates had brought him to America, not to discover gold, but to take gold from the whites the way they had taken it from him today. Nan-Yung would use white man's ingenuity against him. Just as the Englishman, Ambrose Duke, and his British East India Company had brought opium to China, Nan-Yung would bring opium to San Francisco.

Nan-Yung bent down and prostrated himself on the ground. "I thank the earth, the wind, the air and water for keeping harmony in my life. All will be balanced in the universe again. The House of Su will again be revered."

He stood with resolve and courage coursing through his muscles. Quickly, he gathered his camp tools and packed them away. He untied his mule, allowed him to drink the icy, fresh creek water and then drank deeply himself. Nan-Yung looked to the blue sky with a winter sun rising in the east. This was the greatest day of his life, he thought as he headed back down the hills toward San Francisco.

Today was the first day of his new career as a businessman.

* * * *

Yin Ch'u had been abandoned by her husband. Snared in the web of her romantic fantasies about Nan-Yung, Yin had not faced the truth about her predicament for nearly a month. He told her he was going to prospect for gold. He told her he would come back a rich man. He took all her jewels and left her with only enough money to pay the bill at the tiny hotel on Dupont Street that was now her home. It was reality that slapped her awake that Sunday morning when she made her decisions. Yin had always been taught to desire nothing, and yet secretly she had. She believed that her desire not to be part of the emperor's harem had brought her to America. Yin's mother had taught her to swallow her bitterness, to take on the suffering of others and to give her entire life to her husband. Yin had done this since the day she ran off with Nan-Yung. Now she saw that her mother had not spoken the truth. She'd done these things, but Yin discovered that when she defied her mother's teachings, Yin was much happier. Yin harbored the rebellious thought that she could make a life for herself.

Yin rose and went to the window, contemplating the gray winter light masking the sandy hills. She gazed out at the windmill-like contraption on the summit of Signal Hill, which raised its slatted arms to a three o'clock position, announcing an incoming ship. In the hotel lobby downstairs, a diagram chart had been posted on the wall that described each signal and which type of ship it identified. Yin had memorized the entire chart in less than an hour and had despaired at the time that she'd learned the chart so easily. Boredom was a more difficult foe in America than depression over her abandonment. Yin strained her eyes to see the formation. Today the slatted arms were raised at right angles signifying a sidewheel steamer.

How different and strange everything in America is. Even the boats. I miss the private gardens of home. I miss floating lotus blossoms in my reflecting pool. I miss my hours of meditation and contemplation of the universe.

And everything is so expensive here!

The Chinese spoke of the infusion of gold coming down from the hills. Word was that the city officials expected the tally to reach fifty million American dollars. Yin watched the price of a laundered shirt for a white rise to two dollars. She'd heard of the influx of gamblers, prostitutes and con artists who had overrun the white sectors of the city.

"Foreigners" from Australia brought the most degenerate "floozies" with them. The whores from Peru, Chile, Mazatlan and San Blas erected red-lighted shanties along the wharf. Yin noticed that San Francisco seemed to attract those humans who lived on the edge of their cultures, and on the dark side of morality. In Chinatown, she found a different kind of life. Here, nearly all the men were married, and daily she learned of another child being born. It seemed to her that only in Chinatown was a stable base being built for the new city. Then, even this last of her illusions was shattered.

Yin heard tales of "Shanghai" and smuggling. Murder was for sale and prices fluctuated daily like ordinary commodities. She learned that the Chinese thirsted for power just as much as the whites. Men were no different the world over, she thought. She wondered idly if women were all the same, too.

Desperately, Yin wanted to be different from the kind of woman her mother had been. She didn't want to eat her tears when she felt sad. She wanted the freedom to open her mouth and release grief and anger. She wanted to say aloud the thoughts that bombarded her mind. Yin wanted to be a person in this new city.

For nearly a month, she had stupidly resolved herself to the path her husband had furrowed for her. Today, she realized that she need not walk his path. He did not exist for her anymore. He had shamed her by leaving her. In her community, she'd lost face. In China, she had no choices. Now, in America she had many choices. She could cry or smile. She could starve or eat. She could wait for her husband, or she could furrow her own path.

Yin believed Chinese women were not prepared to make decisions for themselves. She was unsure if she was making correct choices. The thought processes were so difficult, Yin's head pounded with the strain. However, after a time, she found a peculiar energy darting down the corridors of her veins. She felt lightheaded and realized with a giggle that no matter where she looked on this dreary winter day, she saw silver. It was the color of her future, bright, shining and surprisingly within her grasp. Yin put the world of China and her past behind her that day, and as she dressed in plain black wool trousers and wool tunic, she believed she was as powerful as any man. She would pave the streets of her own future with silver and gold.

The *hulihudu*, the dark fog in her brain, had lifted. Yin smiled to herself as she went downstairs to the reception desk. "I would like an audience with the proprietor," she said to the Chinese desk clerk.

"Chang Wu is too busy," he replied.

"An audience or I don't pay."

The meeting was arranged swiftly.

Chang Wu was an old man who had bought a parcel of land on Dupont Street during the gold rush and erected the hotel. It was painted Chinese red on the outside of the pagoda roof, with adequate but sparsely furnished rooms throughout that catered to Orientals only. A kitchen downstairs served meals twice a day, breakfast and supper, for a fee.

Chang Wu sat erect with his neck and chin tilted forward like a goose. As Yin approached him, bowing as was expected of her, she noticed he was able to look down at his papers with one eye and with the other look straight at her. It was the oddest-looking accomplishment, and she was certain he used it to frighten others, but it only amused her. Because she wasn't intimidated by him, he was intrigued, as she knew he would be. He focused both eyes on her. He gestured to the black-lacquered backless stool in front of his desk.

"Please, sit," he said.

Yin sat down, still keeping her eyes on the floor as was expected of her.

Chang Wu spoke in Chinese. "Why do you come here?"

"I'm seeking employment."

"My kitchens are full. So are the linen commissaries. Ask the laundry across the street. They always need washing girls."

"I'm not a servant," she said flatly.

Chang sniggered. "There's no other work for Chinese women here. I have nothing for you. Go to the white man."

Slowly, she raised her head, and it sat proudly on her slender shoulders. "I'll not be a servant to a barbarian."

A flicker of amusement ignited in the old man's eyes. "You're more naive than most. How long have you been here?"

"Three phases of the moon."

"Ha! You see? You cannot survive in the white man's San Francisco. You must learn to calculate time in days and weeks, and you must speak in English."

She almost smiled as she watched him move about the chessboard of her plan like a pawn. "You speak English?"

"Yes. I am a businessman."

"You could teach me English?"

Chang's neck rocked back on his shoulders, looking more fowl-like than before. "A woman cannot be taught anything!" he replied pompously.

Yin eyed the abacus resting on the desk. "I can cipher faster than any man I knew in China." Coyly, she cocked her head to the side and allowed her body to relax as she continued. "I can read the *I Ching* sticks. I cast your horoscope, read your tea leaves and see your future."

"Prove it," he demanded, pressing one finger against his thick eyebrow that looked like a black caterpillar.

"I can see black flies in your rice bowl. You're having difficulty stocking your kitchens. This will cost you many customers, both Chinese and white." Yin raised her voice an octave, her words fluttered faintly in the space between them like tiny butterflies. Her eyes were as vacant as the ghosts of the women of shame who still walked the earth that came to her giving her the gift of future sight. "You have argued with a strong warrior from Canton. His ancestors were Chiang: great governors with much power. He still has power over you and you resent it."

"Ha!" Chang boomed. "He is only a shipper!"

"But you need him. Tomorrow kowtow to him. But wear your false face. Make great display of your need for him. Then when you have won him to your confidence, make him sign the contract *you* have written on your terms."

"You're foolish like the fox who believes in himself too much, only to be eaten by the bear."

Yin's eyes reflected back only Chang's own image. He saw nothing in their depths. She continued, "I see this man as your servant. He treasures shallow displays of respect. Yet he respects nothing. You can win him with deceit."

Chang Wu sat immobile for nearly half an hour. His mind made mazes of each path his decision would take him. No matter how much he didn't want to believe anything a woman would tell him, he was wise enough to ascertain truth when he heard it. He could not allow his enemy to tear down his business. This tiny sparrow-bird woman was showing him the way out of the maze. He chose to believe her.

Chang glanced down at his hands, which he had tightened in a gnarled ball. He loosened his hold on himself and flexed his fingers. Yin watched this and knew that she'd just checkmated her opponent. She kept her true feelings hidden behind her face. "I'll make money for you."

"Explain, please."

Yin did not miss a beat. "I need a table and two chairs set up in the lobby just inside the door as patrons come in for a room or meal. Also, I need a small sign announcing my presence placed in the corner of the front window. In one week, I promise I'll bring you more money than all the meals you serve here. I'll keep half the money for myself. You get half."

Chang raised his caterpillar eyebrows. "Preposterous! I make over a hundred dollars a week in my kitchens. Impossible!"

Yin remained calm. "Either I conduct my business in your hotel or I find another patron. Do you want half my profits or should I give them to your neighbor across the street?"

"You're too certain of yourself. I should teach you a lesson. If you don't bring me one hundred dollars in one week, I'll rent your room to someone else."

"There are no other hotels in Chinatown. I'll have no place to live," she said very calmly. "I believe in my gift. I know that today I've already made you money by showing you the manner in which to vanquish your enemy. Still, you treat me as the *hwai dungsyi*—the bad little thing. I'm not."

"That's my bargain. I will test you on many scores." Chang's old eyes glared at her.

Yin rose slowly and gracefully the way she'd been taught. She knew she looked like a swan rising from her perch. She had confidence in her beauty as well as her talent. "It's a good bargain." Yin bowed reverently, the way she knew he expected. She backed out of the room, and when she reached the door she turned her back to him.

Chang raised his arthritic finger and choked faintly on a lump of curiosity. "A moment." He paused as she slowly turned her head and peered at him over her shoulder. "I am old. I have not met a woman like you."

Yin's upper lip gave way to a trace of a smile. "You never will. I can see your future, and I'll make you rich."

Within one hour, a table and two chairs were set up in the yellow-wallpapered hotel vestibule. Yin made a sign on a piece of brown paper and tied it to the leg of the table. She made another sign in the beautiful Chinese script she knew so well. She assembled the necessary tools of her trade: teapot, cups, tea leaves and a bowl of water for lack of a crystal stone in which to gaze. To their side, she placed her astrology books she'd brought from the Celestial City. In a black silk bag she'd hidden her yarrow sticks and the *I Ching* book.

For three hours, Yin sat at her table with no customers. She kept her hands folded neatly in her lap and kept her eyes down and prayed. She never lost patience, never lost faith. She noticed the cut of the clothes of the hotel patrons that day. Some of the Chinese men wore beautifully sewn silk trousers and delicate kid slippers. Conversely, the women's clothing was worn, the dyes had washed out and the hems were patched and repaired. In China, women of rich men were elaborately dressed and bejeweled. She realized that Chinese women in America fared less well than they had in China.

Yin heard the rustle of silk before she saw the tall golden-skinned woman pause at her table.

"How much?" asked the woman, in Chinese, with the nightingale's voice.

"One dollar. American."

"Too much," the beautiful young woman replied and turned to walk away.

Yin raised her head and stared glassily at the emerald green silk tunic the woman wore. Yin was already in trance.

"Your name is Ming. You're twenty years old. You're mistress to Lee Wang who buys this green silk for you to sew."

The beautiful girl turned around and moved quickly back to Yin. She reached inside her wide sleeve and pulled out a small red silk pouch. She opened the drawstrings and withdrew four quarters. She plunked them down on the table and then sat in the chair.

Yin smiled. "Do you wish the tea leaves or should I cast your horoscope? Horoscope cost more."

Ming leaned over conspiratorially. "I'll buy the horoscope later. Tell me."

Yin didn't use a single divining device.

"Tomorrow a new benefactor will come into your life. You will go with him, but you must be wary of him. He has the power to own you. There will be tears over your departure from Chinatown."

Ming looked at the sorceress sitting across from her with great disbelief in her eyes. "Lee Wang has been good to me. Why would I go with another?"

"The new benefactor is a white man."

"Ahhh!" Ming sucked in her breath, now fully understanding this augury. "Where will I go?"

Yin uncurled her hand and let her open palm rest on the table. "This is an empty hand. It needs to be filled."

Ming started to reach for her purse.

"No," Yin stopped her and waved away the money. "I need your help. Tomorrow, after this event has happened, tell everyone you know that I have foretold this. Ask them to come to me. Then I will tell you the rest of your future."

Ming placed her delicate golden hand inside Yin's open palm. "I promise." She rose gracefully, her eyes filled with a newfound awareness. "You have shown me much. But greatest of all is that we can help each other."

"Until tomorrow." Yin waved her away and pocketed the four quarters in the pocket of her wrinkled black trousers.

By nine o'clock on Monday night, Ming saw to it that the story about her chance meeting with the ship captain, Thomas O'Malley, spread to every man, woman and child in Chinatown. She explained to everyone how she had gone to the back door of the emporium to collect the needles and threads she had ordered from Caroline Mansfield. There she had met Thomas O'Malley, who had just anchored his ship, the *Boston Beacon,* at Yerba Buena. Ming understood little English, but some words she knew. "Beautiful" was one of them. Ming could only talk to him with her eyes and listen with her heart. She knew that twenty-seven-year-old, brown-haired, blue-eyed, white-skinned Thomas O'Malley had fallen in love with her. He'd even gone so far as to escort her home.

Like white-bellied magpies, the birds of joy, eager customers came flocking to Yin's table in the hotel lobby. Some of the patrons were difficult to read and Yin had to resort to an assortment of all her devices. Some were much like Ming, and she read their futures as if they were imprinted on their faces for all the world to see. Some futures were tragic, and Yin could only brace them against the truth with pretty lies and gentle warnings to soften life's blows.

She kept her promise to Ming and foretold that she and Thomas would sail away at the end of the month, marry, and that Ming would bear him a son. Yin also saw tragedy, but she knew Ming was strong and so she explained that to her, too. Ming would meet much prejudice in Boston, but she must be careful not to allow Thomas or any others to overtake her own power. Ming would outlive Thomas, and one day she would come back to San Francisco and live the life of a rich woman.

"Will I be happy?" Ming asked.

"That is a question I never answer."

At the end of the week, Yin went to Chang with her profits. She did not report the extra five dollars she had collected as bonuses.

Chang's head moved slowly from Yin's face to the pile of coins and paper that totaled $116. "Is this all there is?" he asked suspiciously.

Yin smiled. "Of course not. You didn't expect me to be honest. I have fulfilled your expectations."

Chang's face was expressionless as he nodded his head and reached his arthritic fingers across the desk and fondled the money.

"You'll be a good businessperson," he said as he divided the money in half and pocketed his share. "I've signed a new contract with my supplier." Chang was unused to deferring to another's superiority. It was his way of thanking her.

Yin tipped her head forward with only the slightest of movements. She knew not to gloat, nor to be effusive. Such manners would destroy his confidence in her and break up the blocks of his ego that men value so greatly. She moved away from the thoughts she heard in his mind and brought out her own thoughts.

"How much will you charge me for English lessons?"

With a quick jump like a cricket, a smile sprang onto Chang's dour face. "You wish to speak with the heavy tongue?"

"Yes."

"Five dollars," he replied.

Yin smiled. "You know how much money I kept back?"

"Yes. I know many things, too," he said, tapping his gnarled index finger to his temple.

Yin lost her smile. "I believe you can only know things that your desk clerk tells you. Perhaps you instructed him to count my patrons and the money they spent at my table."

"Perhaps."

Yin rather liked the repartee they volleyed back and forth. Her mentor was the first person in this life who respected her. It was a valuable gift. She promised herself deep in the shadows of her silent mind not to abuse this gift. "Now teach me the English."

Their lesson lasted over two hours. Chang commented tersely that Yin learned quickly. She did not reply, which told him that she expected him to see this quality in her. Yin bowed deeply when she left the room, not because it was expected of her, but because she wanted to. She wanted him to know that she respected him for his kindness. She told him these things with her thoughts. But Yin knew he was the kind of man who listened with his eyes. Not his heart.

* * * *

Nan-Yung tied his mule to the hitching post outside the red-painted hotel where he had left his wife. During the journey home, he had conjured various tales about his sojourn into the hills, but none had pleased him. Nan-Yung knew he did not owe Yin an explanation, she was his wife. Hers was a role of acceptance of all life's tragedies. What he needed now was money to buy the opium he would sell to anyone who would pay the price. Nan-Yung was not prejudiced when it came to business. He intended to sell opium to anyone who was willing to pay.

Nan-Yung breezed into the hotel lobby and walked straight past his wife who was reading the palm of a middle-aged Chinese woman. Just as he reached the bottom step of the pine staircase, he realized it was Yin's voice he heard in the whispers from the corner.

His eyes took it all in. He saw the hand-painted sign on the table leg; he saw the older woman's entranced face and his wife's earnest eyes as her lips mumbled and rolled against each other emitting sounds that brought joy to the other woman's face.

Furious at the scene, Nan-Yung thumped his thin leather-soled foot on the pine floor ready to pounce upon his wife and berate her for the disgrace she had brought upon his name, when suddenly he saw two glittering gold coins on the table.

He halted mid-stride. Next to the gold coins were a dozen silver coins. As he looked around the lobby, he realized that the people sitting on the black-lacquered bench and on the plump silk cushions against the wall by the fireplace were waiting in line for a reading from his wife. His eyes shot back to the gold coins.

Fortune has smiled on me once again, Shining Girl!

Nan-Yung stood off to the side, patient now to see her. His future unfurled before him. Once again, Yin was his passage to his destiny. With this money, he would buy the land he needed to build a street-side shop, a restaurant or a laundry perhaps. It didn't matter. Because below the earth he would build his opium den, just like the Joss houses in China. He would be proprietor. He would become rich and powerful just as he'd always known he would be.

Yin felt his eyes on her, though she had not seen him enter the lobby. She finished the reading for her customer and then slowly lifted her jubilant, shining eyes to her husband's face. Nan-Yung glowed with triumph. She could see it. She nearly blushed thinking how lucky she was to be wanted this much by her husband.

Yin believed she saw pride for her in his eyes. She believed that it was her ingenuity, her cleverness and her talent that delighted him.

Nan-Yung didn't see her beauty anymore. He didn't take in the delicate lotus-white skin, the tiny hands and feet, the glorious silken hair nor the incredibly shining eyes.

She rose, went to him and he took her hand. They smiled at each other through eyes misted with chimera.

Suddenly, Yin realized she was not seeing her husband at all. She was merely seeing herself reflected in his eyes.

When she'd been on her way to the Forbidden City and seen Nan-Yung for the first time, she'd seen a vision of him becoming her husband. He had been her opportunity for freedom from the harem. She realized now she had moved too quickly in making her decision to help him out of China.

Yin realized she should be furious with him for leaving her for months. His ego caused him to believe that no matter how he treated her, she should abide by the treatment. She realized his mind thought too much about the gold she was making.

She kept smiling at him, letting him think she was duped by him.

Yin knew she wasn't meant to be anyone's fool. That included Nan-Yung. She'd be careful with him from now on. She'd weigh her decisions very carefully before taking actions that would affect her life. She was smart enough to know that she could control her opportunities. After all, she had formed the business relationship with Chang Wu. She'd had one English lesson with Chang. She'd negotiate for many more so that she could give readings and chart horoscopes for the rich whites. She was wise to befriend old Chang Wu, who now looked upon her as a daughter.

Already Yin had observed Nan-Yung's tendency to jump headlong into action without thinking things through. From what he had told her about his father, Luang Su, and what she'd heard about the Su family's disgrace when she'd lived in Peking, she realized that her husband was a fool.

She had to be cautious with such a man.

One who rubs one's shoes in the muck of fate too many times will not achieve one's destiny.

Yin would let her husband think she was submissive just as her mother had taught her all women should be. But she would make certain that no man, no husband, would ever totally control her.

I'll be what the whites call an independent woman.

twenty-three

Even so my bloody thoughts, with violent pace,
Shall ne'er look back, ne'er ebb to humble love,
Till that a capable and wide revenge
Swallow them up.

—WILLIAM SHAKESPEARE
OTHELLO, III, III, L. 454

Word of Yin Ch'u's divination abilities crept slowly to the *waigoren*, the foreigners. They came to Chinatown in fancy black-lacquered carriages and, like night beetles, lined the street in front of Chang Wu's hotel. In those days of 1852 when gold flowed through the city like yellow lava, instantly altering the city and its civilizations forever, those who once had been poor became rich. Those with no lineage invented backgrounds and began dynasties. Gamblers metamorphosized into bankers. Con artists evolved into merchants, businessmen became politicians, whores became ladies, then wives and mothers. Society was born out of the ashes of the gold rush.

French women from the boulevards in Paris flounced into Chinatown on the arms of prospectors to be entertained by the pretty Oriental women they'd heard about. Chang Wu's kitchens served up platters of Peking duck, mounds of fluffy rice and intoxicating plum wines. Yin provided the entertainment as she spun the *I Ching* sticks and described the visions she saw behind her eyes. She told the rich that they'd find happiness, told the poor they'd be rich and always found the positive, yet provocative to say to her patrons.

The heavily made-up women would laugh at Yin's predictions and yet would entice their benefactors to pay for detailed horoscopes. The men plunked down gold coins as if they were worthless trinkets while exacting a lingering kiss from their mistresses. Yin passed no judgment on her clients. She kept her thoughts inside her head behind her face where no *waigoren* nor husband could visit.

Yin charged the *waigoren* triple her fee because Nan-Yung hated them with great force. Yin had listened to his tale about the hills and his stolen gold, but all she heard was his hate. She watched with her eyes how his face contorted and grew lines beside his mouth. She saw his eyes burn like white coals and his lips become thin and stretch themselves over his teeth as curses hissed from his throat.

Yin was frightened when she was around Nan-Yung. She found she was unable to see into his future. When he spoke of the riches he would amass someday, she saw nothing but a black abyss.

When he told her he would dress her like the empress in China, she envisioned herself in rags. Yin began to understand that her talent had limitations. She could help others see their fate, but her own future was perpetually lost in the black fog.

Yin realized with a heaviness in her heart that Nan-Yung carried no remorse for abandoning her. He didn't care that she'd been lonely or afraid. She didn't like this quality in him. She chose to address him about it.

He was counting the money she'd made as they sat in their hotel room together.

"Do you not realize that I'm a resourceful person?" she asked.

"I don't see this," he replied without looking at her.

She pressed on. "You've done nothing to earn this money. I've done all the work. It's my talent that brings you good fortune."

"Nonsense. It was my destiny to come to America. I've known this for a long time."

Yin frowned as she realized how self-centered her husband was. "I thought our destiny was together. To help each other."

Nan-Yung looked at his beautiful wife whose head was filling with dangerous thoughts. How could he control her if she thought she was his equal? "You do help me, that's true. However, it's *my* fate that brings this gold to me. You're merely a channel through which I am forced to work for the time being."

Yin didn't like what she was hearing. Nan-Yung's soul was not as pure as she'd thought when they met. He was a man of two heads. One head thought that she was good for him only because she brought him money. The other head thought her a demon because she used her brain to get this money. Yin's *chuming*, her inside knowing, told her that Nan-Yung's hatred for the *waigoren* had seeped out of his pores and was covering her.

Yin didn't want her life to flow into the pattern like other Chinese women lived. The shining colors she'd painted onto her dreams might fade. She hadn't told Nan-Yung that she was carrying his child. And she would not do so for the time being. This secret gave her power.

She had to make plans for herself and her child. Tomorrow she would start by meeting with Chang.

* * * *

Yin sat across the desk from Chang. "I'm a good businessperson. I've proved this to you."

"Indeed."

"I have further business I wish to conduct with you. I wish to put aside a small portion of money from each of my clients without my husband's knowledge."

Chang shook his head. "It's not my practice to upset the balance of harmony in a man's home."

Yin's eyes narrowed. "I shall upset the balance of harmony in your hotel by leaving if you do not grant my wishes."

"You don't trust your husband. That's very bad."

"Bad men don't deserve trust."

Chang nodded. "Very well. I'll help you. I'll speak with him and tell him I'm taking another, say, 10 percent?"

Yin nodded without smiling. "That will be adequate. Then I need another favor."

"You press my friendship greatly."

Yin's smile was sarcastic. "We're not friends. We are in business. There is greater loyalty when money is involved."

"You learn quickly, for a woman," he paused. "What is the favor?"

"I wish to learn even more English. All you can teach me."

"That's all?" He was surprised.

"It's enough," she replied. "More than enough."

* * * *

In America, time moved more quickly than other nations, Nan-Yung thought as he counted his coins and paper dollars in the tiny hotel room owned by Chang Wu. When the trees stood naked, he had only needed to hold his money. Now that the trees were fully clothed, he had filled seven bags with money and started an eighth bag. He hoped tonight he would fill this bag to the top with his wife's earnings. Nan-Yung had discovered ways to skim money from Chang Wu's share, despite the old man's insistence that he get an additional 10 percent. Nan-Yung had found ways to hide Yin's tips and her private horoscope fees. More importantly, he'd found where he intended to spend her profits.

Three blocks down on Dupont Street, Yan Tsing owned a small laundry. It was two stories tall, fashioned out of pine that he had painted yellow with green trim. Streetside was a small receiving area with a counter where laundry was received. The wall behind the counter had been partitioned into 210 cubbyholes made of pine and varnished. Each cubbyhole had a number painted in Chinese where freshly laundered shirts and linens were placed. A cotton curtain covered the narrow doorway that led to the back room where irons, tables, wash basins and scrub boards and ovens to heat ironing bricks had been installed. A backdoor led to the alley and an open yard area where the laundry was dried and more wash basins stood in rows. Here the washwomen worked twelve hours a day washing clothes.

Yan Tsing was old and overworked, which attributed to his death the night before. He left no surviving children to run his business. Yan Tsing's widow was an excellent washerwoman but she had made it known to her neighbors that she wanted to sell the business. She wanted to go live with her sister in Monterey.

Nan-Yung carefully placed his money bags in the down lining of his satin jacket, which he carried over his arm when he left the hotel.

A sign painted in Chinese stated that the laundry of Yan Tsing was closed due to a death. Nan-Yung looked past the sign through the hazy glass window to the interior. He saw Yan Tsing's widow standing behind the counter waiting for him. She waddled on rickety legs toward the door and unlocked it. She bowed.

Nan-Yung followed her through the curtained doorway to the back rooms. On the left was a huge rolltop desk where Yan Tsing kept his records, accounts and legal papers. Nan-Yung sat in the armless wooden chair next to the larger mahogany chair where he'd seen Yan Tsing sit.

"Madame Tsing, I extend to you my sympathies." He bowed his head again.

She did not look up at him, but kept her eyes down as she had been taught by her mother.

"I have heard that you wish to sell this land and building. I have heard you wish to live with your sister. I have come here to help you attain your wishes, Madame Tsing." Nan-Yung noticed that her head bobbed slightly. It was a good sign. She obviously was not prepared to negotiate a business deal.

"I am willing to pay your passage to Monterey and to arrange for your living fees once you arrive. I have money, Madame Tsing," he slowly pulled out one of his black silk money bags. He plunked it down on the desk. The coins rattled against each other. Nan-Yung saw her eyes dart to the bag and remain there.

He pulled out a second bag and made a great show of the noise these coins made. He watched her fingers unfold. She wanted to touch the money, he thought. It was another good sign.

"I am prepared to pay you four thousand dollars for your husband's business," he said calmly.

This time her wrinkled face wafted in front of him for a moment as she gazed into his eyes. Then she looked directly at the money sacks.

"I know nothing of the value of my land. I must think about this."

Nan-Yung nearly smiled, but kept his face placid. "Excellent. Think also about your alternatives. How do you intend to manage this business? You're in the winter of your years. Your days of washing clothes like the young girls are over. You should spend the twilight of your years with your sister just as you dream. I do not wish for the widow of my neighbor to die as he did from hard work. I'm young, Madame Tsing. I'll carry on the business. I'll not even change the Tsing name on the sign."

Madame Tsing's tiny head cocked to the left. This gesture was obviously important to her. Nan-Yung marveled at his own acumen, for this had been simply an afterthought. "Four thousand dollars is a lot of money for an old woman, Madame Tsing."

"Open the bags. Let me see this money."

He did as she asked. "It is white man's money, every last quarter of it," he said as he poured gold twenty-dollar pieces and silver dollars into a huge pile on her desk. Just as he'd thought, however, it was the sack that rustled with the sound of paper money that piqued her interest most. Together they counted the money. Satisfied that every cent was accounted for, Madame Tsing opened a long drawer, pulled out its false bottom and withdrew the land deed her husband had signed eight years ago. Nan-Yung pulled out a paper on which he had stated the terms of their agreement. It was written in Chinese.

Madame Tsing signed his paper, handed Nan-Yung the deed to her land and the key to her husband's desk. She raked the coins and paper money into a large laundry bag and returned the small silk bags to Nan-Yung. She told him she would sell most of her belongings and move to Monterey by the end of the month.

When Nan-Yung left the laundry, he was fully aware he had paid Madame Tsing only a quarter of its value. It had been imperative she not take any time to consult with anyone about her sale. Since the transaction was completed, few would inquire about the details. She was leaving San Francisco and would be forgotten by the residents of Chinatown. There was only the formality of the transfer of title at the Alcalde's office. For this Nan-Yung would have to hire Chang Wu's English-speaking nephew to interpret for him. Once Madame Tsing was gone, Nan-Yung would rehire her washerwomen and then he'd begin excavating underneath the laundry.

He calculated that six months' construction time was necessary to complete the opium dens he envisioned. During that time, he would insist that Yin continue her readings now that her clientele was increasing. They would live in the apartment above the laundry just as Yan Tsing and his wife had done. No longer would he have to pay rent to Chang Wu, and most important, he would never share his profits with anyone ever again.

* * * *

Jefferson Duke turned his back on the bay, which was so crammed with tall-masted ships it looked like a forest of burned-out trees. He climbed to the driver's perch of his wide open-bed wagon thinking he felt exhausted.

"Dog-tired is what I am," he said, wiping the sweat from his forehead with his sleeve as he took up the reins.

Unlike many of his competitors, Jefferson had not overstocked his warehouse this past year with lumber and building materials. He'd kept his inventories lean. Theoretically, the surge of gold running through the city should have meant high profits for him, but he'd been wiser than most merchants. Common sense told him that the greed that gold fever bred would bring not only more prospectors, but more merchants . . . more competition . . . more mouths to eat up the pie. Jefferson believed in San Francisco's future and with that premise in mind, he began diversifying. His ventures into real estate had been the first step. He was one of the original developers and home builders of South Park, which had this year overtaken Rincon Hill as the most fashionable and elite area in which to live. South Park had been the brainstorm of George Gordon, an Englishman and the owner of the city's first sugar refinery. South Park was to imitate the "refined residences" of London with their elegant facades and parklike settings. South Park was the twelve-acre area enclosed between Second and Third, Bryant and Brannan Streets. These houses were two stories high with French windows opening onto iron balconies.

Architectural detail was all-important in these houses. William M. Gwins constructed the first ballroom in South Park. Planked with wood, the unpaved Third Street boasted a line of omnibuses running up and down the street. Jefferson, like the residents of South Park themselves, anxiously awaited the beautifully sculpted iron fountain George Gordon had commissioned from the Coalbrookdale iron works in England.

With his eye to the future, Jefferson still believed that Nob Hill would be the next and ultimately most sought-after building site of all. With the profits from his South Park residential construction, he'd bought a one-and-a-half-acre lot nearly at the summit of Nob Hill facing California Street with the side entrance of the house to face Mason Street.

However, Jefferson found that with his new warehouse on Montgomery Street, he needed more money to build the kind of mansion he envisioned.

He looked everywhere for potential investments. When Peter Donahue and his brother, James, created the Gas Works on Natoma, Howard, Freemont and First Streets and then followed with a foundry at Market, First, Bush and Battery, Jefferson became a silent investor. He watched how they imported pipe for the mains from the East Coast and shipped coal in from Swansea, Wales. He immediately began searching the United States for domestic coal. He found a new coal mine in West Virginia and imported it by the shipload.

Next on Jefferson's list was a water works company. He foresaw the city lit by gas lamps and he realized that every home and business would eventually have running water and sewage disposal. Convincing city hall to see the same vision was a frustrating task. Jefferson's relationship with politicians and city politics was a love-hate seesaw from the beginning.

Mayor William K. Garrison believed in the kind of public works and utilities as did Jefferson. However, the city had grown to over fifty thousand residents all needing shelter, food and clothing.

At a wedding reception he'd attended in one of the larger homes on the south slope of Rincon Hill, Jefferson pulled Mayor Garrison aside.

"William, help me out here. This city needs water mains and sewers. Let me get this project going now, before more streets are built, which will all have to be torn up and then remade."

"I hear you, Jefferson. But my God, man! I feel as if I've got my hands full just trying to get the voters to agree to a tax levy to get the streets paved. Did you hear about that young woman falling through the planking on Sacramento Street?"

"Yes, I did. She fainted and had it not been for the nearby apothecary shop, Lord knows when she would have come around."

"Don't be facetious. The city is still half-savage and half-civilized. Three days ago a Frenchman shot a catamount near the Presidio. Eighteen pounds! I heard it was thirty-one inches from the nose to tail tip. Wolves, bears, foxes—they're all still around us. During the rainy season, every street is a mud hole that no wagon nor man can traverse. In the dry season this place is a dust bowl. I've tried my damndest just to get the beaches and dunes matted!" William took a thoughtful sip of Spanish wine. Then, with a twinkle in his eye, he leaned closer to Jefferson. "Did you hear about the German prospector who hit a wide streak? He went to Buckelew's jewelry shop just down the street from your new warehouse and ordered a gold buckle set completely in diamonds!"

"It's a city of paradoxes. That's why I love her. Think how much more I could love her if I could install gas and water pipes in the Mission District, South Park and Nob Hill."

Garrison drained his glass. "You never give up, do you, Jefferson?"

"Never." Jefferson laughed. "So, you might as well join up with me. I'll drive you crazy, William."

"All right. I'll see what I can do. What is it with you? Do you intend to be the richest man in town?"

Jefferson's eyes lit with a deep sense of purpose. "I know this city can be the greatest city in America. I intend to be the one who makes it happen."

William shook his head. "I'd be a fool to doubt you."

"Yes, you would."

"I'm going to find the Madeira bottle. Care to join me?"

"I think I've had enough for tonight. I'd better pay my respects and get some rest. After all, I have a city to build tomorrow."

William slapped Jefferson on the back and excused himself.

Just as Jefferson put his glass down on a table and was about to leave he saw Caroline. She was dressed in a soft-pink silk gown with the fashionable French hoops the women of San Francisco had adopted along with their sisters in New York. She wore her hair in long, silvery, thick ringlets held in place at the back of her head with gold combs studded with sapphires that matched the color of her eyes.

Jefferson thought she looked like a vision from heaven.

She saw him out of the corner of her eye and excused herself from the group. She walked toward the buffet table where mounds of fresh seafood awaited the guests.

Jefferson followed her and pretended to inspect the glass trays of boiled shrimp, smoked salmon and oysters. Slowly, he moved toward her, taking a china plate and filling it with garlic-and-butter-marinated crab claws. "I want to see you tonight, Caroline."

"I can't, Jefferson. I have Lawrence with me."

"Later, then."

She selected a thin round of bread and placed a paper-thin slice of salmon on top. "I have mountains of paperwork that must be finished by morning. You'll have to be patient until Friday."

"I don't want to be patient. I'm a man in love, for God's sake."

She smiled to herself. "I know, my darling. Time seems to grow when I'm not with you."

"I know, my love. If it were up to me, I'd change the way we must live. Just say the word."

The lights in her eyes dimmed for a moment, but because she was so thrilled to be with Jefferson even for this one moment, she smiled again. "Tell me what our mayor had to say," she said, jabbing a prawn with a sterling silver seafood fork.

"Oh," he nodded. "We're moving on to safe subjects now," he teased, and then told her about his conversation with William Garrison.

As they spoke, neither Jefferson nor Caroline was aware that Lawrence was watching them from his hiding place under the white-skirted buffet table.

Lawrence had promised his nanny, Lydia, that he would bring her a piece of wedding cake. It had been Lawrence's decision to delight her even further by stealing one of every single appetizer served at the reception.

Stealing the shrimp had been easy. So had the enormous Alaskan crab claws. Just as he shoved a slippery oyster into his mouth, however, Lawrence heard his mother's voice. He gulped the oyster whole. He lifted the edge of the tablecloth just enough to recognize her dress.

Lawrence immediately recognized Jefferson Duke's voice. Oddly, Jefferson didn't speak in his normal clipped, matter-of-fact tones. Not only was Jefferson whispering to his mother, but his inflection was soothing, even enticing.

Lawrence had never heard his father speak to his mother like this, but he'd heard Charlie Wilson's father sound like this when he spoke to Charlie's mother. Lawrence's eyes widened as the full portent of the situation hit him.

Jefferson Duke was in love with his mother.

Lawrence leaned very close to the edge of the cloth.

"Caroline, please," Jefferson breathed sensuously. "Forget the paperwork tonight. William will be back next week. Come to me."

"I can't."

"You would if you wanted me as much as I want you."

"Don't say that! Nothing could be further from the truth."

"Friday seems an eternity," Jefferson groaned with finality.

"Because it is, my love."

Lawrence lifted the cloth again and watched as their shoes moved away from the table. He should have been shocked but he wasn't. From all his Bible teachings and the moral undertones of every piece of fiction he had been allowed by his father to read, Lawrence knew that adultery was against the laws of God and man. However, Lawrence had swiped his mother's copy of *Madame Bovary* and read about romantic love. He'd even heard Lydia talking about the stories of Emily Brontë. He knew things about men and women. Lawrence and Billy Chester talked about sex all the time on the back steps of Billy's house on Powell Street. Billy knew all kinds of things about sex and even told Lawrence about the whores on the Barbary Coast. Billy was thirteen and he liked the fact that Lawrence was interested in what he had to say.

Knowing that his mother and Jefferson might be doing the things Billy had talked about didn't upset Lawrence. He liked to think they were like the people in Lydia's book, *Wuthering Heights*. Somehow, a curious sense of peace, a veil of right, descended upon him. It was as if everything that had been out of kilter in his life had been finally set straight. His world did not go spinning away from him, but rather came to him with a new solidarity.

Lawrence had always had a difficult time placing the unemotional, bland William Mansfield anywhere in his life. The position of father had perpetually seemed the most unlikely spot of all.

His mother, on the other hand, was full of energy and life. She made an occasion out of everything, celebrating birthdays, Sundays, good weather and good days of business. She made everything fun. The best part of his childhood was that Caroline had always included Lawrence in nearly every aspect of her life.

Lawrence went with Caroline to town meetings, political rallies, buying trips and dinners with friends because William saw no point in idle mealtime chatter. Even at this wedding tonight, he was the only child in attendance outside the immediate relatives.

Lawrence had always felt as if he were his mother's right arm. In his mind, it had been the two of them against the world. Lydia was his nanny now and his friend, but for Lawrence there was no one else in his life but his mother.

Lawrence remembered just last night talking with Lydia about his father.

"Yer mother doesn't seem to miss yer fether so very much, now does she?"

Lawrence had shrugged his shoulders. "I don't know what you mean."

"She doesn't write to him. There's no mail from him to you either. It's a very curious thing."

"Not really." Lawrence looked at her. "I know lots of men in San Francisco. My mother has over twelve men who work for her. But of all my friends at school, there are ten boys who don't have a mother. Their mothers died having babies. I'm very lucky to be so close to my mother. I love her a lot."

Lydia ruffled his hair. "Aye. That you are." Then she hugged him.

No, the fact that his mother had taken a lover did not astonish Lawrence in the least. He was pleased for her and hoped she was happy. He was proud she had picked Jefferson Duke. All the boys at school looked up to him and respected him.

Past memories spiraled across Lawrence's brain as he realized that his mother's association with Jefferson went back over several years. He couldn't remember a time when Jefferson Duke was not part of the holiday celebrations at his house. Before the gold rush the gentry always entertained each other in their homes. Therefore, nothing improper would have been noted about Jefferson's presence. The old guard still stuck together, though they were now forced to admit more families into their circle as the city grew. But the mainstay of the Mansfields, the Richardsons, the Cogswells, the McAllisters, the Parkmans and Jefferson Duke, along with a few others, formed the rock-bed of Lawrence's memories.

Idle curiosity rather than bitterness caused Lawrence to ask himself, *Precisely when did Mother's association with Jefferson Duke begin?*

He shoved a second salty oyster into his mouth, liking its exotic taste and texture. He glanced behind him at the long tunnel of his hiding place. He gathered up his stolen epicurean treasures he'd give Lydia, then lifted the cloth to check his path of escape. Most of the guests had returned to the dance floor. He dashed for the French doors that led to the butler's pantry. Then he made his way back to the salon where he would wait for his mother to join him before going back home.

He sat on a white brocade settee as she walked into the salon alone. Jefferson was not with her, but stood back in the hallway talking to the host. Lawrence couldn't help but notice that his mother's eyes sparkled like he'd never seen before and her cheeks were rosy red as if she'd been outside on a winter day.

He smiled at her. He thought about the fact that once his father was home next week, he wouldn't see his mother quite this happy again.

He rose and put his hand out to her. "Did you have a good time, Mother?"

"Of course, Darling," she said brightly.

"I'm so glad for you, Mother," he said and walked with her out the front door and to their carriage.

* * * *

William Mansfield returned to San Francisco with little celebration, but only because he despised the fuss Caroline always wanted to make of comings and goings, not to mention birthdays.

"The least you could do is let me invite some neighbors for dinner, William. You've been gone three weeks this last trip and we've all missed you. Haven't we, Lawrence?"

"Yes, Mother," Lawrence answered with no enthusiasm as he looked at his father's dour face.

"I want to get straight to my books. I'm sure they are a mess. I have no time for folderol."

Lawrence's shoulders slumped. "But Mother made a homecoming cake with pecans and raisins from the Sanchez rancho."

William waved aside their protests and walked away.

Caroline expelled a sigh. "Some things never change," she said to herself, forgetting Lawrence's presence.

Lawrence went to the kitchen drawer, withdrew a cutting knife and stood next to the three-layer cake. "Do you want a large piece of cake, Mother? I think I shall eat two myself!" He laughed.

Caroline laughed along with her son. "What would I do without you, Lawrence?"

* * * *

Jefferson pulled his team of horses to a halt in front of his warehouse. Three warehousemen came rushing outside to help unload the wagon. Jefferson jumped down from his perch and headed to the side-door entrance to his office.

Just inside the door, Lawrence was sitting on a wooden keg filled with nails. He was holding something wrapped in a white linen napkin.

Jefferson's face lit up when he saw his son.

"Lawrence! What a surprise. Did your mother send you for that floor planking she needs?"

"No, sir. She thinks I'm over at Billy's house. I brought you some home-coming cake. My mother invented it, she says."

Jefferson's smile collapsed. "Your father is home now?"

"Yes, sir." Lawrence's face was equally as dour.

"Looks like you have something on your mind, Lawrence."

"I do, sir," Lawrence slid off the barrel, snagging his woolen knickers on the iron banding around the keg.

"Tarnation!" he hissed as he inspected the damage.

"Maybe Lydia can fix it for you before your mother discovers the tear. She'll cover up for you."

Lawrence spun around to face Jefferson, his blue eyes wide with awe. "How did you know that?"

"I know a lot of things."

"From my mother?"

Jefferson's neck hairs rose in warning. He must always be careful. "Lydia, I've found, can be a gossip when it comes to you, young man. But it is obvious to me that she is very proud of you. So's your mother. And your father."

Unconsciously, Lawrence puffed out his chest. "I know that."

"Good," Jefferson said with a watchful eye.

"I also know that you're in love with my mother."

Lawrence blurted out his thought so fast, he was stunned as he looked at the truth sitting in front of him, jeering at him like a newly escaped prisoner. He clamped his hand over his mouth.

"I beg your pardon, Lawrence. I'm afraid you've been greatly misled. Who told you this?"

Lawrence grappled with his courage and opened his mouth again. "I overheard you and mother at the wedding reception. I was hiding under the banquet table."

Jefferson felt his knees turn to powder. He wavered a bit, then sat on the edge of his desk. Not once in all these years had he prepared himself for this confrontation.

What a fool he'd been to think that no one would ever discover them! At worst he'd assembled ammunition to fight attacking gossips. He had alibis, lies and phantom excuses in his arsenal, but looking into the trust-filled eyes of his son, he never dreamed he would need to pull out the truth.

"I love her. I always have. Does that upset you?" Then he stopped himself. "My God! What am I saying? Of course this upsets you."

"No!" Lawrence held up his hand. "That's what I came here to tell you. It doesn't upset me. I'm happy for her."

Jefferson sucked in his breath. He was stunned, but happily. "Does she, I mean, have you told her that you know?"

"No. I wasn't planning to. I just felt I had to talk to you about it first."

Jefferson smiled. "She worries about you all the time. What you think. How you would feel if you knew."

Lawrence looked off to the side for a moment as if he were considering Jefferson's proposal. When he turned back to Jefferson, he gave no hint as to what was to follow. In his youthful, offhanded manner, he asked simply, "How long have you been in love with my mother?"

"What?"

Lawrence's eyes were steady, but Jefferson felt the tears forming in the young boy's eyes before he actually saw them. "When was the first time . . . I mean . . . when did you know?"

The pain was excruciating for Jefferson as he stood on the razor's edge. If he told Lawrence the truth, he could destroy the boy and Caroline's life. If he lied, he'd destroy any chance he ever had of becoming a real father to his own son. Suddenly, a vision of Rachel's face wafted in front of Jefferson. He saw her copper hair and tawny skin. He felt the warmth of her smile comfort him. In a rush, he remembered every word she had ever spoken to him. Selfishly, he wanted to claim his son, establish his dynasty and carve out his destiny. But as he looked into Lawrence's blue eyes, he sacrificed himself . . . again.

"Well," he said as casually as possible, "I suppose it was just after she came back from Boston carrying you in her arms. You were the spitting image of her and I thought to myself, 'Now there are two of them to love, even if it's from a distance.'"

Lawrence was too young to realize that Jefferson had told him a lie and the truth at the same time. He didn't realize that Jefferson had inadvertently told him that he was in love with Caroline before she'd gone to Boston. Lawrence smiled as he bought and paid for the story with his trust.

Lawrence stuck out his hand. "Thanks, Mr. Duke."

"My pleasure," Jefferson replied with an equal grin and then pulled the boy to him and gave him a bear hug.

Just then, Shamus O'Connor knocked on the door and opened it without waiting for Jefferson's reply. "Mr. Duke? There be a problem out here that needs yer tendin'."

Jefferson followed Shamus into the sun and into the lumberyard where stacks of building timbers were stored under tarpaulins behind a wooden fence.

Curious, Lawrence eased around the doorway to watch.

He decided to follow Jefferson. "I'm coming, too," he said running up beside Jefferson.

Standing next to Daniel Flannery, Jefferson's lumber supervisor, was a young Chinese man dressed in silk tunic and trousers and who was accompanied by a diminutive, beautiful young woman whom Lawrence assumed was the man's wife. Lawrence noticed that the young girl was extremely pregnant. He looked up at Jefferson and saw that he noticed the same thing about the young woman.

Lawrence had never paid much attention to the Orientals who were moving to San Francisco by the dozens. He couldn't help but stare at the golden-skinned, almond-eyed beautiful woman. These people came from China, far across the sea. He'd never thought about it before, but he wondered why God chose to make them look so much different than he.

"She's very beautiful, isn't she?" Lawrence said.

"Yes, she is," Jefferson replied, putting his hand on Lawrence's shoulder.

"What seems to be the problem, Daniel?" Jefferson asked.

"I can't understand what these Orientals are sayin', boss. She speaks better English than he does, but he won't let her do the talkin'."

Shamus bent over and whispered to Jefferson. "When he got here, he was puttin' sticks of lumber on her back and expectin' her to carry it. Her bein' in the family way an' all. Jesus, Jefferson. Them folks got no sense at all."

"Shamus, go get the wagon," Jefferson said.

"Yes, sir," he replied and hurried away.

"I'm the owner. How can I help you?" Jefferson tried to gesture with his hands, but it was a futile effort.

Nan-Yung inspected Jefferson with a wary eye. A vague film of recognition covered Nan-Yung's eyes. This man reminded him of someone, but because he was so preoccupied with the business at hand, he threw off the film.

Nan-Yung waved paper dollars in Jefferson's face and made gyrations toward the stack of beams and then toward the planking. "I pay! I pay!"

Jefferson nodded up and down. "Fine." Jefferson held up his fingers. "How many?" Then he pointed to the beams.

Nan-Yung nodded and held up ten, then fifteen fingers.

Jefferson turned to Daniel. "Put fifteen beams on the wagon." Daniel hurried away to his task.

Nan-Yung turned toward the planking. With his fingers he gestured again indicating twenty-five planks. Then he stuck out his wad of dollars. Jefferson started to take the appropriate amount of money from Nan-Yung, but Nan-Yung immediately snatched the money back.

Without thinking, Yin blurted out in broken English, "He want total bill." Nan-Yung shot her a scathing look.

Yin knew her English lessons from Chang gave her power over her self-absorbed, egotistical husband. She chose to defy him and suffer the consequences later. She looked at Jefferson. "My husband. He want know how much for everyt'ing?"

"Sixty-seven dollars," Jefferson said. He turned to Lawrence. "Run inside and bring me that order pad on my desk."

"Yes, sir," Lawrence replied and ran inside the warehouse.

Yin watched and observed many things even though she now chose to keep her head in a downcast position like her husband preferred. She thought she could almost read the tall owner's thoughts.

That is the owner's son. But I see secrets swirling around them both.

Yin lifted her eyes and observed them more carefully as the boy returned. She shivered.

Someone has walked on my grave. No, it's my own future I'm seeing now.

She scrutinized Lawrence's face. Her heart stopped. Time stood still. She knew she must have turned pale.

Impossible! I can't be seeing what I'm seeing. Not for myself. Not for me. This boy is much younger than I. But when he is a man, our ages won't matter to us.

She felt weak in the knees. She had to be strong. She couldn't let Nan-Yung see her like this. She put her hand on the wagon's side to steady herself.

Nan-Yung was so involved in his barter, he paid no attention to Yin.

"I'll have my man deliver your lumber."

Nan-Yung turned to Yin. "What's he saying?"

She interpreted the English words into Chinese for him. She looked back at Jefferson.

"Are you all right, Madam?" Jefferson asked compassionately.

Can he see my vision? He's got the same powers I do. I can feel it.

She searched Jefferson's eyes. *No, he does not see the connection between his son and myself.*

"I'm fine," she answered.

Nan-Yung was impatient. "What is he saying now?"

She turned away from Nan-Yung saying, "He told us to have a nice day."

The white man has more concern about my well-being than my own husband. Perhaps I'm not wrong to see my own future with another man.

She turned to Jefferson.

"We t'ank you for your kindness," she said with a flutter of a smile.

"Not at all," Jefferson said.

Nan-Yung frowned. He detested her ability to learn this horribly difficult language with such ease. He further despised his dependency on her knowledge. "Stop talking to the barbarian!" He scolded her in Chinese. "Tell him I will not pay his exorbitant prices for delivery."

Yin pretended not to hear his reprimand. She looked only at Jefferson. "No delivery. Too much money."

Nan-Yung started to rush off toward Daniel to interrupt the loading of the wagon.

Jefferson reached out and grabbed Nan-Yung's arm. "Stop! There's no charge for deliveries over fifty dollars."

Nan-Yung jerked his arm out of Jefferson's grasp and glared at him.

Jefferson snapped his hand back, looking at Yin. "Please tell him that I won't take his money for the delivery. It's free. Does he understand the word, 'free'?"

Yin's eyes shadowed with pain. "None of us are ever 'free'," she said. Then she turned to Nan-Yung and translated Jefferson's words.

She looked back at Jefferson with grateful eyes. They both knew that without the wagon, she'd be forced to bear much of this load on her back.

Nan-Yung joined his wife. He bowed to Jefferson. She bowed to Jefferson. Reflexively, Jefferson bowed to them.

"Jefferson Duke appreciates your business," Jefferson said formally, then put his hand on Lawrence's shoulder and walked back inside the building.

Nan-Yung thought the blood had siphoned from his body. "What did he say his name was?"

"Jefferson Duke," Yin replied, feeling the power of the name, feeling her life move onto a new track.

Everything about her life changed that day. The gods had given her a vision of her destiny.

But they'd also revealed the truth about Nan-Yung's destiny.

"He is a Duke?"

"Yes," she replied quietly.

"I have been brought here to avenge my family. Your predictions were true."

"Yes."

They turned away from the lumberyard, keeping their eyes on the road ahead.

"Then I must murder Jefferson Duke," Nan-Yung said with conviction.

Yin glanced at her husband and thought of Jefferson's son. *Where will our futures intersect?*

twenty-four

San Francisco—1857

C aroline ran her hand over the glass-smooth, black-lacquer paint on Jefferson's new carriage, which had just arrived from New York. "Are you rich enough now, Jefferson?"

He grabbed her around the waist and chuckled, "You should know by now I believe in abundance in everything."

Playfully she wrangled out of his embrace. "No one in San Francisco has anything like this," she said, looking at the beveled glass panes in the brass lanterns. The driver's perch was covered in burgundy leather as was the rear "tiger's seat" ostensibly reserved for a footman or bodyguard as was the case in a great many of the gambler's coaches.

"I commissioned it last year. The suspension system has the best elliptical steel springs."

"Always the best," she smiled.

"Of course, my list of modifications was horrendous."

"Like the inside seats being covered in dove-gray velvet?"

"Yes," he said, taking one of her curls in his hand. Her hair was shot with gray now, but it only served to make her look more ethereal than ever. "It was the closest to the silver of your hair they could come," he said, his mouth going dry with desire. He moved a step away, hoping to control his emotions. "I put three times the normal down in the seats."

"Not horsehair?"

He quickly pulled her into his arms again. "Nothing but the best for my lady. And the walls are tufted with silver buttons, not fabric."

Caroline looked at the mahogany footstool made for the ladies, which matched the burled mahogany interior trim, padded with down and covered with gray leather. A removable carpet for the interior floor, which could be more easily cleaned, was provided since San Francisco had few paved streets and mud was a constant of life. The draperies were made of pearl-gray silk, tied back with silver tassels also in silk.

"It's beyond elegant, Jefferson," she said.

"I put as much thought and planning into this carriage as I did the mansion. After I saw H. J. Henseley's blue seashell coach drawn by four white horses, I knew I didn't want anything that theatrical. Milton Latham's brown barouche with yellow wheels, lined with light blue satin and drawn by those two white-as-milk horses, borders on the gauche. Of course, the Donahues have a glass coach, which if we were married would be wonderful, then everyone could see how lovely you are."

"Jefferson . . ."

"I decided to do the one thing I hadn't seen in San Francisco yet."

"Which was?"

"I used good taste."

Caroline burst out laughing. "I swear, Darling, you're the only one who can make me laugh anymore."

"You're so full of life, Caroline. You're the one who puts light in my life," he said.

"I feed myself on the love you give me," she replied, looking deeply into his eyes. "So, you see? It's all your fault."

He lifted her into the carriage, sat next to her and kissed her deeply. Her huge hooped skirt filled the cubicle. She had flopped onto the cushion without care to the position of her skirts. "Nice pantaloons," he said.

"Quit gawking and kiss me again."

"My pleasure."

As his tongue probed the sweet interior of her mouth and as she slipped her gloved hand around his neck inviting his passion, he quickly slid his hand up her thigh, pulled at the waist ribbon that held her pantaloons in place and shoved his hand downward.

"Darling," she groaned. "We can't."

"We can and we will," he replied.

She slid her hips further down on the seat and into his grasp. She couldn't stand the torture. She unbuttoned her Zouve jacket, pulled down her chemise and exposed her soft, aching breast to him. With her gloved hand still on his neck, she pushed his head down to her breast. Electric shocks shot through Caroline. "Take me," she groaned.

"Not yet." Jefferson continued to build a fire in Caroline with his hands, lips and tongue. He played her until she was trembling, then shaking and finally convulsing with her orgasm.

Caroline was panting and gasping for breath. She grabbed the belt around his waist and unbuckled it. Her fingers fumbled at the buttons on his trousers until he was free. He plunged himself into her. She moaned with pleasure.

Jefferson twisted her beneath him until she was lying prone on the seat. He hoisted her hips to him as he sank further and further into her. She locked her legs around him.

He closed his eyes and saw the familiar fireworks display against his eyelids that signaled his explosion. Too many nights without her, too many dreams about her, caused his ejaculation much too soon.

He opened his eyes and found her smiling at him. "I love you, Jefferson," she breathed and touched his cheek lovingly.

"And I you, my sweet."

"I hadn't planned on this. . . ." she said.

"Disappointed?"

"Not in the least. But hadn't we, uh, better put ourselves back together before someone finds us?"

Jefferson kissed her deeply again, his tongue sliding over the edges of her lips, feeling the trace of quivering she was still experiencing. "I suppose we should. It wouldn't take much for me to start all over again."

Her heart was beating so rapidly she could barely think. "I know."

"But you're right. This part of my warehouse is not exclusive. I found two of my warehousemen in here yesterday just staring at the coach."

He buttoned his trousers and rebuckled his belt. Out of the corner of his eye he saw the look of disappointment on her face. He helped her button her jacket as she fussed with her skirts.

"Come to me tonight, Caroline." He knew this request would be refused like most of the others. There was always a reason. He'd heard them too often. But he would ask again. And again. He didn't care; when it came to Caroline, he had no pride.

"All right."

"What?"

The look of astonishment on Jefferson's face was so unexpected that Caroline burst out laughing. "You do want me to come?"

"Yes!" he replied happily. "Of course, it's just that you usually say no."

"Not anymore," she replied resolutely.

His eyebrows crept together suspiciously. "What are you saying?"

"I'm over forty. I could spend the rest of my life denying myself. I have just begun to feel lately that the devil be damned. I've given William nearly my whole life. Sometimes, I think Lawrence even knows the truth."

"He does," Jefferson said flatly.

"What? How?"

"He's known for five years. It hasn't killed him. But I promised him I wouldn't say anything to you. He may have wanted to keep you in the dark. Or maybe he wasn't quite sure about it all. Not since that day when he confronted me with the truth has he said anything else about it."

Caroline pressed her palms to her temples. "Lawrence knows?"

"Yes."

She shook her head as reality sank in. "In a way, this doesn't surprise me. Maybe it's because I've always felt you and I were the only right thing in my life. It was William's presence in my life that didn't make sense. He was never right. I wish Lawrence had said something to me."

"Why?" Jefferson eased back onto the seat. "I think that's the most remarkable, loving and trusting part of your relationship with him. He didn't need to say anything. He knew the facts and he was fine with it. Your love for me isn't something that should be hidden from him. It's only with society that you play cat and mouse."

"Society," she repeated and leaned against the seat feeling defeated. "Have I given it too much due?"

"Perhaps."

Her look was faraway. "I've given William too much."

Jefferson took her hand. "Do you really feel that?"

"I'm beginning to, yes."

Jefferson looked at her as she glared down into the valley of her life. Something was changing in their lives. Lawrence's knowledge of their relationship would bring Caroline around, eventually. Of that, he was certain. Time had shown her that she was wasting her life by remaining married to William. Perhaps now, she would have the courage to move forward and take charge of things. But it had to be her decision, he knew.

Jefferson took her hand and kissed it. "Come, love. We have to get you out of here before one of my employees finds us."

"God forbid," she replied sarcastically.

He stepped down the retractable stairs and then turned to help her down.

Just as she stood, her skirts flicked something onto the interior floor of the carriage.

"What was that?" she asked.

Drawing her skirt up, she screamed. "Oh my God, what is it, Jefferson?" She nearly leapt into his arms.

Jefferson reached inside the carriage and picked up the dead carcass of a nightingale. "What the hell is a dead bird doing in my new carriage?"

He turned it over and Caroline screamed again. "There's a hat pin stuck in its heart!" Her eyes shot to his. "Jefferson, this bird didn't just die. Someone killed it. Someone put it here. But why?"

"It's a warning," he said. "But of what? From whom?"

Caroline turned away. "Bury it, Jefferson. Maybe it's a prank of some kind."

Eerie chills coursed Jefferson's spine. Suddenly, he remembered too many stories his mother had told. Too many incantations. Too many rituals.

This is no prank. I have an enemy. He knows me.

All I have to do is find out who it is.

"I'll get rid of it," he said, taking her arm and walking her through the stacks of imported antiques and goods from India, China, France, Italy and Germany he had bought to fill his fifteen-thousand-square-foot mansion.

"Maybe it's from one of the workmen at your house. They've made no bones about the fact that your house has taken six years to build instead of two."

Jefferson's mind was reeling. He'd never had an overt enemy before. Only the specters of his past. Maureen. Hunting hounds looking for runaway slaves. The stuff of nightmares. But this was different. This was present. This was dangerous.

Jefferson knew it was most important to keep Caroline calm and in the dark. He made light of the matter. He would begin his inquiries later. "You have a point. They've been grumbling a lot this past year."

"And who can blame them? Why do you need two ballrooms? The dining room can now seat over fifty people. What are you planning to do with that house, Jefferson?"

"Entertain presidents," he said flatly.

"You're kidding."

He stopped abruptly. "I'm serious. I think our son would make a fine president."

She gasped. "What?" Suddenly, it all made sense to her. Jefferson had pressed himself to the limits ever since she'd returned to San Francisco with Lawrence. He built fortune after fortune, and she'd never asked why. She'd assumed he was ambitious. So was she. But she'd never dug into his motivations behind his work. It made sense. Jefferson had planned every pane of glass, every floor board, plank of burled oak paneling in the library, the furnishings for eight bedrooms, the gold fixtures for each of the ten bathrooms, the Tiffany gas light chandeliers, the marble fireplace mantles and the brocade wallpapers. The house was Greek Revival in architecture, but purely Jefferson Duke in spirit. It sat atop Nob Hill alone, aloof and yet bestowing a majestic aura especially at night when all the lights were burning. Caroline, like many other San Franciscans, could look out at night up to the hill and see those lights blazing and feel as if she could nearly touch the edge of his dream.

Jefferson made no bones about his aspirations for San Francisco's future. He wanted the city to push itself to the pinnacle of beauty, elegance and feast of spirit. He wanted Caroline to accompany him in his journey.

Now she knew precisely where he was heading. She wondered if she was truly ready to accompany him.

They walked out of the warehouse's side door and around to the front that faced Montgomery Street. Three masons were applying brick and framing out new windows for the façade. Jefferson had found that with the increase in retail trade, more fashionable shops were moving into the area. He moved his lumber stock to a location three blocks away and had begun subdividing his building into small shops. This side would soon be rented to a milliner from Paris. The shop next to it would be rented to a men's haberdasher. The third and final section he hadn't leased as yet. In two weeks, he intended to have the last of his things moved to the mansion and his shining carriage ensconced in his newly finished carriage house behind the mansion.

"A new restaurant just opened yesterday across the street. How about risking lunch with me?"

She smiled, forgetting about murdered nightingales and political futures. At this moment, she wanted only to be with Jefferson. "I'd love it."

Just as Caroline stepped off the wooden sidewalk, a black stallion came bolting down the unpaved street.

"Caroline, look out!" Jefferson yanked her back.

From a distance, Jefferson could see the rider. It was a woman, dressed in black. But this woman was not in mourning. There was no veil over her black hair and her dress was not a day dress, but a perilously low-cut ball gown.

The stallion's hooves pounded against the dried mud and bed of crushed sea shells and gravel in the street. The horse raced straight toward Jefferson and Caroline.

"The rider is out of control," Jefferson said to Caroline.

"She's not pulling to a halt at all. Why, she's even spurred the horse on!" Caroline said in shock as she backed into one of the bricklayers behind her, nearly knocking him over.

"What the hell?" The bricklayer then saw the rider, too. "She's heading straight for us!"

"Jefferson!" Caroline screamed. Her back was plastered against the newly bricked wall. The rider was obviously out of control. "We're going to be killed!"

Jefferson bolted around the hitching post hoping to run alongside the horse, grab its reins and stop the runaway steed.

Suddenly, the rider reined the horse to a perilously abrupt halt where it reared up on its hind legs and punched the air with his forelegs. Lather poured off the head and back of the abused horse. He neighed and whinnied and fought for control. But the rider was relentless and kept jerking the reins.

The stallion tried to unseat his tormentor, but she was obviously an expert horsewoman. Finally, the horse surrendered. He dropped his forelegs to the ground.

"Dolores!" Jefferson shouted when he saw her. "What in God's name are you trying to do?"

Though Jefferson had almost no direct encounters with Dolores over the years, he knew of the few occasions when she had come to San Francisco. The day she left for Spain, she'd come to his lumberyard and left a note for him since he was away on business. She remained in Spain for five years. Upon her return again, she'd come to visit, but Jefferson had been with Caroline that evening. She never wrote to him, he never communicated with her. Then last month he'd received a letter from her—a lengthy letter filled with pain, regret and anger. He realized that for Dolores, time had stood still.

She was obviously still in love with him.

He guessed he'd be seeing her, it was only a matter of time.

"You nearly got yourself killed!" he scolded her.

"As if you cared!" she spat.

Her hair was wild and blew in long tendrils around her face. Her eyes wore dark circles and her pale skin with its blue network of veins, so coveted by the Spanish, was puffy and lusterless. Her beauty had long ago abandoned her. Her head bobbed on her shoulders as if her neck had been broken. Her eyes were glassy and unfocused.

"Jefferson," Caroline called, coming away from the building, "help her. She looks—sick."

He went to her to help her down from her horse. She nearly fell into his arms. Then he knew.

"You're drunk," he said as he tried to steady her.

Dolores leaned into his embrace, making certain her breasts rubbed his chest. The thrill of his touch after all these years was more intoxicating than the wine she drank.

"Wine is my only friend," she said with slurred speech. "It's the perfect nunnery. I can go in and not be forced to speak with Father, who as everyone knows, I hate more than the devil. Besides, the wine helps me weave my past with you."

"Fantasies," Jefferson corrected.

"Yes, I'm drunk," she said, carefully forming her words on her thick tongue.

Caroline started to move closer, then thought better of it. This was a situation better handled by Jefferson.

"Why are you here?" he asked.

She looked up into his eyes. "Still the color of spring—those eyes. Haunting me all these years." She paused as a tear formed. Then, just as suddenly, her face contorted as her rage spewed from inside her. "You bastard!"

Crrrrraaaacckkk!!! She slapped him across the face.

Jefferson didn't flinch under the assault. He glared at her and when her hand came back for a second strike, his right arm snatched her wrist. "I think you've had enough. And so have I."

"Ha! You have no idea what I've been through. Or what's happened to me. You never cared about me!"

"I wanted you as a friend. You wanted something I couldn't give." He leaned forward, glaring into the angry dark pits of her eyes. "I think you've used me, Dolores."

"I? Used you?"

"Yes. You needed an excuse not to face life, and I won the honors." He thrust her hand back to her. "Why have you come here now, Dolores?"

She faltered. Her anger began to fizzle. Remorse took its place alongside self-pity. "It's your fault that my life is so unhappy." Soft sobs fluttered inside her throat. Then the pendulum of her mood swung back to hate again. She whirled on her foot. She faced Caroline, who straightened her shoulders, preparing herself for Dolores's attack.

"It was your slut who kept us apart." Dolores began walking toward Caroline. "You still sleep with him, don't you?"

Caroline walked boldly toward Dolores. "You're drunk, Dolores. You don't know what you're saying."

"Drunk or sober. It makes no difference."

Caroline walked up to her adversary and stood nearly nose to nose with her. "I love him. He loves me. He always has. I would give my life to be with him, but that hasn't been an option. But I don't go around using that as an excuse to destroy myself. You don't care about Jefferson. You tried to start vicious gossip about us years ago and it didn't work. You can't love anybody, Dolores, because you can't love yourself."

"Ha! I finally have it! From your own lips. A confession!" Dolores leaned toward the German bricklayers. She pointed to Caroline. "You hear what she says? She is his lover!" Dolores raised her arms in the air and shouted her words as she turned her head to the sun. She felt triumph blast through her brain like a trumpet.

"Go home, Dolores. Go back to Monterey."

Dolores grabbed Caroline's face in her hand and squeezed very hard.

Caroline's hand jerked Dolores's arm away from her just as Jefferson jumped to her defense. Caroline shot him a cautioning look.

"You bitch!" Dolores hissed.

Caroline kept her voice calm. "Go home. Leave us alone."

"I'll tell everyone what you have confessed!"

"Go ahead. Do that. That's what you're best at, isn't it? Or is it?" Caroline kept her voice steady as concern crept alongside her intonation. "Maybe you can love. Maybe I have underestimated you. Maybe you do love Jefferson so much you don't want to destroy him, and all that he has built for himself."

Dolores paused for a long moment as if she pondered Caroline's words seriously. "Destroy?" she whispered to herself. "I don't want to destroy anybody," she said to Caroline and then turned away. "Except myself."

Just then Jefferson took the reins of the horse and handed them to Dolores. "I'll help you back on the horse."

Dolores looked at him wistfully through alcohol-clouded eyes. She nodded her head and then took the reins. She allowed Jefferson to put his hand around her waist and hoist her onto the horse. She stuck her foot in the stirrup. She raised her head and Jefferson was reminded of the once-haughty beauty who had dazzled many a caballero. But that had been a different woman, a different world.

To Jefferson, Dolores symbolized the end of the romantic Spanish era. No longer did festivals or feast-day parades paint the city with bright colors. No Sunday picnics where the young girls would peer out from lacy mantillas and flirt with young men behind the backs of their duennas. The sound of castanets, sad Spanish guitars and the arrogant heels of flamenco dancers had faded completely in the past decade. Even the old bear fights and bullfights that took place at the Mission Dolores had been outlawed. What remained of the half-brutal, half-genteel aristocracy lived like Dolores and her family in Monterey. Or they were assimilated into the new "elegant" culture of San Francisco.

As Jefferson looked into Dolores's tears, he saw his own regret mirrored there. There was much beauty and wisdom in the old ways, yet men like Jefferson, impatient men, empire builders, had always been so willing to sweep away the old to make way for the new.

They all had all made mistakes.

"I wish we could have found a different way," he said when Dolores interrupted him.

"Never," she replied and bent down and touched his cheek. "I wanted it all. It was not mine to have." She peered at him for a long moment, then sat upright again and tugged on the horse's reins. As she cantered down the street, her back was straight and proud. She spurred her horse to a gallop, sped around the corner and then headed toward the hills. For a flash of a moment, she was young Dolores again, proud, independent and certain of her direction.

Jefferson went to Caroline. For a long moment they looked at each other, feeling the depth of their regret, but unable to speak. Words were inadequate.

"I'll take you back to the emporium."

"I can drive the buggy myself." She glanced over at the workers. "They may need you."

Jefferson was always surprised at Caroline's ability to read him like a book. He wanted time alone. This encounter with Dolores unlocked a cavern in his mind he'd long ago believed had been sealed. "Will I see you tonight?"

"Yes," she whispered, then went to the two-wheeled buggy with the black leather fold-down top and took the reins. She nudged the dray away from the hitching post and out into the street. She didn't turn her back, but only lifted her left arm in a controlled wave.

Jefferson couldn't help but to compare the two women. Both were proud of their heritage, their intelligence, their beauty, and both were independent as hell. *Spunk* was a word invented for both of them. So what twist of fate was it that made him fall in love with Caroline, already married, rather than Dolores? With Dolores he could have had a normal life with many children. She would have been equally as loving as Caroline, perhaps even more so. He would still have built the same business, invested in the same ventures, had the same friends, perhaps even more friends if the truth be known.

Why was it then that he'd had the misfortune to love a woman he could never have? Had he made a mistake? A dreadful mistake that not only caused Dolores to drink herself into oblivion, but also brought himself nothing but pain? And what of Lawrence? His decision had affected his son, too.

Jefferson watched Caroline's buggy disappear around the corner. At that moment, he believed no man had ever sinned as greatly as he.

A horse whinnied, then snorted loudly. The pair of drays prancing down the street pulling a new "turnout" suddenly stopped their canter and reared up on their hind legs as if they'd been spooked by a snake. Like a chain reaction down Montgomery Street, every horse whether tethered or not began snorting or bucking or both.

"What the hell is going on?" Jefferson asked aloud.

Dogs barked and raced past Jefferson, nearly knocking him over.

A woman screamed as a German shepherd shot past her and knocked a sack of brown-paper-wrapped packages out of her arms as she came out of Wilson's General Store. A little boy ran after the dog shouting his name.

"Come back here, King!" he yelled.

Just then, a roar like an awakening lion rumbled beneath the earth.

Jefferson felt the earth move, the ground shake, and his legs seemed to dance beneath his torso of their own volition. He looked at the sky. There was no thunder or lightning. No storm approached.

"Damnation!"

The barometer hanging on a nail next to the warehouse door fell to the ground and the precious glass shattered. The blue splattered tin mugs that sat on a display table outside Wilson's General Store across the street tumbled to the wooden sidewalk with a clatter and rolled into the street.

A church bell clanged irregularly.

Then like a chorus, the pedestrians began shouting and screaming en masse.

Jefferson's eyes shot back to the ground. Pieces of gravel and shell rolled back and forth and gyrated against each other. The earth quivered again.

The roar grew louder with a distinct chugging sound almost like the sound coming from the sidewheel steamer boat that came to dock twice a year. The earth moved again, and then just as abruptly as it began, it stopped.

Jefferson dropped to his knees and felt the earth with his hands. It was still as if nothing had happened. For a split-second he wondered if he were having one of his strange dreams again.

His eyes shot to his two bricklayers who were also on their knees with their arms over their heads. The last layer of uncemented brick had fallen to the wooden sidewalk. Otherwise, little else on his property had been disturbed.

He scurried to the two men. "Are you all right?"

"Yes, sir. We're fine."

"Check down this side of the street. Every shop. Make certain there are no fires. One building goes, we all go together."

"Yes, sir!"

"I'll check this side. Then we start with each house all the way up to Nob Hill. You got that?"

"We'll get others to help us."

"Do that," Jefferson said and then raced across the street to check on the boy with his dog and the woman with the packages. He went from store to store making certain no one was hurt. There were no fires.

Jefferson spent the rest of the day checking on friends and inspecting his new home on Nob Hill.

It wasn't until two days later that the residents of San Francisco received information that the most severe earthquake in recorded California history had hit in northern Los Angeles County. Three-story brick and wood build-ings and two-hundred-year-old trees had been felled. What San Francisco had experienced was a slight tremor and nothing more.

The earthquake made a lasting impression on Jefferson. He thought that for as long as he lived he would never hear a sound so frightening as that peculiar roar he heard. He knew there would never be a feeling as unsettling as the movement of the earth beneath his feet. For that split moment, and surely the tremor lasted no more than that, it was as if hell would open and devour him.

"Have I been judged and tried for loving Caroline?"

Or is it something else? A warning?

"Two warnings in one day. Obviously, one is man-made, the other is from God. But what are they telling me? And which should I fear most?"

Jefferson bounded down the hall to his private library. He unlocked the door hastily. The room was three times the size of his locked study in the old house. The burled oak shelves were waiting to be filled with books.

Right now there was only one thing Jefferson wanted to read. Over the fireplace hung his painting of Rachel.

Jefferson went to the portrait and looked up into his mother's eyes. As always happened, goose bumps covered his flesh. "I can feel you with me now, Mother."

Pressing the gilt edge of the frame, the painting sprung away from the wall and revealed a wall safe.

Jefferson spun the dial to the right and then to the left. A little door popped open. Gingerly, he withdrew a steel box that was locked with a padlock. He took a tiny brass key from his key ring and unlocked the box.

"The Rachel Papers," he said with awe.

Jefferson sat in the hunter-green leather wing chair, turned up the cranberry-colored gas lamp and read his mother's inscriptions and stories about his ancestry.

"The answers have to be in here," he said desperately to himself. Somewhere in the mists of his memory, he'd heard a story about a dead nightingale. But he couldn't remember if Rachel had written it down or if she'd simply told him.

The parchment was getting old. He had to be careful not to tear the pages or smudge them. Translations could rest on a single word blotted out.

In the section about healing herbs and voodoo spells, he saw nothing about a nightingale.

He pressed his fingers to his pounding temples. "But I remember something. What was it?"

Wafting back to his mind was the specter of truth. "It was Andrew Duke. And his wife Brenna. Yuala had seen the dead nightingale. But what did it signify?"

Suddenly, he remembered his mother's visitation in the mountains.

An enemy from across the sea. That's what she'd said.

He hates me because I'm a Duke.

"My God," he sucked in his breath. "I can feel this hatred. This is more than just one man's jealousy of another. This man thinks he's waging a holy war."

Sweat broke out across his forehead. "How can I fight this kind of evil? I'm only one man."

Contemplating this, he lit a fire in the fireplace. He glanced about the nearly empty room. He'd spent a king's ransom on furnishings but the house was so huge, it would take two more fortunes to finish it out. Someday, this house would be filled with the proper furnishings. He'd hoped that someday he'd hear Caroline's voice as she laughed at dinner guests' jokes.

He'd dreamed of watching Lawrence's children, his grandchildren, playing on the Persian rug or sitting at his feet while he read them stories.

Someday he would understand why Rachel gave her life for him to achieve his destiny. Someday he would know what his destiny was.

Today's events taught him that life was more precarious and precious than he'd thought. He was guilty of a false sense of security.

Quickly, Jefferson locked the papers back in the strongbox and put them in the wall safe.

"Safe," he said.

He thought of Caroline.

"If this devil wants to kill me because of my bloodline, then if I were to openly declare that Lawrence was my son . . . then I would jeopardize his future, possibly his life as well."

He looked at Rachel's portrait. "What kind of destiny is this, Mother? At every turn, when happiness is within my grasp, it's taken from me. If this foe is out there, then I have no choice but to keep my secrets secure."

If I marry Caroline, I'll have to watch my back and Lawrence's, too, for the rest of our lives.

twenty-five

Hither and thither spins
The windborne, mirroring soul;
A thousand glimpses wins,
And never sees a whole.

—MATTHEW ARNOLD
EMPEDOCLES ON ETNA, I, II, L. 82

Caroline inspected the muddied hem of her black watch-plaid wool skirt as she hurriedly entered her house. She pulled off her gloves thinking that only moments ago Jefferson had held them and begged her to stay with him. Lost in her thoughts of Jefferson, she unbuttoned her three-quarter-length black wool coat as she went to the fire to warm herself.

She didn't see William sitting in the wingback chair, his balding head bent over a thick stack of papers in his lap. His breathing was so shallow that half the time Caroline didn't know if he were dead or alive.

She glanced at the silver teapot on the tray next to him. "Is there any tea left, William?"

As usual, he didn't greet her with a welcome, not even a grunt or grumble. He was unnervingly silent.

"William?"

"If you'd returned at a more proper time, you would have been able to share tea with me."

Caroline's jaw dropped. This was the most articulate response she'd received from William in twenty years.

"I was unavoidably detained. I've been checking on the competition. Did you know that Pandolfini is importing alabaster statuary, oils, vases, tripods and mantle ornaments? Bonestell and Williston have the most beautiful paintings I've seen in ten years. If I could just go to Italy myself and see some of these things, I could make wonderful purchases."

"Stop it, Caroline!" William growled, still not lifting his head.

"What?"

"You'd drive us into ruin in an instant." Finally he raised his head and peered at her over the edge of his pince-nez. "If there are any trips to be made, I'll do the buying."

Caroline nearly bit her tongue to stifle her rage. More than anything she wanted to pick up the silver pot and smash it over his head. "You spend nights looking for errors in the accounting books I've already reconciled. You double-check inventories I've already counted. You can't wait to find a mistake I've made. It's your passion, William. You're so full of yourself and so insecure you can't breathe. You demean my abilities with every move you make. Do you have any idea how foolish you look to me? To others? You act as if I don't have a brain in my head. And after all these years you have never, ever found one single fault in my figures or in my business strategies. You do not run this business, William, I do!"

Carefully, William took off his glasses and poured out the last dregs of tea. "You think that because I allow it."

"You exasperate me beyond everything!" She threw her hands up in the air and let them fall heavily to her sides.

"No more than you tire me. If I'd let you have your way, you would have run us into the ground years ago. You think this spending spree will go on here forever? Don't you pay attention to the newspapers? The North and South are at each other's throats. I predict there will be a war."

She rolled her eyes. "You're stating the obvious."

"Everything will come to a standstill. War does that to a country, you know."

"Not out here it won't. San Franciscans will still be going around the Horn to Europe. People who want to avoid the war will flock here. We're neutral ground. The city will grow beyond our imaginations. Women will still want Paris fashions. Their teas, spices and silks will still come from China. This is an international city, William. Your problem is that you have no vision, William."

"And you do, I suppose?"

"Yes. I read other papers besides the stack in your lap. I don't suppose you caught the small mentions in the *Alta California* that silver has been discovered?"

William yawned. "What's silver got to do with us? This is insignificant."

"There are six mines now, not just the Fraser River mine. You've got to prepare for the future, William."

"I suppose you are preparing for the future?" he said in that tone of exasperation and half-boredom that perpetually set Caroline's nerves on edge.

"I want a divorce." Caroline blurted out and then stared at him waiting for a reaction. She'd been planning to say this for quite a while, actually, though she didn't know why she'd said it just then.

Suddenly, she saw her life for what it was, a dowdy, ill-constructed affair with little to claim that was redeemable. She gave nothing to William except an old worn-out hatred that should have been applied to her father. It was time she attached her emotions to their proper owners.

His small eyes narrowed beneath the shadows of overgrown graying eyebrows. "You may not have one."

"Pardon me?" she gasped. She couldn't possibly have heard him correctly.

"There will be *no* divorce." He stood with a stiff, ramrod-straight back. He gave his chin a jerk like a military tyrant just before sending men off to a fatal battle. "There has never been a divorce in the Mansfield family, and I don't intend to be the first to carry that stigma to my grave. What's more, it was your father's dying wish that I care for you all your life, not just the part of it that was convenient for you. Though it's obvious to me that nothing is sacred to you. No promise is too great to break."

He tossed down the stack of papers he'd so carefully and painstakingly perused earlier. "Isn't it enough you've been the laughingstock of this town for your outspokenness on women's rights? You've campaigned for everything from an arboretum to cleaning up the Bowery, to the necessity of sanitation and paved streets. You stick your head into politics when you should be at home caring for your child."

"I take care of Lawrence. He wants for nothing."

"I didn't say he did."

"You insinuated. You're the one who hasn't given him an ounce of affection since the day he was born."

"He's a Mansfield. That's enough!"

"You arrogant fool! Lawrence is a person. So am I! You can't go through life treating people as if we're like the china vases you sell."

"Why not?" he bellowed. "My father did!"

Caroline stared at him, her blue eyes blazing. Suddenly, when she realized the impact of his admission, William saw pity film over her eyes. He was ashamed.

"William . . ."

He heard the pity in her voice and it sickened him. "No divorce. Everything will go on as it has. Nothing will change. I'll make the business decisions. You and Lawrence will continue to live under this roof." He paused, picked up his papers, shoved them into a leather valise and thrust it under his arm. He looked at her. She saw the tremendous mountain of unspoken words in the depths of his eyes. Her heart nearly broke for this man she barely knew. "Even if you walked out of here, Caroline, I'd never allow Lawrence to live anywhere but in this house."

She'd never counted on the fact that William would make a demand for Lawrence. He'd never wanted her son before. He was doing this just to control her. "William," she said softly, "he's fifteen. It won't be long until he finishes school and goes out to lead a life of his own."

His lips formed a smirk. "He won't leave. He's loyal to me. Believe me, Caroline, he won't follow you to your lover's house."

Caroline felt her knees quiver and the floor seemed to shake beneath her. She wondered if another earthquake had hit. She watched him. She felt a searing jab rend her heart in half, then slice through her stomach.

He knows? What a fool I've been! I thought Jefferson and I had been discreet.

Dolores! That's how he knows. The whole town knows.

A huge burning coal seared her throat closed so she couldn't speak. Her heart rammed itself back and forth between her ribs, bent on annihilation. She'd never wanted him to know. She had wanted to spare him the pain.

She looked into his eyes.

But William has no pain. He feels nothing. My God, he's just as empty as I'd suspected.

Most frightening of all, she saw there was not a shred of love. None for her. None for Lawrence.

They had always been William's possessions. He was telling her they always would be.

"How long have you known?"

"For a week."

"A week?" Caroline repeated hoarsely.

A week? But Dolores only came to town today.

"What happened last week?"

"I had a visit from Dolores Sanchez the day you went to the seamstress about your 'white work.' That was probably a lie, too."

"No! I ordered those petticoats and undergarments for the new ladies section in the emporium. I told you that."

"Liar!"

"William, listen to me. Dolores is a drunk. She's unbalanced."

He waved his arm at her. "It doesn't matter. I believed her when she said you were with Duke then."

"She's jealous."

"For God's sake, give me some credit. I can't stand it when you lie. You do it so badly. You've already confessed to your sin. Leave it at that."

Sin? She'd never thought her love for Jefferson was a sin. Her pain was deep, biting and swarming inside her, but it was not directed toward her relationship with Jefferson. "You're wrong. It's our life, William, that is the sin. You don't love me and never have."

"Love? What's that got to do with it? This is a marriage!"

She leveled her eyes at him. "That's why I had to find love someplace else!"

"Fine. Just make certain you keep it there." He glared at her for a moment. Then he turned and left the room.

Caroline watched after him. She shivered, thinking a cold wind had rushed through the room. Then she realized the icy feeling came from the emptiness in William's heart.

"Don't worry, William, I'll make certain none of my love invades your territory," she said quietly to herself. She bent over, took the brass shovel and scooped up fresh coals and tossed them on the fire. She held her hands close to the glowing red stones, but felt no warmth. Something told her it would take more than a fire to thaw the curtain of ice she'd drawn over her heart.

Chinatown

Lon Su was five years old when he received the first words of praise from his father, Nan-Yung. It was not his ability to speak English, nor his expertise with the abacus, nor his ability to distinguish colors that pleased his father. Lon Su won honors and accolades because he had bested eight-year-old Lu Wang in a fistfight behind the Oriental Hotel.

Lon Su's right eye wore a small bruise, but Lu Wang returned to his parents with a bloody nose and a bruised eye.

"You've made me proud," Nan-Yung said to Lon Su as he watched Yin place a cheesecloth filled with soaked tea leaves over the bruise. "One day you'll lead my bodyguards. I've always known you'll be worthy of running my business for me. Now you've shown me this."

Lon Su was unsure of all that his father was saying. He'd spent most of his time with his mother, Yin. She was the one who had taught him English, to read Chinese characters, and to add and subtract. But as the years passed and Lon Su's hopes for a brother became slim with each of his mother's drops, he, like his father, had less and less respect for her.

These drops, or miscarriages, were always male, Lon Su had overheard the midwife say to his father. And always, he heard the many curses his father placed on the fates and the gods of the new world for denying him sons.

Many times, these curses made Lon Su feel bad, as if he were not good enough to be the only son. Many nights Lon Su went to bed and wondered why he was not worthy. What was missing inside him that made his father want another son, a different son, a better son?

Then Lon Su made up his mind to find the things that would make his father think he was worthy. Lon Su learned that as long as he clung to his mother's side, he would know nothing of the world. He learned to eavesdrop. He learned how to slip down into the catacombs that were built beneath the city and investigate his father's business. He learned that the House of Su had built extensive opium dens that were frequented by many Chinese.

More important, Lon Su learned that his father had constructed a new opium den that was smaller than the others though furnished more elaborately. This was a special place in Chinatown, because here Nan-Yung was the first Chinese man to sell opium to the whites.

Lon Su crouched behind a huge potted fern as he eavesdropped on his father and one of his den managers.

"See that their pipes contain twice the opium as we give the Chinese."

"But Nan-Yung, you will lose profits."

"You have little vision, Lu Tang. In the future, the whites will demand even more opium to take them to heaven as their addiction grows. I've seen this happen in China."

"You are wise, Nan-Yung."

Nan-Yung nodded. "Cater to the whites. Do not steal from them when they sleep. Treat them well."

"I'll do this, Nan-Yung." He bowed.

Nan-Yung started to walk away and then stopped. "You put the nightingale in the home of Jefferson Duke?"

"His home is guarded by Irish thugs he employs from his lumberyard. His possessions, they say, are very expensive. I found a way into his warehouse. I put the bird in his new carriage."

"And you left the stake in the bird's heart?"

"Yes. Do you think he will understand that his death is imminent?"

"It doesn't matter. He will be dead soon. Remember that if he comes to the den, cater to him. Then come get me immediately."

"He is special, Nan-Yung?" he asked, malevolence filling his eyes.

"Very special. I wish to kill him myself."

Lon Su gasped. He could hardly believe his ears. His father wanted to kill this white man Duke. Lon Su knew he could not ask his father about Jefferson Duke and what he'd done to anger Nan-Yung. Lon Su had been forbidden to go to the catacombs, and he certainly would be punished for eavesdropping. But his curiosity swirled inside his brain like trapped bats.

Duke's crime against my father must be terrible and greatly forbidden by heaven to deserve death.

Backing away from the scene, Lon Su was filled with fear. He couldn't get out of the catacombs fast enough.

Down the dirt-walled tunnels he ran and then scampered up the ladder to the street entrance.

His chest heaving and out of breath, he looked up at the sun. "If I were to discover the truth about Jefferson Duke and why he must die, I would know as much as my father. I would have power."

He smiled to himself.

"I am very good at hiding myself. I know many of my father's secrets. I could find a way into the Duke house. I could kill nightingales and leave them for my father. I could be of value to my father."

Lon Su slipped down the alleyway, darting between lines of drying clothes from the Chinese laundries. He was in a hurry. He knew precisely where to go and how to steal nightingales from the vendors.

Breathing deeply, he felt strong.

Lon Su was only a young boy and already he'd discovered his destiny.

twenty-six

I acknowledge the Furies, I believe in them,
I have heard the disastrous beating of their wings.

—THEODORE DREISER
TO GRANT RICHARDS

Dolores Sanchez's heart was slashed, bleeding and in desperate need of healing. She believed she'd done everything in her power to make Jefferson love her. She'd thrown herself at him for years, then alternated with long, painful absences hoping he'd yearn for her the way that she pined away for him. She felt a wringing of her soul, a deep guttural pain that ached more intensely with the passing of each hour. When she was away from him, time seemed to stand still. She felt suspended in a place of continual emptiness.

Jefferson's latest rejection had nearly sent her over the edge of sanity. She tried not to drink these days, realizing that dulling the pain with alcohol was only a temporary healing. She needed to go to the source of herself, dig out her demons and crush Jefferson's image from her mind and heart once and for all.

The only thing that could cure her now was hope, hope that she could make a life for herself without him in it. Dolores had spent so many years of her life wanting a man she could never have that she was afraid she'd become a slave to pain. She didn't understand why she wasn't meant to be happy, only that she was miserable. For the first time, she wanted to end her misery.

However, Dolores didn't know where to turn or how to find the cure she needed. She needed a friend.

While Dolores was in San Francisco, she stayed with her sister-in-law, Angelica Peralta Sanchez, who, like many other daughters of the old Spanish barons, had left the rancheros when she married and now lived in a huge mansion on Rincon Hill. Dolores sat in the plushly decorated salon with Angelica, who was droning on about the changes in the city.

"Have you been to the City of Paris yet? It is the most fashionable store in San Francisco, on Geary and Stockton streets. It is owned and managed by the grandson of Felix Paul Verdier and, of course, the Verdiers are identified with the modern movement to join French and American welfare and economies."

Dolores frowned as she lifted a cup of hot tea to her lips. "Since when do you care about the French?"

"Since they make only the most incredible clothes in the world. You can be such an ostrich, Dolores!" Angelica said defensively. "Things are changing in San Francisco. I've been to Washington Hall to see both *The Wife* and the marvelous farce, *Sentinel*, performed."

Dolores put her teacup on the marble-topped table and sighed heavily as she looked out the window. Nothing had changed for Dolores. Jefferson's handsome face and flashing green eyes haunted her wherever she looked. "Tell me about the other amusements in town," Dolores said, hoping to find even a moment of distraction from her obsession.

Angelica looked to the hallway to make certain none of the servants were about, then she leaned over conspiratorially toward Dolores. "The newest rage is found in Chinatown."

"Truly?"

"Yes. There's a woman there by the name of Yin Ch'u in one of the laundries who tells fortunes so accurately, half the ladies in San Francisco swear by her. The other half are afraid of her and say she's a witch."

"And what do you believe?"

Angelica's brown eyes twinkled. "I know for a fact she's a treasure. She told me over a year ago I was to have another child. Last week I discovered I'm carrying again."

Dolores looked at her happy sister-in-law who lived in a beautiful home and had a husband who, once married, seemed to have found happiness in being married. He loved her and they had two beautiful and healthy children. Life wasn't fair, Dolores thought and then burst into tears. "I'm happy for you," Dolores lied. She was crying for herself. Crying for her unborn children. She'd been young, foolish and stupid on a long-ago day: the day she fell in love with Jefferson.

Angelica went to Dolores and put her arms around her. Angelica was wiser than Dolores gave her credit. "You must learn to let him go, Dolores. If you don't, no other man can come along to take his place. And I know there's someone waiting for you. San Francisco is filled with handsome, exciting, and these days very, very rich men."

"I'm too old. Haven't you heard? I'm an old maid. It was one thing to convince Father to abandon his plans for my marriage to my cousin. Then once he agreed to let me go to Spain and I came back unmarried, he realized my will is stronger than his. I want Jefferson. I'll always want him."

"Shhh. Let me take you to Yin. She can tell you all sorts of things that might make you happy."

Dolores wiped her eyes and sniffed. "Do you really think she can help?"

Angelica smiled. "I think anything is possible in this world. It couldn't hurt, could it?"

"I suppose not."

The two beautiful Spanish women rode in a black-lacquered carriage that had been used for two years by one of the city's newest gold barons. It was lushly upholstered in rich cream-colored velvet seats, quilted cream-colored brocade walls with solid gold handles and carriage lights. The four horses were black-as-night stallions wearing bronze and gold tassels and head-dresses. Dolores thought the livery was ostentatious and in bad taste, but she was pea-green with envy. If she were married to Jefferson, she'd be riding in his new black carriage, she thought woefully, looking out the window at all the new construction.

San Francisco was growing by leaps and bounds. Street after street boasted gas lamps now, though nothing had been paved. They rode past the post office and Dolores saw a woman wearing hoop skirts so large they would not go between the posts. She looked like a parachute dangling from a Montgolfier Brothers' balloon caught between tree branches. Dolores laughed at the sight.

They rode up the narrow streets of Chinatown to the laundry on Grant Avenue owned by Nan-Yung Su.

Yin was reading a fortune for a particularly portly San Franciscan matron who wore more yards of strung diamonds around her fat neck than Dolores wore of silk over her French hoops.

Nan-Yung nodded to Dolores and Angelica as they entered the laundry. He knew they were not maids from one of the big houses because they were dressed too expensively, but neither were they the English. Women of the old Spanish gentry did not come to his shop often, because fortune-telling was considered a sin against the Catholic Church, he'd been told. It wasn't the first time he'd witnessed sin.

"You want see Yin?" he'd learned to ask in English.

"Yes, very much," Angelica said to Nan-Yung and then looked over at Yin, whose eyes were filled with a look of recognition. The last time Angelica had come to the shop, Nan-Yung hadn't been around. She felt uncomfortable in his presence, but she didn't know why. She liked and respected Yin, but this man was strange. Unsettling.

"Perhaps we should come back another day."

"You stay!" Nan-Yung made a gesture to Yin and she nodded.

The fat matron was demanding that Yin tell her more about her husband's gold mine. She wanted to know precisely how much more money she could count on and how could she get him to stop drinking.

"The river of money you have enjoyed will run dry in less than a year. Your husband spends a great deal more than he tells you. Save your money or you will have to sell your jewels. Put them away. In ten years, you will only have the money you have secreted away. Use your wits to save yourself," Yin slid a surreptitious glance at Nan-Yung, who was still studying the two Spanish women. Not knowing as much English or any Spanish, as Yin had learned, Nan-Yung was at a disadvantage. Yin made certain he didn't learn the advice she gave others.

Yin closed the woman's palm.

"Is that all?" the fat woman asked angrily.

"It's enough." Yin opened her own palm for payment and the woman pressed a gold coin to her flesh.

"Thank you. I'll be back."

"Yes, you will," Yin smiled.

The fat woman barely glanced at Dolores and Angelica as she walked out, thinking in her mind that her Anglo-Saxon heritage was superior to the Latin women, and not once did she see the disdain in their eyes for her crude manners and lack of nobility.

Dolores approached Yin warily. Suddenly, she was quite unsure about this decision. Soothsayers were forbidden by the Church, the padres had always told her. Dolores hadn't paid attention to their warnings because she'd never thought she'd have need for a fortune-teller, yet here she was.

"Don't be afraid. I won't charge too much," Yin said as she watched Nan-Yung go back to his file keeping behind the front counter. She knew the only reason he was out front today was because two of their day workers had taken ill with the influenza that seemed to move from family to family in Chinatown like a stealthy, silent serpent. She was glad the evil disease had not come to visit the house of Su.

Dolores sat down and looked at Yin. She saw clear silver lights dancing in Yin's dark eyes. Dolores had never experienced such a sensation of calm and anticipation at the same time. She was intrigued. "What do I do first?"

"Ask what's in your heart," Yin said. "But first I'll tell you that you've had great sadness in your life. You have no children, though you want one."

"First, I must have a husband, wouldn't you say?" Dolores laughed cryptically.

"You're married in your heart but not on paper?" Yin asked.

"You know this?" Dolores was shocked as Yin nodded. "Then can you tell me if I'll ever be wed to Jefferson Duke?"

At the mention of the name of her husband's most dreaded enemy, the air current in the room seemed to freeze.

Nan-Yung had not been listening to this silly woman's fortune being told. All he ever cared about was that the stream of women coming to his wife kept moving and that they all had money. But to hear Jefferson Duke's name mentioned by this beautiful woman must properly be hailed as fate shining upon him once again. Good fortune had made his employees sick in order that he would be in this place at this very hour in order to hear these all-powerful and life-altering words.

Nan-Yung pretended to make his characters on the laundry cards, but all the while he was listening intently to every word Dolores said.

"You love this man?" Yin asked.

"With all my heart. I'd give my soul to be married to him. To have his child. To know what it's like to be loved by him. What I don't understand is why I feel this way. It's as if I'm possessed."

"Not at all. It's just that you have memories of him from a past life together when you were married. But in that life you were not faithful to him. You denied him children. Therefore, he denies them to you this time."

"A past what?"

"Life. In another place. A hundred or more years ago. France, I think it was. Yes. You like things like that. Fine, golden furnishings and clothes."

Angelica laughed. "She spends fortunes on clothes. Elaborate gowns and jewels."

"Yes, I see you were part of the French court. That's why you are so attached to this man. You think you're still married to him."

"I don't understand any of this."

"It doesn't matter. Facts are facts. Your soul understands. I can teach you these things in time."

"And how much will that cost?" Dolores asked.

"I'm only asking for gold. Not your soul. That you seem to be giving away for free."

Dolores sighed. "What can I do?"

Yin knew Nan-Yung would beat her if she didn't ask as many questions as possible, and yet she already knew this woman's fate. "He loves another, but he is not married to her. In that you must take solace. He belongs to no woman."

Dolores slammed her fist on the wooden table. "But I want him!"

Yin closed her eyes to the wave of angry energy she felt shooting toward her from Dolores's heart. "He's not your destiny."

Tears filled Dolores's eyes. She hadn't realized until that very moment how much store she'd put in this woman's words in such a short period of time. When she'd gone to Angelica's house she'd been filled with hopelessness. Then for a brief moment she'd felt hope again. Now, even the fortuneteller was saying that she and Jefferson would never be one. Dreams of holding Jefferson in her arms, having him make love to her, plant his seed inside her, vanished into a bittersweet haze. Dolores looked at Yin through the fog of her broken dreams and the wall of tears. Her life was over.

"Is there nothing I can do?"

"You must be very careful when you leave here. You're sad now, but you will become angry. Because anger is familiar to you, you are not wary of it. This anger will cause you to take chances, and you must not do that. Take heed and caution this night. When you're tempted to walk in the moonlight, don't. When you are tempted to race through the forest on your mighty horse, don't. Watch the shadows around you. I see much danger wherever you go." Yin's eyes were vacant and her voice had dropped an octave deeper, making her words sound as if they were spoken from the bottom of a well.

Dolores was frightened and her hands began to shake. Her mouth went dry as she stared at Yin with fear-filled eyes.

Suddenly, Angelica could stand it no more. She reached out and put her hand on Dolores's shoulder. "I think we should leave."

"I've heard enough bad things to last a lifetime. I came here because Angelica said you would help me, Yin," Dolores said with a quiver to her voice.

Yin nodded. "I'm trying to help you."

Dolores took out a gold coin and put it on the table. "Jefferson and I may not be married, but I know that if he searched his heart, he'd find deep feelings for me. No one will ever be able to tell me otherwise."

Yin's eyes were pleading when she looked at Dolores. "Take caution with your actions. Guard against your impetuosity. It'll be your ruin."

Dolores stood and turned away from Yin. "Please take me out of here, Angelica. I wish I'd never come here. Promise me you won't come back, either."

Angelica simply nodded as they walked quickly through the door.

Nan-Yung shuffled his leather and silk slippers against the wooden floor as he moved rapidly out from behind the counter and locked the door behind the two women. He turned to Yin. "Tell me all you saw."

She looked away from him as he scooped up the gold coins and deposited them in his trouser pocket. "She's the most unhappiest of all women I've ever seen."

"Jefferson is not good to his woman," Nan-Yung smiled.

"She's not his woman."

"Bah!" Nan-Yung trusted nothing his wife said. "I know that he must have a woman. This is the one."

Yin decided right then it was time to mislead Nan-Yung. Perhaps if she told him what he wanted to hear instead of telling him the truth, then she could control her own destiny with more power, more force, more assurance. "And if she were Jefferson's woman?" She baited him.

Nan-Yung realized he'd been right all along. He was not pleased that Yin would choose to deliberately lead him from the path of truth. He realized he must be more careful with his own wife than with even his enemies. "As his woman she would share in his destiny, would she not? Just as you do?"

"Yes," Yin replied, not knowing where he was leading with his questions.

Nan-Yung went to the door and locked it. He put out the *Closed* sign.

"Come, wife. Let us rest and eat. This work is taxing for you as it is for me."

* * * *

Dolores couldn't sleep that night. As always, visions of Jefferson invaded her dreams and kept her from the rest she needed. She went to the window and gazed at the full moon. Huge dark clouds scudded across the silver-drenched night sky like flocking birds on the wing.

"Jefferson," she said his name softly, reverently, making herself conjure his face yet one more time.

She touched her breast and felt her sensitive nipple harden. Like a flash-fire, her body heat spread in thick waves down her chest to her belly, then down her legs and up her thighs like a lover's tongue. She spread her legs ever so slightly and then opened herself to her own hand. She imagined it was Jefferson touching her there, feeling her wetness as it slipped out of her body and onto her fingertips. Her heartbeat increased and like the strong muscle it was, it slammed against her chest wall, pulsing then ramming.

"Just like you should be doing inside me, my love," Dolores said to the vision of her ghostly lover.

Dolores knew she couldn't keep a bridle on her passion much longer. She needed a drink. She went to the cabinet beside her bed where she'd hidden the bottle of port that everyone in the household knew she drank almost nightly. It wasn't the days that were so difficult for her, but the nights when she could pretend her visions of Jefferson were real.

She swallowed a mouthful of the sweet, thick Madeira port and went back to the window. She flung her head back and sucked the neck of the bottle letting the alcohol slide down her throat. How she wished it were Jefferson she were drinking.

Angry at herself, angry at life, she flung the empty port bottle to the floor.

She peeled the silk nightgown from her swollen and untouched breasts and threw it over the chair. She dressed quickly in her dark chocolate-brown velvet riding skirt and a white long-sleeved blouse. She tied her waist-length black hair with a brown ribbon and shoved her feet into a pair of brown leather riding boots.

She left her room, raced down the carpeted spiral staircase and out the back door of the house to the riding stables where her brother's stallion was bedded down for the night.

Nocturnal rides were not unusual for Dolores. She often went riding, but that was in the country. She was in town now. She would ride in the park down the hill and then perhaps out to the Presidio where the eucalyptus trees scented the sea air.

She saddled the horse and mounted him easily. This horse was stronger than the one she was used to on her father's ranchero. Her brother had always liked his horses with spirit. She rode down the gravel-covered drive and out into the street. The horse seemed to know the way, and so she let him have full rein.

As she rode, Dolores's mind was still filled with thoughts of Jefferson. She could still feel his hands on her breasts as they strained against the fabric of her blouse. Even though she'd never done more than steal a kiss from Jefferson, her imagination made her believe she knew what it was like to make love with him.

So immersed in her fantasies was she that she did not see the sinister dark shadows following her. She did not notice the smallness of the men, nor their black clothing nor the queues at the back of their heads.

Dolores rode to the Presidio and raced the horse, challenging him with jumps over the enormous eucalyptus tree trunks that seemed to snake out of the ground and back inside like undulating sea serpents.

From out of nowhere three of Nan-Yung's henchmen appeared and frightened the stallion. The horse jerked to a halt, reared up on its hind legs and batted the air while whinnying loudly. Still Dolores did not see the men, their dark silhouettes fading easily into the shrubbery.

Dolores fought for her balance, but the horse was strong and determined to rid himself of his rider. Finally, she fell to the ground.

Stunned, Dolores did not see the three men circle around her until it was too late. The ugliest one with the menacing black eyes and foul-smelling breath approached her from the front with a knife. She didn't realize he was just the decoy.

It was the largest of the three who padded up from behind her, grabbed her by the throat and snapped her neck as easily as one cracks a wishbone at Thanksgiving.

Dolores's eyes dropped shut.

She found happiness in oblivion.

She found a world where she didn't have to wait for Jefferson Duke to return her love anymore.

—twenty-seven—

When it came night, the white waves paced to and fro in the moonlight, and the wind brought the sound of the great sea's voice to the men on shore, and they felt that they could be interpreters.

—STEPHEN CRANE
THE OPEN BOAT

San Francisco—1857–1865

Jefferson stood over Dolores's grave on the day of her burial. Though the authorities deemed Dolores's death an accident, Jefferson's intuition warned him that there was more to the story than they all knew. He had no evidence. He had no theory. It was simply that something about her death didn't sit well in the marrow of his bones.

Jefferson had no claim to the woman except that he considered her a friend. He wondered idly if her spirit was strong enough and determined enough to "visit" him the way his mother did from time to time.

"Your daughter will always exemplify 'The Beautiful Days' to me," he said to the aging Don Miguel.

Don Miguel nodded sadly as he shook Jefferson's hand. "I wonder, do you think I was wrong?"

"Wrong?"

"She made no secret of her love for you. I believed as my father did and his father before him. We are Castilian. But now my daughter is dead. The old ways cannot bring her back, can they?"

"No, Don Miguel," Jefferson looked past the eucalyptus trees. "She will never come back. But she lives, if only in our memory of her."

The old man turned away from Jefferson and led his family away from the grave. Jefferson waited while a procession of the old dons, their wives and children followed Don Miguel.

Jefferson couldn't help remembering how life used to move more slowly and was savored like fine wine by them all when he'd first come to California.

Thunder rolled in the distance as lightning struck the ground not far from the cemetery. It seemed befitting that the heavens cried down on Dolores today, he thought.

"Mr. Duke," Brian Kelly called, racing up to him. "We have to leave before it starts raining, sir." Brian handed Jefferson a newspaper to shield his head from the rain.

"Yes, we must hurry," he replied, walking quickly behind his driver to the carriage.

Jefferson shut the door and opened the rain-splattered newspaper. "My God, the war is only getting worse."

Jefferson remembered that on April 13, 1860, the Confederates took Fort Sumter. The pony-express rider who brought the news to San Francisco made the trip in three hours less time than normal. He jumped from his horse and in chalk letters he scrawled out the message on the blackboards in front of all the newspaper offices. The Confederate sympathizers in the city were in the minority and though they created two secret organizations, The Knights of the Golden Circle and the Knights of the Columbian Star, they never stood a chance to grab a foothold because Jefferson Duke spearheaded the Union sympathizers.

The heavy rains that spring were more a topical issue than war to most of the city. The "Willows" pleasure gardens at Mission, Valencia, Seventeenth and Eighteenth streets, were washed away, causing most families a great deal of distress because so many had enjoyed the lawns, gardens, willow-bordered stream, aviary, merry-go-round, sea-lion pond and zoo. There was more concern over where families would take their leisure than which side of the Civil War struggle to support.

Through the war years, Jefferson's roots were never unearthed, but when he spoke at a public meeting or political rally, there was no mistaking his sentiments. By the Fourth of July, 1860, there was no question the city was overwhelmingly Union. The city was festooned in red, white and blue banners, flags and flowers for the big parade that Jefferson helped organize.

Few men took up the war cause, and most San Franciscans only read about the battles across two sets of mountain ranges or around the Horn, depending upon the mode of travel chosen. San Francisco was busy building itself up while the rest of the country tore itself apart.

Of more importance to San Francisco than the war was the construction of the Central Pacific, Western Pacific and Southern Pacific railroads. The four chief railroad builders, Leland Stanford, Mark Hopkins, Collis Potter Huntington and Charles Crocker, had the vision to realize the vastness of the new wealth they would bring to the state.

Jefferson Duke was not only one of their strongest supporters, but he was a very quiet silent partner.

In 1859, Jefferson bought two lumber mills in the Oregon Territory two days after he had attended a ball at the home of General and Mrs. Irwin McDowell where he'd met all four of the railroad tycoons and learned of their plans.

Jefferson easily secured a contract from them to supply railroad ties and lumber for the building of the railroad. Because he arranged for the lumber to be directly shipped to the railroad building sites, few in San Francisco knew about Jefferson's sideline business, which stood to make him nearly as rich as the railroad barons themselves. Purposefully, Jefferson told no one, not even Caroline. He wanted to speak to Lawrence first.

Lawrence was twenty-two years old when Jefferson approached him about working for him. In a hotel dining room, Jefferson said, "I think steaks are in order, Lawrence."

"And a Bordeaux, don't you think?"

Jefferson smiled and slapped him good-naturedly on the back. "You're learning, son. With half the Atlantic sea coast under blockade, it seems anything and everything French or Italian finds its way to San Francisco."

"Damn the bad luck," Lawrence laughed. "But I've nothing more I'd rather spend my money on."

"Good, then we'll toast your graduation from Harvard. It seems only yesterday I was standing on the dock, watching you sail away on the *Alta California*."

"I'll never forget Mother crying. I've never seen her cry."

"She's a strong woman, but she missed you tremendously. You were her life."

"I missed her as well."

"But not as much," Jefferson offered.

"Probably not. I was busy," Lawrence smiled.

Jefferson remembered watching Lawrence leave from a distance. He had waited alone in his carriage at the end of the pier near the warehouse, out of sight to avoid detection. Caroline and William had left once the ship moved away from the pier, but Jefferson had remained.

Just as the anchor was hoisted and they were ready to leave, Lawrence spotted Jefferson's carriage hidden from his father's view. Lawrence purposefully stood at the ship's side and waved to Jefferson. Jefferson got out of his carriage and stood in the sunlight, his eyes locked on his son. Lawrence did not move but remained in Jefferson's full view, letting him know he appreciated his loyalty and love. From a distance, Jefferson hadn't seen the tears in Lawrence's eyes, but he'd felt them. They shared a deep bond that went beyond blood and parentage. They were one in their hearts.

Jefferson had waited until the ship had sailed out of the harbor and into open sea. It was nearly sunset when his driver finally asked him if he cared to leave. Jefferson had leaned wearily back against the velvet cushions where he remembered making love to Caroline when the carriage was new.

"Yes, take me home."

Jefferson hated the distance that society and propriety put upon himself and his only son. His inability to tell Lawrence the truth was a more painful bondage than slavery. But he loved Caroline so deeply, he complied.

"I have a business proposition for you, Lawrence," Jefferson said with a smile as he looked at the gleaming head full of brown hair Lawrence wore long around his clear-skinned face. He had a strong jaw, straight nose and a high forehead, and though he somewhat resembled Jefferson, as a grown young man, he no longer resembled Caroline as much as he had as a child. Lawrence was his own individual, and it showed in his face and his personality. Except for the green eyes, which were an exact match for Jefferson's, Lawrence looked as if he'd fashioned himself by his own hand.

Lawrence lifted the wine glass, twirled the red wine against the sides of the glass, inhaled the bouquet and then carefully tasted it. "I'm not interested in running your stores, Jefferson. I want to see the world. *All* the world. Now that I've traveled away from San Francisco, I realize how much travel appeals to me."

Jefferson laughed. "But you've only been to Boston. What could you know of travel?"

"I didn't stay in Boston all the time. Between sessions I went to Washington, New York, Baltimore. Why, last August I even traveled as far as Nova Scotia."

"What on earth for?" Jefferson inquired.

"I had a chance to visit the home of one of my classmates. His father owns a very lucrative fishing business there. I wanted to see what it was like."

"And?"

"It was rugged, cold, gray and fascinating. The people were as warm as it was cold. The sea is like a thrashing monster there. There's nothing tame about it. I've never felt such power as the sea has when I'm on a ship and navigating through dangerous rock."

"You'd better not tell your mother any of this," Jefferson advised as the waiter brought two huge steaks lathered with golden streams of butter.

"Don't worry," Lawrence laughed. "She has apoplexy if I mention New York, much less anything else."

"She's just glad to have you back. I suppose she'd like to have you around for a while and already you're talking about leaving again."

Lawrence cut off a huge hunk of steak, chewing hungrily. He nodded. "I know. Last night at supper I was telling Mother and Father that I want to go to China and find precious porcelains and antiques, and I thought she'd drop through the floor or go through the roof. One or the other. I don't know what to do to calm her down. I just can't stay in San Francisco *all* my life, Jefferson. She just doesn't understand. There's this incredible world out there, and I want to see it all. Taste it all. Live it all."

Jefferson smiled and downed a huge mouthful of wine. "I think I have the solution to your problem."

Lawrence leaned back in his chair and regarded Jefferson intently. "I'm open to your suggestions."

"Perhaps the best thing for right now is to make a compromise with yourself and with your mother. You may have to curb your impatience a bit. The world will still be there waiting for you six months from now. A year from now."

Lawrence rolled his young, idealistic eyes, but he was still listening. "Go on. I want to hear how you intend to placate my mother. I've never known any of us to get our own way once she has decided what she wants."

Jefferson laughed. However, he was thinking how Caroline made love to him and how she did, indeed, "get her own way." Caroline could be forceful when she wanted. Even powerful. But Jefferson didn't care because he'd always gotten his way with Caroline. Because she loved him, she was always willing to bend for him. "What your mother wants is not best for you now that you are grown. However, we need not hurt her feelings, either. What I propose is to set you up as the president of my new lumber company. I need someone I can trust implicitly to make certain that as little news of my venture leaks out to the public as possible. San Franciscans adore their gossip, and this is a very small town. My comings and goings are marked by far too many curious eyes already."

"Why do you want to keep a company a secret?" Lawrence asked.

"For many reasons. I have a signed agreement with Charles Crocker and Leland Stanford to supply all of the lumber needed to build the railroad from the Pacific as far as the Midwest, if I want it."

"Wheeeew!" Lawrence whistled appreciatively. "You'll be richer than all of them combined."

Jefferson smiled proudly. "Not quite, but pretty damn close. I've observed other men and their downfalls over the years, and I don't wish to make the same mistakes with this opportunity. If word were to get out what I'm doing, every Tom, Dick and Harry would be buying up lumber mills and outbidding me. I've got a contract, but contracts can be broken. I need someone to go to Oregon and oversee the shipment of all the lumber to the building sites at least for the first six to nine months, which will get me established with these men as a punctual supplier. Once I have their confidence and, eventually, friendship, no one will be able to take their business from me. You'd be away from home, yet not an ocean separating you from us. You'd see your parents once a month at least and yet still be in the very rugged wilds of Oregon. Since Nova Scotia's hardiness appealed to you, perhaps the beauty of Oregon's forests will touch your soul as well."

Lawrence was silent.

Jefferson poured them each another glass of wine. He said nothing, knowing that Lawrence needed the time to let the idea take root in his mind.

"Six months, huh?" Lawrence asked.

"To a year. No more than that. Then, you can slowly get your mother used to the idea that you will be sailing to Canton and Singapore or wherever it is you want to go. She'll get used to your absences. And once you prove to her how good you are at what you do, she'll have more confidence in you, too. That's an important consideration. You're very young, Lawrence. There's no need to plunge yourself into the deep blue sea and then find out you can't swim. Take life a bit slower. Savor each bite in its own good time. You'll come out the winner that way."

Lawrence nodded his head. "You know what I've always admired about you, Jefferson?"

"What's that?"

"Your wisdom. You seem to get more done in a given day than half the men in the city, and yet, you make everything look effortless. How do you do that?"

Jefferson chuckled. "You want all my secrets, don't you?"

"Not all. Just that one," Lawrence said, focusing eager eyes on this man he not only respected but loved.

"I plan everything as carefully as I can. I weigh all the issues and look at every side. Then, after I've done all that, I sit silently in my den and go inside myself and see what's in my heart. It's the heart that truly decides for us, Lawrence. If you don't feel it in your heart, it's not worth doing. It's not right for you. May be right for someone else, but it will never make you happy. Make yourself happy first and all the rest will fall into place."

Lawrence's eyes were filled with awe. "Jefferson, of all the things in the world you could say to me, that is *not* what I expected to hear from you."

Jefferson propped his elbows on the table and laced his fingers together and placed his chin on them pensively. He looked off to the distance for a moment and then back to Lawrence. "Ordinary men live ordinary lives. I've known since I was a child that I'm not ordinary. I'm different. Peculiar, some folks say. But I know myself. That can be hard to do . . . and it can be the easiest thing to do, if you accept the good with the bad. An ordinary man would never take risks. I thrive on them. And risks are generated by the heart. The mind can talk you out of just about anything if you let it. Listen to your heart, Lawrence. You go to China and India and Africa if you want. You see the world. You experience everything you can. You have an intelligent mind, strong constitution and the vision to live more than an ordinary life."

"I'll do it!" Lawrence said enthusiastically.

"Good. I'm already proud of you. You'll make yourself proud of you. And that's better than money in the bank."

Lawrence stuck out his hand to Jefferson. "I guess the only thing for me to do is report to work as your new president. When do I leave for Oregon?"

Jefferson took his son's hand and then covered the handshake with his left hand. He gave his son the fondest of looks and said, "In the morning."

* * * *

Lawrence rode a chestnut-brown stallion to the felling sight up the mountainside from the lumber mill that Jefferson Duke had purchased the month before. He had expected to be bored to death by the mundane work, simplistic paperwork and the dull conversations of the woodcutters. But from his first day at the mill, he found more challenges than he'd faced in that Nova Scotian sea storm. The old-timers resented taking orders from someone who knew nothing more about the lumber business than what he'd read in books. They disliked Lawrence because he was young, college educated and wealthy. They intended to run him off by making life miserable for him.

"What's the problem, Hardesty?" he asked the fifty-year-old, weathered-skinned, lean foreman.

Hardesty lifted his right arm to his face and even with the slight movement his rock-solid biceps strained at the confines of the wool shirt he wore. "Nothin' I can't handle," he said, cockily looking over at the three Chinese men who sat on a felled log staring at the ground.

One of the Chinese men got up and pulled his black cotton shirt away from his shoulder revealing a festering welt that Lawrence knew instantly was from overwork hauling logs or possibly even from beatings. From what Collins, the assistant to Hardesty had told him, Hardesty could be "meaner than a hungry coot." Lawrence hadn't trusted Hardesty since his first night in camp when Hardesty tried to cheat him at poker. Lawrence hadn't said anything at the time since the rest of the men didn't seem to mind.

However, the reports on Hardesty were all coming back to him with ominous overtones. It was time Lawrence did something about his foreman.

"You just take your prissy, baby ass back there to the mill and tell Mr. Chickasee that Hardesty has everthin' under control."

Lawrence ground his jaw. He looked off at the golden sunlight streaming through the tall pines, dappling the earth with long autumn shadows. This was one encounter too many with the belligerent Hardesty, and Lawrence had just about had enough of his crap. Lawrence's eyes looked like hard green flint when he glared back at Hardesty. Lawrence quickly slid off his horse and stalked over to Hardesty.

"Collins says the Orientals won't work for you, Hardesty, because you ride their asses too hard. They aren't slaves, you know."

"The hell they ain't," Hardesty growled menacingly. "And I don't need no fancy-pants city boy comin' up here and tellin' me how to run my business."

Lawrence was eye to eye with the man, both of them being well over six feet. "It's not your business, asshole."

Hardesty's temper was short, and Lawrence knew it.

The older man pulled back a fist and threw it at Lawrence. Lawrence ducked quickly, circled around the man and instantly assumed a pugilist's stance with his knees bent, feet dancing lightly on the ground as he bobbed and weaved away from Hardesty's impotent attempts to land a blow.

"Stand still!" Hardesty demanded as he missed Lawrence's face once again.

Lawrence's agility and youth stood him in good stead until Hardesty quickly figured out Lawrence's pattern of bobbing to the left, weaving to the right.

Beneath the crunching blow to his jaw, Lawrence fell backward to the ground. Hardesty broke out laughing. "Get up, fancy pants. Let a real man show you what life's all about."

A searing pain shot through Lawrence's jaw, down his throat and across his head. He wondered if his jaw was broken. He smiled at Hardesty. He needed that punch to let him know it was time to pull off all restraints.

Lawrence sprang to his feet and bobbed and weaved just as Hardesty expected him to. But then he faded right when Hardesty had thought he'd go left. Lawrence landed a series of punches to Hardesty's belly and then sank one into the man's liver area since he knew the man couldn't get through a morning without a lot of whiskey. Lawrence didn't stop when the man groaned. He continued battering his face and head with so many punches, the Orientals on the log couldn't tell which hand was leading or retreating.

Hardesty tried to back away, but Lawrence was having none of it. He intended to pulverize the man. Hardesty fell to the ground covering his face with his upraised hands. He was crying and begging for mercy.

"Don't hit me!" Hardesty's right eye was already swelling shut.

"I'll knock your ass to kingdom come if I ever see you on this land again. Now get your things together and get out. You're fired."

"Fired? Who the hell is going to run these goddamn Orientals for you anyway? Who's going to drive this shipment to the station at Sacramento?"

Lawrence was breathing so hard, his lungs felt like they were on fire. He had to put his hands on his thighs just to hold himself up. The truth was, he did need Hardesty, but he would never tolerate mutiny. And that's what he'd been fighting. None of the cutters at the mill, the office personnel, the woodsmen, hell, not even the Chinese laborers had given him one iota of respect. Well, today, he would get his respect. If he had to fire every single man at this mill, he'd do it. He'd start over. He didn't know what Jefferson would think about all this, but in his heart, Lawrence knew he had to take a stand.

"I will," Lawrence said flatly.

Hardesty started laughing. He spit a mouthful of blood on the hard earth. "The hell you will. You don't know shit."

Lawrence smiled and the effort sent a shooting pain to his jaw. "I know enough to beat your ass. Now get out of here."

Hardesty slowly pushed himself up from the ground. On weak and trembling legs, he walked over to his horse and mounted it. Angrily he spurred the horse and galloped down the mountainside to the camp where he kept his change of clothes, whiskey bottle and two poker decks of cards. He'd find another job at another mill. He always had before.

Lawrence turned to the three Oriental men who were now standing up, staring at him with cool distrust in their eyes. Lawrence went over to the long pine tree and picked up a sharp hatchet which was used to trim the last of the limbs and branches. He hacked off the limbs and cleaned the log. Then he slid a long leather strap onto the tree that was used to haul the felled trees to the slide which led down to the mill at the base of the mountain.

The Chinese men gave each other puzzled looks. They nodded to one another and then walked up behind Lawrence and put the straps over their shoulders. One of the men pushed Lawrence aside. He watched as they pulled the log to the slide and then gave it a shove. It went careening down the slide to the mill.

Lawrence smiled to himself as the crew continued working, and he couldn't help but to remember Jefferson's advice. Lawrence had never hurt anyone in his life. Boxing had been a sport at college, but nothing more.

Today, he'd needed those skills to keep the mill running. If that first shipment of lumber didn't make it to the railroad site on time, Jefferson stood to lose his entire contract. It was the first time Lawrence realized the enormity of the small cogs in the big wheel of business. He realized how important every single person's role in life was during his conflict with Hardesty. And it humbled him.

It was a lesson he promised himself he would never forget.

twenty-eight

San Francisco—1866

Jefferson stood on the dock waiting for Lawrence's steamer to anchor. After Lawrence had given him eighteen months as president of the Duke Lumber Company and helped to firmly establish Jefferson as one of the richest men in San Francisco, Jefferson knew he couldn't hold the young man back from his dream of seeing the world. Nor could Caroline.

In China, Lawrence found irreplaceable antiques, which Caroline sold in her emporium at exorbitant prices when the Silver Era surpassed the Golden Days of forty-nine. He sailed clipper ships to the Bay of Bengal and then he scoured the marketplaces of Calcutta and Rangoon in Burma. He trekked into the mountains of Bali and watched exotic dancers wearing golden trousers and blouses and elaborate headdresses like towers on their heads. He was seeing the wonders of the world, but Jefferson missed him as much as Caroline did.

Lawrence shielded his eyes from the sun as he climbed down to the launch that would carry him to shore. From this far out, he could see

Jefferson waiting for him in his sparkling carriage.

"Just like always," Lawrence said, waving exuberantly.

Once ashore, he dashed over to his friend and threw his arms around Jefferson. "How wonderful to see you, Jefferson! How are you? How is my mother?"

"Both of us are happy now that you're home."

Lawrence's smile dropped. "And my father?"

"William," Jefferson replied, "is well."

"You know I find it interesting, Jefferson, that in all my returns, you're the one who comes to the dock to fetch me. Could it be my father can't be bothered?"

Jefferson's expression darkened. "You want the truth?"

Lawrence smiled. "I've figured out the truth. He couldn't care less. And Mother?"

"She knows this is a special treat for me. She allows me this indulgence. We have so much to discuss, what with business and all," Jefferson said.

"Liar. You just want to stop for red wine and steaks!"

Jefferson slapped him on the back. "You're right about that!" He turned. "Are they coming with your luggage?"

"Here, I'll see to it," Lawrence said, sprinting back to one of the deck-hands who was already unloading bags.

Lawrence didn't see the line of Chinese merchants who'd lined up along the west side of the dock to receive goods and smuggled family members until he turned back to wave to Jefferson.

His arm dropped like a rock as his eyes met Yin's. He held his breath. "I know her."

But how? From where?

Lawrence racked his brain as she continued staring boldly at him.

So beautiful. So exotic and so damned familiar.

Lawrence was more than mesmerized, he was spellbound.

Yin returned his gaze, intuition for intuition, energy for energy.

He's like the sun. And I am the moon. But what does this feeling I have mean?

I curse this gift of prophecy that lets me help everyone but myself.

Had she known she was to meet her destiny on this day she would have been prepared. As it was, she felt as if she'd turned to stone. She couldn't move nor did she want to.

Yet he frightened her as he walked toward her.

Is he the one the astrologer told me about so long ago? How will I know for certain? And why is he a white man? Why must my life be complicated?

Lawrence continued walking toward her.

This is dangerous! Yin's wits returned in a flash. The other Chinese watched the white man approach. They looked from him to her with suspicion rimming their eyes.

Yin stared at Lawrence and shook her head ever so slightly. She dropped her eyes.

Suddenly, Lawrence made the connection. He was only a boy when he'd first seen her. She was the beautiful woman in the lumberyard. She'd been pregnant.

How can that be? She doesn't look any older at all. In fact she's more beautiful than I remember.

Scrutinizing his memory he realized that at the time this woman must have been nineteen or twenty.

Suddenly, she turned away from him and ducked through the throng of Chinese. They all wore black trousers and tunics, making it difficult for Lawrence to follow her.

He started toward her, thinking he could inquire about her from the others. Perhaps someone knew her.

Suddenly, her face popped out of the crowd, scowling at him, warning him with fear-filled eyes not to follow.

She vanished.

Bombarded with a plethora of questions and emotions, he walked back to Jefferson's carriage.

"Did you see someone you know?" Jefferson asked.

"Yes."

"An enemy?"

"Why do you say that?" Lawrence asked.

"Because you're white as a sheet."

Lawrence wiped his forehead. "I had no idea. Sorry."

"Don't be. What was that all about?"

"I'm not sure. I saw a woman I remember from childhood. It was nothing," he replied, looking out the window. He didn't want to search for her. But he did. She was nowhere to be seen. "It's as if she was a ghost."

Jefferson leaned back. "Was she?"

"What?"

"A ghost," he said.

Lawrence laughed. "Come now, Jefferson, there's no such thing."

Jefferson's expression was unwavering. "You're old enough to know that there are."

"What?" he guffawed, then seeing Jefferson's seriousness, he dropped his lightheartedness. "You don't believe . . ."

"I most certainly do. All wise men do. I have several whisking in and out of my mansion."

"And they talk to you?"

"Periodically, yes. Mostly, they predict things that will happen in the future."

Lawrence's eyes rounded. "This is incredulous."

"Why, because your father told you there was no such thing as ghosts?"

"He did. But that's besides the point."

"My dear boy," Jefferson said. "You will find that most corruptions in life come from the teachings of our so-called well-meaning relatives."

"Is that why you don't have any?"

"Only dead ones," Jefferson smiled, amused. "But your ghost today was quite real, I'll wager."

"She was. I could feel . . ."

"What did you feel?" Jefferson asked, leaning forward.

"I don't know. She stunned me with her eyes. I knew I knew her. But it was more. She was beautiful, yes, but I saw beautiful women in Burma, Morocco. All over. This was different. She reminded me of something delicate. I don't know. A nightingale."

"Nightingale?" Jefferson felt his neck hairs prickle. "Odd you'd say that."

"Why odd?"

"Oh, it means nothing to you. So, tell me, was she so intriguing to you that you would search her out?"

"Well, I don't know that I'd go that far. Besides, I'm only home for a fortnight. Then I'm off again."

"So soon?" Jefferson was clearly disappointed.

"I must. Mother tells me that no matter how much I purchase, she sells it faster than I can bargain for it."

Jefferson laughed. "Well, I'm going to increase the strain. I have a stack of orders myself I'd like you to fill."

"Oh, ho! The competition is getting intense, is it?" Lawrence laughed.

"It has to! The last Bordeaux we shared set me back plenty."

Lawrence burst out laughing. "Gads, I've missed you, Jefferson! You have no idea."

"Oh, I can imagine," he said good-naturedly. "Now, let's get to those drinks!"

* * * *

Yin threw the yarrow sticks. Clearly, a new lover was coming to her. Yet, she sensed it was within her power to stay away from him. He would never find her in Chinatown. He didn't know his way around. She could stay hidden for a long time if necessary.

She went to the window of her small apartment and gazed out at the night sky. But she did not see stars, she saw her reflection in the glass staring back at her.

My life is loveless. I have married the wrong man. I could change my destiny if I went back to the docks. I could find Duke's son.

Shivers raced over her skin. She hugged herself.

What kind of fate would I bring this man, my husband's mortal enemy, if I were to seek love from him? Nan-Yung would kill him. Despite my attraction to him, I must fight my feelings with all my soul.

Yin stared out the window wishing the stars could speak to her. What they told her was unsettling.

They told her that her destiny had been made before she was born. She would have joy. But she would also have pain. Her life was to be no different than any other human being. Her only choice was to live it.

San Francisco—1881

Lawrence sailed around the world five full times before he was thirty-nine years old. He never married.

He searched for love, but he never seemed to have the time. There was always another exotic country to explore. Another trip home. Another trip away. His mistress was the sea. He couldn't imagine any other kind of life.

Society in San Francisco had altered drastically since Lawrence's youth. Gone were the rowdy gold-rush miners who roared into the city with pockets full of gold. Through the seventies, the silver rush made even the fog off the bay sparkle.

The fashion in houses was Arabian in design and decor. There were fantastic towers, silver balustrades and doorknobs, and Oriental carpets, half of which Lawrence had brought back from Morocco, China and India.

These were not houses, but palaces a sultan would envy. Lawrence was more than delighted to be part of the flow of money that traveled from the silver mines, through his mother's emporium, and back to the Orient. However, he was getting older. The sea was losing her siren's call. The nights on board ship were not intoxicating as they were when he was young. Now they were just lonely. Lately, he'd begun thinking about what it would be like to fall in love and have children.

Caroline was reading the *Daily Morning Call* at breakfast one day when Lawrence arrived fresh from a horseback ride on the beach near the Presidio. The years of sun, wind and sea had crinkled the edges of his eyes and put deep furrows on either side of his mouth. He had no gray hair, though the sun had bleached the crown of his head with strands of gold. He was incredibly handsome, and with the kind of money they were making these days he was a rich man in his own right.

"Come join me for some coffee," Caroline said, putting her hand in his as he bent down to kiss her cheek.

"I'll do more than that," he replied, marching over to the hunt-board, taking a gold plate and filling it with scrambled eggs, sausages, Italian pastries and a mountain of grilled potatoes. "It's been awhile since I've had a home-cooked meal."

Caroline laughed. Her kitchens boasted three of the best chefs in San Francisco. It had been over a decade since she'd cooked a meal for anyone. These days, her dinner parties were considered the crème de la crème in San Francisco society. One had to be either part of the old guard, of which she and Jefferson, the Richardsons and a few others still claimed, or they had to be members of an elite civic-minded corps who not only were fantastically wealthy, like the Crockers, but were intensely dedicated to building a city for the future.

Caroline was a patron of the arts as was Mayor Thomas H. Selby, the Athertons, the Eyres, the Stanfords and the Mark Hopkinses. "I've bought season tickets to the Grand Opera House. Since you're in town for a few weeks, perhaps you'd like to see something special before you sail off to . . ." She looked up at him. "Where are you going on your next trip?"

"St. Petersburg."

She shook her head. "Do you suppose you'll ever light in one place, Lawrence?"

He flashed her a charming smile, not wanting her to worry about him. It was enough he was worried about precisely the same thing. "I doubt it very seriously," he said flippantly.

She sighed heavily and sank her chin into her hand, which she'd propped on the table. "I'll never have grandchildren, will I?"

Lawrence grinned wickedly. "What makes you think I don't have little tykes all over the globe by now?"

Caroline's blue eyes flew open. "I'd never thought of that. Good Lord! You don't, do you?"

Lawrence howled with laughter. "Not that anyone's told me about. I could check next time I'm in Canton."

Caroline waved both hands in front of her face and shook her head. "Please! Don't say anymore. I don't want to know."

"Oh, Mother. I'm only teasing you. You're so predictable. Do you realize every time I come home you try to push me onto some defenseless young maiden, who in turn bats her eyes at me and heaves her breasts up and down in a very low-cut gown trying to make me drop to my knees and propose to her? Mother," he reached out his hand to her and held her soft hand in his, "I love you. But I'm not interested. Society flirts have no personality. No heart. They're husband hunting because their mamas have told them they are doomed to a life of misery if they don't marry someone rich like me."

Caroline slammed her palm down on the table. "They aren't all like that! I was never like that!"

Lawrence shoved a forkful of eggs into his mouth. "There you have it. It's your fault I can find no one to please me. Being brought up by a woman with a brain and a personality has spoiled me for every other woman on earth. Mother, face it. There's no one who can hold a candle to you."

"You say the sweetest things to me." Then she frowned. "But this time it won't work. I'm having a party tonight to welcome you home." She rose from the table and pulled her morning gown together. "Be here at eight o'clock."

"Very well."

"What? You mean you won't put up a fuss? You'll be on time?"

"Yes," he replied soberly.

Caroline saw through his act. She put her hand over his. "You look sad," she said.

"I've been thinking a lot about my life lately. What I'm going to do with the rest of it. And quite frankly, I'm not quite ready to rush back across the world. I've been thinking . . . well . . . that perhaps—"

"I'm right?" She interjected.

"Perhaps." His smile was wan.

She kissed his forehead. "Let nature take its course, Lawrence. If love is meant to come to you, it will, but you have to be ready for it."

"I guess that's what I'm saying. I'm ready."

She smiled consolingly and rose. "I have a hundred details to attend to. Please go up and see your father. He's been ill again. He's never quite re-covered from the pneumonia I wrote to you about."

Lawrence nodded. "I'm surprised he even knows I'm home."

* * * *

Lawrence knocked on the dark burled wood door to his father's bedroom, which had been converted to a study over ten years ago.

"Who is it?" William's voice was raspy, weak and irritated.

"Lawrence."

"Who?"

"Your son," Lawrence replied with an equal measure of ire.

"Come in," William said as Lawrence opened the door.

The room was nearly black in darkness though it was morning outside. Heavy, dark, royal-blue drapes covered the windows and only a meager light from a very old, cheap, whale-oil lamp illuminated the chair in which William sat with a blanket covering his legs.

Lawrence approached his father and nearly gasped at how the man had aged in the past eight months since Lawrence's last visit. His mother had been right, the pneumonia William had endured last winter had ruined his health. It was Lawrence's guess that William's lungs had not healed at all.

An accounting book rested in his lap and a stack of papers and bills lay at his feet.

How strange and sad. All my life this is my only image of my father. At least he's steadfast in his ways. Cold-hearted, but changeless.

"Hello, Father."

"Hello, Lawrence." William glanced at his son momentarily, as one does a bird that flits by a window, and then went back to his work.

William had nothing more to say to his only child whom he hadn't seen for over eight months. He was not interested in where Lawrence had gone, not interested in the bountiful shipload of goods he brought from Japan, and he wasn't interested in anything Lawrence thought, felt, dreamed or wanted.

God, he's pathetic. How has Mother stood it all these years?

Suddenly, as he stood there staring at the shell of the man who had sired him, Lawrence was shocked to realize that in some ways, many ways perhaps, he was becoming just like his father.

The revelation was fantastic but true!

I've spent my life pursuing places and things. Not people! Father's relationship is with numbers. Mine is with things. If I don't make some changes, I'll end up just like him . . . never using my heart.

Lawrence's hands were shaking. "Father, I can see that I'm disturbing you. I suppose I'd better move along. I'll come back this evening for Mother's party. Will I see you at dinner?"

"What? A party? Dad blast it! Doesn't she realize how much those fool things cost?"

Lawrence's forehead furled. "Cost? Have you no idea that I've helped to make us one of the richest families in the city? Don't you look at your own books? We're millionaires ten times over! She can give a party seven days a week and never spend all the money I've made. My God, man! She's enjoying her life!"

William raised his thin face and focused his pale eyes on Lawrence. "What are you talking about? We're as poor as church mice."

Lawrence was horror stricken. "My God, man, you're insane. Or the most miserly man in existence."

"Get out!" William screamed.

"Gladly," he said politely and left.

Shutting the door behind him, Lawrence pulled out his handkerchief and wiped the icy sweat from his brow. He felt as if he'd just seen his future. He'd always believed he was the master of his own destiny.

"I won't end up like him. I won't!" he vowed to himself as he descended the staircase. "And my changes start tonight with Mother's party."

twenty-nine

*Love is the state in which man sees things
most widely different from what they are.
The force of illusion reaches its zenith here, as
likewise the sweetening and transfiguring power.
When a man is in love he endures more than
at other times; he submits to everything.*

—FRIEDRICH WILHELM NIETZSCHE
THE ANTICHRIST, APHORISM 23

My God, Mother, this is incredible!" Lawrence said to Caroline as they gazed out at over two hundred guests who filled their ballroom.

"Look at those boys," she said. "They're smitten by the faintest smile from these debutantes."

"At least they're taking a chance," he mumbled more to himself than to her. "Your glass is empty," he said, looking around the room for another gold-and-white–liveried servant carrying gold trays filled with fine Venetian glasses slopping over their rims with French champagne.

"Thank you, Dear," she said, turning her eyes to Jefferson who just entered the ballroom.

Lawrence retrieved a glass from a passing servant and stopped mid-motion. "Heaven."

Descending the royal-blue–carpeted marble stairs to the ballroom was the most beautiful girl he'd ever seen.

Lawrence held his breath.

So did the young man standing next to him. "She's an angel," the young man managed to say.

"At the very least," Lawrence whispered, taking in the blue-eyed, dark-haired beauty.

He watched as she regarded the room and its inhabitants like a queen oversees her subjects. Her carriage was both regal and possessive as if she knew she deserved such admiration. She wore her hair in old-fashioned curls down her back that moved seductively in the gaslight from the brass chandeliers overhead. The light caught in her hair like a myriad of stars against the night sky. Her face was perfection, a soft oval with high aristocratic cheekbones blushed with a natural pink glow. But it was her smile that nearly brought Lawrence to his knees when she looked at the adoring faces of the young men, mere boys in his estimation and then her eyes met Lawrence's.

He sucked in his breath.

She smiled softly, parting her pink, luscious lips over straight teeth that looked like white pearls from the rarest, deepest parts of the China Sea.

Lawrence swallowed hard.

Her deep indigo-blue silk gown reminded him of expensive sapphires he'd traded for in Africa, and because the fashion for the young girls was to wear pale colors, her boldness and outrageousness put the other young girls to shame. The gown was cut in a scandalously low décolletage that dramatically displayed a swell of creamy breasts which were neither too small nor overly large. Her waist was small, and he could tell from the tight fit of the sleek silk over satin bodice that she did not wear a corset like the rest of the women. Drop pearl earrings rather than the standard diamond earrings and a cameo necklace on a royal blue velvet ribbon were her only jewelry. He noticed that her only compromise to current fashion was the miniature ballroom muff.

"Why, she looks like Mother when she was young, except for her hair, of course."

Could she be any more perfect?

She was an enigma. Her long-lashed eyes were not flirtatious in the least. Instead of batting her eyes and looking demurely away from him, she focused her concentration on his face, regarding him as audaciously as he watched her. She matched his stare and allowed herself to be affected by his power and energy. She smiled at him again, but this time her lips were ever-so-slightly mischievous.

Lawrence was more than intrigued.

"Who is she?" he inquired of the young man next to him.

"Eleanor Baresfield," the young man breathed her name with awe.

"I don't know this family."

The young man turned to Lawrence with a shocked look on his face. "Her father made money in both gold and silver and left his wife everything when he died four years ago. However, word has it that his debts were greater than his assets. Eleanor is most exclusive about whom she even speaks with. She's haughty and reclusive. She only came here this evening on a lark. I can tell by the gown she chose. Most of the town believe she is much too rebellious for society, yet they continue to invite her to their soirées."

"I can understand why. She's the most beautiful woman here."

"They say she turned down a Prussian prince last year when he fell madly for her." The young man said tugging on his white gloves. "She tossed his feelings aside without a thought when she discovered he had been disinherited by his family . . . some disagreement with his family over politics."

"That doesn't seem unreasonable," Lawrence said, thanking Dame Fortune for giving Eleanor the good sense to wait for someone better to come along. The whole idea of marrying a foreigner and then going off to live in Europe for the rest of one's life simply to have a title had always seemed preposterous to him, despite his own obsession for travel. He supposed it had to do with a man's need to possess a woman.

The young man lifted his small boned face in the air and sniffed. "Eleanor thinks too well of herself, if you ask me," he said snobbishly.

Lawrence couldn't help the wry smile that crept over his lips. "And when did she turn you down?" Lawrence walked away as the orchestra began playing a waltz.

His strides were long and purposeful, the kind of gait a man used when approaching a goal he intended to accomplish. With each step as he drew closer to Eleanor he could feel another pair of eyes watching him until he knew that over half the guests were staring at him.

Eleanor never took her eyes from Lawrence from the minute she saw him. She waited for him patiently, not giving one inch of ground to him. She felt like the princess on the glass mountain. He would have to scale the dangerous precipice to get her prize. And it would cost him.

Though she was tall for a woman, he loomed over her. He stood very close to her, invading the space that propriety demanded men and women keep. He wanted to be as close to her as he could without taking her in his arms. He wanted to feel her heartbeat against his chest, which was why he asked, "Would you like to dance with me, or is your dance card already filled?"

"You know perfectly well that I just arrived, Mr. Mansfield."

"You know who I am? We haven't been introduced yet."

A shadow passed over her blue eyes, but she kept her face placid. "You break my heart, sir. You don't remember me at all, do you?"

"Remember you?" Lawrence knew the only vision that had come close to this kind of beauty was solely in his imagination. "We've met?"

Her laughter was like gently falling rain. Her eyes sparkled at him like shimmering rainbows. "Why, Lawrence, I've been in love with you since the first time I saw you in your mother's emporium over twelve years ago."

"In love?" He was stunned. Then he smiled. Perhaps this was a new kind of coquette's ploy with which he was not familiar. He chose to be wary. "You were just a child then. And now you're being more outrageous than I've been told."

"Truthful, Lawrence. I'm truthful. There's a difference."

"Tell me how I have so callously passed you over," he urged.

"You were home from some exotic trip and I was shopping with my mother. I pretended to be inspecting the boxed chocolates from England."

"Belgium," he corrected.

She smiled. "What I was really doing was listening to your fascinating conversation with your mother. I was enthralled with your tales of the Orient and that trip you made to the Himalayas. Lord! But you've led an exciting life."

"I like to think so," he breathed seductively and moved his face a fraction of an inch closer to her where he could inhale her perfume.

"But you're right. I was just a child. You were twenty-seven. I had no alternative but to grow up and hope that one day when I saw you, I would make you fall in love with me."

"My God, you're audacious. What does your mother say about that?"

"She doesn't know. Besides, you're just saying that because you realize that I'm different."

"Well, yes. I have little truck with most of these self-absorbed society people who put a higher price on what others think than on what they want for themselves."

"Then you and I are just the same," she said.

"I guess we are," he agreed.

Eleanor continued. "I heard you were in town and then when your mother's invitation came, I knew that the time had come for me to see you before you left on another voyage. Frankly, I didn't think I could wait any longer for you."

"Any longer? Just how old are you, Eleanor?"

"Nineteen."

"As old as that?" he teased, knowing she was moving beyond the age that was fashionable for young women to marry. However, she was so incredibly beautiful and possessed that timeless kind of beauty that even when she was old she would still be desired by men.

"You taunt me, Lawrence, when you should have your arms around me and dance with me."

"Are you always this forward, Eleanor?" He put out his arm to her, turned and walked her toward the dance floor, realizing that his gesture had crushed over two dozen young, pimply faced boys.

"Yes, I am," she said proudly, holding her aristocratic straight nose in the air. "I mortify my mother on a regular basis, I'm happy to say."

Lawrence howled with laughter and then pulled her firmly into his arms as they joined the other dancers. He held her close and nearly made himself crazy with sexual need. He breathed in her perfume and let it fill his head. Along with the music and the wine, he was intoxicated with Eleanor.

As they danced, he wondered what it would be like to hold her naked next to him. He wondered if she would be daring enough to make love to him under the stars on a hot summer night with the breeze caressing their flesh. He wondered if she would open to him as willingly in bed as she was doing right now.

"Don't look at me like that, Eleanor."

"And how am I looking at you, Lawrence?"

"As if I were the only man on earth."

"And why is that a problem?"

"Because I'm not a kid. I'm a grown man and I don't have time for games."

"Good. Then again, we're alike. I'm not playing a game. I'm playing for keeps."

"I've never liked the idea of living in San Francisco with all the town watching my every move. I've liked adventure. Craved it."

"I crave a lot of things, too, Lawrence," she replied seductively. "But this is where I live. I don't want to live anywhere else. So, if that's what you want, leave now."

"I like holding you," he said, pulling her closer. Feeling hotter.

"I like it more," she whispered, pressing her pelvis into his.

She's challenging me.

Suddenly, a vision of William sitting in his dark room counting his pennies and losing his mind spiraled across Lawrence's mind.

He looked down into the dancing lights in Eleanor's incredible blue eyes and asked, "If you could go anywhere in the world, on say, well, a honeymoon for instance, what would your fantasy be?"

Her eyelids fell demurely over her eyes, her lashes casting long shadows on her cheeks. Then she raised her head and gazed intently into Lawrence's face. She met him on the field of his soul. "Tahiti," she replied. "I'd like to see the sunset in Tahiti."

He pressed the palm of his hand into the small of her back, causing her breasts to flatten against him. "I'd like to see you tomorrow, Eleanor."

She laughed lightly, her voice mingling with the violin strains. "What? And not the day after that? And the day after that?"

Lawrence's face was serious and he hadn't realized his eyes had become possessive. "Those, too."

Caroline, dressed in a French couture ball gown of deepest wine-colored burgundy silk over taffeta, smiled at Jefferson when he brought her a glass of champagne. As usual, William remained in his rooms, refusing to host his own party.

Over the years, most of Caroline's society friends had grown accustomed to Jefferson's taking over the role of escort and host. No longer did they gossip about an affair between the two. There was such a long-standing depth of caring and emotion that many of the Old Guard considered them in a way to be married. The New Guard simply accepted their relationship as quirky.

"Your eyes betray too much emotion, Caroline," Jefferson warned as she watched the interplay between her son and Eleanor Baresfield.

Caroline touched Jefferson's hand and as always he felt a shot of electricity career up his arm. She was as beautiful as the first day he'd seen her. Her platinum-colored hair looked no different, though she claimed it was now gray. Her eyes still radiated with love when she looked at him, though fine lines washed her face with character, sadness and joy. She was sixty-four years old, and looked twenty years younger. She'd told him she'd begun using expensive French lotions on her skin when she was twenty and because she bought them at wholesale, she lavished herself with them. He had to agree that her personal indulgences had not only kept her the envy of even the younger women of the town, but had brought a great many sales to the emporium.

"I wish Lawrence had picked someone besides Eleanor Baresfield to lust after," Caroline spoke her thoughts aloud to Jefferson.

"My love," he whispered quietly. "We both know Eleanor set her sights on Lawrence a long time ago."

Caroline didn't like it but she had to agree with him. Whenever Eleanor came to the emporium and Caroline happened to see her, the young girl had always inquired about Lawrence. Caroline had indeed noticed how the young girl reacted to her stories of Lawrence's travels with curiosity and at times insatiable fascination, asking a myriad of questions. Lawrence had never shown any interest in any women from San Francisco. The invitation to Eleanor had been an afterthought, a fleeting gesture one commits in reaction to a small but distinct voice of inspiration.

Eleanor, however, was no longer wealthy, and several of the women of the town had told Caroline that Eleanor plotted out her flirtations like a general maps out a war. Since her parents were now both dead and her father's estate long having been spent by her tasteless, avaricious mother, Gertrude, Eleanor had taught herself how to budget what little money she had, invest it as wisely as possible and live on a stipend allowed her by her solicitor. Caroline had to admire the young woman for being responsible, but she was also wary of the gossip about Eleanor.

"She has a heart as cold as stone," Mrs. James Flood had said.

"She's a plotter. She thinks of no one but herself," Mrs. Charles Crocker had told Caroline last year. "She's broken dozens of hearts because she measures men by the size of their bank accounts."

Caroline believed that Eleanor was in love with Lawrence and so, of course, she would reject all suitors. She was waiting for Lawrence. Caroline remembered retorting to the accusations with the truth. "She's a survivor. She must be sensible and think about her future. I see nothing wrong with that."

Caroline wanted happiness for Lawrence. However, her intuition told her that of all the eligible bachelors in the room, Lawrence was one of the wealthiest, and, though he was twenty years older than Eleanor, he was the handsomest.

"Think of it, Jefferson. If they marry, we'll be grandparents."

"Of course we will, my love. And it will be a girl. And they will name her Barbara."

"Yes," she said, looking away from Jefferson and back to Lawrence. "It will be just as Rachel told you it would be. Everything is in divine order, isn't it?"

"Always, my love. Always."

Book Four

The House of
Many Mansions

thirty

The sun and the moon and the stars would have disappeared long ago . . . had they happened to be within the reach of predatory human hands.

—HAVELOCK ELLIS
THE DANCE OF LIFE

On December 11, 1881, Barbara Mansfield was born to Eleanor and Lawrence Mansfield after a nearly painless delivery for the mother.

"Here, Jefferson," Lawrence handed him a cigar. "It's from Havana. And the cognac is Louis XIII. The best. Nothing but the best for me tonight."

"I'm so proud of you, Lawrence. She's incredible." *Just as I knew my granddaughter would be.*

Lawrence drained his brandy. "How about some champagne? I brought it back from Paris."

"You'd better go a little slow, Son. Don't want to get stinking the night your daughter is born."

"And why not?" Lawrence asked, popping the cork and slopping wine over the rim of his glass.

"I know you better than this," Jefferson said, taking the flute. "What's wrong?"

Lawrence gulped the champagne. "You won't tell Mother?"

"Of course not."

"Really? I thought you told her everything."

"Everything? No. I have secrets she doesn't know about." Jefferson lowered his eyes. This time he was the one to bolt back the wine. "I'll have another."

324

Lawrence poured. "Eleanor hasn't slept with me since our honeymoon. That's when she got pregnant. She's been angry at me about it ever since."

"Good God, why?"

"She says the baby will ruin her figure. It seems her pretty Paris gowns are more important to her than the baby." He looked solemnly into his wine. "Or me."

"I see."

"Ironic, isn't it? You've loved Mother all your life and couldn't marry her. And I marry Eleanor but can't sleep with her. . . ."

"Or love her?" Jefferson probed.

"That either," Lawrence answered morosely.

"This isn't good," Jefferson said.

"Got any advice?" Lawrence smiled wryly.

Jefferson held his gaze steady. "Not one frigging scrap."

"I guess my only choice is to be philosophic about the whole thing. Barbara is my one chance to put my stamp on the world. I guess that's something, isn't it?"

Affection welled in Jefferson's eyes as he looked at his son. "It's a mighty big something, Lawrence. You have no idea."

* * * *

Caroline rushed too quickly up the staircase on her way to give William the news about the baby. Suddenly, her chest began aching as if someone were sitting on her heart. She couldn't catch her breath. She stopped halfway up the stairs and clung to the railing. Her knees gave way and she quickly found herself sitting on the step. She pressed her hand to her forehead and found it covered in cold perspiration. *What's happening to me?*

It was late at night and the kitchen staff had gone home. Only the butler and the housekeeper lived in the mansion with them, but they had been asleep for quite some time since Caroline had ordered them to bed while she waited for her grandchild to be born.

"Babies can take a long time to be born."

Since the servants' quarters were located at the far end of the house and another two stories up, even if she'd the strength to call out to someone, she doubted they would hear her.

She took a deep breath and then another. It was as if everything was in slow motion. She watched the dust motes dance in the moonbeams that shot through the leaded stained glass window at the top of the landing. She could hear the ticking of the grandfather clock in the upper hallway, but it sounded strange, as if someone were banging a gong slowly. She felt as if the staircase were undulating beneath her the way the ground moves during an earthquake.

This eruption was not from without, she knew. It was inside her. For the first time in her life, Caroline knew fear.

She wasn't afraid of death, she was afraid of not having one more day to love Jefferson, Lawrence and now . . . the baby.

Caroline pressed her hand against her heart and willed it to heal itself. "I can't die now! Not when I have everything I've ever wanted!" She leaned her face against one of the spindles and felt a rush of tears fall down her cheeks. "I'm not ready to go," she said. "I won't go. Not yet."

Caroline gave herself over half an hour to calm her heart and for the pain to ease. Then she pushed herself back to her feet. She was surprisingly surefooted, she realized. "Perhaps it wasn't my heart at all," she told herself as she continued toward William's room.

She opened the door and found him slumped over in his chair, the light still on.

She walked into the room and before she made it halfway across the room, she knew something was dreadfully wrong. There was a chill to the air that touched her soul, but not her skin.

"William?"

Silence.

She lifted his hand. It was still warm. She replaced it atop his accounting book. She looked down at his lifeless body. "He looks the same in death as he did in life. Poor soul. He never lived at all."

She felt no emotions for William. She'd given up a long time ago trying to reach him on an emotional level. He had given her nothing, and she had given him nothing in return.

The lone tear that trickled down her cheek surprised her. She hadn't expected to cry over him. Then she realized she was not crying for William, but for herself because she'd wasted her life staying married to William, when she could have married Jefferson, the man she loved.

She walked out of the room and closed the door, leaving the light on.

She'd be forced to rouse the servants after all.

But I'm not staying in this house for one more night. I want to wake up in the morning in Jefferson's arms. Finally, I'm going home.

Chinatown—1881

At precisely the same hour and within five minutes of Barbara Mansfield's birth, deep in the catacombs of Chinatown, Chen Su was born to Lon Su and Ling Yutang. No one was in attendance at the birth except Yin.

Yin performed her duties as both midwife and mother-in-law. She'd told her son that his seventh child would not be the son he'd hoped for and needed.

"I'm sick of your predictions, Mother," Lon Su said. "If this child is not a son, then you can dispose of it for all I care. I have more important matters to attend to. My father needs me."

"Your father uses you."

"He would respect me more if I had a son," he said angrily.

"When will you understand that your father respects no one? Not even himself. His heart is filled with hate. And you are following his lead quite nicely. I see unhappiness in your future."

Lon Su's face contorted with frustration and bitterness. "I don't want to hear your predictions, old woman. I need a son!"

"This child is a most important person. It is because of her that I came to this country. She is my destiny. And yours."

"Bah! Women's words. Save them for your customers!" He shot out of the house before Yin could reply,

Just as Yin had foretold to Ling, Chen was born with the "veil" over her face, marking her with the gift of prophecy that had steered the course of Yin's life.

Ling Yutang had none of the resourcefulness that Yin had cultivated all her life. She was nearly a slave to Lon Su, his demands, desires and control. "I admire you, Yin," Ling said when she heard the argument between Lon Su and Yin, "but what good does it do you to plot and plan against Nan-Yung, when you can never escape the house of Su?"

"Slavery is a condition of mind," Yin warned Ling Yutang many times. "No one controls what I think or do. No one can stop my visions from happening. I am blessed that way."

"It is difficult for me to understand," Ling Yutang said.

Yin smiled down at the tiny newborn baby girl. "Chen will understand. Perhaps it's not your fight to wage. When she grows, Chen will understand a great many things. Perhaps she'll be able to make a difference for our people and help them understand that fear and hatred do indeed cause disharmony in the earth as the ancient wise men have always said. I'm old and unsuccessful in my struggle with Nan-Yung. He generates his own evil. He thinks he's powerful, but he doesn't realize he is dying."

She looked down at the baby once again. Chen seemed to sense her grandmother's eyes and gazed back at Yin. Yin knew the baby could not see with her eyes yet, but she knew the baby was already "seeing" with her heart. "This child brings me new hope that *my* lineage not only lives, but thrives and will outlast the evil that runs in Nan-Yung's blood. You'll see, Ling, that Chen is no ordinary child. She'll have no equals in her life. She'll be unique among women."

Ling turned away from the mesmerizing stare of her baby daughter. "My only wish for her is that she be happy."

Yin nodded. "She'll find happiness, but not with an Oriental. He will be white."

Ling began to cry. "This is the worst thing you could have said to me."

Yin merely smiled. "You're like my own daughter, but your vision rides only the surface of the waters." Yin laid the baby next to Ling and touched Ling's forehead softly. "Have no fears about her fate. It's yourself you must protect. Now, rest."

Yin sang an old lullaby she remembered from her days inside the walls of the Forbidden City. When Ling slept, Yin left the room and closed the door quietly.

February 14, 1882

Jefferson Duke chose to host an elaborate party when Barbara was christened. Because Eleanor was overtaxed and overtired from the birth and caring for an infant despite the house servants and English nanny Lawrence had hired, she allowed Jefferson to take over party planning for 450 guests.

Jefferson's mansion on Nob Hill was eclipsed by none in size, elegance and furnishings. Never having an excuse to entertain this lavishly since he'd never married, Jefferson believed his turn had finally arrived to be extravagant.

For the christening he imported wines from France, Scotch whisky from

Scotland and vodka from Russia. He enlarged his kitchen staff to fifteen to prepare the many pastries, cakes and pies they would need. Quail, venison, turkeys and duck were smoked and grilled, hogs were roasted and three entire steers were cooked over open pits behind the mansion. Bushels of fresh vegetables and fruits were sailed in by boat from Southern California. Over three wagon-loads of ice were needed to keep the Alaskan crab and salmon fresh.

Nearly every hothouse in the Bay region was commandeered to produce floral bouquets, fern trees, rare palms, mossy beds and long ivy and rose garlands that were used to drape the round white-linen–covered tables, the staircases and the ceiling of the ballroom.

The household staff spent weeks cleaning every crystal prism on the mansion's twenty-six crystal chandeliers, polishing the parquetry and marquetry, and dusting the gilded frames surrounding Jefferson's extensive collection of new French artists like Edouard Manet and Pierre-Auguste Renoir.

The only thing marring Jefferson's high spirits and joy was the fact that he could not openly declare that Barbara Mansfield was his first-born grandchild.

Because William Mansfield had been a recluse for over fifteen years, most of the town barely acknowledged his passing. Therefore, few in San Francisco commented on Caroline's lack of adherence to mourning rituals. Caroline did not wear black, she did not restrict herself from parties, dinners or balls. In fact, she flagrantly immersed herself in the gaiety of the holiday season, wearing her newest French party gowns and winter ball gowns and indulged Jefferson's every request to show her off.

When he hosted the christening party, she chose a particularly impressive gown of rich bronze silk with gold silk rosettes on the bustle and around the hem. She wore her platinum hair piled high on her head with bronze and gold beads encircling her chignon. She danced till nearly midnight, allowing Jefferson's arms to hold her as tightly as he pleased.

Being too young to have been exposed to all the old rumors about Caroline and Jefferson at the time, Eleanor was shocked.

Eleanor was dressed in an English rose-pink satin and silk gown trimmed with hand-painted garlands of deep purple violets around the hem and edge of her short train as she listened to the Sperry girls and their mother discussing the scandalous assignation of their host.

Eleanor politely excused herself and went straightaway to her husband.

"Lawrence," she said in a flustered voice while fanning herself with a gilt fan painted with pink roses. "I've just heard the most outrageous gossip about your mother and Jefferson."

Lawrence nonchalantly slipped his arm around Eleanor's waist and kissed her beautiful cheek. He smiled to himself. "It's true," he said proudly.

"What?" Eleanor's shock escalated to abhorrence. "You can't be serious."

"She's loved him since I was a baby. And he's loved her. I was just a boy when I confronted Jefferson about the matter. He confirmed his feelings for Mother," Lawrence replied.

"This is outrageous! How will we survive such a scandal? And look at them. They're acting like lovesick youths. And at their age. It's disgusting!"

"It's beautiful," Lawrence retorted with a trace of growing anger at his wife's intolerance. "I think of their love as enduring, deep and loyal. Mother sacrificed her love for my father, who was probably the most selfish, mean-spirited man I've ever known. She deserves the happiness I see in her eyes tonight, Eleanor." His voice grew stern. Commanding. "If you do or say anything to take this moment from my mother, I'll personally remove you from this house."

Eleanor was incensed. "You act as if Jefferson's feelings are more important to you than mine."

Lawrence downed the remainder of his wine and glared at her. "You keep me from your bed, even now. You've closed me out of your heart, and it makes me wonder if I was ever a part of you. I admit my good sense was momentarily dulled by your incredible beauty and forthrightness when we met. Marrying you so quickly was no one's fault but my own." He paused thoughtfully and then continued. "But hear me well. His feelings and those of my mother *are* more important to me than your ego."

Eleanor stuck her beautiful nose in the air and threw back her exquisitely rounded alabaster-white shoulders. "Don't forget, if it weren't for me you wouldn't have your precious daughter, who, by the by, is the cause of this celebration."

"Point taken, Eleanor. But she's my daughter, too. Don't forget that."

Eleanor's eyes narrowed as her mind whirled with formulating plans of evening out the score between herself and her husband. She wasn't about to let him get away with saying such mean and hurtful things to her. "I won't forget it, Lawrence. Be assured of that!" She turned on her slippered foot and walked away from him, searching the room for one of the handsome young swains she'd dismissed over the past few years, all of whom were most eager to dance with her.

Jefferson held Caroline close and whispered, "You can't imagine how much I want to take you up those stairs, and one by one, undo the hooks on the back of your gown. I want to see you in the moonlight. I want to be inside you, where I belong."

"What about our guests?"

"I was teasing. But later . . ." He kissed the crook of her neck. "Marry me, Caroline. There's nothing to stop us now."

She clutched his back and felt a rush of happy tears. "Yes, Jefferson. I'll marry you."

So used to her refusals, Jefferson stopped dead in his tracks so abruptly that the next couple waltzed right into them. "I'm sorry, excuse me?" he said not to the man, but to Caroline. "You will?" he asked.

Caroline laughed. "I want nothing more."

He lifted her off the floor. Had he been younger, he would have twirled her around. "You will! You'll marry me!" He shouted the words loud enough that he could be heard over the orchestra. Half the dancers stopped, exchanged curious glances and once the impact of Jefferson's proposal registered with them, they began applauding. Those on the perimeter of the dance floor received the news from those close to Jefferson. Soon the story had circulated throughout the ballroom. The applause was thunderous.

Caroline turned and smiled to her friends and when she looked back at Jefferson, he took her in his arms and kissed her long, deep and with all the passion and love in his heart. Caroline languorously slipped her arms around his neck and indulged herself in their first public kiss.

The only person in attendance who cast disapproval on the happy couple was Eleanor. Her disdain was not missed by her husband, who ignored her, walked away from her and up to his mother and Jefferson and embraced them both, publicly granting them his blessing.

Lawrence turned to the crowd and said, "My only wish for my mother and Jefferson is that they wait not a minute longer to marry. Is there a minister in the house?"

The crowd broke into laughter and then walked up to Jefferson and Caroline to congratulate them.

Eleanor was incensed that Caroline had stolen the spotlight from herself and her baby, Barbara, who'd been presented at nine o'clock for all to see and then taken back upstairs by the nanny. Eleanor had been left behind, even by her husband, and she didn't like it.

"I'll make you pay for this, Jefferson Duke," she vowed to herself as yet another couple pushed past her on their way to offer best wishes to Jefferson and Caroline.

* * * *

Jefferson hungrily plunged his face into Caroline's breast and devoured her nipple. She sank her hands into his thick crop of hair and pressed him to her. "How can you make me always feel like a young girl, Jefferson?" she asked as his hand slipped down her belly.

"I love you," he said earnestly. "I'll love you till the day I die and beyond." Then he moved over her and entered her. He buried his face in the crook of her neck, feeling the mountain of her silver hair fall over his shoulder like water rushing over a mountain cliff. He brought her to the peak of ecstasy and together they cried out their rapture.

Jefferson cradled Caroline in his arms. "It's so wonderful to know we don't have to lurk in the shadows anymore. You can stay in my arms all night and all the next day if you want."

"I know," she sighed. "It's funny how life works out. I never thought I deserved this much happiness."

"How sad, my love." He swept a lock of hair from her cheek. "Maybe that's why we haven't been together until now. Remember what my mother always said? Thoughts are things."

"Maybe there's something to that," she yawned.

"Sleep well, darling. And have happy dreams." Jefferson closed his eyes.

Deep in the altered dimensions of his dream state, Jefferson found himself sitting beside the Jamaican waterfall his mother, Rachel, had described to him when he was a boy. The water sang in whispers as it cascaded over the rock. At the base of the rock sat his grandmother, Yuala, now just a child. She lifted her hand to him and beckoned him to come to her.

"You're my own flesh and blood," she began, "and because we are one heart, I have chosen to be with you at this moment of sadness."

"You're mistaken," Jefferson smiled. "I've never been so happy in all my life."

Yuala's dark eyes were filled with deep sorrow when she looked at him.

She lifted her hand to touch his cheek. "I only come to you so that you'll know you're not alone. You'll never be alone. Your mother is with me, too."

Suddenly, Rachel appeared at the waterfall adorned in a gown of sparkling golden light. He sucked in his breath. It had been a very long time since Rachel had visited him.

"I've come to tell you that I love you, Jefferson," Rachel said. "Listen to my mother."

Then Yuala lifted her other hand and stretched it out to the right. From the shadows of the edge of his dream walked Caroline. She was young again, like the first time he'd seen her. Her hair was radiant like the light from a full moon and her blue eyes sparkled with starlight. She smiled at him with a peacefulness he knew was not of the earthbound.

"I love you, Jefferson. Like your grandmother and mother, I'm with you, too. Never doubt my love for you. Never. Take great care to watch over Lawrence and Barbara for me."

Jefferson bolted awake and sat upright. Sweat beads of icy fear covered his body. "Caroline!" He screamed and then looked down at his sleeping lover.

He scooped her up into his arms and held her to his heart. Tears filled his eyes as every word from the dream engraved themselves on his memory. His tears fell on her cheek, but she didn't flinch. She didn't stir. He rocked her body back and forth as his hysteria mounted.

"My love! My love!" he cried.

But Caroline couldn't hear him.

Caroline's spirit had left her body.

thirty-one

The dream is the small hidden door in the deepest and most intimate sanctum of the soul, which opens into that primeval cosmic night that was soul long before there was a conscious ego and will be soul far beyond what a conscious ego could ever reach.

—CARL GUSTAV JUNG
PSYCHOLOGICAL REFLECTIONS: A JUNG ANTHOLOGY, COLLECTED WORKS,
VOL. X, THE MEANING OF PSYCHOLOGY FOR MODERN MAN

The news of Caroline Mansfield's death the night of her engagement to Jefferson Duke shook the souls of San Francisco. The story of Caroline's nearly forty-year love affair with Jefferson Duke was discussed with appropriate reverence and sentimentality.

Both Lawrence's house on Sutter Street and Jefferson's house on Nob Hill were flooded with flowers and sympathy messages.

During the twenty-four hours after Caroline's death, Jefferson refused to come out of his bedroom, choosing to remain in the bed where she had died.

"It's as if she's still here," he said to Mrs. Kilcarney, the housekeeper. He touched the sheets. "It's still warm here. I can smell her perfume on the pillow," he said, his eyes welling again.

Mrs. Kilcarney couldn't stand the sadness that wafted through the room. "Maybe later you'll feel like eatin'," she said, closing the door reverently.

Jefferson finally emerged the next day when Lawrence brought Barbara to visit.

"I thought seeing the baby would cheer you, Jefferson."

"It's I who should have called on you," Jefferson said. "Here, let me hold her."

Lawrence handed the tiny infant over. "Eleanor is still fatigued. . . ."

"You don't have to say anything, Lawrence. I understand."

Lawrence shook his head. "I wish I did. She's already hired a wet nurse. She won't have anything to do with Barbara."

Jefferson looked into the infant's face and beamed. "Well, we're not going to bother with that now, are we, my love? Between your Papa and I, we will spoil you with all the love you can take."

The baby cooed.

Jefferson looked at Lawrence. "I thought babies didn't smile until they were several months old."

Lawrence looked at his daughter. "Must be an old wives' tale. She's smiling." He glanced at Jefferson's red-rimmed eyes. "And so are you."

They exchanged a long look.

"I miss her, Lawrence. With every breath I take. It's so . . . painful."

"I know. I miss her, too. She was the only person who's ever really loved me."

A tear fell down Jefferson's cheek. "You're wrong. I've loved you."

Lawrence held his breath. "I think I knew that."

"You're my family, now, Lawrence. You and Barbara. Is that all right with you?"

"I wouldn't want it any other way," he said, wiping his cheek with the flat of his palm.

While Jefferson and Lawrence visited, Mrs. Kilcarney sneaked into the master bedroom and changed the bed linens. She slipped down the back staircase, handed the sheets to Maria, the upstairs maid, and told her to take all the household linens to the Chinese laundry on Grant Avenue that Mrs. Hutchinson's maid, Eloise, had recommended.

"The Su laundry is the best there is. Tell them to scent the linens with this lavender water and that you'll return for them tomorrow. I want no smell of death in this house," Mrs. Kilcarney told Maria.

"Yes'm," Maria bowed and took the bundles out the back door.

The Duke carriage pulled to a stop outside the Su laundry. Maria got out of the carriage and carried two tied bundles of soiled table and bed linens into the laundry.

The air was moist, hot and smelled of soaps and lye, Maria thought as she walked up to the fifty-year-old Yin who was standing behind the counter. Maria didn't know many Orientals, but this woman was particularly beautiful with sparkling, friendly almond-shaped eyes and a countenance that radiated an almost unearthly glow.

Maria didn't notice the middle-aged man in the hallway at the back of the shop as he walked back and forth from one desk to another, deeply engrossed in paperwork.

"I'd like to have these linens cleaned and pressed. I was told you would scent the sheets with this lavender water." Maria handed Yin the bottle Mrs. Kilcarney had given her.

"We do this," Yin said and made Chinese characters on a small piece of paper. "The name?"

"They belong to Mr. Jefferson Duke, but my name is Maria."

Just then the tinkling bell over the door sounded as another maid entered the shop. At the same time, Nan-Yung walked up to his wife and placed his hand on her neck and eased her back and away from the counter.

Nan-Yung had heard the name of his enemy. Many was the day Nan-Yung thought of his riches and how his fortune could buy the best assassins money would buy. He could buy anonymity in Chinatown, but not in San Francisco proper. Jefferson was incredibly prominent. His death would raise many eyebrows and many more questions than he cared to fuel. If the assassins were traced back to him, Nan-Yung could go to jail. That he worried about. He needed to buy more white politicians to protect himself, to ensure his one day getting revenge.

In the meantime, Nan-Yung was content to continue on his path of simply killing every person whom Jefferson Duke loved.

Nan-Yung smiled at Maria. "You from the Duke big house?"

"Yes," Maria said, as the other maid walked up to the counter.

"I know you!" the young girl exclaimed. "Mrs. Kilcarney told me about you. I'm Eloise. You've only been in Mr. Duke's employ for a week now?"

"Yes," Maria replied. "And if ever there was a bad time to start. First that big party the other night, I thought I'd drop from all the work. Then Mr. Duke announces his engagement to Mrs. Mansfield, and then Mrs. Mansfield dies in his bed! I can't tell you all the scandalous things I've heard since I've been in that house!"

Eloise prided herself on always knowing the indiscretions of the town. She'd worked in the city's finest mansions. Her work was so superior that a bidding war had erupted when she'd announced to Jefferson Duke she was leaving his employ three years ago. She didn't have any truck with Jefferson Duke, it was simply that since he seldom entertained and kept to himself so much, Eloise had little to do. She believed it was impossible to build a reputation for herself at such a dull household. Now here was this newcomer, Maria, taking full credit for the juiciest gossip San Francisco had seen in twenty years. "There's more to the story than you'll ever hear in that house," Eloise said.

Maria slapped her hand to her cheek dramatically, but her eyes belied her impatience to hear more. "No! Tell all!"

"Since I worked there for so many years, I saw with my own eyes that Mr. Duke has a very, very special bond with Lawrence Mansfield. Have you seen the two together? Notice their eyes are much the same. I'm not the only one who thinks Lawrence Mansfield is Jefferson Duke's son!"

"No!" Maria was shocked.

Eloise nodded firmly. "Take my word fer it. That affair goes back further than anyone knows. Lawrence has known about his mother and Jefferson for a long time. I used to catch Miss Caroline sneakin' out of the house at dawn. If you ask me, that new baby is Jefferson's granddaughter."

Maria was awestricken by Eloise's superior knowledge and insight. "I wonder if the new Mrs. Lawrence Mansfield suspects that her husband is a bastard."

Eloise grinned at Maria's audacity. "I like you, Maria. I think we'll become good friends."

"I'd like that," Maria said and left the shop while Eloise turned to Nan-Yung and requested the Hutchinson linens.

Nan-Yung ordered Yin to retrieve the mountains of linens for his good customer, Eloise. Yin helped Eloise carry the linens out to the Hutchinson's new phaeton and deposited them in the boot for her, but all the while her eyes were glued on Nan-Yung. She knew he didn't understand enough English to know all the conversation she so clearly understood, but he knew Jefferson Duke's name when he heard it.

The death of Duke's lover will be a sign to Nan-Yung that his hatred is justified. For me it's a sign that I am to reach for the stars.

Yin took a deep breath before reentering the shop. She waited until she saw Nan-Yung rush to the back of the store where a secret door led to his real office in the catacombs.

While he descended a ladder that deposited him on the now stone-paved tunnel floor, Yin grabbed her yarrow sticks and threw them for herself.

Just as I thought. Lawrence's child is finally here. Now we can be together.

Nan-Yung's underground tunnel was dug deeply so that he could stand erect as he moved down the corridor to the elaborately hand-carved door that led to his office and counting rooms.

Inside his office, the pungent smell of burning sandalwood incense filled his nostrils. Nan-Yung had spent a fortune on the furnishings in these rooms. Because he'd seen firsthand what an emperor's palace in Peking was like, he'd promised himself the indulgences he so rightly deserved for being the emperor of the opium trade in San Francisco.

The walls were brick, and over the brick hung intricate silk tapestries woven in gold, silver and red threads. Priceless antique porcelain vases a man's-height high stood on either side of the door. His desk was made of gold, carved ivory and black-lacquered wood. A seven-foot-high daybed with carved rosewood sat nearly in the middle of the room. Huge, round, log-shaped pillows were covered in black velvet and rested against the head-board and footboard. The bed was mounded and draped with Russian sables and Indian silk bedding, and like an emperor, Nan-Yung's harem was comprised of the youngest, most beautiful maidens in Chinatown.

In most cases, Nan-Yung traded the deflowering of these girls for the drug and gambling debts of their fathers. Once one of the girls entered his harem, she was never allowed to return to her family again. If a girl displeased him in his bed by not submitting to his depraved needs and desires, he'd banish her to the lowest catacombs where he kept many of his slaves.

The slaves he used as laborers to continue building tunnels and catacombs under the city. Others he used on his ships to sail to China and India where he purchased opium. Some of the women he put into prostitution on the Barbary Coast in secret opium dens and gambling houses.

As the years had passed, Nan-Yung's sexual needs had become insatiable. He was always on the lookout for his next mistress. He watched the young children play in the streets of Chinatown, knowing his patience would be repaid in time with an ever-ripening crop of virgins. It was his wish that someday his reputation as a powerful lover would entice young girls to come to him for lessons in sexuality and lovemaking.

Nan-Yung did not realize that his narcissism had warped his mind. His hatred and need for revenge had created a dark and sinister universe in which his intense power drew in everyone who came into contact with him.

He sat in the straight-backed elaborately carved black-malachite throne that had once belonged to an emperor of the Ching dynasty. He lifted a velvet-covered mallet and hit the brass gong next to his desk, which summoned one of his henchman.

From the room next door, a six-foot-tall Chinese man with an expansive chest, enormous arms and muscular legs walked in. Lee Tong was seventeen years old and wanted nothing more in the world than to serve Nan-Yung because he believed that one day, his loyalty to his employer would be rewarded.

Nan-Yung did not tell Lee Tong he thought loyalty was akin to naïveté. "My desires need fulfillment," Nan-Yung said.

"What do you desire?" Lee Tong asked, thinking he would be asked to kidnap another young girl from her parents' home. Suddenly, he felt his own arousal in his groin. Thirteen-year-old girls were no match for Lee Tong's brawn. They kicked and a couple scratched him, but sometimes Lee Tong would grant himself a few sexual indulgences of his own before he brought the virgins to Nan-Yung. The girls never told Nan-Yung about Lee Tong's molestations because they were afraid of both men.

As long as Lee Tong did not break their maidenheads, he knew he was safe. Often he stood in the dark shadows behind the partially opened door to Nan-Yung's throne room and watched as Nan-Yung took the girls with so little finesse and imagination, it was an insult to the Chinese race. Lee Tong often rubbed himself off as he watched his employer and then when Nan-Yung was no longer pleased with the girl, Lee Tong would visit her in her cell night after night and show her how to pleasure him with her tongue, lips and mouth.

Lee Tong believed in his heart that someday he would outsmart both Nan-Yung and even his son, Lon Su, and take over Chinatown. His own greed enabled him to do anything for Nan-Yung, even murder.

"Fate has delivered my greatest enemy to me once again. I want you to find Lawrence Mansfield. Find his house. Discover his vices. Then I will prey upon him. If he needs opium, sell it to him. If he needs women, give him the most accomplished we can find. If he gambles, rid him of his fortunes."

Lee Tong did not reply, only bowed deeply and turned to leave the room.

"When he has no self-respect left . . . kill him," Nan-Yung ordered.
Lee Tong only smiled. Broadly.

* * * *

For nearly three years, Jefferson's grief locked him in a mental haze from
which he didn't want to be released. Here he could visit with Caroline any
time he wanted. He still tended his various business concerns and met with
politicians about state and local matters, but for the most part, his heart died
that day with Caroline.

The only time he resurrected himself from his daydreams was when he
visited with his granddaughter, Barbara.

Jefferson's favorite pastime was to fetch Barbara early in the morning,
leaving Eleanor the day to herself so that she could shop and attend the
many luncheons and teas to which she was invited.

Barbara was a precocious child, independent, extremely bright and more
beautiful than any child Jefferson had ever known. He loved to buy clothes
for her and take her for rides in his carriage to show her off to his friends.

He called her "stardancer" because the platinum flecks in her china-blue
eyes reminded him of Caroline's eyes. Her rich, dark-brown hair was
Eleanor's, but her strong oval face, straight nose, thick lashes and arched,
expressive brows were more Jefferson than they were even Lawrence. To
Jefferson, the family resemblance was unmistakable. At only three, Barbara
was taller than her playmates and Jefferson could tell she was destined to be
athletically built when she matured. She could already ride a horse side-
saddle with ease, but when he took her to the rolling countryside to the north
of the city and allowed her to ride astride, Barbara confidently galloped
alongside Jefferson.

One day as they rode along the hillsides where Jefferson remembered the
Spanish fiestas, Barbara abruptly pulled her horse to a halt.

"May we stop here, Jefferson?" Barbara called him by his familiar name
ever since she could remember. She remembered that "Duke" had been an easy
name for her to say, but Jefferson had pressed her to struggle with his first
name. She'd tried so hard to say it correctly, and in the beginning she remembered calling him "Jabberson." He'd loved the nickname, but she was
proud she'd learned to say his name correctly.

"Of course," Jefferson said, dismounting and holding Barbara around her waist as he lifted his small granddaughter off her horse.

They stood under a particularly large spreading oak. Suddenly, Jefferson realized that it was on this hill where Caroline had sat on the same blanket as Dolores Sanchez so many years ago. Jefferson felt his knees go weak, and he abruptly sat on the ground indulging himself in his memories.

Barbara put her little hand on Jefferson's cheek. She felt a tear. "Jefferson, why are you crying?"

"I didn't know that I was."

"Yes. See?" She opened her tiny fingers and showed him the tear.

"I was thinking about your grandmother, Caroline."

There was so much sadness in Jefferson's voice that Barbara put her arms around his neck to comfort him, but they did not reach. "You love her," she said as a statement, not questioning him in the least.

"Yes. Always."

"I know," she sighed and put her head on his shoulder.

"Did your father tell you that?"

"Oh, no! Papa doesn't talk about Grandmother. Mommy won't let him. She gets a snarly face when he talks about Grandmother Caroline."

"Then how do you know, little one?" He smoothed her long brown curls down her small back.

"Grandmother told me that she loves you, too."

Jefferson chuckled to himself and shook his head. "You must be mistaken. Caroline died when you were a baby. On the night of your christening party."

"Don't be silly, Jefferson. She talks to me all the time. Sometimes when I get very lonely when you're too busy to see me and Mommy has to go out again, I just ask Grandmother Caroline to visit me and she does."

Jefferson was stunned. He felt chills creep up his back and cover his skull. "She, she visits?"

"Yes." Barbara slipped her hands from his neck and then turned to put her back against his chest. She pulled one of his arms around her. "I like it when we sit like this. It feels safe to me."

"Caroline used to say that," Jefferson whispered. "What has she told you?"

"Only that she's happy in heaven. She's with my other grandmothers, she said. She told me that she loves me. She doesn't usually say very much. I do most of the talking. I tell her about my toys and show her my dolls. She likes that."

Jefferson didn't doubt for one minute that Barbara was telling him the truth. His own experiences in the realm of dreams and netherworlds would never be believed by most people, but it was part of his reality. He remembered when his dreams used to tell him what project to pursue, what business to invest in and what dangers to avoid.

But it had been three years since he'd remembered any dreams at all. With his arms around Barbara, he realized he'd cut himself off from the dream world because he knew deep in his heart that if he met Caroline in another dimension, he would have to admit to his rational mind that she was dead. He could never bring her back.

Jefferson lifted his face to the afternoon sun and let the warm spring breeze dry his tears. "Caroline is dead, Barbara," he said to convince himself.

"I know," she replied and patted his hand comfortingly.

Jefferson tightened his embrace around his granddaughter. He was alive, and so was Barbara. It was time he focused his mind on the future, for her sake. It was time he put his grief behind him and give his love to this little girl. Though she would never know he was her grandfather, that was no reason to stop himself from building a better world in which she would someday live.

Jefferson remembered his mother's long-ago dream that foretold of a beautiful young woman, his granddaughter, Barbara, whose destiny was as much a part of San Francisco as his own.

There were a great many changes taking place in San Francisco. Jefferson wanted Barbara to have the best education money could buy. He wanted her to have all the advantages a cultured city could give her. He'd been approached by several of society's leaders to help establish the Bachelor's Cotillion Club. To date, there had been too much license given to young girls, and many of the city's founders were worried about the hooligans that gained entreé into San Franciscan society and absconded with or ruined their daughters.

Jefferson didn't want anything like that to happen to Barbara. He wanted her to make a good marriage someday. He hoped she would find the kind of love he'd had with Caroline, but with none of the heartaches. Perhaps it was time he became more involved in such pursuits, he thought. For him to be one of the determining factors in San Francisco's social life could be important to Barbara someday.

Mrs. Eleanor Martin and Ned Greenway proposed the Bachelor Cotillion Club to build up the social structure, debutante by debutante, basing choices on the father's wealth and achievements. The girls were to be well-educated, gracious and charming. Chaperones were to be restored. Perhaps it was time for stronger leadership and more rigid censors, he thought.

After all, Barbara was a headstrong child already. He could tell from the way she rode her horse that she was much like Dolores in some ways and he didn't want her to reach a tragic end as Dolores had. He would never be as strict with Barbara as Dolores's father had been with her, keeping her locked inside a house most of her life. No, Barbara was different in many ways. She had Caroline's intelligence and even his overly active imagination. Because she was always willing to try new things, sometimes without thinking things through, he believed he needed to protect her.

Barbara was his most precious treasure, and it was time he concentrated on the living.

San Francisco—1892

Lawrence was always torn apart inside whenever he had to leave Barbara for one of his buying trips overseas. Because business in San Francisco was still flourishing despite many of the economic downturns on the East Coast, Lawrence found the emporium's inventory dwindling faster than he could replenish it.

By the time Barbara was ten years old, Lawrence had replaced himself. He'd found a wonderful man by the name of Jasper Akins, who not only knew the Orient and the Middle East as well as Lawrence, but he was an even better negotiator. As a result, Lawrence made more money than ever.

And Eleanor spent money with abandon. She demanded the best French gowns and the trips to Paris to buy them. Lawrence obliged. She wanted jewels from Harry Winston in New York. Lawrence bought sapphire bracelets, diamond tiaras, ruby stomachers and emerald waterfall necklaces that were the envy of czarinas. When they went to Platt Hall to hear Oscar Wilde lecture dressed in his short breeches, velvet coat, silver-buckled shoes, lace shirt and gloves, the journalists expounded on Eleanor's beauty to the exclusion or merest of mention of any other women.

The next morning, Barbara would sit at the breakfast table while her mother, wearing one of the revived Empire dressing gowns and feather boas, read the article in the *Argonaut,* the *Daily Morning Call* or the *Chronicle.*

"Look here, Barbara, Mr. Benet is describing what I wore to the Literary Club! And here," she picked up yet another section of the paper, "is where someone else talks about me . . . with Mrs. George Hearst, the founder of the new Century Club." She put the paper down and placed a glum-looking face in the palm of her hand.

"What's the matter, Mommy? It all sounded wonderful to me. Someday, I'll be a famous journalist and I'll write stories about you going off to Europe to see the Queen of England," Barbara said, trying to cheer her mother.

"I *must* talk with your father again. It's time for us to move out of this house."

Barbara looked around her at the lavishly hand-painted murals on the dining room walls and above to the Waterford chandelier. "What's wrong with this house?"

"It's the wrong address."

"Huh?" Barbara couldn't figure out how they could be living in the same house all her life and suddenly be at the wrong address. Sometimes her mother just didn't make any sense at all. No wonder Jefferson didn't have time for "Eleanor's twaddle," as he called such nonsense.

"Right here, Dixon Wecter shrewdly says that it is time for the plutocracy of San Francisco to become aristocracy. It's time for a weeding out of nouvelle riche and firmly establish the old guard. That's us, Barbara, the old guard. You remember that. Anyway, the nouveau riche will supplant us if we don't dig ourselves out of stagnation."

"We're in stagnation?" Barbara was horrified, but she wasn't sure why.

"Geographically, society's boundaries are Nob Hill, Taylor Street, Bush and Pine, Rincon Hill, and a few vara lots near the Mission and Presidio hills and Jefferson Square to Pacific Avenue." Eleanor looked her daughter square in the eyes. "I want to move to Nob Hill."

"Hooray!" Barbara jumped to her feet. "Can we go to live with Jefferson now?"

Eleanor frowned. *That's not what I had in mind*, she mused to herself as her daughter danced around the room.

"I'll go ask Papa!" Barbara went racing up the stairs.

Eleanor dipped a silver spoon in her china coffee cup. "Don't bother, Barbara. He's a tightwad. He won't give me a new house."

Barbara tapped on the door to her father's bedroom and before she heard his reply, she went dashing inside. She rushed up to her father, who was tying his tie at the mirror over the bureau, hugged him quickly and then jumped on the unmade bed. Barbara would never act in her mother's bedroom the way she did in her father's. Here she was free to be herself.

"What are you up to today, Pet?" Lawrence asked Barbara with a smile as he came over to the bed, leaned down and kissed her forehead.

"Mommy says we have to move. It's not socially acceptable to live here anymore," she said, testing the waters.

"I'll bet she says a lot more than that," he frowned while sticking his arms through his waistcoat.

"Can I come to the emporium with you, Papa?"

"Not today."

Barbara pouted. "Why not? I miss you all day and sometimes you get home so late now. Why is that?"

"Business," Lawrence lied.

"Oh. Well, I could wait for you. Then we could talk."

Lawrence shook his head. "Talk to me now."

Barbara crossed her arms over her chest. Her blue eyes flashed with fire as she lifted her dainty chin to her father's face. "I've decided I want to be a journalist, Papa, and I've written some stories that are better than anything in the *Call* or the *Chronicle*."

Lawrence laughed aloud. "I'm sure they are, Pet. And I'd love to listen to them. Perhaps tomorrow."

"But, Papa. I want you to help me sell my stories to the *Call*."

Lawrence howled with laughter, went to his daughter and put his arms around her. "You, my dearest, are a delight. However, you are only ten years old and until you finish your schooling, I doubt I could convince the owner of any newspaper to hire you . . . just yet."

"Papa, I want—"

"Please do not use that word, Barbara. Your mother uses it all too much in this house." He put out his hand to her. "Now come with me downstairs and give me a kiss for the day."

Barbara bounced off the bed and gladly took her father's hand.

"What about a new house?" Barbara asked.

"Tell your mother to forget it," he replied sourly. "Even if we built a new house, she'd never be satisfied."

Barbara sighed heavily. "I know."

Lawrence didn't bother to see his wife before he left. Instead, he hugged his daughter and accepted her little kiss. "Good-bye, Pet. I love you."

"I love you, too, Papa," Barbara said brightly. "And I'll wait up for you tonight. No matter how long it takes."

Lawrence took a hired carriage to the flat he'd rented in the Italian section of the city. Few people knew him here. Even less questioned the Chinese woman who delivered the laundry to the apartment with a bay view.

Hearing the key in the door, Lawrence's heart jumped. He rushed to the door and opened it.

"Did anyone see you?"

"No," Yin answered. "But I'm always afraid."

Taking her in his arms he kissed her tenderly. "Don't be afraid. I'll keep you safe."

"You don't understand. I was afraid I would miss you. I was afraid of living another day without your touch," she replied, caressing his cheek.

He held her close. "I can't believe how painful it is not seeing you. Now I know the agony my mother and Jefferson endured all those years and so needlessly."

"Perhaps they were wise not to push fate," she said, moving out of his embrace. "Perhaps the time has come that we should . . . take greater care."

"What?" he went to her.

She hugged herself. "I came here today to tell you that it's become too dangerous for us. I sense death around us and I couldn't bear it if anything happened to you. If I didn't warn you."

"Yin, please. You were the one who came to me at the emporium. You sought me out. When I think what courage that took . . . "

"Courage? I should have let you find me that day on the dock when you first came back to San Francisco. I never should have waited to love you. Sometimes I listen to the stars too much. But the *I Ching* sticks told me I had to wait until after your daughter was born. Then I would be free to love you. When your mother died, I sensed you were as lonely as I. My heart went out to you. I thought you needed me."

"And I did. When you came to the emporium, you didn't have to say a word. Just the look in your eyes. I knew I'd found you again. For so many years, I thought you were an illusion. Sometimes I think I spent my whole life looking for you. It was your spirit that lured me overseas. You were right. We are of one mind."

"You're my one true love," she said softly.

"Let's not talk about being apart. I wanted to see you to tell you that I'm going to ask Eleanor for a divorce. We can find a way for you to divorce Nan-Yung and then we can marry."

Yin's eyes widened. "You want to marry me? Your people would never allow you to wed a Chinese. This is impossible."

He shook his head. "I watched my mother waste her entire life because she was either too guilty, too scared or too worried about what society thought. I've learned from her life. I've learned life is not a dress rehearsal. This is all there is. And damn it, I deserve some happiness. So do you."

Yin felt her fears melt. "I never dared to think like this."

He grabbed her arms. His enthusiasm rushed through his veins. "We can do anything. We can take Barbara and we can sail around the world. I can show you the Nile. London. The Parthenon. I can even take you back to China."

"No, I don't want to go there," she smiled happily at him. "I want to be with you, my love. Wherever that takes me."

He held her close. "I'll make an incredible life for us, I promise. I can arrange everything with the lawyers about your divorce. You can stay here. Don't even go back there to get your clothes. I'll buy you new clothes."

"Western clothes?"

"Not unless you want them. I like you just the way you are."

"Good. I don't want to change the way I dress or think."

"I'm not asking you to. I'm only asking you to live with me . . . forever."

She took a deep breath. "I'll stay here. You will see the men who can do this for us today?"

"Yes."

"Oh, my love. I did not dare to dream I could be this happy."

"Then it's all set?" he asked anxiously.

She nodded. "Before you go, will you make love to me first?"

"Will I make . . . ?" Chuckling, he picked her up in his arms and carried her to their bedroom.

* * * *

Lawrence walked out of the building after being with Yin that night. The night fog was as thick as soup. Lawrence couldn't see a foot in front of him. Too, his mind and heart were occupied thinking and yearning for Yin. It hadn't occurred to him that he was in danger.

He didn't see the carriage coming toward him through the thick fog, but he heard the horses' hooves thundering around him. Not being able to discern their direction, he started to jump back onto the sidewalk, when the horses came up from behind him.

He had not even turned when he felt the blow to his body. With a thud, he fell to the ground. Pain crushed him. Hooves trampled him as if the horses from Hades had stopped intently to crush him over and over. To finish him off.

"Barbara," he uttered her name over the rising blood in his throat. He raised his hand hoping to grasp something, impotently struggling to save himself.

He clutched at the air. "Must tell . . . Barbara . . ." he choked, but there was no one to listen.

"Your . . . grandfather . . . Jeff—"

Lawrence opened his eyes one last time, thinking he saw a bright light. "Yin?" He realized it was only the fog.

He exhaled and died.

* * * *

Lawrence Mansfield never returned home that day. His body was found the next morning outside a brothel on the Barbary Coast, an apparent victim of a hit-and-run by a runaway carriage.

Barbara had waited all night for her father to return so that she could read him the stories she'd written.

When the police came to the door to give Eleanor the news of Lawrence's death, Barbara was still in the salon waiting.

She crept into the hall.

"What are they saying, Mommy?"

Eleanor's face was a mass of confusion. "That's impossible. Lawrence doesn't go there. Would never go . . . there! My God, what are you saying?"

"He's dead, ma'am."

Barbara looked at the officer. "No, he's not! He said he was coming home! He said he would listen to my stories! He said he would help me sell them! He's not dead! He's not!"

"Quiet, Barbara!" Eleanor shouted.

"But they're lying!" she screamed back, tears streaming down her cheeks.

"I said, be quiet! I can't think." She turned a charming smile to the policeman. "Now, I don't know who this person is that you've found, but it's not my husband."

"That's why we'd like to have you identify the body, Mrs. Mansfield. Make a positive identification."

"I'll get my wrap," Eleanor said, pushing past the crying Barbara. "Lawrence would never degrade us by going to the Barbary Coast. Never in a million years."

"I want to go with you," Barbara said, still crying.

"No, you stay here until I get back."

"Mommy, please, I want to see for myself."

"Stop it this instant, Barbara. The morgue is no place for a child. When I do find out where your father spent last night, he's going to wish he were dead."

Eleanor stormed out of the house.

Barbara turned and saw the ashen faces of the servants. It was all the proof she needed.

Crying, she raced up the staircase clutching her sheaves of paper to her chest. She went to her bedroom, closed the door and locked it.

She put the carefully written pages in the metal trash can, lit a wooden match and ignited the bundle. Mesmerized by the flames she watched her words curl, turn into ash and die.

Now they're dead. Just like Papa.

thirty-two

Thus the whirligig of time brings in his revenges.

—WILLIAM SHAKESPEARE
TWELFTH-NIGHT, V, I, L. 388

Jefferson Duke considered bribery as a solution to the inability of the city police to find Lawrence's murderer.

"It was an accident, Jefferson," Chief Ned Phillips said for the umpteenth time.

"I tell you, Lawrence was murdered. He never went to the Barbary Coast."

"I beg to differ with you. I haven't let any of this information out of my office, Jefferson, because I know how close you are to Eleanor and her little girl. But I've got witnesses that will testify on the Bible itself that Lawrence had become a frequent visitor to that brothel for nearly a year."

"I don't believe it," Jefferson argued, running his hand through his graying blond hair.

Chief Phillips shoved his hands onto his hips. "Fine! Let's go down there, and I'll let you talk to some of those people."

"You think I would believe them?"

"Why the hell not? This idea of yours that he was murdered is just insane. What have you got to base your allegations on, Jefferson?"

Jefferson stared at Ned. How could he tell him the truth? How could he tell a grown intelligent man he'd been visited in a dream by an apparition of his mother, Rachel, and she'd told him Lawrence was murdered? "Nothing. It's just a hunch of mine."

"Hunches don't count in this office, Jefferson." Ned went to the window and looked out at the city. "Goddamn it, you've been to this office every day for two weeks, Jefferson. You're obsessed with this case. I realize you've built practically one half this city, but that doesn't allow you to take my time away from real issues. Real crimes. You get my drift?"

"Yes, Ned. I understand," Jefferson replied, feeling deflated.

"Go home and get some rest, Jefferson. You look like you haven't slept in a month of Sundays." Ned slapped Jefferson good-naturedly on the back.

Jefferson had not slept at all since Lawrence's death. He'd had not one dream but several in which he'd been told Lawrence's death was far from accidental. What he didn't understand was why.

Why Lawrence? Why the connection to the Barbary Coast, and why now? Something was happening in Jefferson's life that didn't make sense.

The police flatly refused to help him any more, and the only thing Jefferson could do at this point was to conduct an investigation himself.

When he walked out of the police station, he told his driver to take him directly to the Golden Door, the brothel where Jefferson would begin looking for the mistress the police claimed his son kept.

The Barbary Coast was a string of ill-constructed gambling houses, saloons, brothels, sweatshops and shanties. It smelled of human and animal excrement, sewage and hopelessness. Jefferson had heard many stories about the crimes, the depravity, even Shanghais and white slavery that were part of life along the Barbary Coast, but he'd always been too busy with business, too concerned with society affairs, the erection of yet another opera house to pay attention to the poverty and social ills of his beloved city.

Now his inattentiveness had come home to haunt him.

The Golden Door was not gold at all, but weathered brown siding with two windows on either side of a single white-painted front door. The house had an upper story, a second-floor balcony and porch and a tar-paper roof. It was the least imposing of all the structures in the area.

Jefferson told his driver to wait for him. The man not only nodded, but displayed a pistol he'd hidden under the driver's perch.

"I'll be right here, sir," he said.

Jefferson went to the door and knocked. It was a long moment before the door was opened by a handsome, rather large woman in her mid-forties. She wore no makeup, her hair was combed into a tight, matronly chignon and her only jewelry was a cameo pin she wore at the collar of her very prim white blouse which she'd tucked into a black bombazine skirt. She looked like a schoolteacher, not the mistress of a bordello.

"Good day, sir," she said pleasantly enough.

"My name is Jefferson Duke. I was wondering if you could tell me about the night my son—" he stopped abruptly, surprised that he'd nearly let the truth slip out for the first time in his life. "About the night Lawrence Mansfield was killed."

"Sorry. I don't know anyone by that name."

"Mansfield. He was run down by a team of horses right outside your bordello here."

She shook her head. "Don't know what you're talking about."

"Lawrence—"

She interrupted him. "Look, mister. Somebody dies down here every night. Nothin' new or strange about that. I never ask names or questions."

"You don't understand. The police have refused to help me. I've tried. They think I'm crazy. I was thinking that maybe you could tell me about a particular Chinese girl he was said to be seeing. I thought maybe she might be working for you."

She folded her arms over her chest. "I only have one Oriental girl here. Her name is Mei Su."

"I was hoping you could tell me about her."

"She's dead."

"What?" Jefferson thought the earth had swayed, her comment unsettled him so much.

The prim woman bit her bottom lip fighting back anger and pain. "Some big brute-type Oriental came in here two days ago. Said he had to have her. Well, he did. She was bleeding from every orifice in her body by the time I found her. There wasn't anything we could do."

"You didn't call a doctor?"

The woman started to laugh. "There aren't any doctors down here. This is the Barbary Coast. Nobody cares if the world loses a prostitute!" She started to slam the door.

Jefferson smashed his hand against the door keeping it open. "Please, try to remember. Lawrence was tall, eyes like mine, very handsome, well-dressed. His carriage was black lacquered and had brass appointments."

The woman looked up the street and then down again, making certain no one was watching. She was careful to watch her facial expressions. "He came here twice a week for the past several years. But he and Mei didn't stay here. They went somewhere else. One of the girls told me that Mei wasn't his mistress at all. That he was using her as a cover for his real lover."

"Do you have any idea who she is?"

"No, only that she was older, much older. I heard one of the girls gossiping that Mei was this woman's granddaughter. But that's pretty far-fetched."

"Not really. How old was Mei?"

"She said she was fifteen. I think she started when she was twelve."

"How could her family let her do that?"

She shrugged her shoulders. "Chinese girls are nothing more than chattel. For them, this is a step up in life."

"What else can you tell me about that night?"

"There was a team of horses all right, but I hear they went gunning right for him. On purpose-like."

"He was murdered," Jefferson said icily.

"The police say it's an accident because they don't want to go snooping around in Chinatown. I saw those four Chinese thugs setting up the whole thing. I've got no truck with the Chinese either. But I sure as hell don't want to borrow trouble. I'm telling you this because you've got a kind face. But take my advice. Don't ever come back here. Mei is dead. I may be dead tomorrow for telling you any of this. Keep what I've told you to yourself."

"What else do you know about these Chinese? Who is their leader? Why would they want to kill Lawrence?"

"I don't know. You tell me."

"Please, isn't there anything else you remember about that night?"

"No. And if you want any more information, try Chinatown." Then she glared at him. "But if you go there, don't expect to come out alive." She shut the door and slid a bolt into place.

Jefferson went to Chinatown, riding through the narrow streets in his black carriage. Purposefully, he wanted to make a statement. He was Jefferson Duke and he knew the truth.

I will not allow this cat-and-mouse game to go on forever.

Watching suspicious eyes watch him, Jefferson recalled his mother's story of the feud between Andrew Duke and his Chinese enemies.

How ironic that Lawrence found love with one who has sworn to be our enemy. Perhaps he was healing our families without even knowing it.

Eerily, Jefferson felt as if he'd traveled into another space and time. Even the energy in Chinatown was ominous. It had been a long time since Jefferson felt like taking on the world.

This time he didn't have anything to lose.

Except Barbara.

For Barbara, I'd fight Lucifer himself. No matter what it takes, I will keep her safe.

Finally, he rapped his cane on the roof. "Driver, take me home."

* * * *

Chaos reigned over Eleanor's financial affairs. "With my inheritance, I can build any kind of house I want, wherever I want," she said to Jefferson.

"You need to save Lawrence's estate for yours and Barbara's future."

"It is precisely her future I'm thinking about. In a few years she will be coming out and it's imperative she make a good marriage. I can't arrange that without the proper address, parties and gowns for both of us."

"Barbara loves this house. It's her home."

"She'll love the new house even more."

"You are a mindless woman, Eleanor," Jefferson said flatly, donning his top hat.

"I'm being more practical than you can imagine, Jefferson. I have to do something to stop the gossips from slandering my good name around town."

"What are you talking about?" Jefferson feigned ignorance of the scandal. He was used to turning deaf ears on gossip all his life.

Jefferson and Eleanor did not see Barbara creep down the staircase and hide behind a large potted palm in the main hallway next to the open salon doors. Barbara could hear every word they said.

"I'm talking about my husband's mistress! I received this note three days ago." Eleanor reached in her skirt pocket and pulled out a piece of paper that was written in a very scrawled hand, as if the hand were unfamiliar with a pen and paper.

Or unfamiliar with the English language, Jefferson thought. "How did you come by this?"

"The maid found it slipped under the front door. You see that? Her name was Mei."

"I know."

"You *know*? How could you know? Did you see them?"

"No. It's rumor. I won't believe it. Lawrence wasn't like that."

"I'm sure this little whore enticed him!"

Jefferson glowered at her. "How long ago did Lawrence move out of your bedroom, Eleanor? How long did you make him wait for you? Did you ever make him happy?"

"Be quiet!" she shouted. "How dare you ask me such intimate questions!"

"I'm sorry. I was just making a point."

"You've certainly done that." She folded her hands across her chest. "I've told every journalist in town that Lawrence had never been to a brothel, and they've laughed at me. Every day I'm scared to death to pick up the newspapers for fear I'll be the cartoonist's next victim. You have no idea the pressures on me now. The employees at the emporium think I should be helping them. I suppose they think I should be more like Saint Caroline. Hard working. Interested in commerce. But I'm not. I don't know anything about business and don't care if I ever do."

"I told you I would help you with the emporium."

"I don't need your help. I've appointed Jasper Akins as president."

"Oh, for God's sake," Jefferson turned away from her. "Jasper is a buyer, not a businessman."

Eleanor was appalled that Jefferson disapproved of her decision. "Jasper and I see eye to eye."

"I'll bet. He'll rob you blind if you don't watch out. He's of the same ilk as you, Eleanor. You spend money lavishly and foolishly with no regard to where the profits must come from. Lawrence and Jasper worked well together only because Lawrence kept a tight rein on things."

Eleanor threw her hands up in the air. "Oh! Lawrence was so perfect, he knew everything!" she ranted.

"Not everything."

"He certainly knew how to find a mistress. Why did he have to disgrace me by sleeping with a Chinese? Everyone knows they live like rodents under the city."

"Who told you that?"

"I hear things. From the journalists mostly. I've discovered a few other things in my dealings with my newspaper friends," she said.

Jefferson didn't like the way her voice dropped an octave and picked over her words as one does before they are about to deliver a threat.

She snatched the piece of paper from Jefferson's hand. "This is only one in a series of unsolved mysteries about you, my husband and his mother. I know you think I'm ignorant. That's obvious. You think I'm spoiled, but I'm not. I simply want the best for my daughter, is all." She walked slowly to the white marble fireplace mantle and slid her hand along the smooth surface. "I've been told that your concern for my daughter is unnatural."

"What?"

Barbara's ears piqued. *Unnatural? What does that mean?*

She leaned in closer.

Eleanor continued. "Now that Lawrence is dead, I don't want even the first breath of scandal to influence Barbara's life."

"Neither do I," Jefferson protested.

"Good. Then we understand each other. I don't want you seeing Barbara. I don't want you taking her for carriage rides on Sundays. Or buying her clothes and bonnets. Certainly not ever, ever taking her to your house alone."

Jefferson grew pained and angry. "You're a sick woman if you think for a single moment I would harm a hair on that child's head. I love Barbara. I would do anything for her."

Eleanor's eyes narrowed suspiciously. "I really think you would. But I don't know why. Why? She's just someone else's child. What is it? Because she reminds you of Caroline?"

"Of course!" Jefferson felt his heart cracking under Eleanor's assault. "And Lawrence."

"Ha! He has little to do with it, I'll wager," she replied.

Jefferson's anger nearly exploded but he kept himself in check. He was being told he could not see his own granddaughter. To him, the very idea was unconscionable.

His grieving for Lawrence was something he could never show Eleanor because he believed she would never understand the depth of his emotion for someone who was "just a friend." Being with Barbara kept Lawrence alive to him. She eased his pain and together they shared their memories of Lawrence. It was Jefferson's way of avoiding the emptiness in his heart. Barbara had become his reason for living. "I loved Caroline more than you'll certainly ever understand."

"Ha! And you think I'm sick? You commit adultery for over forty years with a woman and you dare to tell me I'm sick?" Eleanor was furious as her anger spewed forth. "I want you out of my house! Out! Now!" She slammed her fist down on the mantelpiece.

Jefferson went to the doorway. Looking up he saw Barbara, blue eyes swimming in a bath of tears, watching him from behind the long fronds of the potted areca palm.

She was shaking her head back and forth, her brown curls catching in the palm leaves.

"No, Jefferson! Don't leave me," she pleaded in a whispered croak. Her cheeks were beet red as she fought to hold back her protests. Her eyes glanced to the interior of the room and when she saw her mother approaching, panic enveloped her face. She raced for the staircase and climbed the steps two at a time so Eleanor would not see her.

Jefferson turned back to Eleanor and stalled her, hoping to give Barbara enough time to disappear at the top of the landing. He glanced up and saw Barbara as she crouched down at the top of the stairs. She stuck her head between the spindles and a single tear fell to the first floor. It made a tiny puddle on the parquet floor.

A tiny teardrop. So small no one would notice it except me. One teardrop. The sign of a child's broken heart.

Courage surged through his veins. He faced off with Eleanor. "Barbara has already lost her father. I'm her friend. If you keep me from her, she'll feel abandoned. She won't have anyone to turn to."

Eleanor laughed a high-pitched sound that assaulted his ears. *She's drunk with her own power*, he thought.

"Barbara has me," she said. "I'm all she needs."

"If you keep me from this house and that's your prerogative as her mother, then so be it. However, if she wants to find me, she'll find a way. She has a lot of Caroline in her. She's got spunk. She'll see me."

"Don't be too sure of yourself, Jefferson. You may rule half this city with your wealth and influence, but you're not going to run my life anymore. Now, get out of my house."

Jefferson fought the impulse to look up at his granddaughter. To do so would give her away and gain him nothing. All he could hope was that Barbara understood his message to her. He'd be there for her always. All she had to do was seek him out.

As he left the house, Eleanor slammed the door behind him emphasizing her censure.

I love you, Barbara. You're all I've got.

thirty-three

I ran against a Prejudice
That quite cut off the view.

—CHARLOTTE PERKINS GILMAN
IN THIS OUR WORLD, "AN OBSTACLE," ST. I

San Francisco—1901

Until the turn of the century, San Franciscans were the single largest segment of retail spenders on the continent. Whole businesses and legions of commerce were kept going by the unstoppable flow of cash coming from the City by the Bay. As the city grew in size and numbers, so did the need for houses, schools, businesses and shops.

City hall and the city commissioners found many ways in which to line their pockets with what they believed at the time were "slight imperfections," "cost cutting" and "elimination of wasteful procedures" on municipal building projects, infrastructures and long-neglected cisterns needed to fight fires. The truth of the matter was that poverty and crime continued to grow. Because money was easily made and spent, few people chose to look at the dark side of the gaiety. Few people took the challenge to cast their eye to the long-range future.

Jefferson Duke was one of the handful of men who chose to go against the easy flow of cash being made as the city built a high number of wooden buildings on unstable landfills with no pilings for support. He believed, along with the chief of the San Francisco Fire Department, Dennis Sullivan,

358

"If the city doesn't burn to the ground, it'll fall apart in a good wind."

Ever since Jefferson's venture to the Barbary Coast where the squalor and sense of hopelessness indelibly impressed him, he realized it was time to change the focus of his life. Rather than building new businesses, Jefferson used his dinner parties and the club meetings he attended as a forum to voice his concerns about the lack of fire prevention, water mains and fire hydrants within the city. He was appalled at the squalor in Chinatown and the Barbary Coast and wrote letters to the editors of the newspapers that it was his belief poverty and lack of hope bred criminals.

The city laughed at him. As the years passed, Jefferson was labeled a "kook"; an "eccentric." He went to Sacramento and spoke before the state senate about the problems his city was facing. The state officials listened. Finally, he ran for state senator and won. He went to Washington, D.C., and met with Vice President Theodore Roosevelt in March 1901 hoping to bring national attention to the violations of the National Board of Fire Underwriters and the corruption in San Francisco's City Hall that was the cause. The vice president was greatly impressed with Jefferson Duke and promised that when he traveled to San Francisco, he would be a guest in Jefferson's home.

Still, the city commissioners thought Jefferson was a lunatic. It was to their benefit to convince everyone else in the city of the same. Nearly every city commissioner was on the take for graft, and they could not afford Jefferson Duke's meddling. Jefferson was relentless, but age and time were taking their toll on him. He wondered why he loved his city so much when her people had begun to turn on him. His only joy was seeing Barbara.

Ever since the day Eleanor had kicked Jefferson out of her house, Barbara Mansfield used every chance she got to defy her mother. Barbara met Jefferson Duke in the park near the Presidio. She shared ice cream with him on a hot summer day at her favorite soda fountain on Powell Street. She waited for him after school at the Pacific Union Club, when she prearranged meetings by sending a messenger to his home with her little notes. Jefferson always gave her pocketfuls of change so that she could pay a messenger boy anytime she felt she needed.

Barbara kept the money in an inlaid mother-of-pearl box Jefferson gave her for her twelfth birthday. Inside the box she kept small mementos of Jefferson: tickets to ride the merry-go-round, a winter rose he'd bought for her one Valentine's Day and a miniature Kewpie doll he won for her at the state fair. There were no rings or bracelets in her cache box.

"I don't want anything money can buy, Jefferson. I just want to spend time with you."

"Yes, time," he said. "It's more precious than gold."

"You aren't old to me, Jefferson," she'd say touching his withered cheek. "We'll always be together."

"We always have been," they said together.

"Since before time," Jefferson added.

Time, Jefferson gladly gave his granddaughter, along with sentimental poems he wrote about her from his heart. He gave her love and his own unique view of the world. Because they met in secret, Jefferson was often reminded of the clandestine nature of his love for Caroline. He supposed he could have eliminated intrigue from his life, but then he would not have built his friendship with Barbara. Jefferson believed that the love he received from Barbara was the greatest gift of all. She wanted to be with him not because she felt obligation for an aging grandparent, but because she loved him.

* * * *

Barbara arranged to meet Jefferson at the Palace Hotel because it was Jefferson's prototype on how a structure could be built to defy earthquakes and fire. At nineteen, Barbara was Jefferson's champion. She'd written a school paper on the Palace Hotel, citing the building statistics Jefferson had given her. Built on massive pillar foundations twelve feet deep and with outer walls two feet thick, over three thousand tons of reinforcing iron had been woven into the walls for strength. Besides an enormous reservoir tank of water in the basement, over 130,000 gallons of water had been placed on the roof to drown out fires through a five-mile-long piping system throughout the hotel.

Barbara knew that if Jefferson had his way, all buildings in San Francisco would be made to similar specifications.

However, she called this meeting with Jefferson today not to discuss his newest crusade against Mayor Schmitz, but to tell him that she was going to get married.

Jefferson's brand-new carriage pulled to a stop in front of the hotel. The new driver, a young and handsome Irish boy by the name of Patrick O'Shea, jumped down from his perch like a gazelle and opened the door for his eighty-six-year-old employer. Jefferson was not as spry as he'd been even two years ago. He stooped a bit when he walked and his feet didn't want to move in the purposeful fashion they once had. He allowed the young, strong Patrick to help him out of the carriage and on to the sidewalk.

"Jefferson!" Barbara said in her naturally exuberant voice. "How good to see you." She went to him and embraced him.

Jefferson patted her back and let her young arms surround him. "It seems like years since I've seen you."

"It's only been three weeks," she pouted.

"Three-and-a-half. Much too long at my age."

"Oh, Jefferson. You aren't old. You told me so yourself."

"Did I say that?" He laughed.

"Yes. You said the only reason you allowed yourself to move slower was so that others could catch up."

He took her hand. "That's quite true," he laughed again and smiled at her sparkling blue eyes.

Barbara slid her arm around his waist and though she wanted him to lean on her, he did not. He walked proudly through the front door with his arm wrapped affectionately around her shoulder. The valets and bellboys shot sidelong glances at them and then exchanged smiles among themselves.

"They think you are my mistress, Barbara," Jefferson whispered with a mischievous twinkle in his green eyes.

Barbara lifted her chin proudly. "Good. I wouldn't mind letting them think you have a young lover."

Jefferson couldn't help laughing. "Thank God you have Caroline's sense of humor. And coming here today to such a public place is quite daring of you, my dear. I'm glad you've stood up to your mother all these years."

Barbara looked away from him hoping he didn't see her frown as they were escorted to a table for lunch. "That's what I have to talk to you about, Jefferson," she replied, unable to hide the morose tone in her voice.

They sat at a square table covered with fine damask linen and appointed with heavy English sterling silver, gold charger plates and a crystal bud vase holding three English tea roses. Barbara smoothed her skirts before the waiter snapped a large dinner napkin in the air behind Barbara's head and then with one crisp movement placed the napkin on her lap.

"Would you care to speak with the wine steward, Mr. Duke?" The waiter asked.

Barbara didn't reply or make one of her comical facial gestures as she had when she was a child. As he looked at her he realized there was nothing in the least childish about Barbara anymore.

"Bring us a bottle of Perrier Jouet champagne," Jefferson said, looking at her as the waiter nodded and left.

"Why are you looking at me like that?" Barbara asked, unused to his scrutiny.

"You've grown up," he said a bit sadly.

"Jefferson, I'm no older than I was three weeks ago."

"I understand that, but it's that you're beautiful. More so than even Caroline, if that's possible."

"Well, it's not, so don't say that."

"No, it's true," he replied, observing how her dark rich hair fell in luxuriant shining waves down her back and there were small curls around her cheeks and under the brim of the perky royal-blue velvet hat that framed her face. Her blue eyes were the color of the ocean on a bright summer afternoon, and he noticed that the iris was ringed with navy blue that enhanced the glow of the sparkling lights that seemed to radiate from her soul. When she looked at him, he felt a power emanate from inside her as if she were giving him a piece of herself each time she blessed him with a glance.

Of all the things he wanted to do, Jefferson wished he could take Barbara's hand in his, look into her captivating eyes—Caroline's eyes—and tell her that he was her grandfather.

But he didn't. The time wasn't right.

He wasn't precisely sure why at this point he was unwilling to explain the truth to her, but he would know. Or Caroline would come to him in a vision and tell him.

Barbara buttered a hunk of sourdough bread. "I don't think of you as old at all," Barbara said.

"Liar."

"Am not."

"You can barely fight your tears thinking that I'm slipping away from you. My time is getting short. That's certain." He patted her hand. "Let's make every moment count."

"I don't want you to leave me . . . like Papa," she choked out the words.

"You miss him."

"So much. And sometimes when I'm with you, you remind me so much of him. Of the times we had together. I remember that day when the police came to the house like it was yesterday."

He reached out and squeezed her hand. "I miss him, too. We were very close. Even when he was a little boy, he used to come to me when I had the lumberyard and warehouse and he'd tell me his dreams of sailing away to foreign lands. He was a man of vision, Barbara. He lived his dreams. He created fantasies in his head when he was your age and younger, and before he was out of his twenties he'd done most of the things people only read about in books and periodicals. He was amazing," Jefferson said wistfully.

"You loved him, too," she said.

"As if he were my own son." Jefferson wondered if this were the time, but Barbara interrupted him.

"That's why it's so hard for me to say what I've come here to say to you."

"Don't fret over it. Just say it," he urged her with loving confidence.

Barbara took a deep breath. "I know that you and Mother don't get along. In fact, she hates you."

"But I don't hate her, Barbara. I simply disagree with her methods of dealing with problems, and from what I hear, I was right about her overspending. Is she in as much trouble as I've been told?"

Barbara nodded. "She's put the house up for sale."

"God in heaven! I didn't know it was that bad. And of all times to sell! The stock market crash in May has sent the economy into a tailspin. This is a time to hang on to her real estate, not sell. Why, she'll be lucky to get fifty cents on the dollar."

Barbara sat back in her chair with a concerned look on her face. "I've heard that kind of talk myself. So, it really can be that bad for us?"

Jefferson shook his head and rubbed his chin thoughtfully. "If Eleanor weren't so stubborn I'd loan her the money she needs. Or thinks she needs. The problem is she'd never take charity from me, and frankly, I doubt I could trust her because she'd spend it all on some damn frock she wants! On second thought, I won't lend her money," he said grumpily. He leaned forward. "Now, if you need anything from me, all you have to do is ask."

Barbara covered her laughter with her hand.

"I'm being funny?" he asked.

It was a long moment before she composed herself. "Jefferson, your feud with my mother is so funny to me."

Jefferson was indignant. "I don't see why! She threw me out of her house and has done her damndest to keep us apart. The woman is as foul as stink on a goat!"

"Jefferson, really!" Barbara kept laughing. "But you're right."

Jefferson's laugh tripped over his pursed lips. He howled and held his stomach. "So, tell me what else she's up to these days."

It was if he'd thrown a glass of cold water on Barbara. Her face instantly sobered. "She wants me to marry Donald Pope."

Jefferson nearly choked on his wine. "What?"

"One of the reasons she claims she needs money is to bring me out properly so that I can make a good marriage. Now that I've lost my baby fat, grown three inches since last summer and my skin isn't burned and peeling, I guess she decided to take a good look at me. She thinks I can make a good match. She says I should be able to 'snare any man of the town' I want. She says we'll both be 'set up' for the rest of our lives."

Jefferson was stunned. "And what do you want?"

She put her elbow on the table and rested her chin in the palm of her hand. She didn't try to hide the gloomy look in her eyes. "I wanted to go to Paris like Papa did. I wanted to write stories for a newspaper, maybe. I wanted . . . Oh, what's the difference?"

She was positively the picture of melancholy, he thought. "What's the difference? This is your life we're talking about here! What happened to my headstrong, independent little girl who was going to help me change the world?"

"She got smart. She realized women don't do that sort of thing."

"Really?" He ground his jaw angrily.

"That's what Mother said."

"To hell with Eleanor! You go back and tell your mother that Caroline did just fine without marrying for money. In fact, the truth be known, William married her for her money! At least for her potential to make money. You tell Eleanor you have twice as much of Caroline's moxie in you as you do of her selfish, conniving manners."

"Oh, I'll do just that, Jefferson," she said facetiously.

"I was getting carried away, wasn't I?" he asked sheepishly.

"A little," she replied.

"I overreacted. I never asked you what you think of this Donald Pope."

"He's a nice enough fellow. I met him at a party last Christmas when St. Benecia's was on break. Actually, my friend, Meredith Winters, likes him more than I do. But Donald told his mother he's in love with me. Then his mother talked to my mother, and now my mother is spending all her savings on this huge party for me at our house this Saturday night and, oh, Jefferson! I just don't know what to do!"

He drummed his arthritic fingers on the table. "This is a fine kettle of fish, Angel. It seems to me you're in a very tight spot. If you want to make Donald happy, you'll lose your friendship with Meredith. If you make your mother happy, you'll make yourself miserable. If you make yourself happy, your mother will be angry, Donald will be broken-hearted but Meredith will be happy."

"That's the way I see it." She threw her hands up in the air. "What can I do?"

Jefferson leaned over conspiratorially. "Get out of town. Fast!" He laughed.

A smile broke across Barbara's face. "Would you be serious?"

"I am being serious. Come with me to Washington, D.C. Since McKinley died and Teddy Roosevelt has taken over as president, things there have been in a whirlwind. Our new president has asked me to be one of his advisors. On several issues. I could use the company."

"Me? Go to the White House? Are you sure? I mean, well, this is nothing short of a journalist's dream come true!" Barbara was ecstatic.

"I thought you'd see it that way. Tell your mother you need to think things over. She doesn't need to spend the money on a party. At least not now. What do you say?"

"I say, I'm with you, Jefferson!" She lifted her wine glass and clinked her glass to his in a toast.

He smiled. "Sometimes it's just best to stand back and let things take their own course without getting involved," he said. "As you get older, you'll find I'm right."

"I don't care what Mother says about my leaving. I'm going. Besides, maybe I will decide to marry Donald, and if I do, who knows when I'll be able to make an exciting trip like this?"

"So, what will you tell your mother?"

"That you can't possibly make this trip on your own. At your age," she said teasingly. "I'll tell her that you need me."

"I always have. Always will."

thirty-four

To have known love, how bitter a thing it is.

—ALGERNON CHARLES SWINBURNE
"LAUS VENERIS," ST. CIII

"This trip of ours across the country has transformed me, personally, Jefferson," Barbara said, looking out the windows of the observation car of their train.

"And how is that?"

"I've never seen you in action. Watching you address the State Assembly last week was inspiring. Why, you kept every person spellbound. I had no idea about these deals you've cut with Rockefeller, J. P. Morgan and Andrew Carnegie. Didn't he just retire this year?"

"Yes, he sold his company to United States Steel."

"I thought so."

"So, you like my political friends, too."

She rushed on with enthusiasm. "I knew you'd met with the president before but to see all this firsthand . . . well, I'm more than impressed. You have incredible power and influence, Jefferson. Do you know that? Of course you know that. What am I saying?" Finally, she took a breath and said sincerely, "You've shown me that I can try to change the world, too. Make it better."

"Then this has been a fruitful trip," he said.

"And we're only halfway to Washington," she said.

Barbara had noticed when they went to the dining car or the observation car to watch the Rocky Mountains, not only was the crew effusive in their deference to Jefferson, but the passengers asked to be introduced to him,

366

struck up conversations with him and simply wanted to orbit around him.

Barbara was not surprised that Jefferson treated everyone with polite equanimity, though he told her he preferred his privacy on trips like this.

"When we get to Washington, there'll be nothing but throngs of people day and night. While I have the chance to be alone with you, I want to indulge myself."

In the evenings he liked to rest by himself, dressed in an old Indian-print wool robe that was the style twenty years ago and not what one would think a multimillionaire would own. He requested she pour him a brandy, sit with him in their private car and read poetry or verse to him by the light from a Tiffany reading lamp.

She was surprised at the bittersweet romantic poems and stories he chose as his reading material. She'd never realized how incredibly sentimental he was. She thought she'd been the sensitive one. It was a revelation to her that a man's heart was woven with the same kind of heartstrings as a woman's.

> *For winter's rain and ruins are over,*
> *And all the season of snows and sins;*
> *The days dividing lover and lover,*
> *The light that loses, the night that wins;*
> *And time remembered is grief forgotten,*
> *And frosts are slain and flowers begotten,*
> *And in green underwood and cover*
> *Blossom by blossom the spring begins.*

Barbara read the stanza from *Atalanta in Calydon,* by Jefferson's favorite poet, Swinburne.

Jefferson sipped the last of his brandy and leaned his head on the back of the chair. He rolled the brandy over his tongue, savoring every drop and remembering when Caroline read him exactly the same verse.

"Even your voice is like your grandmother's. Your perfume, your energy. I can almost trick myself into believing she's alive again."

Barbara watched him close his eyes, and for a moment she thought he might have fallen asleep. But a tear trickled down his cheek. "Why do you make me read these sad poems? They only upset you."

Slowly he righted his head and looked at her. His eyes blazed with the kind of passion and life Barbara saw in her own eyes when she looked in a mirror. Instantly, she was able to glimpse at the kind of fire he must have had

as a young man. She almost wished she'd known him back then, one of the
first settlers to come to San Francisco. Chills erupted on her skin as she
thought of all the things this man had seen and done in his lifetime. She realized that for a very long time, Jefferson had been her hero. She wanted to be
like him, but she knew that was impossible . . . or was it?

"Never fear pain, Barbara. If you do, you'll never live. To live this life,
you must take risks. They are all sorts of risks, I suppose. I've been lucky in
that mine usually went my way. But not always."

"You mean Caroline."

"Yes," Jefferson said.

And Lawrence. Rachel.

"You loved her deeply, didn't you?"

Jefferson placed his hands on the arms of the chair as he opened his heart
to his granddaughter. "I like to believe that once in each of our lives comes
a special person to love and who will love us in return. And that isn't easy.
Dolores Sanchez loved me and as wonderful and as beautiful as she was, I
didn't have the same feelings for her. There's a special electricity that comes
from the soul when love is really right.

"Again, I was lucky because I fell in love with Caroline from the instant
our eyes met. I lived my life for her and yet, I never lived with her. We were
as married in our hearts as two human beings could ever be, Barbara. That's
what I want you to know. I never felt our affair was wrong or sinful. I sacrificed everything for her and she for me. My only consolation in getting old
is that my time alone is coming to an end. I believe she is just over there,"
he pointed off to the distance, "waiting for me."

Barbara's heart clutched. She scooted across the floor and rested her head
in Jefferson's lap. "Who will love me then?"

Jefferson touched her hair.

"I'll never leave you alone, Barbara, any more than Caroline has left me.
Most people don't understand that about life. Life goes on. I'll just be in a different place is all. But you'll feel my love come to you. I promise you that."

"Oh, Jefferson. Please," she said, drying her tears with the tips of her fingers.
"Let's not talk about this anymore. I want to be happy and gay on this trip."

"And so you should be. Next year, I'll take you to New York City for your
birthday. We'll go to a play and have lunch near Central Park and shop for
all the new clothes you want."

"Jefferson! How you dream!" she laughed, feeling her tears subside.

"You must dream, my child. Without dreams, you'll never make your reality."

"I never thought of it that way," she replied pensively.

"Remind me to introduce you to a friend of mine. Thomas Edison."

"You *know* Edison? Do you know everybody?"

A mischievous smile quirked the edge of his mouth. "Just about." He took the book from her and put it on the table next to his chair. "Now, I think it's time this old man got some sleep."

Washington, D.C.—December 23, 1901

Barbara stepped out of the luxurious Pullman coach car with its inlaid burled wood, green-velvet–draped windows and room dividers, sterling silver wall sconces and heavily tufted rosewood chairs into the chaos of the train station in the nation's capital.

The head conductor, along with two valets and a stevedore to assist with their trunks and a mountain of luggage, was overboard with his ministrations.

"This way, sir," the conductor said, taking Jefferson's elbow and leading him down the narrow corridor to the end of the car. "Be very careful, sir, these steps can be quite unsteady." He pulled back the etched glass and burled wood pocket door. "Here we go, sir."

Washington was still in a state of mourning over the death of President McKinley. However, concessions were made because of the Christmas season. The train station was festooned with garlands of pine and holly branches with huge, red-velvet bows and clusters of shiny, red apples over the main entrance.

The carriage they hired to take them to the hotel was decorated with clusters of spruce on its shiny brass lamps and bay-leaf wrapped wreaths around the horses' necks. The impish-faced driver wore a sprig of mistletoe in his top hat.

Though there were automobiles in San Francisco and even a newly formed "Automobile Club," Barbara had never seen the likes of all the automobiles there were in Washington. Fords, Stanley Steamers, curved-dashed Oldsmobiles, touring cars, a Daimler, grand touring cars and Mercedes Specials congested the streets along with the usual horse-drawn hacks, four-in-hands, rockaways, pole buggies and phaetons.

The carriage took them past the theater district where she saw Ford's

Theatre where Lincoln was shot and others whose marquees advertised *Aïda* and *Floradora* being played.

The carriage halted at the Washington House Hotel. A bevy of bellboys and even the concierge rushed to welcome Jefferson Duke.

"Mr. Duke! How wonderful to see you again, sir. Welcome back to Washington."

"Thank you, Reynolds. It's good to be back."

"Things have been a bit dull without you, sir," Reynolds the dark-haired, thirtyish, tall, bearded man said with the kind of effusive flattery Barbara was coming to expect when she was around Jefferson.

Then Barbara poked her head out of the carriage. Reynolds drew in his breath. "What a ravishingly beautiful woman!" He clamped his hand to his breast theatrically and then bowed to Barbara. He smiled broadly as he offered his hand to her. "Washington has never seen such beauty," he went on. "Why just the other day I was reading in the *New York Sun* a comment that the blue-blooded Southern woman's beauty could only be eclipsed by a cosmopolitan California woman and that the New York woman of fashion was commonplace. That journalist must have seen you, Miss. . . ."

"Mansfield," Jefferson replied tersely, suddenly realizing that Barbara's reputation might be in danger among the notorious Washington gossips. Men like Reynolds were the circuitry the rumor mills fed upon for news. "Barbara, this is Harold Reynolds, concierge here at the hotel. He'll fetch you anything you need while I am in meetings." He turned to Reynolds and with confident aplomb said, "Barbara is the granddaughter of my deceased fiancée, Reynolds. She's my most precious treasure. See that she is treated like the princess she is."

Reynolds prided himself on having the sharpest of wits and the keenest of insightful minds. He realized that if a single derogatory remark or aspersion about Miss Mansfield were to find its way back to Jefferson, he'd be a man without a job, possibly even a country. Reynolds dropped his smile and clapped his hands together, summoning a new round of bellboys. "Consider her wish our command," Reynolds replied respectfully.

Jefferson held out his arm for Barbara as they walked toward the Art Nouveau iron-and-glass–worked front doors. Reynolds followed like a puppy. He pulled out a small notepad and pencil.

"Whom will you be meeting while you are in town, Mr. Duke? And what arrangements do you wish for me to make on your behalf?"

"I'll be seeing the president in the morning, Reynolds. Eight o'clock sharp. I would like a hack at 7:40 exactly. Barbara will need to shop for a gown for tomorrow night's dinner at the White House. See that she has assistance at the best dress shop in town. See that all the bills are sent to me."

"Yes, sir."

"Tomorrow I have a meeting with several senators at noon. I'll need a hack. I've arranged for Barbara to have luncheon with Alice."

Barbara stopped abruptly. "Not the president's daughter?"

"Yes, the president's daughter. Who did you think I meant?"

"Why didn't you tell me this before we left?" she asked.

"I thought you'd get too nervous. Maybe not come with me."

Barbara swallowed nervously. "You're right."

Jefferson pulled her along as he glanced back at Reynolds. "I'll let you know further plans later. Christmas, you know. I wouldn't want to spoil my surprises."

Barbara was aghast. "You mean there's more?"

Jefferson smiled enigmatically. "I told you. Dreams are meant to become reality, Barbara."

They stepped into the brass elevator. The elevator operator closed the door behind them, and they ascended to the fifth floor where Jefferson had booked two suites of rooms for them.

* * * *

Barbara was poked, pinned, pushed and plied by three seamstresses who acted as if they would be led to the guillotine if they didn't produce a spectacular gown by 5:30 that evening.

Barbara stood on a foot-high round-carpeted riser in front of six mirrors watching bolts of cream-colored French crepe de chine, cream-colored overlay silk and deep panels of matching lace being tossed and draped over her body. She especially loved the deep royal-blue velvet that was to be used for her cape and lined in heavy, cream-colored satin and edged with midnight blue and gold braid. There was even a muff to match.

The seamstresses were young and apprenticed to the older head seamstress, a woman from Paris by the name of Veronique who abhorred the new slang the young girls used when describing their own work among themselves.

"She'll be the nattiest dresser at the party," Carrie said.

"The *Washington Post* columnist will be at the White House dinner. It's the Christmas Party all the town is talking about," Mary said turning Barbara around to face her again and pinning yet another dart under Barbara's full breasts. "All the swell-elegants will be there."

"High-stepping, that's what you'll be, Dear," Jane said. "What I wouldn't give to be a fly on the wall there."

"You know," Carrie popped her head up from the hem where she was working and looked Barbara in the eye, "that Alice will be wearing one of our creations. But take it from me, she don't hold a candle to you, even if she's the president's daughter."

"Alice's debut is scheduled for the third of January. You wouldn't believe all we have to do for her," Jane said.

"Lord! But I don't believe there's one as fierce beautiful as you in all of Washington," Carrie said as the girls finally stood back and looked at Barbara standing in the floor-length gown.

Barbara had never seen a gown this beautiful, and she'd never seen so much of her ivory skin exposed either.

Veronique walked into the room to inspect the draped folds of the low-cut neckline, the transparent lace leg-o'-mutton sleeves and the lace overskirt. She shook her head disapprovingly. *"Non!"*

The three seamstresses stared at each other in horror.

Veronique circled Barbara staring at every stitch, tapping her cheek with her forefinger as if she were trying to ascertain where her calculations had gone awry.

Suddenly, she brightened and then rushed out of the room. She returned with several huge panels of beaded lace. *"Maintenant! C'est magnifique!"*

"But that's for Alice's debut gown!" Jane blurted with high-pitched horror in her voice.

"Oui. But now, ees for Barbara!" Veronique smiled and then ripped the overskirt from the waistline. With scissors, she cut a V-shaped panel out of the overskirt which would lay tightly against the abdomen section of the skirt.

The three girls instantly went to work, knowing already the effect Veronique was after. They stitched encrusted lace appliqués at the hem of the skirt and when they were finished, Barbara was stunned at the result.

When she twirled in the light as she would hopefully twirl on a dance floor, the beads and crystals on the hem sparkled like dewdrops.

"I feel like a princess!" Barbara said.

"*Oui. C'est vrai*," Veronique smiled and kissed each of her cheeks.

Barbara realized she was about to have a debut of her own.

thirty-five

Music I heard with you was more than music,
And bread I broke with you was more than bread.
Now that I am without you, all is desolate;
All that was once so beautiful is dead.

—CONRAD AIKEN
"BREAD AND MUSIC"

Washington, D.C.

Flags at half-mast and black crepe had a difficult time casting their funeral pall on the Christmas visitors to the White House for President Theodore Roosevelt's private party. Deprived of the traditional social season that fall due to the assassination, Washington society was looking for an excuse to revel.

The women were dressed in the most elegant gowns Barbara had ever seen. Though there was little of the San Franciscan penchant for ostentation, and not once did she see a diamond-studded stomacher or jeweled tiara, there was a refined cosmopolitan sophistication she found she liked.

The older statesmen wore tails, and the younger men like the president, who was only forty-two, wore tuxedos. Jefferson wore a black tuxedo with black straight-cut pants, snowy white shirt and a white tie. His top hat and black wool evening cape, lined in heavy, cream-colored satin—much like Barbara's midnight-blue velvet cape—were set off by the gold-topped black cane he carried.

Jefferson held her hand on the ride through the lightly snowing streets of Washington. It was a wet snow, Jefferson explained, which was why it clung so voraciously to the bare limbs of the cherry and apple trees down Pennsylvania Avenue. Lamplight fell in golden puddles illuminating the snow. When Barbara stepped out of the carriage and put her satin-slippered foot on the snow-covered walk, the hem of her dress sparkled like the icy crystals underfoot. She was awed by Veronique's insights and attention to detail.

As they walked into the White House and were ushered to the State Room where the party was being held, Jefferson leaned over to whisper to Barbara. "Remember, these people have never been exposed to a real San Franciscan beauty. Be gentle with them, Barbara."

"Oh, Jefferson!" she laughed. "You tease me too much."

"I was speaking the truth," he said, when a portly man walked up behind them and clamped his hand on Jefferson's shoulder.

"Jefferson Duke! By God, old man! I can't believe you made it!"

Jefferson turned around. "Charles Fuller, you should know better than to ever doubt my word!" Jefferson laughed and exchanged pleasantries. He introduced Barbara to Charles Fuller and his wife, Sylvia.

"I'm so very pleased to meet you," Barbara said as Charles took her hand and kissed it.

"Enchanted," he said appreciatively and then turned to Jefferson. "Now I wish I had known your grandmother," he said with deep sincerity.

Sylvia had known about Jefferson's betrothal to Caroline and she knew how Jefferson still grieved over her. She chose to bring the conversation back to lighter matters. "Is this your first visit here, my dear?"

"Yes," Barbara replied. "I'm overwhelmed with the history and the power I feel here."

"Washington is all that and more," Sylvia agreed.

As Jefferson turned to more political matters involving himself and Charles, Barbara felt her head buzz with the sound of an orchestra playing and the ever-escalating noise of people conversing, but it was the realization that she was inside the home of, now, twenty-six different presidents of the United States that gave her the headiest of all sensations. Champagne at this point would bring her down, she was so high, she thought.

Huge crystal chandeliers lit the red velvet furniture, red floral carpeting and hundreds of potted palms. The furniture was a disappointment, she thought, most of it looking like leftovers from Lincoln's reign, which it was. The air was filled with the fragrance of fresh-cut pine and spruce, and fires roared in every fireplace.

Waiters passed among the crowd offering wines, bourbons and whiskeys. The guests were in a lively, holiday mood. Barbara sipped a glass of champagne and smiled to herself.

It doesn't get any better than this.

Michael Trent despised these affairs. People crushing shoulder to shoulder while they got slightly or greatly inebriated was a ridiculous pastime. Christmas for Michael was not the time for merry-making. In his business, it was the deadliest time of year. Michael was President Theodore Roosevelt's special agent. He scanned the crowd of guests looking for an imperceptible raise of an eyebrow, a wink, a hand signal, a shrugged shoulder or the kind of glance that signaled danger to him.

Michael didn't trust anyone or anything. His deep-set golden-hued brown eyes observed things most people never noticed. The tall, thin-shouldered senator from Illinois carried a flask in his jacket pocket and from the way in which the man absentmindedly touched his breast every seven and a half minutes, Michael believed the man felt he needed more than the pre-dinner drinks the kitchen staff was serving. It was not just Michael's business to know that the senator was a drinker, but why. Why did he need a drink? Was he nervous? Was he upset? Was he power-hungry enough to want to assassinate the new president for his own personal gain?

These were the kinds of thoughts that filled Michael's head day and night. Tonight was one of those nights.

Not until all the guests were accounted for as specified by the invitation list, which had been checked and double-checked months ago, could Michael relax. These first hours of a party like this kept him nervous as a cat.

It took three days of briefing with his men to set up this party. Nothing was left to chance. In thirty minutes, when the president was brought into the room to meet his guests, he and his men would go on alert. Michael had left nothing to chance. The positioning and seating of each guest had been scrutinized and planned like a play with actors' places. Because people were basically like dumb sheep, they could be steered into certain directions without being aware of the manipulations he performed.

On the main floor itself were over two dozen bodyguards like himself, who were so highly trained they could almost read minds. Almost. Michael *knew* he could read minds.

Fortunately, there was little to be alarmed about this evening. Most of these people were not politicians with even a motive for murder. Rather, they were heads of industry, favorites of the president he'd invited to Washington simply because he liked them or they'd helped him in the past. Some were Roosevelt's hunting buddies. Some were conservationists like the president who were pushing for the National Parks. Some were the wealthiest men in the country who practically owned whole cities.

Men like . . . Jefferson Duke. Now there's a man to admire.

Michael had met Jefferson Duke three years ago when Michael had only been twenty-five and new to Washington himself. He'd had the privilege of sitting in on a meeting with Jefferson and Roosevelt when Teddy was governor of New York.

Michael had been impressed with old Jefferson, who made it implicitly clear that no one could ever bribe him, buy him or manipulate him. Jefferson was old, but he was ornery and determined to clean up the corruption he'd found in San Francisco.

Roosevelt had told Michael that Jefferson was probably the least greedy man he'd ever known. "He's an anomaly, Michael. Honest to a fault and richer than Croesus. Protect him and you'll do our country a real favor."

Michael straightened his wide shoulders and flexed his muscular arms. He felt the building tension of the night. He rubbed his square jaw, which signaled to Jake Patterson that so far everything was going well. Patterson's eye caught his gesture, but there was no response from him other than a tiny flicker of recognition Michael saw in his eyes. He'd trained Jake well.

Standing at over six feet, two inches tall, Michael was able to see over the heads of most of the crowd. His height was a prerequisite for this kind of work, as was his athletic body, which he kept in shape with workouts at the boxing gymnasium both lifting weights and hoisting himself arm over arm up hemp ropes to the ceiling. He rode his horse every morning at dawn and practiced archery, rifle- and pistol-shooting weekly as forms of self-defense rather than simply exercise.

Michael kept his life as tightly planned as did the president. He left little to chance.

Barbara found herself being asked a myriad of questions about San Francisco.

"Are there Indians?"

"Don't you feel removed from civilization being so far west?"

"How did people cope with getting the news?"

Finally, she'd had enough. "We've had the telegraph since its inception."

"Heavens," Mrs. Milton, the wife of a lobbyist said. "We weren't talking about national news, but our insider's news here in Washington."

Mr. Milton concurred. "Matters of state and commerce are discussed freely at parties just like this one long before anyone thinks to make them policy."

"Be careful what you say, Dear. You may set precedent and never know it!"

"I'm beginning to understand," Barbara answered. This evening alone, she'd overheard several state senators discussing Theodore Roosevelt's private plans to use his executive powers to sue a number of business trusts. Now she knew why Jefferson was invited here. Now she knew the connection between Jefferson and the president. Jefferson was quietly feeding the president information.

What a wily fox he is!

"I've heard enough stories to fill my journal front to back," Barbara said. "I've harbored a secret desire to be a journalist since I was a child. Any more evenings like this, I may have to publish what I hear," she teased.

"Well," Mr. Milton said. "If you lived here, we could guarantee you excitement on a daily basis," he laughed.

"I'm certain of that. It's a good thing I've never given up completely on my writing. I kept a journal of our trip across the country. My only regret is that I didn't let Jefferson buy me one of those new 'Brownie' cameras. Photographs say so much, don't you think?"

"Perhaps on the return trip you can use your new Kodak."

"What a good idea," Barbara said, looking around the room not wanting to miss a single detail of the most incredible evening of her life.

Michael was standing behind Barbara with his back against the walnut-paneled wall when she noticed him for the first time.

A bronze wall sconce above his head dropped golden light into his thick, brown wavy hair. His eyes had locked with hers, and they pierced her so fiercely that she rocked back on her heels just enough that she almost spilled her champagne.

Who is he? And why is he looking at me like . . . that?

Nervously, she drained the last few drops, but refused to be intimidated by his bold and bloodless stare.

"Mrs. Milton, who is that man over there by the wall?"

"What man?"

"The one staring at me as if I'd committed a crime."

The matron drew in a deep breath and exhaled dismissively. "He's just a guard. They all look the same."

"They do?" Barbara's eyebrow cocked. *They can't all be that handsome.*

Feeling a blush rise from her toes, she dropped her gaze and pretended to listen to the conversation.

I can feel his eyes on me. It's as if he were undressing me with his mind.
She faced him.

He was still staring at her.

She glared back at him.

He didn't move a muscle.

Not even a twitch! Oooo! He's making me crazy!

They stared at each other. Challenge for challenge.

She walked toward him.

He watched as she approached, cheeks flaming, eyes full of censure. The crystals at the hem of her gown and across her belly twinkled in the chandelier light. The skin on the long column of her throat, her softly rounded shoulders and her half-exposed highly rounded breasts were flushed.

Uh-oh. She's mad.

He didn't know why he couldn't take his eyes off her. He'd seen beautiful women before. Washington was filled with them. *But not a face like this.*

Get a hold of yourself, Michael. You're trained not to respond to lust. You'll snap out of it.

He noticed that, as she moved toward him with more purposeful strides than most women took, her hips moved quite sensuously, and he couldn't help wondering how far below the V-shaped panel of pearls and crystal the crook of her legs began. He was barely aware that he opened his fists and then clenched them again.

Skin is skin. Hers is probably no softer than any other.

When she drew near he was engulfed in the heady fragrance of an exotic sandalwood and musk he remembered from his trip to China during the

Boxer Rebellion when he was part of the secret forces going to Peking to help break out the hostages.

He noticed she wore none of the powder, rouge or lip stain that most of the other women wore. The pink of her sweet lips was natural, and he wondered what they would taste like if he were to touch his mouth to hers.

"I want to know why you keep staring at me, sir," Barbara lambasted him angrily. "And if you don't tell me right now . . ."

"You'll what?" he retorted without revealing the first sign of emotion, just as he'd been trained to do.

Barbara stood very close and whispered, "You need to be taught some manners." She flipped her fan open and whirled around, the white plume in her chignon swiping across his face.

One of the feathers stuck to Michael's lip.

He spit it out.

Barbara started to walk away when she felt a very strong hand grab her upper arm at its most tender spot.

"Where did you learn those manners?" Though he held her firmly, he didn't hurt her.

"In charm school." She yanked her arm and he let her go.

"Go practice your charms on somebody else. I have a job to do."

"Job?" Suddenly, Barbara realized the enormity of what she'd done.

What's come over me? This is Washington. These people eat intrigue for breakfast.

"Oh, my God," she put her gloved hands to her flaming cheeks. "This isn't like me," she gushed.

"Good, go on about your business," he said gruffly, inhaling her heat and closeness. His lips brushed her ear. If she continued to brush her backside up against him any longer, she'd feel his hardness.

This is embarrassing. And whose idea was it to invite goddesses to this function?

Sheepishly, Barbara turned around to apologize, but when she did, she found he was staring right down her bosom with the most lust-filled pair of smoky eyes she'd ever seen.

Taken aback, she blurted, "They need to put you in a cage somewhere, Mister."

Michael blinked, suddenly remembering himself. She was right.

"I'd better get back," she said.

"Not so fast," he said gruffly. Michael grabbed her arm and ushered her out the side door and to the adjoining anteroom.

She slapped his arm sharply with her fan. "See here, what do you think you're doing? You unhand me or I'll scream!" she threatened.

"Don't even think about it. I'll have to knock you out," he replied coldly.

She slapped his face. "You wouldn't darc."

"It wouldn't be the first time," he said, his cheek stinging from the slap. But while he was bantering with her he kept thinking that what he really wanted to do was kiss her.

That would keep her quiet. And do me a world of good.

She glared at him. "I'm glad I hit you."

"Happy to oblige."

"Oooph! You're the most insolent man I've ever met."

"Then you've led a sheltered life."

She balled her fist. "Why, you're proud of your lewd looks."

"I think you at least owe me an explanation why you assaulted me."

She bit her lower lip forcing herself to speak slowly. "I told you. I didn't like the way you looked at me."

"I wasn't looking at you."

She threw her hands up in the air. "I've got to get out of this city and back to San Francisco where people are sane, at least."

"San Francisco?" Suddenly, it hit him. The only person here from San Francisco was Jefferson Duke.

Of all the people to have an altercation with, I pick Jefferson Duke's mistress. What an idiot I am!

"You're with Jefferson Duke, aren't you?"

"Yes. He's my friend."

"I'll be more than happy to take you back to him." Michael tried to hide his smirk, but failed.

Barbara saw it. Her heart slammed against her chest. She held her ribs and started laughing. "That Jefferson and I—!"

She howled until a tear formed in her eye. "That's so silly."

"In my line of work, I see it all the time," Michael replied pompously.

"Oh really? And what line of work is that?"

"I guard the president's life," he said flatly with an icy tone to his voice that unnerved her.

Shock riddled her. *Oh, God. What have I done?*

"You're telling me I hit a government official?"

"Yes," he replied smugly.

"Does this mean you're going to lock me up?"

"For eternity."

"I won't go back home?"

"Doesn't look like it," he said, biting back a chuckle.

"I'm sorry. I didn't know. I thought you were some kind of pervert."

"Really? And what do you know about perverts? Do they have those in San Francisco?"

"Not after I get through with them," she said proudly, thinking of the boys she'd "straightened out" at family parties when she was in the seventh grade at St. Benecia's convent school.

Michael rubbed his cheek. "I believe you."

She watched the achingly slow movement of his hand over his handsome face. She also noticed that below his tuxedo jacket, his pants fit rather tightly against very muscular thighs. She tried not to look at the bulge between his legs. She lifted her face quickly and looked into his eyes. She couldn't wait to get out of there. "I'm sorry," she said very fast. "Now can I go?"

"No."

"What?" *I am going to jail!*

"Tonight you caused a real disturbance. The president is due here in fifteen minutes. It's my job to make certain there are no incidents this evening. You can understand that, after the recent assassination and jailing of Leon Czolgosz. People here are very nervous about such things. Your behavior was inappropriate this evening."

"I'm sorry," she said softly, her hands now trembling.

"My men will want to question you."

"Question?" Her eyes darted to the door at the right. "I'm not an assassin. I just thought you should be taught a lesson for staring at me. That's all. I didn't really mean any harm."

Michael was torn between wanting to keep her with him and his duty. "If you promise to meet with me personally for just a few more questions, and if you promise not to cause any more trouble tonight, I'll let you go. It's imperative I get back to my post."

"I understand. And I promise. I'll do whatever you say," she replied.

Michael had a list of things he'd like her to do for him, beginning with taking the pins out of her chignon and letting that long, dark hair spill over his bare chest. But that was fantasy. Michael Trent didn't deal in fantasies. "What's your name?"

"Barbara Mansfield."

"I'm Michael Trent. Once I know the president is safe and the dinner is over, I'll send a message to you about a further meeting. All right?"

"Yes. Anything you say."

"You can go," he said finally.

Barbara didn't waste a moment. She slipped back into the brightly lit room. She walked up to Jefferson, who smiled at her. He'd been so engrossed in his conversation, he hadn't noticed she'd been gone.

Barbara breathed a sigh of relief. She'd be more careful about allowing her impulses to rule her actions.

Michael went back to his post. Jake gave the signal that the president was about to enter the room. The orchestra began playing "Hail to the Chief" as Michael gave the signal to all his men that everything was well.

Theodore Roosevelt greeted his guests with enthusiasm and the good-natured, open friendliness for which he was best known.

Barbara shook his hand and accepted his thanks for accompanying his friend, Jefferson, to Washington. She was doubly pleased that she and Jefferson were seated very close to the president during dinner in order that the president could converse with Jefferson on several political matters. It wasn't until the soup was served that Barbara dared look back to the wall where Michael had positioned himself.

She didn't realize that some of the lights in her eyes faded when she realized Michael was gone.

thirty-six

Not with a Club, the Heart is broken
Nor with a Stone—
A Whip so small you could not see it
I've known
To lash the Magic Creature
Till it fell.

—EMILY DICKINSON
"POEM NO. 1304," ST. I

Barbara clutched the tiny note Michael had sent her as she had finished dessert at the White House. She'd thought the request odd at first because she still feared he thought her capable of intrigue against the president. But as the conversations wound down that evening and she glanced again and again at the note in her lap, she realized she'd been right about the look she'd seen in Michael's eyes. It was the look a man gives a woman when he wants her.

Behind the hotel a gazebo stood underneath spreading chestnut trees. The trees were frosted with a two-inch layer of sparkling snow. The pathways to the gazebo had not been swept as Barbara walked out of the back door of the hotel toward her midnight rendezvous with Michael.

The full moon cast a silver glow over the still city, making Barbara think about fields and shepherds nineteen hundred years ago. She could hear the faint sound of carols being sung at the midnight services at the church around the corner. It was Christmas Eve, the holiest night of the year. It was a magical night, she thought, as she neared the gazebo and found Michael was already waiting for her.

"I was afraid you wouldn't come," he said, taking her hand and pulling her to the bench.

"I thought you were going to put me in jail," she said teasingly.

Michael was earnest as he spoke. He purposefully kept an arm's length of distance between them. "I'm the one who owes you an apology, Miss Mansfield. You were right that I was staring at you, and it was most inappropriate of me. I honestly don't know what came over me. I've never acted like that. I pride myself on controlling my thoughts and my emotions when I'm at work."

"And what about when you aren't working?" she challenged him with an intensely probing look.

"I don't know. When I'm not on duty, I'm usually by myself on holiday. I go up to the Adirondacks a lot and practice my photography. I like taking pictures of nature. Not just a few birds and trees, but awesome, incredible waterfalls or snowfalls on mountain peaks. I like to hike to places where no one's been. Have you ever seen the thunderclouds over the Grand Canyon?"

"No."

"Old Faithful at Yellowstone or the redwoods at Yosemite?"

"No."

"They look like they could grow straight to God. I'd like to show you my photographs of them. In fact, some of my work has been instrumental in convincing the president to pursue the national parks idea. Even your friend, Jefferson, has seen my work."

"He has? When?"

"On his last visit to Washington. I was in San Francisco last year and showed him some of the land the president wants to restrict as a park. Jefferson knows me." Then he looked into her eyes again. "I'm surprised I didn't see you when I was there."

"I've known Jefferson since the day I was born. He was engaged to my grandmother. She died before he could marry her. I'm like a granddaughter to him. I love him very much, Michael. But not in the way you suggested."

"I apologize for that, too." He wanted to touch her hand, but she imprisoned them inside her muff, a gesture, he was certain, meant to keep him at a distance.

"Why did you say something so crude and unfounded? I should think in your job it's important to seek out the facts before you make such a bold statement."

"I was jealous," he interrupted her.

"That's ridiculous. You don't know me. You don't own me. Nobody ever could or will."

He nodded his head and chuckled. "Believe me, you can deliver a mean punch. No one would dare cross you in any way." He paused and then looked in her eyes. "I guess what I'm trying to say is that I was infatuated with you. You were the most beautiful person I'd ever seen. Then you looked at me, as if you'd sensed my eyes on you somehow. I wanted to believe there was some kind of, I don't know, a connection between us." He looked away and took a deep breath. "I'm not doing this very well. I came here to say that I was sorry for putting you through all that tonight. I don't want you to worry that anything is going to happen to you or to Jefferson. But the truth of the matter is I wanted to see you again. I wanted to look into your eyes and see for myself that you were real."

"No one's ever talked to me like you do. Flirtations aren't in my history."

"I'm not flirting," he said brusquely.

"What are you doing?"

"It's only a start, but I'm making love to you."

Barbara sucked in her breath. "And you thought I was bold."

"You are. You're here, aren't you?"

"I should get up right now and leave."

"But you won't," he said.

She took her hand out of the warm muff and touched his icy fingers. She squeezed them and then drew his hand to her lap where she put it inside the muff with both her hands. She didn't realize how intimate and sensual the gesture was. She didn't realize that such an overture could be taken as a sexual advance worthy of a courtesan. All she knew was that she wanted to hold him and when she touched his cold hand, she wanted to comfort him. It was a sincere gesture. It was from her heart.

Michael looked at her and smiled. "I've never met anyone like you, Barbara. You impress me as vulnerable, yet incredibly courageous and strong all at the same time. I make a living reading people. You are very different. Very special and I'd like to get to know you better."

Barbara could see the golden light in his eyes, and she remembered that Jefferson had told her that the light in people's eyes was the passageway to their souls. She wanted to travel down that road and see where it took her. She wasn't afraid of him as she thought she might be. She wasn't afraid of herself, which she thought she should be. She wanted to go exploring. Jefferson would have told her to follow her heart, as he always had. "I'd like to get to know you, too," she said in a near whisper.

Michael expelled a sigh of relief. "Oh, good. I was afraid you still thought I was a pervert."

"And what if I did?"

He took his hand out of the muff and put one warm hand and one cold hand on either side of her face. The moonlight cast a silver luster over them both as he raised her lips to his. The hood of her blue cape fell back and dislodged a long dark curl. "I can't wait until I see you with all your hair down," he said touching the errant lock. "I don't deny I want to kiss you, Barbara. That and so much more, but I'm not a pervert. I don't have designs on you that aren't honorable. Tomorrow, I intend to go to Jefferson since he's your guardian and tell him I want to court you."

"No! Please don't do that!"

"Why not?"

"It's hard to explain. Jefferson thinks of me as a little girl sometimes. I don't want him to think that anyone else is more special to me than he is."

"I don't think you give him enough credit."

"Well, maybe you're right. But not tomorrow. Not on Christmas. Perhaps later in the week."

"All right. I'll let you decide the when and the where. But, honestly, Barbara, I have to see you tomorrow. Even if it is Christmas. How are you going to get away?"

"I could meet you here again," she offered.

"I was thinking of something warmer," he said with a shiver and smiled at her. His eyes grew smoky and intense. "Don't worry, I'll think of something and send you a message."

Before she could answer him, he pressed his lips to hers gently at first and then with a possessiveness that caused her to moan. He pulled her body into his arms and leaned her head back on his arm that encircled her shoulder.

His lips were passionate and commanding, yet tender and so sensual, she felt bolts of heat shoot through her body and by the time they reached her loins, they'd turned to a liquid fire that intensified the deeper they went. She felt as if she were floating as he suckled her bottom lip. He plunged his tongue into her mouth, caressing her with long strokes.

Sliding her tongue against his, she accepted even more of him inside her. She had no concept of what was to follow since she'd never been kissed before. She simply followed his lead and did what came to her naturally.

She gave herself to him fully, openly and totally. She wanted to feel goose bumps, every deep breath, every heartbeat in her body. She memorized the sound of the carolers in the frigid night as they exited the nearby church. She wanted to remember the smell of snow melting on Michael's wool coat and the scent of the bay rum cologne he wore. Mostly, she wanted to remember the taste of him, the satin feel of his tongue in her mouth and the deep yearning he created down deep in her belly, and further to the secret place between her legs where she already felt a strange pulsing begin.

He breathed in short, hot, steamy puffs of smoke as he kissed her over and over again. She didn't feel a rush of cold air as he pulled the ribbon at the throat of her cloak and slowly peeled the cloak open to reveal her satin flesh that had seemed to swell even more over the top of her ball gown.

He tore his mouth from hers and pressed his lips to the hollow at the base of her throat. "This is where I can feel your pulse beat, Barbara. I can feel your heart, the heat and temperature of your blood." He moved his lips further to the narrow valley between the round swells of her breasts. "This is where you give me comfort with your passion." Pressing his lips to her, he inhaled her perfume. His kisses became more intense.

Barbara didn't realize she'd thrown her head back so far until she felt an incredibly intense tingling slide from her breasts down over her ribs to her abdomen and then plunge deep, deep inside her. She raised her head and realized he'd lifted her breast out of her gown.

She'd never felt anything so delicious, so comfortable in her life. She didn't know what was happening, but she knew she wanted to discover more.

She sank her hands into his thick hair and pressed his lips deeper into her breast and massaged herself against his face. Shock waves of pleasure nearly sent her over the brink of reality.

It was Michael who pulled away from her. Before she realized what was happening, he'd replaced her rosy, swollen breast inside her bodice. "Barbara, I'm sorry. I got so carried away."

She didn't understand it. "Why are you stopping?"

He chuckled to himself. "Right now, I honestly think you haven't the slightest notion what happens next, do you?"

She shook her head innocently. "No."

"Good. That's why I'm stopping. I want it to stay that way. *You* to stay that way." He tied her cloak for her and pulled up her hood.

She smiled at him. "Your kisses make me feel lighthearted," she giggled.

He cocked an eyebrow and looked down at her. "Your kisses do a whole lot more to me than that." He stood up and then pulled her to her feet.

"I'll send a message for you. Tomorrow evening after Jefferson is asleep, I'll be with you again. If you want to see me."

"Yes, Michael. I very definitely want to see you."

* * * *

On Christmas morning, Barbara walked into Jefferson's suite and found the drawing room decorated in pine garlands, pine cones and shiny apples and red velvet ribbons. He'd arranged a special brunch to be served in his rooms for them both. Next to the roaring fire in the fireplace was a stack of brightly wrapped presents, all for Barbara.

"Jefferson, you've already bought me that fabulous ball gown and cloak. You've done too much," she said, hiding her gift for him behind her back.

"Indulge me, Angel. This is the first time in nearly ten years I've not been forced to deal with your mother."

She smiled broadly at him. "I know what you mean," she said, handing him the gift she'd brought with her from San Francisco.

"What's this?" he said, gingerly taking the gift from her hand. "I don't need anything."

"You need this," she replied and kissed him on the cheek. Then she sat down in the French bergère chair next to the fire.

Jefferson sat in a Hepplewhite chair opposite her while he opened the box. He took off the gold ribbon and green paper and lifted the lid. Beneath a wad of tissue was a small carved ivory Chinese pagoda. On the back side, in English, were the words: "Son of Heaven."

"Where did you get this?" he asked.

"When Papa died, I found a wooden box at the back of his closet that Mother still knows nothing about. There were several things in there like that. Mother would have sold them by now for the cash, but I knew they were worth something to Papa and because they were special to him, I kept them. I wanted to share this with you. What do you suppose it means? Son of Heaven?"

Jefferson shrugged his shoulders. "Son of Heaven is the name the Chinese use for their emperor. But other than that, Lawrence went to China so many times, he could probably tell us. But why this particular piece? There were others you say?"

"Yes. I remember four distinct jade pieces all made to look like gates. One said T'ai Ho Men. For a long time I thought it was English. Something to do with men, but I had it translated by a Chinese laundress Mother used once. She said it meant Gate of Supreme Harmony. I thought it sounded so pretty."

"It does sound lovely. Sometime I'd like to see those other pieces." Jefferson put the ivory pagoda in his pants pocket. "This is too special not to keep with me always."

Barbara smiled, reached in her skirt pocket and pulled out a white silk scarf with intricate drawn work and long, silk fringe. "I made this for you."

"I had no idea you were so domestic," he teased, knowing Barbara would rather read a book, play lawn tennis or write in her journal than sew or cook.

"I did it for you. I'd take good care of it if I were you. I seriously doubt I'll ever make another."

"Done!" he said and put it around his neck. "Now, it's your turn. The one with the red bow first."

"When did you do this?"

"I didn't. Santa Claus did," he said mirthfully.

She opened the box and found the "Brownie" camera she'd wanted. "Now I can chronicle our trip back to San Francisco in photographs!" she squealed delightedly. In the other boxes were perfumes, sachets, gloves, a new blue velvet reticule with cream satin lining to match her cloak, which was a special order filled by Carrie with a new bonnet Jane had made.

"The seamstresses at the shop liked you a great deal, my dear. They brought those over this morning on their way to church."

"How very sweet," Barbara said as she put her presents away and gave Jefferson a big hug.

Barbara served their brunch from the cart the waiter had left in the room. She chatted with Jefferson about her first night in the White House. He told her that he would be returning to the White House for meetings every day until they left four days hence. At noon they dressed and went to church services. Afterward, they were guests at the home of Senator Peter Mannering and his wife, Estelle, along with all the Mannering's family and friends.

Barbara was amazed at the people who knew Jefferson and the stories she heard about his generosity, loyalty and patriotism. It seemed he'd spent a lifetime trying to make the United States a better place to live. In her mind, he was even more important than the president.

Michael hired a coach at ten o'clock to drive himself and Barbara around the city. He wanted to show her some of the beautifully decorated houses on this festive night. Mostly, he wanted to be alone with her. He wanted to hold her. He needed to kiss her.

As he pointed out each home and related a brief history of the building of the house and the family that lived there, Michael used the time to tell Barbara more about himself.

"I was born in a house much like these Greek Revival homes, in Cleveland, Ohio. My father is active on the Cleveland Stock Market Exchange. We used to have picnics by the lake in the summer, and I sailed toy sailboats I made myself. My mother died when I was fifteen. I miss her tremendously. She was a wonderful woman, loving Dad and me more than she loved herself. He's never been quite the same after she died. He mourns her still, I think."

Barbara nodded her head, thinking of Jefferson, still in love with Caroline. "Then you think it's possible to love one person with all your heart?"

"I know that it is," he replied sincerely. "I think we're given chances to love at different times in our lives. I think it's the choice we make that makes the difference, not the other person."

She turned to him. "At the White House, you had chosen to not feel anything, ever. Hadn't you, Michael?"

"Yes," he said solemnly. "It was safe."

"It hurt you a great deal when your mother died, didn't it?"

"Yes."

"And how do you feel now, Michael?" she asked, nearly holding her breath as she awaited his answer.

"Feel?" He looked at her. "I feel everything. I feel the bite of the cold like I never have before. I feel a strange emptiness when I'm away from you, and yet that's impossible because I don't even know you."

"Yet," she said with a smile and a twinkle in her eye.

The carriage halted at a street corner, and through the window Michael spied a small family restaurant he knew. Though it was Christmas, the owner was inside busily serving hot coffee and cakes to a room full of shabbily dressed men and women.

Michael put his arm around Barbara and pulled her to the window. "I want you to see the real spirit of Christmas."

Barbara saw the dark-haired portly man of about sixty wearing an apron over his formal shirt and pants. He was merrily instructing a woman to cut another pie and serve another cake to the lean and very hungry-looking people.

"Do you know him?"

"Mr. and Mrs. Patelli are wonderful people. I eat here as often as I can."

"Michael," Barbara stuck her hand into her reticule and pulled out several gold coins Jefferson had given her as her spending money during her trip. "Do you think he'd mind if we overpaid for two cups of coffee?"

Michael kissed her cheek. "Splendid idea," he said and ordered the driver to let them out.

They walked to the restaurant and tapped on the door. Michael waved at Mr. Patelli, who put down his coffee server and waddled to the door. He unlocked it.

"Michael! How good to see you! It's rather late for you, eh? And who is this beautiful lady?"

"This is Barbara Mansfield, Mr. Patelli. She wanted to buy a cup of coffee and perhaps you'd give the change to your friends?"

Barbara handed Mr. Patelli the gold coins.

Mr. Patelli's gratitude was in the mist in his eyes. "I'll make you a very special coffee," he said and ushered them inside.

Michael and Barbara sat at the back of the restaurant at a wooden booth where they did not interfere with the merry-making. Barbara told Michael more about herself and her home in San Francisco. She told him about her dreams to become a journalist one day and perhaps even travel to Europe.

Without making a show, they slipped out of the restaurant so that Mr. Patelli could distribute the money she'd given him without anyone knowing it came from her, as she'd told him she wanted.

Michael put his arm around Barbara as they rode through the streets watching the lights in the houses dim and then go out as the city slumbered.

"I'm falling in love with you, Barbara," Michael said as they circled around Pennsylvania Avenue for the second time.

He pulled her to him and kissed her. This time when Michael sank his tongue into the sweetness of her mouth, Barbara didn't want him to stop, ever. She wanted him to explore her body as much as she wanted to experience all the sensations he was creating within her.

"Touch me like you did last night, Michael," she pleaded with him. "Take my breast into your hand—"

Michael put his lips next to her ear as he pulled her breasts to his chest crushing her against him. "God, Barbara, don't talk to me like that. You have no idea how the sound of your voice arouses me."

"Michael, I want to feel you."

He kissed her again if for nothing more than to stifle her words. Had she been experienced he would have guessed her words were calculated, but he knew she was an innocent. And she was driving him out of his mind.

He filled his hand with her breast and rubbed the nipple between his thumb and forefinger, bringing it to full erection. Blood thundered in his brain as he closed his eyes and saw a crashing of white lights behind his lids like the primordial igniting of energy. He thought his lungs would burst with the burning from breathing so hard. Finally, he grabbed her face in his hands and looked into her eyes. "Barbara, I can't do this," he almost growled angrily.

"Michael, what's wrong?"

"Nothing is wrong. Yet, nothing is right. Since the moment I met you, I haven't slept or eaten. I can't think of anything but you. Thank God it's Christmas and I didn't have to work! My powers of concentration, of which I've always been so proud, have abandoned me completely. Tell me, what kind of temptress are you?"

"I'm not. I'm just myself," she said as he clamped his mouth down over hers once again. She allowed the capture and reveled in the sweet taste of him. She understood his hesitation that perhaps there was only some kind of animalistic attraction between them and that once she was away from him for awhile, he'd forget. Or worse, she'd forget him.

"I am *not* myself," he said between kisses. "God help me from perhaps what all this truly is—that I'm finding myself at last."

"What do you want me to do, Michael?"

"I don't want any more clandestine meetings. You're a free woman. I'm a free man. I respect Jefferson. I want him to know about how I feel about you. I must talk to him tomorrow."

"If that's what you want," she replied in throaty tones.

Michael gazed into her eyes believing that somehow he could carry her lovelights with him always. "I want so much more." Then hungrily, he kissed her again.

His kiss was soul-wrenching as he pulled her close. He slid back on the seat, pulling her down on top of him. Lying across his body, her pelvis melted into him and she felt his full erection. Startled, she lifted her hips away, but he put his hands on her buttocks and pressed her into him. He ground his hips into hers, rubbing himself against her.

She felt his body heat soar at the same dizzying speed as her own temperature escalated. She wanted to lie with him. She wanted to feel everything there was about him.

"I wish you didn't thrill me so much, Barbara. I wish I didn't want you so desperately," he said. "Barbara, I want you more than I've ever wanted anything in my life, but not like this. You don't know what you're doing to me."

She slid her arms around his neck and buried her face in the crook of his neck. She felt as if she'd been caught in an undertow at sea. She was glad he was stronger than she, because she *didn't* know what was happening to her. She only knew it was incredibly sensual and that with Michael she felt comfortable enough to allow herself these pleasures.

"Have I embarrassed you?" she asked.

"Lord, no!" he replied and helped her straighten her clothing. "It's that— I want to marry you, Barbara. I want you to come to Washington and be my wife. I want to live with you and grow old with you. I want to share everything about myself with you."

"Michael."

"I'm not asking you formally. Yet," he said sternly.

"You're not?"

Then he grinned seductively. "Tomorrow," he laughed and pulled her into his arms as she laughed with him.

When he brought her back to the hotel, it was after two o'clock in the morning. There was no one about except the doorman and the night clerk, who'd fallen asleep in the chair by the fireplace. The doorman told Barbara not to wake him. The doorman had double-duty as the elevator operator that evening, since it was Christmas.

Michael promised Barbara he would meet her the following night at 10:30 in the gazebo behind the hotel. By that time he would have carried out his plan to talk to Jefferson about their plans to marry.

As Barbara dressed for bed that night and climbed between the clean linen sheets the maid had changed that morning, all she could think about was Michael's kisses and the promises he made.

At ten-thirty the next night, Barbara waited until she knew Jefferson was asleep before stealing away to see Michael. She got to the gazebo five minutes early. He was not there.

She waited in the cold for thirty minutes. It began to snow. She waited another fifteen minutes. Then another twenty. Michael never met their rendezvous.

She went back to her room believing that if he'd been detained, he would send a message to her hotel. She sat by the fire, fully dressed until dawn. Still, Michael didn't come for her.

The next day she asked Jefferson if Michael Trent had met with him.

"About what, my dear?" Jefferson asked.

And then she knew. Michael had lied to her. He'd used her to play his game. She was a silly, stupid girl from the West. He'd not only taken liberties with her body, but he'd stolen her heart to boost his ego.

Barbara never told Jefferson about Michael; there seemed no point in it. After all, what were three days out of one's life? She hadn't lost her virginity.

Michael's tryst with her would forever remain a secret. She'd go back to San Francisco, and life would return to normal.

She'd learned a valuable lesson, however. She'd forgotten that her first night here she'd reminded herself that this was not home. This was Washington, D.C., a city of intrigue.

She had committed the greatest crime possible, according to her rules by Jefferson Duke.

I didn't listen to my heart when it tried to warn me.

thirty-seven

*Days decrease,
And autumn grows, autumn in everything.*

—ROBERT BROWNING
"ANDREA DEL SARTO," L. 35

Barbara lost the will to search for exoneration for her broken heart. Jefferson observed her melancholy on their trip back to San Francisco. Though she snapped a bevy of pictures with the new camera he gave her, there was little animation in his granddaughter.

"Why are you morose, Angel?" he asked.

"I'm just tired after all that revelry in Washington. I don't know how you do it, Jefferson."

"Yes, I know. At my age."

Had Jefferson's mind not been preoccupied with the enormity of being President Roosevelt's advisor, he might have pursued questioning Barbara. However, Jefferson knew that upon returning to San Francisco, he was about to become a right arm to the president, advising him on the lawsuits against big business, the graft and corruption in San Francisco itself and even his suggestions for turning lands around San Francisco into national parks. It was a heavy task even for a young man. For a man of eighty-six, it should have been overwhelming. However, Jefferson was exhilarated by the prospect.

When Barbara arrived home, she found Eleanor knee-deep in packing barrels and crates. Nearly everything they owned was being carted out of the house.

Jefferson's driver, Patrick, deposited Barbara's bags on the floor in the vestibule. "I can take these upstairs for you."

Barbara shook her head as two maids stuffed excelsior into wooden barrels covering French porcelains her father had bought nearly twenty years ago at a small, out-of-the-way shop on the Left Bank in Paris. "It looks like I'll just be putting them on the wagon later, anyway. Thank you, Patrick," she smiled.

He tipped his tweed hat. "Anytime," he said and left.

Barbara walked into the salon where Eleanor was giving instructions to two burly men lifting a large curio cabinet. "Hello, Mother," Barbara said. "I take it you've sold the house."

Eleanor glared at her daughter. There was no welcome-home hug or kiss. Barbara knew better than to expect affection from Eleanor. "No thanks to you."

Barbara sighed as she realized that her day of reckoning with her mother was here. Because of the deep emotional turmoil she'd been going through over Michael, Barbara hadn't given a second thought to the ramifications of her quick and headstrong departure from San Francisco two weeks ago. She'd forgotten how much store Eleanor had put into giving Barbara her debut party. "Did you get a good price?"

"Yes, thank God. My solicitor handled the negotiations and even found us a small but affordable home not far from Union Square."

"It sounds lovely," Barbara tried to assuage her mother.

"It's hideous. Absolutely the worst place I've had to live. But it was all I could afford. And after having all this." She spread her arms wide, gesturing to the exquisitely appointed room. "It's like falling off a cliff."

"It's not as bad as all that."

"No, Barbara, it's worse. When you left so abruptly, your friend, Meredith Winter, moved in on Donald Pope and they announced their engagement just yesterday."

"They don't seem well matched at all," Barbara surmised, thinking of sensitive, caring Donald, whom she thought of as a dear friend despite her flight to Washington. Even though she cared for Meredith, no one understood Meredith's failings and insecurities more than Barbara did. The problem with Meredith was that the girl possessed not the first ounce of humility, but Barbara knew her bravado was a smokescreen for her insecurities. Meredith felt she always had to be the best in school, the prettiest among the girls and the most popular girl with the boys. It was right in character for Meredith to make a play for Donald at a time when she knew Donald would be upset about Barbara's canceling her debut party.

"All our chances to get you married off are gone!" Eleanor said with an overly dramatic hand to her forehead.

"What a ridiculous statement. I'm only twenty!"

Eleanor dropped her hand and went to the mantel. "This invitation came just yesterday. Mrs. Pope is giving a party for Donald and Meredith on Saturday. I've already told her you'll be there."

Barbara took the invitation from her mother. She knew Eleanor was challenging her, maybe even hoping she would openly defy her again. Right now, Barbara didn't care if the czar himself were coming to San Francisco. She didn't care if she went to this party or to a hundred parties. She didn't have the energy to argue with Eleanor any more. "I'll be there. In fact, Jefferson bought me a lovely gown that I wore to the president's dinner party. We won't even have to spend money on a ball gown."

"Well, bully for him!" Eleanor glowered.

Just then the maids came back into the room with the moving men. "Pardon us for interrupting, but what do you want moved next, ma'am?"

"The divan and then the rest of the china barrels." Eleanor turned back to Barbara. "You might as well change into a day dress. I could use the help."

"Certainly," Barbara said and left the salon. As she entered the vestibule she realized that a young Chinese girl was standing at the front door.

Chen Su had turned twenty years old on the same day as Barbara, though neither of them realized that fact about the other. Chen had openly defied her grandfather, Nan-Yung, by refusing to work in the laundry rooms and out back in the alleyway where linens and shirts were boiled, scrubbed and rubbed till they were clean. Chen listened to her grandmother, Yin, who told her to go among the whites and learn to be a housemaid. Then when she was paid money, she could learn to pocket some of the money for herself rather than being a slave to the House of Su. Yin taught her favorite granddaughter to think for herself. Yin taught Chen how to use the intuitive gifts she'd been given.

"You are the most gifted of all my grandchildren, just as it was foretold to me in China. You are the seventh child. As you mature, your sight will increase. Use it with wisdom. Remember your dreams, but keep your feet firmly in reality. This is the earth-plane, and spiritual dictates many times are not what they seem in this plane. Choose caution over impetuosity and you will never be wrong."

"Yes, Grandmother. This family you want me to seek out is special to me?"

"Yes. Go to this house." Yin had given Chen a house number and street. "The young woman who lives there will be kind to you."

"You saw her in a dream?" Chen asked.

"No, I've watched her all her life. I knew her father."

"Her father was my sister Mei's lover?"

Yin frowned. "I have never believed that story. Mei was a good girl. She was loyal to me. She hated Nan-Yung as much as I do. Your grandfather will not have you murdered if you become a housemaid. He will think the work is worthy of you. Never tell him all you learn."

"Learn?"

"I want you to learn the ways of the whites. Read their books. Listen to their music. Incorporate our wisdom with their knowledge and you will create a better world for yourself than I have."

Chen nodded. "This young woman. I sense things about her before meeting her. She is powerful?"

"Yes. But no more so than you or I. I want you to watch after her as I guard against evil around you. Pray for her as I pray for you. Be her helpmate."

"But I won't be her friend."

Yin smiled at her granddaughter and caressed her silken hair. "I feel that, in time, you will. Trust my words."

"I do, Grandmother."

That night, Chen had slept fitfully. She dreamed of a young white girl. She saw her clearly, the dark lashes, the oval face. The apparition even spoke to her. "My name is Barbara."

Now Chen stood outside the etched glass door of Barbara's house, watching the blue-eyed white girl walk toward her. Chen was shocked at the power of her own dreams. This was the first time Chen had taken one of her dreams seriously.

"Hello," Barbara said, opening the door. "Is there something I can help you with?"

"I here about a job?"

"Really? I didn't know my mother was hiring any more people." Barbara opened the door all the way and motioned for Chen to step inside. Just then the moving men rounded the corner with the very heavily carved, pecan-wood divan with white silk upholstery.

Chen and Barbara quickly moved out of their way.

"Come with me," Barbara instructed as the men exited the front door. She glanced over her shoulder at the pretty and petite Oriental girl with the mysterious dark eyes. "What's your name?"

"Chen," she replied sheepishly as she knew whites expected of one of her race and station.

"Mother, this is Chen. She came about the job you have."

Eleanor shook her head. "I'm not hiring any more staff," she said, exasperation etched on her face. "But, judging from all the work we have, I suppose we could use the help." She looked Chen square in the eye. "It's only for a day or two and I'm only paying two dollars. But it's yours if you want it."

Chen had been taught fluent English by her grandmother. She had also been taught never to use her precise English in front of the whites and never in front of her father, Lon Su, or her grandfather, Nan-Yung. "That good." She bowed politely.

"Take her to your room, Barbara. She can help you get your drawers cleaned out and pack your clothing."

"Very well," Barbara replied and turned to Chen. "I guess you work for us now," she said.

Chen smiled happily. Little did Barbara realize that the two of their destinies were linked. Chen's gift of prophecy had allowed her to see into the future. Even as a little girl, Chen had dreams in which she and a white girl were running through fire. She had cried over the dreams, knowing the danger around her might even kill them. The dream was so real, she'd told her grandmother. Yin had comforted Chen, but the most frightening thing about the dream was that it returned to her over the years again and again. Chen knew that she and Barbara were meant to fulfill some sort of divine plan, but she didn't know what the outcome would be. She could only trust in her own instincts, her own visions and pursue them.

Mounting the staircase, Chen smiled to herself. She knew her job would last longer than two days.

Much longer.

* * * *

Barbara and Eleanor rode in a hired coach to the Pope mansion on Nob Hill for Donald's engagement party. Because Meredith's family was not wealthy, Harriet Pope insisted upon hosting the party. "Besides," she told Barbara, "this will give me another chance to make the social columns in the newspapers. Such things must be considered."

Barbara had agreed with her. After all, Eleanor had once been the darling of all the society reporters. If she didn't pull off a coup with Barbara soon, they'd forget about her. Barbara knew her mother could stand anything except being ignored.

Barbara took the footman's hand as she got out of the coach. The front steps to the Greek Revival mansion were crowded with fabulously jeweled and gowned women. When she entered the house and the butler took her cloak, several of her friends commented on her stunning gown.

Ordinarily, Barbara's eyes would have twinkled as merrily as the crystal beading on her gown, but tonight all she could think about was Michael.

She walked into the ballroom and was introduced by the butler. As she watched a room full of admiring gazes turn her way and smile appreciatively, she barely heard their greetings. Instead, her mind was filled with visions of Michael.

"You look lovely tonight, Barbara. How was Washington?" Sally Ann Jefferson asked.

"It was all right," Barbara answered.

"I knew it would be stuffy and boring. I never want to go there."

Barbara didn't hear her old school friend. She heard Michael's voice. *I want you, Barbara. I want to marry you. I'll speak to Jefferson about it. You don't know what you do to me.*

Had she been a weak woman, she would have cried. *But I'm not weak. I'm only a fool.*

Never will I choose a man with my heart again. Next time, I'll be smarter. I'll use my head.

Barbara went to Meredith and took her hand and offered her best wishes.

"I couldn't be happier that my two friends have found each other," Barbara said sincerely and then kissed Donald on the cheek. When she realized his hands were trembling, his eyes told her she was standing too close to him.

She backed away. She didn't want Donald to be in love with her, because she couldn't return his feelings. He was her friend and that was all. But her heart went out to him because she knew what it was like to love and not be loved in return.

Barbara told herself that some of the best marriages did not start out on the best footing. Perhaps Meredith's would be one of those marriages. Barbara could only hope their life together would grow in happiness as the years progressed.

Barbara had just turned away from Donald and glanced back at the entrance to the ballroom when the butler announced an unfamiliar name.

"Mr. Peter Kendrick," the butler said loudly.

A tall blond man with tremendous shoulders, narrow hips and long legs walked into the room.

"Who is he?" a woman asked.

"An angel, of course. No man can be that handsome," Barbara heard her companion say.

"Why, he's almost beautiful," Barbara said.

Though he had the same stature and well-toned physique as Michael did, Peter's blue eyes were riveting in a tanned and aristocratic face.

"His clothes are impeccable. So expensive. He looks like . . ."

"A fairy-tale prince," Barbara finished, watching him move toward the Popes, Meredith and herself.

"My God, I have never seen a man move like that . . . or wear such tight breeches. Why I can almost see . . ." Meredith whispered to Barbara with a distinct sensual undertone to her voice.

"Meredith! He'll hear you."

"I hope so!" she giggled.

Barbara swallowed hard. Ordinarily, she never thought about such things, but Michael had opened up the carnal world to her. He'd taught her to be sensual. He'd taught her to feel life through all of her senses. What she wouldn't give to go back to being the Barbara she'd been less than a month ago when she hadn't known such intense feelings.

"He's coming this way," Meredith whispered again.

"I can see that," Barbara said as she moved aside in order for Peter to greet and thank his hosts.

Harriet Pope leaned over to Barbara and said, "Peter has just moved here from Chicago. He's a new builder in town. He's only been here three weeks, and Mr. Pope says that all his cronies at the Union Pacific Club think Peter Kendrick is going to do quite well here. He's already a millionaire, but he told Mr. Pope he intends to quadruple his income, this year alone."

Barbara stood next to Harriet Pope as Peter introduced himself.

"I'm pleased to meet you, Mrs. Pope. Your husband has been singing your praises since I arrived in town. I can't tell you how grateful I am to be invited this evening." He paused and glanced at Barbara out of the corner of his eye. "It's been rather lonely for me in a new city."

"We're delighted you could come," Harriet said, introducing Peter to Meredith and Donald. Then she turned toward Barbara. "I don't think you've met Barbara Mansfield. She's recently returned from our nation's capital, which is why you probably haven't met her at any of the local parties or opera outings."

Peter Kendrick turned to Barbara and took a step closer to her. "I saw you the moment I walked in the room," he said. "May I say that is a most exquisite gown. It deserves breathtaking beauty to display it properly."

Barbara glanced at Meredith who looked as if she'd swoon from his kind of obsequiousness, even though it was Barbara he was praising. Meredith gave her a nudging look when she realized Barbara was not responding to Peter's overtures.

"Thank you," Barbara said politely. She gave him no encouraging looks. She didn't return his flattery.

"I'd like to dance with you tonight. Is your card full, Miss Mansfield?" Peter asked.

When Barbara hesitated for a hairsbreadth of time, Meredith stepped in. "She just arrived! She hasn't seen a soul in weeks!"

Peter laughed. "Then may I see your card?"

Barbara handed it to him, all the while glaring at Meredith. Peter handed the card back to her after scribbling something on the card. He put out his arm to her. "I think this dance is mine," he said and placed her arm through his when she still hadn't responded.

Barbara allowed herself to be led to the dance floor while she thought of a thousand excuses to leave this party.

Peter took her in his arms and held her close as he smoothly executed perfect dance steps. The cologne he wore reminded her of Michael. He was the same height as Michael and so her body fit next to his in much the same way she had fit with Michael. The curve of his neck where it met his shoulder was at her eye level just like Michael's.

She looked at the ceiling and tried to concentrate on the Venetian crystal chandeliers overhead and the hand-painted frescoes of heavenly skies filled with cupids. She thought of a million excuses to get away from Peter Kendrick.

I could say I was sick to my stomach. No, he'd probably just fetch me some seltzer water and bitters.

I could tell him my maid is in childbirth. No, that won't work, either.

I'm stuck dancing with Peter tonight and that's that.

As they danced, Barbara watched the faces of the young girls around the perimeter of the dance floor practically drooling over Peter. She wondered what they saw that she didn't.

It's not them. It's me. Peter is not Michael. That's all.

And that's the hell of it.

After the first half of the evening was over, Peter turned to Barbara and chuckled to himself. "You know, Miss Mansfield, I've never met anyone quite like you."

Michael said that.

"Boring, huh?" she replied, looking over the buffet table.

"I feel you are a challenge. You barely know I'm here. Usually, I've had my choice of any woman I want," he said flatly, honestly and without conceit, though it was a vain statement.

"Maybe your time would be more wisely spent on someone else."

"But I want you," he said.

I want you, Barbara.

And she had believed him. Worse, she had wanted him, too. She frowned at herself for thinking about Michael when he so obviously didn't want her at all. She smiled cryptically at Peter. "You're telling me you want me because I'm a challenge? That's rather silly, don't you think?"

"Not to me, it's not," he said, leaning close.

Barbara had the impression he wanted to kiss her. Now that she'd been thoroughly kissed by Michael, she knew what it was like to be wanted by a man. She knew the heated, musky smell that emanated from them when they wanted to make love. She knew the smoky glaze that covered their eyes as they moved in to take their prey.

And that's all I am. Prey.

She backed away from him. "It'll take a lot more than a few fancy words to win me, Mr. Kendrick." She threw down a gauntlet of her own.

"I don't doubt that for a second. But I'm willing to do whatever it takes to win you."

"Really?"

"Yes," he replied firmly.

"Do you think you could accept a woman who worked as a journalist?"

"Pardon me?"

"I've talked to the city editor at the *Call* and he says he'll hire me, based on my writing abilities, which I gave him a sampling of a few days ago. Not even my mother knows of my plans to work at the newspaper. But you see, I've always wanted to be a journalist, and I've decided this is something I need to do for myself."

Peter smiled mirthfully. "It's going to take a lot more than some articles about garden parties to dissuade me, Miss Mansfield."

"Garden parties? I'll be working for the city editor, covering news stories."

"Wonderful! I'm sure that in no time you'll be the best writer they've got," he replied and leaned his body closer to hers.

Barbara raised her chin proudly. "I will be. You'll see."

"I don't doubt it for a minute," he said and led her back to the dance floor for yet another waltz.

Eleanor Mansfield spent the evening learning everything she could about Peter Kendrick.

She discovered from one of the officers at the First National Bank of San Francisco that Peter Kendrick had wired over a million dollars to the new account he'd set up. Then he'd arranged for a loan of half that amount to buy a parcel of land on the north side of the city where he intended to build a tract of homes. He applied at City Hall for a building permit to build a new nickelodeon theater just off Powell Street.

As far as she could tell, Peter Kendrick had dug his feet into San Francisco soil with a vengeance. There was no doubting he was more than enamored of Barbara. Eleanor could tell from the tiresome look on Barbara's face, she was going to have a difficult time convincing her daughter that Peter Kendrick was the answer to their prayers.

It wasn't the first time Eleanor had fought the odds against her.

thirty-eight

*And fire and ice within me fight
Beneath the suffocating night.*

—ALFRED EDWARD HOUSMAN
A SHROPSHIRE LAD, ST. IV

San Francisco—1905

Barbara married Peter thinking she'd forget Michael.

She was wrong.

Peter's attentiveness died the instant the ring was on her finger After her quiet ceremony in the small chapel decorated with English ivy and white calla lilies, there was apathy in Peter's eyes as the couple walked through the doors to the bright sunlight. Jefferson had hugged Barbara tightly as she stepped into his black-lacquered carriage he'd lent them for the ride to the Fairmont Hotel for their reception, but there had been incredible sadness in his eyes.

"Be well," he'd said.

Barbara was struck at the time that he'd not wished her happiness. It was as if he knew she'd made a dreadful mistake. "I'll be fine," she replied.

"Of course you will," he said, kissing her cheek.

Jefferson had helped her lift her voluminous veiling into the coach. She watched him glance derisively at Peter, who was receiving congratulations from the many business associates he'd insisted be invited to the wedding. Barbara had been concerned that Eleanor was spending far too much money

406

on the wedding and insisted the ceremony and reception be drastically reduced. The flowers and carriage had been a gift from Jefferson. Because Peter wanted only the most influential people at the reception, he insisted upon paying for the requisite cake and champagne.

Barbara was already learning that Peter was all show and no substance.

But it was on her wedding night that Barbara learned only one man would ever hold her heart. Each time Peter touched her she pretended it was Michael. Every effort he made at romance, she thought of Michael. In a way, she pitied Peter because he could never measure up to a memory who was destined to remain a phantom in her life.

Barbara's marriage was doomed. She knew it. Peter sensed it.

In less than a month, she realized she could find an escape through her writing.

Landing the job at the *Call*, she worked long hours, pushing herself harder than her editors did.

"If I have to cover one more society bash, I think I'll throw up, William," she said to the city editor.

William Melton ignored her.

"On your desk. Will that get your attention?"

"Be quiet and let me finish this piece you gave me."

"Oh," she sank sheepishly into the chair opposite him. "Sorry. Go ahead."

He turned the page over and looked up. "Is this crap true?"

"You bet it is."

"How'd you get this councilman to admit to what's going on?"

"I told him if he didn't give me the scoop I'd print the interview I got from Sheldon Ash who owns West Coast Concrete and Shell. Ash admits to selling his third-grade concrete to the city. Ash says that's all the city paid for. To quote Ash, 'city council knew this concrete wouldn't hold back a creek bed much less hold up a building.' The council members pocketed the bulk of the budget. Ash told me there's no water mains under the street he installed down in the Mission District."

"Those hydrants?"

"Are phonies."

"Whew!" he whistled. "How'd you get so good so fast?"

"Easy. Jefferson Duke."

He shook his head. "You realize every reporter on this paper is going to hate you."

"I don't care."

"They can make life miserable for you. And that's the upside."

"And the downside?"

"Have you got any idea how easy it is to hire an assassin in this town? If this is true, you'll have half the city council and all of the shysters in the construction business after your hide. What are you thinking? That you're impervious?"

"I'm banking on the fact that I'm a woman."

William laughed. Then he stopped. "It might work."

"I'm willing to take the chance." She leaned forward. "Frankly, I figured you wouldn't have the guts to print it. Once this is out, the paper could be vandalized. Bombs set. Stuff like that."

William rubbed his very tired eyes. "Yeah, well, maybe it's time we fired the first round."

"Thanks, William." She started out the door.

"Barbara, I still want you to cover the ball."

Her shoulders slumped. "Why?"

"Think of it this way, it'll make your husband happy."

Frowning, she faced him. "He's pretty transparent, huh?"

William nodded. "He's taking the social ladder three rungs at a time."

"What are you saying? I should watch my back?"

"In more ways than one. Just a word to the wise," he said.

Smiling wanly, she answered, "Point taken. See you tomorrow."

* * * *

Knowing that because of Jefferson, Barbara moved with the most monied and powerful forces in the city, Peter's entrée into society was accepted with no questions asked.

"I was blessed the day I met you, Barbara," Peter said, tying his bow tie.

Chen reheated the curling irons while Barbara watched Peter in the reflection of her vanity mirror. "That was a sweet thing to say," she said.

"Well, it's true," he replied charmingly. "I'm going downstairs for a drink while you finish dressing."

"I won't be long," she said, watching him leave. Then she turned to Chen. "Take as long as you want, Chen."

"You are tense this night," Chen said. "I could rub your shoulders."

"Oh, please do, Chen. You have magic hands."

"Not magic. Education. I learned from my grandmother how to increase the flow of energy up the spine and through the meridians of the body."

"Thank God for her. How is she these days?"

"She's very happy for me. She gave me a lotus blossom to give to you," Chen said, pulling the delicate flower from her trouser pocket. "It's exquisite," Barbara said. "But she didn't need to do that for me."

"She said to thank you for giving me the room upstairs and for not sending me away." She knew she could never go back to Chinatown once she'd gotten away from Nan-Yung. Seldom did she venture out of the Kendrick house for fear of meeting someone from the catacombs who would recognize her. Pursue her. However, Chen knew she could never stand up to the Su power and evil by herself. She would have to make a great deal of money to topple the House of Su. All she could do was fend for herself and make certain she never became one of the slaves who lived in the bowels of the catacombs.

Such a life was living death.

Chen knew her grandfather, Nan-Yung, was the devil who sold little boys into prostitution and tortured Chinese girls for the entertainment of demented whites. She knew about the money Nan-Yung made in the Shanghai business: selling whites and Chinese into slavery off the China coast. When the House of Su dealt in drugs and opium dens, Yin had tricked herself into believing she could work her way away from her greedy husband. Instead, as the years passed, Nan-Yung's perversions had become diabolical.

Chen wasn't sure if she would ever be able to do more than save herself. It was still her dream to go back to Chinatown and save her grandmother, Yin, and mother, Ling, and any of her sisters or friends who wanted a new life away from the evil tentacles of the House of Su.

Only with great caution and planning did she visit Yin. They communicated through their minds, and though Chen's gift was not as practiced as her grandmother's, she was learning.

Outside the Kendrick household, at the markets or when she accompanied Barbara shopping, Chen pretended to speak only Chinese. The English language she saved for Barbara, who relished being her teacher.

Chen realized she was a prisoner of her own making, but to her, incarceration was a state of mind. There were all kinds of prisons. This one was paradise.

"Why would I ever want to send you away? Why, I rely upon you to keep the household going. To keep me going. Lord knows no one else seems to care as much about me."

"Mr. Kendrick doesn't like me."

Barbara's back instantly stiffened. "Sometimes I think he doesn't like me, either."

Chen was silent.

Barbara watched her reaction in the mirror. "You sense it, too?"

"It's not my place to say such things," Chen replied, wishing she could say the things she saw. The things she heard.

"Such things?"

Chen stopped massaging and picked up the curling irons. "Mr. Kendrick would want you to be the most beautiful at the ball."

Barbara watched Chen's reflection in the mirror as she expertly curled her hair. "You know that Peter has been unfaithful to me, don't you?"

Chen's hand faltered only a fraction of a second. But Barbara saw it.

"Do you know who it is?"

Chen burned her finger. "Ow!" She put her finger to her tongue, then said, "You and I have no secrets. You must know that by now. I know that you lost your heart to another long ago, though you've never told me so. I can see his face next to yours."

"What?"

"There in the mirror. If you look long enough, you'll see him."

"I don't need a mirror," Barbara replied hollowly. "I see him everywhere I go." She dropped her eyes. "Does Peter know?"

Chen drew in a breath for courage. "He's too selfish to see anything concerning you."

"Oh, God. How did my life get so mixed up?"

Chen halted mid-motion. "Your life is in perfect order. Everything is this way for a reason. Your destiny was to be with Mr. Kendrick. For now."

"But why? Why couldn't I just be with Michael and be happy? Why didn't he want me?"

"But he did want you. Someone else got in the way."

"Someone?" Barbara felt the first flicker of hope since she left Washington several years ago.

Chen's eyes focused on the distance. She looked as if she were in a trance. "I don't see the person. Only the energy. A selfish person. Like your husband in many ways. One who puts their own greed ahead of all others. This person has no heart."

Barbara grabbed her arm pleadingly. "You can't see who it is?"

"No. I will try for you."

A knock on the door interrupted them as Meredith Winters Pope rushed into the room wearing a canary-yellow gown and capelet. "Aren't you dressed yet?"

"Meredith! You're early." Barbara glanced at the clock. "Look at the time. I had no idea. I won't be a minute."

Meredith pulled on her new lace gloves. "I left Donald with Peter. Men talk. It's so boring."

"Chen, see to Mr. Pope. He's not much of a whiskey drinker. Some tea, I think."

Chen bowed and left the room.

Stepping out of Chen's path, Meredith waited until she'd left and said, "She doesn't understand you, does she?"

For a moment Barbara had almost forgotten the ruse she and Chen played. "She understood 'tea' and that we have guests. She'll figure it out."

"Why you don't hire suitable help is beyond me, Barbara. Everyone knows these Orientals aren't smart enough to do anything more than laundry."

"Really?" Barbara said, patting her elegant curls. "I think they're highly trainable." *Unlike you.*

"Well, I'll give you that Chen is an exception. She's a master at hairdressing."

"You don't know the half of it," Barbara chuckled as she slipped into her dressing room. "Believe me, I'm the one who learns from her."

"Don't be ridiculous, Barbara. What could you ever learn from her?"

"Oh, things." *If I'm lucky, Chen might see a vision of Peter's lover. At least I'd know what I was dealing with.*

Downstairs, Peter paced. "What is taking Barbara so long? I swear, Donald, the woman thinks only of writing and forgets the important matters."

"You needn't apologize, Peter," Donald said. "No one is ever on time for these things."

"Don't I well know it," Peter said, lighting a cigar. "I love these Havanas, don't you?"

"Well, yes," Donald said, blowing out the aromatic smoke. "But who can afford them?"

Peter chuckled to himself. *Thank God I got to Barbara in time before she married some nitwit like Donald.*

Peter thought well of himself and his accomplishments. And why shouldn't he? Methodically and with painstaking attention to his every move, Peter Kendrick had infiltrated San Francisco's society and politics with the silent stealth of a viper. Once he'd earned their trust, he began robbing them bit by bit.

Peter won municipal building bids over every other construction company in town because he was well connected to the crème de la crème of society thanks to Barbara's connection to Jefferson Duke.

Peter made friends with Mayor Eugene Schmitz and his crony, Abe Ruef. He skimmed hundreds of thousands of dollars off the new post office building he erected on the north side of town. He cleared nearly a million dollars on a hospital he built on the west side. He put away another half a million dollars building a new theater. Because he was so very clever and so aligned with the town, no one ever suspected his dirty way of doing business. Not even his wife.

The butler appeared at the salon doors. "I'm sorry to disturb you, Mr. Kendrick, but there's a Mr. Clancy at the door who is making rather a ruckus and won't come back tomorrow. He says it's urgent and must speak with you."

"Clancy?" Peter frowned. "Show him to the library. I'll be there directly."

"Very good, sir."

"I'm sorry, Donald. Construction, it seems, is a perpetual bother. Help yourself to some whisky."

"I don't drink."

"I'm sorry. I forgot."

As Peter started out of the room, Chen appeared in the hall. "Ah! Chen.

Please see to Mr. Pope. He needs something to drink," Peter said using more hand and arm gestures than words to convey his meaning to the servant girl whom he believed didn't understand English.

She bowed as she crossed the hall to the library and shut the mahogany doors behind him. As Chen entered the salon she could hear a man's voice shouting at Peter Kendrick.

She suppressed a smile, then proceeded down the hall.

Donald Pope stood next to the east windows near the wall of bookcases, looking at a leather-bound version of Longfellow, when Chen entered the room.

She'd read the poet from cover to cover. She wondered if Donald Pope had done the same.

Chen had met Donald Pope when she'd first come to work for Barbara. The Popes had been guests of the Kendricks shortly after Peter had completed the construction of this house. Chen had helped serve the meal that night since one of the Irish maids had taken ill. Chen prided herself on being a keen observer of humans.

She realized while the first courses were being served that Meredith Pope paid far too much attention to Peter Kendrick, flattering him on the elegant mansion he'd built and the great amount of money he'd spent on the furnishings. Chen witnessed a quiet pain in Donald's eyes as he watched his wife throw herself at another man. Chen's heart went out to Donald Pope because she saw that he was a good man. Though he was quiet, he was not lacking in depth of emotion or width of his heart.

That first night Donald had looked at her, and she believed he saw her empathy in her eyes.

At that moment, she'd felt a connection between them as if she'd been hit by a thunderbolt. She knew then that all the things her grandmother had told her about finding the other half of her soul were true.

The only problem was, Chen could never do anything about it. Donald Pope was white. He was wealthy. He was married. And as she observed the way he looked at Barbara that night, she knew that Donald was in love with her mistress.

Chen felt sorry for these wealthy but very unhappy people. They had homes as beautiful as an emperor's palace. Their carriages were gilded with gold and their clothes were worthy of a king's coronation ceremony, but their hearts were empty and sad. How badly she wanted to tell Donald Pope that until someone else gave him the love he needed so desperately, he would not be able to release Barbara.

Knowing Barbara's heart had been stolen by another didn't help Donald, either.

"I bring tea," Chen finally said, getting Donald Pope's attention.

He closed the cover of the book and looked at her with his soft brown eyes. "That would be lovely," he replied and watched her as she gracefully padded across the marble floor and out into the hallway.

Chen returned a few minutes later with a steaming pot of tea, a china cup and a small plate of cakes and scones. She put the tea on the tea table and poured the tea while he watched. She added a heaping teaspoonful of sugar and floated a paper-thin slice of lemon on top. She handed it to him, her eyes still cast down.

"You remembered how I took my tea?" he asked, suddenly aware of the delicate scent of jasmine soap. The gaslight struck her lustrous hair.

"Yes," she replied wanly as all Chinese servants were instructed to do.

"And you understand English. Does Barbara know?"

Gasping, she realized she'd been tricked. "Yes," she replied confidently. "But Mr. Kendrick does not."

"That's good," he said conspiratorially. "Your secret is safe with me."

"Thank you."

He observed her delicate ministrations with the tea. He wondered why she didn't leave the room quickly the way servants were expected.

Chen read his thoughts. She knew she tarried too long. She wanted to talk to him. To tell him that she'd dreamed about him at night. Wished for him to come to call on the Kendricks during the day. She wanted to tell him that each time she shopped with Barbara, she hoped they would see him in a restaurant or at the perfumers both he and Barbara frequented.

Instead, she kept her head down where her eyes could not betray her.

Donald put his tea cup down and sat in the huge Chippendale wing chair where his vantage point was such that he could see her face, even when she was trying to avoid his gaze.

"What other secrets do you have, Chen?"

"None," she replied flatly.

Donald uncrossed his legs and leaned his elbows on his knees. Something

told him this dainty girl who weighed no more than an apple blossom knew
a great deal.

"I sense a mystery about you, Chen. Are you like the fortune-tellers on
Grant Street?"

"You've been to them?"

"Yes. But don't tell anyone." He shook his finger in front of his face.
"Others might not understand."

"Understand what? Are you afraid they would think you foolish? Or desperate?"

"Both."

"You want to know if your wife has not been true to you. She has not."

"I already know that. What I want to know is who."

"You know that as well."

Donald glanced across the hall to the closed library doors. "I'm afraid I
do. It's obvious, isn't it?"

"Only to those who have eyes to see."

"And does Barbara know?"

"In her way."

"She doesn't know it's Meredith, does she?" he asked.

"Not yet," Chen said honestly.

He leaned back in the chair and exhaled. "Poor Barbara."

"You love her still?"

His eyes flew open. "You don't miss a trick, do you?" He looked at the
lovely golden-skinned girl. "They say that Barbara's father had an affair
with a Chinese girl and that she was murdered because of him. And that he
was murdered because of her."

"I've heard the same," she said, lifting her eyes to look at him directly.
"But you think the Chinese are unclean?"

"No," he replied, holding his breath. "I would never think anyone as
beautiful as you—I can understand why a man like Lawrence Mansfield
could fall in love that deeply."

With graceful hands, Chen placed a tea cake on a porcelain plate. When
Donald took the plate from her, their fingers touched.

"Thank you, Chen," he said, feeling a tingling sensation go up his arm.
He imagined it went straight to his heart. "I won't tell anyone you know
English so well. It will be our secret."

She nodded but made no reply.

"I don't want to cause any trouble for you, Chen." He looked away from her then, thinking this was insane to even be considering these feelings he had as anything more than lust. He was Donald Pope, after all, crown prince of the town. His family practically ruled San Francisco society. They would never understand how he could feel this way. Hell! He didn't even know what he was feeling. Only that he *was* feeling.

She still made no reply. She sensed the turmoil in his mind. She didn't know exactly what he was thinking, but she knew he'd realized she was in love with him.

I could make her my mistress. Yes, isn't that what one does in a situation like this? If I could just touch you again . . .

He reached out to touch her hair and then snatched his hand back.

She was like a perfect lotus blossom. She was young and no doubt still a virgin. Barbara had told him she and Chen had been born on the same day, at the same hour. He found that fascinating. Mysterious.

But is it fate?

There's no such thing as fate. I've just lost my mind is all. I'm upset about Meredith and Peter.

"I . . . I should be going," he said, putting down his plate.

"I'll get your wife for you."

"My wife?" *God, I've lost track of time. Where I am. What's wrong with me?*

"Chen, tell my wife and Barbara that I'll be in the carriage waiting for them. I need some fresh air."

She lifted her face to him and stared at him boldly, letting her love shine in her eyes. "Don't be afraid."

She stunned him. She overpowered him. She changed his life with one look.

"Chen, I . . ."

"I'm not afraid," she said. "Not anymore."

Slowly, he rose. "You don't mind if I take some time?"

"No."

Moving past her he halted. Without looking back at her, he lifted his hand. She took it.

He felt his nerves ignite. "I'll be back tomorrow. Alone."

"I know," she replied as he left.

thirty-nine

I fled Him, down the nights and down the days;
I fled Him, down the arches of the years;
I fled Him, down the labyrinthine ways
Of my own mind; and in the midst of tears
I hid from Him, and under running laughter.

—FRANCIS THOMPSON
"THE HOUND OF HEAVEN," L. 1

December 1905

For the first time since Barbara's christening party, the Duke mansion was being readied for a celebration.

Jefferson was entertaining President Theodore Roosevelt.

Every member of the town spent weeks readying themselves for what was to be the social event of the decade. Caterers bid for the party, undercutting each other like vultures. The florists were employed by the dozen to fill the house with red roses, white poinsettias, pine garlands and swags of magnolia leaves over every doorway.

Jefferson hired a string quartet for the vestibule, an orchestra for the third-floor ballroom and a trio of violinists for the main salon. He wanted music, laughter and gaiety everywhere in his house.

"Barbara, I will finally admit to you now that I'm ninety; I'm old."

"Hallelujah! Now, will you slow down and rest?"

417

"Good God, no! Now I have to run twice as fast. I have so little time left!" He joked.

"At least you're finally giving the kind of party this house was built for. Grandmother would be proud," she said, kissing his cheek.

"I was thinking the same thing myself. And to honor her, will you be my hostess?"

"I'd be honored."

Barbara hired a Russian seamstress whom everyone claimed was impeccable in her designs and execution. She chose a winter-white, heavy satin for the skirt of her gown and a midnight-blue velvet for the bodice. The deep V-neckline of the gown was encrusted in silver bugle beads, round crystals and white pearls. The sleeves were long and tight fitting and the pointed cuffs were beaded as well. The heavy satin skirt fell in two layers each with six-inch-deep beading on the hemlines.

Her new gown was about the only bright spot in her life.

Barbara's story on graft in the city council was taking twist after turn. One lead after another pointed to the fact that Mayor Eugene Schmitz was on the take. But each time she got close to actual proof, she found another blind alley.

Looking over her notes, Barbara did not look up as Chen entered the room.

"It's late. You should be asleep."

"Is Mr. Kendrick home yet?" Barbara asked.

"No."

"Good. Then I can keep working," she said. After a minute she put her notes aside. "I don't know what I'm doing wrong. I've got to find a new angle."

"What is 'angle'?"

"It's . . . something earth-shattering. I need a story that turns this city upside-down and shakes everyone up. Opens up their eyes to the truth."

"Truth?"

"Yes," she sighed. "I've gotten used to being labeled 'Muckraker Jane.' I like it."

Chen bolstered her courage. What she was about to do could be dangerous. Life-threatening. For them both. "I have such a story."

Barbara's head jerked up. "You do?"

Chen nodded. "I want to tell you about my grandfather and the well-holes."

"Well-holes?"

"That is where they torture the young girls. Prostitution is considered a fine job by many girls in Chinatown."

Barbara was shocked. "God! That's so hard for me to understand."

"All the prostitution in this city pays money to the city hall. Even the Chinese."

"Go on," Barbara said, remembering a fellow worker, Larry, who uncovered a story about the prostitution rings being supported by city hall.

The French restaurant on Jackson Street applied for permits to build and all the while the city commissioners knew full well the second floor was to be used as a brothel. When Larry finally convinced one of the young girls to talk, she told him that she and the other girls had been coerced into prostitution by unscrupulous men who masqueraded as their beaus. Once they'd raped them, the young girls were too ashamed to go back home. All the newspapers or police knew was that another girl had disappeared from San Francisco.

What Chen was telling Barbara could very easily be true.

"Is there any way I could prove all this, Chen? Could I get an interview with an eyewitness?"

"My grandmother, Yin. She's very old, but she would help. It's been two years since I visited her. She could even be dead. If I go back to Chinatown, I'll be killed for running away. I've been hiding here for so long. Almost four years."

"And you think your grandmother would talk to me?"

"She's an honorable woman. She doesn't want this pain in Chinatown. There's too much hate and evil there. She told me years ago that it comes from my grandfather."

"Come now, Chen. One man isn't responsible for all the hate in a city."

"If he's powerful enough, he is. He rules people's lives. He teaches them to hate by his cruelties. One begets another, my grandmother told me. Even you have said this."

Pensively, Barbara looked at her. "I do believe that."

"You told me you would stop at nothing to find the source of greed and evil in San Francisco. I'm telling you Nan-Yung is as powerful as Jefferson Duke."

"Good and evil . . ." Barbara whispered. Chills shot down her spine. She rubbed her arms. "You're right, Chen. This could be very dangerous for us. But you'll do it?"

"Yes," Chen replied.

"I'll go to Jefferson for help."

* * * *

"Are you insane?" Jefferson bellowed. "You've gotten too carried away with all this. There are just some things that a young woman can't do. Going headlong into a Chinese prostitution ring is one of them. You'd never get out of there if you're discovered. And what's worse, I'd never find you."

"But Jefferson, this is important."

"You aren't going down to Jackson Street, Grant Street or anyplace else. What do I have to do? Hire a bodyguard to watch over you?" He ranted. "I suppose next you'll tell me you want to investigate the Barbary Coast!"

"Well, I . . ."

"I was right. You are insane. That's where they killed your father!" He put his hand on hers. "Barbara, you're all I have left. Please, for my sake. Stay out of harm's way."

"I'll try."

"No. Promise me."

Underneath the table she crossed her fingers. "I promise."

"Good. I want to know you'll be alive long enough to hostess my party.'"

"Aha! I should have known. You have an ulterior motive."

"My dear," he said, lifting a sherry. "I'm an old man. I wouldn't be alive if it weren't for ulterior motives."

* * * *

The night of the party, Barbara had still held off on her story. She'd kept her promise to Jefferson and stayed clear of Jackson Street and Chinatown.

She hadn't told William, the city editor yet, but she wanted to compile enough information so that charges could be filed against Mayor Eugene Schmitz and Abe Ruef. She wanted the charges to stick and get an indictment. Barbara wouldn't be happy until they were both in jail.

"If I could do that," she said aloud to herself. "I'd make history."

"It's good to see you smiling," Chen said, filling the rosebowls in Barbara's room with tight buds.

"Was I?"

"Yes. Are you thinking about that man?"

"Never a man, anymore, Chen. Only my work."

"Your writing is not your life. Life must be lived."

"I'm living."

Chen stopped and faced Barbara. "No, you're not."

Barbara exhaled. "I hate it when you put me on the hot seat."

"Hot seat? I don't know this."

"You know too much about me," Barbara said, picking up a sheaf of notations from her last interview. "It's unnerving."

"That's only because you're afraid of the truth."

"Who? Me? Muckraker Jane? Never!" She laughed nervously. "Okay. So, I'm scared to death. I have reason to be. I still want to see your grandmother, and we both know how dangerous that is."

"That's not what you were thinking about just now."

"It wasn't?"

"I said your 'life.'"

"Oh, that. Well, it scares the pants off me, as well. My husband is carrying on some torrid affair and tonight everyone at Jefferson's party will be talking about it. I hate gossip. I really do."

"But you hate their pity even more."

"How did you know?" She waved her hands in the air. "Never mind. Don't answer that. I don't want to know."

"You're so funny. You're the mysterious one. You search and search and face terrible, dangerous men to write your stories about evil in San Francisco, but you're afraid to burn out the viper in your own home."

"Gutless, huh?"

Chen clutched her hands in front of her. She'd thought about doing this for months. She'd had dreams and visions of Barbara's future for so long, the information was like a lit fuse. To honor her friendship with Barbara, she'd never said anything unless asked. But the more entrenched Barbara had gotten with her work, the less she'd looked at her life. It hurt Chen to see Barbara walking through her life with blinders. Chen was afraid Barbara would miss her one chance at happiness.

"Do you remember that I told you we were born on the same day at the same time in the same city?"

"Yes."

"It's important because that means our lives are on a similar path. Tonight, my life will change forever."

"How?" Barbara was incredulous.

"The man I love will claim me tonight."

"The man . . ." Barbara rushed to her and held her arms. "You're in love? Who is he? Did you meet him in Chinatown?"

"No," Chen swallowed hard. "I met him here."

"In this house? I don't understand. I don't know any . . ."

"He's white," Chen said.

"But all our friends are married. . . ."

"After tonight, his wife will demand to stay with her lover. He will finally oblige."

Barbara heard the words. It took a long moment for her to slip names and faces into the spaces where Chen's words had been. "Donald?" She breathed. "You're in love with Donald?"

Suddenly, Barbara grasped the back of the mahogany chair. Her knees buckled. She felt lightheaded. Pressing her hand to her forehead, she whispered, "Meredith . . ."

Chen quickly put her arm around Barbara's waist to steady her. She remained silent while the truth settled into Barbara's mind.

"My God . . . My God! Why didn't I see it? It's all so clear now!" Perspiration broke out on her forehead and upper lip. The room whirled then abruptly stopped. "I feel cold."

Chen rubbed her back.

"Meredith and Peter," she said aloud. She laughed. It was a personal chuckle at first, the kind that one uses when they are not willing to share their joke with another. As the sting of betrayal slit into her, Barbara's voice rose in pitch to a final cryptic shriek.

"Barbara, are you all right?"

"Yes."

"I shouldn't have told you."

"No, you were right. Meredith and Peter are perfect for each other. Perfect. I honestly can say I don't know two more vain and selfish people. Why, he and I have been mismatched from the beginning. Any fool can see that."

"Fool? You're not a fool."

"Oh, yes, I am! I was a fool in Washington. I've been a bigger fool here." Barbara stood straight. "Not anymore," she said with resolve. "After tonight, Chen, you and I are leaving Peter's house. I'll file for divorce first thing Monday morning. I don't know where we're going, so don't even ask, but it won't take me long to find us a nice flat. My job at the *Call* will feed us both."

She patted Chen's hand as if Chen were the one who needed comforting. "You go see Donald. You tell him he has my blessing."

"I'll tell him," Chen replied.

"Now, help me with my gown. I want to make sure no one pities me tonight. Envy, yes. Pity, no."

* * * *

Jefferson's mansion blazed with lights when Barbara arrived an hour before the guests. As hostess she wanted to make certain every candle was lit, every electric light burned and the flowers were in place.

She was setting the stage, but she didn't yet know how the play would end.

She sensed a tension in the air, an ominous energy that existed when one's life is about to switch tracks. She'd thought she'd made that change when she met Michael. But she'd been young and impressionable then.

She'd allowed life to happen to her back then.

This time, she was in charge.

Barbara stood at the top of the massive white marble staircase with its midnight-blue runner bordered in gold hand-painted fleur-de-lis. The caterers swarmed over the inlaid cobalt blue and white marble foyer like bees, making certain everything was ready. The florist was inserting tall stalks of hothouse-grown, brilliant blue delphiniums into the arrangement of white and red roses in the Waterford vase on the round Sheridan table in the center of the rotunda-like vestibule. Though it was Christmas, Barbara had ordered certain arrangements to be executed with a touch of midnight blue in deference to the president and in keeping with the cobalt blue, white and gold decor of Jefferson's formal areas.

The mansion was a revival of the French Empire period with an abundance of regal blue-velvet drapes, gold fleur-de-lis accent motifs and white silk sofas. Rich dark-paneled walls were a perfect backdrop for the gilt mirrors in the ballroom and for the ceiling-to-floor book stacks in the massive library. Everywhere else, the walls were painted a rich off-white. Bronze and crystal electric chandeliers illuminated the mansion and on this night, there was not a single window that did not pour forth an abundance of light into the gardens outside.

A dozen footmen stood at the front door to assist the guests as they arrived by both carriage and automobile.

Barbara could feel the excitement in the air. Everyone was moving a bit more quickly, the smiles were just a bit wider, the eye contact from employer to staff a trace more intense and exuberant. Just then the front door opened and the vestibule floor was filled with a new wave of tuxedoed men who moved efficiently around the room and then barked orders to each other. Half of them scurried to adjoining rooms as the president's bodyguards stationed themselves in the library, dining room, salon and music rooms. The tallest man stood in the center of the vestibule next to the rose and delphinium arrangement and pointed to various spots in the house as each of the men in his charge rushed away.

Hearing the commotion, Barbara moved to the edge of the staircase overlooking the foyer.

Barbara saw him.

His dark-brown hair gleamed in the light from the chandelier overhead. Suddenly, his shoulders ceased moving up and down. He was holding his breath as he cocked his head minutely to the left, like an animal suddenly alerted to a new danger.

Barbara held her breath.

Michael thought he could feel the heat of a pair of eyes on the back of his neck. It was not the chilling sensation of danger, but a distinct heat. One he'd not felt for a long time.

Since the day the president had told him they were coming to San Francisco, he'd hoped to see Barbara again.

When he wrote to Jefferson about the security arrangements he'd need to make if Jefferson were to be allowed to give this party, Michael couldn't help thinking about Barbara. Michael had purposefully requested that Jefferson give Michael's regards to Barbara. However, when Jefferson wrote back, there was no mention of her.

Michael knew then that Barbara had never told Jefferson about him. It was just as he'd thought. He was nothing more than a romantic fling for her. He wondered if she ever thought about him since then. Probably not. Women with this kind of money and surroundings didn't need men like Michael Trent.

But God almighty, he'd fallen for her fast. It was as if there was some kind of magic between them. Over the years he told himself it was timing, that the spirit of Christmas had duped him somehow into thinking dreams did come true or maybe there was a Santa Claus. Something had happened to him that night, and ever since then he hadn't been the same.

Sometimes when he'd been stuck on a freighter in the middle of the Indian Ocean or under the stars in Algeria, Barbara came to him like a phantom, haunting him like the harpies with memories of how she felt and tasted—like champagne and honey.

He felt her presence behind him. *All I've wanted for weeks is to see you, Barbara.*

He closed his eyes.

He opened them.

Do you still smell like jasmine?

Will you still haunt me at night?

He inhaled deeply for courage.

My hands are shaking. Just remember, old man, she left you. She never made the first move to contact you. No letters.

He turned around. *Don't do this, Michael. She's a heartbreaker.*

Michael did the bravest thing he had ever done in his life. He faced her.

Barbara felt her breath catch in her throat. She saw nothing of the impeccably tailored tuxedo he wore, nor the concealed pistol he carried. She looked past the stone-set jaw and the taut lay of his lips. She saw the golden lights in his eyes. It was all she needed.

"Michael," she whispered to herself.

She's dazzling. And I'm opening Pandora's box. Aw, hell . . .

"Michael," she said aloud, descending the steps and never taking her eyes off him.

He was riveted to the spot.

The lights from above danced in the beading on her gown. She sparkled like a celestial being.

But as she drew nearer to him, he realized that her ethereal look had nothing to do with her gown or the glittering luster in her dark curls. Her eyes were filled with the same emotion he knew she could see reflected in his eyes. He was looking into the eyes of love.

Double hell.

She moved up to him and stretched out her hand. "Michael," she said his name like a prayer with a tentative, but giving smile on her lips.

Chen, you were right. My life is changing. Please, God. Make it for the better.

"Barbara, I didn't think you'd remember me." How could he have misjudged her? How could he have thought she had merely dallied with him? No wonder he'd fallen in love with her. She was as genuine as he'd thought her to be. But something had gone awry. What?

"Not remember you?"

A wounded look crossed her face. He felt his heart toss itself against his rib cage. "Why, yes."

"Mr. Trent," a man called to him.

Michael glanced at the two sentries he'd posted at the door. In moments, the first guests would be arriving. The place would be packed in fifteen minutes, he knew. He needed more than that to talk to her. He turned to the man to the right of the entrance. "Smithers, I'll be awhile. You know what to do. The President won't be here for an hour. Everything seems to be in order. I'll be in the conservatory if you need me."

"Yes, sir," Smithers replied with blank eyes as he kept his back ramrod straight and looked back at his partner across the vestibule.

Michael took Barbara's hand.

"What are you doing?" she asked as they rushed quickly downhall to the glass conservatory.

He whirled her around to face him. "We have to talk."

"You bet we do. You left me, Michael! Why did you do that?" Barbara demanded, deciding to throw pride out the door . . . this once.

"But you know why!"

"I know nothing of the kind," she retorted angrily.

"I told you in the message I sent to your hotel."

"What message? I never got any message." Shock filled her eyes.

"Sure you did. I gave it to the Chinese messenger when he brought me your note."

"What messenger? I never sent you a note."

"Yes, you did. I kept it for the longest time. You asked me to meet you at nine the next night in the park across from the White House in the grove of trees."

"I don't know about any trees. And I'd certainly never go to a park late at night. That's too dangerous, Michael."

Barbara had no more uttered the words when she shivered. Her hands flew to her cheeks. She trembled.

Illumination hit Michael like a thunderbolt. "We were set up."

"Someone was going to harm us that night, Michael."

His mind was racing. "It's making sense to me."

"Well, then please explain it, because it makes none to me."

"When I got to my apartment, Captain Jeffers was there to take me to the train. I took a ship out of Boston Harbor the next morning. I had the ship's purser send a telegraph to the hotel before I set sail." He was shaking. "Barbara . . . I went to China."

"What?"

"I can see now that telegram was intercepted somewhere."

"But by whom?"

"Obviously, the Chinese faction who didn't want me to get to China."

"What do you think they wanted with us in the park?"

"Shanghai, I'd say."

"Slavery?"

"It's the reason I was going to China. I was tracking down a ring we'd linked to Washington."

"They wanted you out of the way. They were using me to do it."

"It looks that way."

Her eyes probed his. "What was in the note you sent?"

Putting his hands on her shoulders he said, "In the note I had begged you to send a message to the ship before I left about how you felt about me. I guess I needed reassurance. I figured the room steward would put the note under your door at the hotel. Even if you read it during breakfast, there was time to telegraph the ship before I sailed. When there was no reply I got to thinking that you had thought more about what we were doing. I mean, it wouldn't be an easy life for you, with me, I mean. Always taking off to God knows where for the President. It's not the kind of life a beautiful woman like you could ever want. I'm just a guy. I'm not rich or powerful like Jefferson."

Barbara put her fingers to his lips. "I don't care about all that."

"But you must have, Barbara. You married Peter Kendrick."

"Did Jefferson tell you that?"

"No. He still doesn't know anything about us. When I got back from China, I came here and met with Jefferson. I asked a few questions and discovered you'd gotten married. God! I even hired a hack to drive by your house. I knew I could never give you a life like that. That's when I knew that you'd been wiser than I. You were right to leave me."

"But don't you see, Michael? It was all a mistake! You almost lost your life. But you never lost me. Not really."

"What about Peter?"

"That's an even more terrible mistake. I married Peter because I thought you'd been playing a game with me. I never loved him. In fact, I doubt he's ever cared for me at all. He wanted me to bring him up the social ladder. He's made his wealth off construction contracts with the city government. What's worse is Peter's having an affair with my best friend," she said flatly as if discussing the facts in one of her newspaper stories.

She was surprised at the lack of her own emotions.

She was glad.

Michael touched her cheek. "So much unhappiness. And it's all my fault."

She put her hand over his and brought his fingers to her lips.

"It's no one's fault. It's the way things happened. We can't do anything about the past, but we can change the future." She pressed her lips into the palm of his hand.

He pulled her into him and wrapped his arms around her. He put his hands on the small of her back, pressing her closer, tighter into him. He felt himself get hard. He thought he was losing his mind as he sank his face into the crook of her neck and kissed her tender skin. "God! Barbara. I love you. I don't want to spend another second of my life without you."

"Michael, just hold me. Let me feel you." She slid her hands up his arms to his shoulders and then splayed her fingers over his chest pulling her hands down over his jacket where underneath she could feel his heart beating. Feel his love for her. "Your heart is racing as madly as mine," she said.

"No. A million times more," he replied.

She melted into him.

Michael lifted his head and sought her mouth. He pressed his lips against her mouth, feeling its pliable softness. Without hesitation, Barbara opened her lips to him, allowing his tongue to plunder the interior of her mouth. A fiery heat swirled inside her. This time she didn't know if she could wait. She needed to feel him inside her.

"Michael, I want you," she said, kissing him back with a desire that threatened to overwhelm her.

Michael pulled away from her lips, but only with a great deal of effort. "I want you, Barbara. But not like this, not here. Not now. I want to spend the whole night making love to you. I want to be with you at a time when you don't have to sneak away to see me. I want Jefferson to know, because he's the only person you love and care about. I want nothing to be profane about my love for you. I want to look into your eyes when you tell me you love me. I want you to give me your soul. I don't want an affair with you, Barbara. I want you. All of you. Now. Forever."

His words took her breath away. She couldn't help but remember that just tonight she'd told Chen they would be leaving Peter's house right after the party tonight. It was as if her heart was already preparing the way for Michael to come.

"I want the same thing, Michael," she said as she rested her head on his shoulder. "Jefferson told me how he and my grandmother had to keep their love hidden. I don't want that for us. Chen, my maid and my friend, told me my life would change tonight. I told her that I'd file for a divorce on Monday."

"Is that true?" Michael couldn't believe his ears.

"Every bit."

"I never dared think I'd hold you again, much less this. My God, Barbara, are you sure?"

"Yes, I'm sure, Michael."

"There's something blessed about your having already decided to leave Peter."

"There is, isn't there? It's as if fate is smiling on us."

"Don't go to him tonight, Barbara. I couldn't bear it."

"Are you anxious to be with me, Michael?"

He squeezed her tightly. "I've waited four years. Yet, one more day seems an eternity. But yes, I am quite anxious to be with you."

Barbara heard the orchestra begin to play the repetoire of music she'd selected while the guests entered the house. "I suppose I should see to my guests."

Michael smoothed her curls that had become mussed from his love-making. When he touched her cheek, he noticed that a sense of melancholy had invaded her happy eyes. "Barbara, what is it? What are you thinking?"

Boldly she lifted her chin and looked at him. "How long till you leave this time, Michael? A night? A day? What?"

He placed her chin between his thumb and forefinger. "Believe it or not, this is my last assignment. I spent a great deal of time coming to this decision, but I'm tired of the danger. The risks . . . Do you remember I told you about my love of photography?"

"Yes."

"Well, it's an explosive new field, I believe. I've saved some money and I've procured a job as a photographer for a New York publisher who wants me to chronicle the West before there isn't any untamed area left. My new salary is quite handsome. Then, I've written to some men in Southern California who are forming a movie production company. They were pretty successful in New York. Samuel Goldwyn was one of their names. I'd like to learn more about these moving pictures."

"Don't you think moving pictures are just a fad?"

"I have a feeling they're here to stay. Anyway, I'll be living in San Francisco until my job here is finished."

"Living? You mean you're not just here for the party tonight?"

"God, no. I can't give you all the details, but the President had put me on a special task force to rout out Mayor Schmitz and his cronies. I want to put his ass in jail."

Barbara's eyes were huge with surprise. "But that's my job!"

"What are you talking about?"

"It's taken me over a year to talk the city editor into letting me do the story on Schmitz. I want to be the one who puts him in jail."

"Is this guy insane? This is dangerous, Barbara. You can't go poking around ruthless men like that."

"Don't you see? Because I'm a woman, I can get away with things that men can't. I can be places that won't attract suspicion. Besides, I have some excellent leads that may tie in the prostitution in this city if not to Schmitz's office directly, then certainly to his city commissioners."

He passed his hand over his forehead. "Is there nothing that will stop you?"

"Absolutely not," she said resolutely. "We better get this straight right now, Michael. I'm not the type of person to sit at home and darn your socks for you. I want to be a part of history, just the way my grandmother was."

"I'll bet she didn't try anything this dangerous."

"She did a lot more than this," Barbara said.

Michael saw the determination in her eyes. She'd be relentless in her work.

She was courageous and because of that she was a special kind of woman. She was the only woman he wanted. "Okay. Here's the deal. We work on this together," he said, thinking he could do the bulk of the investigative work and she could do all the writing she wanted. "I'll give you all the information you want. Okay? But the deal is, if it gets too nasty and I think your life is in danger, you agree to pull out and let me take over."

She considered this for a minute. "I think we should define 'nasty.'"

"Barbara," Michael was in no mood for negotiations.

"Okay. We both agree the goal is to get Schmitz?"

"Agreed," he said and extended his hand to confirm the deal, but as Barbara took his hand, he pulled her into his arms and just as his mouth was about to clamp down on hers he said, "Barbara, don't you know that lovers seal bargains with kisses?"

"I've never heard that," she said and let him devour her mouth.

forty

With hue like that when some great painter dips
His pencil in the gloom of earthquake and eclipse.

—PERCY BYSSHE SHELLEY
THE REVOLT OF ISLAM, CANTO V, ST. XXIII

January 1906

I 'm in love, Jefferson," Barbara said, riding down Union Street in his carriage with him.

"I know."

"What?" she gaped at his wise smile.

"You haven't looked like this since Washington. Are you finally ready to tell me about him?"

"I can't believe this."

"Do you think you're the only investigator in the fam—around here?" Realizing he'd almost slipped, Jefferson kept his eyebrows crouched together accusingly.

"Did it show back then? Really?"

"Absolutely." He looked away and then back at her. "I had wanted so much for you to take me into your confidence. I had wanted to know who it was that made you so radiant. And then so quickly, you were sad beyond measure. I wanted to be there for you for that. I could have helped."

"Jefferson . . . I was thoughtless. I'm sorry."

He put up his hand. "Don't be. I am guilty myself of doing precisely what

432

you've done. We all must have our secrets, Barbara. Sometimes I think it's our secrets that keep us going."

Caring spilled from her eyes as she stared at his lowered head. "Jefferson, is there something you want to tell me?"

Though feeble, his head popped up with agility. His eyes pierced hers. She felt her nerves ignite. Something was dreadfully wrong.

He parted his lips to speak.

Silence hung in the air between them.

He exhaled heavily. "No. Not yet."

"But there is something?"

"Yes. But now is not the time. It's your turn to speak today."

"How mysterious you are, Jefferson. Yet," she leaned across the distance and touched his hand, "how dear you are to always put my needs before everything else."

"That's what life and love are about."

"I'm learning that," she nodded. "His name is Michael Trent."

"My God! I knew it was." He slapped his thigh and smiled. "I approve."

"But you don't know anything about him."

"I know more than you, I'll wager. He's been with Roosevelt from the beginning. He's a fine young man. Dedicated. Honest. Loyal. I've dealt with Trent myself directly when making the plans for the reception. When I met him in Washington years ago, I thought to myself, 'now that's the sort of young man for Barbara.'"

"You didn't."

"Mmm. I did." His expression turned morose. "And Peter?"

"I've filed for divorce and moved myself and Chen out of the house."

"What was Peter's reaction?"

"He was about as apathetic as he was on our wedding day. I've served my purpose for him. On all counts."

"So, it's true he was having an affair," Jefferson said.

"Yes."

"Well, that's one time I wished I'd paid attention to the gossips. All those years of being the butt of their cackling, I've learned to turn a deaf ear. I thought it was just jealousy."

"No, it was truth this time. But I'm glad it turned out this way. I'm so happy now. Michael is helping me with my investigations for the newspaper. I really think I'm onto something, Jefferson."

He squeezed her hand as concern riddled his face. "Your earnestness is commendable, Angel. But it's your naïveté that frightens me. I'm too old to be your hero anymore and that bothers me. Please call on me to help you whenever you can. I want to help. More importantly, I want you to stay out of harm's way."

"I'll be fine, Jefferson. Michael won't let anything bad happen to me."

"I'm sure he won't," he said firmly, not feeling an ounce of the reassurance he was trying to convey to her. If Jefferson knew one person well, it was his granddaughter. She was high spirited and a crusader.

If she continued poking around in the muck of San Francisco he was certain she would find the path to the one destiny he'd been foretold but never wanted for her. He didn't want Barbara to be Joan of Arc.

Fights between good and evil could only be waged by an indomitable will.

Though he'd been one of San Francisco's founders, he knew that when it came to facing demons, he wondered if he'd have the strength to fight.

Barbara beamed at him, her eyes sparkling with the love she carried for Michael.

Jefferson remembered that he'd seen that same light when Caroline used to look at him.

"On second thought, Barbara," he said, choking back his emotions, "You do everything you feel you must. Don't waver. Give it your best. God is on your side. You'll win."

"Oh, thank you for that, Jefferson," she replied, taking a deep breath. "I have this feeling, in here," she touched her solar plexus, "that this is what I'm meant to do. I don't know why, but every step I take leads me to the next and the next. I can't go back or stop. I just have to keep going."

"And you're not frightened?"

"Terrified," she laughed nervously.

"Then I'll pray for you. I'll wrap you in angel's wings every night in my prayers. You'll be fine."

Her face glowed with confidence. "I will."

April 17, 1906

Police officer Leonard Ingham awoke in a cold sweat.

"My God, it's happening again, Bess," he said to his wife.

"Not that dream about the Palace Hotel burning to the ground?"

"Yes."

"Leonard, these dreams have been going on for over two months. That can only mean one thing," she said.

"It's going to happen," he replied morosely.

Officer Ingham was forty years old and though he was still pounding a beat on Dolores Street where he lived, he was proud of his work. However, the recurring dreams of fire were a warning. The only problem was, no one would believe him.

The dream was haunting and always the same.

The Mission district, a crowded group of wooden houses, factories and railroad yards, was always the first to be destroyed by the hungry appetite of the imaginary fire. Then the fire swept up Market Street, then across it taking the Palace Hotel and most of the city's principal buildings as well.

"What are you going to do, Leonard?"

"Two things. Tomorrow I'm going to see Chief Dinan. Maybe Jeremiah can show me how to stop these thieves like Peter Kendrick who are filling in the old sea bed with trash and old furniture instead of using sand and gypsum to make our streets. Look at Union and Battery south of Market Street. He built all that area. There's not a single fire hydrant around Montgomery Street."

"But why would anyone be so negligent?"

"Are you kidding? The city paid him a fortune to build those streets. He built crap on top of crap. He as good as stole that money. You've seen the shabby hotels, boarding houses, warehouses and factories he's thrown up. Same scenario. They're an arsonist's dream. All it will take is a minor shift from one of a hundred small earth tremors we get every year to topple one of Kendrick's shacks. But does Kendrick care? Not a whit. From what I've heard on my beat, he throws his money away on some society mistress."

"But his wife writes for the *Call*. I read Barbara's column all the time. I wonder if she knows?"

"Well, tomorrow, I'm going to do some reporting myself. She'll know soon enough," he replied gruffly.

Bess leaned against her pillow and looked at her husband. "What's the second thing you're going to do?"

"I'll stop at the Hartford Fire Insurance Company on California Street and talk to the company's Pacific agent. I think his name is Adam Guilliland. I think a two-thousand-dollar policy on our house ought to do it."

* * * *

Michael Trent bounded into Mayor Eugene Schmitz's office with a thick manila folder under his arm. He was still battling for the president.

"What is it this time?" Mayor Schmitz growled impatiently.

"Just this," Michael said evenly, tossing the folder on Schmitz's desk for emphasis.

"That's from Fire Chief Dennis Sullivan."

"Right. He sent me an intriguing report." Michael jabbed his finger on the folder. "It seems that potential fires are on everybody's mind these days."

"What else is new?" Schmitz said dismissively.

"I read in the *Call* that you've refused to fund the building of new water cisterns. Sullivan's report says that on numerous occasions, he's requested money from your office to build a supplementary salt-water system. You turned him down. He then asked for money to reactivate scores of long-neglected cisterns, even in their deplorable state they'd be better than nothing. He's also asked for money to buy high explosives and to train his men on how to use them to check a major fire."

"So?"

"Why?" Michael demanded.

"There isn't enough in the city budget for that nonsense."

"I see." Then Michael took out another document. "I have here a request from the War Department in Washington in which they consent to furnish a competent corps of engineers and sappers, with the necessary explosives to be always in readiness at the Presidio. The War Department requested the city to provide one thousand dollars to build a brick vault in the Presidio grounds to house the explosives. You refused that money, too."

"So what? I told you, we didn't have it."

Michael ignored him and continued. "Then I have here the report from the National Board of Fire Underwriters dated October of 1905, that's last fall," Michael said condescendingly, "and it states, 'San Francisco has violated all underwriting traditions and precedents by not burning up. That it has not already done so is largely due to the vigilance of the Fire Department, which cannot be relied upon indefinitely to stave off the inevitable.'"

"I suppose you're going to tell me something I don't know," Mayor Schmitz said.

"Brigadier General Frederick Funston, the acting commander of the Presidio, has been putting pressure on Washington to have you either change your mind or run you out of town. Washington puts pressure on me, Mayor Schmitz." Michael leaned his palms on the desk, leaning close to the mayor's disgruntled face. "How does it feel down there in that hole you've dug for yourself?

"Get out."

Michael was intractable. "Thirteen years ago, geologists discovered this city lies along the San Andreas Fault. Andrew Lawson, who by the way is the best geologist there is, tells Washington the tilting and movement around this area is still active. In a nutshell, it means we're ripe for earthquakes. Big ones. Every building I check out stinks of bribery and graft by you and Abe Ruef and your pal, Peter Kendrick. Why is that?"

"I don't know what you're talking about. And if you had a leg to stand on, you'd be talking to the district attorney, William Langdon."

Michael smiled. "He and I are collating the evidence together."

Mayor Schmitz swallowed hard. He thought of his gingerbread house at the select end of Fillmore Street, a house far beyond the scope of his mayor's salary. He liked having nice things. He deserved them.

"I've got some nails for your coffin. Looks like you've been double-crossing your own partner, Mayor. You granted a franchise to construct an inter-urban rail line to Santa Cruz. Isn't that Downey Harvey's pet project? Isn't he the major shareholder in the Ocean Shore Railway? Seems you forgot to collect the regular bribery fee from Harvey. Now your buddy Ruef is a bit miffed."

Mayor Schmitz was stone.

Michael waited a long moment for a reaction, but got none. "You know, Eugene, you can screw the government for awhile, you can screw the city for awhile, but sooner or later we're gonna getcha. I just hope your buddy, Abe Ruef, doesn't beat us to it."

Michael saw the beads of perspiration spring up on Schmitz's brow. Once Michael knew he had Schmitz where he wanted him, he left.

April 17, 1906

Leonard Ingham wasn't the only San Francisco resident experiencing dreams about the city in flames. Chen dreamed identical scenes. Screams of humans being burned alive and the sound of crashing buildings jolted her awake night after night.

Chen also knew that recurring dreams were not always about the future.

Chen believed that sometimes they were thought communications between two minds.

That's how she heard her grandmother calling out to her. Ever since Barbara had moved out of Peter's house and into this cozy flat where Chen now occupied the basement floor with three spacious rooms, Chen's nightmares had become more real than her waking hours.

Something horrific has happened to Yin.

In her mind's eye, Chen saw the truth.

She looked out the window of her bedroom on the lower level of the house where the bay window looked out onto a brick wall. At the halfway level was the sidewalk. She was only half underground. She was not in a well-hole like her grandmother.

Nan-Yung has put Yin in the well-holes! But why?

What has she done?

Suddenly, she knew. Every intuitive nerve in her body was electrified. Yin had done the one thing she'd always warned Chen not to do. Never tell Nan-Yung the future. Never tell him the truth.

Chen focused her thoughts on her grandmother. Yin felt no remorse. She was happy she'd stood up to Nan-Yung. However, Yin's mind was filled with thoughts about death.

No, Grandmother. You must not give up. I'll find a way to save you.

But how?

The way Chen saw it, there was no solution but to go down to the catacombs herself and find Yin.

Am I being a fool? How will I ever get past Nan-Yung's bodyguards?

What if I confront Lee Tong? There's no henchman as vicious.

There was no question in her mind that Lee Tong would kill her because she'd run away not just from Chinatown, but from him. He was the reason she'd lived in fear all these years. He was the reason she was afraid to leave

Barbara's house. Chen had hoped now that Michael lived with them, they would be protected.

But Chen didn't feel safe. She felt as if danger were closing in on her. Coming into her circle.

She was beginning to realize that if she didn't go into Lee Tong's lair, he would come to hers.

Either way, she might never survive.

Just thinking about Lee Tong gave Chen eerie chills. Lee Tong was a madman, and he'd wanted her for a wife.

"Lee Tong," Nan-Yung had said when Chen was eighteen, "I want to reward you for your feats of bravery in my behalf. I will give you one of my granddaughters in marriage. Which do you choose?"

Lee Tong turned to Chen who was the last of six girls standing in a row for presentation like slaves at an auction.

"Chen."

"Why the youngest?" Nan-Yung asked.

"Because she has always laughed at my bravery."

Impulsively, Chen believed she had but this one chance to save herself. "Ha! You call snapping necks of little children for sport and strangling women who were half-dead from being raped by you a brave act? These are heinous acts of a devil. I will not ever be your wife!"

"You will. Your grandfather wishes it."

She closed her eyes. "I have looked at my future. I don't see myself with you. There is another."

Lee Tong grabbed her by the arm and pulled her face up to his. Their noses touched. She could smell his foul breath from chewing opium and drinking plum wine. "Mark this. You became mine today. Your grandfather gave you to me. I'm the mightiest of his warriors."

"This is not China."

"Yes. This is America, where I have a chance to be an emperor. Royal blood or not."

He tossed her to the ground so hard, she'd bruised her hip.

"I'm glad to see you taking a firm hand with her, Lee Tong," Nan-Yung said, rising then looking directly at Chen. "Defy me and I'll put you in the well-holes."

Chen sucked in her breath, but said nothing.

All her life she'd heard about the well-holes, those round bins dug deep in the earth for only the space of a human body. Buried to their necks, no prisoner escaped the well-holes. Ever.

All six granddaughters and his wife, Yin, bowed to him as he left the room. Lon Su stood upright, while his wife, Ling, bowed the lowest.

"See that your daughter is readied for her wedding," Nan-Yung said to Lon Su. "Come Lee Tong, I have an assignment for you today."

Lee Tong followed Nan-Yung out of the room.

It took Chen only seconds to devise her escape plan.

It was simple. She followed her sisters up the ladder to the shop, walked to the front door and started running.

No one in Chinatown could run as fast as Chen.

She regretted not telling Yin and Ling about her plan. To save herself she had to run. She knew they'd understand.

Now, however, it was time for Chen to make it up to Yin. She was going back to Chinatown.

And Chen was very, very afraid.

Barbara and Chen met with Police Chief Jeremiah Dinan in his office.

"I want you to raid the opium club," Barbara demanded.

"I'm not going to Chinatown. That labyrinth down there is endless. What would closing down one club do anyway? The answer is nothing. And nobody gives a damn about the Chinese."

Barbara shot him a scornful look as she moved a protective step closer to Chen.

"Look, I'm on your side, Barbara. I think you've done one hell of a job in that series of articles you're running over there at the *Call*."

Barbara frowned, thinking how she and Michael had worked four months on getting their facts together. They were both ready to hone in on their targets. She was about to explode from the frustration of not seeing any action, real action take place. "The Jackson Street brothel, then," she changed subjects to an equally controversial one. "Make a stink. Shake people up," she argued.

"Sure, sure. And then what? Vice isn't new to San Francisco, Mrs. Kendrick. Life is cheap in San Francisco. In the Tenderloin and on the Barbary Coast a man can get murdered for the price of a bottle of whiskey. Just this morning my officers rescued a fifteen-year-old boy from being snatched on Dupont Street."

"Shanghai," Chen nodded.

"Yes," Dinan agreed. "Look, this city is a flesh pot. Protection rackets abound. Sometimes I think that to curb vice here would be like throttling the image of the city. People come here to buy sex, drugs and alcohol in that order. To raid the Jackson Street brothel would be more than my job is worth. Nobody ever really wants San Francisco cleaned up. I send my men out time and again and then the city ho-hums my efforts. Look, I've got the force up to seven hundred men. We're using photography here to detect crime and get convictions. I've increased the number of street boxes where the officers can summon help, but it's like pissing in the wind."

"You're doing an admirable job. I just want more done."

"Don't we all?" Dinan expelled an exasperated sigh. "Do me a favor, Mrs. Kendrick, go drive somebody else insane."

She smiled. "Do me a favor? Peter and I'll be divorced next month. Call me Barbara Mansfield again."

"Divorce? That's good. I don't like him. You know very well I think he's in cahoots with Ruef. I just wish I could prove it."

"Don't worry, I already have," she said flatly.

"What?"

"I turned my findings over to the district attorney yesterday. But I can't testify until I'm divorced."

"Who made you so smart?"

"I had good advisors," she replied with a wily smile.

"Looks like it," he said, crossing to the window, looking out at the city. "I love this city, Barbara. I'm doing the best I can, considering who I'm up against. It's getting late and I'm taking my wife tonight to see Caruso at the Grand Opera House. Let's call it quits for now, shall we?"

Barbara nodded. "I'll be back."

Dinan ushered Barbara and Chen out of his office and then closed the door.

Chen looked at Barbara. "He won't help free my grandmother?"

"Not tonight," Barbara patted Chen's back as they walked out into the April dusk. "He's going to the opera instead."

"We have to do something," Chen said.

Barbara put her arm around her friend. "I know we do. I just wish I knew what."

* * * *

Barbara lit the gas stove with a wooden match and put a pot of tea on to boil.

Green tea was Chen's favorite. She hoped to cheer the girl; she'd seemed so hopeless when they'd shared supper that evening.

Sitting at the table Barbara looked at the small pots of paper-white bulbs she was forcing in the windowsill, the dish drainer with a clean stack of inexpensive dishes upon which she and Michael had shared their breakfast.

There were no crystal chandeliers, no gold faucets, no electric lights like she'd had in Peter's mansion. Except for her concern for Chen's grandmother, Barbara had never been happier in her life.

Looking at the legal documents she and Michael had helped the prosecuting attorney to compile against Mayor Schmitz, she realized she was not only becoming a part of history, but that she was a shape-changer.

Barbara was making her life make a difference.

She would do the same for Chen.

But it might take time.

For months, Barbara and Michael had worked together digging into the convoluted cover-ups Abe Ruef and Eugene Schmitz had used to conceal their crimes.

Her biggest shock had been when she'd discovered Peter's role in the graft. Inadvertently, she'd packed a box of Peter's business receipts among her personal belongings when she moved out of the house. She was able to prove that Peter had filled the sea bed with trash and old flotsam. He had falsified receipts for sand and gypsum he'd never purchased.

"I can put him in jail," she said to herself, not realizing Chen was standing in the doorway.

"Put who in jail?"

"Peter," Barbara replied as the tea kettle whistled.

"I was hoping you meant Lee Tong," Chen said, taking cups and saucers out of the cabinet. She put them on the table next to the evening edition of the *Call*.

Chen was more than proficient in English with Barbara as a teacher. She read Barbara's article covering the Spring Ball.

"Mr. Peter Kendrick was accompanied by Meredith Pope." Chen could not conceal her surprise. "You wrote that?"

"It's about time everyone knows what I know."

"But Donald . . ."

"Is in New York to relocate his family's funds in order to build a new retail department store near Central Park," Barbara finished. "I don't want to hurt Donald but Meredith has been flaunting this affair for too long."

Chen sliced a lemon. "He knows."

"He what?"

"He's moved out of the house and hired an attorney to get it back for him. He's taking the police with him tonight while they evict her."

"You're kidding? How do you know this?" Barbara smiled and put her hands up. "No, never mind. I know how you know. When did he come back?"

"Three days ago," Chen replied sheepishly.

"Why, that rascal. He didn't tell me any of this."

"He said you had enough on your mind."

Barbara lowered herself into the chair. She looked at Chen with new insight. "And how many times have you seen him?"

A blush crossed Chen's face. "Every day. Every night."

"He loves you?"

"Yes. And I love him," Chen sat down. Her words came in a rush. "That's why it's so important I confront Lee Tong. I don't want him to know about Donald. If Lee Tong finds me and discovers Donald coming to see me, he'll kill us both. I don't want that."

Fear filled Barbara's voice. "We have to be incredibly careful, Chen. I had no idea Donald's infatuation had become this serious."

"Now you understand my urgency to find my grandmother? Once I know she is safe, I will leave San Francisco. I'll go somewhere else."

"But what about Donald?" Barbara asked.

"He doesn't know about Yin or Lee Tong. I can't tell him. He would want to come with me, and Lee Tong would find us. I love Donald too much to put him in this danger."

Barbara put her arms around Chen. "Promise me you won't set foot outside this house again until I think of something to do. Make a plan. And promise me you won't see Donald again until we can figure out what we're going to do."

Chen felt a stinging pang in her heart. "He won't understand, but I'll do it."

"It's his life we're saving, Chen."

Chen nodded sadly.

Barbara rubbed her forehead. "We can't do this on our own. We need help. But who? It's obvious I have to tell Michael. Maybe I should talk to Jefferson." She looked at Chen. "I saw him just today in my office, but it was such a strange meeting. He gave me a folder of very old papers to read." She looked through the doorway into the living room where she'd left the "Rachel Papers."

"How can he help? He's so old."

"Jefferson has money and influence. We might need money to bribe some of your old neighbors," Barbara said.

"I thought we were against bribery."

Barbara shook her finger. "Not when it's warranted."

"Ah," Chen nodded.

"And you have to tell Donald the truth. It's only fair he knows the dangers."

"All right," Chen said, expelling a heavy sigh. "I'll do it, but not tonight. Tomorrow." Chen rose, taking her tea with her. "Michael is due home soon, isn't he?"

"Yes," she replied, looking at the clock. "His meeting was over twenty minutes ago."

"I'll say goodnight," Chen said.

Tracing her fingers over the legal documents on the table, Barbara said, "The truth will always set you free, Chen. Remember that."

Chen turned back to look at Barbara. "There are many truths. I'm afraid this time truth may be too late."

forty-one

I see on an immense scale, and as clearly as in a demonstration in a laboratory, that good comes out of evil; that the impartiality of the Nature Providence is best; that we are made strong by what we overcome; that man is man because he is as free to do evil as to do good; that life is as free to develop hostile forms as to develop friendly; that power waits upon him who earns it; that disease, wars, the unloosened, devastating elemental forces have each and all played their part in developing and hardening man and giving him the heroic fiber.

—JOHN BURROUGHS
ACCEPTING THE UNIVERSE

T*ruth.* Barbara breathed the word reverently as she read the last of the "Rachel Papers."

Her head pounded with the onslaught of information she'd taken in that night.

So much truth. She thought of Jefferson. *Grandfather. My grandfather. How sad you couldn't tell me the truth about yourself. How sad you were afraid to let me love you that much more.*

She put the papers aside and stumbled into the bedroom.

"Michael?" Her eyes burned with tears. Her chest felt as if an anvil had just landed on it.

He rolled over. "What is it?" he asked groggily.

"Michael. Please hold me," she said, rushing into his arms.

He enfolded her. "Barbara, tell me."

"I read the 'Rachel Papers' that Jefferson gave me," she said between sobs.

"My God, Darling." He swept a lock of hair from her cheek. "What did they say that upset you this much?"

"Jefferson is my grandfather."

"What?"

"I should have known. As a child, I should have realized . . . I never felt about anyone in my life like I did Jefferson. We were so close. Just as much as with my father. How could I have been so blind?"

"But why in the world wouldn't he tell you something like that?

"He's a quadroon. He's a runaway slave. He's been battling his fears all his life."

Michael shook his head. "But you, of all people, haven't a bigoted bone in your body."

Barbara gazed out the window at the flickering predawn lights of the city. "I've always felt people were people. I guess it's because my mother is so prejudiced. She hates everyone and everything that isn't like her. Actually, she's equally magnanimous about that. In my way, I was rebelling against mother and her limited vision of life. I just never wanted to be like her in the slightest way. Eleanor has never loved anyone but herself. Not father and certainly not me. There was never any room in her heart for us, so how could she have any room in her heart for someone like sweet Chen?"

She continued. "Poor Jefferson. To be ashamed of his heritage. He thought I would be ashamed of him and reject him. If you love someone you can't reject them, can you, Michael?"

He lifted her chin and peering into her eyes, he said, "I love you, Barbara. All the parts of you. I don't care if you're purple and blue, you're you." He kissed her tenderly. "I've never been a petty person. Considering all the real ills of this world, racism is pointless. What does it gain anyone? If people would only realize that we are the sum of all our parts and it's something we build on, not become, the world would grow up. Each of us can be what we want to be. We can choose good or evil. Our faults and successes are ours alone. We're responsible for our own lives. Not our ancestors."

"Yes, maybe that is what Rachel was trying to say in her journals. Maybe that's the lesson she wanted Jefferson to learn. And me."

"Sounds like it."

"Now I understand why Jefferson fought Eleanor all my growing-up years to see me. I wonder if Eleanor sensed his territorial instincts to be part of my life. Their feud still persists, you know." She paused. "There's something else, Michael. Jefferson's drive to eradicate the corruption in San Francisco goes back a hundred years."

"What?"

"Jefferson discovered that Chen's family, the House of Su they call themselves, vowed revenge against Jefferson's ancestors, Andrew and then Ambrose Duke in China years and years ago. The Sus emigrated to America. In the last pages I read, Jefferson wrote that when the police wouldn't help him find my father's killer, he hired a private detective. Jefferson not only discovered that Nan-Yung Su ordered my father's death, but that his assassins caused Dolores Sanchez's death as well."

"Who is Dolores?"

"A tragic woman. She was deeply in love with Jefferson but he loved Caroline. Dolores was forbidden by her Castilian father to marry outside their lineage. She died while riding one night, but certain circumstances about her death always puzzled Jefferson. According to Jefferson's journal, his affair with Caroline began almost the day she arrived in San Francisco. My father is Jefferson's son. But, she was married to William Mansfield and wouldn't leave him."

"She didn't believe in divorce?"

"Apparently not."

Michael hugged her. "Thank God times have changed. I'm glad you do, otherwise we wouldn't be together."

She kissed him. "I'm glad, too, Michael." She rested her head against his chest.

Stroking her hair, Michael said, "You want me to help Chen, don't you?"

"How did you know that?"

"I pay attention," he chuckled.

"These men are killers, Michael. Jefferson said the strangest thing to me today. He said that he knew he was going to die very soon, but he didn't know if it would be by God's hand or man's hand."

"What do you suppose that means?"

"After reading these papers I think he still feels guilty for never telling Caroline the truth. I think he feels that in some ways his life was a sham because he was afraid. That's why he fears God's retribution. The other is clearly the hatred the Su family had against him. I find it curious how close I am to Chen. I love her like a sister. I'd do anything for her. Yet, her grandfather has based his entire life upon hating my grandfather," she paused to reflect. "Jefferson told me once there's no such thing as coincidence. I told Chen that, and she said that when we have intense emotional bonds with another, it's because we knew each other in a past life. We've come back to be with that same person again."

"Or maybe we came back to right the wrongs against us," Michael said cryptically.

Barbara shivered. "I'm not so sure we should do anything about Nan-Yung and the Su family, Michael. My father was murdered by them," she said, swallowing hard. "I believe the Su family is directly linked to the mayor's office. Chen said there's more than prostitution going on in those catacombs. She said Nan-Yung pays bribes to Schmitz to keep his drug dens open."

"She's right," Michael said flatly.

"You know this?"

"I don't tell you everything. It's too dangerous."

"If we could get hard evidence on Nan-Yung, we could put him and Schmitz out of business for eternity."

"I've thought of that."

"I'll talk to Chen in the morning," Barbara said yawning.

Michael rolled over and looked at the clock.

It was twelve minutes after five.

"It is morning, Barbara." He moved over her. "Let's not talk about Jefferson anymore," he said, kissing her deeply.

"What then?" she smiled up at him.

"The only story I want to talk about is the one we are making right now, together."

April 18, 1906—5:00–5:12 A.M.

On the edge of Chinatown, five peals from the tower bell of old St. Mary's Church rang across the San Francisco hills. The sound did not penetrate the earth where Chen Su faced Lee Tong and her grandfather, Nan-Yung.

Beneath the dirty streets and deep within the catacombs where the Chinese lived in tenement houses, Nan-Yung lifted his nearly skeletal finger and pointed it at Chen.

"You dare to disobey me!"

Lee Tong slapped Chen across the cheek with a force than sent her to the floor. She felt the imprint of his fingers rise on her flesh. She refused to cry out. She'd do more than eat a few tears. She would fight them both to the death with her will.

Tossing back her long black hair, she stood defiantly. "Where is Yin?" She didn't care if they beat her to death. They'd never kill her spirit.

Nan-Yung's withered face showed no compassion, no mercy as he nodded at Lee Tong.

Lee Tong slapped her again, and she felt as if her neck would snap off from her spine, but it didn't. She remained standing. Slowly, she lifted her face to him. Her eyes were shot with icy shards of pure hate. All the love she'd ever felt for Donald, all the respect she'd ever felt for Barbara and all the loyalty she'd felt for Yin shifted on an inner axis and became hate.

Taking all her emotions, she honed them into weapons that she would use one by one to fight her enemy.

Nan-Yung was aghast at what he saw in her eyes. "You cannot fight me."

"I can and I will," she growled lowly like an animal about to strike.

"Ha! You're only a woman! Lee Tong can snap your neck like a twig. I only have to give order," Nan-Yung retorted proudly.

She glowered at Lee Tong. "He's nothing. He knows he is nothing. Ha! Lee Tong is like a eunuch. He fights against only the defenseless. He has no testicles!"

Lee Tong's face was devoid of any emotion as he pulled back his mighty fist and sent it plunging into Chen's abdomen. She crumbled, doubled over with pain and almost emitted a cry of pain. She felt as if she were ripped in two inside. She knew he'd broken her ribs. She couldn't breathe. She gasped and tried to fill her lungs with air, but nothing happened.

I have to stay alive. I have to find Yin.

"Killing you will be like pinching an insect," Lee Tong finally said. "No more than a gnat."

Her hair was splayed over her face, hiding her menacing eyes, eyes that were beginning to close from the welts he'd inflicted. "But like a gnat, I'm a nuisance. Too small to catch. Too quick to imprison. But what you really fear, Lee Tong, is what I see." She straightened.

Lee Tong looked at Nan-Yung.

Chen saw the look. "You both fear me. You should. If you were to blind me, you know that I'll still see. I see the future. Everyone's future. I'm more gifted than Yin. That's your fear. The gods of wind and earth speak through me. The ancient spirits of the dead speak through me. The forces that make the future find my voice to speak for them."

She passed her hand through her hair, flipping it away from her face so they could see her eyes in all their fury. "You can never own what I have, because it's a gift. You think you can silence me? I'll speak from the grave and haunt you for eternity."

Lee Tong's vacant eyes filled with terror. A thousand warriors he could face on a battlefield, but the superstitions of his forefathers frightened him. Dream demons had haunted his nights for years. With every murder he committed, he'd believed he could feel the life force leave his victims. He'd always wondered where they had gone. Was it possible they were lying in wait for him for the time when he was dead and his spirit was forced to do battle with their spirits? He didn't know how to fight in the unseen world.

He feared no man in the real world. He feared everything in the spirit world.

Nan-Yung knew she was trying to intimidate Lee Tong. "Fool! Don't listen to her!"

Suddenly, Chen knew she was winning. "There is time to save yourself, Lee Tong, before the forces unite to kill you. Tell me where I will find my grandmother! And I'll tell you how to escape death tonight."

Lee Tong sucked in his breath. "I am to die tonight?"

"Yes." She looked at Lee Tong. "Your death will be slow and painful. It will be as if all the forces of nature and earth have come together to rid this world of you, Lee Tong. And of my grandfather. There will be no stopping the gods of heaven and earth. There will be fire and chaos," she said.

Her eyes were black as the night sky and reflected a vast emptiness as if one were looking into eternity. Her face was blank and her mouth moved as if it were being manipulated by a puppeteer. Her voice had dropped to such a deep octave, she sounded like a man.

Lee Tong believed Chen, but he feared Nan-Yung's retaliation against him if he gave in.

Chen was in a trance. She was unaware of her body or her whereabouts. It was as if she were floating above the world, looking down on strangers.

"Fulfill her request, Lee Tong! Take her to her grandmother. Show her the well-holes where I put all those who defy me!"

Lee Tong was glad to have the sentence passed. He grabbed Chen's arm and dragged her from the luxurious apartment in which Nan-Yung lived and worked. Lee Tong was just about to the ornately carved door when Nan-Yung stopped him.

"I have another request for you, Lee Tong. Before the dawn finishes its rise, I choose to avenge myself against my enemy."

Suddenly, Chen came out of her trance. She thought of Barbara and of Jefferson. She felt the need to protect them. "Revenge?"

Nan-Yung's smile was malevolent. "By dawn the House of Duke will fall."

Chen smiled to herself. "The House of Duke has secret passages you know nothing about. It's your blood that will spill today."

"I don't want to hear any more ravings!" Nan-Yung swatted the air with his thin arm, dismissing his henchman.

When they were gone, Nan-Yung shuffled his elderly body across the floor to his elegant desk where stacks of gold coins awaited his attention. He smoothed his withered hands over the folds of his richly embroidered scarlet robe and sat in his throne-like chair.

Once Lee Tong killed Jefferson Duke, he would order Chen's death. And he supposed, absentmindedly, it was time to be rid of Yin as well. He'd been smart to have Ling Yutang killed last month when she proved to be a nuisance to his son, Lon Su.

Ling Yutang had tried to turn Lon Su against Nan-Yung.

She'd pestered Lon Su for details concerning Yin's whereabouts.

Lon Su was good at evasion. The only reason Nan-Yung had allowed Ling to live as long as she did was because Lon Su claimed he loved her and needed her.

It sickened Nan-Yung that his only son was sentimental. Sentiment was weakness. Nan-Yung would never tolerate weakness of any kind for long.

Lon Su was a disappointment. Too much opium had turned his mind to mush. Two days after Ling Yutang was killed, Lon Su had gone to his very own opium den, laid down on one of the pallets and purposefully consumed enough opium to kill three people.

There were times when Nan-Yung told himself that Lon Su's weakness was not good for business. The den keepers had often commented on his gluttonous appetite for opium. They accused Lon Su of consuming all the profits. He supposed it was just as well that Lon Su had committed suicide. It kept peace among Nan-Yung's employees.

Nan-Yung picked up the first gold coin. He had ruled all of Chinatown for over fifty years and he'd enjoyed every day of it. But the greatest power came from knowing he could have killed Jefferson Duke on any given day of any given year. As Nan-Yung looked back over his life and thought of each morning when he'd made the decision to give Jefferson one more day to live, he'd thought there was no more heady experience.

It was not the cowering bodies of the Chinese who begged him for mercy, nor the terrified eyes of the young girls he raped and then sold into slavery, nor was it the trembling hands of the opium addicts he'd purposefully addicted that gave him joy.

To rule lives with fear was power.

But to rule death was the greatest opiate.

As the dawn rose on this April morning, Nan-Yung was joyful.

forty-two

*The goal of life is living in agreement
with nature.*

—ZENO

DIOGENES LAERTIUS, LIVES OF EMINENT PHILOSOPHERS, BK. VII, SEC. LXXXVII

April 18, 1906—5:00–5:12 A.M.

Meredith pulled the sheet up to her naked breasts and watched as Peter shoved his legs into his trousers and buttoned them up. "I'm not finished with you, yet!" she shrieked angrily.

"Well, I'm sure as hell finished with you," he said coldly.

She scrambled out of the bed pulling the sheet with her. She nearly stumbled.

Peter glared at her. "You look ridiculous. Why the attempt at modesty? I see nothing but a whore."

She slapped him. He turned his face away. Then he glared at her again. She slapped him again.

"Bastard!"

He grabbed her shoulders angrily. The sheet fell to the floor in a puddle. "Oh, I'm the bastard. You think I'm impressed with your conniving ways, your lies and tricks anymore? Maybe those things worked with Donald to divest him of his money, but I'm smarter than he is."

"You said you'd marry me!"

"Well, I changed my mind," he replied callously and rammed his fists into a clean white shirt. "You married poor Donald for his money. Now you think you're going to get your hands into my honey pot? I think not."

"Oh, I understand now. You're going back to Barbara. Sweet, giving Barbara."

He paused for a fraction of a second.

It was long enough for Meredith to see that Peter had regrets.

It pained her more than she imagined.

He glared at her. "I wouldn't dream of it any more than you'd go back to Donald. I got what I wanted out of her. She introduced me to all the right people. Now that those people do business with me and she's nothing more than a twenty-dollar-a-week newspaper reporter, no one gives a damn about her."

"She's got a settlement from you."

"The courts can only give her a portion of what I told them I had," he laughed to himself as he ran a brush through his thick hair and regarded his handsome face in the mirror.

Meredith wasn't used to battling with men of the world, men who knew how to play games. She was used to Donald who was easily duped. For the first time, she realized how smart Peter truly was. How conniving. How dangerous he was. She was out of her league. She was so angry she wanted to break something. Throw something. She forced herself to contain her anger, otherwise she couldn't think.

She realized only her wits would turn this situation around. "You can't do this! It's breach of contract," she said haughtily.

"My dear, I hardly think that proposals whispered between adulterers would stand up in court. You weren't divorced when I asked you that."

"Why did you ask me to marry you, Peter?"

He lifted his face to the ceiling as a look of total exasperation fell over him. "To get you into my bed. Why else?"

"You can't use me like this, Peter!"

"I just did," he said, slipping his stockinged feet into his shoes. "Now, if you'll excuse me, I'm going out for my morning constitutional. See that you're gone when I return."

Rage seethed through Meredith's marrow. Never had she known the kind of anger that drove a person to kill. But at that moment she wanted Peter Kendrick dead. "You'll never get away with this!" She screamed and lunged at him with her hands outstretched to claw his face.

* * * *

Donald Pope rolled over in bed, thinking someone had just sat down on his bed. "Meredith?"

He bolted awake with a start. But there was no one in his bed or in the room with him. "Thank God."

The bed moved again.

Then he felt and heard a deep rumble, a terrible rumble. The ground began undulating. It was if he was riding a raft on waves in the ocean.

Earthquake!

I'm going to die!

* * * *

Eleanor Mansfield nearly dove across the room to catch the hand-painted Sevres vase as it tumbled from the mantlepiece. The chandelier overhead shook of its own accord as if being tickled by ghostly fingers.

What's happening? Eleanor shrieked to herself.

Suddenly, every plate and cup in the china cabinet began moving. French crystal shattered. The sound of the rumble from inside and outside the house was deafening. Eleanor would have put her hands over her ears, but she'd never let anything happen to her vase.

It's worth a small fortune. Lawrence told me so.

* * * *

Forty fathoms below the surface of the sea, ninety miles north of San Francisco at Point Arena and traveling at two miles a second, the earthquake ripped open the ocean bed and then shot out of the sea at seven thousand miles per hour. The one 110-foot-high Point Arena lighthouse swayed like a stalk of sea grass in the wind. In seconds, the lighthouse was a pile of shattered glass and rubble.

The rip shot south, shifting billions of tons of earth and hurtling masses of rock up and over itself to form new cliffs where moments before had been nothing but flat land.

It smashed through the coastline at Humboldt County. It demolished forests of redwoods and flattened black shale bluffs. It plunged itself back into the sea at False Cape Cliffs where the tail of the earthquake lashed like an angry Chinese dragon and spilled millions of tons of shale into the ocean, resculpting the coastline.

A shudder wrecked the small town of Fort Bragg, before it inhaled and smashed itself into Point Arena again. At Bodega Head, a hotel was flattened in the blink of an eye. At Point Reyes Station, it tossed four rail cars into the air and buckled the track from the force of its subterranean pressure, smashing the poppies along the track with jack-knifed rail cars.

The farms and ranches were realigned in the wake of the earthquake. Cypress trees spun into the air like Roman candles.

At the fishing village of Bolinas, boats snapped from their moorings, and the wharf dropped into the water. On down the coast it scourged the land like the talons of a demented harpy, split centuries-old redwoods in half as if they were no more than matchsticks, redirecting ridges and plowing up valleys.

In Salinas, Rudolph Spreckels's sugar factory was destroyed along with the Elks Hall, the Masonic Temple and the Odd Fellows Building. The lash killed twenty-one people in San Jose.

At Hinckley Gulch, hundreds of thousands of tons of earth were sent rolling into the gulch, burying nine men. As a cruel joke, the earthquake deposited a hundred-foot-high redwood tree, erect, on the spot where the men lay buried.

* * * *

Jefferson Duke did not hear the lock on his back door being pried open. He did not hear the fall of black-satin–slippered feet as they padded up the royal-blue–carpeted marble staircase to his bedroom.

But he did hear the long, low, moaning sound of the earthquake as it shot into the city.

The earthquake snaked up Washington Street. A few blocks away, John Barrett sat at his desk in the *Examiner* building working on an article for the newspaper when he heard the unnatural moan and then saw neighboring buildings pirouetting on their foundations like clumsy ballerinas. Then the *Examiner* building swayed and plunged the early morning staff onto their faces.

The building swooped out into the street and then back again as if some deity had descended from heaven and was pulling it to and fro like a string toy. When they rocked back and heard the frightening roar, they knew it was the god of the earth.

And he was angry, indeed.

At the top of Russian Hill where Bailey Millard was painting the dawn's light, the trembling earth smashed his easel and sent Bailey to the ground. From this highest peak, Bailey watched as the brick walls of Nob Hill mansions began swaying and then falling into piles of rubble. Stunned, he saw the whole city rocking and rolling and then look as if it were moving out to sea.

Crack! The whiplash sound reverberated again and again and with each sound another chimney fell, another spire snapped and houses turned inside out.

In utter disbelief, Bailey watched the enormous and fashionable Kendrick mansion crumble to little more than a pile of dust in the blink of an eye.

Peter turned in time to see Meredith plunging toward him, ready to strike like a viper. But the oddest thing happened. A strange sound like the snapping of a whip cut the house in two. Meredith opened her mouth to scream, but all he heard was a thundering roar that drowned out even the sound of his own voice.

"Peter!"

Meredith fell flat on her face, missing her target by inches, and then by feet as the bedroom was severed in half. Meredith looked up at him as she continued to be borne away from him. There was no panic in her eyes, only curiosity. Then the roof caved in and crushed her.

Her eyes closed.

"What in the name of . . ." Peter looked up just in time to see the other half of the ceiling fall in on him. He couldn't help but remember Meredith's last words to him, "You'll never get away with this." *No, I guess not.*

* * * *

Michael was kissing Barbara when a roar like the sound of mountains colliding filled the house.

"Earthquake!" Michael bolted to his feet and grabbed Barbara's hand, yanking her out of bed just as the overhead alabaster lamp fell to the center of where they'd been lying.

"My God!" she screamed. "We were almost killed!"

"Here!" He tossed her the white blouse and skirt she'd worn that day. Quickly, he rammed his legs into his pants.

Barbara didn't know what to do first. "Michael?"

"Get your notes. I'll get mine. Then let's get out of here. You can dress in the street once we're safe!"

She nodded and quickly raced to the salon and gathered all of Jefferson's papers and her notes she'd made during her investigation of city hall. She started for the door.

Then she remembered Chen.

"I have to get Chen," she shouted to Michael.

"Hurry!"

She raced down the backstairs to Chen's room. She found the bed empty. "Chen! Chen!" She rushed back to the small room Chen used as a salon. She saw Chen's books, her writing paper, ink and charcoals. But there was no sign of Chen.

"Barbara! For God's sake what are you doing down here? We've got to get out of here. The roof just caved in!" Michael stretched out his hand.

Barbara raced from the house half-naked. Once she was in the street she stepped into her skirt and finished buttoning her blouse. As Michael helped her dress, they looked around them.

"Holy heaven!" Michael whistled.

The street was ripped apart and the cable-car tracks were intertwined straight up in the air like crystalized spun sugar. Trees sat inside houses as if they'd grown there. Other houses were flattened to the ground, the inhabitants not as lucky as Barbara and Michael. People ran screaming into the streets carrying photographs and silly mementos along with valuables. Dogs barked at the eerie moaning sound of the earthquake. Children cried and women wept. And yet, an eerie silence hung in the air. It was the absence of birds chirping, of insects crawling, of horses hooves and commerce starting for the day. It was the sound of the end of the world.

Barbara turned terrified eyes to Michael. "Jefferson!"

"Come on!" Michael grabbed her hand and they started up the street on their way to Nob Hill.

"He's got to be alive," Barbara mumbled to herself over and over like a litany as they made their way over buckled sidewalks, felled telephone poles, severed lamp lights and debris. "He's just got to be alive."

"Don't think like that," Michael warned.

"Look out!" Barbara screamed, looking up in time to see a telephone pole falling.

"Run!"

The telephone pole crashed to the ground, narrowly missing them.

"Michael, we have to hurry. Every second counts!"

Racing against time, Barbara jumped over a wide fissure in the street. Rock and shale moved beneath her feet.

She screamed.

"Grab my hand!" Michael shouted reaching for her arm. Just as the earth sank into a cavernous hole, Michael lifted Barbara away and swung her in close to him.

"We'll never make it," she said, her adrenaline surging through her one more time.

"Yes, we will," Michael grunted. "Come on."

Jefferson knew this was going to happen. He knew about the earthquake. That's why he feared God would take him soon. But how did he know? Was it Rachel? Yuala?

And if he knew about the earthquake, why would he fear a murderer?

Suddenly, Barbara knew.

Every nerve in her body ignited. Then quick-froze.

"Michael, I know what Jefferson was saying now. Nan-Yung is going to have Jefferson killed today."

"I figured that out," Michael said, hurtling a fallen tree limb.

Barbara dodged a flying shard of metal roofing. It crashed to the warped pavement and spun in a circle.

The cacophony of babies crying and mothers screaming filled the morning air. More people ran into the streets, running for their lives in all directions.

Some ran to the sea. Others ran from house to house looking for friends and neighbors. Twenty became a hundred. Then two hundred.

All of them it seemed were running down Nob Hill as Michael and Barbara were running up it.

A hysterical woman ran toward Barbara and grabbed her. "Have you seen him? Have you seen him?

"Who, your husband?" Barbara asked.

"No!" the woman replied. "Have you seen the Lord?"

"It's an earthquake. It's not the end of the world," Barbara tried to reason with the woman and set her at ease. She was inconsolable.

Michael grabbed Barbara's hand. "Jefferson," he reminded her.

"Oh, Michael, all these people. They all need help."

"And we'll help them. But later."

Tears filled Barbara's eyes as she cried for the world.

A chimney crumbled to the right of them and the bricks fell like bombs, each bursting upon impact with the ground. Flecks of mortar shot through the air, stinging Barbara's arms and neck.

"Cover your face with your hands!" Michael shouted, steering them around the falling rubble.

Barbara didn't think of the danger to herself. All she thought of was Jefferson.

What if I'm too late?

Who will save him?

You've let him live this long, God, let him live a bit longer. Give me enough time to tell him that I love him. That I'll always love him. Let me have the chance to tell him I'm not ashamed to share his blood.

forty-three

And now I have finished a work that neither the wrath of love, nor fire, nor the sword, nor the devouring age shall be able to destroy.

—OVID
METAMORPHOSES, BK. XV, L. 871–872

April 18, 1906—5:12–5:30 A.M.

Bailey Millard's panoramic view of the San Francisco skyline dancing an eerie ballet was accompanied by a senseless cacophony of church bells clanging, giving the entire play a malefic tone. Surely, he thought, the devil had come to town.

The area south of Market Street moved in earth waves two- to three-feet high. The waves undulated through the ground like a monstrous sea serpent bursting from its subterranean womb. Foundations trembled, buildings rocked and masses of brick walls fell as if a highly powered vacuum had sucked out all the mortar. What was once a house, a store, a warehouse was now ash.

The prima donna of the ballet was City Hall. In seconds, it lost over seven million dollars worth of hand-carved stone and carefully laid brickwork. The frame stood against the morning sky like an enormous birdcage.

Suddenly, the trembling stopped.

Bailey counted to ten. He pushed himself up on all fours, not certain if his frightened legs would hold him. He stood.

461

It was a terrible mistake.

The second tremor started with an even stranger sound than the low moan of the first big rip. Like nails being pulled out of a packing crate, the sound signaled the collapse of thousands of roofs all over the city. Rafters were spread and then they kicked out the walls as buildings collapsed in a deafening roar.

It sounded like the orchestra pit in Hades as the violinists vied with each other to create discordance.

As chimneys fell on the sleeping inhabitants below, the sound of human screams of agony, pain and death mingled with the cadence of the clanging church bells.

Plaster showered everywhere, creating voluminous columns and clouds of dust. It looked as if the avenging angel of death had risen from beneath the earth.

But as Bailey watched people scrambling out of their falling houses, horses being crushed by falling brick walls and the wagons and carriages being overturned by the undulating riptide of the earthquake, the greatest evil of all finally surfaced.

It was truly Judgment Day.

The Lord of Hell Fire had appeared.

Within seventeen minutes of the earthquake, over fifty fires in the downtown area alone were reported, though not a single fire bell clanged. Housed in a building in Chinatown, the fire department's central alarm system was annihilated.

The first whiplash tremor had knocked out 556 of the 600 wet-cell batteries needed to operate the system.

Dennis Sullivan, the fire chief, had not been able to sleep that night because of a nightmare he'd had that the city was burning. He sat in a chair in his front parlor when the first tremor woke him. His first thought was to save his wife who was sleeping in the rear bedroom of their home above the fire station on Bush Street.

The high ornamental tower of the adjoining California Hotel broke through the firehouse roof, split the bedroom and carried half the room away. Dennis fell along with avalanching bricks through the opening down three floors and landed across a fire wagon. He fractured his skull, ribs, legs and arms.

The firemen crowded around him and lifted him clear of the debris. They placed him gently in a cart and raced him through city streets that looked like a war zone to the Southern Pacific Hospital.

Dennis Sullivan was the twenty-seventh emergency case admitted to the hospital since the first tremor began. The nurse logged the time of his admission at exactly five-thirty in the morning.

Eleanor Mansfield raced to the safety of the doorjamb of her front door, still holding the Sevres vase. On her way through the foyer, she managed to grab her sterling silver samovar. She only had two arms. She failed to secure any of the accompanying pieces.

How many times did Lawrence tell me that an incomplete set was worthless at auction. Oh, what will I do?

"My things! My things!"

Refusing to leave her valuables and her home, Eleanor steadfastly stood in the doorway and watched in shock as the roof caved in, crushing her silk sofas, Chippendale dining chairs, French armoires, Waterford chandeliers, four sets of Limoges china and the remainder of the priceless antiques Lawrence had spent his lifetime accumulating. The walls fell in on each other like a child's construction toy. The sound of the destruction was one Eleanor knew she'd never forget. She didn't want to forget.

"My God, what did I do to deserve this?"

My insurance can never replace a genuine vanity mirror that belonged to Marie Antoinette.

"How do I replace the Chinese bowls Lawrence gave me for our fifth anniversary?"

Another crash broke the air. "My crystal bird collection! Lawrence so loved those birds," she wailed, her eyes filling with tears.

The north wall caved in.

Eleanor felt the life draining from her body. Her knees buckled and she sank listlessly against the door. "My birds. My precious birds," she moaned. "Oh, Lawrence, they're all I have of the time when you once loved me. In the beginning . . ."

Eleanor's mind reversed time. She was standing in the ballroom. Lawrence had just walked up to her.

She'd wanted him all her life.

She still did.

It was the first time Eleanor realized that her need for possessions went deeper than the simple acquisition of things and their ownership. For her, each article had been a tangible witness to Lawrence's affection for her.

"I'm sorry. I'm so sorry, Lawrence." She raised her eyes heavenward. "I never gave you the love you deserved. I see that now."

Eleanor realized she'd been duped by society or her upbringing to think that men were above sentimental feelings and a need to be loved.

She looked mournfully at the Sevres vase. "I did love you, my dear, in my way. How I wish you were alive."

Suddenly, she envisioned Barbara's face. Assaulted by a profusion of missed chances she'd been given in her life to show kindness and love to her only child, Eleanor could almost feel herself slipping into hell.

"All the things I could have done. All the nights I could have hugged her." Her skin crawled with chills.

Sinking her face into her hands, Eleanor knew the earthquake had come to seek retribution. It was telling her she'd been a miserable mother and that Lawrence would never come back to her again.

How can I ever make it up to Barbara?

How will I survive this grieving for Lawrence?

How can I face myself ever again?

A mountainous cloud of dust enveloped the house, looking like the fog off the bay on a winter's day. It obscured her vision and mercifully kept her from seeing the devastation: the death of her old life. She was glad for the momentary respite.

* * * *

A wall of smoke rose from Union Square barring passage from *The Examiner* building to the Postal Telegraph office near the corner of Market and Montgomery streets. Flames roared like medieval fire-breathing dragons.

There was no St. George to slay them.

The fire stretched sinewy arms from building to building, embracing each like a lover. Slaking the walls with enticing kisses, the fire devoured timber frames. Then it expelled the torrid heat of its breath to melt glass. The passion of the fire grew at a monstrous rate. It was an insatiable lover, intent on feeding its desire with every building in the city. Its roar turned to laughter as it watched futile bucket brigades try to fight it. But they were no match for its lust. Soon, the fire would feed its greatest need, the fever for human flesh.

Jefferson Duke sat upright as the tremors ceased. Because he'd spent twice as much money on the foundations, pilings and walls of his mansion than anyone else in the city, the tremors did not devastate his fortress like his neighbors.

Only tiny fissures erupted in the ceiling plaster. Slowly, a minute webbing of cracks splayed themselves across the ceiling of the bedroom above him. Jefferson looked overhead and watched as the chandelier above him finally stopped swaying.

The roar of the crumbling houses around his property drowned out all other sounds in his own house.

On the top landing, Lee Tong paused for a moment as he surmised which of the expensively carved doors led to the master suite where he would find his prey.

Beads of perspiration had broken out on Lee Tong's forehead while the earthquake struck. All he could remember was Chen's dire predictions about his own death.

Was Chen right? I thought she was stalling for time. Hoping not to be tortured. But what if she has "the gift" as Yin does after all?

He swallowed hard, searching for courage.

Lee Tong had always been afraid of Yin and the things she could see. Sometimes, he thought that people, even a woman, who conjured visions in their minds were the kind of magician whose minds were so strong they were able to create the future with their thoughts. Lee Tong was a man of strong body. His talents were found in the set and size of his muscles, the mammoth size of his hands and power in his arms and back. He knew little of the workings of the mind, and his ignorance of such things filled him with fear.

All these years, Nan-Yung had told him he would be the avenger who would put his father's spirit to rest. Lee Tong believed that the golden moment of his life would be reached the day he finally sank his jeweled dagger into the heart of Jefferson Duke.

Generations of injustice would be set right by his act. The honor of the House of Su would be restored. Even if the emperor in China knew nothing of Lee Tong's bravery, the gods would know.

Jefferson Duke and the legends about the man and his power had created a formidable enemy in Lee Tong's mind. Jefferson embodied everything about the white man's world he despised. Lee Tong was a man of violence and he used murder to balance the odds against himself, odds that the fates had cast against him from birth. He thirsted for the kind of riches and power

Nan-Yung possessed. Once he killed Jefferson Duke, his place in Nan-Yung's debt could never be usurped. He believed Nan-Yung would reward him with the gift of his opium empire when he passed into the next world.

Lee Tong listened to the crashing sounds of houses falling inside themselves as he crept down the hallway toward the largest door. He reached under his tunic and pulled out the gold dagger with the carved jade-serpent handle. He depressed his thumb against the two rubies set in the eyes of the serpent.

Outside the Duke mansion, four fires ignited independently of each other deep in the bellies of the rubble where cinders from fireplaces and furnaces spit sparks onto dry timbers and roof shingles. Like gleaming fairies, they pranced from timber to timber, spewing glittering fairy dust in their wake. Innocent in their infancy, they grew to enormous heights as their need for nourishment grew into voracious appetites, devouring draperies, furniture, wood paneling and very old, very dry antique wood mantles. They spun together, twisting and gyrating like fornicating lovers and then, bringing their climactic heat into an explosive finale, they threw themselves onto the roof of the Duke mansion.

"This house will stand," Jefferson said aloud as if willing the walls of his mansion erect.

But the roof?

It was strong, but it could not stop the hand of God.

Suddenly, the door to his bedroom opened. Lee Tong stood in the morning shadows. His Oriental features looked demonic as his huge body moved toward Jefferson.

"It's you?"

Lee Tong said nothing.

"Let it be," Jefferson whispered to himself.

For weeks Jefferson had believed that to die by the hand of God would mean that he had displeased God.

The revelation came to him in a flash. He looked at the ceiling as the plaster crumbled and allowed the fire to seep through the cracks and lick the flat surface.

God is not angry with me. He never was.

He's always loved me. Just as you said, Mother. He's always smiled on me.

God had given him Caroline's love all his life. God had given him Lawrence and Barbara.

It was Man who'd robbed him. Man who made the rules that had duped Caroline into believing they were more important than the love in her heart.

"You took Lawrence from me," Jefferson said to his assassin.

Silence.

"Now you want to kill me."

Craaaack!

Jefferson's eyes flew to the enormous section of ceiling breaking away.

A light flashed across the blade of the Chinese dagger.

Jefferson's eyes went quickly to Caroline's portrait.

"My beloved. I am with you," he said.

He wanted her face to be the last thing he saw.

The ceiling fell and crushed Jefferson.

He died instantly.

Lee Tong jumped back. Stunned, he realized he had not avenged the House of Su. "This cannot be! It cannot!"

Other sections of the roof began falling into the room. Tongues of fire dropped into the room.

Lee Tong's mind snapped.

This murder was the one act in which he would establish his own reign on earth and his immortality in the next world.

I've been robbed! In the eyes of the gods, I'm the fool!

He lunged toward the bed and began frantically scraping off the plaster. He raised the dagger and with both hands and all the power in his muscles, he plunged the knife into Jefferson's heart.

"I will still win this battle!"

Lee Tong stood back and laughed uproariously. "No one cheats me of my day at glory. Not even the fates!"

Slick, hot and like drops of liquid, the fire dropped from the ceiling onto the carpet and then onto Lee Tong's black satin hat, tunic and trousers.

His queue smoked and then ignited. Because there was so much of it, his flesh sizzled at first before it burned.

Lee Tong's mind had always been weak and so it did not recognize that his strong body was fighting the fire by itself. Lee Tong laughed and danced around the room flaying his arms about as if he were embracing the fire.

He burst from the bedroom and down the hall giving the thirsty flames the life-supporting oxygen they craved.

Lee Tong danced and rolled down the staircase and out the door before being hit by a wall of smoke from the burning houses around the Duke mansion. Lee Tong had become a human torch by the time he fell into the street looking like an enormous cinder.

* * * *

In the postal telegraph office, the chief operator was on duty. Flames were licking the walls of every building around him. Frantically, he tapped out what he thought would be his last message to the outside world. He sent the message to New York City.

"There was an earthquake at 5:15 this morning, wrecking several buildings and wrecking our offices. They are carting dead from the fallen buildings. Fire all over town. There is no water, and we have lost our power. I'm going to get out of the office as we have had a little shake every few minutes and it's me for the simple life."

The operator in New York City took the message. In less than thirty seconds, he received a second message.

"We are on the job and we are going to try and stick."

The New York operator marked down the time. It was six o'clock in the morning.

Michael held Barbara's hand as they dodged falling brick and plaster. Dust clouds mingled with the growing number of thunderclouds of black smoke. They ran through the centers of smoke, feeling like ghosts walking through walls not knowing what they would find on the other side.

The noise of crashing walls sounded like the dueling sabers and cannons between the forces of good and evil, Barbara thought as timbers fell in their path, barely missing them.

"Is no place safe, Michael?" She looked at the inside of houses whose foundations had been ripped out from under them. The streets still moved and shook and the alleyways were strewn with fallen trees.

They were in hell.

They had no choice but to continue on.

Michael had been through war zones, been in the line of sniper fire, and been the bull's-eye target of a Chinese gang who'd surrounded him in Peking, but he'd never been through anything like this. When his opponent was a man, he always knew he could outwit him. But the forces of nature didn't know logic. Nature didn't have a brain. It was either loving like a warm summer breeze or wrathful.

Michael's senses were on alert.

He shut down his human brain and gave his instincts full throttle. He smelled the fire before he saw it. He heard the splinter of wood before he saw the timbers fall. He sensed the next tremor in the earth through the muscles in his legs. His nerve endings were electrified and, like the hair trigger on a gun, could go off at any second. He had to know when to dodge left to avoid falling debris, when to weave right to miss a newly formed crater in the earth.

Nob Hill was a mess. Fire spewed across the street like the flaming torches of jugglers in the circus.

Barbara screamed. "Oh my God, Michael. We're too late."

"Don't think. Just keep moving," he said after holding her a moment, but he knew nothing would calm her until they saw Jefferson.

By the time they got to the mansion, the neighboring houses were tinderboxes of incredible heat. The house across the street exploded from within and sent shards of glass flinging through the air like flying razors.

Barbara covered her face with her hands, ducked her head and continued toward Jefferson's front door.

In the street outside the house, Michael saw the body of a man, charred beyond recognition. He'd seen a body like that once before in India when a woman threw herself on her husband's funeral pyre.

Michael was glad Barbara hadn't seen it. But the sight filled him with fear of what she might see inside.

Michael raced after her. "Let me go first," he said.

He spied a large secretary off to the side in the library by the front door. Michael slipped inside the room and opened the secretary lid.

"What are you doing?"

"Give me those notes. And Jefferson's papers," he said, pulling out one of the two drawers. "Just as I thought, there's a false bottom. And here's the key to the secretary."

Quickly, he deposited papers in the drawers of the desk. "Safekeeping," he said. "Given human nature, during a crisis like this it won't be long before the looters come."

"Looters? I hadn't thought of that."

Michael closed the secretary lid, locked it and put the key in his pocket. "Let's go."

Barbara rushed up the staircase. The house seemed virtually intact, and oddly calm.

"Grandfather!" She cried and suddenly realized she'd barely breathed until she reached the front door. Tears filled her eyes. "Grandfather!"

I don't hear him.

Her heart froze.

Dread raced through her marrow.

"Grandfather! Are you here? Are you all right?"

Smelling fire and smoke, panic shot through her. She bounded up the last stairs.

"Grandfather! Grandfather!"

She raced down the carpeted hallway, not noticing the pieces of burned black satin or the remains of a Chinese queue.

She burst into Jefferson's bedroom. "Grandfather!"

She halted.

"Oh, my God! Grandfather!"

The fire in the room had extinguished itself. There was nothing left of the dancing fairy lights except small charred speckles in the deep-blue carpet. A light dusting of plaster covered the tops of the furniture.

The only sign that the house had been damaged was the large section of plaster that surrounded Jefferson's bed and the floor next to the bed.

Jefferson lay face up with a huge gold dagger sticking out of his chest.

Michael burst into the room behind Barbara. He grabbed her protectively and put his arms around her. "Don't look," he said.

She closed her eyes thinking she could fight her tears, but they were too strong, too persistent, too determined. "Please, I must see him."

"Barbara, he's dead. Don't torture yourself."

Her eyes swam in tears. "But he's my grandfather. He's my friend."

"I know."

Michael kept his arm around Barbara as they walked over to Jefferson's body together. She slipped her arm around Michael's waist and hugged him before she let go and then knelt beside the bed.

She thought her heart would explode. "How I will miss you." She touched his hand. He was still warm.

"He was always warm. His heart was warm," she said with a burning catch in her throat. "I love you, Jefferson."

Michael caressed her shoulders. "He knows, Darling. He can feel your love. Just like I do."

She touched Michael's hand. "I hope so," she sniffed.

Barbara couldn't take her eyes off the dagger. "It's not fair. They killed him, and it wasn't his time. He might have had one more day left. One more hour. And that's all I needed. Just another hour."

Michael dropped to his knees beside her.

Barbara dropped her head on Jefferson's arm. "Oh, Grandfather. Why didn't you tell me sooner?"

Then she lifted her tear-streaked face and let Michael hold her. He caressed her back and whispered soothing sounds in her ear. He smoothed her unbrushed hair away from her cheek. "Darling, please don't cry."

"You just don't understand, Michael."

"I think I understand a great deal. You've lost your best friend. That's the most difficult loss of all. But I have a feeling that Jefferson would ask you a question right now."

"What's that?"

"If you had known the truth before, could you have loved him any more? Any differently? Wasn't your relationship with him as special as either of you could make it?"

Barbara nodded. "We were special, Jefferson and I, weren't we?"

"Yes, Darling. You were."

"He and I had—"

"Magic, Barbara. That kind of love is unique. Nothing and no one can take it away from you."

She felt Michael's arms give her strength. Michael was right. Love was strength and its power was in knowing it was yours to keep and yours to give.

forty-four

It ended . . .
With his body changed to light,
A star that burns forever in that sky.

—"The Flight of Quetzalcoatl" (Aztec)

Michael glanced down at Jefferson's head. There were bruises everywhere. "Barbara, I don't think Jefferson died from the dagger wound."

"What?"

"No." Michael got up and inspected the plaster around them. He looked at the ceiling. Then he looked down at Jefferson's body, the odd twist to his head on the pillow. "Barbara, I think he was already dead by the time the assassin got here."

He saw the dark streaks where the fire had singed the ceiling and bubbled the paint and then died out. He saw the pockmarked carpet. He backed up a few steps. He saw pieces of charred black satin on the floor. The ornate Chinese dagger proved to Michael that the murderer was Oriental. However, if Michael was right, the murderer did not get away. Somehow, there had been enough fire in this room to catch the murderer's clothing on fire.

The human cinder in the street was the murderer.

Michael turned to Barbara who grabbed his arm. "Michael, one of the Su henchmen did this."

"I believe so."

"I just had another thought. Remember when we first met in Washington? I was with Jefferson. The Su must have followed us there. It was one of them who intercepted and deliberately did not deliver our notes to each other. They were planning to kill Jefferson then."

"You could be right. But in the meantime, I was there. I would have been a threat."

"But how could they manipulate events to have you assigned to China?"

"Maybe they didn't. Maybe they did."

"My God, how terrifying that their power could reach to the White House."

He shook his head. "It wouldn't have had to go that far. Only far enough for a letter to be written to be sent to my superior. But it's possible. However, my work there was important."

"You think it was coincidence?"

"No, what I'm saying is, it's just as much my destiny as yours to stop evil. Wherever we find it. Your fate and mine are one. That I do know. I believe Jefferson's stories about being visited by his ancestors. I believe they're helping us. We may not understand the reasons for the timing they choose for certain events, but they're there."

"Watching us?"

"Guiding us," he said, touching her cheek. "Just as Jefferson is probably watching and guiding us now."

Barbara shivered. "You're absolutely right, Michael. Funny, just talking about him keeps him alive to me. Think how wonderful it would be if I could see him again."

"Then that's what we'll wish for," he said.

Barbara looked back at Jefferson's body. "I'll lock up the house to protect it from . . ." Her eyes darted back to Michael. Her voice was filled with fear. "Chen! We forgot about Chen!"

She picked up her skirts and started for the door. "We have to hurry."

He was next to her in a flash. He grabbed her arm, pulling her back. "Are you crazy? What if Chen is part of this Su plot to bring down the Dukes? What if they knew the truth about you and Jefferson? You'd be in mortal danger. I won't let you go."

Shaking her head, she put her hand on his chest. "No, Michael. Chen isn't like that. She's like a sister. She's my friend. My heart tells me that. If I can't follow my heart in this life, then why am I here?"

"Barbara . . ."

"Don't you see?" she protested. "Jefferson followed his heart when it

came to building this city, but when he didn't follow it, like not telling
Caroline about himself, he lost." Her eyes were pleading. "I have to go."

"But where will you go?"

"I know this sounds crazy, but I can hear her calling me. In here," she
said, tapping her finger on her temple. "She's got to be in Chinatown. She
told me about the prostitution and even the well-holes where people are kept
and tortured. She's been obsessed with finding her grandmother."

"We can't go there. Have you any idea how massive Chinatown is? Those
catacombs . . ."

"Are right beneath her grandfather's laundry on Grant Avenue. I know
where it is! I went there once with my maid to pick up laundry. I didn't think
anything of it at the time. I was jotting notes for an article and waiting in the
carriage. But I've been there, Michael."

"Barbara, this is too dangerous. Half the city is in flames, the other half
is demolished. Someone sent an assassin here to kill Jefferson and now you
want to go hunting for Chen?"

"I love her. I love you, too. I'd crawl through glass to find you."

"Crawling through glass will be the easy part," he groaned. "But I can see
that reasoning with you isn't going to work. If I go, will you stay here until
I come back?" Michael asked.

"Two of us are better than one. We can cover the same ground in half the
time."

"I can't let you go."

She started walking out of the room again. "Don't order me, Michael. I'll
just have to lie to you and then go on my own. I hate to lie."

He ground his jaw. *You'd do it, too.* "Okay, but you stick close to me," he
relented.

She smiled wanly and then glanced back at Jefferson. Michael knew what
she was thinking. "As soon as we find Chen, we'll put Jefferson to rest."

"Okay," she sighed.

When they left the house, Barbara retrieved a key to the front door from
a hiding place where Jefferson had shown her several weeks before the party
when she'd been working with the florists and caterers. Michael made certain all the doors and windows were locked against intruders.

They headed for Chinatown.

* * * *

The chief operator at the postal telegraph building sent the following message at 2:20 in the afternoon:

"The city practically ruined by fire. It's within half block of us in the same block. The Call *building is burned out entirely, the* Examiner *building just fell in a heap.*

Fire all around us in every direction and way out in the residence district.

Destruction by earthquake something frightful the City Hall dome stripped and only the frame work standing. The St. Ignatius Church and College are burned to the ground. The emporium is gone, entire building, also the old flood building. Lots of new buildings just recently finished are completely destroyed. They are blowing up standing buildings that are in the path of flames with dynamite. No water. It's awful. There is no *communication anywhere and entire phone system busted. I want to get out of here or be blown up."*

For six hours the jets on the roof of the Palace Hotel sprayed their streams. Abe Ruef, along with half the city, watched the Palace fight for its life, a symbol of their refusal to admit defeat.

The mighty A. Ruef Building had cracked under the force of the tremor; a dynamite squad completed the destruction later that day. But that was nothing compared to the shock he had received earlier that day when one of his informants came to his house after the earthquake and told him that the task force set in motion by Rudolph Spreckels and President Theodore Roosevelt was bringing an indictment against him for corruption.

Ruef's golden glory years were over.

Many a devil has found God in the face of the demon. Eugene Schmitz found salvation during the earthquake.

At midday, Mayor Eugene Schmitz invited a cross-section of fifty of the city's most prominent businessmen to form a committee in whose hands the civil administration of San Francisco would rest. As the still-shaking city burned, the mayor made certain that neither Ruef nor any of the city commissioners was invited.

Schmitz told the men that during the thunder of the earthquake he realized that his "life had really begun again."

Schmitz looked as if he were in a trance all day. He watched as the flag over the Palace Hotel fought for glory. He convinced everyone he had a change of heart and had seen the error of his ways.

Abe Ruef thought Schmitz was lying to save his own neck.

Reporter James Hopper of the *Call* blended into the crowds of refugees as they streamed down Market Street. He felt like the Israelites marching through the parted Red Sea. Walls of fire on either side of Market Street roared over the silent hordes as they came out of the Mission Hills on their only escape route to the Bay. Later, James Hopper would write, "People spoke little, or if they did it was in hushed tones. The silence was acute. Everybody seemed to be overwhelmed by the terrible magnificence of the spectacle being enacted all around."

Donald Pope was one of those silent humans who plodded mechanically down the street. Donald had risen as the quake had first bolted through the city. He'd escaped death by racing out of the house before the roof fell in. Briefly, he thought about his treasures inside, but then he remembered that everything had been chosen by his wife, Meredith, and he'd always thought she had tawdry taste. Their divorce would be final next month and he had no doubt they would never reconcile. His marriage to her had always been a sham.

He looked at his house and realized that for the most part it was still intact. The walls were strong and holding their own. The roof could easily be rebuilt. He would discard the furniture and he would begin anew.

He supposed it was idle curiosity that urged him to work his way through the debris and fires to Peter Kendrick's house where he knew instinctively Meredith would be. Somehow, it didn't surprise him that Peter's house was completely demolished. Peter was a user. He'd skimmed money from the city for years. He'd used those same ethics when he built his own house. Ornamentation had abounded, but there was no solid foundation.

Donald stood in the street looking at the pile of Kendrick rubbish. "If I dug through the rubble, all I'd find is Meredith in Peter's arms."

He glanced away. "I already have my truth."

He shrugged his shoulders and walked away. "Let the looters have them."

Donald fell in with the masses of homeless. "Where are you going?" he asked the man beside him.

"To the park."

"What for?"

"To wait," the man replied as if that should explain everything.

"To wait," Donald mused. "Yes, that's what I'll do. I'll wait."

But for what?

Suddenly, Donald smiled to himself. Revelation filled him with joy. "I'll wait for my new life to begin."

"Precisely," the man nodded.

In Golden Gate Park bedding and tents were being brought in by the troops from the Presidio for the refugees. Army rations, water and donated food were being put into wagons in Los Angeles for shipment to San Francisco that afternoon.

Donald Pope sat down next to a man who had stretched out on a blanket and propped his head on his bulky briefcase. Donald noticed the British Foreign Consul's emblem.

"Walter?"

"Huh?" The man groaned.

"Aren't you Walter Courtney Bennett, the British Consul General?"

"Yes."

Proclamation by the Mayor

The Federal Troops, the members of the Regular Police Force, and all Special Police officers have been authorized by me to KILL *any and all persons found engaged in Looting or in the Commission of Any Other Crime.*

I have directed all the Gas and Electric Lighting Companies not to turn on Gas or Electricity until I order them to do so. You may therefore expect the city to remain in darkness for an indefinite time. I request all citizens to remain at home from darkness until daylight every night until order is restored.

I WARN *all Citizens of the danger of fire from Damaged or Destroyed Chimneys, Broken or Leaking Gas Pipes or Fixtures, or any like cause.*

E. E. Schmitz, Mayor
Dated April 18, 1906

* * * *

Like a mass of crawling beetles, the Orientals streamed out of Chinatown in black-suited hordes carrying their belongings on their backs in black bundles.

Barbara stood with Michael on the corner of Dupont and California streets as they scanned the crowd for any sign of Chen.

"I don't see her anywhere," Barbara said.

"Neither do I."

Barbara glanced to the wall of a building where she saw scrawled in English, *"I hate the African 'cause he's a citizen, and I hate the Yellow Dog because he won't be one."*

"That's the intolerance I can never tolerate," she said angrily.

Barbara knew the Orientals as a race in San Francisco had been denied an education, were constantly harassed by the police and were exploited by the white business community. It was no wonder they stayed to themselves and lived in shanties as they did. As the fires blazed, she realized there wouldn't even be shanties for them to return to.

They fought the crowd on their way toward the laundry where Barbara hoped to find Chen.

Surprisingly, the Su family laundry was largely intact. Fires blazed a block away and though the building two doors down had been toppled, there was not the imminent danger here they'd thought they would find.

Barbara peeked through the front window. "It's empty."

Michael tried the door and found it was open.

"Chen?" Barbara called.

Silence.

"There's a trapdoor in the back of the shop floor, Chen told me," Barbara said to Michael.

"I found it!" Michael lifted the door and found the ladder that led to the tunnel below.

Barbara followed Michael down the ladder. "My God, it's just as Chen described."

They walked down the tunnel, then turned into a larger area that looked almost like a city square but not as large. Dozens of doors opened onto the area. "It's like a whole city. I've never seen anything like it."

"I have," Michael said. "On the Barbary Coast. It's where they smuggle men, women and booty every day of the year. Only there they have names for their tunnels," he explained as they walked through the empty cata-combs.

"It's as silent as a tomb." Barbara looked at the bricked walls, the doors that led to tenements, opium dens and dark, unholy places. She shivered. "I don't even want to know what happens behind those doors."

Michael took her hand. "You bet you don't."

She guessed that in the first hours after the earthquake everyone had been too frightened of the tremors to remain below the street. Once the danger had passed she knew the looters and muggers would come back to ravage the shops and apartments.

Her heart was racing. Her mouth went dry.

"Okay," she said to Michael. "You were right. I shouldn't have come."

"Well, it's too late now. Just stay close."

"Don't worry," she said, looking back over her shoulder.

"I know you're afraid, Darling, but I'm glad you're here."

"You are?"

"Yes. The looters are surely out in droves by now. People will be beaten to death for a simple wedding ring. I'm afraid that life in San Francisco is not very precious at the moment."

"Tell me about the names of the tunnels on the Barbary Coast, Michael," she said, hoping that the change in subject would calm her fear.

Michael thought it was good that Barbara was scared. If she were frightened then her senses would be keen and her responses quick, should they get caught. "Dead Man's Alley, Murder Point and Bull Run Alley."

"Charming," she replied.

"Chen believed her grandmother was in prison, right?"

"Well-holes, she called it."

"Then I have the feeling we need to drop down another level."

"You mean these tunnels are multileveled?"

"If they're anything like the Barbary Coast they are. They use a second level expressly for keeping prisoners. And it's my guess they used the same architect," he said, racing ahead to a black-painted door with a red rooster painted on it. The rooster had a light in its beak. He tried the door and found it locked.

"Why this place?" Barbara asked.

"Because its sister house is a brothel on the Barbary Coast, the Red Rooster. It has the same logo. Some of the girls there are Chinese. It's my guess this is where the girls come from." He rammed his shoulder against the door and burst the lock open.

The front room was no more than a chair and table. There was no one else around. Michael went to the back of the room and parted a pair of dingy cotton curtains and found they covered a second door which he easily opened. It led to a hallway with half a dozen rooms.

Barbara opened doors on one side of the hall and Michael opened the others. Each room was equipped with a cot, cotton-ticking–covered soiled mattress, a chair, a table and a porcelain chamber pot.

Barbara was in shock. "This is a . . ."

"Brothel. Yes. Not very fancy, but then the management probably doesn't have to charge for frills."

They got to the last door and still there was no sign of Chen.

"Michael, where do we go now?" Barbara asked.

Suddenly, Michael realized he had overlooked something. He raced through each room and lifted the mattresses off the floor. In the middle room on the right, he found what he was looking for. A second trap door.

"I'm going down and this time you *are* staying here," he said firmly holding Barbara's shoulders. "I don't want anything to happen to you. And I don't want you to see this."

"Okay." She didn't feel like arguing.

Michael opened the door and the stench of human urine and excrement was overpowering. Barbara put her hand over her nose and mouth to keep from vomiting. It was as if Michael were descending into hell.

"Be careful," was all she could say.

Michael took off his shirt and tied it around his face. He had to bend over to make it through the low-ceilinged tunnel, which was little more than shoulder wide. He hadn't gone three feet when he heard human moans.

He stepped on a wooden grate.

"Chen?"

Another moan and then a louder groan.

"Chen?" He yelled as loudly as possible.

Chen's mind had left her body hours before. She knew her life was over. Lee Tong had beaten her about her head and shoulders, the pain rendered her unconscious. She'd been deposited in the well-hole, a six-foot-deep, round grave no wider than her own slim body. She couldn't sit or lie down. She could only stand. Here she was left to die. She would either starve, dehydrate or drown in her own filth.

Hope flitted briefly through her brain when she slipped into her dreams. There she saw a vision of the fire that would consume the city. In her dreams, she saw her grandmother who was being held in one of the cages in the tunnel next to the well-holes.

But never in her visions did she see herself being rescued by Michael and Barbara.

The sound of Michael's voice was familiar to her, but because she lived so much in a dream world, she didn't think it was real.

"Chen! For God's sake, answer me. It's Michael! I know you're down here!"

Then he heard a cacophony of pained voices cry out to him in a language he'd often heard, but still didn't understand.

He stepped on another grate. The light from the room above was gone. He couldn't see. "Chen!"

Reality snapped a long lash against Chen's face. She felt its sting. She opened her eyes. So long accustomed to the dark, she could see where Michael could not. She saw the shape of a man's shoe over her head.

"Michael," she barely whispered.

"Chen?" Michael turned around. He still wasn't sure where the sound had come from. "Chen, where are you?"

"Here. Beneath you."

Michael dropped to his knees and felt the floor. He felt like a blind man. "How do I get this grate off?"

"A wooden peg to the side," she said. "Lift the peg."

Michael pulled off the grate and stuck his hands into the darkness. "Give me your hand."

"My arms are locked on my sides. I can't lift them. You must pull me up by my hair."

"I don't want to hurt you."

"I won't be hurt. Not anymore. Please, pull."

Michael realized the best thing to do was to yank hard and fast. Chen was as light as a feather. She was fully out of the well hole before his biceps had even felt her weight.

"Can you walk?"

"No," she said, feeling her legs melt beneath her.

Michael picked her up and carried her to safety.

On the other side of the tunnel, Barbara was frantic. "Did you find her?"

"Yes," Michael said as he reached the opening. "She can't walk. I'll push her up and you pull her. But be careful. I think her arms are broken."

"Chen! Oh, God! Oh, God! What have they done to you?" Barbara burst into tears when she saw Chen's mutilated body.

Chen flopped onto the floor like a rag doll, her face swollen beyond recognition. She had bruises everywhere. "My grandmother. Please. She's in the cage. There's a tunnel just past my well-hole. Her name is Yin. She speaks English. Please, Michael."

Michael smoothed Chen's black hair from her face. "Don't you worry, I'm not leaving here until all these people are free." Then he looked at Barbara. "Find some clothes for these people. Some rags to help them clean up. Water especially. They're all half-dead. Break into one of the apartments if you need to. Try that shop next door."

"There's a shop next door? How could you tell?"

"Without windows it isn't easy, but the sign was the one Chinese symbol I recognize. It's a tailor's shop. I used to have my shirts made by a Chinese tailor."

"Okay," she replied as she cradled Chen's head in her lap.

Michael started down into the tunnel again. Then he stopped. "Hand me that candle on the table. Do you see any matches?"

Looking around she saw a box of wooden matches on the shelf above the table. She handed the whole box to him along with the candle.

"This will help a lot."

Michael went back to the tunnel and quickly found his way down to the well-holes.

"Yin! Can you hear me? My name is Michael."

"The name of the savior," a woman's weak voice replied.

Michael crouched toward the sound. "I thought his name was Jesus."

"That, too. And Mohammed to some. Allah to others."

"Those are illustrious folks," Michael said, coming up to the cage.

A pair of flashing eyes shone out of an elderly woman's face. "I am Yin. Not so illustrious," she smiled. Her face lit like the sun. Michael blinked, wondering if she'd lit another candle somehow. "I'm here to take you to Chen."

"I know," she replied, nodding.

Michael looked down at the huge padlock on the cage door. "I didn't bring any tools. How will I get you out?"

Yin smiled again. "One always travels with everything one needs in this life." She pointed at the matches. "Those will do."

She reached in her pocket and withdrew a small fistfull of black dust. "Gunpowder," she said.

Michael was aghast. "And you didn't use it?"

"I was waiting for you. And those," she said.

Quickly, Michael put the gunpowder in the lock and lit his match.

It was just enough gunpowder to blow the lock apart. He opened his arms. "Come."

Yin weighed less than Chen. When he saw the water and food bowls, Michael surmised that the only reason she was alive was that someone had wanted her alive. Chen, on the other hand, was expendable.

Michael carried Yin to the surface and reunited her with her granddaughter.

"I'm going back," Michael said.

"Be careful," Barbara replied, kissing him, but not stopping him.

From the six well-holes, only two people remained alive. There were four more cages, Michael discovered, and he rescued all four women who were being held for ransoms, Yin said.

While Barbara helped the women put on new clothing and deposited their filth-encrusted rags in a heap in the corner of the room, Chen cried as she embraced her grandmother.

"I will never eat my tears again," Chen sobbed.

"Neither will I," Yin promised.

As battered as she was, Chen realized her arms were not broken. She lifted them to hold Yin's face and kiss her.

"He hurt you this badly?" Yin asked.

Chen only nodded. "But he could never break my spirit," she smiled with bruised lips.

Yin's eyes were filled with fire, the kind of light Nan-Yung had seen on that first trip to Peking when she'd been riding in the sedan. Her eyes shone like the sun and the moon and the stars. She would forever be the girl with the shining face. "Nor could they break my soul," she said proudly with all the defiance and deep self-love Nan-Yung had feared and hated.

"We were too much for them."

"You are the blood of my blood, Chen. You will always have the power to be victorious, as I am," Yin replied.

Chen smiled gently as Yin's face beamed at her. Chen put her forehead to Yin's forehead. "I knew you were alive. I saw you in my visions. I would not rest until I found you and brought you to safety." She looked up at Barbara. "I should be ashamed to use my friends. It was very dangerous."

Yin looked at Barbara and put a withered hand on Barbara's smooth cheek. She gazed into Barbara's eyes and saw the silver lights. "You have the light of God in your eyes. Just like Chen."

"Thank you."

Chen held her grandmother and they shared information about themselves they had both missed in their years apart. Yin told Chen that Ling-Yutang, Chen's mother, was murdered by Nan-Yung the previous year.

Chen burst into tears and then clung to her grandmother. "That's why I could never find her except in my dreams."

Michael found food and water and while Barbara fed everyone, Michael began carrying each of the prisoners to the surface.

Barbara decided they would all go to Jefferson's mansion where there were enough beds, food and room for everyone to be comfortable.

Barbara sensed that Yin might not live much longer. Of them all, she was the most fragile. Malnutrition had taken its toll, and Barbara guessed that the festering flesh on her arms was leprosy. One of the other women, Mei Yin, was in similar bad health. The others had not fared as badly. It would take weeks of care to bring them all back to health, but she wanted to believe they would make it.

By the time Michael managed to get everyone to the street, Chen was able to walk on her own. "I'm bruised, but I'm determined to help my grandmother," Chen said.

"I can't get a carriage through the streets in order to take these people up Nob Hill. I'll have to carry them one at a time."

"We could take the mattresses and make a stretcher out of them. Then we could take two at a time and I could help you pull them up," Barbara said.

"Good idea."

With rope and the mattresses, Michael and Barbara took Yin and the other sickly woman, Mei Yin, to Jefferson's house.

"I'll wait here with others until you return," Chen said.

"Just stay out of sight," Michael warned.

"Don't worry," she replied. *I'll be well out of sight.*

Chen turned around and went to the back of her grandfather's laundry shop and descended the ladder. She knew not even an earthquake could make him leave his golden lair.

forty-five

There's no such thing as chance;
And what to us seems merest accident
Springs from the deepest source of destiny.

—JOHANN CHRISTOPH FRIEDRICH VON SCHILLER
THE DEATH OF WALLENSTEIN, II, III

April 18, 1906—3:00 P.M.

Chen thought it apropos that she kill her grandfather at the precise hour many Christians claimed their god died on the cross. *Three o'clock. A fateful number.*

San Francisco, the only world she had ever known, lay in ruin. She believed her grandmother would not live long. There was only one person to blame for both: Nan-Yung.

She went to one of the joss houses where she'd attended Nan-Yung's men several years ago, taking them meals and their cleaning. She went to a desk in the front room and felt the underside. Smiling to herself, she found the hidden dagger one of the men had placed under the desk in case of an emergency. She'd always thought it strange that Nan-Yung's entourage thought of defending one's self as the only kind of emergency that arose in life. During her years living with Barbara, she learned their were other kinds of crisis and there were other ways of defending one's life and honor without using physical violence.

She left the joss house and went back down the tunnel.

Chen placed her hand on the solid-gold handle on the black-lacquered door that led to her grandfather's throne room.

Just as she was about to open the door, one of the wooden beams overhead shifted. Impacted dirt slipped over the edges of the beam. Another beam shifted. A rock fell loose. Then a brick.

"I don't care if I'm crushed alive by all the earth in California, as long as I kill Nan-Yung first."

Then I'll rest.

Nan-Yung heard the door creak.

"Who's there?"

He held his breath.

The hairs on the back of his neck stood on end.

Death passed over him.

I was right. It's happened. The day of my revenge has come. The House of Su has endured because of me.

"I'm here," he said anxiously to the shadows.

He'd waited a lifetime for this moment to arrive. Lee Tong had been gone since daybreak and Nan-Yung was impatient. He needed to hear from Lee Tong's lips that Jefferson Duke was dead. Not since the day his father, Luang Su, was executed had Nan-Yung felt such emotion.

All his life, Nan-Yung had prided himself upon his ability to remain "balanced" in his emotions about all things. He did not become elated when he learned of a particularly large shipment of opium that would make him piles of gold. He didn't feel regret or remorse when he took the virginity of the young girls whom he later sold into prostitution or slavery. They were commodities after all: sources of profit and for that he needed them in his life, but certainly for no other reason. He taught himself not to become attached to Yin, or to fear her dire predictions, or to put the feelings or needs of his granddaughters or son, Lon Su, over his own needs and appetites.

Even his hate and desire for revenge against the House of Duke had been properly channeled into a long-standing game of cat and mouse, a game that Nan-Yung played for many years against himself since Jefferson Duke knew nothing of Luang Su's death. However, the day Dolores Sanchez was killed, Nan-Yung indulged himself in pleasurable feelings.

The day Lawrence Mansfield was murdered, he allowed himself to smile. *Patience increased the tension. The tension of purposefully delaying one's pleasure heightens the climax.*

Today, he'd immerse himself in an explosion of self-satisfaction. Jefferson Duke's death had been worth the torturously long wait.

"Lee Tong?" Nan-Yung said as the dark figure emerged from the shadows by the door.

"No." Chen moved closer. "Not Lee Tong."

Instantly, Nan-Yung realized his mistake. He could smell the lingering stench that clung to the clothing of one who had been in the well-holes.

Then he knew.

"Chen," she said and walked into the light that puddled from the antique oil lamp on his desk. Her lips were swollen from Lee Tong's beating, but she didn't feel pain. She wanted to grin at him but decided to wait until later.

He looks like a skeleton.

The light cast hideous shadows on the deep hollows of his eyes and cheeks. His long white mustache hung limply on either side of his mouth. She noticed his hands were palsied as he lifted his precious gold coins to count them. Without Lee Tong's brutish strength, Nan-Yung's power was extremely diminished.

She knew better than to underestimate him. She could tell by the icy glint in his dark eyes that Nan-Yung's mind was just as evil as ever. Theirs would be a fight to the death.

"How? How did you escape?" Nan-Yung was truly shocked to see her, though he struggled to remain both calm and unaffected by her presence.

"I have many friends now. They rescued me."

"No one in Chinatown goes to the well-holes without my knowledge."

"My friends are white."

Nan-Yung spat on the floor. "That is disgusting!"

"Why?" she asked.

"It sickens me you are so stupid. Whites only use the Chinese. We are beasts of burden to them. Nothing more. Bah! You are less than I thought you to be. My disgrace with this family is keen."

Chen glared at him with eyes filled with red-hot hatred.

"You! You are the one who brings us disgrace. You have never accomplished one thing in your life that would make me proud of you."

"Who cares what you think? You're a woman. Excrement. Go back to the well-holes. At least you have purpose there."

"The well-holes are no more. My grandmother was rescued by my friends as well as all the others there. Your reign of terror is over. When the Chinese come back to Chinatown, I'll tell them I rule the House of Su now. Many things will be changed in the new world my friends and I will build here."

"Silence!" He threw his hands up to stop her. Immediately, he dropped them.

She smiled crookedly through bruised lips. "You hear it, don't you, Grandfather?"

"What?"

"The ring of truth in my words."

"Bah!"

"You realize you have neglected to acknowledge the closing of your own life. You've waited, even planned Jefferson Duke's death, but you never anticipated your own. You see you've created your own demise. Without the mouse to pursue as prey, you have no purpose."

"Shut up! I have more money than three emperors."

"Who cares, old man? You can't sire children anymore. You're too old. You don't even feel lust in your loins anymore. I know this. The well-holes speak. You have only lived these last years to inflict pain."

"Get out of my sight!" Nan-Yung hissed.

"You will hear me. Be silent." He covered his ears, but Chen only spoke louder.

"You've despised women all your life because we are the creators. You create nothing. You sent Yin to the cage because she served no purpose in your life. Well, old man, you serve no purpose in mine."

"Women are emotional. Weak. They disgust me."

"Weak? Not Yin. I see it in your eyes. You're surprised she's still alive. That she had the will to live despite all odds. She has always amazed you, even frightened you with her intuitions and visions of the future. You have none of her powers."

"She's not so special."

"Really? She told me that before you came to America she told you all her visions, but as the years passed, she told you less and less. You thought her disloyal. You punished her with many beatings until the pain no longer affected her. Then you realized you could hurt Yin by torturing your grand-daughters. Yin tells me they're all dead now."

"All except you," he said defiantly.

"He's not coming back," Chen said coldly.

"Who?"

"Lee Tong," she said his name slowly, allowing each syllable to reverberate in the chambers of Nan-Yung's mind. She got the reaction she sought.

Nan-Yung's lower lip quivered, not with emotion but disbelief. He tried to talk but couldn't. The truth hit him like a death wound. He buckled at his waist as if someone had punched him and his spine hit the back of the chair. "Not . . . coming back."

"He's dead."

"How do you know?"

"I saw it in a vision."

"Ha!"

"You know I have the power. You believe I have the power. That's why you wanted to destroy me."

Nan-Yung's eyes rattled in his head. He blinked. He lifted his hand to his forehead and then let it drop back to his lap. It was as if the life force had seeped out of him. Had he been standing, she was certain he would have collapsed.

Chen had never liked seeing anyone in pain. However, Nan-Yung's torture was well-deserved. She didn't smile, but kept her cold eyes focused on him. She didn't trust him for a split-second.

It's a trick. Nan-Yung never feels emotions. He's overreacting to dupe me.

She wrapped her fingers around the dagger.

Nan-Yung's left foot felt for the spring at the bottom right side of his desk that would release the drawer in which he kept his gun. If Chen's friends had rescued her, they might still be around. Somehow they had killed Lee Tong.

He felt no sorrow over learning of Lee Tong's death. Nan-Yung was an old man, and he needed Lee Tong to protect him.

His only true regret was that he didn't know if Lee Tong had carried out his mission or not. Was Jefferson Duke alive or dead? How was he ever to know?

And now here was his granddaughter filled with the fire of revenge in her eyes. He had no doubt she would kill him because he'd seen the same look in his own reflection. He must rely on his wits and the hidden pistol to save himself.

"And so you have come to kill me?" Nan-Yung taunted her.

"Yes." She turned the dagger around in her hand and crooked her arm behind her back.

"Nonsense. What you really want is for me to turn over my empire to you since you are my only living relative."

"There is Yin."

"She's old. Sick, no doubt. She doesn't have your ambition. And that is what I see in your eyes. And desire. You want the power I have built all these years."

"You're so very wrong, Grandfather. What I want is something you can't give me."

His grin was cold and enigmatic. "And that is?"

"I want the House of Su to be put to rest. Totally and completely. No white man can avenge you because our disgrace comes from within. Not without. Andrew Duke was not the cause of our ancestor's death. Your grandfather chose the opium that brought murder and suicide to our house."

"How do you know?"

"I told you. My power is greater than Yin's. I see the past lives of all. I can see our ancestors standing in this room. They are telling me the truth. The truth, Grandfather. Not distortions. They're telling me it was not Ambrose Duke who ordered Luang Su's death. His own greed caused his execution. You never accepted this truth. You spent your life blaming someone else for the Su disgrace. Instead of building a new life, your life is one of hate and revenge built on a lie. How pathetic!" She laughed.

"And what's more, it was a lie you told yourself. Only a Su can right the wrong of a Su." She stepped forward. "Face me, Grandfather. I'm your avenger."

Nan-Yung depressed the pedal that opened his desk drawer. With an imperceptible move, he lifted the gun out of the drawer and had it leveled at Chen's forehead before she realized what had happened.

"You are only a woman. Your sentiments prevent you from taking action." He pulled back the trigger.

Chen didn't blink as she hurled the razor-sharp dagger at Nan-Yung's heart, sinking it deep into his chest.

"What?" he groaned.

Blood seeped onto his gold satin tunic. His eyes held a look of disbelief and his jaw dropped open.

The gun dropped to the floor beside Nan-Yung and fired.

The bullet stuck in the wall as Nan-Yung fell face first onto his desk.

A beam overhead shifted again. Dirt trickled down on top of Nan-Yung's head.

"I'll never come back to this house," she vowed, as she left the room and the tunnels—forever.

* * * *

Donald Pope handed a blanket to his longtime friend, Mrs. Claudia Grant. She was still in shock over the burning of her house on Nob Hill. Donald rubbed her arms and held her hands. She was icy cold.

"Everything is going to be just fine, Claudia. You'll see."

She shook her head. "We're in the middle of Golden Gate Park, Donald. I have no home, no possessions left. I'll never get that back."

"But you're unharmed. And your daughter lives in Santa Barbara. You can live with her for a while until you rebuild."

"I'm fifty years old, Donald. Why would I start all over?"

Donald smiled. "Why would you not?"

She pondered his comment for a long time as she looked around at the hundreds of refugees like herself. These were the same people she'd sat on chairing committees with for charity organizations. She couldn't begin to count the balls and parties she'd given over the years to raise money for hospitals, churches and the needy. Never, ever did she think she would become homeless or in need of help from anyone. She'd always been able to take care of herself. Now she only had one choice in her life, and that was to turn everything over to God and let him provide for her.

She smiled at Donald. "Yes. Why would I not?"

Donald kept rubbing her hands and smiled back at her. "What news do you have of your neighbors?" he asked to change the subject.

"It was the strangest thing, Donald. My house, the two on either side of me and two across the street all burned. Yet, Jefferson Duke's house was barely scratched. There was no foundation damage, just a bit of roof damage. His house looks as if . . ."

"As if what?" Donald asked suddenly, raising his eyes toward Nob Hill and the Duke mansion. He thought of Barbara and how beautiful she'd looked the night that President Roosevelt came to Jefferson's house. He thought of how close she'd always been to Jefferson. To him.

He was happy for her that she had found Michael Trent and that Michael appeared to love her so deeply. She was his dear friend. Even though he'd wanted to marry her when they were younger, he realized now that the relationship they shared was very special in its own way.

Thinking of Barbara reminded him of Chen. Lovely, delicate Chen. He thought of the way his hand touched hers when she served him tea the last time he had gone to Barbara's house she shared with Michael.

He thought of the way Chen looked at him with eyes so full of . . .

"Are you sure it was unscathed?"

"Yes," Claudia said. "It was like his house was protected by the angels."

"Or love." Donald kept his eyes raised toward the hill.

"What?" Claudia wondered what had come over Donald.

"I went by Peter Kendrick's house. It was demolished. I went to Barbara Kendrick's new flat, but it was destroyed as well. I didn't think about Jefferson's house."

"What has Jefferson got to do with Barbara?" Claudia asked.

"They were very close."

Donald dropped his gaze. He rubbed her hands again. "How are you doing there, Claudia?"

"I'm much better, thank you, Donald."

Donald stood up. "Good. I have to go, Claudia. But I'll come back for you. I think maybe we might have a roof over our heads tonight after all. But first," Donald stopped abruptly.

Claudia thought Donald's face had the most curious smile. It was as if he'd discovered something quite pleasant. Quite pleasant, indeed.

Donald began walking very fast.

"Where are you going, Donald?"

"To find someone."

"I thought you might still be in love with Barbara," Claudia said.

"It's not Barbara," he said, turning back and smiling. "Her name is Chen Su."

Claudia glanced at the billowing smoke annihilating the only life she'd ever known. Then she looked back at Donald. "You better run, Donald. You wouldn't want to lose her." Her smile filled her face.

Donald broke into a run.

* * * *

Chen Su helped Barbara bathe Yin with the water they heated out of the large tank reserve in the basement of Jefferson Duke's solidly built house.

"Thank God," Chen said to Barbara. "She doesn't have leprosy at all."

"I agree. I think it's a type of scurvy from lack of fruits and vegetables. You may have several years left to enjoy each other," Barbara said with tears in her eyes. "I only wish my grandfather were alive, too."

Chen put her hand on Barbara's shoulder. "Jefferson hasn't left, Barbara. He's still in this house. I can feel his love."

"So can I, Chen. So can I."

Chen went into one of the bedrooms where Yin rested in a huge, burled-walnut bed. She propped a pillow behind Yin's head.

Looking at her granddaughter, she asked, "You killed him, didn't you?"

Chen nodded silently.

"It was your destiny. Don't feel guilty, ever. You were guided by the fates and had no choice. His evil heart had to be stopped."

Chen laid her head on her grandmother's lap. "It was like I was not myself. I barely remember it and it only happened hours ago. I'm not a murderess."

"No one will ever know the truth except you and me. But there are times when you must give yourself up to destiny. It was a good thing you did. When Nan-Yung sent me to the cages, I knew one day I'd be saved. I saw you kill him in a vision one night. I knew I had to stay alive, just to tell you that you did the right thing. There are so many wonderful things ahead for you, my child. Love. Children. Even respect from those in Chinatown. One day, you will be a great leader in your own right. But you will rule from goodness." Yin touched Chen's satin smooth hair. She picked up a lock and let its silkiness caress her fingers.

"I want to believe all that, Grandmother."

"Believe and you will make it happen."

"Is that really true, Grandmother? We're not just p·⸱ ⸱ ; for the fates?"

Yin lifted her eyes to the ceiling and took a deep breath. "I had planned to tell you a story someday, yet I never knew quite when the right time would be."

"Right time for what?" Chen was puzzled.

Yin turned to her side, reached under the pillow and retrieved a small, leather-covered book. The leather was old and sweat-stained. It was marked with dark spots as if it had been water splattered or struck by tears. She handled the book with great care as if it were some precious jewel. Her eyes misted as she looked at it. Lovingly, she passed her hand over the top. "I have kept this with me day and night nearly all my life. Except for the gun-powder, it's the only thing I took with me to the cages. The guards never saw it because I kept it hidden under my clothes."

"What is it?"

"My poems. Love poems. I wrote these when I was young, like you, and very much in love."

"You wrote poetry to Grandfather?"

"No," Yin said as her face softened and Chen could tell her mind was drifting back to another day. To another life she shared with some other man than the one to whom she was wed.

"He was white. And he was much younger than I. The first time he saw me was at a lumberyard. Nan-Yung had gone to Jefferson Duke's lumber-yard to buy the timbers with which he would build the catacombs and his opium dens. Nan-Yung insisted that I carry the lumber back to Chinatown on my back, but Jefferson came to my defense and refused to pile the heavy wood on my shoulders. Instead, he ordered his men to deliver the lumber. Nan-Yung was indignant.

"My love later told me that he had watched the encounter, thinking I was the most delicate and beautiful woman he'd ever seen. I remembered him, the little boy with the sparkling green eyes. I knew instantly that he was Jefferson Duke's son. Because the Dukes were the Sus' sworn mortal enemy, I kept these things in my heart.

"When my love was older and world traveled we found each other again, but he was already married. I just wanted to walk with him and talk with him. We shared stories about Peking since he'd been there. He touched my hand and I knew we'd be lovers.

"We remained lovers for years. I became afraid Nan-Yung would dis-cover our love. It was the happiest time of my life and yet it was the most painful. I had to tell my love I could not see him anymore; not because I was married, but because it was too dangerous for him and for me.

"He understood, though it pained him a great deal. I knew I'd broken his heart. He was angry with me for a while."

Yin's eyes were full of tears and Chen held her hand silently, giving her grandmother courage to continue her story.

"Please tell me the rest, Grandmother," Chen urged.

"I could not live without him in my life. I missed him so tremendously, my insides were hollow without him. I felt a burning in my stomach when I was not near him. I thought in time my feelings would abate, but they never did. In fact, time away from him only made my need for him more acute. The hours dragged. The days were eternity. Finally, when you were about two and his daughter was the same age, he came to me. We devised a plan to throw off suspicion.

"He told me that everyone knew he was not sleeping with his wife, because the maids in San Francisco have lax tongues. I was now in charge of delivering linens to the prostitution house on the Barbary Coast that Nan-Yung supplied with young girls. There was little I could do to save them, but I could use the trips to see my love.

"I had an accomplice, your sister, Mei, who hated Nan-Yung with a vengeance. She'd do anything to hurt him, including act as my smokescreen so that I could be with my love.

"The night my love was murdered, Nan-Yung had discovered that Mei had betrayed him. He ordered her death as well. Two people died protecting me," Yin said as her tears washed her cheeks.

"What did Grandfather do to you when he discovered you'd taken a lover?"

"He beat me and tortured me. He ordered his henchman Lee Tong to castrate me."

Chen's hands flew to her face in abject terror. At that instant she was glad she'd killed Nan-Yung. What traces of remorse she felt vanished. "He was more than cruel, he was diabolical!"

"Yes," Yin said. "With my love gone from me forever, I didn't care. I had little to live for." She touched Chen's cheek. "You were only ten years old, yet the visions of you as a grown woman came to me. I saw you murder Nan-Yung. I saw you being the force that righted the scales of justice. You and your destiny were the only reasons I made myself go on."

Barbara did not intrude upon the intimate scene between Chen and Yin. She waited by the slightly opened door. Yin had started her story in Chinese but as she spoke more about Jefferson Duke and Lawrence, she spoke in English. Barbara heard just enough to put together the missing pieces of the mystery surrounding Lawrence's death.

Barbara knew her father well enough to know that his caring personality was not the kind that bought sex for an hour or two on a Saturday night from a stranger, no matter how abominably Eleanor treated him. Though she never got along with her mother, she knew that Lawrence had loved Eleanor in his own way. She had been his wife. She had been the mother of his child.

Barbara also knew that the well of his heart was too deep to never be plumbed. Lawrence would have had to give his love to a special person.

Yin is very special, indeed. I don't know that I have that kind of courage and strength of will to stay alive through decades of mental and physical abuse.

"And her only sin was loving my father."

Barbara slowly closed the door and let them have their privacy.

Chen touched her grandmother's tired cheek. "You must rest now, Grandmother. I'll be back later with a thick potage to make you healthy."

Yin merely nodded as her eyes slowly closed in sleep. Chen kissed Yin's cheek and slowly left the room, her mind still pondering all that Yin had told her.

* * * *

Michael tossed the last shovelful of dirt onto Jefferson's grave in the back garden beneath the flowering apple tree as Jefferson had requested in his will, which he'd given Barbara along with his journals and the "Rachel Papers."

Barbara cried unabashedly in Michael's arms. She wiped her tears with her fingertips as she felt Michael's arms tighten around her. "I miss him already," she sobbed.

"I know, Darling. I know."

"There should have been a big funeral. A party. He would have liked that. Lots of flowers. But with half the city burning and hundreds of dead to bury, he's just one of the numbers."

She paused. "It doesn't seem right. If it weren't for Jefferson Duke and a few other men of vision, there might never have been a San Francisco. He was one of its sturdiest foundations. He was like a . . ."

"God?" Michael offered.

"No. He was just a man with a divine vision. I wish there were more like him."

"There are," Michael kissed the top of her head. He put his arm around her and nudged her toward the house. "I think Jefferson's funeral here, with just us, is what he would have wanted. He loved you, Barbara. You're his legacy to the world. You're the only one who has the right to be here."

"You're right," she sighed and laid her head on Michael's shoulder as they walked inside the back door.

Chen looked in on the sleeping, and now well-fed, Chinese women they'd brought up from the well-holes and cages.

Chen had just descended the staircase on her way to the dining room where Barbara and Michael were serving cold sliced turkey and fresh vegetables, when she heard a knock at the front door.

Chen opened the door and found Donald Pope almost out of breath, leaning against the doorjamb. The minute he saw her swollen face and bruises, he stood upright, stepped inside the house and took her face tenderly in his hands.

"Who did this to you, Chen?"

She didn't miss the anger and protective tones in his voice. "It's not important any more. They're dead."

"They? God in heaven, why would anyone want to hurt you?"

"I wouldn't bend to their will." She dropped her eyes not wanting him to see the pain in her eyes.

"I wish I'd been there to save you."

She looked up at him. "But you're here now, Donald."

"That I am."

She put out her hand to him. She could feel that same tingle she always felt whenever they touched. There was a spark, a connection that was exciting, yet familiar. "Did you feel that?"

"It's always like that when we touch," he said. "It's as if two souls have found each other."

"Perhaps we were together in heaven before coming to earth."

"Perhaps there's no such thing as heaven. Perhaps heaven is to be found on Earth," he said, leaning down to kiss her. "Perhaps you are my heaven."

* * * *

Late that night after everyone in the house was asleep, Michael cradled Barbara's head in the crook of his shoulder. He laid his hand on her softly rounded hip.

Through the lace curtains, they saw fires blazing across the city. Black smoke billowed in columns blending with the dark night sky.

"Golden Gate Park is filled with refugees," she said.

"They'll need our help tomorrow."

"Oh, Michael, it's going to take so much work to rebuild San Francisco. I just think of all that Jefferson did. His whole life was spent making this city great."

"We'll make it greater," he replied, kissing her tenderly.

"We will, won't we?"

"Of course," he said, taking her hand. "You will marry me, won't you?"

Surprised, she smiled. "Michael, I've felt married to you since the day we met."

"Come to think of it, we should have been married in Washington. I should have popped the question then."

"What?" She feigned shock. "Why, I would have been pregnant twice over by now."

"And what's the matter with that?" he asked.

"Michael, you wouldn't really have wanted to deprive me of being part of your bringing an indictment against Abe Ruef and Mayor Schmitz, now would you?"

"I like the part about you being pregnant," he teased. "I love you."

"I love you with all my heart," she said and kissed him. Then she nuzzled her face into his neck where she planted tiny, affectionate kisses.

"I was reading over Jefferson's will, Barbara. He's left absolutely everything to you. The house, the fortune, the businesses. That's quite a lot to handle, isn't it?"

She touched his lips with her fingertip. "Not for two people, it isn't. After all, Jefferson did it all by himself. I have you."

"We have each other," he said.

"When I was a little girl, Jefferson told me he'd built this house out of love. Now that I know all the story, I realize how very special this house is. Donald said the angels protected the house from the earthquake and fires."

"Yes," Michael said and pulled her into his arms. "And now there's one more angel watching over us."

"Jefferson," she whispered. "I like knowing that. I don't feel quite so alone."

"Barbara, Darling, don't you see? None of us is ever alone."

Barbara looked up to the sky and in that moment she thought she saw Yuala, Rachel, Caroline, her father and Jefferson smiling down on her and Michael. She could feel her heart filling up with an abundance of love.

She was filled with wonder and awe.

"Do you see them, Michael?" she asked.

Michael knew instantly what she meant. He didn't need to look up. He gazed at Barbara. "I see them every time I look at you."

Barbara knew she could never really be sure about what she saw in the sky.

But she had faith.

epilogue

*There is only one happiness in life,
to love and be loved.*

—GEORGE SAND
LETTER TO LINA CALAMATTA

San Francisco—October 1906

The special task force appointed by President Theodore Roosevelt had collected enough evidence to prosecute. The crimes fell into three main categories.

Police graft—money for protection of illicit enterprises (for example, the French Restaurants);

Franchise graft—money received for obtaining franchises or special privileges (for example, the Home Telephone franchise, the United Railroad's overhead trolley franchise, the prize fight monopoly, in which money was paid to ensure that a certain body of promoters could receive the rights to stage lucrative boxing matches);

Rate graft—money received for procuring advantageous rates for quasi-public corporations (for example, the gas, water and electricity rates).

The jury was sworn in on November 9, 1906. By November 15, 1906, five joint indictments on extortion charges were filed against Ruef and Schmitz. Ruef immediately surrendered himself to Sheriff O'Neal. By this time Schmitz was on his way home from his unsuccessful trip to Europe on which he had hoped to persuade the German insurance companies to pay the monies due to the earthquake victims. When Schmitz crossed the California state line, he was arrested.

The trial was delayed until March 4, 1907. Abe Ruef pleaded "not guilty" and was allowed bail by Judge Hebbard, who was drunk at the time. Ruef disappeared.

After a three-day search by Ruef's cronies, the sheriff, the coroner and the police, Ruef still had not been found. A special task force was appointed by the court. Michael Trent and William J. Burns found Ruef in two hours at Ruef's comfortable roadhouse, the Trocadero, six miles from the center of San Francisco.

The grand jury returned 65 indictments against Ruef on bribery of the supervisors in regard to the Franchise graft. There were over 305 indictments in connection with the French Restaurants case.

On June 13, 1907, Eugene Schmitz was found guilty of extortion in the matter of the French Restaurants and he was sent to jail to await sentencing.

Not until December 10, 1908, did the jury return a guilty verdict in Abe Ruef's case. He was given the maximum sentence of fourteen years in San Quentin.

He spent the next year in the county jail. In December 1909, he was released on six-hundred-thousand-dollars bail. He did not enter San Quentin until March 7, 1911.

In 1912, Eugene Schmitz was brought up on another bribery charge and was acquitted. Later, he had the audacity to run for mayor and lost. He was elected to San Francisco's Board of Supervisors for a two-year term . . . twice. He died, forgiven and loved, on November 20, 1928.

Abe Ruef was released from prison on August 23, 1915, after serving only four-and-a-half years of his sentence. He was not allowed to return to the bar and died on February 29, 1936, in San Francisco. He was bankrupt.

Michael Trent and Barbara Mansfield Kendrick were married three days after the earthquake in Jefferson Duke's mansion, which Barbara inherited. Only Eleanor Mansfield, Yin Su, Donald Pope and Chen Su were present. Due to the massive destruction in the city, there were no flowers, no music and no refreshments.

Immediately following Michael and Barbara's ceremony, Donald married Chen with the same Judge Allen Chesterfield officiating.

Eleanor cried throughout both ceremonies. "It took an earthquake to put me back on destiny's path," she said, and told Barbara her tears were happy tears.

They were the first of her life.

Geological and Historical Notes

The geological sections of this book are both historically and scientifically accurate.

The Chinese section of this book is completely factual except for the main characters. The beheading of a Chinese man, upon whom the character of Luang Su is based, actually took place by the Emperor in the presence of emissaries from the East India Company.

All sections about San Francisco are historically accurate. During the earthquake period, great effort has been made to depict the actual occurrences. The investigation into corruption took place exactly as depicted, though the chief investigator was William J. Burns, not Michael Trent. Burns was employed directly by President Theodore Roosevelt.

As a matter of record, the instances of psychic dreams as much as two months prior to the 1906 earthquake and fire were recorded by journalists and magazine reporters. The fire chief and police chief both reported having dreams of a "great fire" two weeks before the earthquake.

The mayor of San Francisco, Eugene Schmitz, and his promoter, Abe Ruef, both went to prison for graft. Over half the city supervisors were brought to trial for graft and convicted.

About the Author

The first time author Catherine Lanigan ever submitted a manuscript was to a creative writing professor during her freshman year of college. Following a terse review of her work, he squinted his eyes, grimaced and told her point-blank, "Your writing stinks. You'll never make a living as a novelist . . . but I'll make a bargain with you. I'll get you through this class if you promise never to write again." Catherine still remembers the impact of that crushing blow. Fortunately for her hundreds of thousands of fans worldwide, that moment was the spark that ignited a graceful determination which fuels her remarkable career today.

One of the publishing community's most prolific and eloquent literary voices, Catherine Lanigan is the author of over twenty books, including the wildly popular *Romancing the Stone* and *The Jewel of the Nile*, which preceded the blockbuster films of the same names. Her newest title, *The Legend Makers* (MIRA Books), is already a hot topic with industry insiders, who anticipate an enthusiastic reception from the publishing community and loyal fans alike.

In addition to the commercial success of her books, Catherine Lanigan's work strikes a profound visceral chord with her readers. Many of them write her frequently, sharing deeply personal insights about their own lives and why the female characters in her books inspire them. Unlike the self sacrificing heroines of most traditional contemporary fiction, Catherine Lanigan's protagonists are self-empowering women who, despite stunning obstacles, build an internal arsenal of wisdom, courage and dignity that enables them to finally be true to themselves. They embrace change with aplomb, grit and grace, even though deep down they may be frightened stiff.

For Catherine Lanigan, these are the characteristics of the "evolving woman," a new breed of heroine she's introduced to contemporary fiction. The "evolving woman" is someone who, given a certain set of circumstances, makes choices that enrich who she is inside and, as a result, the world around her. This passionate perspective comes from powerful experience. The trials and triumphs of her characters are engraved with her own initials. Unfulfilling marriages, the tragic birth and loss of a child, single parenthood, financial struggles, career disappointments, personal and professional betrayals, and her self-made rise as an author comprise the fertile soil of her own life from which Catherine creates her stories.

"I would like to believe that if a woman whose life is in turmoil or chaos picks up one of my books, something in the book will help guide her through the turmoil," says Catherine Lanigan. "I hope my books are a catalyst, a gentle yet firm push in the right direction."

Catherine Lanigan lives in Houston, Texas.

Visionary Fiction from HCI

"She watched him closely as he slept, aware that Matt couldn't see her or feel her presence. It was hard to see him in so much pain and not be able to simply "fix it" or show him the way. Yet she knew that she had to let him make each step on his own. She could not interfere by helping him until he was ready. She could help him become aware of what he already knew, and that was all."

Jim Britt, *Rings of Truth*

Code #7249 Paperback • $12.95

A profound tale of a man's journey to discover his true self. Matt, a motivational speaker, has it all, until a spiritual apparition allows him to see that his material success means nothing if his soul is empty. Follow him on his transformative journey of awareness and awakening as he develops a greater understanding of who he his and teaches those around him, one truth at a time.

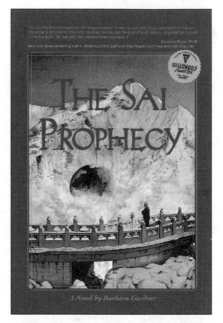

A New Season of

Chicken Soup for the Soul

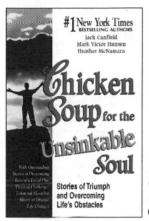

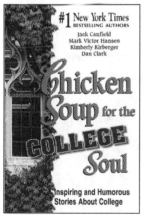
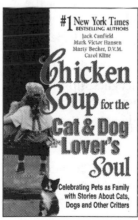

Get Some Soup to Warm Your Heart

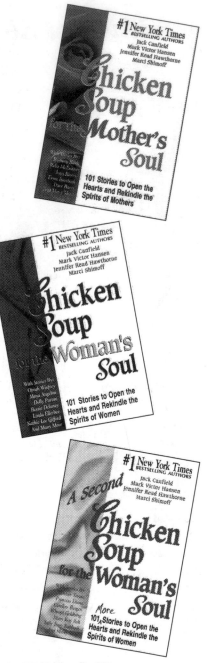

There are many ways to define a woman: daughter, mother, wife, professional, friend, student. . . . We are each special and unique, yet we share a common connection. What bonds all women are our mutual experiences of loving and learning: feeling the tenderness of love; forging lifelong friendships; pursuing a chosen career; giving birth to new life; juggling the responsibilities of job and family, and more.

These three volumes celebrate the myriad facets of a woman's life.

Chicken Soup for the Mother's Soul
Code #4606 Paperback • $12.95

Chicken Soup for the Woman's Soul
Code #4150 Paperback • $12.95

A Second Chicken Soup for the Woman's Soul
Code #6226 Paperback • $12.95

A Classic is Born

"It all began at a glitterati dinner party in the chic part of Philadelphia. A cluster of women, all wearing shapeless haute couture satin dresses our mothers would have worn as negligees, were sipping white wine and talking about men and sex. It was getting a little late. We were holding the last sparkling remnants of the party in our eyes."
Wendy Keller, *The Cult of the Born-Again Virgin*

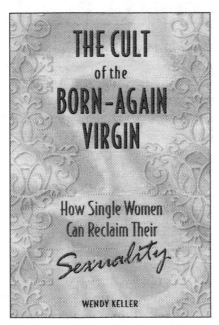

Code #7249 Paperback • $12.95

This candid, intimate, sometimes funny, sometimes poignant book will show you how to reclaim your soul by reclaiming your body. Through firsthand accounts of real-life "Born-Again Virgins," learn the events that acted as catalysts for choosing abstinence, the repercussions of the choice, the effects on self-esteem, ways to deal with abstinence or celibacy on a daily basis, the effects on relationships and how to handle resuming sexual activity.

The Love of Knowledge

Code #7206 • $10.95

From its birth in ancient Greece to the present day, philosophy has inspired us with insightful questions and thoughts to help us live life to the fullest.

This book will give you the basics tenets for many of the most important thinkers throughout history and show you how they relate directly to our everyday life. From advertising slogans to celebrities, to familiar phrases, you'll be amazed at how much of our popular culture results from the teachings of the great philosophers.